KUSHIEL'S JUSTICE

JACQUELINE CAREY

KUSHIEL'S JUSTICE

TREASON'S HEIR: BOOK TWO

www.orbitbooks.net

ORBIT

First published in the United States in 2007 by Warner Books,
Hachette Book Group USA.
First published in Great Britain in 2008 by Orbit

A CIP catalogue record for this book
is available from the British Library.

ISBN 978-1-84149-362-6

Papers used by Orbit are natural, recyclable products made from
wood grown in sustainable forests and certified in accordance with
the rules of the Forest Stewardship Council.

Typeset in Adobe Garamond by Palimpsest Book Production Limited,
Grangemouth, Stirlingshire
Printed and bound in Great Britain by
CPI Mackays, Chatham ME5 8TD

Orbit
An imprint of
Little, Brown Book Group
100 Victoria Embankment
London EC4Y 0DY

An Hachette Livre UK Company
www.hachettelivre.co.uk

www.orbitbooks.net

Dramatis Personae

House Montrève

Phèdre nó Delaunay de Montrève—Comtesse de Montrève
Joscelin Verreuil—Phèdre's consort; Cassiline Brother (Siovale)
Imriel nó Montrève de la Courcel—Phèdre's foster-son (also member of the royal family)
Ti-Philippe—chevalier
Gilot (*deceased*), Hugues—men-at-arms
Eugènie—mistress of the household, townhouse
Clory—niece of Eugènie
Benoit—stable-lad, townhouse

Members of the D'Angeline Royal Family

Ysandre de la Courcel—Queen of Terre d'Ange; wed to Drustan mab Necthana
Sidonie de la Courcel—elder daughter of Ysandre; heir to Terre d'Ange

Alais de la Courcel—younger daughter of Ysandre

Imriel nó Montrève de la Courcel—cousin; son of Benedicte de la Courcel (*deceased*) and Melisande Shahrizai

Barquiel L'Envers—uncle of Ysandre; Duc L'Envers (Namarre)

House Shahrizai

Melisande Shahrizai—mother of Imriel; wed to Benedicte de la Courcel (*deceased*)

Faragon Shahrizai—Duc de Shahrizai

Mavros, Roshana, Baptiste Shahrizai—cousins of Imriel

Members of the Royal Court

Ghislain nó Trevalion—noble; Royal Commander; son of Percy de Somerville (*deceased*)

Bernadette de Trevalion—noble, wed to Ghislain, sister of Baudoin (*deceased*)

Bertran de Trevalion—son of Ghislain and Bernadette

Amaury Trente—noble, former Commander of the Queen's Guard

Julien and Colette Trente—children of Amaury

Nicola L'Envers y Aragon—cousin of Queen Ysandre; wed to Ramiro Zornín de Aragon

Raul L'Envers y Aragon—son of Nicola and Ramiro

Marguerite Lafons—Marquise de Lafoneuil

Childric d'Essoms—ambassador to Ephesium

Maslin de Lombelon—lieutenant in the Dauphine's Guard

The Night Court

Agnés Rame—Second of Alyssum House

Mignon—adept of Alyssum House

Janelle nó Bryony—Dowayne of Bryony House

Simon nó Eglantine—adept of Eglantine House

ALBA

Drustan mab Necthana—Cruarch of Alba, wed to Ysandre de la Courcel

Breidaia—sister of Drustan, daughter of Necthana

Talorcan—son of Breidaia

Dorelei—daughter of Breidaia

Sibeal—sister of Drustan, daughter of Necthana, wed to Hyacinthe

Hyacinthe—Master of the Straits, wed to Sibeal

Firdha—Cruithne *ollamh*

Galanna, Donal—children of Sibeal and Hyacinthe

Grainne mac Conor—Lady of the Dalriada

Eamonn, Mairead, Brennan, Caolinn, Conor—Lady Grainne's children

Brigitta—Skaldic wife of Eamonn

Aodhan—Dalriadan *ollamh*

Urist—commander of the garrison of Clunderry

Kinadius, Deordivus, Uven, Cailan, Domnach, Selwin, Brun—members of Clunderry's garrison

Morwen, Ferghus, Berlik—magicians of the Maghuin Dhonn

Kinada, Kerys, Trevedic, Murghan, Hoel, Cluna—folk of Clunderry

Leodan mab Nonna—lord of Briclaedh

Nehailah Ansout—priestess of Elua

Milcis—beekeeper

Girard—D'Angeline chirurgeon

Corcan—captain of the Cruarch's flagship

SKALDIA

Adelmar of the Frisii—ruler of Maarten's Crossing

Yoel—Yeshuite pilgrim

Halla—innkeeper

Ernst—wool-merchant

Ortwin—harbor-master of Norstock

Ditmarus and Ermegart—members of the Unseen Guild

VRALIA

Iosef—trade-ship's captain
Ravi, Yuri, Ruslan—sailors
Micah ben Ximon—commander of Vralian army
Tadeuz Vral—Grand Prince of Vralia
Fedor Vral—Tadeuz' brother; rebel
Jergens—fur-trader
Ethan and Galia of Ommsmeer, son Adam—Yeshuite pilgrims
Kebek—Tatar horse-thief
Avraham ben David—Rebbe of Miroslas
Skovik—seal-hunting boat's captain

OTHERS

Lelahiah Valais—Queen Ysandre's chirurgeon
Emile—proprietor of the Cockerel
Quintilius Rousse—Royal Admiral, father of Eamonn
Favrielle nó Eglantine—couturiere
Bérèngere of Namarre—head of Naamah's Order
Amarante of Namarre—daughter of Bérèngere
Morit—woman of Saba, astronomer
Eleazar ben Enokh—Yeshuite mystic
Raphael Murain—priest of Naamah
Diokles Agallon—Ephesian ambassador; member of the Unseen Guild
Tibault de Toluard—Marquis de Toluard (Siovale)
Isembart—steward of the Shahrizai hunting manor
Lucius Tadius da Lucca—friend of Imriel's
Claudia Fulvia—Lucius' sister; member of the Unseen Guild
Domenico Martelli (*deceased*)—Duke of Valpetra
Canis (*deceased*)—member of the Unseen Guild; emissary of Melisande

HISTORICAL FIGURES

Benedicte de la Courcel (*deceased*)—great-uncle of Ysandre; Imriel's father

Baudoin de Trevalion (*deceased*)—cousin of Ysandre; executed for treason

Isidore d'Aiglemort (*deceased*)—noble; traitor turned hero (Camlach)

Waldemar Selig (*deceased*)—Skaldic warlord; invaded Terre d'Ange

Necthana *(deceased)*—mother of Drustan

The Mahrkagir (*deceased*)—mad ruler of Drujan; lord of Daršanga

Jagun (*deceased*)—chief of the Kereyit Tatars

Gallus Tadius (*deceased*)—great-grandfather of Lucius

Cinhil Ru (*deceased*)—legendary leader of the Cruithne

Donnchadh (*deceased*)—legendary magician of the Maghuin Dhonn

NORTH

GOTLAND

Eastern
Sea

JUTLAND

Innisclan

Clunderry
Bryn Gorrydum

ALBA

THE FLATLANDS

Norstock

Maarten's
Crossing

SKA

TERRE D'ANGE

City of • Elua

CAERDICCA

ILLYRIA

THE

ONE

BY THE TIME I WAS eighteen years of age—almost nineteen—I'd been many things. I'd been an orphan, a goatherd, and a slave. I'd been a missing prince, lost and found. I'd been a traitor's son and a heroine's. I'd been a scholar, a lover, and a soldier.

All of these were true, more or less.

Betimes it seemed impossible that one person's mere flesh could contain so many selves. Mine did, though. I was Prince Imriel de la Courcel, third in line for the throne of Terre d'Ange, betrothed to wed a princess of Alba and beget heirs to that kingdom with her. And, too, I was Imriel nó Montrève, adopted son of Comtesse Phèdre nó Delaunay de Montrève and her consort, Joscelin Verreuil.

Imriel. Imri, to a few.

When I gained my age of majority, eighteen, I tried to flee myself. My selves. I went to the University of Tiberium in Caerdicca Unitas, where no one knew me, and played at being a scholar. There I found friendship, passion, and intrigue. I found myself targeted by an enemy not of my making, and I dealt with it on my own terms. I found myself caught on the wrong side of a siege, and learned of grief, courage, and loyalty. I discovered that few people are wholly good or bad, and all is not always as it seems, including the very ground beneath our feet.

And somewhere along the way, I found a little bit of healing. It wasn't enough to undo all of the damage done to me when I was a child; that, I think, cuts too deep. But enough. Enough to lend me a little bit of wisdom and compassion. Enough to face the responsibilities of my birthright like a man. Enough to let me come home, even if it was only for a while.

Enough to face one last self.

My mother's son.

My cousin Mavros claims we must all face two mirrors, the bright and the dark. Perhaps it is true. I never thought I would confront the mirror of my mother's legacy. When I was fourteen years of age, she vanished from the temple in La Serenissima where she had claimed sanctuary for long years. No one has seen her since, or no one living who will confess it. Before that time, I had seen her only twice. The first time, I thought her beautiful and kind, and I loved her for it. I didn't know who she was; nor who I was, either.

The second time, I knew. And I hated her for it.

I thought she was gone from my life forever, but she wasn't. In the besieged city of Lucca, a man spent his life to save mine. Canis, he called himself; Dog, in the Caerdicci tongue. I'd known him first as a philosopher and a beggar, and last as a mystery and a bitter gift. On the streets of Lucca, he flung himself in front of a javelin meant for me, and it pierced him through. He smiled before he died, and his last words stay with me.

Your mother sends her love.

So I came home. Home to Terre d'Ange, to the City of Elua. Home to Phèdre and Joscelin, whom I loved beyond all measure. Home to Queen Ysandre to agree to her political machinations; to Mavros and my Shahrizai kin. To Bernadette de Trevalion, who hired a man to kill me in Tiberium. To my royal cousins, the D'Angeline princesses; young Alais, who is like a sister to me, and the Queen's heir Sidonie, who is . . . not.

To my mother's letters.

For three years, she had written to me. Once a month the letters came, save when winter delayed their delivery; then a packet of two or three would arrive. I threw the first letter on the brazier, but Phèdre rescued it. After that, she saved them for me in a locked coffer in her study.

I read them in single sitting, well into the small hours of the night. The lamps burned low in Phèdre's study until they began to sputter for lack of oil. I refilled the lamps and read onward. Beyond the door, I could hear the sounds of Montrève's household dwindle into soft creaks and sighs as its members took to their bedchambers.

When I had finished the last letter, I refolded it and placed it atop the others. I put them away and closed the coffer, locking it with the little gold key. And then I sat for a long time, alone and quiet, my heart and mind too full for thought.

By the time I arose, it seemed it must nearly be dawn; but I'd grown accustomed to doing without sleep during the siege of Lucca. I blew out the lamps and made my way quietly through the townhouse.

"Imriel?"

There was a lone lamp burning in the salon. On the couch, Phèdre uncurled. She reached over and turned the wick up a notch. The flame leapt, illuminating her face. Our eyes met. It was still too dark to see the scarlet mote on her left iris that marked her as Kushiel's Chosen. But it was there. I knew it was.

"I'm fine," I said softly.

"Do you want to talk?" Her gaze was steady and unflinching. There was no mirror in the world into which Phèdre feared to look. Not anymore. Not after what she had endured. I thought about what my mother had written about her.

"No," I said, but I sat down beside her. "I don't know. Not yet."

Phèdre had read the letters. It was four years ago, when my mother vanished. Because I couldn't bring myself to face the task, I'd asked her to do it, to ensure there was no treason in them, nothing that might divulge her whereabouts. There wasn't. But I remembered how she had looked afterward, bruised and weary. I felt that way now.

She watched me for a long moment without speaking, and what thoughts passed behind her eyes, I could not say. At length, she reached out and stroked a lock of my hair, a touch as light as the brush of a butterfly's wing. "Go to bed, Imri. You need sleep."

"I know." I swung myself off the couch, leaning down to kiss her cheek. "Thank you."

Phèdre smiled at me. "For what?"

"For being here," I said. "For being *you*."

In my bedchamber, I pulled off my boots and lay down on my bed, folding my arms beneath my head and staring at the ceiling. When I closed my eyes, I could see the words my mother had written swirling in my head.

The first words, her first letter.

You will wonder if I loved you, of course. The answer is yes; a thousand times, yes. I wonder, as I write this, how to find the words to tell you? Words that you will believe in light of my history? I can tell you this: Whatever I have done, I have never violated the precept of Blessed Elua. It is in my nature to relish games of power above all else, and I have played them to the hilt. I have known love, other loves. The deep and abiding ties of family. The fondness of friends and lovers, the intoxicating thrill of passion, the keen, deadly excitements of conspiracy.

All of these pale beside your birth.

I began to know it as you grew within me; a life, separate yet contained. Our veins sharing the same blood; my food, your nourishment. And then the wrenching separation of birth, the two divided and rejoined. When they put you in my arms, I felt a conflagration in my heart; a love fiercer and hotter than any I had known.

You will remember none of this, I know. But in the first months of your life, I suffered no attendant to bathe you, no nursemaid to suckle you. These things, I did myself. Like any fatuous mother, I counted your fingers and toes, marveling at their miniature perfection, the nails like tiny moons. Your flesh, a part of mine, now separate. The veins beneath your skin where my blood flowed, the impossible tenderness of it all. In the privacy of my chambers, I held you close to my breast and said all the foolish things mothers say.

I remember the first time you laughed, and how it made my heart leap. And yes, I dreamed great dreams for you—dreams you will call treason. But above all I knew I would never, ever suffer anyone to harm you. I, who had never acted out of spite (although you may not believe it), would gladly have killed with my own hands anyone who harbored an ill thought toward you.

When I sent you away . . . if you believe nothing else, I pray you will believe this. I believed you would be safe in the Sanctuary of Elua. Safe from my enemies, and safe from the intentions of the Queen. Safe and hidden, the secret jewel of my heart. If I had known what would happen, if there was any way I could undo what was done to you, I would do it. I would humble myself and beg, I would pay any price. But there is none, none the gods will accept.

Instead, I am afforded a reminder harsher than any rod, that cuts deeper than any blade: Kushiel's justice is cruel.

You will wonder if I loved you. The answer is yes; a thousand times, yes.

One may be wounded in battle without feeling it. After we retreated from the first onslaught in Lucca, I was surprised to find a gash on my thigh, a gouge on my arm. And I was surprised now to find tears leaking from my closed lids. I'd known the letters had bruised and battered my heart. I hadn't known my mother's words had touched something deep and aching within me, something I had buried since I was ten years old and I learned who I was. Now it was cracked asunder.

It hurt.

It hurt because I had believed myself unloved, a political expedient; a cog in my mother's vast ambitions. It hurt with a deep, bittersweet ache. For the laughing infant in his mother's arms, for all that she had understood too late. I had spent so many years despising her, knowing only the proud, calculating monstrosity of her genius. It was hard to feel otherwise.

Alone in the darkness of my bedchamber, I pressed the heels of my hands against my closed eyes and sighed. I couldn't love her. Not now; likely not ever. But I could begin to forgive her, at least a little bit, for the things that had befallen me.

In time, I slept without knowing it, sinking into the depths of exhaustion. At first I dreamed I was reading my mother's letters still, and then the dream changed. For the first time in many months, I dreamed of Daršanga. I dreamed of the Mahrkagir's smile and the sound of a rusty blade being scraped over a whetting stone, and I cried aloud and woke.

A figure at the window startled. "Your highness?"

I sat up and squinted at her. There was light spilling into my bedchamber. It had been the sound of the drapes being drawn, nothing more. "Clory?"

Phèdre's handmaiden bobbed a quick curtsy. "Forgive me, your highness!"

"It's just me, Clory." I ran my hands through my disheveled hair. "Is it late?"

Her lips twitched. "Late enough, according to messire Joscelin. He thought you might want a bite of luncheon."

"Luncheon?" My belly rumbled. "Tell them I'll be down directly."

No one mentioned the letters when I appeared, still yawning, and took a seat at the table. Joscelin gave me a quick assessing glance, and Phèdre merely smiled at me. Ti-Philippe and Hugues were there, bickering good-naturedly about who had neglected to fill an empty charcoal-bin in the garrison.

"I thought we might spar later," Joscelin offered after I'd filled my plate. "I'm out of practice since you've been gone."

Ti-Philippe snorted. *"You?"*

"Well." Joscelin looked mildly at him. "Somewhat, yes."

I didn't believe it any more than Ti-Philippe did. Hugues laughed. "'Alone at dawn the Cassiline stands,'" he declaimed. "'His longsword shining in his hands. Across the cobbled stones he glides. Through the air his bright blade slides' . . . Oh, all right," he added as Joscelin rolled his eyes. "I'll stop."

I laughed, too. Hugues was kindhearted and loyal to the bone, but his poetry was notoriously dreadful. "I'd like that," I said to Joscelin. "Indeed, why not now?"

He glanced at Phèdre.

"There was a messenger from House Trevalion this morning," she said quietly. "The Lady Bernadette wishes you to call upon her at your earliest convenience."

"I see." I nodded. "Well, good."

Ti-Philippe raised his brows. "A clandestine affair? That's swift work, young Imriel. You do know she's old enough to be your mother?"

"Hmm?" I scarce heard the comment. This wasn't going to be an encounter I relished, but it was necessary and I'd be glad to have the matter resolved. I was weary of being persecuted for my mother's sins.

"It's not what you think. It's . . . a family matter, that's all. She *is* my cousin, you know."

"Ah, well." He grinned. "That never stopped anyone."

"Shall I go with you?" Joscelin asked.

"No," I said slowly. "It's . . . somewhat I'd rather do alone."

He gave me a long, hard look. "All right, then."

After our luncheon was concluded, I borrowed Phèdre's study to make a fair copy of a letter in my possession. Not one of my mother's, this one. It was brief and inelegant, scrawled on a single sheet of parchment, a signature and a smeared thumbprint affixed at the bottom. It had been written by a man named Ruggero Caccini. In it, he divulged the details of his arrangement with Lady Bernadette de Trevalion, who had paid him a considerable sum of money to ensure that a deadly mishap befell me in the city of Tiberium.

I'd found out about it. And I'd extorted the letter from him using a combination of blackmail and bribery.

I daresay my mother would have been proud.

I had the Bastard saddled and rode to the Palace. There was a sharp chill in the air, a harbinger of winter. It made the Bastard restless. I kept him on a tight rein and he chafed under it, tossing his head and champing at the bit. He was a good horse, though. Tsingani-bred, one of the best. I patted his red-speckled hide, thinking about Gilot and how much he'd wanted the spotted horse we'd seen together in Montrève the day I learned my mother had vanished.

I wished I'd bought it for him, now.

Gilot was dead. He'd been one of Montrève's men-at-arms, the youngest of the lot and the closest thing to a friend I had among them. He'd gone with me to Tiberium, where I'd been a plague and a trial to him. He was killed in Lucca. He'd gone to protect me, and I brought him home in a casket. It was only two days ago that I had arrived in the City; two days ago that we had buried him. I missed him.

At the Palace, I gave the Bastard over to an ostler with the usual warnings. The footman on duty swept me a low bow.

"Prince Imriel," he said. "How may I serve your highness?"

"I believe Lady Bernadette de Trevalion is expecting me," I said.

He bowed again. "Of course."

I followed him down the marble halls. The Palace was a vast place. The City of Elua is the heart of Terre d'Ange, and the Court is the heart of the City. Betimes it seems half the peers of the realms maintain quarters there. Others maintain lodging elsewhere in the City, but spend their days loitering at Court—playing games of chance in the Hall of Games, partaking of entertainment in the Salon of Eisheth's Harp, begging an audience with the Queen or a chance to present a case before the Parliament when it is in session.

The young nobles play the Game of Courtship, testing out dalliances and angling for marital alliances. I'd never played it; nor would I, now. I was betrothed to a woman I barely knew; Dorelei mab Breidaia, a princess of Alba.

House Trevalion's quarters were on the third floor of the Palace. I'd visited them often when Bernadette's son Bertran and I were friends. That had all changed the night he believed he'd caught me out at a treasonous intrigue, and I hadn't been back since. The footman knocked for admission, exchanging low words with the attendant who answered. In short order, I was ushered into a private audience with the Lady Bernadette in her salon.

"My lady." I accorded her the bow due an equal. She sat upright and rigid in a tall chair. Her mother had been my father's sister; Lyonette de Trevalion. The Lioness of Azzalle, they used to call her. She was dead, convicted of treason, along with her son Baudoin. They had conspired to usurp the throne. He had fallen on his sword; she had taken poison. My mother had betrayed them both, and it was her testimony that had convicted them. "You asked to see me?"

Bernadette's sea-grey eyes narrowed. "Do me the courtesy of playing no games with me, Imriel de la Courcel. My son Bertran said you had a message for me. What is it?"

"As you wish." I handed her the copy of Ruggero's letter. "I hold the original."

She scanned it, then nodded once, crisply. "So. What will you?"

I sighed. "My lady, what would you have me say? I am sorry for the death of your mother and brother. I am sorry for your time spent in exile. But I am not willing to die for it."

Her hands trembled, making the parchment quiver. "And with this, you could destroy me. Destroy House Trevalion, or what is left of it." Her voice hardened. "So I ask again, *what will you?*"

I sat, uninvited, on a couch. "Forswear vengeance."

Her eyes widened. "That's *all?*"

"More or less," I said, studying her. Looking for lies, looking for the fault-lines of bitterness and anger and pride that lay within her. "Tell me, did Bertran know? Or your husband, Ghislain?"

"No." Bernadette de Trevalion closed her eyes. "Only me. It would kill them."

"Then why did you do it?" I asked her. *"Why?"*

Her eyes opened; her lips twisted. "You have to ask? Because I *hurt*, Imriel. I miss my brother. I miss my mother. I grieve for my father's disgrace, my husband's disgrace. You?" She shrugged. "I was willing to abide. When my son befriended you, it galled me. Still, I tolerated it. But when Bertan caught you in the midst of conspiring treason, it brought it all back." Her cheeks flushed. "All the old hurt, all the hatred."

"And so you thought to kill me for it," I said softly. "Despite the fact that the Queen herself declared me innocent."

"I wanted you to suffer like Baudoin did!" Her voice rose. "And I wanted your *mother*, your cursed mother, to know what it felt like. To feel her actions rebounding on her and know her role in them. To *hurt* like I do."

My old scars itched. "You have no idea," I said. "None."

Bernadette de Trevalion looked steadily at me. "What will you?"

At least she had courage. She made no effort to lie, no plea for undeserved mercy. I returned her regard for a long moment. "First, understand this. What Bertran overheard that night was a lie." She opened her mouth to speak and I cut her off. "Duc Barquiel L'Envers was behind it, Bernadette," I said wearily. "There's proof. That's how he was pressured to relinquish the Royal Command your husband now enjoys."

Her mouth worked. "Why would he—"

"Elua only knows." I spread my hands. "L'Envers has wanted me dead since I was born. And you very nearly obliged him."

She turned pale. "I didn't know."

"Now you do." I stood. "My lady, I'm no traitor. I never have been.

You, on the other hand, conspired to murder a Prince of the Blood." I nodded at the letter she held. "You ask me what I will. Ruggero Caccini's letter stays in my keeping as surety. But if you forswear all vengeance against me for my mother's misdeeds, I promise you, it will never come to light. I will never speak of this incident."

Bernadette hesitated. "Why would you make such a promise?"

"Because your son Bertran was a friend, once." I smiled grimly. "Not a very good one, as it transpired, but a friend. Because your husband is the Queen's loyal Commander and a hero of the realm. Because the Queen ardently desires peace among her kin. And mostly because I am sick unto death of being caught up in the bloody coils of things that happened long before I was born. Do you swear?"

She raised her chin. Oh yes, there was pride there. "In the name of Blessed Elua and Azza, I swear to forgo all vengeance against you, Imriel de la Courcel."

Her voice was low, but it was steady. I nodded once more. "My thanks, my lady."

"Imriel." Bernadette rose and caught my elbow as I turned to go. Old anguish surfaced in her sea-grey eyes, complicated with guilt and dawning remorse. "I didn't know, truly. I'm sorry."

I gazed at her. "Good."

After I took my leave of her, I visited one other place within the Palace. The Hall of Portraits was a long, narrow room on the second floor. A row of windows along the outer wall admitted a wash of wintry light. The interior wall was lined and stacked with portraits of the scions of House Courcel, rulers of Terre d'Ange for some three centuries.

I'd never set foot in it before. But after reading my mother's letters, I reckoned it was time. I made my way toward the far end of the hall. Family members were clustered together, stacked in groups. There; there was Ganelon de la Courcel, Ysandre's grandfather, and his wife above him. There was no portrait of Lyonette de Trevalion, his sister. I daresay that had been removed after her execution. But there, beside him . . .

I read the name on the frame's brass plaque: Benedicte de la Courcel.

My father.

You will wonder about your father. There are few left, I think, in Terre d'Ange who knew him well, well enough to speak of him. He spent long years in La Serenissima, and there were things that happened to poison him against his own legacy. You may hear that it made him bitter, and it did. We D'Angelines are not a people who take well to exile, even though it be for political advantage. This I know all too well.

But this I will tell you: He was a brave man, and a noble one in his own way. He fought for his country as a young man. He believed what he did—what we did together—was in the best interests of Terre d'Ange. He believed in the purity of the bloodlines of Blessed Elua and his Companions. He believed the nation cried out for a pure-blooded D'Angeline heir.

You.

I stared at the portrait. I didn't remember my father. He died when I was only a babe, killed in the fighting in the Temple of Asherat where my mother's final treachery was revealed. He'd been an old man, then. She had played on his prejudices. He'd been willing to condone the assassination of the Queen, his own grand-niece, to pave the way for a pure-blooded heir. Me. If he'd lived to stand trial, I daresay he would have been convicted of treason.

As for my mother, she'd already been convicted, long ago. Her life was forfeit if she ever set foot on D'Angeline soil.

The portrait depicted a serious-looking young man. It was formal and a bit stiff, and I thought it must have been painted when he was scarce older than I was. I could see a little of my own face in his; only a little. The strong, straight line of the eyebrows, the angle of his jaw. He didn't look like a man who laughed often, but he didn't look unkind, either. Mostly, he looked like a stranger; someone I'd never met.

There was no portrait of his first wife, the Serenissiman. No portraits of the children they had borne together, disowned by House Courcel due to other intrigues. But there was a second painting hung above his, veiled with drapes of sheer black muslin. It was there because of me; because Queen Ysandre insisted on acknowledging me as a member of House Courcel. It was veiled because of the death-sentence on her. I pulled back the drapes and gazed at my mother.

Melisande.

She bore the unmistakable stamp of House Shahrizai. I bear it, too. The blue-black hair that grows in ripples, the deep, deep blue of the eyes. It was a good portrait. Her eyes seemed to sparkle with untold secrets and her generous lips were parted slightly, as though in the next instant she might laugh or smile, blow a kiss. I touched my lower lip with two fingers, thinking of the portrait I'd allowed the artist Erytheia to paint of me in Tiberium, lounging in the pose of Bacchus. Same mouth, same shape.

There was a click-clicking sound. "Imri?"

I tensed at the intrusion and turned my head to see Alais, with her pet wolfhound padding beside her, nails clicking on the marble. A pair of the Queen's Guardsmen hovered discreetly in the doorway behind her. I relaxed. "What are you doing here, villain?"

Alais pulled a face at the nickname. "I come here sometimes. But I heard you were here. You know how it is in the Court, everyone keeping track of everyone else's comings and goings. What did Lady Bernadette want of you?"

"Oh, she was hoping that Bertran and I would make up our quarrel now that I'm back," I said casually. "We never really did, you know."

"Well, it might help if he apologized for the way he behaved to you!" Alais came alongside me. "Your parents?"

I nodded. The wolfhound Celeste pushed her muzzle into my hand. I'd known her since she was a pup. She had been my gift to Alais. I scratched absently at the base of her ears, watching Alais contemplate the portraits. She'd grown up while I was gone. A little lady, now, almost fifteen years old. Her small face was dark and intent. Alais took after her father, Drustan mab Necthana, the Cruarch of Alba. Mixed blood. There were those in Court who still thought as my father had done.

"What do you think?" I asked her.

"Of them?" Alais tilted her head. "He looks . . . uncomfortable. Like his skin's too tight. That's what I always thought. And she . . ." Her expression turned wistful. "I never dared look at her before. But she doesn't, does she? The world fits her just right."

"I read her letters," I said softly.

Alais shot me a startled glance. "What did she say?"

"A lot," I said. "A lot that added up to nothing."

She nodded somberly. "Adults talk that way, don't they?"

I nearly laughed, then thought better of it. Though I was an adult now, we had been children together. Alais was wise beyond her years, and she had dreams that came true sometimes. She'd dreamed I met a man with two faces and it came true, in Lucca. "Yes," I said. "They do."

Why?

You asked me, and I will try to answer. It is a child's question, the first and last and best of all questions that may be asked. Why? Why did I do what I did? Did I know it was treason? Yes, of course.

So . . . why?

Ah, Imriel! Son of mine, I will say to you what I have said to others: Blessed Elua cared naught for crowns or thrones. It is a human game, a mortal game. I imagine you will say it was not worth the cost of innocent blood spilled in the process, since it is what Phèdre nó Delaunay once said to me. Mayhap it is true. And yet, countless numbers of those she would deem innocent never hesitated to engage in a death-struggle for these things, these mortal tokens of power.

What does it mean to be innocent? It is impossible to move through this life without making choices that injure others. My choices were bolder than others'; and yet. If they had not chosen as they did, they would not have suffered for it. We are all driven by desires, some simple and some complex. In the end, we all make choices.

In the end, no one is truly innocent.

I shook my head to dispel my mother's words. Her betrayal of House Trevalion was the least of her sins. Long before my birth, her machinations had brought Terre d'Ange to the brink of conquest. Thousands had died fighting against the invasion of the Skaldi that she had orchestrated, D'Angelines and Albans alike. And yes, it was their choice to struggle against it, but . . . ah, Elua! Surely the choices were not equal in weight.

Small wonder there were those who longed to see her suffer.

"Imri?" Alais' brow was knit with concern.

"Yes, my lady." With an effort, I gathered myself, smiling at Alais and closing the muslin drapes. My mother's face vanished. My father's continued to gaze somberly from the wall. I bowed to Alais. "I place myself at your service. What will you?"

She looked away, one hand buried in the wolfhound's ruff. "Please don't make mock of me, Imriel."

"Alais!" Startled, I went to one knee. "I wasn't."

"All right." She stole a sidelong glance at me. "Do you ever think . . . do you ever wish she had succeeded? Or think they might have been right?"

I gaped at her. "My *mother*?"

Alais nodded at the portraits. "The both of them."

"No." I took her free hand and squeezed it. "Never."

TWO

"AGAIN!"

In the gloaming, Joscelin's teeth flashed as he took a stance opposite me, his wooden sword angled before him. I grinned in reply and launched a fresh attack.

Our blades flicked and clattered as we circled each other in the courtyard, testing each other's defenses. There was hoarfroast beginning to form on the slate tiles and I placed my feet with care as we revolved around each other. Out of the corner of my eye, I watched Joscelin's feet move. Hugues' bad poetry not withstanding, he *did* seem to glide. His footwork was intricate and impeccable.

He was good; better than I was. I daresay he always will be. At ten years of age—the age at which I was learning to beg for mercy in the Mahrkagir's zenana—Joscelin entered the Cassiline Brotherhood and began to train as a warrior-priest. Day after day, he had trained without cease.

It wasn't just the training, though. There were other Cassiline Brothers. But none of them had ever made his choice. None had ever been tested as he was.

I pressed him on his bad side; his left side, where he was slower. His left arm had been shattered in Daršanga. He relinquished ground in acknowledgment, step by gliding step, and I pressed him. And then, somehow, he leaned away from my thrust with a subtle twist of his torso and I found myself overextended. The sharp point of his elbow came down hard on the back of my reaching hand.

"Oh, hell!" My sword fell and my hand stung. I shook it out.

Joscelin chuckled.

"Show me?" I asked.

"Here." Setting down his blade, he placed one hand on my belly and the other on my lower back, applying pressure. "Weight on the rear foot, knee flexed. See?"

I leaned as he'd done. "I feel off balance."

"Widen your stance." Joscelin nudged my forward foot. "Better." He patted my belly. "It all flows from here, Imri. You can't be stiff. Have you kept up your practice?"

"No," I admitted. "Gallus Tadius didn't approve. He had us training with—"

He wasn't listening. He was smiling across the courtyard. Nothing had changed, but his face was alight. Since there was only one person in the world who made Joscelin Verreuil's face brighten so, I knew without looking that Phèdre was there.

I looked anyway. She stood before the doors that opened onto the courtyard, hugging herself against the cold as she watched us spar. There was so much love and gladness in her eyes, I had to look away. What I wanted wasn't meant for me.

"Show me?" she asked, teasing.

Joscelin laughed, low and soft. He crossed over to her and placed his hands on her, as he'd done to me, only not. Not at all the same. She twined her arms around his neck, the velvet sleeves of her gown falling back to lay them bare, white and slender. He bent his head to kiss her, his wheat-blond hair falling forward. For the span of a few heartbeats, nothing else in the world existed for them.

I stooped, picking up our fallen swords. It shouldn't hurt. When I was younger, when I was a child, it wouldn't have. I loved them, I loved them both so much. They rescued me out of hell and they paid a terrible price for it. Together, we found healing. We reknit our broken selves as a family, and their love lies at the core of it. I will never, so long as I live, begrudge either of them the least crumb of happiness. They have earned it a thousand times over.

It did hurt, though. I never thought it would, but it did.

Ah, Elua! Jealousy is a hard master. I'd known love and I'd known desire, but never the two at once; not this kind, the kind that shut out the world. And there was a darker strain, too. Like it or no, I was my mother's son; Kushiel's scion, albeit a reluctant one. It was there, it would always be there. Phèdre was Kushiel's Chosen, born to yield; Naamah's Servant and a courtesan without equal. It was there between us, it would always be there.

My mother had written of it.

When, I wonder, will you read this? Not soon, I think. You are too angry now. I think you will be older. I think you will be a man grown.

I should speak of Phèdre nó Delaunay.

You will wonder, did I love her? No . . . and yes. I will tell you this, my son: I knew her. Better than anyone; better than anyone else.

I let out my breath in a sigh, wondering what Phèdre had made of those words. When all was said and done, I do not think she disagreed. Still, whatever lay between them, it was Joscelin she loved. And he knew her, too. I watched her withdraw from him, smiling. In the lamplight spilling from the open doors, I could make out a faint flush on her cheeks.

"Are you coming, love?" she called to me. "It's perishing cold out here."

"I'm coming," I said.

How is it that two people so unlikely, so unsuited, find one another? I thought about it that night, watching them at the dinner table. And I thought about the fact that I was unlikely to do the same. I had met my bride-to-be, Dorelei mab Breidaia, the Cruarch's niece. She was a sweet young woman with a lilting laugh, and I couldn't possibly imagine sharing the kind of all-consuming passion that I craved with her.

I heaved another sigh.

"Why so somber?" Hugues asked me. "Did Messire Cassiline give you a drubbing?"

"No," I said, then amended it at Joscelin's amused glance. "Well, yes." I flexed my bruised hand. "It's not that, though. I think . . . I think I would like to go to Kushiel's temple on the morrow."

"*What?*" Joscelin stared at me in disbelief. "Are you mad?"

I hadn't known what I was going to say until the words emerged from my mouth. I mulled over them. "No," I said slowly. "I think I need to make expiation."

"For *what*?" He continued to stare.

I thought about my recent excursion into extortion and blackmail. I thought about the soldiers I had killed in Lucca, about Canis with the javelin protruding from his chest and Gilot after the riot, battered and broken. I thought about cuckolded Deccus Fulvius and mad, dead Gallus Tadius standing above the maelstrom, meeting my distant gaze as he dropped his death-mask. I thought about the night Mavros took me to Valerian House and the morning after, when I grabbed Phèdre's wrist and felt the pulse of desire leap.

"Things," I said.

Joscelin shook his head. Phèdre rested her chin on one hand and fixed me with a deep look that gave away nothing. I returned it steadily. "You're sure?" she asked. "It's like to stir memories. Bad ones."

"You go," I said. "What do you find in it?"

She smiled slightly. "Oh, things."

I nodded. "I'm sure."

I wasn't, not really; at least not on the morrow. I couldn't even say of a surety what had prompted the urge. After Daršanga, I would have said I would never voluntarily submit myself to any man's lash, nor any woman's. And yet, the idea had fixed itself in my thoughts.

By morning, Joscelin was resigned. "You know, betimes I think you *are* a little mad, Imriel nó Montrève," he said to me in the courtyard outside the stable, holding the Bastard's reins.

"You never said that to Phèdre," I reminded him.

"Ah, well." He grinned despite himself. "In her case, there's no question." His expression turned sober. "Imri, truly, I know the dead weigh on you. I know it better than anyone. And I may be Cassiel's servant, but I don't deny Kushiel's mystery. It's just that it may be different for you."

I swung astride. "Because of what happened to me?"

"Yes." His eyes were grave.

"I know," I said. "But Joscelin, I'm tired of having a terrified ten-year-old boy lurking inside me. And I need to deal with my own blood-guilt and . . . other things. You told me I'd find a way, my own way. So I'm trying."

"I know." He let go the reins. "You'll see him home safe?" he said to Hugues. Ti-Philippe had offered to go, too, but I'd rather it was Hugues. If the ordeal took a greater toll on me than I reckoned, I trusted him to be gentle.

"Of course."

It was another cold, bright day in the City of Elua, the sky arching overhead like a blue vault. All the world seemed to be in high spirits. Hugues brought out his wooden flute as we rode and toyed with it, then thought better of it, tucking it away.

"It's all right," I said to him. "Play, if you like."

He shrugged his broad shoulders. "It doesn't seem right."

"Have you ever been?" I asked.

"No." His face was open and guileless. "I've never known the need."

It had been a foolish question; I couldn't imagine why he would. I had known Hugues since I was a boy, and I'd never known him to say an unkind word. I wondered what it would be like to be him, unfailingly patient and kind, always seeing the best in everyone. I tried to look for the good, but I saw the bad, too. The flaws, the fault-lines. I was of Kushiel's lineage and it was our gift. My mother's gift, that she had used to exploit others.

But I was Elua's scion, too.

I wondered, did Elua choose his Companions? Nothing in the scriptures says so. They chose him as he wandered the earth; chose to abandon the One God in his heaven to wander at Blessed Elua's side until they made a home here in Terre d'Ange, and then a truer home in the Terre-d'Ange-that-lies-beyond.

He loved them, though. He must have. And if Blessed Elua found somewhat to love in mighty Kushiel, who was once appointed to punish the damned, then mayhap I would, too.

Elua's temples are open places; open to sky and grounded by earth. In the Sanctuary of Elua where I grew up—until I was stolen by slavers—the temple was in a poppy-field. I used to love it there.

I'd never been to one of Kushiel's temples. It was a closed place.

Though it was located in the heart of the City, it sat alone in a walled square. There were no businesses surrounding it; no shops, no taverns, no markets. The building was clad in travertine marble, a muted honey-colored hue.

"Funny," Hugues mused. "I'd expected it to be darker."

"So did I," I murmured.

The gate was unlocked and there was no keeper. We passed beyond it into the courtyard, hoofbeats echoing against the walls. I thought about the wide walls of Lucca, so vast that oak trees grew atop them. A young man in black robes emerged from the stables.

"Be welcome," he said, bowing.

We gave our mounts over into his keeping. I watched the Bastard accept his lead without protest, pacing docilely into the stable, and thought once more about the Sanctuary of Elua and an acolyte I had known there.

Hugues nudged me. "This way."

The stairs leading to the entrance were steep and narrow. The tall doors were clad in bronze and worked with a relief of intertwining keys. It was said Kushiel once held the keys to the gates of hell. House Shahrizai takes its emblem from the same motif. The door-knocker was a simple bronze ring, unadorned. I grasped it and knocked for entrance.

The door was opened by another black-robed figure: a priest, his face covered by a bronze mask that rendered his features stern and anonymous. Or hers; it was almost impossible to tell. The sight made me shiver a little. He—or she—beckoned without speaking, and we stepped into the foyer. He waited, gazing at us through the eye-holes of his mask.

"I am here to offer penance," I said. Save for a pair of marble benches, the foyer was empty of all adornment and my voice echoed in the space.

The priest inclined his head and indicated the benches to Hugues, who took a seat, then beckoned once more to me. I followed, glancing back once at Hugues. He looked worried and forlorn, his wide shoulders hunched.

I followed the black-clad figure, studying the movement of the body beneath the flowing robes, the sway of the hips. A woman, I thought. I wasn't sure if it made me more or less uneasy. She led me through another set of doors, down a set of hallways to the baths of purification.

Although I'd never gone, I knew the rituals. I'd asked Phèdre about it once. It used to bother me that she went, betimes. I was fearful of the violent catharsis she found in it. The dark mirror, Mavros would say.

And now I sought it.

The baths were stark and plain. Light poured in from high, narrow windows. There was a pool of white marble, heated by a hypocaust. The water shimmered, curls of steam rising in the sunlight. The priestess pointed at the pool.

"Do you know who I am?" I asked her.

She tilted her head. Sunlight glanced from the mask's bronze cheek. In the shadows of its eye-holes, I could make out human eyes. The bronze lips were parted to allow breath. I thought she would speak, but she didn't answer, merely pointed once more.

I unbuckled my sword-belt, pulled off my boots, and stripped out of my clothing, piling it on a stool, then stepped into the pool. It was hot, almost hot enough to scald, and yet I found myself shivering.

"Kneel."

A woman's voice, soft and sibilant, emerging from between the bronze lips. I knelt, sinking shoulder-deep in the hot water. It smelled vaguely of sulfur. She took up a simple wooden bucket, dipping it into the pool. I closed my eyes as she poured it over my head in a near-scalding cascade; once, twice, thrice. When no more water came, I loosed the breath I'd been holding and opened my eyes.

The priestess beckoned.

I clambered out of the pool, naked and dripping. Water puddled on the marble floor. She handed me a linen bath-sheet. I dried myself and looked about for a robe, but she pointed at my piled clothing.

"Seems a bit foolish," I muttered. She said nothing, so I put on my clothes and followed as she led me out of the baths, feeling damp and anxious.

We entered a broad hallway with a high ceiling and another pair of massive, bronze-clad doors at the end of it. The temple proper. The doors clanged like bells as they opened. My mouth was dry.

Kushiel's inner sanctum.

All I could see at first was the effigy. It towered in the room, filling the space. I wondered how they'd gotten it through the doors, then realized the entire temple must have been built around it. His arms were crossed on his breast, his hands gripping his rod and flail. His distant face was stern and calm and beautiful, the same visage echoed in the mask of the priestess who led me, and those of the priests who awaited us.

One held a flogger.

I couldn't help it, my throat tightened. At the base of the effigy was the altar-fire. A few tendrils of smoke arose. The stone walls of the temple were blackened with old soot. The flagstones were scrubbed clean, though. Especially those before Kushiel's effigy, where the wooden whipping-post stood.

"Damn it!" I whispered, feeling the sting of tears. I thought about Gilot. No more tears, I'd promised him when we set out for Tiberium. Impatient at myself, I strode forward. I made an offering of gold and took up a handful of incense, casting it on the brazier.

Fragrant smoke billowed. I'd offered incense to Kushiel in the ambassadress' garden in Tiberium; spikenard and mastic. This was different. This was *his* place.

A bronze mask swam before me. A priest, a tall man. He bent his head toward me. "Is it your will to offer penance?"

"Yes, lord priest." I blinked my stinging eyes, rubbing at them with the heel of one hand. "Do you know who I am?"

"Yes."

A single word; a single syllable. And yet there was knowledge and compassion in it. Behind the eye-holes of his mask, his gaze was unwavering. The decision was mine.

I spread my arms. "So."

Hands undressed me; unfastening my cloak, unbuckling my swordbelt. Anonymous hands belonging to faceless figures. Piece by piece, they stripped away my clothing, until I was naked and shivering in their black-robed midst. A heavy hand on my shoulder, forcing me to my knees. I knelt on the scrubbed flagstones.

Hands grasped my wrists, stretching my arms above my head. I willed myself not to struggle as they lashed rawhide around my wrists, binding them tight to the ring atop the whipping-post. The incense was so thick I could taste it on my tongue, mingled with the memory of stagnant water, rot, and decay.

The chastiser stepped forward, his bronze-masked face calm and implacable. He held forth the flogger in both hands, offering it like a sacrament. It was no toy intended for violent pleasure, no teasing implement of soft deerskin. The braided leather glinted and metal gleamed at its tips. It was meant to hurt.

My teeth were chattering. All I could do was nod.

He nodded in acknowledgment and stepped behind me.

I braced myself.

Ah, Elua! The first blow was hard and fast, dealt by an expert hand. White-hot pain burst across the expanse of my naked back. I jerked hard against my restraints, feeling my sinews strain near unto cracking. Again and again and again it fell, and I found myself wild with panic, struggling to escape. I flung myself against the coarse wood of the whipping-post, worrying at it with my fingernails. And still the flogger fell, over and over.

I saw Daršanga.

Dead women, dead boys. The Mahrkagir's mad eyes, wide with glee.

Phèdre, filled with the Name of God.

Brightness.

Darkness.

All of the dead, my dead. Daršanga, Lucca. Everyone's dead.

Kushiel's face, wreathed in smoke.

"Enough." The tall priest raised his hand. I had ceased to struggle, going limp in my bonds. On my knees, aching in every part, I squinted up at him. "Make now your confession."

I craned my neck. "I'm sorry," I whispered. "And I will try to be good."

There was a pause; a small silence. I let my head loll. From the corner of my eye, I saw the tall priest gesture. There was the soft sound of a dipper sinking into water, and then another voice spoke. "Be free of it."

A draught of saltwater was poured over my wounds. I rested my bowed head in the crook of my elbows, sighing at the pain of it.

It was done, then. My penance was made. The anonymous hands untied my wrists and helped me to stand. Patted dry my lacerated back, helped me to dress. Though I stood on wavering feet, strangely, I felt calm and purged.

"So." The tall priest regarded me. "Is it well done, Kushiel's scion?"

If I had wished it, I thought, he would have spoken to me as a man, mortal to mortal, both of us grasping with imperfect hands at the will of the gods. I didn't, though. I bowed to him instead, feeling the fabric of my shirt rasp over my wounded flesh. It was a familiar feeling. I'd known it well, once. This was different. I had chosen it.

"It is well done, my lord priest," I said.

He nodded a final time. "Go, then."

Hugues leapt to his feet when I entered the foyer. "Are you . . . how are you?"

I ran my tongue over my teeth, thinking. I could taste blood where I'd bitten the inside of my cheek, and the lingering taste of incense. Nothing else. I hurt, but no worse than I'd hurt after a rough training session with Barbarus squadron. The weals would fade. And I wasn't scared inside. "I'm fine," I said, surprised to discover it was true. I smiled at Hugues. "Come on, let's go."

THREE

SOME DAYS AFTER MY visit to Kushiel's temple, the Queen threw a fête to celebrate my return to the City of Elua.

It was a small affair as such matters went. Given free rein, she would have thrown a larger one—and I daresay Phèdre would gladly have aided her—but I had left the City under a lingering cloud of suspicion and recrimination, and as glad as I was to be among my loved ones, my return was tainted by what had gone before. I preferred a smaller engagement.

Duc Barquiel L'Envers would not be in attendance, which was good. My unwelcome nemesis was the Queen's uncle on her mother's side. The plot he had conceived against me had been simple and effective. A mysterious messenger, a whispered password, a note indicating a clandestine meeting. That was all it had taken to convince far, far too many peers that Melisande Shahrizai's son plotted treason, including some I counted as friends. Some of them had apologized after the Queen publicly proclaimed my innocence.

Others had not.

Bertran de Trevalion was one of those, and despite my wishes, he would be attending. I'd greeted him civilly upon my return. I was glad to know he'd been ignorant of his mother's intrigues, and I'd made my uneasy truce with her. Still, I'd rather not have to be polite to them at the dinner table just yet. Being targeted for murder had that effect.

"I'd truly prefer it if House Trevalion wasn't in attendance," I said to Phèdre.

"I know, love." There was a slight furrow between her brows.

"Believe me, so would I, and Joscelin, too. But there are blood-ties between House Trevalion and Courcel, and other ties, as well. You know how Ysandre can be about such such things. This is the price of the choice you made, and unless you wish to change your mind, you'll have to bear it."

I shook my head. "I made a promise."

I'd made my choice, in part, because of the Queen. Ysandre de la Courcel, the product of a contentious marriage and inheritor of a throne plagued by treachery, had a fierce determination to heal old wounds and unite the members of her family in harmony. It had not, however, extended to holding her uncle accountable for his actions in the public milieu. It still galled me, and all the more after learning that Bernadette de Trevalion had tried to have me killed because of it. Somehow, I blamed him more than I did her.

"At least Maslin de Lombelon won't be there," Phèdre commented.

"He's still in disgrace?" I asked. She nodded. "Why did he do it, anyway?"

Maslin de Lombelon was a minor lordling because I'd made him one. I'd given him an estate, Lombelon; the smallest of my holdings. I'd done it because I knew he loved it, and I thought we understood each other, at least a little bit. His father had been a traitor, too. I'd been wrong. He'd left Lombelon to enlist in the Queen's Guard, where he glared daggers at me at every opportunity and later disgraced himself by administering a beating to one Raul L'Envers y Aragon, who was also distant kin to the Queen.

Betimes, returning to the City made my head ache.

"Raul challenged him," Phèdre said dryly. "Maslin carried it too far."

The first time I'd seen Maslin, he'd been attacking pear trees with a pruning hook. I wouldn't have cared to cross him then, and that was before he learned to wield a sword. By all accounts, he was very, very good. And for some obscure reason, my cousin Sidonie was fond of him. Even before I left, there were rumors they were lovers and that she'd promised him the captainship of her Guard one day.

"I wonder why," I mused.

Phèdre shrugged. "Some slight Maslin offered to Colette Trente. An ungentle rebuff, mayhap. Lord Amaury was angry, too."

"Hmm." I tried to peer at the wax tablet on which she was scratching a list. "So no Maslin, which is all to the good. Who else is attending?"

"You'll see." She covered it with one hand and smiled at me, one of those heart-stopping smiles that no poet could hope to describe. "There's a surprise, somewhat I didn't tell you in letters. You'll like it," she added when I looked dubious.

"Will I?"

Phèdre nodded, her eyes sparkling. She was still in the prime of her beauty, and when she smiled like that, she scarce looked older than Claudia Fulvia, whose husband I had so thoroughly cuckolded in Tiberium. "Don't you trust me?"

I smiled back at her. "Always."

It was true. There were only two people in the world I would trust with my life and beyond. If I were standing on the edge of a cliff and Phèdre or Joscelin bade me close my eyes and step off it, I would do it. It was why I struggled so with my feelings.

"What about . . . the other matter?" I asked.

"The Unseen Guild?" Phèdre lowered her voice, glancing at the door of her study. I rose and closed it. "I've not had time yet. But I found the reference to the blind healer's notation you mentioned. I was thinking of asking Ti-Philippe to make a discreet inquiry at the Academy of Medicine in Marsilikos. They should have a copy in their archives."

That was the other thing I'd learned in Tiberium; that games of power and influence were played out across the face of the earth by a hidden consortium of players. I'd been recruited to be a part of it, a choice I had refused. I wasn't entirely sure of the extent of their influence, nor was Phèdre.

But whatever it was, my mother was a part of it.

"Do you think it's safe?" I asked.

The frown-lines were back between her brows. "Nothing's certain. But all the world knows I keep a vast and extensive library. There's naught anyone should find amiss in one of my retainers seeking to add to it. And Ti-Philippe's not a green lad, he knows what he's about, even if he needn't know why."

"True." The healing welts on my back were itching. I worked my shoulders, feeling the scabs tug and crack. Phèdre's expression changed, touched with rue. "What?" I asked.

"Ah, love!" She shook her head. "'Tis nothing, only that you've grown so. I remember worrying, after Daršanga . . . you were so small, so thin. Bird-boned."

"Not anymore," I said lightly.

"No," she agreed. "Not anymore."

We were silent a moment. We had been victims together in that place, that dark place. We understood each other. But Phèdre had entered it willingly, knowing what she would face. It was worse, I think, than she could have guessed; but she endured it and survived. And after my visit to Kushiel's temple, I understood us both more than I had before. His mercy was harsh, but it was not without purpose.

"Well." I leaned down to kiss her cheek. "I look forward to my surprise."

The days passed swiftly. I spent long hours sparring with Joscelin, feeling my skills return. Betimes I set aside the trappings of the Cassiline style and sparred with him using a sword and buckler, the way old Gallus Tadius had insisted we train. I surprised him a few times, too. Gallus had made a passable soldier out of me.

I began brushing up on my Cruithne.

I spoke the Alban tongue well enough, but I wanted to be fluent beyond reproach. Come spring, Drustan mab Necthana would set sail to Terre d'Ange, bringing my Alban bride. We would be wed in the summer, Dorelei and I. And when the Cruarch of Alba set sail in the fall, I would go with them. I would leave behind Terre d'Ange to become a Prince of Alba and beget heirs to a foreign kingdom.

All my days, I thought, would pass swiftly until then.

I spent time in the salon of Favrielle nó Eglantine, Phèdre's terminally ungrateful couturiere. I'd travelled light to Tiberium, and most of what I'd brought back with me was unsalvageable. The clothing I'd returned to was ill-fitting now. I'd put on muscle through the shoulders and I'd lost weight elsewhere due to short rations. Despite Eugènie's best efforts to fatten me, I remained leaner than I'd been.

So it was that I attended my own fête in smart new attire: a sleeved velvet doublet and breeches of Courcel blue, a deep midnight hue. The doublet was adorned with silver stitching and the buttons were silver with an impress of lilies on them, which I thought was a bit much. It was open at the throat, revealing the pointed collars of the white cambric shirt beneath, lace protruding at the sleeves.

At the fête, Alais gasped to see me, clasping her hands together. "Oh, Imri! You look so—"

"Silly?" I suggested, offering her my arm.

"No." Her small, dark face was very serious. "You look beautiful."

It was a beautiful gathering; we D'Angelines are a pretty folk, as my friend Eamonn was wont to say, conveniently forgetting that he was half D'Angeline himself. I wished he was here with me, but he was off on a quest of his own, pursuing the Skaldic bride he'd wed and lost, taken away by her disapproving kindred.

The fête was held in one of the Palace's smaller banquet halls, with no more than a few dozen peers in attendance. At one end, a long dining table was laid with white linens and gilded plates, awaiting our pleasure. At the other end, where people were milling and talking, a fire roared in the tall hearth and there were couches set about for sitting and conversing.

I paid my respects to Queen Ysandre, who was holding court before the hearth. She waved off my bow and rose to give me the kiss of greeting.

"Well met, young cousin," she said with a smile. "Tonight we rejoice to have you home and safe."

"My thanks, my lady," I said politely.

Ysandre de la Courcel was tall and slender, with an elegant, clean-cut profile that looked well on the side of a coin. Alais looked nothing like her, except for the violet hue of her eyes. I wondered where Sidonie was. I hadn't seen her yet.

Phèdre and Joscelin were following in our wake, and I moved aside to let them greet the Queen, marking how Ysandre relaxed in their presence, her demeanor warming. I had been taught to observe such things.

"Imriel de la Courcel!" a light voice remarked. I turned to see Julien Trente. He had been a friend once. He was one of those who had apologized, and I had resolved to set my lingering resentment aside.

"Julien." I clasped his hand. "How goes the Game of Courtship?"

"Well enough." He studied my face. "*You've* been having adventures, I hear. Will we be hearing tales of derring-do tonight, I hope?"

"I hope not," I said.

"Such false modesty!" Another voice, warm and teasing. Mavros Shahrizai slid an arm over my shoulders. "It's unbecoming, cousin." He gave me an affectionate squeeze, then greeted Alais with a deep bow. "Well met, your highness. I'll wager you know a few of our reticent prince's secrets, don't you? Imriel's often spoken of your friendship."

Alais glowed under his attention. It made me smile, albeit sadly. Too few of the peers of the realm paid heed to Alais, and now that her betrothal to the Alban prince Talorcan—her Cruithne cousin and the brother of my own bride-to-be—had been announced, I doubted it would change for the better.

"Imriel." Bertran de Trevalion hailed me cautiously. "Well met."

I clasped his hand. "Bertran."

He took a deep breath. "I understand . . . my mother said you had a very good talk the other day and certain matters were made clear. And I'm . . . if I wronged you, I'm sorry for it."

"Yes, we did. And yes, *you* did." I glanced over at at Bernadette. She stood beside her husband Ghislain, who was deep in conversation with Joscelin. They had fought together during the Skaldi invasion. I used to wish I'd been born earlier, in an era that called for heroism. After Lucca, I felt differently. "Thank you, Bertran."

"You're welcome," he mumbled. "I *am* sorry, Imri."

To my relief, he made a hasty retreat. Bernadette looked in my direction once. There was a combination of apprehension and guilt written on her face. I gave her a brief nod of acknowledgment.

"Here, cousin." Mavros slid a goblet of red wine into my hand. "Mayhap this will help remove that look that says you'd rather be elsewhere."

"My thanks." I took a sip and felt the hair on the back of my neck prickle. I glanced over at the door and met Sidonie's eyes as she entered the hall.

"What—?" Mavros followed my gaze. "Ah. Still?"

"No." I shrugged. "It's just . . ."

"An itch begging to be scratched, is it?" he mused. "You've got to watch out for the brittle ones, Imri. It's not always pretty when they break."

"Shut up, please," I muttered.

Mavros raised his hands. "As you wish, your highness."

I liked Mavros, I truly did. Our relationship had been uneasy at first, but I'd come to terms with my Shahrizai kin. House Shahrizai was loyal to family above all else and he'd stood by me without flinching when I was under suspicion. But why on earth I'd told him about my furtive feelings for Sidonie—which I barely understood myself—I cannot fathom.

One of her attendants accompanied her: Amarante of Namarre, whose mother was the head of Naamah's Order. They bowed their heads together, whispering as they strolled.

"Imri!"

I nearly jumped at Phèdre's call. She approached me with a strange woman in tow. I frowned, trying to place her. Not D'Angeline, neither young nor old. There was an olive cast to her skin that could have belonged to any one of half a dozen nations, and her gown was plain and somber, though well-made. Phèdre's face was alight with anticipation.

The woman bowed her head. "Shalom, your highness."

Her accent and the sound of her voice made me think of stars, a vast field of stars, hanging over an endless lake. Habiru. She had greeted me in Habiru. *"Morit?"* I whispered incredulously, dredging the name from my memory.

She smiled. "You remember."

"Name of Elua!" I found myself laughing. "How not?"

I learned that there were a dozen of them, an entire delegation of Sabaeans sent to Terre d'Ange to study among the Yeshuites here; and too, to study D'Angeline theology. Only Morit had been invited to attend the fête tonight, owing to the service she had done us, but Phèdre had met the others.

I forgot about everything else, listening avidly as Morit described the chaos our visit had sown in Saba, a land forgotten by time. It was far away, far south even of distant Jebe-Barkal, and the descendants of the Habiru Tribe of Dân who had lived there for isolated centuries practiced customs that scarce existed elsewhere.

They had not known of Yeshua ben Yosef, whom their brethren elsewhere had acknowledged as the *mashiach*, their savior, after he was slain by the Tiberians.

And of a surety, they had not known of Blessed Elua, who was conceived in Earth's womb, engendered by the mingled blood and tears of Yeshua and Mary of Magdala, who loved him. Earth-begotten Elua, claimed by no god, who made Terre d'Ange his home.

At the time, I'd been too young—and too haunted—to imagine what it must have been like to have all of one's beliefs turned upside down, to learn one's people had moved on to hold new truths, new beliefs. To find that the world was so different. But since then, I'd stood atop a building in flooded Lucca and watched Gallus Tadius open a portal onto the underworld and send the floodwaters straight to hell, just as he'd promised.

It must, I imagined, have felt somewhat the same.

"What now?" I asked Morit. "Will your people become Yeshuites, do you think?"

"Or D'Angelines?" She looked thoughtful. "No. I do not think so. But perhaps some Yeshuites will become Habiru again." I wanted to speak more with her, but the call to dine came and she was seated too far away to allow for conversation. "We will speak later," Morit promised. "Lady Phèdre has been very gracious."

I had been given a place of honor next to Sidonie, who sat at her mother's right hand.

"Cousin Imriel," she said in her cool, measured tone. "We're so pleased to have you here with us tonight."

I kissed her proffered cheek. "Are you indeed?"

"Of course." A faint smile curved her lips. Unlike Alais, Sidonie resembled the Queen. The same fair skin, the same fine-cut features.

There was a time she had feared me, and there was a time I had found her unbearable. And then there had come a hunting accident, and I'd flung myself atop her in the woods, thinking to protect her. The danger turned out to be imagined, but in the space of a few heartbeats, everything had changed. Now the danger lay between the two of us.

There was desultory small talk at the table while course after course was served: veal tarts, suckling pig, stewed cabbage and quinces, and more. I applied myself to my food and ate with a good will, conscious of Sidonie's amused gaze.

"Did they not feed you in Tiberium?" she asked.

"In Tiberium, yes." I wiped my mouth with a linen serviette. "In Lucca, no."

"Tell us about Lucca, Imriel." There was a conciliatory note in Bertran de Trevalion's voice. "We're all eager to hear about your heroics."

I gave him a long look. "I survived a siege, that's all. There were no heroics."

Across the table, Alais said, "But what about when you cut off—"

"My lord Bertran." Sidonie's clear voice carried over her sister's. She glanced at her mother, who made a gesture of acquiescence. "My lords and ladies, fear not that you will lack for tales of heroism this evening. In honor of our cousin's safe return, and in honor of our admired Sabaean guest, Gilles Lamiz has composed a new tale, a familiar one from an unfamiliar perspective."

The Queen's Poet entered the hall to a round of applause and bowed deeply. "I am indebted to the Lady Morit for this tale," he said, then began.

"My thanks," I whispered to Sidonie.

She nodded without looking at me.

Gilles Lamiz told the story of how Phèdre and Joscelin and I had gone to Saba, seeking the Name of God. Only this time, he told it from the perspective of the Sabaean women; how they had marveled at the news we brought, how they had debated whether or not our appearance among them was an omen. How they had decided among themselves to aid us, and Morit had taught us to read the stars and chart a course across the Lake of Tears to find the hidden temple.

I rubbed my palms, remembering the blisters. We had rowed for hours that night, hours and hours. Mostly Joscelin, but Phèdre and I had taken turns, too.

He didn't tell the part about the temple and what had transpired there. No one truly knew except Phèdre and the tongueless priest who tended it. But he told of our return, and how the light had shown from her face and the Sabaeans had known that the Covenant of Wisdom was restored.

"Thus did the words of Moishe bear fruit, a fruit at once wondrous and bitter, for we were restored in the world, though a stranger led the way; and yet did he not bid us to aid the stranger among us? For we were strangers ourselves in the land of the Pharaohs, and their hearts are known to us," he concluded.

The applause that followed was thoughtful, and I was glad to hear it. D'Angelines are a proud folk, but we can be insular. It was brought home to me in Caerdicca Unitas that we think too seldom about our role in the broader world.

That has changed under Ysandre's rule, but change comes slow. There are still those who look askance at Sidonie and mutter about a Pictish half-breed heir.

I stole a glance at her, thinking about the unfettered laughter she had loosed in the woods. It was the only time, I think, I had truly heard her laugh. Brittle, Mavros said. I didn't believe it.

She raised her brows slightly. They were a burnished gold, almost bronze; darker than her hair. The same shape as mine, the same shape I'd seen in my father's portrait. Cruithne eyes, Pictish eyes, black and unreadable. I could read most people's eyes. But my sixteen-year-old cousin had been raised from birth to inherit a nation and keep her thoughts to herself, and I could not read hers.

"Did you like it?" she asked.

"Very much," I said.

Her smile came and went. Dark currents, stirring. "I'm glad."

Ysandre ended the dinner with a pretty speech welcoming me home and reaffirming her gratitude for my decision to wed Dorelei mab Breidaia and ensure a peaceable succession in matrilineal Alba. I made a little speech of thanks, which Phèdre had insisted I prepare. And then cordial was served and we were given leave to depart or mingle, according to our pleasure.

We stayed, of course. I was the guest of honor and it would have been an insult to leave before the Queen did, and she was still conversing. Morit left, and the members of House Trevalion, too; as early as protocol would allow. For that, I was grateful.

Alais and Sidonie left. I watched them go, Sidonie holding her younger sister's hand. Her lady-in-waiting went with them.

"Ye gods!" Mavros flung himself down on the couch beside me. "My bollocks ache. I'd like to get that priestess' daughter alone in a room for a few hours."

"You waste your time, my friend," Julien Trente advised him, leaning against the couch. "She's loyal to the Dauphine."

Mavros gave him a slow, smoldering look. "Well, I'd not mind trying." He slapped my knee. "Come, Imri! Let's take ourselves off to the Night Court and ease our aches with Naamah's sweet succor." He gauged my expression. "Not Valerian House, no fear. I've somewhat lighter in mind."

"You go." I nodded at Ysandre. "I'm honor-bound."

"What of you, young lord Trente?" Mavros cocked a brow at him.

Julien blushed. "I'm game."

"Good." Mavros swung himself upright. He gazed down at me with an odd mixture of predatory affection and concern. "Next time, mayhap?"

Come spring, my bride would arrive. Come summer, I'd be wed. And come fall, I'd depart Terre d'Ange for Alba, a country still wild and half civilized. I didn't fear it. Already, I'd travelled farther in my life; much farther. But I was D'Angeline, and the blood of Blessed Elua and Kushiel ran in my veins. However damaged I might be, even a stunted tree may seek the sunlight. And in Terre d'Ange, that meant love in all its forms.

Whatever lay between Sidonie and me, it was not to be. It was a foolish infatuation, the lure of the forbidden. Nothing more.

And I wanted more.

So much more.

"Next time," I promised. I stretched out my hands, warming them at the hearth. I thought about Claudia Fulvia, who had driven me half mad with desire in Tiberium. I thought about her brother, too; Lucius, who had kissed me on the eve of battle. And I thought about Emmeline nó Balm who had been my first, and all the girls and women I'd known, and Jeanne de Mereliot, who had welcomed me home with love and healing. "All of them," I said recklessly. "All the Houses of the Night Court. I want to visit them all ere I'm wed."

Mavros grinned. "*All* of them?"

"Well." With the weals of my visit to Kushiel's temple still healing, I amended my boast. "All save one."

FOUR

IN THE WEEKS THAT FOLLOWED, the good news was that Bernadette de Trevalion made an unexpected decision to return to Azzalle for the winter, taking her son Bertran with her. I didn't blame her, though I wondered what she told Bertran and Ghislain. Once they had gone, it seemed easer to breathe at the Palace.

The bad news was that I spent less time than I might have wished in the Houses of the Night Court, and a good deal more immersed in foreign cultures.

One, of course, was Alba's.

The matter of succession in Alba had been a point of contention for as long as I could remember. Now, at last, it was settled in a manner pleasing to everyone. In accordance with matrilineal tradition, Drustan mab Necthana had named his nephew Talorcan his heir. I was to wed Dorelei, Talorcan's sister, and our children in turn would be named Talorcan's heirs.

And Alais had consented to wed Talorcan to satisfy the demands of concerned peers that Terre d'Ange might wield influence in Alba in every generation. Although she would not rule nor her children inherit, one day she would be a Cruarch's wife.

Since the agreement was made, Alais had been appointed a Cruithne tutor that she might learn more about the country, and we agreed that I would benefit from taking part in her lessons.

The tutor's name was Firdha, and although she was small, she was imposing. When I first encountered her, she cut a fierce and upright figure, standing in the center of the well-lit study that had once served as the royal nursery. Her iron-grey hair was as thick and coarse as a mare's tail, caught at the nape of her neck by an elaborate pin, and her eyes were like polished black stones. In one hand, she held a golden staff in the likeness of an oak branch.

Behind her back, Alais mouthed the word "bow" at me.

"*Bannaght*, my lady," I said, bowing deeply.

Her black eyes flashed. "Daughter of the Grove."

I straightened. "Your pardon, my lady?"

"Firdha is an *ollamh*," Alais informed me. "A bard of the highest rank. That's the proper greeting. Even my father uses it," she added. "An *ollamh* is the king's equal."

"And my superior, I take it?" I asked. There was the faintest glint of amusement in the bard's eyes. I bowed a second time. "*Bannaght*, Daughter of the Grove."

Firdha inclined her head. "Greetings, Prince."

So my studies began. There were no books, no scrolls. Alba had no written tradition. Everything worth knowing was committed to memory. Firdha had studied for twelve years to gain her rank, and she knew hundreds upon hundreds of tales—a vast history of Alba and Eire, encompassing all manner of lore and law.

The islands were a strange place. Once, I daresay, our people wouldn't have found them so. We share a distant ancestry in common, or at least some of our people do. There were dozens of tribes in Alba, but they reckoned themselves divided roughly into four folks: The Tarbh Cró, or people of the Red Bull; the Fhalair Bàn, the White Horse of Eire; the Eidlach Òr, or Golden Hind of the south; and the Cullach Gorrym, or Black Boar.

Those were the true Cruithne—Drustan's folk, and Firdha's, too. Earth's oldest children, they called themselves. They had borrowed many customs from the others, but they had held the islands first.

"Many thousands of years ago, we followed the Black Boar to the west," Firdha said with a certain satisfaction. "Long before you D'Angelines learned to count time on your fingers, the Cullach Gorrym were in Alba. The Tarbh Cró, the Fhalair Bàn, the Eidlach Òr; they all came later."

Mayhap it was true, but then had come the Master of the Straits and his curse. For almost a thousand years, there was little exchange between the islands and the mainland. Alba and Eire were sealed, and they had grown strange to us. The curse is broken now. It is a lengthy tale, but Phèdre broke it for all time with the Name of God she found in distant Saba. There is still a Master of the Straits—Hyacinthe, who was her childhood friend—but the Straits themselves are open, and he is an ally.

"What of the others?" Alais asked. "Did they come later, too?"

"Others?" The bard's creased eyelids flickered.

"Somewhat I heard my father say once." Alais frowned. "The Mag . . . Maghuin—"

"Hush." Firdha raised one hand. "The folk of Alba are divided into four," she said, repeating her lesson. "And the Cullach Gorrym are eldest among them."

There followed a lengthy tale of how Lug the warrior led his people to follow the mighty Black Boar, and the boar swam the Straits, and the hump of his back was like an island moving toward the setting sun, and Lug and his people built hide boats and covered them with black tar, and followed. And then more, about how Lug stood upon the shore and cast his spear, and where his spear struck, a spring of sweet water bubbled from the earth to form a river, and there Bryn Gorrydum was founded.

It was a fine tale and one of many such as I would hear over the course of the following months, filled with ancient heroes, magical beasts, and sacred springs. I listened to it with pleasure, but with a nagging curiosity at the back of my thoughts, too.

"So who are these *others*?" I asked Alais afterward, when Firdha had departed. "And why didn't she want to speak of them?"

"I don't know." Alais leaned down to scratch Celeste's ears. The wolfhound was lounging at her feet, content to doze in a patch of sunlight. "I remember the name, though. It was Maghuin Dhonn, Brown Bear. That's why I thought mayhap he was talking about a different people, and not just another tribe among the Four Folk."

"What did he say say?"

Alais shook her head. "I couldn't hear, really. He was talking to Talorcan and they were being quiet. When he saw me, they talked of somewhat else." She regarded Celeste, who thumped her tail obligingly. "There's unrest in Alba, you know."

"Still?" I asked lightly. "I thought I'd settled all that."

There was a touch of amused pity in Alais' smile. "Not all of it."

"So tell me."

She shrugged. "Talorcan says it's only old clan feuds and that there's always fighting of that sort in Alba. But Dorelei says there are some who feel Father is too beholden to Terre d'Ange."

"Funny," I said wryly. "That sounds familiar."

"I know." She smiled again, but sadly this time. "Are other countries truly so different, Imri?"

"Yes," I said. "But people aren't." I kissed the top of her head. "Don't worry, Alais. They'll love *you*."

"I hope so," she said softly. "I had a bad dream about a bear, once."

"A true dream?" I asked.

"No," she said. "A nightmare."

"We'll protect you," I said. "Won't we, Celeste?" The wolfhound lifted her head, brown eyes clear in the slanting sunlight. Her tail thumped again, stirring gleaming motes of dust.

"I hope so," Alais repeated.

The time I spent among the Sabaeans and the Yeshuites was more pleasurable. Phèdre had indeed been a gracious hostess, opening her house for a series of salons where they might meet and converse.

There were not as many Yeshuites in the City of Elua as there once were. Their numbers have dwindled during my lifetime as hundreds, then thousands, set forth toward the distant northeast in accordance with a prophecy. Far north, farther even than the farthest reaches of Skaldia. It was the one thing above all others that perplexed the Sabaeans.

"North!" Morit exclaimed. "If this Yeshua was the *mashiach*, why would he send the Children of Yisra-el *north*? Did Moishe toil for forty years in the desert to win our people a berth of snow and ice? I do not believe it."

There were nods and murmurs of agreement from the Sabaeans. It was strange to see Phèdre's household filled with so many somber scholars all at once, when she was wont to entertain more colorful gatherings. It pleased her, though. In deference to their ways, she wore an unadorned gown of brown velvet with a modest neckline, her hair caught in a plain black caul. She still shone, though. I do not believe Phèdre could look drab if she tried.

"I did not say I believe it." Seated cross-legged on the floor, Eleazar ben Enokh spread his hands. His thin face was lively with interest. "There are passages in the Brit Khadasha that suggest it, and there are passages that suggest otherwise."

"Bar Kochba," another of the Yeshuites murmured. " 'And he shall carve out the way before you, and his blades shall shine like a star in his hands.' "

Phèdre and Joscelin exchanged a glance. He touched the hilts of his twin daggers. There was a story there about young Yeshuites he'd taught to fight in the Cassiline manner. Ti-Philippe told me once. He knew, he'd been there.

"But why *north*?" Morit asked in frustration.

"Yeshua spoke of making a place in cold lands to await his return," Eleazar said to her. "For my part, I believe he spoke in parable, and the place of which he spoke is the wastelands of the human heart. It is there that we must await him."

"You believe he was the *mashiach*?" one of the Sabaean men challenged him.

Eleazar was quiet a moment. He was a mystic, and Phèdre had befriended him many years ago in her long quest to break the curse that bound the Master of the Straits. He had heard the Name of God when she spoke it. "I do," he said slowly. "For I have found beauty and goodness in his words, and the promise of salvation. And yet I believe there is much that is hidden to us. What is it, this thing we call *salvation*? Who are we to discern the will of Adonai?"

"So." Morit smiled. "We are not so different, perhaps."

"No." He smiled back at her. "Not so different."

It was true, what I'd said to Alais.

True, and not true.

They debated this and many things. I liked listening to them. It was much like the conversations we had in Tiberium under Master Piero's guidance, seeking to define the nature of salvation, of goodness, of justice. Only they spoke in Habiru, not Caerdicci, and I stayed quiet and listened as best I could.

"What of this *Elua*?" one of the Sabaeans inquired. "You are silent, Lady Phèdre, and yet you alone among us have come closest to touching the mind of Adonai. Do you believe Elua, then, was the *mashiach*? Why do you not speak?"

"It is too big for words," Phèdre said simply. "Ask your own untongued priests, for I can speak of it no more than they can."

Some of them were put out by her refusal, but Eleazar nodded. "You were given a gift," he said. "Gifts do not always come with understanding; or not one to which we may give voice. Is it not so?"

"My thanks," she said. "Yes."

"I'll say it, then." Unexpectedly Joscelin lifted his head. His fair hair gleamed in the lamplight. "Yes," he said firmly. "I believe it. I do not claim it is true for all folk, but for me, at least, Blessed Elua is the *mashiach*."

It surprised me a little, and yet it did not. Alone among Elua's Companions, Cassiel followed Blessed Elua out of a belief that the One God had been wrong to turn his back on his misbegotten son. The Yeshuites called Cassiel the Apostate. They believe he will relent one day and return to the One God's throne, and Elua and his Companions will follow. The Cassiline Brothers believe it, too. But Joscelin had passed through damnation and beyond, and he believed otherwise.

I did, too.

We spoke of it after our guests had left, after a fashion. There was somewhat I'd heard that I'd never asked him about, and I was curious.

"Is it true you nearly converted to Yeshuism?" I asked him.

"Where did you hear that?" Joscelin eyed me.

"Gilot," I said. It was true, although I knew he'd gotten it from Ti-Philippe.

"I thought about it," Joscelin said. "It was a long time ago."

"Why?"

He got up to prod the fire, squatting with effortless grace. His unbound hair curtained his face momentarily. I knew it hid the place on the upper curve of his right ear where a chunk of flesh was missing, taken out by a bandit's arrow by the Great Falls above Saba. "Salvation," he murmured. "What, indeed, does it mean? At the time, I thought I knew. I thought myself in need of it, and the Yeshuites offered it. And all it cost was faith."

"But you didn't," I said.

Joscelin shook his head. "No," he said. "In the end, the cost was too high. I was unwilling to lay love on the altar of faith. Instead, I found my faith in love."

We would have spoken further, but there was a commotion at the door. I thought it was one of our guests returning, but it proved to be Mavros calling on me.

"Name of Elua!" He laughed. "I saw your guests leaving. What a dour lot!" He bowed graciously to Joscelin, which he didn't have to do. "Messire Cassiline."

"Lord Shahrizai." Joscelin inclined his head. He tolerated Mavros, but he had little fondness for any member of House Shahrizai.

"My lady." Mavros' expression changed, and I knew Phèdre had returned.

"Hello, Mavros." She gave him the kiss of greeting with serene composure. A little shiver ran through him as he returned it; I could see the myriad braids of his hair quiver. I could have punched him for it, even though I knew what he was feeling.

"Ah, well." He cleared his throat. "You did promise to come with me, Imri. And I've got both the Trentes in tow, and a fair escort to keep us safe."

My face felt hot. "Where are you bound?"

"Alyssum House." There was a wicked challenge in Mavros' eyes. "I thought we'd follow the alphabet. Do you have a better idea?"

There were Thirteen Houses in the Court of Night-Blooming Flowers, known more familiarly as the Night Court. Each of them catered to a different taste. The patrons of Alyssum House fed their fancies on illusions of modesty. It might not have seemed a titillating notion elsewhere, but D'Angelines were not known for their modesty, and that which is rare is always prized.

I glanced involuntarily at Phèdre.

"Go." She sounded amused. "You'll come to no harm at Alyssum. Go, with my blessing."

I wasted no time in obeying.

The night was cold, but it was warmer in Mavros' carriage. Julien and Colette Trente were there, huddled under fur blankets. As the carriage lurched into motion, Colette squealed and threw herself in my arms.

"Imriel!" She kissed me effusively. "I'm sorry I couldn't attend the fête."

"No matter." Her soft warmth was dizzying. I hugged her, forgetting I'd ever been wroth with the Trentes. "'Tis good to see you."

"And you." She ran her hands appreciatively over my shoulders.

"Oh, it's *Imriel*, now, is it?" Julien inquired. "What will Raul say?"

Colette looked sidelong at him. They were cut of a piece, the children of Lord Amaury Trente, who was one of Queen Ysandre's most trusted nobles: eager, friendly faces, topped by curling brown hair. "He knows who he's wedding. He's half-D'Angeline himself, you know."

"Now, now, my loves." Mavros wagged a lazy finger. "Tonight's for honoring Naamah's pleasures."

"So it is." I set Colette from me, gently but firmly. "You're wedding Raul?"

"I am." She looked defiant. "But he's in Aragonia now. And anyway, it needn't mean—"

I raised my hands. "I know," I said. "Believe me, I do."

Mavros chuckled.

Outside the confines of the carriage, the horses' hooves clopped steadily along the frosted flagstones. I drew back the curtains and peered out. One of the outriders saluted me. We crossed the Aviline River, the hoofbeats sounding hollow over the bridge, and passed soon through the district of Night's Doorstep. All the taverns were alight and lively, and a part of me yearned to tarry there. But we passed onward and began to ascend Mont Nuit.

"So what passed between Raul and Maslin of Lombelon?" I asked Colette. "I heard Maslin gave you insult and Raul challenged him."

"Maslin!" Julien nudged his sister. "Tell him."

"He was rude." She crossed her arms. "Very rude. I merely expressed the thought that I found him appealing in a certain brooding fashion. His response was quite ungracious. Raul took offense on my behalf when I told him. It was all very foolish."

"Mayhap Maslin's interests lay elsewere," Mavros said smoothly. "Mayhap he had an *itch* in need of scratching."

As much as I liked my cousin, betimes I hated him.

"The Dauphine," Julien affirmed. He withdrew a flask of brandy from the inner pocket of his doublet and drank deep before offering it to the rest of us. "Dear Sidonie. That's where Maslin's aspirations lie."

"Oh, Sidonie!" Colette said scornfully. "She wouldn't."

"No?" Mavros tipped the flask and drank. "I heard she did."

"No, no," Julien said drunkenly. "She's got the priestess' daughter. And *she* took her to the Night Court, just as we're going. All very discreet, but that's the rumor *I* heard."

"*What?*" My voice rose.

"Well, what would you have her do?" Mavros' tone was logical, but his eyes gleamed in the dim light of the carriage. "Grant her favors to one of the dueling cocks of the walk that hang about the Court and watch the feuds ensue?" He wagged his finger at me. "Ah no, dear cousin! Our young Dauphine is far too cool-headed to be carried away by passion. If she was of a mind to take a man into her bed—and why shouldn't she?—she'd sooner trust to the discretion of Naamah's Servants."

I glared and snatched the flask from him, swigging brandy.

"Was it Alyssum House?" Colette asked her brother, who opened his mouth to reply.

"No, wait." Mavros forestalled him. "Let me guess." He tilted his head back and pursed his lips in thought. "Not Dahlia," he said. "It's too obvious, isn't it? She's haughty enough as it is, she'd not seek more of the same. No. Camellia, mayhap? Nothing less than perfection should suit a princess. But no, she might not care to be reminded that her lineage renders her less than perfect in the eyes of Camellia House. And I think we've already seen that our Dauphine favors unwavering devotion. So." He narrowed his eyes. "Heliotrope."

Julien shook his head. "Jasmine."

"Jasmine!" Mavros' brows shot upward. "Well, well!"

I laughed softly in the darkness. Among the Thirteen Houses, Jasmine catered to sensuality, pure and simple. Phèdre's mother had been an adept of Jasmine House. Ti-Philippe had once said there were adepts there would leave you limp as a dishrag, half drowned in the sweat of desire.

"Well, well," Mavros repeated.

"It's just a rumor," Julien said. "It may not be true."

I believed it. I had caught a glimpse of what lay beneath Sidonie's surface. It wasn't brittle and it wasn't cool. And I half wished we were headed for Jasmine House. It was a mortifying thought, but I wanted to study the adepts and guess which one she'd chosen, which one bore the memory of her naked skin against his. But then came the sound of one of the outriders answering the gatekeeper's query, and we passed through the gates and arrived at our destination.

Alyssum House had a deep courtyard lined by tall cypress trees. It had twin entrances with high pointed arches, both deeply recessed.

"Which one—" I began to ask. No sooner had the words left my lips than a pair of adepts emerged; a woman, robed and veiled, and a man, clad in a long surcoat with a high collar. He bowed to Colette without meeting her eyes and beckoned her toward the left-hand entrance. She giggled and went with him.

The veiled woman ushered us into the right-hand entrance. I felt at once uneasy and aroused. She led us into a private salon. With a shy gesture, she drew back her veil to bare a lovely face, though her gaze remained averted.

"Be welcome, my lords," she murmured. "I am Agnés Ramel, the Second of Alyssum House." A light flush touched her cheek. "We have all manner of adepts to serve you. You may whisper your desires to me."

I felt a fool when my turn came, bending to whisper into her delicate ear. *I seek a woman.* Surely there was naught out of the ordinary in it, and yet her flush deepened and her eyelids trembled.

Amid hushed apologies, her steward brought the contracts. We all signed them and paid our patron-fees, and one would have thought there was somewhat unnatural in the transaction for all the embarrassment it caused.

"This way," she whispered.

I had been to only two Houses of the Night Court, and they were very different. Here, there was no easy commingling. What Mavros and Julien had chosen, I couldn't say, but I had to await my turn before I was ushered into a room filled with female adepts, standing in a line. All of them were robed and veiled, but the robes they wore were of sheer linen, almost transparent in the lamplight. I could make out the shapes of their bodies; tall, slender, plump, short, firm. At a word from Agnés, they unveiled and stood with eyes downcast.

The remembered odor of stagnant water haunted me. It was too much like the Mahrkagir's zenana, the women awaiting his summons in dread. I did not like the way it stirred me. "I'm sorry," I said thickly. "I fear this is not for me."

Agnés Ramel twisted her hands together in an agony of embarrassment. "My lord, please! Do not be cruel."

Near the end of the line, one of the adepts glanced up at me. A quick glance, swift and darting, and then her gaze was lowered once more.

"All right," I said recklessly, pointing. "Her."

Her name was Mignon, and once I had chosen, she led me to a private chamber. There, I gazed at her. Her limbs beneath the sheer linen were soft and rounded, and she made me think of a dove. She looked away.

"Will you put out the lamps, my lord?" she whispered.

"No," I said. "Mignon, this is a game, is it not?"

"Would you have it be so?" She did look at me then, her eyes full of soft wonder. "No, my lord. There are those among us who believe that Naamah trembled at what she did when first she lay with a mortal man—at the audacity of it, at the shame of it, at the glory of it."

"Shame," I murmured, sitting on the edge of the bed.

"Shame is a spice, my lord," Mignon said softly. "Why have you come here if you do not understand this?"

"Because," I said, "Alyssum starts with an 'A.'"

"Then I will have to show you."

It was not, I think, the way assignations usually went in Alyssum House; or mayhap it was common. I do not know. Mignon sat on my lap and stroked my face, her fingers quivering. She rained soft kisses on me, her breath quickening, and pressed herself against me. Her body trembled in truth, and yet she radiated heat and the tips of her rounded breasts were taut with desire as they rubbed against my chest. She whispered in my ear, telling me in a broken voice all the things she wished me to do to her, until I groaned aloud.

I understood.

There was pleasure in it, and it was a pleasure akin to the violent ones I had known in Valerian House, though it was different, too. I did all that she wished, and all that I wished, too. And yet I could not relish the shame. For her, it was purging. For me, it was not.

When we were finished, she wrapped herself once more in her linen robes. "I'm sorry, my lord. I wish I could have pleased you better."

"Don't be." I leaned down to kiss her, but she turned her head away. "Mignon!" I said her name sharply and she glanced up involuntarily. I smiled at her. "I have learned somewhat about myself this night, and that is a valuable gift. Thank you."

She gave me a shy smile in return. "You are welcome."

Afterward, in the carriage, the other three compared their experiences. Mavros, as usual, was pleased with himself, and the Trentes had found it a great lark.

"Oh, the way he *blushed*!" Colette laughed. "I bade him take off his shirt, and he went red all over. It was sweet. Did yours blush, Julien?"

"I don't know," he admitted. "She begged me to blow out the lamps, and I did."

"Silly boy," Mavros said. "That's part of the fun." He studied me. "And you, Imri? You didn't care for it?"

I shrugged. "Not as much as you did."

My Shahrizai cousin grinned. "That's true of a great many things."

That night I lay awake for a long time, thinking about Alyssum House, wondering what manner of patron went there as a matter of course, whether they went to purge their own shame or to revel in that of the adepts. Whether Naamah appreciated the reverence done to her there. I supposed she must. Desire, like love, takes many forms.

And I thought about Sidonie, too.

Jasmine House. I wondered if it were true. Somehow I didn't doubt it.

Well, well.

FIVE

DIOGENES," I SAID FIRMLY.

Favrielle nó Eglantine clamped her jaw so hard the crooked little scar on her upper lip turned white. "Can you not talk *sense* into him?" she spat at Phèdre.

"Why not Diogenes?" Phèdre replied. "Can we not do a Hellene theme?"

Due to the distraction of Lucca's siege and my uncertain return, we were late in commissioning costumes for the Longest Night; truly late, and not just in terms of Favrielle's reckoning. That wasn't why she was angry, though.

"Rags!" She loaded the word with contempt. "You want me to adorn a Prince of the Blood in *rags*."

"And a lamp," I added.

"Why?" Favrielle demanded of Phèdre.

"I've no idea," she said tranquilly. " 'Tis Imriel's fancy. And after what he's been through in the past year, I'm minded to let him have his way." She paused. "If you're unwilling, we can always go elsewhere . . ."

Favrielle merely glared at her. It was a bluff, but it was one she wouldn't call. It was ever thus between them. In the end, Favrielle conceived of a notion that pleased her well enough. I would portray asceticism in the persona of the Cynic philosopher Diogenes, and Phèdre would portray opulence in the persona of the D'Angeline philosopher Sarielle d'Aubert, who was renowned in her lifetime for travelling with a retinue of attendants prepared to cater to her every whim.

"I reckon that would be me," Ti-Philippe observed.

There was a reason for my choice. The Cynic's lamp was a symbol of the Unseen Guild, and I was minded to serve notice that I knew it. I'd been caught up in my Alban studies and personal affairs, but I hadn't put the Guild altogether out of mind. It would be interesting to see if anyone reacted to the sign of the lamp. There was a risk, but not a great one. The Guild knew I was aware of its existence; they had sought to recruit me in Tiberium through Claudia Fulvia. In the end, I had refused. Still, I was curious to know if it operated within Terre d'Ange.

We hadn't learned much since my return. Ti-Philippe had paid a visit to the Academy of Medicine in Marsilikos and brought back a copy of the system of notation devised by a long-ago priest of Asclepius who lost his vision; a complicated series of notches and strokes intended to be read by touch. Members of the Guild used it for secret communication. My mysterious protector Canis had given me a clay medallion in Tiberium that bore the Cynic's lamp on its face and a hidden message etched on its edges. It was mere chance—and Gilot's ill luck—that had led me to the temple of Asclepius, where a priest told me its meaning.

Do no harm.

The chirurgeon's credo, the Guild's warning. It was Claudia who confessed that it meant a member of the Guild had placed me under his or her protection. The medallion was gone—I'd crushed it to bits in a fit of anger—but I had made a sketch of it, and I intended to have a silversmith craft its likeness.

Exactly why, I couldn't say, except that it was an unresolved mystery. I wanted to *know*. The Guild had done a good job of shrouding itself in secrecy. Like the folk of Alba, they left no written trail. Still, there was a human trail, and one never knew what inadvertent reaction one might provoke.

The same held true for Alba.

I hadn't forgotten about Alais' Maghuin Dhonn. I didn't broach the subject again with Firdha—her withering glare stilled my tongue—but there were other Cruithne in the City of Elua. Not many, truth be told; the Albans preferred their green isle to our white-walled city. Still, there was the honor guard.

Drustan had left half a dozen of his men to serve as Firdha's honor guard while the esteemed *ollamh* tutored his daughter. They were all proven warriors among the Cullach Gorrym, and they made for a striking sight when one came upon them in the Palace, their faces etched with woad tattoos.

I made it a point to seek out their company. At first they were reticent in my presence, until I had the very good idea of convincing them to accompany me to Night's Doorstep. There was a tavern called the Cockerel there, and it had a long history. It was a Tsingani place, mostly, although young D'Angeline nobles still went there to fancy they were living dangerously. There was no danger for me. It was the place where Hyacinthe had told fortunes when he was still the merry young Tsingano half-breed I knew only from stories, and not the fearsome figure I had met. I had told the story of freeing the Master of the Straits from his curse there more times than I could remember. The owner Emile had been his friend, and he would defend to the death any member of Phèdre's household for what she had done.

"My prince!" he roared when we entered. "Our *gadjo* pearl!"

I suffered his embrace, which rivaled Eamonn's for bone-cracking strength. The Cruithne grinned. "Emile," I wheezed. "These are the Cruarch's men."

"Ah!" He let me go and clapped his meaty hands. "Ale! Ale for the Cruarch's men!"

There was ale, then, and a great deal of it. Emile and I toasted to Drustan and then to Hyacinthe, and the Cruithne drank, too. Other toasts followed, and I made a point of offering a toast to Dorelei, my bride-to-be.

"You are a lucky man, you know." Kinadius, the youngest of them, studied me. "You *do* know this, yes?"

"Yes," I said honestly. It was true, in its own way. "I do."

They exchanged glances among themselves. "Few of your countrymen would feel the same," murmured their leader, Urist. He was old enough to have fought at Drustan's side in the war of the Skaldi invasion, and I understood the Cruarch regarded him highly.

I shrugged. "There are always those who fear change. Is it not the same in Alba?"

"A great deal of change has come swiftly to Alba." Urist took a deep draught of ale. "Some think too swiftly, yes."

"The Maghuin Dhonn?" I asked.

Kinadius, startled, dropped his tankard. Several of the Cruithne cursed and leapt up to avoid the spreading pool of ale, and a barkeep hurried over with a rag. Urist folded his arms and stared at me. His features were hard to discern in the intricate patterns of blue woad that made a mask of his face, but his eyes were as black as stones. "What do you know of them?"

"Only the name."

"It's ill luck to speak it." Kinadius shivered.

"Why?" I asked.

"Because they did a very bad thing long ago, and brought shame upon themselves and upon Alba." Urist's unblinking eyes held mine. "We do not speak of it. We do not speak of them."

"The *ollamh* refused to, but the Cruarch spoke of them," I said. "To Talorcan."

They exchanged another round of glances. "The Cruarch has a country to rule," Urist said firmly, "and Talorcan is his heir. There are matters that must be addressed. But among ourselves, we do not speak of them."

"The bear-witches still have the power to curse," Kinadius muttered. "At least the women do. Shrivel your loins, they will."

"Or make 'em burn," another offered. Someone laughed.

"Aye, and change shape in the middle of the act and devour you whole!" Deordivus poked a finger at me. "Starting with your manhood. You stay away from 'em, Prince."

Another jug of ale arrived, and with it came Emile to ply me to tell him about the siege of Lucca. So the conversation turned, and I was obliged to tell the tale. The Cruithne had not heard it—I had not spoken overmuch of it in public—and they listened with interest as I told of arriving in the city of Lucca to celebrate the wedding of my friend Lucius Tadius, only to find the bride kidnapped and, within a day, the city besieged by her captor.

They nodded when I described how Lucius came to be inhabited by the spirit of his dead great-grandfather, the warlord Gallus Tadius, who organized the defense of the city. Such tales were not strange in Alba, where a woman might eat of a salmon and give birth to a bard.

When it came to the battle, I made much of Eamonn's role. In truth, it needed no exaggeration—Gallus Tadius had appointed him the captain of our squadron, and Eamonn had acquitted himself with honor. But he was a prince of the Dalriada, of the folk of the Fhalair Bàn, and it pleased the Cruithne to hear it. The Dalriada were a sovereign folk unto themselves, immigrants from the island of Eire who maintained a foothold on the far western shores of Alba, but there was a long history of alliance between the Cruithne and the Dalriada.

They were pleased by my deeds, too. "You're not so green as I reckoned!" Deordivus slapped my shoulder. "You're owed your first warrior's markings, Prince. Or at least once you're wed and dedicated as one of us."

"Oh?" I said.

"Right here." Kinadius touched the center of his brow, which bore an elaborate design of an inverted crescent containing trefoil circles, pierced from below by a V-shaped symbol. "The warrior's shield and spear."

"Ah, no!" I gazed at him in dismay.

"Do you not wish to declare kinship with the Cullach Gorrym?" He grinned. "They'll look a treat with your big blue eyes."

"You *are* jesting?" I asked.

They laughed. "Not really," Urist added.

"I'll think on it," I muttered, and beckoned for more ale.

At any rate, the evening ended amicably and they seemed to like me better for it by the time it was over. We rode back toward the Palace together, and Deordivus began teaching me the rudiments of a Cruithne drinking-song. When I made to part company with them and head for the townhouse, Kinadius insisted on escorting me.

"Drustan would expect us to do it for Talorcan," he said to Urist. "If Imriel is to be a Prince of Alba, should we not treat him as one?"

The older man's face was unreadable in the starlight. "As you will."

"Come, then." Kinadius blew out his breath in a plume of frost and gave me a sidelong look. "Let's race. Unless you're scared?"

"Care to wager?" I asked.

It wasn't a wild race. I'd done that once with Gilot and nearly run down a party of merry-makers, and it was early enough that folk were still abroad, torch-escorted carriages clopping along the streets. We rode vigorously, though, weaving in and out among them. I kept the Bastard well in hand. He was quick and surefooted and fearless, and I'd ridden him almost blind in the darkest nights of Lucca. I could have won handily, but I was mindful of what Phèdre had taught me of diplomacy, and I let Kinadius draw abreast of us at the end.

"Well run!" he said cheerfully. "At least Dorelei's wedding a man knows how to sit a horse."

"You're fond of her," I said.

Kinadius nodded. "We grew up in the same household. I'd thought to court her myself one day."

I didn't know what to say, so I said, "I'm sorry."

"Ah, no!" He shook his head. "'Tis for the best, and those of us who are the Cruarch's men know it. I bear you no ill will."

"My thanks." I put out my hand.

He clasped it firmly. "You'll be mindful of what we said tonight?"

"About the warrior's markings?" I grimaced. "Oh, yes."

"Not that." Kinadius smiled, but only faintly. "I was jesting, you know. Urist holds to the old ways more than some of us. No, I meant the other thing." He squeezed my hand, cutting me off when I opened my mouth, then leaned over in the saddle, speaking in a low tone. "They sacrificed their *diadh-anam*. That's why the *ollamh* will not speak of them."

"Their *what*?" I asked, bewildered.

He let go my hand and placed two fingers over his lips, shaking his head once more. "I've said too much. Ill luck. Good night, Prince!"

I watched him take his leave, then shouted for Benoit to open the gate. He came out grumbling and sleepy-eyed to admit me, then led the Bastard into the stables. I went inside the townhouse and found Phèdre still awake in her study.

"Hello, love." She set a paperweight on the scroll she was studying and lifted her chin when I leaned down to kiss her cheek. "You smell like the bottom of an ale-barrel. Did you learn aught tonight?"

"Mayhap." I sat cross-legged at her feet. "What's a *diadh-anam*?"

Phèdre's beautiful lips moved soundlessly, shaping the word. I gazed up at her face and watched her search her memory. She had studied Cruithne as a child, long before it was commonplace in Terre d'Ange. Anafiel Delaunay, who had been her lord and master, had taught her. As it transpired, he'd been a man much ahead of his time. "God-soul?" she hazarded at length. "I don't know, love; it's not a word I've heard before. Why?"

"Because whatever it is, the Maghuin Dhonn sacrificed theirs," I said. "Phèdre . . . I'm not so sure what I've gotten myself into with Alba."

"Nor am I," she said softly. "But we will find out."

I leaned my head on her knee, as I had done since I was a child. She stroked my hair with gentle fingers. It wasn't the same; it never would be. But it was enough, and I could endure it.

"I don't want to leave you," I whispered.

"I know." Her voice broke. "Imri—"

I bowed my head, resting my brow on one upbent knee. Unwanted desires racked me; my own, the echo of my mother's words. "You know I have to?"

"Yes."

It was implicit; there was a compact between us. I could not stay in this place. I had debts of honor to fulfill and desires that would never be sated. The kind of love with which the gods had blessed Phèdre and Joscelin wasn't destined to be mine. But if I couldn't be happy, truly happy, I could at least try to be *good*. I sighed, straightened, and stood. "Tell me what you learn?"

"Always." Phèdre's dark eyes were grave. "And you?"

"Yes," I promised. "Always."

SIX

"BEHOLD!" MAVROS FLUNG UP his arms. "Bryony House."
Even from the courtyard, it stood in marked contrast to Alyssum. It was a grand structure, three stories high, with steep gables. Every window was ablaze with light, and the mullions were adorned with ornate reliefs of bryony vine. When the door opened, laughter and music and the rattle of dice spilled out.

We were ushered into the receiving salon, which was modeled after the Hall of Games in the Palace. A throng of D'Angeline nobles played at games of chance and skill—dice, cards, rhythmomachy, and other, more obscure games. The atmosphere was sharp and charged.

"Lord Mavros!" A tall woman with black hair piled in a high coronet greeted us with a curtsy. Her black gown was cut low in the back, showing off her marque. Delicate tendrils of bryony climbed her spine, sprouting pale flowers above the spade-shaped leaves. "It's been too long." She straightened and appraised me with unabashedly calculating eyes. "Prince Imriel. Welcome to Bryony, your highness."

"Imri, this is the Dowayne, Janelle nó Bryony," Mavros said. "Watch your purse."

She tapped his arm with a folded fan. "Never wager what you can't afford to lose, for Naamah will take all you have and more. What are you after, you naughty child?"

Mavros smiled lazily. "Tokens."

On the Longest Night, there are two fêtes of note in the City of Elua. One was at the Palace, and the other was held at Cereus House, first among the Thirteen. It is a night Naamah's Servants celebrate among themselves, and no one, not even a Prince of the Blood, may attend without a token.

"Is that so?" Her wide mouth curled. "And what do you offer for them?"

Mavros spread his arms. "What would you wager?"

"A challenge!" Janelle nó Bryony flung back her head. "Let's put it to the crowd, shall we?" She gestured toward the corner, and an attendant there struck a massive bronze gong. The sound reverberated and an expectant hush followed. "A challenge!" she repeated. "Lord Mavros Shahrizai and Prince Imriel de la Courcel come begging a wager for tokens! How shall we judge them worthy?"

"Mavros," I muttered under my breath.

He nudged me. "Hush. You wanted this."

True and not true. I had argued that we bypass Balm House, next in the alphabet, for I had already been there and experienced Naamah's healing grace. But I didn't understand what gambit Mavros was playing, and whatever it was, it had me on edge.

Patrons shouted out suggestions, profane and amusing and vile. Janelle nó Bryony listened, nodding, until she heard one that took her fancy echoed a number of times. "The hourglass?" she murmured. "That would suit. Indeed, so well that I'll take the challenge myself. And *I* shall choose the contestant." She pointed at me. "Are you minded to accept, your highness? If you lose, I win a forfeit of my choosing."

"I'm sorry," I said, feeling foolish. "I don't understand."

" 'Tis a simple matter, sweet prince." Janelle stepped close to me, caressing my cheek. Her grey eyes shone. "I seek to please you in the time allotted," she breathed in my ear, making the hair at the nape of my neck stand on end. "And you seek to outwait me. Will you play?"

"Here?" I glanced at the avid crowd. "I think not."

"No, no, I'll not put you on display." She pointed toward the second story, where a specially constructed chamber overhung the balcony, lined with silk curtains. "There."

Behind her, Mavros was shaking his head in warning, looking dubious. Elua knows what he had expected, but it seemed he didn't like the odds of this wager the Dowayne had conceived. But I thought about

Claudia Fulvia and what she had made me endure, and I smiled at Janelle. "All right," I said lightly. "Why not?"

"Oh, *very* good!" Her nails trailed down my throat and over my chest. "Come."

It was something, it seemed, for the Dowayne of Bryony House to take on a challenge personally. She led me up the sweeping staircase while the throng cheered and laid wagers. From what I could hear, none or few of them favored me. We entered the dais chamber, strewn with cushions and hung with fretted lamps. A pair of adepts closed the drapes behind us, and Janelle opened those facing the salon. Below us, the crowd milled.

"Bring the hourglass!" she called.

A bare-chested male adept with the Bryony mark brought forth a tall, slender hourglass capped with silver at both ends and wreathed in trailing vine. The crowd parted to make a space for him.

Janelle nó Bryony raised her hand. "Let it begin!" The adept overturned his hourglass. Sand began to trickle through its narrow neck. Janelle closed the drapes and turned to me, letting her gown slip from her shoulders. Her skin was white in the lamplight, and there was rouge on the nipples of her high, firm breasts. I swallowed at the sight. "You were unwise, sweet prince," she said, her voice soft and mocking. "Have you not heard the first rule of Bryony House's patrons? Never wager against its Dowayne. I will enjoy choosing a forfeit."

I wanted her, badly. But I didn't much like her. I bared my teeth at her in a cold smile. "A Dowayne should gauge her patrons better, my lady."

"Defiance!" One eyebrow arched. "This will be fun."

All of Naamah's Servants are adept in her arts. As the crowd below chanted and clapped to mark the passage of time, Janelle sank gracefully to her knees before me. Her hot breath penetrated through my breeches. My phallus leapt in response, stiffening.

I stared at the draped ceiling.

The Dowayne of Bryony House performed the *languisement* on me. She did it with excruciating skill. I could feel the muscles of her cheeks and throat milking my phallus. I thought of Claudia and nearly lost all control. No. So I did the only thing left to me and thought of Daršanga.

It went on for a long time. The unseen crowd's roar grew louder, clapping turning to stamping. I felt her hands, growing urgent, cupping my testes, squeezing and rolling them; her urgent finger probing my anus. My body went rigid with shock and pleasure, and I overrode it.

"*Duzhmata,*" I whispered. "*Duzhûshta, duzhvarshta.*"

Ill thoughts, ill words, ill deeds.

The gong sounded and the crowd of patrons erupted in cheers, demanding to know the outcome. On her knees, Janelle released me. She bowed her head for a moment, then gazed up at me, and there was no mockery in her face, only puzzlement. "Why are you crying?"

I rubbed away the tears with the heel of my hand. "I told you. You should gauge your patrons better." I pulled up my breeches and fastened them. My arousal had faded, leaving behind a dull, unfulfilled ache. I extended her hand to her, then retrieved her gown. "Here."

She dressed without comment and made to draw back the drapes, then paused. "Tell me, highness. Was the victory worth the cost?"

I thought about it. "Probably not."

Janelle nó Bryony inclined her head. "Well, then."

With that, she opened the drapes and presented me to the shouting throng, sinking low in an elaborate curtsy of acknowledgment and defeat. I looked down at their upturned faces and listened to the sound of my name being chanted. Wagers were settled, coins changing hands. Mavros, his cupped hands overflowing, winked up at me. Janelle fished a pair of ivory tokens from her purse and tossed them to him, and the crowd roared some more before turning to other pursuits and fresh pleasures, fueled by avarice and desire.

Afterward, during the carriage ride homeward, I was quiet. Mavros hummed to himself in contentment, dividing our spoils. "Here." He poured a handful of coins into my lap, making a point of showing me the ivory token. "Mind you don't lose this."

I tucked my share away. "I didn't think you'd wager on me."

"Ah, well." He shrugged. "You're a stubborn one. I know that much about you."

"Too stubborn, mayhap," I mused.

"Mayhap." Mavros considered me. "Imri, listen. I was all for this idea. After two Houses, I'm not so sure. Me, I can find pleasure in anything, but you've got a way of battering yourself to pieces against your own desires."

"You know why," I murmured.

"I do." He nodded. "Some of it, at any rate. But listen, beneath the trappings of pleasure, these are Servants of Naamah, sworn to her service. When we indulge ourselves in the Night Court, we make reverence to Naamah in the ways we like best. When you choose instead to wrestle with your own despite, you do Naamah a disservice."

I looked away, knowing Mavros was right. "What would you have me do?"

"Stop picking at scars," he said laconically. "Scratch the itch."

"Easier said than done," I said.

He shrugged again. "You asked."

I thought about his words in the days that followed, and we didn't visit any more Houses. I went instead to the Temple of Naamah, to make an offering and beg forgiveness lest I had offended. To my surprise and pleasure, Phèdre and Joscelin elected to accompany me.

It was an unpredictable day, with an unseasonable warm breeze blowing. Everywhere in the City, people had exchanged heavy winter garb for lighter attire. Dense clouds scudded across the sky, broken by patches of brilliant blue.

I bought a dove from the vendors outside the temple, carrying it in a gilded cage. The Great Temple of Naamah was a modest place, a round marble building surrounded by gardens. Even in winter, it was green with cypresses and yew trees, filled with the cooing of sacred doves.

"My lady!" The acolyte at the door bowed low at the sight of Phèdre. "We are honored."

Phèdre was one of Naamah's Servants, too, and she has taken it to places farther and more terrible and wondrous, I think, than any adept of the Night Court might dream. It has been many years since Naamah called her to service, but if she did, I daresay Phèdre would answer. But today was not that day. She merely looked calm and peaceful as we entered the temple. I showed the acolyte my dove and told him my desire, and he went to fetch the priest.

"So." Joscelin tilted his head, gazing at the statue of Naamah that stood beneath the oculus at the apex of the dome. "You were dedicated here?"

"Twice," Phèdre agreed. They stood side by side, hands entwined. Naamah's arms were open as though to embrace the world. Her face was soft with compassion and desire, bathed in a shaft of sunlight from above. After a moment, a slow-moving bank of clouds passed overhead, dimming the light. Joscelin laughed softly and shook his head, and I thought about what he had said about being unwilling to lay love on the altar of faith.

"Prince Imriel."

I started at the priest's voice. He stood waiting, hands folded in the sleeves of his scarlet surplice, attended by a pair of acolytes carrying the implements of his office. I guessed him to be around Joscelin's age, although he had the sort of smooth, tranquil features that made it hard to tell. His hair was ash-brown and it fell straight and shining to his waist.

"My lord priest." I approached the altar and knelt, setting down the birdcage. "I come to make an offering."

"Why?"

The priest's eyes were a sooty grey, long-lashed and disconcerting in their openness. I rubbed my palms on my thighs. "Because I fear I may have transgressed unwittingly," I said slowly. "And I wish her grace upon me."

"Do you?" he asked steadily. "It may come at a price."

"I know." I glanced involuntarily at Joscelin. "Yes."

"Then let it be done." The priest took an aspergillum from one of his acolytes and dipped it in a basin of water, flicking me with droplets, then smeared chrism on my brow. "By Naamah's sacred river, be cleansed of all transgressions," he intoned. "By the touch of anointment, be blessed in Naamah's sight." He nodded at me. "Make your offering."

Kneeling, I opened the cage. The dove huddled at the bottom, round eyes wary. I cupped her in my hands, mindful of the fragile bones, the swift-beating heart. "Forgive me," I whispered to her. "I know how it feels."

When I stood and opened my hands, two things happened. The

dove launched herself in frantic flight toward the oculus, and the cloud-bank overhead passed. An unexpected blaze of sunlight once more streamed down upon us, broken only by a wild flurry of beating wings as the dove winged its way free of the temple. I felt my heart soar and laughed aloud for the sheer joy of it.

"Naamah is pleased." The priest's grey eyes crinkled. "Are you?"

"Yes," I said simply.

"Good." He bowed to Phèdre. "Well met, my lady."

She smiled at him. "Do you not remember me, Raphael Murain? Somehow, I'm not surprised to find you here."

The priest laughed. "I didn't think you'd remember *me*."

Something passed between them; a shared memory. Joscelin raised his brows and offered no comment. We took our leave of the temple and lingered for a moment in the gardens outside. I gazed at the roosting doves and tried to guess which one was mine, but they all looked more or less alike.

"I could never tell," Phèdre said, guessing my thoughts.

"It's funny, isn't it?" I mused. "The vendors breed them in order to sell them to supplicants to set them free. And yet, if there were no temple, there would be no need for cages in the first place."

"True," Phèdre agreed. "The will of the gods is strange."

I glanced at her. "Was he a patron?"

"Raphael?" She looked surprised and amused. "Oh, no. *I* was. He was an adept of Gentian House." She laughed at my expression. "Ah, love! It was a long time ago, and I'd need of counsel in the matter of a dream. Speaking of which, I think I've found somewhat that you and Alais might find of interest."

"Oh?" I said. "What?"

"A story about a bear."

When we returned to the townhouse, she showed me. It was in a text by the Tiberian historian Caledonius, who had served as a military tribune in Alba during the uprising of the Cruithne under the leadership of Cinhil Ru. I knew *that* story, of course. Cinhil Ru was the first Cruarch of Alba. He united the multitude of warring tribes and made a pact with the Dalriada. They defeated the Tiberian forces occupying Alba and drove them out, across the Straits, never to return. Drustan mab Necthana was descended from his line; and so, for that matter, were Sidonie and Alais.

This began earlier, though.

It was an account of entertainment gone badly awry. The Governor of Alba had staged public games to keep his men entertained, and bear-baiting was a common sport in those days. Caledonius wrote with enthusiasm of its bloody merits. In this instance, the bear was to be chained in the amphitheatre and pitted against a handful of captive Pictish rebels armed with short spears.

I read about how the bear was the size of three ordinary bears, how it tore the stake to which it was chained from the ground and slaughtered the Picts. How it clambered into the stands and slaughtered scores of spectators, and tore apart the Governor's box with its claws, then took the Governor by the scruff of the neck and shook him like a dog, nearly severing his head. It took Caledonius' men over an hour to slay it, though they shot it so full of arrows it bristled like a pin-cushion.

When it was done, they skinned it, and found a human body inside its pelt.

I shuddered. "Not a pretty tale."

"No," Phèdre said thoughtfully. "The rest is all about Cinhil Ru and the uprising and there's naught in it that's not written elsewhere. Caledonius survived the battles and and the retreat. He spent the rest of his days in a country villa outside Tiberium, eschewing war and politics. And to the end of his life, he had nightmares."

"About the bear?" I asked.

She nodded. "It's all I could find."

I debated whether or not to tell Alais the story. In the end, I decided not to. She'd already had one nightmare, and there was no need to feed her fancy with bloody tales. I thought about asking the *ollamh* about it, too. I daresay Firdha suspected—or mayhap she'd heard I'd been asking her honor guard about the Maghuin Dhonn—for she fixed me with a challenging stare at our next session, black eyes glittering.

"Did you have a question, Prince?" she asked.

I returned her gaze without blinking, until her knuckles whitened where she gripped her gilded oak branch. There were fault-lines. For all her lore, for all the hundreds upon hundreds of tales she knew, one unspoken truth could render so much a lie. I could say so, and humble her with it, earning her enmity in the bargain.

Or I could wait and ask Drustan mab Necthana, whose business it was to speak of such matters. There was no hurry. My wedding was months in the offing, and if the Cruarch truly wished for it to take place, he would deal honestly with me.

"No, Daughter of the Grove." I inclined my head, ceding the victory. "No question."

"Good," she said dryly.

For once, I felt wise.

SEVEN

"NAME OF ELUA!"

The feverish whisper of gossip surged through the crowd assembled in the Palace ballroom on the Longest Night: Sidonie de la Courcel, the Dauphine of Terre d'Ange, had usurped the costume of the Sun Prince.

I laughed aloud when I heard it. It was the last time in years, mayhap, that I would celebrate the Longest Night on D'Angeline soil, and I felt strangely lighthearted. Doubtless some of it was due to my own costume, for there was a certain freedom in being clad in rags—albeit rags of coarse, undyed silk—barefoot and unmasked, my hair unkempt and tangled. It was scandalous in its simplicity, and Favrielle herself had evinced a certain grim satisfaction with it.

But Sidonie had outdone me.

"Is it true?" Phèdre asked Ysandre, her eyes alight with mirth.

"Oh, yes." The Queen laughed. "Don't you think it meet?"

"Why not?" Phèdre raised a glass of cordial. *"Joie!"*

They drank; we all drank. The clear cordial burned a pleasant trail down my throat and made my skull expand. Ti-Philippe shook his head to clear it, and the absurdly unnecessary gilt-fringed parasol he held for Phèdre bobbed dangerously.

I steadied his arm. "Careful, chevalier."

He gave me a lopsided grin. "Found an honest man yet?"

I held my silver lamp aloft. "Still searching."

"Be careful with that, love." Phèdre kissed my cheek. Her gown was a shimmering column of crimson silk, draped with gold netting into which a thousand tiny mirrors were sewn, and she scintillated with every movement, casting myriad points of light around her. Opulence, indeed. It wasn't Favrielle's finest work, but it would serve.

"I will," I promised.

It was already hot and crowded in the ballroom, redolent with the aroma of fresh-cut evergreen boughs, beeswax, and a hundred competing perfumes. Soon the odor of roasted meats joined the fray as the Queen's kitchen staff began loading the massive table with all manner of savories. I decided to make a circuit of the room before I found myself swept into the merriment. I had my lamp and I wore the medallion I'd commissioned from the silversmith, my sole adornment. If anyone was going to react to either in a suspicious manner, it would likely be earlier than later. Or at least I was likely to note it earlier; wine and *joie* were flowing in abundance.

As it proved, the response revealed little.

My costume drew reactions aplenty; for its daring lack, not its accoutrements. I began to give up on my plan when Mavros nearly fell down laughing at the sight of me.

"Oh, Imri!" he gasped. "It's, it's . . ." He caught himself and gave his head a shake. "Well, it's quite fetching, in a unique way." His blue eyes gleamed behind his mask, an ornate affair of black leather with tall, spiraling horns. "Tell me, have you seen your sweet cousin?"

"Not yet," I said. "But I've heard."

"Look yonder." He slid one arm around my waist and pointed with his free hand.

I looked.

By tradition, the Sun Prince awoke the Winter Queen to youthful rebirth in the Midwinter Masque we enact every year on the Longest Night. It is an old ritual, with roots going back to before the coming of Blessed Elua, and there is a distant connection between the Sun Prince and the ruler of the land. Mostly that is all forgotten and it's only pageantry, nowadays. But Baudoin de Trevalion resurrected it as a symbolic gesture when he was plotting to usurp Ysandre's inheritance. I remembered how Sidonie asked me last year, when I came attired as a Skaldic deity of light, if I thought to play the Sun Prince. In answer, I'd offered her my oath of loyalty.

She must have remembered, too. And she was using the costume to serve notice to the peers of the realm that she had no intention of being supplanted as the heir to Terre d'Ange.

Gold; cloth-of-gold. Her gown was gold, her shoes were gilded. The half-mask that hid her upper face was gold, and the sun's rays burst outward gloriously from it. Lest anyone should mistake the symbolism, she carried a gilded spear in her right hand.

Sidonie's head turned as though I'd called her name. I raised my lamp in salute. I could see her lips move in a smile beneath the half-mask, and her spear dipped briefly in reply.

"Well, well," Mavros murmured in my ear.

"Oh, hush." I shrugged him off me. "Is Roshana here?"

"No. There's a Kusheline fête. Most of the family in the City is there." He read my expression. "I was supposed to invite you, but trust me, Imri, you wouldn't have liked it. And anyway, we're going to the Night Court later, yes?"

I was still watching Sidonie. "Right."

Mavros gave me a shove. "Go on, I'll find you."

I hadn't gone more than a few steps in her general direction before I was waylaid by an older woman with a beaked mask and a towering headdress of feathers. "Prince Imriel!" She inclined her head, surveying me with a disapproving gaze. "What costume is this, pray?"

"Diogenes," I said. "My lady . . . ?"

"Marguerite Lafons, Marquise de Lafoneuil." Her lips thinned. "My estate lies on the western border of the duchy of Barthelme. You *are* aware of your holdings, are you not?"

"Yes, of course." I'd visited it exactly once. "Well met, Lady Marguerite."

"Are you aware that now that you've reached your majority, you're entitled to a hereditary seat in Parliament as the Duc de Barthelme?" She didn't wait for my answer. "No, I didn't think so. No one's claimed it since your father went off to La Serenissima. Young highness, I want a word with you." One hand clamped firmly on my elbow. "You'll do me the kindness of filling a plate for me while you listen, will you not?"

The habit of politeness was too deeply instilled in me to protest.

I escorted the Marquise de Lafoneuil to the Queen's table, where I procured a pair of seats and directed the serving staff to fill two plates, reckoning I might as well eat in the bargain. Meanwhile, Marguerite Lafons filled my ear with the inequities of taxation on the Namarrese wine trade. It went on at great length, but it seemed the gist of it was that there was a tax on the wine itself and a cooper's tax on the barrels, both of which the vintner was forced to pay.

I sat, chewing and nodding, as she expounded on it, thinking about Canis in his barrel. I thought about Gilot, too. I'd planned to make him steward of one of my two estates. He would have liked it, I thought; and he would have done a good job, too.

"Well?" the Marquise demanded. "Does that not seem unjust?"

I swallowed a mouthful of squab. "It does, my lady."

"You're wasting your time, Marguerite," a familiar voice drawled. "Yon princeling is bound for Alba, as surely as his father was for La Serenissima." A booted foot descended on the edge of my chair and a male figure leaned over me, arms propped on one knee. "Isn't that right, your highness?"

"Duc Barquiel." I glanced up at him. "What a pleasure."

Barquiel L'Envers, the Queen's uncle, snorted. He wore the same Akkadian finery he'd worn to the last Midwinter Masque, and he hadn't bothered with a mask either, only a turbaned helmet. "Lies don't become you, lad, any more than those rags do." He stroked my hair with a gauntled hand. "Nor this tangled mane. I thought you might keep it short. It was quite becoming."

I went rigid with fury and stared at my plate, afraid I might strike him. I hadn't the slightest doubt he'd strike back, and a good deal of doubt over which one of us would prevail. I had youth on my side, but Barquiel L'Envers had a name as a formidable fighter. He'd been Commander of the Royal Army for a long time, before Ysandre made him step down.

"Barquiel!" Marguerite Lafons said tartly. "Leave the lad be. You always were a bully."

A chair scraped. "Hear, hear," a new voice said.

L'Envers straightened. *"D'Essoms?"*

I raised my head to see who had put that incredulous note in Barquiel L'Envers' voice. There were two men: one tall and D'Angeline, one slight and foreign. The D'Angeline smiled at me. He had dark hair and hooded eyes. "You must be Imriel de la Courcel. Well met, your highness. Childric d'Essoms, formerly of the Court of Chancery, lately ambassador to Ephesium."

"Well met, my lord." I stood, ignoring L'Envers, and reached across the table to clasp d'Essoms' hand. I didn't know who he was, but if Barquiel L'Envers didn't like him, I did. My silver medallion swung forward as I leaned over, and I heard d'Essoms' companion take a sharp breath. At the same time, there was some commotion a few yards away; a fresh swirl of gossip, the crowds parting.

"Pray, your highness, come and—" Childric d'Essoms stopped. A muscle in his jaw twitched. "Phèdre nó Delaunay," he said softly.

There she stood, her cheeks flushed. "My lord d'Essoms."

A patron, a former patron. Elua knew, he couldn't be aught else. It wasn't anything like the priest in Naamah's Temple. The air between them fairly crackled. Ti-Philippe, a step behind Phèdre, looked worried and a little foolish, holding her parasol. D'Essoms dismissed him without a second glance.

"Where's your Cassiline?" he asked her. "I've heard stories."

"Keeping Elua's vigil." Flushed or no, Phèdre kept her voice steady. "'Tis the Longest Night, my lord."

"So it is." He reached for a glass of cordial and downed it. "*Joie!* Phèdre nó Delaunay, Comtesse de Montrève, this is Diokles Agallon of Ephesium, on embassy from the Sultan."

I murmured apologies to the Lady Marguerite and brushed past L'Envers. He was standing with arms folded, a look of distaste on his features. There was a story there, no doubt, but I didn't care at the moment. I made my way around the table and put myself between Phèdre and Childric d'Essoms, ostensibly that I might be introduced to the Ephesian ambassador.

Diokles Agallon bowed. "My very great pleasure, your highness," he said in heavily accented D'Angeline. There was somewhat familiar about the accent; and yet, not quite.

"And mine, Ambassador." I fingered the medallion on my chest, feeling its notched edges. "Will you be with us long?"

"Not long, no. Only until the spring, when I return to serve the Sultan." He glanced downward. "Is that a part of your costume, highness? It doesn't look like D'Angeline workmanship."

"No," I said. "It was a gift from a fellow Cynic. It seemed fitting I wear it tonight."

"I see." Diokles touched it lightly, tracing the edge. He nodded gravely. "Treasure it well. All gifts have merit."

"Yes," I said. "They do."

I wanted more from him; ah, Elua! I always wanted more. I wanted to wring his neck until he talked freely and openly, admitting himself a Guildsman without secretive insinuations, and I wanted to shake Phèdre until she stopped looking at Childric d'Essoms that way, and I wanted to punch d'Essoms for looking at her like a bird of prey eyeing a rabbit. I especially wanted to punch Barquiel L'Envers, who had stalked away from the table and was lounging against a column with an insouciant look on his face.

But none of it would avail anything.

". . . like to see you," Childric d'Essoms was saying to Phèdre. "Although I suppose many things have changed in the years since Delaunay's *anguissette* became the Comtesse de Montrève."

"A few, yes." Phèdre caught my eye. "Ah, Imri. Princess Alais was looking for you. Shall we—?"

"Please." I grabbed her arm and steered her unceremoniously away from d'Essoms. "Who is he?" I demanded when I had her alone.

"It's a long story." Phèdre closed her eyes briefly. The flush began to fade from her cheeks. "I'll tell you later." She opened her eyes and regarded me with a hint of amusement. "Love, listen. Believe it or not, I've managed to pass the Longest Night without betraying Joscelin for a very long time now. The last time I was with anyone else on this night . . ." She stopped, her color returning, and I knew with absolute certainty it had been my mother. Melisande.

A Kusheline party; a diamond and a velvet leash.

Trust me, Imri, you wouldn't have liked it.

"I know," I said.

"Well." Phèdre cleared her throat. "Joscelin honors Blessed Elua in his way, and I in mine. And none of that will change tonight. All right?"

"All right," I muttered.

"Good." She rubbed her arm where I'd grabbed her, looking absent for a moment. Beneath the crimson silk, I suspected there were bruises. "Now go see Alais, will you? She really is missing you."

I found Alais amid a gaggle of attendants. At almost fifteen, she was old enough to have her own ladies-in-waiting; daughters of the peerage, nearly old enough to play the Game of Courtship in earnest. They giggled with one another, flirting and making eyes at the young noblemen. Alais looked lonely and forlorn in their midst.

"Hello, my lady." I bowed to her. "Joie to you on the Longest Night."

"Imri!" Her expression brightened, dispelling my bad mood. "Where's your lamp? I thought you were supposed to have a lamp."

"I left it on the table," I said, extending my hand. "All the better to dance with you, if you'll do me the honor."

Her face glowed. "Of course."

We took to the floor, moving smoothly among the myriad costumed couples. It struck me anew how much Alais had grown in the past year. She was a studious dancer, following my lead with care, as though she feared to do aught that might make her look foolish. In the past, she wouldn't have cared.

"You look beautiful tonight," I told her. She was clad as a forest sylph in dark winter hues, and her mask was adorned with ebony brambles, clusters of garnets gleaming like berries in her black curls.

"Do you think so?" Alais asked.

I nodded. "Truly."

She turned her head. "Have you seen Sidonie?"

"Oh, yes." Out of the corner of my eye, a flash of gold. Mavros was talking to her. I prayed he kept his mouth shut. "Tell me, do you like your ladies-in-waiting?"

"Sometimes." Alais' tone was noncommittal. "It's different."

"Why?"

She sighed. "You know."

I did. It was different because she was half-Cruithne and looked it;

because she was betrothed to an Alban prince and wouldn't be playing the Game of Courtship. Because she was Alais, proud and clever, and not terribly good at flirting.

"Will you stay with me a while?" Alais asked hopefully, her hand tightening on mine.

"Of course," I promised. "As long as you like."

It was a promise I had cause to regret. In Lucca, surrounded by soldiers, I'd yearned for the company of women. After ten minutes amid a horde of adolescent girls, I'd have traded their giggles and shrieks for the grunts and bellows of the training ground in a heartbeat.

Still, I'd promised.

At Alais' pleading, I told a story about the siege. They got round-eyed, oohing and ahhing, and begged to see my scars until I relented and pushed up the rags draped around my right arm to let them see the shiny pink mark where a deep gouge had healed. The squeals were deafening, and all of them insisted on touching it. Some were more insistent than others.

"You're so *strong*," one of them breathed.

"Greetings, cousin."

I glanced up to meet Sidonie's amused gaze. Her gold dress had a low décolletage, and a sun-shaped pendant nestled above the swell of her breasts. Her skin was fair and smooth as new cream. I stammered a greeting and attempted to pry Alais' young attendant off my arm.

"I'd thought we might have a dance." It was hard to tell behind the half-mask, but I thought Sidonie was trying not to laugh. "Later, mayhap? If it doesn't inconvenience your plans with Lord Mavros."

"Of course." I inclined my head.

"Later, then." Her voice softened to a tender note. "Are you enjoying yourself, my heart?" she asked Alais.

"Oh, yes!" Alais' violet eyes shone. "Now I am."

"I'm glad." Sidonie smiled at her sister and turned away. She tapped her favorite attendant, the priestess' daughter, with the tip of her gilded spear. They exchanged a glance of unspoken complicity and strolled back into the throng, masked guardsmen hovering discreetly. I sighed, the sound lost in the general uproar.

"Prince Imriel?" There was a small hand on my thigh, resting just below another long-healed gash I'd taken in the battle of Lucca. I glanced down at the very young lady-in-waiting to whom it belonged. She batted her lashes at me. "Do you not have *another* battle-scar you might show us?"

"No," I said shortly. Alais giggled. "And it's not funny."

She wrinkled her nose at me. "Yes it is."

It seemed like ages before I was saved by Night's Crier, entering the hall and sounding his bronze tocsin. The stern sound and the pall of darkness that fell over the ballroom made me shiver, stirring echoes in my memory; the sound of bronze wings clashing inside my skull, and Gallus Tadius standing over a dark abyss, the broken mask in his hands. The ritual played out as it had done a thousand times before, year after year. The cunningly built mountain crag behind the musicians' grotto split apart to the sound of a crashing drumroll and the Winter Queen hobbled forth as an aged crone; an answering drumroll sounded as the doors were flung open to admit the Sun Prince's chariot.

There was one difference this year. After he'd pointed his spear at the Winter Queen, after she'd let fall her tattered robes to reveal herself in her youth and beauty. After the wicks were relit and light returned in a glorious rush, and the Winter Queen ascended the chariot. The chariot made its slow turn, and they both bowed to Queen Ysandre. This time, the Sun Prince saluted Sidonie, too; one glittering figure to another.

It was a small gesture, only a symbol. Mostly people cheered, but a few murmured. I hated them for it. As the musicians struck up once more, I decided I wanted very much to claim the first dance of the reborn year of Sidonie.

"Will you be all right on your own?" I asked Alais. "I promised your sister a dance."

She nodded. "Do you think they have anything like this in Alba?"

"I don't know, villain." I kissed the top of her head. "We'll find out."

"Don't call me that."

Now the revelry began in earnest. I caught sight of Mavros looking impatient and made a forestalling gesture. Servants were circulated with freshly laden trays of *joie*. I snatched a glass in passing and drank it at a gulp. The lamps seemed to burn brighter. I slid easily through the crowd, winding past bulkier figures, agile in my rags and bare feet. A gilded spear-head, a glint of cloth-of-gold.

"Sidonie." I held out my hand to her.

Beyond her, Barquiel L'Envers was watching us, arms folded over his Akkadian robe. Sidonie ignored him. "You do keep your promises, don't you?" she mused.

"I do," I said. "Yes."

She gave her gilded spear to Amarante of Namarre and took my hand. I led her onto the dance floor. The musicians were playing a galliard. I wished it was a slower tune. I wished half the room, including L'Envers, wasn't watching us.

"You look absurd, you know." Sidonie touched the ragged neckline of my tunic, her fingertips brushing my skin.

"Do I?" I asked, not caring.

Her lips curved. "No," she whispered. "Not really."

We drifted closer toward the far end of the floor, dancing beneath the looming form of the Winter Queen's mountain, its hidden opening closed once more. The musicians ended their tune and shifted into the opening bars of a quadrille. Lines of dancers began to form, a dense wall of costumed backs presenting itself.

"Here." Tugging my hand, Sidonie darted behind the mountain.

It was dark and cramped and wonderful. We stared at each other; masked and unmasked, rag-clad and golden. I caught her other hand, pinned them both against the false mountainside, pinning her there with my body. Our fingers interlocked. My blood was roaring in my ears, and I could see the pulse beating in the hollow of her throat. I couldn't see her eyes, only dark glimmers behind the radiating sun-mask.

"Sidonie." My voice sounded raw and strange.

Her head tilted and our lips met.

Wrong, so wrong! And ah, Elua! Glorious. I felt her lips, impossibly soft, part and I made a sound I'd never heard before. I kissed her, and it was a delirium of kissing; avid mouths, darting tongues. It felt as thought it could go on forever, more and more and more, all of it new and undiscovered. Her mask scraped my cheek, and I didn't care.

I pressed harder against her and felt her shudder, our intertwined fingers spasming. Deeper and deeper, I kissed her. If I could have crawled down her throat, I swear to Elua, I would have.

"*Sidonie!*"

An urgent hiss. She tore her mouth away from mine, gasping. I leaned my brow against the mountain and groaned.

"L'Envers is on the lookout, cousin."

A different voice; Mavros, wry and warning. I let go of Sidonie's hands and stepped back, breathing hard. My body was one single quivering ache of desire. Mavros glanced over his shoulder, then beckoned to Sidonie.

"Here, your highness. Quickly."

She adjusted her mask, then took his hand. He led her around the curve of the crag, shielding her gilded figure with his height. My legs were trembling, and I sank down to sit, resting my back against the mountainside.

Amarante looked down at me. "Prince Imriel?"

"Give me a moment." I pressed the heels of my hands against my eyes.

"It's all right now." Her voice had regained its usual composure. "Anyone who noticed will think it a foolish game, nothing more."

I dropped my hands and squinted at her. She was arrayed as Spring, in a gown of pale green with a crown of flowers. I knew the costume. Sidonie had worn it last year. "It's not, you know. A game."

"I know." Her mother was the head of Naamah's Order. Of course she knew. And I had asked for Naamah's blessing, knowing the risk. I was at the mercy of my own desire. Genuine desire, fierce and real. I was an idiot.

We waited until the musicians began a stately pavane, then slipped back onto the dance floor. By the time the dance ended, my pulse was nearly normal and I felt steady on my feet. I thanked Amarante, who merely nodded and went to find Mavros.

"Shall we go?" he asked.

"I think we'd better."

I made my farewells. The royal family was together. Alais, who was beginning to look sleepy, hugged me and kissed my cheek. Sidonie and

I exchanged cordial nods. She was as cool as ever, her back as straight as the spear she'd reclaimed, but the sun-pendant on her breast trembled. I felt a quiver in the pit of my belly.

"Imri?" Phèdre gave me a long, quizzical look. She suspected, I thought; surely, she must. But if she did, she didn't say anything. "Be careful," she said instead, smiling ruefully. "I know, I'm always telling you that."

"And I'm always careful," I lied.

Outside, the air was bracing. The unseasonal warmth had given way to a cold snap and there was ice on the streets. I shifted from foot to bare foot on the courtyard as we waited for the carriage to be brought around. It was only an hour or so past midnight. The stars were distant and frosty, and a full moon stood high overhead, washing everything with silver. Mavros flung back his head and howled at it. I laughed, and he thumped my shoulder with one fist.

"You were right, cousin," he said. "You were oh so right. She *wants* you."

"I don't want to talk about it," I said.

"Why?" he asked.

I shook my head. "I don't know."

Mavros eyed me. "Are you going to be any fun tonight?"

"I don't know," I repeated.

"Ah, well." He shrugged. "*I* am."

By the time we arrived at Cereus House and gave our tokens at the door, the festivities had gone well beyond revelry and into sheer license. I daresay at the outset the panoply outshone the Palace, but by now costumes were disheveled, and those masks that had not yet been discarded sat askew. Still, it was an amazing thing to see all the adepts of the Thirteen Houses in one place. So much beauty! Many of them came from a long lineage of Naamah's Servants, and their blood was as pure as any peer's.

On the Longest Night, there were no assignations allowed in the Night Court, no contracts. Only such liaisons as the adepts themselves chose. And this they had commenced to do with fervid enthusiasm. Everywhere one looked, in every corner or nook that afforded a measure of privacy, couples were entwined; couples and triads and groups of all manner. Alyssum's modesty and Bryony's avarice were abandoned, Heliotrope's marque blossomed beside Jasmine's.

"Elua!" Mavros took a deep breath. "What a lovely garden."

He plunged into its midst and I lost sight of him almost immediately. I followed more slowly. I felt strange, a beggar at a banquet. I'd never gotten my lamp back, and I daresay I looked the beggar, too.

It was all right, though. I didn't mind.

A ripple ran through the crowd and I heard my name whispered. It seemed my bet with the Dowayne of Bryony House had caused a stir in the Night Court. I was Phèdre nó Delaunay's foster-son and I was welcome among them. Whatever I felt, I'd not go begging; not here.

There were offers.

A lot of offers.

And I turned them down, all of them. I found a perch atop a mostly empty banquet table and watched the glorious swirl of pageantry and lovemaking, the breathless, flushed garden of D'Angeline adepts. A vast tenderness filled me, and the beauty of it all made me ache with longing and loss.

"Are you sad, highness?" An adept with a satyr's mask pushed atop a head of brown curls hopped onto the table beside me. "You shouldn't be, not tonight."

"Not sad," I said. "Thoughtful."

"Oh, well then." He grinned. "That's all right."

I thought about Eamonn teasing me for brooding, and I thought about Lucius, because the satyr's mask reminded me of him. And I thought about where I wanted to be at that moment if it wasn't with Sidonie, which it was. I excused myself and went to find the Dowayne of Cereus House to ask if I might beg the loan of a horse, to which he readily agreed.

The sky was beginning to turn dark grey by the time I reached the Temple of Elua. I was shivering in the saddle, huddled in my rags and cursing myself for a fool. I'd had to saddle the horse myself; there was no one left on sober duty in the stables of Cereus House, and no one from whom to borrow a cloak or footwear.

At least I didn't have to remove my boots. I passed through the vestibule and walked silently into the temple garden, the frozen ground hard beneath my bare soles. My feet made dark prints in the frost. I gazed at the statue of Blessed Elua and thought about what the priest had said about love the first time I'd come here, that I would find it and lose it, again and again. Somewhere in the distance, a horologist's cry announced dawn's first rays breaking the horizon, setting loose a clamor all across the City.

I watched Joscelin raise his bowed head.

There were no other Cassiline Brothers. Joscelin had kept the vigil alone this year. He got stiffly to his feet, turned, and saw me. For a moment, he merely blinked, not quite believing his eyes. "Imri?" After long silence, his voice was hoarse. His hands reached unthinking for his daggers, sure there must be danger. "What are you doing here?"

I hugged myself against the cold. "Greeting the dawn."

Joscelin let go his hilts and swore softly. I smiled at him, and he laughed and shook his head. "Name of Elua! Look at you. I'm not taking the blame for this, not this time."

"No," I agreed. "This time, it's mine."

We rode home together in companionable silence. There was a blaze of gold in the eastern sky. The sun had returned, piercing and lovely. For the first time since I'd left the Palace, I let myself think about Sidonie, reliving every fevered whisper and gasp of our encounter, wrapping the memory around me like a fur cloak, warm and sensuous.

After a while, I didn't even feel the cold.

EIGHT

Once Phèdre had gotten over the worst of her outrage at my admittedly foolish decision to ride unarmed, unattended, and clad in rags across the City on the Longest Night, which took the better part of a day, I told her about how the Ephesian ambassador had recognized my medallion. If nothing else, it served to distract her.

"So they're among us," she mused. "The Unseen Guild."

"So it would seem."

She sighed. "Well, and so. You didn't speak to him of it, did you?"

"No." I shook my head. "Not directly."

"Good." Phèdre frowned. "I'll see what Ysandre knows of his purposes, and try to find out who else he's meeting with. There's not much else we can do without tipping our hand."

"*Your* hand," I pointed out to her. "It doesn't matter what they think *I* know, only that they don't know I've spoken of it. To you or to anyone."

"Are you telling me to be careful?" she asked wryly.

I cleared my throat. "Who's Childric d'Essoms?"

Joscelin, listening without comment, snorted. Phèdre glanced at him. "He was a patron," she said. "Barquiel L'Envers' protégé, once. Delaunay used me to reach L'Envers through him. I don't think L'Envers took it kindly."

"Hence the bad blood between them?" I asked.

She nodded. "Did he recognize the lamp-sign?"

"No," Joscelin said. They exchanged another glance. "I don't care if he recognized it or not," he added adamantly. "You're not doing what you're thinking of doing. Not with d'Essoms. I never liked him."

"I know." Phèdre smiled sweetly at him. "I'm not."

A corner of his mouth twitched. "You're *thinking* it, love."

"Oh, well." Her smile deepened. "Thinking's not doing."

"I don't think he did recognize it," I said. "Only the Ephesian."

I was fairly certain it was true, anyway. In the end, there wasn't much to be done about it. I'd served notice to a member of the Guild, and they would respond or not as they chose. Either way, my future lay in Alba and owed naught to the Unseen Guild. It was one small piece of a puzzle that no longer held the interest it had for me. Once, I would have seized upon it. When I was younger, I'd daydreamed about finding my mother and bringing her at long last to justice. It was the one act of heroism I could commit that would clear away forever the taint of treachery that clung to me.

And now . . .

Now I owed her my life. It was harder to hate her wearing the seal of her protection around my neck, remembering Canis' dying words. It was harder to envision watching her long-delayed execution after reading her letters, reading how she'd counted my fingers and toes when I was a baby.

And I had other things on my mind.

Two days after the Longest Night, I returned to the Palace for another session with Firdha. The *ollamh* treated Alais and me to a lengthy dissertation on Alban law, which we would be obliged to know and honor. It was surprisingly intricate and different from ours. In Terre d'Ange, penalties under the law are the same for everyone, commoner or noble. In Alba and Eire, they differed. A wealthy man who stole a cow from his neighbor would pay pay a far greater fine than a poor one, and the penalty for noblemen convicted of a crime of dishonor was far greater than it was for commoners.

It was interesting, but I had no time to muse on it. There were too many, far too many specific laws we were to memorize, and none of them might be written down. Firdha crammed our heads with law upon law, refusing to dismiss us until we could recite a score of them letter-perfect. I was glad that Phèdre had trained me to use my memory well. Poor Alais looked ready to weep when she garbled an answer.

"Daughter of the Grove," I said wearily when she released us. "Would it not make more sense to set these in a book of law which all could consult?"

Firdha gave me a stern look. "Were it so, then it would be the book, and not the law, that men respected. Were it so, then men and women would no longer need to be wise to be just."

"I see," I said, though I didn't.

The corners of her eyes crinkled. "Perhaps you will, one day."

Pondering the matter, I left the study and found Amarante of Namarre awaiting me. Every law I'd just memorized went straight out of my head and my chest felt hollow. "Well met, my lady."

"Your highness." Amarante inclined her head. "May I speak with you?"

"Of course."

I followed her through the royal chambers. A few guards grinned, and well they might. The priestess' daughter had hair the color of apricots, green eyes, and plump lips, and I understood why she drove Mavros mad. Still, it wasn't her that I wanted, and when she led me to her little bedchamber, I was hoping against hope. It wasn't until I saw the Dauphine of Terre d'Ange curled in a chair beneath the narrow window that I let myself believe.

"Sidonie," I said.

She looked young. Elua, she *was* young, not yet seventeen. But her dark gaze was unwavering. "Thank you," she said to Amarante, who nodded.

"I'll be in your quarters," she said softly, opening the adjoining door.

I watched her go, leaving Sidonie and me alone.

"Imriel." Sidonie knit her brows. They were the same shape as mine, and I wanted to kiss them. "Will you sit?" she asked, nodding at the bed. "We need to talk." I sat cross-legged on the bed. She took a deep breath. "What are we doing?"

"Talking," I said gravely.

"Oh, don't!" Her eyes flashed. "Don't be glib. If there are two people anywhere in the whole of Terre d'Ange who cannot, *cannot* have a casual dalliance, it's us. And you damnably well know it, cousin!"

"Why?" I asked, curious. "Truly, Sidonie? Do you think the sky will crack and fall? And why do you assume there's aught *casual* about it?"

She looked away. "Why are you doing this? You don't even like me."

"That's not true."

"It is." She looked back at me. "You've never liked me."

"Me!" I laughed, stung. "You've looked at me like I was dung on your shoe since you were eight years old. Why are *you* doing this?"

Her voice broke. "I don't know."

We sat for a moment, neither of us speaking. "I do like you," I said at length. "You're right, I didn't, not for a long time. You were cold and mistrustful, and you always said things to goad me. I never understood why."

Sidonie bowed her head, fidgeting with the hem of her gown where it was tucked around her ankles. "You never heard the arguments," she murmured. "Imriel . . . I grew up hearing them. Alais didn't, she's too young." She lifted her chin. "I don't think you have any idea what kind of opposition my mother faced for her decision to see you rescued. I do. I remember. And the first thing you did was throw it in her face."

"Is that why you hated me?" I asked.

"In part," she said.

"Do you have any idea what I'd been through?" My voice rose. "*Any* idea?"

"No," she said simply. "Imriel, I don't. Or I didn't. I was eight years old, and I couldn't begin to fathom it. I'm sorry."

It eased a hurt in me so deep I hadn't known it existed. I drew a shaking breath. "Do you remember the time I was sick, and Alais and I were playing—"

"With the wooden daggers?" Sidonie nodded, her eyes bright with tears. "Yes. I'm sorry for that, too. I was wrong."

"When did it all change?" I asked. *"How?"*

"The hunting party?" She smiled a little. "I don't know. It happened bit by bit. The day with the daggers, when I realized I was wrong. Do you know, we had a nursemaid from Camlach who was certain you meant to poison me and marry Alais? She used to spy on us whenever Mother had you visit in case the guards weren't vigilant enough."

"She did?" I felt sick.

Sidonie nodded. "She gave Alais nightmares. Mother dismissed her when she found out. Alais loved you so much, from the very beginning. It worried me."

"Does it still?" I asked.

"For different reasons." She hugged her knees. "She adores you, Imriel. And this . . ." She shook her head. Her hair was loose around her shoulders, honey-colored in the sunlight angling through the window. "How did we come to this?"

"You laughed." I watched the sunlight play on her hair. "When you saw the deer."

"You should have seen your face," she said.

"I know." We smiled at each other. "Sidonie, it was the first time, I think, that I truly *saw* you. And it felt like the world had turned upside down."

"I remember." She was quiet for another long moment. "And I remember watching you tend to poor Alais' dog, kneeling on the ground with Amarante's embroidery needle, covered in blood. Elua!" Sidonie shuddered. "You won *her* over that day, I think."

"Alais?" I asked, confused.

"Amarante." She said the name fondly. I wished she'd linger over mine the same way. "Mother would dismiss her for conspiring in this, you know."

"Why?"

"Because you're Melisande Shahrizai's son, Imriel." Sidonie's gaze was steady and direct. "My mother is fond of you. She trusts you. She is entirely sincere in her desire to see you an honored member of House Courcel. But if you wonder if she harbors a seed of doubt, yes, of course. She'd be a fool not to. And I daresay the one thing that could truly ignite it would be you in my bed."

I swallowed. "I see. And you, too?"

"No." She raked a rare impatient hand through her hair. "No, I don't. But how am I supposed to explain that I saw a look on your face when you thought you were protecting me, and I *knew*?" She shook her head. "And why am I thinking of doing this? Name of Elua! I could take a *goatherd* for a lover, and Mother would stand by my choice. She wouldn't like it, but she'd allow it."

"I was a goatherd," I said.

Sidonie didn't laugh. "Imriel, tell me truly. How much of what lies between us is just the lure of the forbidden? Can you even say?"

"No." I got off the bed, restless, and paced the room's small confines. "Truly? No. It's a part of it, I know. I do. I didn't reckon . . . I didn't know Ysandre would feel quite so strongly. I didn't think, I suppose. I really *was* a goatherd, you know. I didn't grow up thinking of myself as a Prince of the Blood or Melisande Shahrizai's son. I don't want your throne, I don't even want the estates I have."

"I know," she said. "But—"

"I want you, Sidonie." I knelt before her chair and caught her hands. "You're the most infuriatingly self-possessed person I've ever known, and somehow I've come to admire you for it. And I know there's fire underneath it, and it makes me crazy. I can't help it. If you want me to leave, I'll go, but—"

She tore her hands free of mine and grabbed my head, kissing me hard. Sunlight, liquid gold. I slid both arms around her, hands pressing her slender back. We tumbled onto the floor together, our fall cushioned by a woven rug. I held her down, kissing her. Ah, Elua! My head was filled with a dazzling brightness, my body singing with desire.

"Imriel . . ." Sidonie arched her neck, gasped. "Ow!"

"Sorry." I'd pinned her hair to the floor. I pulled her atop me and sat up, settling her astraddle of my lap.

"I don't—" Her skirts were puddled around us. She rocked against me. "Oh."

With one hand, I undid the laces of her bodice, baring her breasts. Skin like cream, tender with youth. I cupped her breasts, tracing the line of her cleavage with my tongue, then lowered my head to lave her nipples. Sidonie sighed, sinking both hands into my hair. I held her breasts and suckled them hard until she whimpered and ground herself against me, and somewhere there was knocking, and I wanted to stop, but I couldn't, not until she cried out and shuddered, and the fierceness of it made me lose control and spend myself.

"Ah, Naamah!" she panted.

The adjoining door opened. "Sidonie?"

Sidonie glanced up, dark eyes wide and blurred with pleasure, honey-gold hair clinging to skin damp with sweat. "What is it?"

"I'm sorry." Amarante looked apologetic and amused, and not in the least startled to find her half-naked royal mistress straddling me. "Your mother sent a messenger. I told him you were napping, but he's waiting."

Sidonie sighed. "All right." She got up, which Elua knows, I couldn't have done at the moment. In seconds, her bodice was laced and her hair twined in a lover's-haste knot at the nape of her neck. I stared at her in amazement and began to wonder what I'd gotten myself into. Her lips curved, her Cruithne eyes reading my thoughts. "We'll talk later."

"All right," I said faintly.

The women exchanged one of their glances, and Amarante raised her brows. "Don't worry," she said. "I'll clean him up."

"My thanks." Sidonie kissed her and left.

I groaned. Amarante laughed and fetched a linen towel from the washbasin. "Here."

"Give me a moment." I rested my back against the edge of her bed and contemplated her. "Why are you doing this, my lady?"

"Should I be jealous, you mean?" she asked, and I nodded. "Are you?"

I thought about it. "I don't know. But Mavros said you were loyal to Sidonie."

"I am." She sat in the chair beneath the window. "She has a lonely path. I think she deserves to have one person who won't break trust with her for any reason. I think, too, that it will make her a kinder person in turn, and one day, mayhap a gentler ruler. And for so long as she wishes, I'm content to serve in that role."

"And are you always impossibly wise and compassionate?" I asked.

Amarante laughed again. "No."

"That's good to know." I levered myself to my feet and went to use the washbasin, feeling remarkably self-conscious about it. Amarante waited, unperturbed.

"Prince Imriel," she said when I'd finished. "You asked *why*. I was raised in Naamah's worship, and we honor love and desire over politics. If you and Sidonie wish to bruise your hearts on each other, it is your right. But if you hurt her a-purpose, I will call down Naamah's curse on you."

I nodded. "Fairly spoken."

"I'm glad you think so." Her apple-green eyes glinted. "And next time, mayhap you'll make it as far as the bed."

I left the Palace in a daze. Fire, had I said? Name of Elua! More like a firestorm. I should have known. I *had* known, or suspected. Still, it hadn't prepared me for the reality. Sidonie, my cool, regal cousin. My body was quivering like a plucked harp-string and I wanted more, so much more, than this half-thwarted encounter that left me with damp breeches and heightened yearning. I'd known desire before. Claudia Fulvia's ardor had kept mine at a fever pitch for days on end.

This was different.

For the first time, it scared me. She was right, of course. We were the last two people in the realm who could afford a casual dalliance. Only it wasn't casual. It wasn't casual because of the Queen's disapproval and the menace in Barquiel L'Envers' stare, and worst of all, the unnerving ache in the hollow of my chest, a terrible surge of tenderness.

Naamah's curse didn't frighten me.

Her blessing was another matter.

NINE

I ATTENDED MY FIRST SESSION as a member of Parliament some days later, although the Marquise de Lafoneuil would be displeased to know that the matter of the cooper's tax was not addressed. Ysandre had convened the meeting to give ear to Diokles Agallon, the Ephesian ambassador. It was a partial session, as many members would not be travelling to the City until spring, but it would suffice to afford him a hearing.

Sidonie was there. I hadn't expected it, Elua knows why. She had no vote, no official role until she gained her majority. But she was Ysandre's heir, and she'd been learning statecraft at her mother's knee while I was herding goats in the mountains of Siovale.

It made it hard to concentrate. Childric d'Essoms introduced the ambassador, and Diokles spoke at length about the diminishing market in Ephesium due to unrest in realms to the north, and the desire to establish a more fulsome trade with Terre d'Ange. If he had a hidden agenda, I couldn't fathom it.

"Your policies favor Khebbel-im-Akkad, your majesty, though we offer many of the same goods," he said. "Ephesium does but seek the right to compete freely, with the same import fees."

"The cost of transport is higher for the Akkadians," Barquiel L'Envers observed. "Thus, you have the advantage elsewhere." He had a vested interest in the matter, as his daughter was wed to the Lugal of Khebbel-im-Akkad. I was fairly certain she'd tried to have me assassinated when I was a boy.

"And a shipment of Ephesian cotton should sell for a lower price than an Akkadian," Diokles Agallon said politely. "Yet we must pay a higher fee for the right to do so, and are forced to raise our prices accordingly to make a profit. Should Ephesium be punished for its geography? And moreover, should Terre d'Ange be deprived of the right to benefit from it?"

I ceased paying attention to his words and focused on the way he shaped his vowels. His accent was like Canis' and yet, not quite. I'd known Ephesians in Daršanga, but I couldn't remember if it had been the same. It was hard to tell there, where everyone spoke in a polyglot babble. And at times, I could have sworn Canis was Hellene by the things he said, though that wasn't quite right, either.

". . . an obligation to honor alliance through ties of marriage," L'Envers was saying.

"Indeed." Agallon bowed. "The Sultan is well aware of this. In fact, it is a matter he would be interested in discussing himself."

At that point, everyone in the room looked at Sidonie.

"No," Barquiel L'Envers said. "Oh, I think not."

"Oh, let him speak, my lord uncle." Sidonie smiled at the Ephesian ambassador. "I confess myself curious."

"Forgive me." The words were out of my mouth before I had any intention of speaking them. I flushed. "The proceedings are new to me. Is this a fit matter for Parliament to discuss in an open session?"

"No, no." Diokles Agallon raised his hands. "I would welcome a private audience with her majesty, but I fear I overstep here. Trade is at issue. My lords and ladies, pray, think on our request."

Ysandre inclined her head. "We will do so."

There was a rancorous discussion on the question of trade after the ambassador took his leave. L'Envers led a faction arguing against easing the fees, and others argued in favor of it. When the Queen called for a vote, it was evenly divided. I voted for it, mostly because L'Envers was opposed.

"Very well," Ysandre said. "We'll return to the matter in the spring when a full meeting is convened."

"Are you going to hear the Sultan's suit?" someone called.

Ysandre glanced at Sidonie, who raised her brows a cool fraction.

"We may hear it," the Queen said calmly. "There is never any harm in listening, my lord."

Of course, once the session was dismissed, no one could talk of anything else. Members of Parliament clustered in the halls of the Palace, gossiping in hushed whispers. They fell silent when Ysandre and Sidonie drew nigh. I watched them pass, my emotions in a tumult. We hadn't had a private moment since the afternoon in Amarante's bedchamber, and I was losing sleep. I was hoping very much that if I hovered here long enough, the priestess' daughter would come fetch me.

"Prince Imriel." A hand landed on my shoulder. I turned to see Childric d'Essoms. He smiled at me. "Lord Agallon would like a word with you."

I sighed inwardly. "Of course."

D'Essoms escorted me there and left us. The ambassador's quarters in the Palace were quite fine. We met in the tapestry-hung sitting room, where a tall Ephesian servant with a bald head and an imposing beard brought mint tea sweetened with honey. Diokles Agallon dismissed him and poured the tea himself. I thanked him and didn't drink until he raised his own cup and took a noisy sip.

"You're careful," he said. "Wise."

The tea was good. "I try, my lord."

He smiled. "I have been thinking, your highness. Your aid in this matter would not be unwelcome. A youthful prince's voice urging for the vigor of change. Perhaps an exchange of favors might be made."

"Which matter is that?" I asked.

Another noisy sip. "The matter of Ephesium."

"Do you speak of trade or marriage?"

"I speak of both," Agallon said. "Though of course, our hopes are modest."

"I see." I set down my cup. "And what do you offer?"

His smile was a diplomat's, smooth and practiced. "The medallion you wore . . . very interesting. Perhaps if you were to tell me more about it, I might be able to tell you somewhat about where it originated."

I gazed at him for a long moment without speaking. There were no telltales of a lie, but there were cracks in the veneer of his composure, a subtle discomfiture that surfaced the longer I stared. I thought about his careful wording, and I thought about what Claudia Fulvia had told me about the Unseen Guild. There were currents and cross-purposes within it. If this man was my mother's ally, he would have known where the medallion came from. He wouldn't have needed to dig.

It smelled like a trap, though I couldn't have said why. I didn't want to be beholden to the Guild in any way. And of a surety, I didn't want to argue the case for Sidonie's wedding the Sultan's son or brother, or whatever he had in mind. It wasn't just my own feelings at stake. The very notion had the peerage in an uproar. For me to argue in favor of it would have smacked of sedition.

My mother would have known that. And strangely enough, if she had enemies in the Guild, I didn't want to treat with them.

"Thank you, my lord." I inclined my head. "You are generous and I am grateful for it. I will gladly argue on behalf of enhanced trade, for your cause seemed good to me. But as for the rest . . ." I spread my hands. "I fear I must decline."

"Indeed?" Diokles Agallon mused. "Interesting."

"Is it, my lord?" I asked lightly.

He showed white teeth in his diplomat's smile. "I find you very interesting, Prince Imriel de la Courcel. Remember my name, young highness. You may find yourself interested in trading a favor of your own one day. Not many are willing to entertain such an offer."

That, at least, I could be reasonably sure would never happen. "Of course, my lord," I promised. "I will."

Leaving his quarters, I made my way downstairs and decided to loiter for a few minutes in the Hall of Games, listening to the lively buzz of gossip. The rumor had grown in the telling; already, Sidonie was said to be contemplating a marriage with the Sultan's second son. I accepted an offer to play a hand of piquet with an Azzalese lordling I knew by sight, listening to the murmurs and shaking my head to myself.

"Imri!" Mavros manifested, winding through the crowd. He laid his hands on my shoulders and peered at my cards. "You're not going to lead with *that*, are you?"

I batted at him. "Shut up, Mavros."

"You're so unkind, cousin." He leaned over, his lips close to my ear. "The priestess' daughter was looking for you."

I lost the trick and then the hand, paid my wager, and left the table, leading Mavros over to the colonnade. "Where is she?"

"I'm jealous," Mavros said, narrowing his eyes. "Or am I?"

"Mavros!" I shook him.

He laughed. "She left, Imri. Couldn't stay, said she'd look for you on the morrow. Tell me, did you succeed in poaching where I failed? Or does the lady run her mistress' errands?"

A pair of strolling passersby glanced at us with idle interest. I put my hand over Mavros' mouth. "Will you please *shut up*!" I hissed.

"Ooh, forceful." His voice was muffled and his twilight-blue eyes gleamed above my smothering hand. "Do you want me to play Valerian to your Mandrake, cousin?"

He was so impossible I had to laugh. "Mavros, truly. I need you to be discreet."

"As the grave," he agreed. "Will you tell me if I promise not to breathe a word?"

"Swear it," I said.

Mavros raised his hand promptly. "In Kushiel's name."

I glanced around. "Not here."

We went to Lord Sacriphant's townhouse. Mavros' father wasn't in residence, and Mavros, who liked the City rather better than many of my Shahrizai kin, had the run of it. Truth be told, the place made me uneasy. It was very elegant and the servants moved about with hushed grace. They seemed to have pride in serving House Shahrizai, but one couldn't help but wonder what penalties were levied on them for disobedience or failure.

Or at least *I* couldn't. The first time I'd been here, Mavros had gotten me stinking drunk and taken me to Valerian House, where the Shahrizai reserved a private dungeon. The memory of that excursion still made me squirm with pleasure and unease.

Come to think on it, I'd been chafing over Sidonie that night, too. That was shortly after things had first changed between us, and Mavros was still the only person I'd told. Despite his teasing, he was a good listener and I trusted him; or at least I did in this.

He listened without comment while I told him an abbreviated version of what had transpired, leaving out the more embarrassing bits.

When I had finished, he raised his brows. "You really didn't think about how this might appear?"

"Well, yes," I said. "But not as—"

"Conspiracy?" he suggested. I nodded. Mavros steepled his fingers, tapping his lips in thought. "You do have a certain naïve charm, cousin. One thing in the realm I daresay everyone could agree on is the fact that Melisande Shahrizai's laughter would ring to the heavens if she learned her son had managed to seduce Ysandre's heir."

"It's not like that," I said miserably.

"No, it's not, is it?" There was sympathy in his gaze. "Do you want my advice?"

"Please."

"Too bad," he said. "Because I don't have any."

"Mavros!"

"All right." He smiled wryly. "My *best* advice is to make an end of it, because if you're caught—and the odds are you will be—there'll be an unholy uproar and Barquiel L'Envers will want your blood. But . . ." He shrugged. "This itch has plagued you for a long time. The lady knows her mind and at least she's a better sense of the danger involved than you do. If you're minded to pursue it, in Elua's name, be careful. It's only a few months, and then you'll be packed off to Alba with your Cruithne bride."

"I know," I murmured.

"Second thoughts?"

I glanced sharply at him. "Don't tempt me."

On the ride home, I thought about Sidonie and the risk involved; bruised hearts at best and accusations of treason at worst. And I thought about my impending marriage and all the fine advice about duty and honor I'd given Lucius Tadius da Lucca, whose situation mirrored my own. I'd resolved to take my own advice when I made the decision to come home. I would do my duty to Terre d'Ange and House Courcel.

My resolve strengthened on the ride. Mavros was right, I should make an end of it. There was no future in it for Sidonie or me. Like as not she was right, and it *was* little more than the lure of the forbidden that goaded us. I was bound for Alba, and if it wasn't the choice I might have made with my life, it was one that would atone for all the choices my mother had made. In the meantime, I had no business sowing the seeds of chaos.

"I'll end it," I said aloud to the Bastard's flicking ears. "I will."

The Bastard snorted, as well he should.

For all my bold words, my resolve began to falter the following day, the instant I saw Amarante of Namarre waiting for me outside the *ollamh*'s study. In her bedchamber, Sidonie was gazing out the window, standing in a shaft of light. She turned as we entered, smiling at me with unreserved happiness. My heart leapt in my breast, and my resolve crumbled into a thousand meaningless pieces.

"Imriel." She did linger over my name this time.

I bowed to her. "Sun Princess."

It made her laugh, that unexpected, full-throated laugh that had turned my world upside down and made me realize that the private Sidonie de la Courcel was very different from the public one. Amarante shook her head and left us. I sat down on the bed uninvited, fearing we might not make it that far if I didn't start there.

"Do you think we might take this at a slower pace today?" I asked.

"We can try." Sidonie stood between my legs and cupped my up-turned face. I rested my hands on her hips and we gazed at one another. Her hair was pinned in a complicated chignon with looping tendrils, and the sunlight made an aureole of it. She kissed my face, my eyelids, the corners of my lips. " 'The lover showers kisses on the face of the be-loved,' " she recited softly from the *Trois Milles Joies*, " 'like petals falling in a summer rain.' " Her lips brushed mine, once, then again. The tip of her tongue darted, fleeting. " 'The lover seeks to open the beloved's lips like a tight-furled bud.' "

" 'The beloved's lips open like a blossom to admit the lover,' " I whis-pered, and then her mouth was on mine and her tongue in my mouth, my arms hard around her waist. We fell over onto the bed, kissing.

Elua, it was sweet, so sweet! When I could tear myself away from her mouth, I undressed her in between kisses, and kissed every part I uncovered, while Sidonie did the same. She found the scars; the battle-scars and the others. I felt her touch linger over the faint traces of old weals on my back, the brand on my left flank.

She lifted her head, eyes grave. "Will you tell me about these?"

I nodded. "But not now."

"No, not now." One finger brushed along the underside of the rigid arch of my phallus, which quivered in response. "Can we do it like before? Only properly."

I smiled. "You liked that?"

"Mmm." Sidonie kissed me. "Yes. Now, please. I don't want to wait."

She didn't say why and I didn't ask. I knew. It was a threshold. Until we crossed it, we could still go back. We could still tell ourselves it was nothing more than a few feverish moments of kissing and groping. Afterward, it would be different.

"You're sure?" I whispered when she was straddling me, her bare thighs nestled on the outside of mine. My phallus was throbbing in my fist, the swollen head nudging her nether-lips. They were parted and slick with desire, and I thought I might die if she said no.

"I'm sure." Sidonie shifted deliberately, and we both drew in our breath as the head of my phallus slipped inside her. "Oh, yes! I'm sure."

Inch by inch, she took me in, until I was sheathed to the hilt. I felt like laughing and I felt like crying. I wrapped my arms around her as she rocked atop me. And ah, Elua! It was hot and tight and slick, and terrifyingly intimate in a way I'd never felt before. We held each other and leaned our brows together and I watched her eyelids flutter, echoing the steady surge of ripples below that made her pant and gasp, until I couldn't stand it. With her hands wrapped around my head, I clung to her and groaned against her breast, my seed spurting deep inside her.

Everything was different now.

"Imriel?" Sidonie murmured. "Why do we fit so well together?"

I lay on my back, exhausted. "I wish I knew."

She wriggled atop me, clamping her thighs together and preventing my softening phallus from slipping out. I rolled her onto her side, rolling with her. We stayed conjoined, her upper thigh flung over mine. Our entwined limbs slid against each other and I felt the surge of desire returning, sooner than I would have thought possible. Sidonie laughed deep in her throat, legs squeezing mine. "I could climb you like a tree."

"I didn't think you liked climbing trees," I said.

She kissed me. "I don't."

"Do you know what I love?" I whispered. "I love your eyes. I love the way they don't match the rest of you."

"Cruithne eyes." Sidonie smiled. "You don't mind?"

"No." I kissed the outer corners of her eyelids, moving slowly inside her. "I like them. I always did." I dug my fingers into her thigh, moving it higher. I settled deeper into her, and she caught her breath in a long, satisfied sigh. "Why did you tell the Sultan's ambassador you'd entertain his suit?"

"Politics." Sidonie tasted my throat. "You want to talk politics?"

"I'm curious."

"Jealous?" She bit my earlobe. "*You* don't have the right to be."

"I know." I gathered her closer, sliding my arms up her back and sinking my hands into her hair. It was true, we fit together as though our bodies were made for one another. I'd never felt that with anyone else. This was slow and languorous and wonderful, and I didn't want it to end. I wanted to stay inside her, holding her. "I'm curious, that's all."

"Because," Sidonie murmured, punctuating her words with kisses, "it shows good faith on our part. And because Parliament will be sufficiently relieved when I refuse the Sultan's suit, they'll be more inclined to agree to the reduction in import fees despite my uncle's opposition, which is what Mother wants." She lifted her head, black eyes languid and amused. "Does that answer your question?"

"Mm-hmm." I thrust into her, watching her eyelids flutter again. For some reason, it was perversely arousing to hear her discuss matters of state while I made love to her. "You know, I could envision spending the rest of my life—"

"Don't say it." She touched my lips. "Please, don't."

Until that moment, I hadn't been sure that what Sidonie was feeling cast the same fearsome shadow in her heart that I felt in mine. But I saw the pain surface and I knew. We gazed at one another, face-to-face, and saw the vast, impending hurt that awaited us reflected in one another's eyes.

"Too late," I said quietly.

Something else surfaced in her expression; the cool determination with which she faced down whispers in the Court and charted her course to the throne. Sidonie rolled onto her back, pulling me atop her with agile strength. I propped myself on my arms above her. The pins had fallen out of her hair, spilling it over the pillows. "Then let's make it worthwhile," she said, locking her heels behind my buttocks.

I did my best to oblige.

TEN

THAT WINTER PASSED too quickly.

For days on end, I forgot all the things that should have absorbed me. I managed to tend to my Alban studies and I endeavored to learn more about issues of statecraft I'd neglected throughout my tenure as a Prince of the Blood. I consulted with the Queen regarding my upcoming nuptials, which filled me with vague dread. Everything else—the Unseen Guild, the mysterious Maghuin Dhonn, my vanished mother—I forgot.

Sidonie.

We didn't speak of the future, but every stolen moment we could snatch, we spent together. It was never enough. I always wanted more. I wanted to make love to her, and I wanted to talk with her. I wanted to talk about politics and philosophy and what it meant to be good. I wanted to talk about everything under the sun, the way Eamonn and I used to do. I wanted to talk about the endless ways she surprised me.

Sometimes we did. I kept my promise and told her about being abducted, about Daršanga and the Mahrkagir's zenana, and what I had endured there. I told her more than I'd ever told anyone except Eamonn and Phèdre.

"The worst part was that he made us complicit in it," I said without looking at her. "It happened a lot. There was a girl from Ch'in who displeased him. I never knew her name, but she had beautiful hair, hair to her waist. She used to hide her nakedness behind it in the festal hall." I gazed into the distance. "The Mahrkagir grew impatient at it. He gave me a blunt knife and bade me shear her. He said if I didn't do it, he'd do it himself and take her scalp with it."

Sidonie made a sound deep in her throat.

"So I did." My palms were sweating at the memory. I rubbed them on my thighs. "I hacked away her beautiful hair and laid it in his hands. Then he put the knife to *my* throat and bade her plait her own hair or watch me die slow. When she was done . . ." I took a deep breath. "He throttled her with it and made me watch. Took her by force and throttled her, so he could feel her die under him. He liked that."

I told her how I'd gotten the scar seared onto my left flank. How after Phèdre had come, the Mahrkagir had given me as a plaything to the Tatar warlord Jagun. How Jagun had fondled me and beaten me and branded me as his own property. How for long years I'd had nightmares in which I'd awakened screaming, the stench of my own burning flesh in my nostrils.

There were other stories; worse stories.

I didn't tell them all, but I told enough.

Sidonie listened without saying a word, her face stark with horror, streaked with silent tears. It was the only time I didn't touch her, and I couldn't look at her when I'd finished. "I'm sorry," she whispered. She knelt behind me, wrapping her arms around me, her head on my shoulder. "I'm so sorry."

I nodded, unable to speak. Neither of us did, not for a very long time. Sidonie held me, so still she might have been keeping a vigil; and mayhap she was. The sun crept across the floor of Amarante's bedchamber and another knot of shame inside me slowly uncoiled.

At length her warm breath stirred my hair. "Does this mean I shouldn't expect you to do wonderful, horrible things to my helpless body?"

A bolt of mortified desire went through me and my mouth went dry. I turned in her arms to look at her in shock. "Are you jesting?"

Her black eyes were bright with a mix of mirth and sorrow. "No."

"Elua!" I laughed shortly and rubbed my face. "Oh, Sidonie."

She kissed me, soft and tender; a shower of petals falling. It washed away the last traces of shame, at least for a moment. She cupped my face and regarded me with a deep gaze worthy of Phèdre, then kissed me lightly on the lips. "We'll see."

No one else had ever reacted that way, with anything less than unalleviated horror and sympathy; not even knowing a tenth of what had befallen me. Until Sidonie did, I hadn't known I'd wanted someone to. Even a year ago, I don't think I would have. But I wasn't the same Imriel who had shorn his own hair in a fit of self-loathing after Mavros took me to Valerian House. In Tiberium, Asclepius' priest had told me to bear my scars with pride. I was learning.

And wrong and doomed though this affair might be, it helped.

I asked Sidonie about it the next time we were together, lying in the afterglow of lovemaking. "All right, then. Tell me. What sort of wonderful, horrible things did you have in mind?"

She smiled, her cheek pillowed on one arm. "Oh, nothing *too* horrible."

I traced the neat, sleek curve of her back, imagining the kiss of a flogger, welts arising on her tender skin. "Why?"

"I'm curious," she said simply. "I want to."

"You're too young." I smacked her nearest buttock lightly.

Sidonie wrinkled her nose in an expression so like her sister's that it did nothing to belie my observation. "You sound like Amarante when she's being instructive." Her voice took on a tone of unearthly calm. "'Sidonie, if you rush too swiftly through all the pleasures Naamah's arts offer, they will lose their savor.'"

I laughed. "Oh, instructive, is it?"

"Well, not as much, now." She smiled again. "It was."

I ran a lock of her hair through my fingers. It glinted in the light, subtle differences in the hues of gold. "Tell me more about these instructive parts."

"Give me your hand." Sidonie rolled onto her back. I propped myself on my left arm and she took my right hand, guiding my forefinger to her warm, moist cleft and placing the tip of it on her still-swollen bud. "'First and foremost, it is important to understand your own pleasure,'" she said in the same imperturbable tone. She rubbed my fingertip against her bud, and moisture gathered and glistened there. "'Though the pinnacle of pleasure may be gained by many methods, for a woman, its seeds lie always in Naamah's Pearl. This is the ultimate source of your pleasure. That, you must never forget. You see, though I touch you with but the merest tip of one finger, I bring you to—'" Her voice broke and her hand tightened on mine, pressing hard. "'Ah! There, yes, there.'"

"No!" I was laughing almost too hard to let her finish. "So didactic? Surely not!"

"Not exactly," Sidonie admitted breathlessly. "Nearly, though."

I felt a twinge of guilt. "You shouldn't make mock of it. At least not in her own bed."

"I'm not mocking." She sat up, shaking out her hair. "Well, only a little. Only in love. After all, it *was* very instructive. At least in the beginning. I learn quickly." She smiled at me. "And anyway, Amarante doesn't sleep here very often."

"Oh, I see." I caught another lock of her hair, winding it around fingers damp with her pleasure. "The pupil has become an ardent scholar."

"Yes." Sidonie leaned down to kiss me, the tips of her breasts brushing my chest.

No apology; no shame. She was half-Cruithne, but wholly D'Angeline in matters of desire. And strangely, there was no jealousy in me, only fondness. I gazed up at her and understood for the first time, truly understood, the gifts of Blessed Elua and his Companions. Even the heir to the throne, long schooled in the arts of discipline and self-control, was free to lay those concerns aside in the bedchamber. Even damaged goods like me could be healed here. It was a sacred place in which we were free to be whoever, whatever we wished. Such was the grace of the gods we worshipped.

The dark mirror and the bright alike; both reflected our true selves.

"What are you thinking, Imriel?" she asked.

"A great many things," I said slowly. "Not the least of which is that I love you."

It was a violation of our unspoken pact, but Sidonie said nothing, only made another soft sound deep in her throat. She shook her head in impatient despair and kissed me again, over and over. I kissed her back, drowning in gold, her sun-shot hair falling around my face, hearing the echo of the Asclepian priest's words in my memory.

Even a stunted tree reaches toward the sunlight.

Another priest, a priest of Elua, had spoken a different prophecy for me, long ago, when I was still a boy. When I had first undertaken Blessed Elua's vigil on the Longest Night. The priest had spoken to me of love.

You will find it and lose it, again and again.

That, I tried to forget.

I never dreamed there was such a vast difference between loving and being in love. When we were together, it was glorious. I was happier than I'd been since I was a child, since before I was taken. When we were apart, which was far too much of the time, my emotions ran rampant. Betimes I was filled with misery and self-pity, aching with longing. Betimes I brooded and conceived countless schemes wherein I confronted Queen Ysandre and the entire Court and proclaimed our love, challenging Barquiel L'Envers at the point of a sword when he rose to defame me.

And betimes I was angry and struggled against it. I didn't *want* this feeling, and it seemed absurd I couldn't shake loose of it. I couldn't, though. Absurd or no, love had set its hooks in my heart, and they were barbed and deep.

I loved her.

I hated it.

Elua, it was hard, so hard, seeing her at Court! After hours of blissful lovemaking, we'd lost the trick of being cordial with one another in public. Even before, there had been an invisible cord between us. Now it seemed like a living thing, pulsing with intimacy.

Still, we hid it; or at least I thought we did. We were careful and overly cool in the public eye. It spawned talk of ill will between us— over the absent Maslin de Lombelon who had never made any secret of disliking me, over my rumored dalliance with Sidonie's favorite lady-in-waiting, over my aspirations in Alba, over my long-standing favoritism toward Alais.

Betimes I would see Ysandre's gaze linger on us with regret, and all I could think was how much more distraught the Queen would be if she knew I was calculating how many hours or days it might be before I could lose myself in the arms of her naked, nubile heir, whose name ran like a constant refrain through my thoughts. And then I would have to look away for fear it was written on my face.

It was, of course, to those who knew how to read it.

I wasn't so great a fool that I thought I could keep my state from Phèdre; only its cause. As the days wore on and I was mooning and restless, sleeping poorly and picking at my food, I half expected her to confront me. Instead, she merely regarded me with a speculative look and kept her thoughts to herself.

Joscelin was another matter.

"There's somewhat I'd like to see today," he announced one morning as we broke our fasts. "I've been thinking we might try a crop of sunflowers in Montrève, and Tibault de Toluard has invented a means of using a hypocaust sytem to germinate seeds months early. I thought you might be interested, Imri."

I shook my head. "I've a session with the *ollamh*."

"We'll go afterward," Joscelin suggested. "It's right here in the City."

Afterward, I had had hopes of wallowing in tangled bedsheets with Sidonie. I toyed with a hunk of honey-smeared bread. "Seems an odd spot to germinate seeds."

"It's just a trial. If it works, he'll build a larger system in Siovale." Joscelin tapped the table. "You know, Drustan told me about a place in Alba where the springs run warm as blood, summer and winter alike. If Lord Tibault's method works, you might replicate it there. Think of it! A hypocaust that needs no fuel."

All Siovalese are mad for inventions. Joscelin, born and bred in the mountains of Siovale, was no exception. I drizzled more honey on my bread, watching it coil and dissolve in a puddle of amber-gold. "If it's an Alban spring, like as not it's sacred." I'd learned a few things from my studies.

"Still," Joscelin said dryly. "I'd like you to come."

I glanced up at his tone. Unless we were sparring, there was very little Joscelin asked of me. And I owed him a debt I could never repay.

"All right." I set down my bread and squared my shoulders. "Yes, of course."

We spent the better part of the afternoon in a building on the outskirts of the City marketplace, where some enterprising D'Angeline merchant had thought to build a bath in the Tiberian style. The venture had failed, but the Marquis de Toluard had purchased the building and converted the hypocaust to his own purposes.

"See!" he crowed, pointing to the etiolated seedlings sprouting in the trenches of rich soil. "If it works, we'll gain weeks. A month, mayhap."

Joscelin poked at a seedling with a dubious finger. "It wants sunlight, my lord."

"I know." The Marquis steered him to the far end of the trenches, where a patch of daylight bathed the seedlings. "See, here . . ."

His voice trailed away, or at least, I stopped listening. While Joscelin and Lord Tibault debated the merits of his system and whether the benefits of an early harvest outweighed the cost of charcoal to fuel the hypocaust, I lost myself in a pleasant memory of Sidonie crouched between my thighs, performing the *languisement*. Elua knows how, but the incident at Bryony House had reached her ears and we'd made a wager, both of us laughing about it. I'd lost the moment I saw her delicate pink lips engulf the head of my phallus, sliding down the shaft to meet her clutching fist. The mere sight was enough to drive me over the edge.

I'd paid my debt in kisses, tasting my seed on her tongue, thick and salty.

". . . percentage of seedlings don't take root—" Joscelin gave me a funny look. "Imri?"

I shook myself, praying I hadn't groaned aloud. "Oh, yes. I'm listening."

"Ha!" Tibault de Toluard clapped me on the back. "Daydreaming of love, young highness? I remember it well, those days." He patted my shoulders. "Enjoy, enjoy. May she or he be worthy of your reveries."

"Thank you, my lord," I murmured.

Joscelin didn't comment, or at least not then. It wasn't until the ride home when he suggested we share a jug of ale at the Cockerel. Emile greeted us with effusive joy. At Joscelin's request, he secured us a quiet table in the corner, backing away with a finger to his lips and elaborate promises of discretion.

"So." Joscelin poured two foaming mugs of ale and shoved one toward me. "Shall we talk about it? Phèdre and I drew lots, and I lost."

"Truly?" I asked, scandalized.

"No, of course not." He hid a half-smile with a sip of ale. "Well, the part about talking, yes. Since you didn't bring it to her, we both thought mayhap it would be best if I pressed the issue. Love, is it?"

I took a long drink. "Joscelin, would you believe me if I told you you'd rather not know?"

"I would," he said. "Trouble is, I already do." When I didn't say anything, Joscelin continued. "According to Ti-Philippe, there's gossip among the Palace Guard that you've been dallying with one of the Dauphine's ladies-in-waiting," he said, and I relaxed. Joscelin raked me with a sharp gaze. "And the trouble with *that*, love, is that Phèdre doesn't believe it."

"Oh," I said faintly. "Why ever not?"

Joscelin shrugged and sipped his ale. "Naamah's business. She's known the young lady's mother for a long time. Exactly what they've concocted between them, I couldn't say, except that Phèdre's certain the lady in question wouldn't engage in casual dalliance. And therefore, based on your strange and secretive behavior, my love, she has conceived the sort of outrageous notion that I would discredit in a heartbeat if I hadn't spent half my life watching Phèdre nó Delaunay's outrageous notions proved true."

I looked away. "What makes you think it's casual?"

"I don't," he said. "Not by the way you're carrying on. I also don't think it's Amarante of Namarre you're mooning over." Joscelin waited until I looked reluctantly back at him. Puzzlement and disbelief were etched on his face as he lowered his voice to a scarce audible murmur. "Imriel . . . Sidonie?"

I groaned and put my head down on the table. "Oh, Joscelin!"

"Elua's Balls! It's true?"

I clutched my hair. "Yes."

"Why?" He sounded as though he was trying not to laugh. "Name of Elua, Imri! *Why?*"

Dragging myself upright in my chair, I poured out the story to him, starting with last year's boar hunt, the spooked horse, and Sidonie's laughter. I'd not told anyone but Mavros, and once I started, the words tumbled out. Joscelin listened to me in a state of bemused awe, periodically glancing around to ensure that Emile's assurance of discretion was holding.

"Are you quite sure we're talking about the same person?" he asked dubiously as I rambled on about how passionate, uninhibited, and devastatingly funny she was. His voice dropped again. "Sidonie *de la Courcel*? The Dauphine of Terre d'Ange?"

"You don't know her," I said helplessly.

"So it seems." Joscelin refilled my cup. "You know, her mother has a fierce temper, and one rarely sees *that* in public. The women of House Courcel have learned to keep a sharp check on their emotions. I suppose . . ." He shook his head. "You do know this is a disaster in the making?"

"I know." I stared into my ale. "We both do."

"Then why—"

"I can't help it!" I jerked my head up. "I can't."

Joscelin sighed. He looked at me for a long time, and when he spoke, his voice was gentle. "And are you planning to do aught foolish, love? Like break your word to the Queen in the matter of Alba?"

I'd thought about it. I thought about it every day. "No. I don't know."

"All right." Joscelin swirled the ale in his cup. Elsewhere in the tavern, there were Tsingani laughing and chatting. Someone was playing a timbale. "Imriel, we will stand by you whatever you choose," he said in his direct manner. "Know that, but listen, too. You asked me once how I could bear it; knowing what Phèdre is. Knowing how different we are, knowing we're so ill suited it must make the gods laugh. Knowing it, and choosing it anyway. Do you remember what I told you?"

"I remember." I knew what he was hinting at, though I didn't much like it. "You said you'd tried doing without her."

"Even so." There was sympathy in his summer-blue eyes. "Believe me, love, I know your childhood was stolen. I know that in some ways, you haven't been young since you were ten years old. This isn't one of them. You're very young, and so is she. She doesn't even gain her majority for, what? Two more years?"

"She's seventeen in a few weeks."

"A little over a year, then." Joscelin put one gauntleted hand on my arm. "Imri, if it's real, it will endure."

"How would you know?" I asked, then colored. Still, I kept going. "It's not the same, Joscelin! You left of your own will."

"Indeed." He raised his brows. "Whereupon your mother had two of our companions slaughtered and Phèdre thrown into a dungeon so dire that sailors believe it god-cursed. The worst thing you'll have to worry about is that your love will prove inconstant and fickle. Which would you prefer?"

"I take your point," I muttered.

"Good," Joscelin said. He squeezed my arm and released it. "And if a year passes and you both feel the same way, at least she'll have gained her majority. If she wants to defy her mother and the peerage, she'll have the legal standing to do so. And if you want leave Alba to be with her, Elua knows, Phèdre and I will move heaven and earth for you."

I smiled a little. "Promise?"

"Against my better judgment, yes." Joscelin smiled back at me. "You know, in a way, it makes my heart glad to see you like this. There was a time I wasn't sure . . ." His voice faded and I knew we were both thinking about Daršanga. Butchery in the festal hall, the screams of dying women, blood running in channels between the flagstones.

"I know," I said softly. "You, too."

"Elua's grace is a mysterious thing," he murmured. "Still . . . Sidonie?"

I laughed. "Strange to say, yes." I tipped my cup and downed the last swallow. "Joscelin, is love supposed to make you feel like you're sick and dying, and mad enough to hit someone, and drunk with joy, and your heart's a boulder in your chest trying to burst into a thousand pieces, all at once?"

"Mm-hmm." He finished his ale. "That would be love."

ELEVEN

I TOLD SIDONIE ABOUT MY conversation with Joscelin, or at least parts of it. Apart from my single declaration, we still hadn't spoken openly about *love*.

Alarm flashed in her eyes. "He's not going to say anything, is he?"

"No, of course not." I regarded her. "Sidonie, truly. What do you think would happen if we were found out?"

"Truly?" She thought about it. "I think my mother would dismiss Amarante and anyone in else my retinue likely to be the least bit sympathetic. I think she would lock me in my quarters and give me a lecture that blistered my ears, double my guard and fill it with men loyal to her and order them to report on my whereabouts every minute of the day. I think she would pack you off to Alba on the next ship." Sidonie gave me a level look. "And I think my uncle would try to have you killed at the first opportunity."

"I see." Her tone chilled my blood. "Why on earth does he hate me so much? On the long list of people with reason to bear grudges against Melisande Shahrizai's son, he's nowhere near the top."

"No," she said slowly. "He's a strange man and an ambitious one. I think he conceived a plan in Khebbel-im-Akkad to create a dynasty for House L'Envers with ties to other powerful nations. But he didn't know my great-grandfather was plotting the same thing with Alba until it was too late and his daughter was already wed to the Khalif's son. Which, in the end, gained him very little here in Terre d'Ange and cost him his best pawn."

"So his plan failed. Come here." I tugged her down beside me on the bed. "Still, it's nothing to do with *me*."

"No, I know." Sidonie nestled against me. "I don't know, Imriel. It all happened so long before either of us were born."

"It's not fair, is it?" I murmured.

"To you least of all." She took my hand and kissed it, then placed it on her chest. Beneath her soft, warm skin I could feel the steady beat of her heart under my palm. Her dark, lustrous eyes were filled with unwavering trust. "Truly? I think it simply drives him mad to think that after all the spectacular failure of your mother's schemes, you're two heartbeats away from inheriting the throne."

"But I don't want it," I said. "Just you."

Sidonie smiled sadly. "It's a hard case to prove."

"We could demonstrate," I suggested, and she laughed and kissed me until we forgot all about Barquiel L'Envers and the disapproving world beyond the door of the bedchamber, making oblivious love until Amarante had to interrupt us to summon her mistress to dine with the Queen, standing over the bed where we lay sweating and entangled until we realized she was there. It had happened more than the once, enough times that I'd lost all traces of self-consciousness about it. Sidonie had never had any, not here.

"I swear to Elua, Sidonie, someone ought to dowse you with cold water," Amarante said mildly. "Both of you."

"You don't mean that." Sidonie extricated herself from the bed, and I lay watching her. She had a deft way of moving, quick and graceful. "And anyway, haven't you heard? I've got icewater in my veins."

Amarante raised her brows. "Appearances *are* deceiving."

It was common wisdom at Court. I'd believed it, too. I remembered the first time I'd danced with Sidonie. *Mind you don't get chilblains*, Eamonn had said, and I'd laughed. Now, it merely drove me mad and heightened my desire, knowing the depth of wanton abandonment that lurked beneath her cool exterior.

It made me proud of her, too. That was another strange thing about this business of love. All the things that had once irritated me—her imperious manner at Court, her infuriatingly self-possessed demeanor, her dislike of climbing trees—filled me with tender affection.

A bewildering thing, love.

I talked to Phèdre about it. It was a relief, knowing that she knew. I thought surely she would be filled with sage advice, since surely if there was anyone in the world who knew about love in all its myriad forms, it was Phèdre.

On that count, I was wrong. She only laughed. "There's nothing I could tell you about love that you'd believe without learning it for yourself, Imri."

"But you weren't surprised," I said.

"About Sidonie?" Phèdre shook her head. "I grew up in the Night Court. Even as children, we heard stories about patrons. By the time I entered Delaunay's service, there was precious little that would surprise me when it came to desire. And you . . ." She sighed. "Ah, love! The first thing you did when we emerged from the zenana was fling yourself headlong into danger. Why should this be any different?"

I fidgeted at her feet. "It is, though."

"I know." She stroked my hair, her voice gentle. "You still worry me, that's all."

"Phèdre?" I craned my head to look at her. "Did you love my mother?"

In all the years I'd been a part of her household, I'd never dared to ask. Her stroking fingers went still. "Love would be an odd word for it," she mused. "And yet, in the end, yes. Although I hated her, too." Phèdre propped her chin in her hand and contemplated me. "There was no one else quite like her. Betimes I think the qualities that made her monstrous might have vaulted her to greatness in other circumstances."

"Am I like her?" I asked.

"Well, you've a conscience," she said dryly. "That's one difference. And I don't know that your mother ever did aught impetuous in her life, whereas you . . ." Phèdre smiled. "You're another matter."

"I'm not impetuous!" I protested.

"Oh, no?" Phèdre tweaked a lock of my hair. "Truly, Imri? Yes, a little. In a roomful of people, your mother shone. It's naught to do with beauty. For good or for ill, some people seem to love more fiercely, want more powerfully, burn more brightly. She had profound desires and an indomitable will. I see glimpses of that in you."

I swallowed. "I see."

"Does that frighten you?" she asked.

"A little," I said truthfully.

"Ah, love! It's only a part." She smoothed my mussed hair. "In her own unfathomable way, your mother had a good deal of integrity. I see that in you, too."

"I keep my promises," I murmured. Locked away in a cabinet in her study, Phèdre kept a note with those words on it, alongside a diamond on a frayed velvet cord, an ivory hairpin, and a figurine of a jade dog.

"Even so." Having adjusted my hair to her satisfaction, Phèdre kissed the top of my head. "And there's so much more that's yours, and yours alone, most of all a kind heart and a generous spirit. And rather more courage than I'd like, when you come to it," she added. "I'm not altogether sanguine about your adventures in Lucca, and I know you've not told me the half of them."

I laughed. "Eamonn told me his mother said you were the bravest person she'd ever met."

"Did she?" Phèdre, who had walked into the living hell of Daršanga—a place the most hardened Akkadian soldiers held in dread—of her own volition to rescue me, smiled. "Ah, well. 'Tis a different sort of courage. You've not had word from him, have you?"

"Eamonn?" I shook my head, feeling guilty. "No, not yet." Although he was my dearest friend in the world, I'd been too caught up in my own affairs to spare much thought for him. I fidgeted with the dagger-sheath strapped to my left leg. "Before he left for Skaldia, he promised he'd try to come for my wedding."

"Here or in Alba?"

I shrugged. The rites would be held in both places. I was to wed Dorelei mab Breidaia in the D'Angeline fashion here in Terre d'Ange. At the summer's end, we would sail to Alba, where we would be wed in a Cruithne ritual for all of royal Alba to witness. Thus far, outside of my conversations with the Queen, I'd done a good job avoiding thinking about either. Even now, it gave me a horrible pang of loss and longing. "Here, I suppose. I didn't know about the other when last we spoke."

"Imri."

I looked up at Phèdre.

The scarlet mote of Kushiel's Dart floated on the iris of her left eye; a crimson petal on a a forest pool. It was no accident that I'd lost my heart to a dark-eyed girl who was more than she seemed on the surface. Even as the belated realization dawned in my mind, I saw Phèdre smile ruefully, already knowing my thoughts. No girl, but a woman long grown; Kushiel's Chosen with the Name of God in her thoughts. I'd only ever surprised her once, growing up before either of us were ready for it.

"Do you know," Phèdre said lightly, "your mother possessed one trait in abundance that you lack. If you were minded to cultivate aught of Melisande Shahrizai, you could do worse."

I gritted my teeth. "What is it?"

She tilted her head. "Patience."

As winter eased into spring, Elua knows, I tried. It was hard. The days seemed to rush past, each one bringing a new harbinger of spring. Days grew warmer and windy. Blossoms appeared on fruit-bearing trees. Wisteria climbed the trellis in the inner courtyard where Joscelin and I sparred, clusters of green buds forming. Yellow blossoms opened on the thriving coronilla bushes, releasing honey-sweet fragrance into the damp air.

And Sidonie turned seventeen.

There was a fête, of course. I viewed its advent with a mix of dread and longing. It brought her one step closer to her majority, but every day that passed brought my impending marriage closer, too. If I could have held back time's passage with my bare hands, I would have that spring.

Sidonie's birthday dawned fair and clear, boding well for Ysandre's desire to hold the fête in the royal gardens. Silk pavilions were erected between the lilac trees, large enough to hold a number of couches, and braziers were set all around to drive off the evening's chill. This year, the Queen had contracted a number of adepts from Eglantine House to entertain; musicians, tumblers, and poets.

By the time the guests began to arrive, the first hint of twilight was in the air and servants were lighting the myriad glass lamps strung around the garden. Every pavilion held a table laden with food. The Eglantine adepts mingled with the guests, green and gold ribbons twined in their hair. Here and there, laughter or clapping arose in response to a ribald song or a tumbling display. One greeted us with a handspring and a standing somersault.

He came up grinning, ribbons askew in his curly brown hair. "Welcome, welcome, my lords and lady!"

Joscelin nudged Phèdre. "Think you could you still do that, love?"

She laughed. "With a good deal of practice, mayhap."

"I know you," I said to the adept, picturing a satyr's mask shoved atop his curls. "The Longest Night, wasn't it?"

He nodded. "Still thoughtful, your highness?"

I glanced over at the royal pavilion, lit from beneath with so many torches that the Courcel blue silk seemed luminous in the twilight. "Unfortunately, yes."

"Well, come visit me!" He took my hand in a hard, wiry clasp and winked. "Simon nó Eglantine. I'm very good at *not* being thoughtful."

It made me laugh, whereupon Simon grinned again, planted a kiss on my lips, and flung himself backward into another handspring, waving cheerfully before plunging into the midst of the milling guests.

"Charming," Mavros commented, strolling over to meet me. "It's about time."

I shook my head at him. "It's not what you think."

"Pity." He watched the adept Simon. "They're very flexible, tumblers." His voice dropped. "Tell me, are we still going through with your mad scheme tonight?"

"Are you still willing to help?" I asked.

Mavros sighed. "Oh yes, fool that I am! You *are* family." He touched the purse at his belt. "I have the ribbons here."

"Good." I clapped his shoulder. "I have to greet Sidonie."

She was seated on a couch in the royal pavilion, surrounded by courtiers and well-wishers presenting gifts. The wealthier of the young noblemen vied to outdo one another with extravagant tokens, each of which was admired publicly before being handed into a servant's keeping. I lingered for a moment, smiling inwardly at the cool way Sidonie accepted them. The only time I heard her voice warm was when a young scion of the impoverished House Labarre stammered apologies for having nothing more to offer her than a flask of cordial with a limp bunch of violets tied around the neck.

"Imri!" Alais spotted me and broke my reverie. She had Celeste with her, the wolfhound pacing sedately at her side. "See how good Celeste is being?" she asked after I'd kissed her in greeting. "Mother wanted me to leave her."

"Oh no, we couldn't have that," I said gravely, dropping to one knee. "So you've not filched a thing tonight, have you, Celeste?"

The wolfhound regarded me with apologetic dignity. "Only a very small squab," Alais said defensively. "And I didn't let her eat the bones."

I smiled. "Good girl."

"Prince Imriel." Amarante's voice, that calm tone Sidonie emulated so terribly well. I had to own, it made one wonder what she sounded like unstrung with passion. She was smiling as I rose. There was genuine affection in it, and I remembered Sidonie saying I'd won her over when I'd sewn up Alais' wounded dog. "Well met, your highness."

"Well met, my lady." I bowed. "Mavros was hoping to see you."

Her smile deepened. "Oh, indeed?"

It was a part of our plan, though seeing Alais' gaze sharpen, I wondered if Mavros wasn't right about the madness of it, and mayhap it would be wiser not to go through with it. Well, of course it would be *wiser*, but . . . I sighed. "I've got to greet your sister, villain," I said to Alais.

"All right." Alais knit her brows. "Be *nice*, Imri."

"I will be," I promised.

When I approached, courtiers were exclaiming over the gift Phèdre and Joscelin had presented Sidonie. It was a Siovalese music box in the shape of a clamshell that played a sweet melody when opened, a pearl emerging from the bed of the shell through some cunning, unseen mechanism. An apt gift, I thought, remembering her recounting the lesson of Naamah's Pearl, squirming beneath my finger. At that moment, Sidonie caught my eye. I must have been careless and let my face reveal my thoughts, for a pink flush tinted her cheeks.

"Thank you," she murmured to Phèdre. "It's lovely, truly." Sidonie took a deep breath. Her flush faded and she shot me a look that no one else but me would have known was wicked. "Well met, cousin. What have *you* brought me?"

I bowed. "A small token, your highness."

Sidonie accepted the polished ebony box I proffered and lifted the lid. Inside, a pair of gold earrings nestled on black velvet; twin sunbursts, miniature duplicates of the pendant she'd worn on the Longest Night. I knew, because I'd persuaded Amarante to borrow it without Sidonie's knowledge. It wasn't an extravagant gift, but it was a fitting one.

"How clever!" Ysandre, gazing over her daughter's shoulder, sounded surprised. "That's very thoughtful, isn't it?"

"Yes." Sidonie lifted her head. My gift had moved her, and her black eyes were bright with unshed tears. "Thank you, Imriel." Her voice was light, but it lingered over my name, sure as a caress. It made my skin prickle. I couldn't imagine that the whole Court couldn't hear it, too. I couldn't imagine that no one could see that for a moment, there was no one in the world but the two of us.

No one did, though.

"I'm glad you like them." I cleared my throat. "A joyous natality to you."

Ah, Elua! After that, the fête wore on *forever*. Under any other circumstances, it would have been pleasant. We dined, we danced, we drank free-flowing wine and enjoyed the Queen's largesse. The Eglantine adepts were sublimely entertaining. Mavros flirted with Amarante, thoroughly enjoying himself. I spent a good deal of time in Alais' company and danced once with Sidonie because it would have been rude not to. We were both so rigid for fear of giving ourselves away, we tripped over one another's feet, which filled us both with a desperate hilarity we had to struggle to suppress.

All in all I thought the night would never end.

Patience.

At last it did. The assembled guests began straggling into the spring night, accompanied by wavering torches and the lingering scent of lilacs. An end was declared to the fête, and the other members of House Courcel retired to the Palace. I made my way to Phèdre and Joscelin's side to tell them I meant to go to the Night Court with Mavros.

"Oh?" Phèdre cupped my face. "Name of Elua, love! Will you *please* be careful?"

I didn't lie as well as I thought; not to her. Not to Joscelin, either. He eyed me wryly, and I knew I'd not fooled either of them. "Yes," I said. "I will. *We* will."

Joscelin rolled his eyes.

They went, though. I found Mavros, who hauled me behind the lilac bushes. With deft fingers, he braided into my hair the green and gold ribbons he'd brought, creating a cascade of color. "Tilt your head," he ordered. I obeyed, letting the ribbons fall to obscure my features. Mavros sighed. "I must be out of my wits."

"Do you think it will work?" I asked.

"Let's find out."

It *was* a mad scheme, like a scene in a farcical play. I daresay we deserved to get caught, and the fact that we weren't owed everything to Mavros. He played his role to the hilt, trailing after Amarante as she escorted me to Sidonie's quarters, plaguing her with such incessant wooing that I was hard-pressed not to laugh. Amarante was laughing, fending him off with both hands as she bade the guard on duty outside Sidonie's chambers to fetch her mistress. He obeyed with a grin.

Sidonie came to the door. "Lord Shahrizai," she said coolly. "Have you become an adept of Eglantine House? I don't believe I requested *your* presence."

"Take him, take him!" Mavros shoved me past the distracted guard and wrapped his arms around Amarante, nuzzling her neck. "I've come to lodge a complaint. Your lady-in-waiting has skin as soft and white as apple blossoms and a heart as hard as stone. 'Tis cruel and unfair."

"My lord!" Amarante protested, laughing.

Sidonie raised her brows. "Giraud, will you summon someone to escort my lord Shahrizai to the Hall of Games?" she said to the guard, who was still grinning. "And mind, I'm not to be disturbed on any account until I arise."

"Aye, your highness," he said cheerfully. "A joyous natality to you!"

"Unfair!" Mavros shouted, loosing Amarante. "Cruel and unfair!"

"Come on, my lord," the guard said, taking his arm and steering him down the hall. Sidonie pulled Amarante into her chambers and closed the door firmly behind her, throwing the bolt. The three of us were alone in her salon.

"Name of Elua!" I rubbed my face. "It would have been a good deal easier and safer to go through Amarante's room."

"But not as much fun," Amarante observed, sounding less than calm. Whatever else Mavros had accomplished, he'd succeeded in that much.

"No." Sidonie put her arms around my neck. "And this way, if there's talk of a man in my chambers, which there will be, no one will wonder." She kissed my throat, making the ribbons in my hair rustle. "I don't think the guards eavesdrop a-purpose, but they'd hear the timbre of a man's voice. I needed a very good reason to be left undisturbed."

It had been her one wish for her birthday: one night. The two of us alone in her own quarters, her own bed. It seemed absurd that such a simple wish could carry such risk, and yet it did. Unfair, as Mavros said; cruel and unfair.

"I'll leave you," Amarante said. "If there's trouble . . ."

"I'll send my Eglantine adept to you," Sidonie said. She smiled into my eyes. "We'll say I wearied of my gift and chose to share it."

As plans went, it was no better than the first one. Still, it would have to serve. I didn't care. I reckoned it was worth the risk. Whatever else happened, I wanted this. I wanted it as much as Sidonie did. An entire night . . . Elua!

After Amarante departed through the adjoining door, Sidonie took my hand and led me through her salon, which was heaped with gifts, to the bedchamber beyond. I stopped in the doorway, swallowing.

The room was ablaze with candlelight. It held a massive four-posted bed, spread with a coverlet of rich maroon velvet. For a moment, I had a dizzying flash of Claudia's bedchamber. There was one difference, though. Coiled in the center of the bed was a length of silken rope.

I looked at Sidonie.

"Only that," she said gravely. "Only if you truly want to."

My blood throbbed in my veins. I took a deep breath and smelled only beeswax and the spicy fragrance of a pomander ball on the bedside table. Love was here and Daršanga was far, far away. "Yes," I said, gathering Sidonie in my arms. "Oh, yes."

She laughed and kissed me. "Let me take out your ribbons first."

I did. We undressed one another slowly. After so many stolen hours and rushed encounters, there was an unspeakable luxury in taking our time. The shadows gathered in the corners of the room, the vast expanse of the bed, made everything new and strange.

"You look different by candlelight," I murmured.

"So do you," Sidonie whispered.

I trailed one tasselled end of the rope over her bare skin. "You're sure?"

Her back arched. "Imriel . . ."

"Because I *will* make you beg," I breathed into her ear. Ah, Elua! There was a thrill in speaking the words aloud, a thrill in her inarticulate reply. I knelt over her and stretched her arms above her head, pinning her shoulders between my knees. I kissed the insides of her wrists, tasting her rapid pulse. When I tied the first knot with a hard jerk, Sidonie gave a small cry. I glanced down at her. Her eyes were wide and excited.

"Go on," she whispered.

I learned to tie knots aboard a felucca sailing the Nahar River. I lashed one wrist to a bedpost, threaded the rope around the other bedpost and lashed the other wrist. Hard and tight, her arms splayed wide. The sight of her when I'd finished was beautiful beyond words.

Patience, Phèdre had said.

I found patience in myself that night, although I daresay it wasn't the kind she'd had in mind. Then again, mayhap it was. One never knew for a surety. I made love to Sidonie with my lips and tongue and hands, with endless patience. Again and again, I brought her near the crest of desire and abandoned her there. Her hips jerked in helpless frustration when I took my mouth away, hands above her bound wrists clenching and opening. And ah, Elua! It felt so *good*.

"Imriel . . ." Sidonie writhed, almost in tears. *"Please!"*

"Is it this what you want?" Between her thighs, I sat back on my heels, caressing my erect shaft. It throbbed pleasantly in my hand. "Tell me."

She did, ragged and gasping.

"All right," I whispered.

I spread her thighs wider, pushing her knees toward her straining shoulders. No more teasing. I fit myself inside her; deep, deeper than I'd ever gone. Her loins rocked against mine and I felt her climax, over and over. I wanted it to last forever. Patience. I held off for what seemed like hours, stroking her long and slow, until a driving urgency overtook me. Deep, deeper, deepest. I buried myself in her, groaning, and spent my seed with a shudder that ran from the crown of my skull to the base of my spine.

We lay there for a long time, panting.

"Imriel." Sidonie's voice at my ear, low and resonant. "You could untie me now."

"I'll try." I rolled off her, picking at knots grown tighter. "Elua's Balls!"

She laughed; *that* laugh. It made my heart soar. I freed one wrist and kissed it. There were marks where the rope had been. "Better?"

"Yes." Sidonie flexed her arm, watching me work on the other wrist. "I don't want you to leave."

"I'm not going anywhere, Sun Princess," I murmured, taking the time to plant a kiss on the upturned palm on her outstretched hand. "Not tonight, I promise you."

"I don't mean tonight."

I freed her other wrist. "Tell me."

"You." Sidonie tossed off the coils of rope, sat up, and shook her head impatiently. "Imriel, have you any idea how many women of the Court look at you and see somewhat beautiful and damaged and dangerous? Have you *any* idea how many dream of easing that haunted look behind your eyes?" She raked one hand through her hair. "Name of Elua! You don't, do you?"

"No," I said softly. "I . . . no."

"You're so . . ." She shook her head again. "And the damnable thing is, I wasn't one of them. Never. And now you smile at me, and it feels like my heart's on a string and it's being yanked out of my chest."

"I know the feeling," I said. "All too well."

Sidonie sighed, drawing up her knees and hugging them. "I love you," she said in a small voice. "I thought if I didn't say the words, mayhap it would go away. But Elua help me, I do. So much it hurts. So much that I already miss you. I don't know if I can bear it."

I moved behind her, enfolding her in my arms. "Do we have a choice?"

"Not any good ones." Sidonie leaned back, head resting on my shoulder. She gazed at the dancing patterns of candlelight on the ceiling. "Believe me, I've thought about it. I can't step aside as Mother's heir. It would fall to Alais, and that would throw everything into chaos in Alba. I can't do it."

"No, I know," I said. "Joscelin said to wait a year."

"Oh, he did, did he?" She shifted in my arms to get a look at me. "You didn't tell me that part."

"You hadn't told me you loved me," I observed.

"I was hoping it would pass," she said wryly. "Elua! This is so *stupid*."

"True." I tightened my arms around her. "But I do love you. Sidonie, in a year, you'll gain your majority. And if I spend it in Alba, no one will be able to claim I didn't do my best to obey the Queen's wishes. Everything would be different."

"Mayhap," she mused. "A year's a long time."

I smiled. "Not so very long."

Sidonie twisted to look at me again. "What if there's a child, Imriel? That's the whole point, isn't it? To secure the line of succession in a manner agreeable to Terre d'Ange and Alba alike?"

"Yes," I said slowly. "If there is, there is. I'm sure any child born into Drustan's family would be raised with love and care. I've seen how he is with you and Alais."

"I'd hate it, though," she murmured. "Knowing there was such a big part of you that would never belong to me."

"Possessive?" I asked lightly.

"Of you? Yes." Sidonie turned all the way around to face me. "I don't mind sharing your body." She kissed me. "I'm D'Angeline, or at least half. It's the other things that hurt more. Thinking about you laughing with someone else the way we do. Thinking about you sharing your heart. A child would be the worst." She sighed again. "I know you have to try. And ah, gods, I know I shouldn't feel this way, I know it's not what we've all agreed is best for both nations, but I do."

"Let's hope I'm not terribly fruitful," I said.

She nodded. "Let's."

"You haven't . . . ?" I frowned.

Sidonie laughed. "Oh, *that* would be an interesting solution, wouldn't it? No, no. I'm not ready to importune Eisheth, not even on your behalf." She cocked her head and regarded me. "I would, though, someday."

"Truly?" I whispered.

"Yes." She took my face in her hands and kissed me. "Truly. Imriel, let's not talk anymore. I'm tired of talking."

We didn't, not that night. We made love once more, languorous and sweet and slow, altogether different from the first time, and just as nice. The best part was falling asleep together, curled beneath the warm coverlet. It felt so terribly good to feel her body nestled into mine, soft and warm and naked; to hear her breathing slow and deepen into sleep. There was an intimacy to it beyond lovemaking.

And in the morning, when Sidonie awoke and smiled at me, her face soft with sleep and memories of the night's pleasure, hair tousled and the creased impress of her pillow on one cheek, I knew I was wrong.

A year was a very, very long time.

TWELVE

THE RED SAILS OF THE CRUARCH'S flagship were sighted early that spring.

Almost every other year of my life, I'd heard the news with gladness. In the Sanctuary where I grew up, it meant there would be a feast that night with toasts to Drustan's health. In the City of Elua, it meant Phèdre's household would soon depart for Montrève. I'd dreaded it the year Eamonn fostered with us, for it meant he would be leaving, but I'd awaited it in a fever of anticipation the next year, for it meant I'd be free to follow him to Tiberium.

This year, it was like a death-knell.

Worst of all, I was attending a state dinner in honor of Diokles Agallon, the Ephesian ambassador. A full Parliament had convened, and although the Sultan's suit offering alliance through marriage had been declined by House Courcel, Agallon would be returning to Ephesium having secured the trade concessions he sought.

All I cared about was that it meant Sidonie was there.

The hall burst into cheers when the messenger interrupted with the tidings. Sidonie and I exchanged a single stricken glance across the table. We'd hoped for at least another week. I watched the blood drain from her face, watched her square her slender shoulders and begin explaining to Agallon the long-standing tradition of granting a gold ducat to the first person to spot her father's sails.

And then I looked away, because Diokles Agallon was trained in the arts of covertcy, and I didn't want him reading my face.

The next day, I had my final session with the *ollamh*. Having stuffed our heads full with as much Cruithne lore as they could hold, Firdha actually seemed somewhat proud of Alais and me.

"Do not fail to recite your lessons," she said sternly, her tone belied by a hint of a twinkle in her eye. "A memory that is not exercised grows frail. Do this, and you may bring pride to Alba."

Alais was fairly bouncing with eagerness and wanted to talk afterward. I listened to her burble, struggling to rein in my impatience. All I wanted to do was find Amarante and see if she had any message for me.

"Oh, Imri!" Alais clapped her hands together. "Aren't you *excited*?"

I smiled ruefully. "I'm pleased, love. Remember, I don't know Dorelei well."

"I wish you hadn't gone away to Tiberium last year," she said. "You'd know her a good deal better if you'd stayed for the summer. You liked her, though, didn't you? I liked her. Dorelei's not nearly so serious as Talorcan can be."

"I liked her, yes," I said.

"She has the best laugh," Alais reflected, and I winced. My young cousin gave me a sharp-eyed look. "Did you like her as well as you like Amarante?"

"Amarante!" I laughed. "Why do you ask?"

"I'm not stupid, Imri."

"No, you're not," I agreed. "I don't know her as well, that's all. Anyway, I thought you liked Amarante, too."

"I do, only I don't see Sidonie as much since she came to Court. They're always whispering about something. And now you've been acting awfully odd." She shrugged. "I know what people say, but I don't always believe it, you know."

"Nor should you," I said, ruffling her hair. "You're wise beyond your years."

"Don't do that!" Alais jerked her head away from my touch and scowled. "Imri, if I asked you something, would you tell me the truth?"

I felt bad for ruining her happiness and opened my mouth to make an apologetic promise, but somewhat in her expression, at once wary and determined, stopped me. Alais was clever and observant, and she saw a good deal that others didn't. Young or no, she knew me better than almost anyone at Court; and she knew her sister, too.

"I've never lied to you, Alais," I said, picking my words with care. "And I don't mean to start. So if you don't think you'd like the answer, think twice before you ask."

Alais looked away, and I saw her throat move as she swallowed. Although I'd spoken gently, they were harsher words than I'd ever said to her. "Are you . . . do you mean to ask Father about the Maghuin Dhonn and why the *ollamh* wouldn't talk about them?"

"Yes, of course." I relaxed. It wasn't what she'd meant to ask and we both knew it. "Do you, too?"

She shook her head. "I'd rather you did it. He still thinks of me as a child."

"I will," I promised. "And I'll tell you about it."

"That's good." Alais looked back at me, her violet gaze steady and hurt. "I don't like secrets, Imri."

"Nor do I, love," I murmured. "Not this kind."

Days passed in a flurry, each one bringing a new report of the Cruarch's progress as his ship made landfall and his retinue rode toward the City of Elua, carrying my bride-to-be closer and closer. Ysandre fretted over whether or not it was possible to move our wedding to an earlier date, deciding at last that it was impractical. The announcements had been sent long ago, and a multitude of arrangements were in place. The date would stand, some three weeks after their arrival. She bestowed a massive suite of rooms at the Palace on me, laughing with pleasure at my surprise.

"Where were you planning to bring her?" Ysandre asked. "Surely not your tiny bedchamber in Phèdre's household!"

"I'd not thought on it." I gazed around the salon. The high ceiling was recessed and trimmed in gilt, containing a fresco depicting Eisheth gathering herbs. The rooms were hung about with costly tapestries and appointed with heavy, ornate furniture. There was even a small balcony overlooking the gardens.

"I know." Ysandre regarded me with amusement. "Young men can be thoughtless. But Imriel, you are a prince of Terre d'Ange and a member of House Courcel, and the young lady is sister to the Cruarch's heir. At some point, you're expected to live as such."

"My thanks." I bowed. "You're very generous."

She waved a dissmissive hand. "'Tis naught, truly."

It was a bitter piece of irony. I daresay Ysandre would have given me aught I'd asked for in those days, glad as she was to have the matter settled. She was in high spirits, anticipating Drustan's arrival and the forthcoming wedding. And I was in misery, because the only thing in the world I wanted was the one thing she would never give me: her daughter.

We had almost no time together. My own birthday arrived, and the Cruarch's party was gauged to be two days away from the City. Between that and the coming wedding, there would be no natal festivities for me this year. No chance to hatch another mad scheme, no gift of a second night spent together.

The best we could manage was a few stolen moments. That afternoon, Sidonie and Amarante contrived to pay a visit to view my new quarters while I was there, bringing armloads of blue and yellow irises from the garden. They made a pretty picture, both of them fresh-faced as flowers. The guard attending them lingered outside my door, near enough we didn't dare throw the bolt for fear of raising suspicion. Amarante found a tall vase of Serenissiman glass in one of the ornate cabinets—more of the Queen's largesse—and began arranging the irises.

"Mind you tell one of the servants to refill the ewer on the bathstand," she called to me. "I'm using all your water!" Tilting her head toward the bedchamber, she added in a low voice. "For Elua's sake, please be *quiet* in there."

We managed, barely.

It was a hushed, hurried encounter. In the zenana, there were women addicted to opium, the only pleasure the Mahrkagir ever afforded us. Betimes he took it away to see them suffer. I never saw such profound, aching relief and gratitude as on the days when the opium was restored, even the merest crumbs of it. One would have thought the release it provided was life itself. It scared me, for I never understood it.

I understood it better now.

Sidonie and I kissed and grappled with frantic haste, tearing at each other's clothes with urgent whispers. I sank into her with a gasped prayer of thanksgiving and she bit my shoulder to stifle a whimper. We ground against one another, clutching and thrusting and shuddering our way to a rushed climax.

"Wait." Sidonie caught my arm as I made to rise. "I have something for you." She knelt and rummaged in the purse tied to the girdle of her abandoned gown. "You gave me the idea for it. I didn't have time to have a box made."

I knelt opposite her. "What is it?"

"Give me your hand." She took my right hand and slid a ring onto my fourth finger. It was heavy and warm. I glanced down at our joined hands and laughed. Gold; a knot of gold. Sidonie smiled. "I didn't want you to forget."

"Never," I said. "We're bound together, you and I."

"So it seems," she said wistfully.

I wanted to kiss her until the sorrow passed, lay her down and make love to her until the world crumbled around us, but there was no more time. Instead we rose and donned our clothing, returning to the salon to exclaim over the glorious vase of irises while Amarante regarded us with concern and love in her green eyes. And then there was no more time at all, no reason for them to linger without giving the Guard cause to wonder, for all the Court knew all too well that Sidonie and I were not overly fond of one another, and one thoughtful gesture would do little to allay it.

So they went and I watched them go, a knot of gold on my finger and a knot tightening around my heart.

And two days later, the Cruarch's party arrived.

I'd learned a good deal about dissembling in Tiberium, carrying on an affair with Claudia Fulvia beneath the oblivious noses of her husband, her brother, and my friends. Training in the arts of covertcy, she called it. But that was nothing compared to this. Lying comes easy when one's heart isn't engaged.

As always, we greeted them at the gates of the City and there were crowds and showers of flower petals. The commonfolk of Terre d'Ange loved the ritual. I stood in a place of honor between Alais and Phèdre with a false smile plastered on my face, watching the Cruarch of Alba and his niece ride toward us, surrounded by guards.

Sister of his heir; my bride-to-be.

Dorelei mab Breidaia was much as I remembered her. Cruithne through and through, slight and dark, with wide-set black eyes that appeared at once shy and startled. There were twin lines of dots etched beneath her eyes in blue woad, high on her cheekbones. Thanks to the *ollamh*'s lessons, I now knew they meant she had had true dreams and passed a season studying women's secrets among the Cullach Gorrym. More than that, I was not privy to know, although Alais knew some of it.

The Queen's herald announced her as my betrothed and the crowd cheered. Dorelei caught my eye and blushed a dusky rose. I smiled at her, clenching my right hand into a fist so hard I felt Sidonie's ring dig into my flesh.

In the hours that followed, I did it more than once.

Blessed Elua, the formal reception was *agonizing*. Naturally, I was expected to dance attendance on Dorelei. Even if it hadn't been for Sidonie, I think it would have been difficult. Dorelei and I had gotten to know one another some little bit last spring, but not well. And now, in three weeks' time, we were to be wed. The shadow of it hung over us, reminding us that we were nearly strangers.

It made her shy and it made me awkward, and all the while, I dared not glance in Sidonie's direction. I knew where she was, always. I could feel her presence on my skin, sure as the sun's warmth.

Firdha the *ollamh* attended the reception, small and dignified with her golden oak branch in hand. When she entered, Drustan greeted her with a bow worthy of an equal. "Daughter of the Grove, how did your pupils fare?"

Our instructor returned his bow. "Well enough, Cruarch. You will find the lad sufficient, I think. And it is my recommendation that the lass return to Alba with you come autumn to pass a year among us ere her wedding." A smile touched her lips. "She is a child of Necthana's line and should learn to read her dreams."

At that, Alais let out a squeak of happiness. It was what she had hoped for, although she'd been convinced Firdha wouldn't say it. Dorelei laughed for the first time that day and hugged her. While I was away in Tiberium, they'd become fond of one another. "I'd like that, little sister. Perhaps you could stay with us."

"Oh, Imri!" Alais' eyes shone. "Could I?"

"Of course." I made myself smile at her. "If your father allows it, I'd like nothing better."

It was good, at least, that someone was joyous. And I *was* happy for her. Alais had never been truly at ease at Court and the Cruithne blood ran strongly in her. Back in the days when we spoke often together, she had wondered if she would feel more at home in Alba.

I hoped she would.

I knew I wouldn't.

In the days that followed, my sense of time's passage spun completely out of proportion. Minutes and hours dragged on to eternity, while days passed in the blink of an eye. The Palace was constantly a-bustle with preparations for the wedding. I was plagued on all sides with the demands of courtship that were expected of me, and I couldn't steal a moment alone with Sidonie.

Once, we encountered one another unexpectedly in the halls as I was escorting Dorelei from the audition of a renowned flautist in the Queen's quarters, one of the myriad musicians hoping to play at the wedding. He'd been nervous and played poorly. After he left, I'd declared that Hugues would have done a better job, and then had to explain to Dorelei who Hugues was. I was reciting some of his worst poetic verse to the accompaniment of her delighted laughter when it happened.

I stopped dead. For the space of a heartbeat, Sidonie and I stared at one another, Dorelei's laughter still ringing in the hallway. I clenched my fist, feeling the ring's bite.

"Well met, your highnesses," Amarante said quietly behind her mistress. Sidonie reached back and caught her hand, squeezing it hard enough to hurt. I knew, I could tell.

I said something; I don't know what. We passed and moved onward on our separate courses. Dorelei's slim brown fingers rested on my arm.

"They're very different for sisters, aren't they?" she observed. "Alais and Sidonie."

"Yes," I said shortly.

"I like Alais," Dorelei mused. "Sidonie . . . she's like a house without a door. It's harder to see her as Drustan's daughter, there's so much of her mother in her. Very D'Angeline." She glanced up at me and lowered her voice. "Is it true that the Lady Amarante was brought here to instruct her in . . . in the bedchamber?"

I gritted my teeth. "Yes."

Dorelei shook her head in wonderment. "That's what Alais said! I didn't believe it."

"Why ever not?" I asked.

"I'm sorry." She flushed. "It's not our way, that's all. To teach such things as though they were a fit matter for study, to build pleasure-houses . . . I'm sorry, I've offended you."

"No, no." I patted her hand. "I'm being rude, forgive me."

"No, I was." Dorelei stole another glance at me. "Prince Imriel, please believe me, I'm not . . . that is, I look forward to our nuptials." Her flush deepened. "You do not find me as pleasing, I know. I'm sorry."

I sighed, feeling horrible. "Oh, my lady! 'Tis untrue." I touched her cheek. "Mayhap you have heard," I said gently. "I was stolen as a child and forced to endure a difficult time." She nodded, her wide-set gaze fixed on mine. I had never, ever traded on my history for pity. Now I did, vile and deliberate. "Betimes it makes me cold," I said to her. "And I am sorry for it. But I will do my best to be a good husband to you."

"I understand," Dorelei whispered. "You will, I know you will!"

It was all there in her adoring gaze, everything Sidonie had said. The reflection of myself, the yearning to *heal*, to be the one who made me whole. Too late, I wanted to say; too late. I'd already found it. I'd found it in the last place in the world anyone would expect, in the one person who'd never harbored any such desires.

I couldn't, though.

I patted her hand again. "My thanks, my lady. I will try."

In the midst of all of it, with the wedding hurtling down on me like an avalanche, I had a private meeting with Drustan mab Necthana. I'd requested it at the reception upon his arrival and he'd readily agreed, but then he'd put me off twice, citing pressing affairs. I was beginning to doubt his sincerity, but he sent around a note of apology and we met some ten days prior to the wedding.

It was the first time I'd ever met man-to-man with the Cruarch of Alba. Drustan received me in his personal study at the Palace. I was surprised to find it cluttered with books and letters and writing materials.

"I was beginning to think everyone in Alba held the written word in disdain," I commented, taking a seat at his nod of invitation.

Drustan smiled briefly. "In Alba, I have the luxury of following Cruithne customs. Outside of Alba, it is different. I bear many responsibilities as the Cruarch."

"So I understand," I said.

His gaze sharpened. "What did you wish to speak of?"

"The Maghuin Dhonn." I took a deep breath. "My lord, before I wed Dorelei, there are things I wish to know. Who are the Maghuin Dhonn? What is a *diadh-anam* and why did the Maghuin Dhonn sacrifice it? Exactly how widespread is the dissension in Alba? Is it merely tribal feuding or is is somewhat more?"

My words hung in the air between us. Drustan didn't answer right away. He rose and paced the room with his uneven gait, his hands clasped behind his back. When he was seated or riding astride, one forgot the disability of his clubbed foot. Still, he moved well despite it, steady and deft. I didn't find it so hard to see Sidonie as his daughter.

"It's ill luck to speak the name," Drustan said at length.

"*You've* spoken it," I pointed out. "Alais heard you."

The Cruarch of Alba sighed. "She hears too much."

"She has a right to know," I said. "So do I."

"So be it." Drustan sat down to face me, hands on his knees. "You know that the Cullach Gorrym lay claim to being the first folk in Alba?" he asked, and I nodded. "So do the Maghuin Dhonn. And truth be told, no one knows who has the right of it. Like us, they came from the east, back when the world was young. Their lore holds they came from a more northerly clime." He shrugged. "Indeed, they say all the world was colder in those days, so cold the very Straits froze solid enough to cross."

A shiver brushed my spine. "Do you believe it?"

"I don't know." His face was grave. "Of a surety, they are old. They were a powerful folk before they lost their *diadh-anam*, shapechangers and magicians." I opened my mouth to repeat a question, and Drustan forestalled me with a gesture. "The *diadh-anam*, the guiding and protecting spirit of a people. Theirs was the Brown Bear. It's a sacred word, from the mysteries. It would been taught you after the rites in Alba, when you truly became part of the Cullach Gorrym."

"So the Black Boar is the *diadh-anam* of the Cullach Gorrym?" I asked slowly.

Drustan nodded. "Ever since Lug the warrior followed his *diadh-anam* across the Straits. There is a *geas* on me that I may never hunt boar lest I curse the Cullach Gorrym. When I die, the *geas* will fall upon Talorcan."

I thought about the story in the Tiberian historian Caledonius' writings. "Somehow, my lord, I suspect that the Maghuin Dhonn did worse than hunt brown bears. Does this have aught to do with the bear that slew the Governor of Alba?"

"Yes." Drustan's hands tightened on his knees. He gave me a rueful smile that didn't reach his eyes. "I should have guessed Phèdre nó Delaunay's foster-son would know surprising things. The bear was raised in captivity and fed on human flesh until it grew to a vast size. The magicians of the Maghuin Dhonn did that, fed it on the flesh of their own children. And then they sold it to the Tiberians for sport."

My stomach lurched. *"Why?"*

"No one knows," he said softly. "Not truly. The Maghuin Dhonn said it was to summon a curse on the Tiberians. Cinhil Ru said their magicians had gone mad. After it happened, a pox swept through the folk of the Brown Bear. Many, many of them died."

"But not all of them," I said.

"No." Drustan regarded me. "A handful survived and their line continues. And they do not welcome change in Alba, and they do not welcome D'Angelines. But they are few."

"How few?" I asked.

"A hundred, perhaps?" Drustan shook his head. "Not many. You asked about dissension. They are a wild, fey folk, and they come and go like the wind. They speak against this wedding and seek to stir trouble, spreading whispers of dire consequences to follow. For the most part, they've gone unheeded. There was one small uprising among the Tarbh Cró in the north after the betrothal was announced, easily ended. Nothing more."

"And the tribal feuding?" I asked.

"Oh, well." He grinned unexpectedly, teeth white in his woad-marqued face. "Cattle raids and the like. That's to be expected in Alba."

"I see," I said.

"You will." Drustan leaned over and clasped my forearm. "Imriel, listen. If I could root out the Maghuin Dhonn and destroy them, I would. But as long as they merely *speak* dissension without taking up arms, I can do nothing. Every man, woman, and child in Alba has a right to speak their mind, even to the Cruarch. Firdha taught you as much, did she not?" I nodded and he squeezed my arm. " 'Tis a frustrating rule, but a just one. My father sought to quell voices of dissent and paid a price for it. I will not make his mistake." Drustan looked thoughtful. "Change comes to Alba. Some hunger for it and some fear it. It cannot be forced, nor can it be suppressed. It must come slowly, with wise care and discussion. But I promise you this," he added, giving me a final squeeze and releasing his grip. "If I believed you would be any less safe in Alba than in Terre d'Ange, I would not ask this of you. And of a surety, I'd not allow Alais to go!"

It was a long speech and an honest one; more honest than he knew, since I was carrying on an illicit affair with Sidonie that made me considerably *less* safe in Terre d'Ange. I nodded in acknowledgment. "Fair enough, my lord."

Drustan fixed me with a level gaze. "Do you plan on telling Alais this?"

I returned it without flinching. "I do. She's not a child, you know."

"You think not?" He smiled fondly. "Wait until you have children of your own. They'll always be little girls in my eyes, my daughters."

At that I looked away and twisted the gold knot of a ring on my finger. It was an uncomfortable time to be reminded that I'd tied his other little girl's wrists to the bedposts and made her squirm with pleasure and beg me for release. I cleared my throat. "My lord, what is it the Maghuin Dhonn fear from Terre d'Ange? Surely, her majesty has given them no cause to believe we desire aught but a continued alliance through marriage. Terre d'Ange doesn't even maintain a garrison in Alba."

"Conquest comes in many forms," Drustan said quietly. "I do not like the Maghuin Dhonn, but I understand them. It is my responsibility to do so. The Tiberians came with shields and swords and we fought them off. Terre d'Ange comes with merchants and architects, pleasure-houses, bridegrooms and"— he nodded at his desk—"books. Tell me, Imriel, which do you think is more dangerous?"

To that, I had no answer.

THIRTEEN

IN THE DAYS PRECEDING the wedding, all manner of visitors streamed into the City of Elua. Some came from beyond Terre d'Ange, like the Lady Nicola L'Envers y Aragon and her son Raul, who would celebrating his own nuptials with Colette Trente. Most were D'Angeline, lords and ladies of the realm I barely knew by name. Phèdre, who had spent rather more time during my youthful years training me in the arts of covertcy and allowing me to pursue the study of philosophy than she had teaching me the protocol of the peerage, sought in haste to rectify her oversight. We spent many long hours poring over the list of peers invited to attend.

The one guest I most longed to see, Eamonn mac Grainne, was nowhere in sight.

There was no word from him, no word at all. It worried me when I had time to think on it. I had visions of him lying slain in Skaldia, bright blood staining the snow. And in the midst of my private heartache and the swirl of courtly chaos, betimes I wished I'd gone with him in pursuit of the ill-tempered Skaldic bride he adored for no reason I could fathom, but which I nonetheless understood far, far better than I had in Lucca.

A clean death in the snows of Skaldia might have been preferable to *this*.

Instead of Eamonn, the spring heralded the return of some of the last people on earth I wanted to see. There was Bernadette de Trevalion, of course, and my erstwhile friend Bertran. That, at least, I had expected. I'd made my choice and I was reconciled to living with it.

The other one was worse: Maslin of Lombelon, back from his period of disgrace among the Unforgiven of Camlach.

Oh, I hated him!

I hated him because I'd admired him, once. He was the bastard son of Duc Isidore d'Aiglemort, traitor and hero, gotten on the daughter of the Master Gardener of Lombelon, a tiny estate with a peculiar history. It had been my mother's, once. She had deeded it to d'Aiglemort, no doubt in thanks for conspiring there with her. And d'Aiglemort had died ere he could acknowledge his son, slain on the fields of Troyes-le-Mont, avenging my mother's betrayal of him. Lombelon fell into the Queen's purview, and she deeded it to my father as a gift on his wedding day, when he wed my traitorous mother with all the world unwitting. And then he died as a result of her treachery.

Thus, it fell to me.

I'd met Maslin there. I'd seen his love for the place, his fierce pride. I'd thought I had a chance to right a wrong, to make a friend, and so I did. I did the thing I thought right and best, and I deeded Lombelon to him.

Phèdre had warned me he might resent me for it, but I did it anyway. And I understood, with sorrow, when her words proved true. Maslin left Lombelon to enlist in the Queen's Guard. We spoke of it once. He told me with bitterness that I'd made it small in his eyes. It hurt, but I understood. If it was only that . . .

It wasn't, though.

Sidonie *liked* him.

I saw her brighten at his return. There were rumors; there were always rumors. I knew the truth of them. She hadn't taken him as a lover, though she'd considered it. Was still considering it, or would after I left. She didn't say it, but I knew. And it was true that she'd promised to appoint him as the Captain of her Guard within a few years of reaching her majority, provided he acquitted himself well after being restored to his lieutenancy.

Maslin loved her.

I knew it, *knew* it. I'd seen it in his face the day of the boar hunt, and I saw on his return nothing had changed. He watched Sidonie with what passed for dedicated attentiveness, but there was more in it. A tender surety, a possessiveness. I knew, I saw it.

To her credit, Sidonie did naught to encourage it, beyond making it clear that she was pleased to see him. I daresay she'd no more heart for the Game of Courtship in those days than I did, and although I was forced to play it with my bride, Sidonie wasn't one to do the same out of spite. She knew too well what I was feeling. Still, in a few months, I would be gone and Maslin would be there, a handy balm to soothe an aching heart.

The knowledge grated on me, and I half wished he'd do somewhat to offend me. I would have welcomed a chance to challenge him. Whether or not I could have defeated him, I couldn't say for sure, but I would have been glad to try. But no; Maslin had learned a measure of discipline from his time in Camlach. He was polite and contained, and even made a gracious apology to Raul.

Preparations progressed apace and still no Eamonn.

No time to see Sidonie alone, even for a moment.

On the eve of my wedding, my Shahrizai kindred threw a bridegroom's fête. It was a gorgeous affair hosted by Duc Faragon himself, although Mavros and Roshana had planned it. Suffice to say it was splendid and opulent, and a centerpiece of the festivities was a Kusheline game played with blindfolds. As the musicians began to play a merry tune, the Shahrizai mingled among their laughing, blindfolded guests, directing them to exchange partners and dance until they guessed their identities, forfeiting a kiss for each wrong guess. I was tying my blindfold in place when I felt a hand on my elbow, steering me toward the colonnade along the hall.

"Here," Mavros murmured in my ear. "You've got all of a minute."

Sidonie was waiting, hidden by a tall marble column. The sight of her nearly broke my heart. Her honey-gold hair was piled in a coronet and my sunburst earrings adorned her delicate earlobes. Her black eyes were filled with tears.

"Sidonie . . ." I whispered.

She shook her head. "Don't. Don't say anything."

I took her face in my hands and kissed her instead, long and deep. I pressed her against the column so hard it must have bruised her shoulders. She clung to me as though she were drowning and kissed me back, hands tugging the hair at the nape of my neck, silently urging me for more and more and more.

Shouts of mirth and laughter rose above the music. In the hall, blindfolds were being removed, one by one.

"Time," Mavros said quietly from the other side of the column.

We broke apart. I touched Sidonie's kiss-swollen lips. "I love you."

Her eyes glittered. "I love you, too."

And that was all, all that there was time for. Mavros came around the column to take Sidonie's hand and lead her discreetly back into the crowd. I loitered a moment before following.

Such was the eve of my wedding night. Ysandre and Drustan had made an appearance. They had even taken part in the blindfold game in a display of good-natured sportsmanship. I stood at Duc Faragon's side as they made their farewells, and Sidonie stood at theirs, avoiding my gaze. Everyone else seemed very pleased at this splendid evidence of rapprochement between House Shahrizai and House Courcel. The Queen had proved her generosity of spirit; the truth of Duc Faragon's oath of loyalty was acknowledged with gratitude.

At last, their efforts had borne fruit untainted by my mother's treason.

I wondered what they would have thought, both sides, if they'd known that for me, for Sidonie—and for Mavros, who was complicit in it—the entire evening existed for the purpose of one last, desperate kiss. One last yearning press of bodies, crush of lips, and starved tangle of tongues that could have brought the whole edifice of rapprochement and goodwill crashing down if we had been discovered.

It would have been worth it.

Almost.

I nearly wished it had happened. But there was Alba; there was Drustan's honesty and his faith, and promises I'd made. There was Dorelei, sweet and trusting. There was youth, Sidonie's and mine, and Maslin of Lombelon, and the fact that I couldn't say, not with utter, absolute certainty, that in a year's time, I would feel as I did now, that my heart was being yanked from my chest at the thought of being parted from her. It would have been simple, so simple, if we were com-monfolk. It wouldn't have mattered, then.

But we weren't.

We were the Dauphine of Terre d'Ange and a Prince of the Blood, soon to be a Prince of Alba. And we could not afford to be any more young and foolish than we were. The stakes were too damnably high.

So I stood beside barrel-chested Duc Faragon, the head of House Shahrizai, his hair silver with age. Stood and watched Queen and Cruarch depart, their guards escorting them, their daughter beside them, her carriage erect and proud. Her slender back upright as a spear, giving no sign that I'd bruised her shoulder blades against the cold, unyielding marble column, pinning her with my passion.

Elua! I could have wept.

I didn't, though I wanted to. I watched them go, dry-eyed.

And on the following day, I married Dorelei mab Breidaia.

The ceremony was held in the Palace gardens, site of a thousand fêtes. Drustan and Ysandre's own wedding had taken place there and I was meant to be honored by the gesture, though of course it only served as a bitter reminder of Sidonie's birthday and the pangs of loss and resentment that consumed me.

Indeed, the entire day felt like a wake. It was strange to arise in my room in Phèdre's townhouse—my tiny bedchamber, Ysandre had called it—knowing I wouldn't be returning to Montrève's household. Oh, I'd visit, of course, but it would all be different. No more days beginning with Ti-Philippe's teasing at the breakfast table, no more of Eugènie's efforts to spoil me with heaping platters of food, no more afternoons sparring in the courtyard with Joscelin, no more nights ending with a quiet word of love from Phèdre.

The mood in the household was somber. Phèdre and Joscelin, knowing full well my heart was heavy, made no effort to lighten it with false merriment. The rest of the household took their cues from us, and in truth, I think no one was lighthearted that day.

I dressed slowly and reluctantly. My wedding attire was Courcel blue, this time adorned with gold embroidery. I'd thought it foolish to have new clothing commissioned when I already had a suit much like it, but Ysandre had insisted. The brocade doublet fit close through the waist, with a high collar that closed at the throat with golden frogs. It was going to be hotter than hell, and I was already stifling.

"Imri?" Phèdre knocked lightly at the door and I admitted her. She regarded me with a complex mix of emotions. "Ah, love! You look splendid."

"Feels like I'm choking," I informed her.

She reached up to fuss with my collar, her fingers cool against my skin. Whatever she did, it felt better afterward. I caught her hands and kissed them. "Thank you."

"You're welcome."

There are never any words to suffice when one wants them. We stood there for a moment, hands joined. After a while, Phèdre sighed.

"Time to go?" I asked.

"I'm afraid so." She touched my cheek. "Imriel, be kind to the girl. I know what you're feeling, but remember, none of it is her fault. And don't . . . don't expect her to share all of your desires."

"I won't," I said. Once, it would have made me appalled and uncomfortably aroused to contemplate such a thing, to hear Phèdre give voice to it. Now I merely smiled sadly, remembering the shocked thrill of delight that had run through me at Sidonie's unexpected words, and ah, Elua! the sight of her in bonds, naked and writhing. "Still, I suppose one never knows."

"I do," Phèdre said quietly.

"Always?" I asked.

"Always." She returned my smile, filled with fond sorrow. "Oh, Imri! All I ever wanted was for you to be happy. And happiness isn't always where you think you'll find it. Promise me you'll at least try?"

"I will," I said. "I promise."

Downstairs, Joscelin was waiting. I watched them exchange a wordless glance that racked me with a helpless blend of love and envy. I couldn't begrudge them what they had together; not now, not ever. But oh, I could envy them!

The hours that followed passed in a waking daze. We travelled by carriage to the Palace, and the streets were lined with people, cheering and throwing flower petals, for Ysandre had decreed a day of license in the City. Hugues and Ti-Philippe served as our outriders, acknowledging the shouts and bawdy jests with cheerful waves.

I slumped in my seat and stared at the roof of the carriage, tugging at my collar, sweltering in my finery.

"Imri!" Joscelin said sharply. "Name of Elua! Stop moping."

A thousand angry retorts were born and died on my tongue. Phèdre had walked into a living hell of her own volition to rescue me, and Joscelin had gone with her. When all was said and done, his role may have been the hardest of all. I was acting like an idiot and it reflected badly on all of us. I sat up straight and did my best to make them proud of me. After all, it was only a year; and no one need die for it.

I married Dorelei.

It was hot in the Palace gardens, hotter than anyone had expected it to be that day. Dorelei and I stood side by side, our damp fingers entwined, before Elua's priest, barefoot in his blue robes. I was sweating in my doublet and there was a sheen of perspiration along her hairline, beneath the wreath of flowers that adorned her black hair. The priest touched the greensward, lifted his palms to the sky, and invoked Elua's blessing on us. He anointed our brows with oil. He gave us vows to recite, and we recited them. Dorelei spoke hers with a soft, lilting accent. I was surprised by the sound of my own voice, strong and firm. The priest spread his arms in blessing and bade us seal our union with a kiss.

Several hundred people I couldn't have cared less about cheered. Dorelei mab Breidaia, now my wife, raised her face to mine. Dark eyes, Cruithne eyes.

Wrong, all wrong.

Not the ones I loved.

Still, I closed my eyes and kissed her. A chaste kiss, by D'Angeline standards. I didn't love her. I didn't want her. I would do my best to be kind to her. Cheers, erupting. Another pelting of petals. Ysandre's face was happy, Drustan's woad-masked face was happy. Elua, I was sweltering! Overhead, the sun blazed. I tugged at my collar.

It was done.

I looked at Sidonie. Although it bore no markings, her delicate face was a mask, too; smooth and perfect and unreadable. She reached into a basket Amarante held for her and grasped a handful of rose petals, tossing them high in the air. They fell all around us in a gentle shower, settling in our hair. Dorelei laughed with delight, unaware of the silent message I read in the gesture. I closed my eyes again, briefly, hearing Sidonie's voice in a sunlit room.

The lover showers kisses on the face of the beloved . . .

Elua, but it hurt.

The Queen clapped her hands together. "Let us celebrate!"

More than anything, I wished that day that there were no festivities following the wedding rites. I wished we could have departed immediately afterward; for Alba, for Montrève, for Jebe-Barkal. Anywhere but here. But this was Terre d'Ange and because the Queen had decreed it, there must be a fête, lavish and interminable. The silk pavilions must be erected, this time filled with long tables lined with chairs, laid with white linen and set with gleaming dishes.

Servants circulated with flagons of cool white wine. The sun crept across the sky with infinitesimal slowness. I stood sweating and drinking wine, receiving the well-wishes of those guests not deemed sufficiently important to attend the dinner. Dorelei stayed at my side, overwhelmed by the unrelenting attention.

At last the lower rim of the sun's disk slipped below the edge the western horizon and the worst of the day's heat began to dissipate. Palace servants began lighting the lamps and bringing forth an endless stream of platters.

I remember very little of that meal, save for the tremendous effort it took to remain courteous; though in response to what, I couldn't have said. I heard words that held no meaning for me and felt my lips move in reply, uttering equally meaningless pleasantries. I laughed politely at jests and clapped politely at toasts. The food I ate had no taste; the wine I drank had no effect. Inside, I felt empty.

Afterward, there was music and dancing. I danced with my new bride. My wife. Her fingers trembled in mine and her wide-set gaze searched my face, filled with uncertainty. I smiled reassuringly at her.

I danced with Alais, who had little to say to me.

I danced with Phèdre, who said quietly, "I'm proud of you."

I danced with Amarante, and as I did, I caught a glimpse of Maslin in his lieutenant's attire offering Sidonie a glass of cordial, the lamp-light catching his fair hair. For the first time that night, I felt a spark of anger in my breast. "How long do you think before she takes him into her bed?" I asked in a low voice.

Amarante followed my gaze. "Longer than you think, my lord," she murmured. "And not as long as I'd like."

"Jealous?" I asked grimly.

"No." She gave me a long, level look. "I think she's going to hurt him quite badly."

"He's a grown man, let him take his chances." For some reason, her calm, reasonable words fanned my anger. "Name of Elua, Amarante! What about you? Do you care so little for her that you don't even fear getting hurt?"

Her green eyes flashed with rare emotion. "I care a great deal, actu-ally. Love's not always a raging tempest, Imriel. It can be a safe harbor, too. I value Sidonie's friendship and trust above all else. I take neither lightly and I do not expect to lose them."

I sighed. "I'm sorry. It's just—"

"I know," Amarante said.

"A safe harbor," I mused. "Surely even your waters must get ruffled at times."

"Oh, well." A smile touched her generous lips. "If Sidonie has her way, you may find out someday. She can be persuasive when she chooses, and she does have a very large bed."

It made me laugh, and it very nearly made me cry. It was a good deal easier feeling empty inside. The song ended and I released Ama-rante. "Take care of her?" I whispered. "Please?"

She nodded. "I'll try."

And then, because it would have been rude not to, I danced with Sidonie on my wedding night. There was no awkwardness as there had been on her birthday. We had gone too far beyond it. I bowed and ex-tended my hand, and she took it without a word.

It didn't need words.

I remembered them all, all the words we'd spoken. The first time, that terrifying rush of intimacy upon entering her, crossing the forbidden threshold together. Her voice, wondering and bemused in the aftermath, legs clamped around my hips. *Why do we fit so well together?*

I hadn't known then and I didn't know now.

I knew only that we did.

We danced without speaking, without exchanging a glance. And when the musicians swung into a new tune, we stood for the merest space of time, no more than a heartbeat, heads bowed against one another. Then Sidonie pulled away from me and I escorted her back to the pavilion.

Maslin of Lombelon was there, waiting. He was playing the faithful guard and companion, but his body was taut and his nostrils flared like a dog's catching a strange scent. He took a step toward me, bristling.

I stood my ground. "Maslin, don't."

Another time, any other time, I'd have welcomed it. I wasn't the fear-haunted boy he'd met in an orchard years ago, threatened at the point of a pruning hook. I'd stood before the onslaught of a Caerdicci mercenary army and I'd seen men die by my own hand. I had a whole new set of nightmares to haunt my sleep.

"Traitor's son!" Maslin spat under his breath. "Can you not leave her be on your own wedding night?"

"It was only a courtesy," I said wearily. It was a piece of irony that he, of all people, could throw that epithet at me. But then, his father had died a hero in the end. Beyond him, I could see Amarante murmuring somewhat with a questioning expression, and Sidonie shaking her head and turning away from the scene. "And I'm only a bridegroom. Let it be, Maslin."

He looked uncertain. I didn't care. It was late. Drustan's men and the Cruithne honor guard had broken out the *uisghe* and were beginning to sing a complex harmony, urged on by the D'Angelines. Dorelei—my wife—appeared lonely and at a loss amidst the gathering. The Daughter of the Grove had long since retired. None of the women of her family were in attendance, having chosen to wait for the Alban rites.

Be kind to her, Phèdre had said.

I walked past Maslin, past everyone, to my wife's side. Dorelei looked at me with gratitude. "Shall we have a last dance?" I asked softly. "Or shall we retire?"

"I don't want to stay here any longer," she whispered back.

I took her hand. "Then we won't."

A group of revelers followed us into the Palace, tossing the last of the flower petals, shouting out good wishes and more bawdy jests. I led Dorelei through the halls to my newly appointed chambers and closed the door in their faces, bolting it firmly.

We were alone.

Husband and wife.

Our rooms had been strewn about with flowers and all the lamps were lit. The Serenissiman vase stood on a sideboard, filled with roses. I remembered Sidonie and Amarante with their arms full of irises and swallowed hard. "Are you tired?" I asked Dorelei. "We needn't . . ."

"No." Her face was set and determined. "I want to do this."

"All right." I smiled at her. "Come here, then." I led her into the bedchamber and sat on the edge of the bed, holding her hands. "'Tis awkward, is it not?" I said gently. "The whirlwind of courtship, the two of us knowing so little of one another. Tell me what pleases you."

Her cheeks flushed. "I don't . . . I don't know."

It startled me. "You're a virgin?"

Dorelei nodded, her flush deepening. "It seemed wiser to wait. I couldn't risk getting with child, not with Alba's succession at stake and Terre d'Ange's interest in it. We're not like you, you know."

"No, I know," I murmured.

"They took me to Eisheth's temple today," she mused. "So strange! I lit a candle to her and said the prayer they taught me. Do you think our children will share her gift?"

"I imagine so," I said. "Alais and . . . Sidonie do. The gifts of Blessed Elua and his Companions run strong in the Great Houses."

"Like beauty?" Dorelei asked gravely, and I nodded. She plucked an errant flower petal from my hair. "You know, you frighten me a little. Here, it seems even beauty can be a weapon."

"I won't hurt you," I said. "I promise."

Her gaze above the dots of blue woad was dark and deep, and I wondered what she saw with it. They dreamed true dreams, the daughters of Necthana's line. But Dorelei only shook her head, her hair black and shining beneath the wreath of wilting stephanotis flowers that adorned it, held in place by pearl-headed pins. "I'm not ignorant, if that's what you're thinking. I've read your . . . sacred texts." Her flush returned. "I do read, you know. But when you ask me what pleases me, the truth is, I do not know."

I reached up to undo the pins, lifting the wreath from her head. "Then let us find out, shall we?"

"I would like that," Dorelei whispered.

I made love to her, slowly and gently. Kindly. I kissed her until her body softened, trusting, and she returned my kisses with ardor. I removed her clothing piece by piece, tasting her brown skin. I removed my own clothing and held myself very still, letting her tentative hands and lips and tongue explore my body. She was eager in some ways, shy in others. Her fingers trembled, wrapped around the shaft of my phallus.

"Will it fit inside me?" she asked in wonderment. "Truly?"

Why do we fit so well together?

"Truly," I assured her. I spread her thighs and performed the *languisement* on her, concentrating on Naamah's Pearl until Dorelei gasped with surprise and clutched at my hair. And then I eased my way up her body. Patience. I fitted the head of my phallus inside her and heard her gasp again. I thrust my hips forward, slow and gentle.

There was an obstruction.

And then there wasn't.

"Oh, slowly, slowly, please!" she gasped.

I didn't want *slowly*. I wanted to bury myself in her, deeper and deeper, I wanted to feel her loins rocking against mine. I wanted her arms stretched tight above her head, or at least her fingernails buried in my buttocks, urging me onward. I wanted to feel her heels drumming against the backs of my thighs, I wanted her uttering sweet, urgent obscenities in my ear.

I wanted Sidonie.

Patience, Phèdre had said.

I propped myself on my arms. I made slow, patient love to my wife.

I felt Dorelei give a little shudder inside, her inner walls rippling. She made a noise deep in her throat, half pain, half pleasure. The sound made my testes contract. I hissed through my teeth and spent myself in her. She had lit a candle to Eisheth. I flooded her womb with my seed, wondering whether it would take root, praying in my guilty heart that it didn't.

Afterward, I held her and stroked her hair until she fell asleep, her head pillowed on my shoulder, her breathing slow and even. It should have been a comforting sound.

It wasn't.

Fourteen

Thus began my new life as the husband of Dorelei mab Breidaia and a Prince of Alba.

I detested it.

Even if it hadn't been for Sidonie, I daresay I wouldn't have been *happy*, despite Phèdre's wish for me. This marriage was a cage I'd entered voluntarily, but it was a cage nonetheless. I felt trapped; trapped into enforced intimacy, trapped into a life I didn't want. There would have been an element of confinement under any circumstances, but I could have borne it with better grace if I hadn't had a taste of the freedom and happiness I might have enoyed otherwise. Now I had, and I detested the prison of my new life with a thoroughness that was profound and unrelenting.

Every day, waking to find Dorelei in my bed, I fought against a black tide of bitterness that rose in me. I forced tender words to fall from my lips. I was gentle, I was kind.

I tried very, very hard not to hate her.

Elua, it was unfair! Unfair to me, and unfair to her most of all. Dorelei was a nice young woman, good-hearted and sweet. It was no fault of hers that *nice* wasn't what I'd desired. And unfortunately, she was perceptive enough to sense my withdrawal and struggle as the days passed.

For a mercy, Dorelei attributed it to the travails I'd undergone. It was yet another piece of irony. Although I'd been the one to plant the thought in her head, for once in my life, my turmoil had nothing to do with Daršanga, nothing to do with old wounds. I wasn't wrestling with cravings I despised. For once in my young, tumultuous life, I knew perfectly well what I wanted.

I wanted Sidonie.

And I couldn't have her.

It drove me mad to be under the same roof with her, albeit a very large roof. I hated living in the Palace, surrounded by people—guards, peers, delegates, supplicants. Someone was always watching. When Firdha the *ollamh* departed for Alba, Drustan shuffled his men around and assigned her honor guard to attend Dorelei and me. It made her happy—Kinadius, the youngest, was a childhood friend. It made me feel more trapped than ever. I watched them laugh and jest together, remembering how he'd entertained thoughts of courting her.

I wished he would. I wished he'd seduce her and take her off my hands. Albans weren't D'Angeline, but they were easy enough in matters of marital fidelity. Oh, but no! Not in this instance, not with the damnable succession at stake.

Betimes I thought the nights were the hardest. A year ago, I wouldn't have thought so. It wasn't long before Dorelei lost most of her shyness in the bedchamber. She was like the Siovalese country girls Eamonn and I had bedded that summer in Montrève, earnest and simple in her ardor. Phèdre was right. If Dorelei mab Breidaia ever gazed into the dark mirror of her own desires, nothing would have gazed back at her.

A year ago, I would have been glad, even if it left me with a vague melancholy yearning for *more*. I would have accepted it with resolve.

But everything was different now.

It made me angry and unreasonable. It made me want to be cruel; to hurt her, to force her past her boundaries. It would have been heresy and I didn't. But betimes the desire showed in my face or in a careless gesture, when I gripped her flesh hard enough to bruise. And then I would see the fear surface in her eyes and I would apologize to her and hate myself. Worst of all, Dorelei would apologize in turn and try to soothe me, gentle and understanding. It only made me hate myself more.

Still, when all was said and done, I think the days were worse; at least the days when I saw Sidonie.

Elua! Why does love come with such deep barbs? It hurt, more than I knew it could. I tried to tell myself that a year was not a very long time, that things would be different in Alba, that Sidonie was my seventeen-year-old cousin whom I had never much liked anyway.

None of it did any good.

Once you cross a threshold, there is no turning back.

I thought, in those days, about my mother's letters; about what she'd written of Phèdre. *I will tell you this, my son: I knew her. Better than anyone; better than anyone else.* I hadn't understood those words when I read them, not truly. I understood them better now. For better or for worse, I *knew* Sidonie. We had bared a portion of our souls to one another, and found, against all odds, an unexpected fit.

Or at least I had.

I wished I could be sure, absolutely sure of her. Sure that her feelings wouldn't change, sure that this was more than a passing fancy. At times, I *was* sure. And then doubt would creep in and I would wonder. It would all be so much easier to bear if there was no doubt. Easier to be kind and gentle, easier to let the days pass in the certain knowledge of the reward that lay in wait. Instead, I was tormented, swinging wildly from doubt to surety.

All in all, it made me unbearable.

I wanted to *see* her, to hold her, to pin her down and make savage love to her. But if anything, Sidonie was avoiding me. When I had the chance, I cornered Amarante and begged her to find a way. She gave me a long, unreadable look and made no promises. A few days later, though, Mavros came to fetch me for a visit.

"I thought you could use an outing with a kinsman," he said blithely, adding to Dorelei, "You don't mind, my lady, do you?"

Her voice was quiet. "No, of course not."

My heart soared. I was so glad, I kissed her farewell with genuine good spirits. On the ride to Lord Sacriphant's townhouse, I badgered Mavros. "It's a pretext, isn't it? Tell me it's a pretext! Did you manage to spirit Sidonie there?"

"Yes to the first, no to the second," he muttered. "Elua! Remind me never to fall in love."

My soaring heart faltered. "What, then?"

Mavros eyed me darkly. "Nothing you'll like."

He was right. It was Amarante who was waiting at the townhouse, her expression somber. I folded my arms. "Tell me."

"I have a gift for you, your highness." She handed me a small leather-bound book trimmed in gilt. "From Sidonie."

I opened it and glanced at the frontispiece. The book was a collection of letters exchanged by a pair of famous lovers, Remuel L'Oragen of Azzalle and Claire LeDoux of Namarre. They'd met in their youth and been parted by their feuding Houses, carrying on a love affair through letters that spanned a score of years, wedding at last in the middle of their lives. "I see." I closed the book with a snap. "Very apt. Is that all?"

Amarante's face was a touch pale. "Sidonie thinks it would be best if you don't see one another, at least for a while. With her mother's blessing, she's decided to make a pilgrimage to Naamah's shrine in Namarre and abide there for a few weeks."

"Praying for guidance?" I asked coldly.

"Mayhap." Her tone was even. "Prince Imriel, you're behaving badly, and Sidonie is miserable. She's quarrelled with Alais, who is very upset and knows a good deal more than one might wish. And then there is the matter of Dorelei, who is becoming manifestly unhappy and deserves better from all of us, myself included. I think it is for the best. And I think it would be for the best if you found a way to remove yourself from the Court before Sidonie's return."

"Oh, so says the oracle of Naamah!" Bitterness made me cruel. "You know, Amarante, you may play at the role of priestess, but whoever your mother may be, you're naught but a Court attendant enjoying a taste of royal favoritism."

She didn't react as I expected. "'Tis hard to lose the habits of a lifetime, my lord."

I blinked, uncomprehending.

"You do know, of course," Mavros drawled, lounging on a couch, "that Amarante was trained from birth to be a Priestess of Naamah and the presumptive heir to her mother's position. She's already served as an acolyte. Why, she was a mere year away from taking her vows when she accepted the invitation to become a lowly Court attendant instead!"

"You were? You did? Why?" I blinked again. "And how do *you* know?" I added to Mavros.

"Because I thought this was more important," Amarante said.

Mavros clicked his tongue. "Imri, Imri! Everyone knows no priest nor priestess of Naamah may swear full vows without spending a year in her service. And *I* know because I asked." He sighed. "It sweetens the bitter pill of rejection to hear, 'Oh, Lord Mavros, if ever I am freed from the inexplicable clutches of the heir to the realm, I will dedicate myself to Naamah's service and you shall be my first patron!'"

"You said that?" I asked Amarante, feeling stupid.

Her lips twitched. "No."

"She might, though," Mavros offered in a helpful tone. "Part of it's true."

I shoved Mavros' booted feet off the couch and sat down, burying my head in my hands, still clutching the book of letters. "Why are you doing this to me?"

"Because you bade me take care of her," Amarante said quietly. "And I am trying."

"Because you're being an ass," Mavros added. "Remind me—"

"Never to fall in love," I muttered. "Truly, don't."

"Imriel." Amarante sighed. "Believe it or not, I *am* trying to help. You need time apart, sooner rather than later. You need to treat the wedding vows you made with respect, or recant them and make atonement."

"I know," I said. "I know, I know!"

"Then do it," she said simply.

"Hear, hear," Mavros added.

I raised my head to glare at him. "Why do you care?"

"Oh, mayhap because the honor of House Shahrizai is at stake." He prodded my legs with one booted toe. "Family is family. It works both ways, cousin. If you wanted to bring this whole mess crashing down on your heads a-purpose, most of us would stand by you. But it seems the young lady has chosen a wiser course, and I'd rather see her wishes honored for all our sakes." Mavros rubbed his chin. "Strong-willed little minx, isn't she?"

"So it seems," I said shortly.

Mavros grinned at me. "You're put out. Come on, let's get you good and drunk and go to the Night Court. Trust me, it will help." He swung himself to his feet and bowed to Amarante. "My thanks, my lady. I'll take him from here."

She knit her brows. "Don't let him—"

"No, no." Mavros shook his head. "I know what I'm doing."

"All right." Amarante hesitated. "This wasn't an easy choice for Sidonie," she said to me. "Please don't make it harder."

I looked away, fiddling with the book she'd given me. "This doesn't mean she wants us to wait twenty years, I hope."

"Oh, I think one will suffice." An unlikely lilt of humor warmed her voice. "By Naamah's grace, I hope so!"

It made me smile despite myself. "Are you that eager to be freed, my lady?"

"No." Amarante stooped and kissed me. "Not really."

Mavros watched her go, eyes narrowed, tapping his bottom lip in thought. "Elua's Balls! You know, I really do like that girl. That hair, that mouth. What I wouldn't give to see her on her knees, wearing nothing but a leather collar, sucking my—" He shook himself. "What a damnable waste. Whose idea was it to throw her into Sidonie's bed?"

My temples ached. "Phèdre's, I think."

"Phèdre's!" He shot me a startled look.

"Don't ask. I don't know. She has a knack for that sort of thing." I shoved the little book of letters inside my shirt. "Come on, let's go out."

True to his word, Mavros got me good and and drunk in Night's Doorstep. When he bade the carriage-driver to take us to Valerian House, I didn't object. In a haze of wine and pent-up emotion, I was ready, filled with residual resentment and self-pity, and too drunk to care about my demons. If I couldn't have *who* I wanted, at least I could have *what* I wanted. In the receiving room, wavering on my feet, I began to tell the Dowayne my desires.

"No, no." Mavros shook his head at me. "We're not here for that."

I stared at him. "We're not?"

Didier Vascon, the Dowayne, bowed low. "Your private Showing awaits, my lords," he murmured. "All has been arranged."

"Oh," I said foolishly. "When did you . . . ?"

Mavros clapped a hand on my shoulder. "I have my ways. Violent pleasures and an angry heart are a deadly mixture, cousin mine, and yours is too angry by far. Betimes 'tis better to let the eyes feast until the heart is purged lest you do harm unwitting. Come and see."

I followed, stumbling, as the Dowayne led us down hushed corridors to a private viewing chamber. It was warm and dimly lit, and hung all about with erotic tapestries. There was a small staging area with a pair of reclining couches placed before it. Four adepts waited there, still as statues. Two women, two men. One pair was from Valerian House, kneeling *abeyante* with lowered heads. One pair was from Mandrake House, faces hidden behind domino masks. The man held a brass-tipped flogger, thongs trailing over the top of one glossy boot. The woman held a tawse paddle with a slit down the middle. From time to time, she twitched it against her thigh. Every time she did, one of the Valerian adepts whimpered.

Mavros stretched his length on one of the couches with a luxuriant sigh, folding his hands behind his head. "A pair to attend," he said to Didier Vascon. "Unclad, if you please. And mayhap a fortified wine?"

"Of course, my lord." The Dowayne bowed low, beckoning with a subtle gesture.

A pair of adepts appeared, naked and unabashed. The male knelt with silent grace beside the couch where I perched uncomfortably, proffering a goblet. His eyes were downcast.

"My thanks," I said awkwardly, accepting the wine. He flashed a quick smile.

"Name of Elua!" Mavros said tartly. "*Relax*, will you?"

"I'm trying."

And much to my surprise, I did. Mavros clapped his hands, bidding the Showing to commence. The adepts in the staging area began a performance that was no less genuine for being rehearsed. We sipped our fortified wine and watched; watched as the Mandrake adept swung his flogger in an intricate rhythm, the brass tips kissing the Valerian woman's skin as she stood with her hands braced against the wall, head lowered and legs wide. Watched the male Valerian adept bend over a padded barrel, strong hands clasping his own calves. His buttocks reddened as the Mandrake dominatrice wielded the tawse, every hard slap of leather against skin making him groan. And then the adepts of Mandrake House exchanged masked glances and traded places, and it all began anew.

It was like a dance, dark and elegant, filled with gasps and sighs and soft commands. It made my throat tight with desire, my rigid phallus strain against my breeches. I glanced over at Mavros. He was smiling at the stage, heavy-lidded. One hand was idly stroking his attendant's hair. Her head bobbed above his groin, her cheeks working.

"My lord?" my attendant whispered. "If it please you?"

"All right," I said recklessly. "Why not?"

"Thank you, my lord!" he breathed.

I closed my eyes, feeling his deft fingers unbutton my breeches. I heard him sigh with pleasure, felt his mouth descend to engulf me, skilled and eager. I listened to the crack of the flogger, the slap of the tawse, the moans and murmurs, the occasional low chuckle. I pushed away thoughts of Daršanga and thought of sunlight.

Sunlight, and tangled hair the color of honey.

And horrible, wonderful things done in the name of love.

Afterward, I felt purged and calm; calmer than I'd felt for days. Mavros had been right, and I was glad he'd done what he'd done, arranging the Showing instead of letting me indulge my worst desires. I told him so as the carriage-driver drew rein in the Palace courtyard, my head lolling on the seat.

"Yes, I know." Mavros patted my cheek. "As I told that damnable priestess' daughter, I do know what I'm doing, cousin. At least when it comes to family." He regarded me with worried fondness. "Elua, you look a mess! Give your lady wife my apologies. And *talk* to her, will you?"

"I will," I promised drunkenly.

"Good," he said.

Entering the Palace, I waved off the footman's insistence on summoning a guard to escort me to my quarters. It was late enough to be quiet, for which I was grateful. I walked slowly through the marble halls, willing my head to stop spinning. The unusual hush helped. By the time I reached my quarters, I was reasonably steady on my feet.

Inside, it was dark. I fumbled with my flint striker, trying to kindle a lamp, and failed to raise aught but a clatter and a shower of sparks. I gave up and took a taper into the hallway to light it from one of the wall sconces. The D'Angeline guard on duty looked amused. I went back inside and used the chamberpot in the privy closet, scoured my face in the washbasin. The cool water felt good.

Carrying my lighted taper, I made my way to the bedchamber. At first I thought Dorelei was asleep. I knelt beside the clothes press that held my things, easing the little book of love letters from my shirt and tucking it away in the bottom drawer beneath an old pair of breeches I wore for hunting. When I rose to unbutton my shirt, I saw her watching me.

She was sitting with arms wrapped around her knees, clad in a thin shift with her shining black hair loose over her shoulders.

"I'm sorry," I said. "I didn't mean to wake you."

"I wasn't asleep."

"Mavros sends his apologies." I raked a hand through my tangled hair. "I didn't know it was so late."

"Where did you go?" Dorelei asked quietly.

"To the Night Court." I sat on the edge of the bed and hauled my boots off. The lone candle flickered. I felt her waiting silence and sighed, turning to face her. "Dorelei, I'm sorry. I've been cruel and unfair. It's not your fault." When there was no response, I swallowed and said the words aloud. "I'm in love with someone else."

She nodded. "I know."

"You do?" I blinked. "How?"

For a long moment, she didn't answer. "I asked Alais," she said at length. "You know, I'm perfectly aware that this is a marriage of politics. I didn't expect you to love me, and I didn't expect you to be faithful to me. But I hoped, at least, that there could be honesty between us. At first I thought it was me, that I was distasteful to you."

"You're not—"

Dorelei held up her hand, forestalling me. "But you can be so charming sometimes, kind and funny. And I thought some of it was real. Alais thought so, too. She says you have a good heart. So I thought it must be because of what you suffered, like you warned me." I didn't say anything and she continued. "But then it seemed like there was always someplace else you'd rather be, someone else you were always looking for, and I began to wonder. And so I asked Alais."

I felt a chill in my veins. "What did Alais say?"

"Alais turned a lot of strange colors," she said steadily. "And told me to ask you. I didn't want to, though. I wanted to see if you'd tell me yourself."

"Well," I said. "Now I have."

"Now you have." Dorelei regarded me, pinpricks of flame reflected in her dark eyes. "I don't know who it is, Imriel, and I'm not asking. Believe me, I don't want to know whose face you're picturing when you hold me so hard it leaves marks. I'm not asking you to break off the affair. All I'm asking is that you stop treating me like I'm an actor miscast in your own personal tragedy through no fault of my own."

"I don't—" I began to protest, then stopped. "That's well said, actually."

"Please don't make me laugh." She shook her head, and I saw there were tears making a gleaming path on her brown cheeks. "I want you to treat me like a person, that's all. To see *me* and not only who I'm not. I don't love you either, you know. I barely even know you. But I might if you'd let me."

It was fair; it was more than fair.

I got to my feet and made a courtly bow. "My lady, my name is Imriel de la Courcel nó Montrève. I have been many things in my short life, most recently what my foster-brother Eamonn would call a right bastard."

Dorelei smiled through her tears. "Well met, my lord. My name is Dorelei mab Breidaia. I am the niece of the Cruarch of Alba, and most recently, your wife. If you are willing, I think we might at least become friends."

"I would like that," I said gravely.

Her eyes shone. "So would I."

It was late and I was tired and still more than a little drunk. I shucked off the rest of my clothing and climbed into bed beside her. A part of my heart ached with loss and longing. A part was glad we had talked. I laid my head on my pillow and closed my eyes, feeling Dorelei's fingers stroking my temples.

"I do wish you weren't so beautiful," she whispered.

"So do I," I murmured.

"Oh, such a burden!" she said, soft and teasing. I opened my eyes to gaze at her. She didn't know, didn't understand that my face carried a constant reminder of my mother's treachery. Although we'd never spoken of it, Sidonie had understood. She'd grown up with my mother's veiled image hanging in the Hall of Portraits. She'd never said such a thing to me, ever. I sighed, knowing I should try to explain to Dorelei, too tired to do it. I lifted one hand and touched her cheek, tracing the dots of blue woad. I'd thought, when first she said she knew, that mayhap she'd seen it in a dream. Stranger things had happened.

"Have you ever dreamed of me?" I asked. "A true dream?"

"Only once."

"Oh?" I closed my eyes again, feeling sleep begin claim me. "What was it?"

"It wasn't one I understood," she mused. "No one did. You were all alone, kneeling in a snowstorm, beneath a barren tree. Holding your sword and weeping."

"Oh," I whispered, and slept.

FIFTEEN

ON THE FOLLOWING MORNING, I slept late. In consideration of my late—and somewhat drunken—return, Dorelei had left orders not to disturb me, and by the time I arose I'd missed Sidonie's departure. It was probably as well that I did, though my heart ached at it.

Still, by the time the day ended, I had to own that it was easier knowing she was gone. Knowing we wouldn't encounter one another in unexpected places, knowing we wouldn't have to endure the grueling ordeal of being cordial to one another in public. Knowing the temptation to take dangerous risks was removed, knowing there was no way of arranging a covert assignation.

I didn't like it, but it was easier.

I had no idea what I'd do upon her return. Amarante was right, of course. It would be for the best if I could find a way to remove myself from the Court. I toyed with the idea of an excursion to Montrève, but something in my heart balked at the notion. It was a special place, a private place. I wasn't ready to share it with Dorelei. Mayhap, I thought, it would be better to tour my own neglected holdings with her. Of a surety, it would be politic to pay a visit, and they held no strong memories for me.

Well, except for Lombelon, which was no longer mine. Though I wouldn't find Maslin there, oh no. He was off to Namarre accompanying Sidonie, second in command of her personal guard, which galled me to no end. The thought of her in his arms, naked and willing, was enough to make the bile rise in my throat. Why she liked him I couldn't fathom, but she did.

She'd do it, too; I was sure of it. It was only a question of when.

I tried not to think about it.

And as matters transpired, for once the gods took pity on me. A few days after Sidonie's departure, the one thing that could serve to lift me well and truly out of the slough of despondency took place.

Eamonn returned.

He presented himself at the Palace, himself and his Skaldic wife. There was no letter, no word of warning. I was sharing a midday luncheon with Dorelei and Alais when the news arrived, delivered by a grinning guard. Alais let out a little shriek.

"Eamonn mac Grainne?" Dorelei asked. "The Lady of the Dalriada's son?"

"The same." I laughed, lightheaded with relief and gladness. "I told you, he fostered with House Montrève for a year. I was hoping to have word from him weeks ago. Have you met?"

"Oh yes, years ago, when I was a little girl. I daresay he won't remember it." She smiled. "I do, though. He was lively."

"Indeed." I held out one hand to her. Alais was already tugging on my other hand. "Well, come on! Let's go."

The Palace Guard had, after some debate, escorted them to one of the Queen's private salons. Brigitta was stalking around the perimeter of the room, eyeing the luxurious appointments warily. Eamonn was watching the door, rocking on the cracked heels of his boots and grinning to split his face, which sported a thick red-gold beard.

"Imri!" he shouted.

My heart rose into my throat; I couldn't even answer. I embraced him hard, thumping his broad back with both fists. Eamonn gave me a long, crushing squeeze, then held me off by the shoulders.

"All right, all right!" he said good-naturedly. "Dagda Mor! You'd think I'd risen from the dead."

I feinted a punch at him. "Elua! You might as well, by the smell of you."

"Eamonn!" Alais hugged him about the waist, then wrinkled her nose. "You do stink. And you're very hairy."

Eamonn laughed. "Sorry, young highness. It's been a long journey." He pried her gently away and bowed, switching to the Caerdicci language. "May I present my lady wife, Brigitta of the Manni."

"Yes, of course." Alais, suddenly realizing she was the ranking member of the royal family present, struggled for composure. Her face reddened as she gazed at tall, blonde Brigitta, who was regarding us all with profound skepticism. "Well met, my lady, and welcome to the City of Elua. I'm Alais de la Courcel."

"Hello, Brigitta," I said to her. "You're supposed to curtsy."

"Hello, Imriel." She smiled slightly. "What are the dues of fealty in a strange land?"

It sounded like one of the questions Master Piero would have posed us back in Tiberium, and it made me laugh. I turned to introduce Dorelei to her, and realized belatedly that they shared no language in common. Brigitta spoke Skaldic and Caerdicci; Dorelei, Cruithne and D'Angeline. Of a necessity, I made the introductions in two languages and the women nodded awkwardly at one another.

At least with Eamonn there was no awkwardness. "Breidaia's little girl!" he exclaimed, hugging her. "Look at you, all grown up. I'm sorry we missed the wedding."

"Never mind that," Alais said impatiently. "Tell us what *happened*!"

I was dying to hear it, too, but it was clear they were both travel-worn and weary. "Mayhap you might extend the Queen's hospitality to them?" I suggested gently to Alais. "I suspect Prince Eamonn and his wife would be grateful for it."

"Oh!" She flushed again. "Yes, of course."

By the time Ysandre and Drustan arrived to proffer their greetings, Alais had summoned the Master of Chambers. Quarters had been located for Eamonn and Brigitta and Palace servants had gone ahead to drawing them a much-needed bath. They would have moved their baggage, too, but there was none.

"Name of Elua!" Ysandre murmured, bemused. "The last time anyone emerged from Skaldia and turned up on my doorstep looking like this . . ." She shook her head, and I knew she was thinking of Phèdre and Joscelin, who had escaped from slavery to bring word of an impending invasion. I was glad Brigitta didn't catch the reference. She was none too fond of D'Angelines as it was.

"Oh, we were robbed, that's all," Eamonn said cheerfully. "Still, here we are!"

An hour later, we heard their tale over our interrupted luncheon. Neither the Queen nor Cruarch were able to attend, but I sent word to the townhouse, and Phèdre and Joscelin came posthaste. They'd grown fond of Eamonn during the time he fostered with us and the feeling was amply reciprocated. Eamonn let out another shout, sweeping Phèdre off her feet in a glad embrace, setting her down to clasp Joscelin's hand with a broad grin.

"This is my lady Phèdre," Eamonn said to Brigitta. "She taught me to speak and write Caerdicci. And my lord Joscelin." He laughed. "He taught me I'm not as clever with a sword as I think!"

"Well met, my lady," Phèdre said graciously to Brigitta, speaking in fluent Skaldi. "We're so very pleased to have Prince Eamonn returned safely, and you with him."

Brigitta nodded curtly; staring at her, staring at Joscelin with his Cassiline daggers and the longsword at his back. I thought of Erich, the young Skaldi man in the zenana. Phèdre had spoken to him in his mother tongue, too. And although he'd given no indication of it for weeks on end, he had known exactly who she was. He'd known her by that and by the scarlet mote in her eye. I remembered what he'd said. *The defeated always remember.* He'd been six years old when it happened. I hadn't even been conceived. Nor had Brigitta, but she'd grown up with the same stories.

"Eamonn," I said in D'Angeline. "Did you ever happen to mention to Brigitta exactly *who* Phèdre and Joscelin are, and their history with a certain Skaldic warlord?"

"Well, of course!" He blinked at me. "Oh, that. No."

I sighed. Everywhere I turned, it seemed I was hemmed in by the past. Heroism on one side, treachery on the other. "Oh, hell! No mind. Tell us what happened, will you?"

"May we eat first?" Eamonn asked plaintively. "I'm perishing."

Between bites of a warmed-over roast with piquant sauce and large chunks of bread, he got out most of the story. Being Eamonn, he made it funny, although I daresay little of it was at the time. Armed with the map Brigitta had drawn for him and copies of maps in the archives at the University, he'd gone in search of her father's steading amid the tribes of the Manni in southern Skaldia.

"I nearly made it, too," he said, cramming another hunk of bread in his mouth.

Eamonn was telling the story in Caerdicci, and I'd been translating for Dorelei. "You didn't encounter any . . . hostility?" I asked delicately at his pause.

He shook his head, mouth full, and Brigitta answered for him. "Once he crossed the border into Skaldia, he told people he was a countryman stolen by the Caerdicci and raised in slavery in Tiberium." She sounded proud. "He could be Skaldi, you know. He almost looks it."

I translated for Dorelei, who nodded. "They share roots from long ago."

"I know." I smiled at her. "The *ollamh* told us at great length."

She laughed her infectious laugh, breaking to end on a giggle. It had grated on me before, when Sidonie was here. Now I only felt my smile turn a little wistful. I caught Eamonn's gaze on me, shrewd and wondering.

"Anyway," he said, swallowing. "I was caught in a blizzard before I reached the steading. Some of Hallgrim's—Brigitta's father's—thanes found me. And I couldn't very well lie to *them*. Brigitta had warned them I would come for her."

Eamonn went on to relate how they'd taken him back to the steading, where he had presented himself as Brigitta's husband. Her father and brother had refused to acknowledge his claim, refused to believe he was a prince of the Dalriada. Her mother had been more circumspect, swayed by political interest and the golden torc he wore about his neck. They'd come to a compromise.

"He agreed to serve as a carl until my father relented," Brigitta told us.

"Dagda Mor!" Eamonn chuckled. "I think he saved the hardest, foulest chores for me. I don't think anyone else did a lick of work that winter, and my hands were cracked and bleeding in a week's time. But it only lasted until the spring."

Phèdre and Joscelin exchanged a glance, doubtless remembering.

"That's so romantic!" Alais clasped her hands together, eyes bright. "How did you know her father would relent?"

"Oh, I knew." Eamonn smiled at Brigitta. "He has a stubborn daughter and a stubborn wife. Stubborn women will wear a man down every time. Come spring, Hallgrim was minded to let me go and let Brigitta go with me, if only to buy a moment's peace in his household. But *then*," he added, "her brother Leidolf got angry and challenged me to the holmgang. Do you know it, Joscelin?"

An uncomfortable silence fell.

"Yes," Joscelin said quietly. He met Brigitta's narrowed gaze. "I fought twice in the holmgang. The second time was against Waldemar Selig. He was a very great swordsman."

"A great *man*," she said stiffly.

Eamonn made a rumbling sound deep in his chest. "Brigitta . . ."

"It's all right." Phèdre reached across the table to touch Brigitta's hand. "Child, you're a scholar. 'Tis better to know the reality than the myth, is it not? Waldemar Selig *was* a great man in some ways. In others, he wasn't. You, too, have set on a course that may better your people's lives, only it is done out of love. I think it is a better way. But having set your course, you must abide by it and accept what comes, including new friends in the shape of old enemies. Surely, you consented to as much when you agreed to wed the son of the Lady of the Dalriada."

Brigitta looked startled. I wondered if she knew Selig had attempted to skin Phèdre alive on the battlefield. Somehow, I doubted that story was oft-repeated in Skaldia. She said somewhat low in reply to Phèdre which I missed, trying to translate for Dorelei.

"So you defeated Leidolf?" Joscelin asked, prompting Eamonn to continue. "In the holmgang?"

"Me?" He gave a wide-eyed look. "Oh, yes, of course."

I wasn't fooled by the seemingly artless way in which Eamonn had introduced the matter of Joscelin and Phèdre's past. Eamonn didn't always think matters through to their conclusion, but he was a good deal cannier than he looked. He'd meant to force the issue. With Brigitta quiet and thoughtful beside him, he told the rest of their story.

How they'd departed from her father's steading, leaving his golden torc behind as a pledge of surety for a generous gift to follow on their return to Alba. How they'd been set upon by brigands near the border and robbed. He'd kept his sword and defended Brigitta's honor, but everything else had been lost; horses, supplies, money. For the better part of a week, they'd hovered near starvation, forced to travel on foot and beg.

"Luckily, we found a trade caravan bound for the Caerdicci coast," Eamonn said lightly. "And I was able to take service with them as a mercenary until we reached Giano."

In the coastal city-state of Giano, they'd found a small fleet of D'Angeline merchant-ships. As it transpired, Eamonn's father, the Royal Admiral Quintilius Rousse, had received the letter his son had entrusted to my keeping, which I had left with the Lady of Marsilikos late last autumn. Although he was an absent father, Quintilius Rousse was a proud one, too. He'd spread word far and wide in the D'Angeline seafaring community that anyone spotting his errant, half-Eiran son was to give all aid possible. Eamonn and Brigitta had sailed aboard a merchant ship to the mouth of the Aviline River, travelling by barge inland to the City of Elua.

"And here we are!" Eamonn concluded, spreading his arms.

I shook my head. "Oh, Prince Barbarus. I wish I'd gone with you."

He grinned at me. "Well, we might have beaten those damned brigands if you had, Imri. But I'm not sure Hallgrim would have been so accommodating. And besides, you would have missed your own wedding."

I couldn't tell him that I wished I had, not with Dorelei at my side. And of a surety, I couldn't tell him what had befallen me betwixt my return and my marriage. That would have to wait.

"I've missed you," I said softly.

Eamonn laughed. "Oh, I daresay you've kept busy without me." He winked at Dorelei. "At least I *hope* so."

She smiled politely, not understanding. This time, I didn't translate.

Eamonn noticed that, too.

Several days passed before I had the chance to speak with Eamonn in complete privacy. They had truly arrived in the City of Elua with little more than the clothing on their backs, and while they were anxious to continue on to Alba, there was a good deal to be done if they weren't to travel as beggars. Ysandre was gracious in the matter of hospitality and insisted that they allow the Palace couturiers to provide new attire. I made him a gift of monies from my own accounts, which Eamonn accepted reluctantly after I convinced him it was a belated token of congratulations on his nuptials.

For the most part, he and Brigitta were inseparable. I knew she was uneasy in Terre d'Ange, and in truth, I didn't blame her for it. There were a good many people at Court who made it clear they didn't relish hearing a Skaldic accent in the Palace halls.

Eamonn, who had never particularly cared for the D'Angeline Court, did his best to insulate Brigitta with his constant presence, offsetting her scowls with his sunny good nature, much to the perplexity of everyone who encountered them.

"What a peculiar pair they are!" Dorelei mused when we were alone together. "And yet they seem to dote on one another."

"Prince Barbarus and his shield-maiden," I said. "That's what Lucius used to call them."

"His mother was a doughty warrior in her youth," she said. "You know, I wish I could talk to her."

"The Lady Grainne?"

Dorelei shook her head. "Brigitta. It must be a frightening thing to be almost alone in the world so far from home. I understand a little bit. Although at least . . ." She didn't finish her thought. "Alais is right. It is very romantic."

"Alais wanted to marry Eamonn when she was thirteen," I informed her.

"She did?" Dorelei smiled. "What a picture! I can see why, though."

I'd met few women able to resist Eamonn's charm. Well, except mayhap Sidonie. *She's a right bitch*, Eamonn had said of her after their first meeting. I'd asked her, once, why she didn't like him. She'd given me a perplexed look. *I do *like* him, Imriel. He's just so infernally loud!* It was unkind and true, and it had made me laugh.

Elua, but I missed her.

"You know," I said to my wife. "When you told me about your dream, the next morning I thought of Eamonn. I thought mayhap that's what it was about."

"The snowstorm?"

"Mm-hmm."

"No." Dorelei was silent a moment. "No, I don't think so."

"I suppose not, since he's here now." I ran a few strands of her hair through my fingers, fine and straight and black, wishing it were otherwise. "What if you offered to teach Brigitta to speak Cruithne and Eiran, you and Alais? Eamonn's been trying, but he's a dreadful teacher. He gets ahead of himself and she gets muddled."

She looked at me. "I don't speak Caerdicci."

"Alais does," I said. "And you might learn some. Anyway, I suspect Brigitta would welcome the kindness. She'd as soon leave on the morrow, but they're staying another week in the hope of hearing from Eamonn's father. 'Tis enough time to make a beginning."

"'Tis a generous thought." Dorelei considered it. "I'll talk to Alais."

I smiled at her. "Oh, good."

Truth be told, it *was* a good idea. Alais took to it with immediate enthusiasm and Brigitta received it with something that very nearly resembled gratitude, well aware that once she reached Alba, she'd be nearly devoid of the ability to communicate. Alais was clever and patient, and I'd no doubt she'd make an excellent teacher. It proved to be true, and Dorelei's gentle guidance an asset in the process.

I was glad, since my motives were selfish.

It gave me a chance to talk with Eamonn.

Once I had it, though, I found myself strangely reluctant. I couldn't help but wonder if that was how my mother had managed to enlist so many allies in her schemes; advancing her own motives by means that pleased them, at least up until the moment she betrayed them or no longer had a use for them. I suspected it was. At least in this, my motive was simple and none too dire. I wanted only a chance to ease my troubled heart by talking to my dearest friend.

And yet . . .

It would burden him. And then there was the memory of his glad exclamation at the sight of Dorelei, the fond embrace. It was all very much at odds with his opinion of Sidonie, and I wondered if it would be better to keep silent. I didn't mind Mavros speaking ill of her; I was used to it and he'd proved himself a friend to us both in other ways. I didn't know if I could bear it from Eamonn.

We went to Night's Doorstep to revisit our old haunts. In the spring before Eamonn had left for Tiberium, we were wont to spend hours there, drinking and talking. Naamah's Servants plied their trade there, too, serving those who couldn't afford the Night Court. A few familiar faces called out merry greetings and invitations to Eamonn, who merely shook his head and grinned.

There were new faces, too. I wondered how many of them were priests or priestesses in training, planning to take their vows in a year's time. I tried to picture Amarante among them, and found the image at once disturbing and arousing. It made me glad she was in no hurry to leave Sidonie's side. Safe harbor, indeed.

At the Cockerel, there were greetings all around. It was a long time before Eamonn eased himself into a chair opposite me, stretching out his long legs. He took a long pull on a foaming tankard of ale and smacked his lips. "Oh, that's good!" He sighed. "It's good to be here, Imri. I feel like I'm being smothered at the Palace."

"I know the feeling," I murmured.

"Oh, aye?" Eamonn drank again and eyed me. "Care to tell me why?"

I shrugged. "There's naught to be done about it."

"Imri, Imri!" He set his tankard down. "We've played this game before in Tiberium. I didn't care for it then, and I don't care for it now. I know you and your brooding and secrecy. So tell me, what new Claudia Fulvia is casting a shadow over your marriage?"

"You know, it's funny." I toyed with the change lying on the table, left over from the purchase of our ale. "I had a similar conversation with Joscelin at this very same table." I smiled. "He said he and Phèdre drew lots, and he lost."

"Very funny," Eamonn said. "So who is she?"

One of the coins was a silver centime, old and worn. It must have dated back to the early years of Ysandre's reign. I studied her youthful profile. Softened and blurred by time, it still held a resemblance to her eldest daughter. "Eamonn, if I tell you, will you do me the courtesy of trying not to laugh?"

"Of course."

I balanced the coin on edge and set it spinning with the flick of a finger. "Sidonie."

Eamonn's jaw dropped. He stared at me, eyes wide. The coin spun, slowed, clattered onto its side. Eamonn closed and opened his mouth a few times, licked his lips and cleared his throat. "You know," he said carefully. "Somehow, that's not nearly as funny as I would have imagined it would be."

I smiled wryly. "My thanks."

"How?" he asked. "And *why*?"

I told him how it had come to pass; the boar hunt last summer, the Longest Night, and the affair that had ensued with all its attendant dangers. Eamonn listened without comment until I was finished. "Does Dorelei know?"

"Yes, and no." I took a gulp of ale. "She knows there's someone. She didn't want to know who."

"How in the world do you manage to do this?" Eamonn shook his head in disbelief. "I swear, Imriel, you stumble into the most difficult things!"

"Oh, thus speaks the man who spent a Skaldic winter slaving to win the hand of his ill-tempered bride!" I observed sharply.

Eamonn grinned and beckoned for more ale. "She's not ill-tempered with *me*. Well, not anymore. Not usually." He fished on the table for coins to pay for the ale, waiting for the barkeep to leave. "So tell me, Imri. Which is she? A Claudia or a Helena?" I looked at him, uncomprehending. "A wanton you long to debauch or an innocent you want to protect?" he clarified. "Oh, come! You tumbled into Claudia's marriage-bed without a second thought, and you lopped off Valpetra's hand to save Helena without even having met her. Surely you've noticed you're drawn to one or the other."

"I hadn't, actually." I thought about it and smiled. "Both."

"You *are* in trouble." Eamonn raised his brows. "What do you mean to do?"

"Hope it passes." I shrugged. "We're both hoping."

"That's why Sidonie went to Naamah's shrine?" he asked. "To get away?"

I nodded. "It was too hard being under the same roof together."

Eamonn gave me a dubious look. "I'm not laughing, Imri, but it *is* hard to fathom. What will you do when she returns?"

"I don't know." I shook my head. "I was thinking of taking Dorelei to tour my holdings to the north . . . I don't know. I hadn't decided, and then you showed up, and I've not made any plans since."

"I've an idea," Eamonn said slowly. "Come with me."

"To Alba?" I stared at him. "Now?"

"Why not?" He grinned. "I'd be pleased to no end to have you, and Brigitta wouldn't mind. She quite likes Dorelei. You could pay your respects to my lady mother before your Alban nuptials. Surely, the Lady of the Dalriada deserves no less from a D'Angeline prince. After all, I was named for her brother my uncle, who died defending Terre d'Ange."

"Yes, I know," I said absently. "She carried his head home in a bag."

"True," Eamonn agreed. "It's buried atop the mound in Innisclan. Pity she didn't get the head of the man who killed him to bury at the foot, he would have rested easier for it. But you could make an offering there. It would be fitting."

"Ysandre would never—" I reflected. "Well, she might."

"There's a debt of honor owed," he said pragmatically. "*She's* never deigned to visit. What better opportunity than to send you, your bride, and a large armed company to escort the Lady's wayward son home?"

It seemed like a mad adventure when he first proposed it, but the longer I thought about it, the more sense it made. Eamonn was right, Terre d'Ange did owe a debt to the Dalriada, and his arrival forged the perfect opportunity to acknowledge it. Dorelei and I were bound for Alba anyway. Our wedding had been witnessed by the peers of the realm here, who could now assure themselves that the line of succession in Alba wouldn't revert wholly to the Cruithne, shutting out Terre d'Ange's influence. Nothing more was needful.

It made sense; it made a great deal of sense. My heart protested at it—ah, Elua! I didn't want to leave D'Angeline soil any sooner than I had to. And yet something had to be done. Mayhap with the Straits between us, Sidonie and I would find our ardor cooling and our infatuation passing. And if we didn't . . . well.

I hoped we would at the same time I prayed we didn't.

"All right, then." I hoisted my tankard. "To the Dalriada!"

SIXTEEN

PHÈDRE TURNED PALE when I told her the idea.

"You don't think it's wise?" I asked.

"No, it's not that." She laughed, but there was sorrow in it. "The opposite, in fact. I think it's an excellent plan. I'm being selfish, that's all. I didn't expect to lose you again quite this soon."

"I know," I said. "I hate it, too. But—"

"No, no." She shook her head. "You're right, it's for the best."

Joscelin, who was sharpening one of Eugènie's kitchen cleavers as he listened, tested it on his thumb and swore mildly when it cut him. "Elua! These things hold an edge. What does she use them for, anyway?"

"Much the same thing you do, my love, only it results in dinner." Phèdre passed him a silk kerchief. "Here."

He wrapped his bleeding thumb. "Why don't we go with them?"

"To Alba?" Her color began to return. "You and I?"

Joscelin gave his half-smile. "We were bound to go for the Alban rites, anyway. It's only a couple months early, and Ysandre might like the plan better with the Queen's Champion riding in attendance. Besides, you could pay your respects to the Lady Grainne."

"And Hyacinthe?" Phèdre's eyes sparkled.

"Yes, and that damned Tsingano." Joscelin caught her about the waist and kissed her. "Exactly how respectful do you plan on being?"

She laughed and kissed him back without answering.

It made me smile. There is no one else in the world, I think, who would refer to the Master of the Straits as "that damned Tsingano." But

Joscelin had the right, if anyone did. They had all known each other long ago, and Phèdre had loved Hyacinthe, too. I daresay in a part of her heart, she still did. To his credit, it didn't seem to bother Joscelin, not really. I hadn't understood before why her feelings for some of her former patrons and lovers bothered him, and others didn't. I understood it better now.

All in all, Eamonn's plan was well received. Dorelei had been delighted by it, so much so that it made me feel guilty to see the happiness that transformed her face and realize I'd never seen her truly happy before. All of us together begged a formal audience of the Queen and Cruarch and presented our proposal.

I could tell by the look of approval in Drustan's eyes that he liked the idea. Ysandre rested her chin in one hand and gazed at us for a long time, considering it. Her gaze rested the longest on Phèdre and Joscelin.

"You know," she mused. " 'Tis a strange day indeed when the two of *you* are to be entrusted as my sensible elder statesmen."

Joscelin smiled. "You've taken far greater risks on us, your majesty."

"True." Ysandre looked at Eamonn, Brigitta, Dorelei, and me. She shook her head in amazement. "Elua! When I think that the four of us were only a few years older than this lot when the Skal—" She caught herself, mindful of Brigitta's presence. "So be it. However, if it is to be done, let it be done properly. A suitable gift of tribute must be found, and my lord Drustan will need to speak with Ghislain nó Trevalion regarding an escort of Alban and D'Angeline guards. Tarry another week."

Eamonn bowed. "Your majesty, we'd thought to leave in two days—"

Ysandre raised one hand. "Ah, no! You've made it clear I've been remiss, and I'll not be rushed in this. Why hurry? You may receive word from your father." She smiled. "Besides, Sidonie will be home by then. It would be nice to have all the members of House Courcel under one roof one last time ere you disperse."

"I agree on all counts," Drustan said in a tone that brooked no argument. "Let it be done properly, or not at all."

So it was decided.

In the days that followed, an armed escort of fifty men was assembled; thirty D'Angeline and twenty Cruithne. Although Drustan could spare no more than a score of his personal guard, it was agreed that the company would be placed under the command of Urist, one of the most seasoned veterans among the Albans. Supplies were commissioned, messengers sent to the coast of Azzalle to arrange for transport across the Straits.

The inventory lists from the Royal Treasury were procured, and Ysandre and Phèdre spent hours poring over them to select appropriate gifts, assisted by Eamonn, who took a surprising interest in the process.

Brigitta applied herself fervently to the study of Cruithne and Eiran, assisted by Dorelei and Alais, who was the only person deeply unhappy about our plan. Alais begged to be allowed to accompany us. Both her mother and her father refused.

A swift courier arrived from the Lady of Marsilikos, bearing a much-battered oilskin pouch containing a missive from the Royal Admiral Quintilius Rousse promising to meet his son and his bride in Alba, pending the Queen's permission. Ysandre penned a hasty reply granting as much, and the courier dashed back on his errand, racing to catch an outgoing vessel to bear the Queen's letter to Rousse.

And Sidonie returned.

Of all the damnable luck, I was there when her party arrived. I'd meant to be gone; they'd been spotted from the walls and I'd known they were coming. I was planning to meet Mavros and a few of my Shahrizai kin at a manor house a half league outside the city, where they meant to ride to hawks. But I'd gotten delayed leaving the Palace and the ostlers were slow in bringing around the Bastard, who could be fractious.

I was waiting in the courtyard, growing anxious and impatient, wondering if I should go saddle him myself, when they arrived.

It was a fine day, bright and clear and temperate. I saw Sidonie before she saw me. She'd forgone the chariot to ride astride, her skirts draped over her mount's crupper. The sun was bright on her honey-gold hair, looped in a soft coronet. Her face was calm and composed, half-turned toward Amarante, who was riding beside her. The exposed line of her white throat was lovely. And oh, Elua! Nothing had changed.

My mouth went dry.

My heart turned into a lead weight.

I didn't say a word, but Sidonie turned her head as though I'd called to her. If she was surprised to see me, it didn't show. Her expression didn't change. Still, somewhat in it deepened, somewhat only I could see. I bowed and stepped forward to hold her stirrup. Her guards clattered into the courtyard around her, led by Maslin.

"Imriel." Sidonie dismounted, allowing me to assist her. "Thank you."

"Welcome home, your highness," I said softly. She was wearing the earrings I'd given her. "I hope your pilgrimage was a good one."

"Yes." She smiled a little, sadly. "Yes, it was."

Her hands were still resting in mine. I could have stood there forever, holding them; I could have listened to her say my name a thousand times. I rubbed the inside of her left wrist with my thumb, feeling the warm, steady beat of her pulse quicken. "There's news," I said with a lightness I didn't feel. "Eamonn's come back."

"Oh?" Her black eyes searched mine. "I'm glad to hear it."

"I'll be . . ." I swallowed. "I'll be leaving with him in three days' time."

Sidonie drew a slow, deep breath, gathering strength. Her fingers squeezed mine. "Well, then. I'm glad I returned in time to bid you farewell."

"So am I," I said hoarsely.

At that moment, the tardy ostler leading the Bastard into the courtyard gave a shout of alarm as the spotted hellion chose to spook at the unexpected sight of so many riders, jerking against the reins and plunging about. Maslin's mounted guards milled and cursed. I dropped Sidonie's hands and ran over to grab the reins. The Bastard gave me a walleyed look, but I glared back at him, and he subsided. I swung myself astride and pointed his head toward the Palace gate.

Maslin blocked my way.

The Bastard checked as I reined him hard. Maslin had dismounted, but he showed no sign of fear. He spread his arms wide, making the

Bastard shy and snort. I wrestled with the reins. "You don't fool me, princeling," Maslin said to me, his dark eyes glittering. "I just want you to know that. You don't fool me at all."

I got the Bastard under control and leaned down. "What's the matter, Maslin?" I whispered to him. "Did you not get what you hoped for?"

The muscles in his lean, handsome face worked. He closed his eyes briefly, making himself strangely vulnerable. As fair-haired as he was, his lashes were dark. I watched him struggle with pride, anger, desire, and dislike. Once, I'd wanted him for a friend. For the space of a few heartbeats, I could see what it was in him that Sidonie liked; a potent mix of caustic honesty and hot-blooded yearning.

It was unnervingly familiar.

"Go." Maslin stepped aside. "The sooner the better."

"Maslin." I hesitated. "Must we always be this way?"

Our eyes met, then he looked past me. "Yes."

I turned in the saddle. Sidonie was mounting the Palace steps, Amarante's arm around her waist. Safe harbor. I sighed. "Fine. Do your duty."

"I am always mindful of my duty," Maslin said stiffly. "*Prince* Imriel. Can you say the same?"

"Believe it or not," I said to him, "I'm trying."

I got over the worst of my anger on the short ride to the manor house. By the time I arrived, it had faded, leaving behind a deep and abiding sorrow. It was good to spend time alone with my Shahrizai kin, especially Mavros. I'd gotten in the habit of thinking of Eamonn as my one true friend, but I'd grown close to Mavros. I would miss him.

In a meadow beyond the manor's mews, I told him about the encounter in the courtyard. He shook his head. "Elua's Balls! Whatever possessed you to give him Lombelon, anyway? You do realize if you hadn't, he'd be spreading dung in an orchard somewhere, not plotting his way into the royal heir's bed."

"I know." I shaded my eyes, watching Mavros' peregrine falcon circle lazily in the blue sky. "I thought it was the right thing to do, that's all."

"No good deed goes unpunished," Mavros observed. "Will you see her before you leave?"

"Sidonie?" I shrugged. "I'll make no effort to. 'Tis too maddening to hope."

"Good lad." Gauging his bird had been aloft long enough without a strike, Mavros whistled shrilly through his teeth and began swinging his lure in looping circles. "Make her come to you."

"It's not like that," I said.

Overhead, the falcon abandoned its gyre and began winging toward us. Mavros whistled again. Something rustled in the long grass and wild chicory. The falcon changed course abruptly and stooped, falling like a comet. There was a thrashing in the grass and a hare's terrible squeal. "Ha!" Mavros looked smugly at me and began coiling his lure. "It's *always* like that."

"We'll see," I said.

There was a formal Courcel dinner that night in celebration of Sidonie's return, with Eamonn and Brigitta attending as guests. I managed to be pleasant and circumspect throughout the evening. I hadn't lied to Mavros. I did want to see her, but it was simply too agonizing to hold out hope where little or none existed. There was too little time and no opportunity I could conceive. I made myself close the door on the possibility, regretfully but firmly, wondering in only a small corner of my mind if Mavros might be proved right.

He was.

I rose early on the day before our departure. Since moving to the Palace, I'd taken to practicing the Cassiline training-drills Joscelin had taught me in the little pleasure-garden beneath my balcony, at least on those days when I rose at a decent hour. I'd neglected them in Tiberium, and it felt good to establish the habit of discipline. I moved through the circular patterns—telling the hours, the Cassiline Brothers called it—slowly, then swiftly, then slowly again. My plain, wellwrought sword glinted in the grey light, marking each quadrant of defense. The dewy grass squelched under my boots, and I concentrated on placing my feet with care.

When I finished, I realized I was being watched.

The garden lay within the Palace walls and there was no guard posted at the little trellised egress that led onto it. Amarante was standing there in the shadow of the doorway, a shawl over her shoulders to ward off the dawn's chill. I sheathed my sword and crossed to her.

"Can you be at Naamah's Temple at noon?" she asked. "Alone and unseen?"

My throat went tight. "Yes."

Amarante nodded. "Please be careful."

"I will be," I promised.

For once, I was. If the risks Sidonie and I had run had been high in the past, they seemed a great deal higher now. Too many people stood to be hurt, too many plans could be thrown into chaos. I wondered, briefly, if it was worth it for the sake of a single assignation. And then I lied to Dorelei and told her I meant to make an excursion to Phèdre's townhouse to retrieve a favorite shirt I'd neglected to bring with me.

I rode instead to Night's Doorstep and begged a favor of Emile. Along with the Cockerel, he also owned a livery stable, started long ago by Hyacinthe.

"Of course!" Emile waved off my coin. "No, no, consider it a wedding gift. You'll need a driver?"

"A discreet one, yes." I hesitated. "And … . a shirt."

He stared at me. "A shirt?"

"Something worn," I said. "Not too fine."

"Secrets." Emile shook his head. "Well, the Tsingani will keep yours, young highness, never fear. We never forget what Phèdre nó Delaunay did for Hyacinthe, Anasztaisia's son." He plucked the coin from my hand. "But I'll take this for the trouble of finding you this *shirt*."

"My thanks," I said.

So it was that a bit before noon, I arrived at Naamah's temple in an unremarkable livery carriage driven by a close-mouthed Tsingano lad named Yanko. The same doves were roosting in the yew trees, but the garden below them was in full splendor. It seemed like a long time since I'd made my offering there, begging Naamah's forgiveness for my transgressions.

To my surprise, I was expected. The acolyte at the door led me past the altar, into the inner sanctum of the temple. There was a courtyard with another garden, this one bright and bursting with geraniums and bougainvillea.

The priest who had been an adept of Gentian House was waiting for me there. I remembered his name: Raphael Murain. His grey eyes were somber. "Prince Imriel, you are neither the first nor the last to seek the clandestine aid of Naamah's Order in this manner. I do this in honor of my vows, in recognition of the blessing you received at my hands, and in accordance with the wishes of her Ladyship in Namarre. However, I pray you understand it is a serious business. We serve Naamah, not the Crown, but no priest relishes the thought of crossing the Queen."

"I understand," I said steadily, although it gave me a little shiver.

Raphael Murain sighed. "Come with me." He escorted me to the far side of the garden and unlocked a door onto a small bedchamber with shuttered windows, prettily appointed and bedecked with flowers. Even the bed was strewn with petals. "As I said, neither the first or the last. Wait here."

I waited.

Sidonie came.

We didn't make it to the bed; we didn't make it beyond the door. The moment it closed, her arms were around my neck, my mouth on hers. Elua, the taste of her! She bit my lower lip, sucked on my tongue. I shoved her against the door, shoving her skirts up. She wrapped her legs around my hips. I clawed at her fine linen underdrawers, tearing them. Only the sound of ripping fabric made me pause.

"We should—"

"No." Sidonie's nails dug into the back of my neck. "Please."

Bracing her with one arm, I undid the straining laces of my breeches. I could feel the wet warmth of her sliding against my phallus, heard her gasp at my ear. Enough; Elua, enough! I shifted to grasp her buttocks with both hands, entering her with a thrust so hard and deep, it made the door bounce.

It was hard and fierce and so, so terribly good! The door creaked and rattled as I slammed into her, over and over, feeling her climax with a wordless cry, her thighs suddenly gripping me so tightly I could barely move. It didn't matter, I was ready. I buried myself in her and spent, the release so dizzying and intense that for a moment I couldn't see.

The sparkling darkness receded.

I held her where she was, breathing hard. "Feel better?"

"Yes." Sidonie smiled. "Carry me to the bed?"

"Can't." I shook my head. "Not with my breeches around my ankles." She laughed, low and enthralling, arms still wound around my neck. The sound made me ache. I released my grip on her buttocks, moving my hands to her waist. Her legs slipped slowly down mine until her feet touched the ground and she stood, her skirts falling into place. "Sun Princess," I murmured. "You break my heart."

"Mine, too," she whispered.

"I know." I stooped to retrieve my breeches, tying them loosely. "Come here." I swept her off her feet, scooping her into my arms and carrying her to the bed.

How long it lasted, I couldn't say. An hour, mayhap, before there was a discreet knock at the door. It wasn't enough. It was never enough. I gazed at Sidonie, naked and disheveled, bruised geranium petals stuck to her damp skin, and heaved a sigh from the depths of my heart.

"I have to go." She climbed out of bed and began pulling on her clothing. "Will you write to me?"

"Yes." I plucked a crimson petal from her collarbone. "Will you?"

"Yes." Sidonie swallowed. "And in a year . . . ?"

I nodded. "We'll see."

She took my right hand and held it to her cheek. Planted a kiss in my palm, then folded my fingers and kissed the gold knot of a ring; soft and lingering, her breath warm against my knuckles. There were tears in her eyes. "Think of me?"

"Always," I said.

There was another knock at the door, more insistent. Sidonie swept her hair into a coil. I helped her pin it in place, adjusted the stays of her bodice. I tugged on my breeches and kissed her one last time before she went to open the door.

And then she left.

Sunlight flooded the little bedchamber. I sat on the edge of the bed, its covers tossed and tangled, turning the gold ring on my finger. I thought about what Elua's priest had said to me about love when I was fourteen years old, spending the Longest Night maintaining Blessed

Elua's vigil with Joscelin, filled with a mixture of bitterness and hope and hero-worship.

You will find it and lose it, again and again. And with each finding and each loss, you will become more than before. What you make of it is yours to choose.

He hadn't told me how much it would hurt.

I wished he had.

SEVENTEEN

ON THE MORROW, we departed for Alba.

It seemed like half the City turned out to see us off. Everyone loves a gala procession. Of a surety, we were that. The Cruithne guards rode bare-chested, displaying their woad warrior's markings. The D'Angeline guards were resplendent in Courcel blue uniforms. The carriage-horses and wagon-mules had been caparisoned with silver head-plumes that bobbed with every step. No one was riding in the carriages, not on such a bright, fine day. Eamonn was grinning, the sunlight glinting on his red-gold hair, Brigitta beside him. Phèdre and Joscelin were there, the Queen's Champion and the realm's most famous courtesan.

And me; a Prince of the Blood, now a Prince of Alba. Riding alongside my wife. Somewhere in the multitude of trunks stowed aboard the wagons there was a truly disreputable shirt in gaudy Tsingano colors and a small leather volume of love letters.

I felt numb.

At the head of our procession rode the royal family, doing us the honor of escorting us to the gate of the City. Ysandre was merry, Drustan pleased. Alais wore a downcast expression. I couldn't bear to look at Sidonie. All I knew was that she sat very straight in the saddle, upright and unwavering.

We filed through the gate. Ysandre made a pretty speech about the Dalriada, and Drustan added a few words. The crowd cheered. A throng of well-wishers flooded through to bid us farewell, including most of Montrève's household. Eugènie and Clory embraced me and wept. Hugues gave me his wooden flute as a keepsake, insisting over my protests. Ti-Philippe listened, nodding, to last-minute instructions from Phèdre. Joscelin watched with amusement, his strong hands resting idle on the pommel of his saddle.

And then it was over.

Heralds atop the walls blew a fanfare on long trumpets. The Cruithne commander Urist raised a battle-horn to his lips and blew a long note in reply. The crowd cheered again. The Bastard pranced under me, reckoning the attention was all for him. Dorelei's eyes were bright, her gaze fixed on the western horizon. The Queen raised one hand in salute.

Urist blew another long blast, and our company began to move.

We were bound for Alba.

I clenched my right hand into a fist, feeling the ring's bite. Knowing Sidonie was somewhere behind me, watching. If she could be strong, I could, too. I squared my shoulders as I rode away from her, feeling her dwindling presence tug at me like a sea-anchor. I wanted to turn the Bastard and ride back, I wanted to take her in my arms and kiss her in front of the Queen, the Cruarch, and the watching City, and let the consequences be damned.

But I didn't.

The first day was the hardest, and all the harder because everyone around me was glad-hearted. 'Tis a lonely business, being miserable when happiness abounds. I did my best to hide it, although the people who knew me well, knew. To my surprise, one of them was Dorelei.

She was the only one who spoke of it. We'd made the village of Hercule in L'Agnace by nightfall. Accommodations had been arranged for the peers among us at a local inn, along with a handful of soldiers. The rest made camp in a field on the outskirts of the village. Dorelei and I shared a private room, as did Phèdre and Joscelin, Eamonn and Brigitta.

Our room had a battered bronze mirror. Dorelei sat on a low stool before it, brushing her long black hair, watching me in the mirror. I sat cross-legged on the bed atop the thin counterpane, toying with Hugues' flute.

"Can you play it?" she asked, curious.

I lifted it to my lips and blew a few notes, soft and low, my fingertips dancing over the wooden holes.

"Oh!" Dorelei's face kindled. "How nice!"

I lowered the flute. "I played the shepherd's pipe when I was a boy."

Her reflected features turned grave. "You don't speak of it often."

"No." I shook my head. "Not often."

"I'd listen, you know." Dorelei hesitated. "Do you . . . do you miss her, Imriel? Was it hard to leave her?" She hesitated again. "It is a *her*, is it not?"

"Would it matter?" I asked, my voice stony. She flinched, and I sighed. "Oh, Dorelei! I'm sorry. Yes, and yes. You did beseech me for honesty. I miss her, and it was hard." I patted the bed beside me. "Come here, I'll play for you." I didn't play well, but I could still carry a tune. I played a simple, lilting melody from my childhood, one of the songs all the children at the Sanctuary knew by heart.

Dorelei sat quietly, listening. "'Tis a pretty tune," she said when I finished. "Are there words to it?"

"Oh, yes." I played the first measure, then sang for her. *"Little goat, brown goat, with the crooked horn. Little goat, bad goat, eating all the corn. If you don't come away with me, I'll lock you in the paddock. Cook will come and chop you up, and stew you like a haddock."*

She laughed with delighted surprise. "That's terrible!"

I smiled. "I know. You shouldn't have asked."

"Will you play it again?" Dorelei asked. I obliged, and she sang the chorus. She had a sweet voice, clear and true. I taught her the rest of the words and played it through. We were both laughing by the time it was over.

"Thank you," I said to her. "That was fun."

"'Twas your doing." She ducked her head with a shy smile and took my right hand in hers. Her slender fingers toyed, unthinking, with the gold knot of Sidonie's ring. It was more than I could bear, and I pulled my hand away gently. "I'm sorry." Dorelei glanced up at me, her wide eyes filled with sorrow and a sympathy I didn't deserve. "Will it be better in Alba, do you think?"

"I do," I said. "Truly."

She kissed my cheek. "I hope so."

After that night, I made a determined effort to master my mood. I sought to live from moment to moment, enjoying the camaraderie of the friends and loved ones who surrounded me, taking pleasure from Eamonn's gladness at going home after his long travail, from Phèdre and Joscelin's delight at embarking on adventure, albeit a small one. From Dorelei's happiness at returning to Alba, from the fierce earnestness with which Brigitta applied herself to her study of Alban languages.

All of us tried to help in her endeavor. We sang a great deal as we rode. With Eamonn's aid, Phèdre translated a handful of Skaldic hearth-songs into Eiran, and we sang those over and over. I began learning to play them on Hugues' flute, which had proved to be a far better gift than I'd reckoned. Betimes I played the song about the little brown goat to make Dorelei smile, and we made up Eiran verses for that, too. Betimes, when everyone was tired of singing, I played simple, wandering melodies of my own invention.

There is healing in music; or so they say in Eisande, which is famous for its chirurgeons, its musicians, and its storytellers. I found it to be true. I poured my grief into the mouthpiece of the wooden flute and turned it into music, refused to let myself dwell on it.

Refused to allow myself to think about Sidonie.

Betimes, my concentration would lapse and my thoughts would drift toward her. The memories that broke through the barriers I'd erected against them were vivid and shocking in their intensity. Love is an irrational force, urgent and animal. Betimes—ofttimes, to be honest—it was memories of lovemaking that pierced me. That, at least, I could understand. It was an endless source of wonder to me that Sidonie managed to effortlessly combine uninhibited ardor, tenderness, and willing depravity.

She was so young, and so sure in her desires.

Elua, I loved that about her.

But it was the other memories that hurt the worst. All the little intimate moments, so damnably precious and few. The way she'd wrinkled her nose at me, so like Alais; and yet so not. The upraised sweep of her arms as she coiled her hair, quick and deft. The way she carried herself in public, stalwart as a soldier and twice as proud. The tears in her eyes when we parted for the last time.

It hurt.

It hurt a lot.

Again and again, I pushed my memories away. There were days when it was easy and days when it was hard. My love for Sidonie was a boulder in my heart. I sought to let go of it and let it sink. Let it sink below the surface, carrying my heart with it. Let it come to rest on the stream's bottom, a vast hidden bulwark, dividing the current. Let it stay there, hidden and unseen. Forgotten.

Betimes it worked.

Betimes it didn't.

It was the best I could do.

The Cruarch's flagship was awaiting us in Pointe des Soeurs, along with a pair of lesser vessels to carry our entourage. I hadn't seen it since I was ten—no, eleven—years old. The sight of it filled me with remembered awe. I watched it bob gently in the harbor, the crimson sails lashed, wondering if it was the selfsame ship I'd known as a child. If it was, I'd stood aboard its wooden decks and watched as Phèdre floundered to her feet atop the waters, and spoke aloud the unspeakable Name of God to banish the vengeful angel Rahab.

"Elua!" Phèdre gazed at it. "It's been so long."

"Not so long." Joscelin leaned over in the saddle to capture her hand, lifting it to his lips for a kiss. His summer-blue eyes danced. "Never *that* long, my love."

I caught Dorelei watching them, a shadow of sorrow in her eyes. She hid it when she noticed me looking, giving me a quick smile.

And then we were at sea, the shores of Terre d'Ange falling away behind us. There were only water and wind, bearing us afloat, bellying our crimson sails as they were unfurled. Wind, caressing our cheeks; wind, ruffling the waters. We crossed the Straits and headed northward up the coast. Our journey was uneventful. How not? The Master of the Straits controlled the winds and the waters.

The waves danced for us, shaping themselves into patterns. Spelling out a message in an alphabet none of us could understand, save one. Phèdre watched the water and smiled to herself, while a green-hued Joscelin avoided looking at the water altogether. Somewhere, Hyacinthe was watching in his sea-mirror.

A day later, we made landfall at Bryn Gorrydum. The city wasn't where Dorelei and I would ultimately forge our lives together—once we were wed, we were to be ensconced in Clunderry Castle, which lay inland—but it was the Cruarch's seat of rule. Bryn Gorrydum was a harbor city, built where the Fayn River spilled into the sea. A sturdy grey fortress flying the Black Boar from its turrets perched above the harbor, surrounded by the sprawl of a thriving city. The innermost center looked to be old Tiberian stonework, but the outer rings gave evidence of a D'Angeline influence.

Phèdre and Joscelin marveled at it. "It's grown," she murmured. "I hadn't expected it to have grown so much."

"Oh, aye." The Cruithne commander Urist sauntered up to the railing and spat over the edge. "Lots of things have grown. You should see Lug's Town."

"Bryn Gorrydum's grown since *I* left." Eamonn sounded wistful. I remembered him gaping at the tall buildings in the City of Elua. "I hope Innisclan hasn't changed."

It felt strange to set foot on Alban soil for the first time. I was a D'Angeline Prince of the Blood, descended from two of the oldest Houses of the realm, Kushiel's scion and Elua's. I felt, suddenly and keenly, that I didn't belong here. It seemed as though the earth itself roiled underfoot in agreement, although I daresay it was only the effects of the sea voyage.

At least I hoped it was.

Compared to others I'd seen—Marsilikos, Ostia, the great harbor at Iskandria—Bryn Gorrydum's harbor was small and sleepy. But there were ships flying D'Angeline and Aragonian flags, a few round-bellied merchant-ships from the Flatlands, even a Skaldic dragon-ship that made Brigitta clap her hands with glee. Twenty years ago—mayhap even ten—few of them would have been here.

Prince Talorcan had sent a delegation to meet us. As we ascended through the city toward the fortress, I tried to gauge the mood of the populace. If they were hostile, it didn't show; but neither did they receive us with great joy. The dark-eyed Cruithne glanced sidelong at us, while other folk stared outright with impolite curiosity. Overall, the mood felt wary and watchful.

Of a surety, I didn't feel I was entirely welcome here.

In the City of Elua, I thought, there would have been cheers. Even if the commonfolk cared for naught but the spectacle and the nobility immediately turned to plotting ways to dispose of the foreign prince, there would have been cheers. Well, and so. Mayhap it would change. Mayhap there would be cheers when Dorelei and I wed in the Alban tradition. It didn't matter—I had no heart for cheers, anyway—but it served to remind me I was once more far from home.

At the fortress, Prince Talorcan received us graciously. He was a serious young man, the Cruarch's heir; Drustan cast in a youthful mold, only without the quiet, intense air of command that made people fall silent and listen when he spoke.

Dorelei wept for gladness to see him and Talorcan smiled, folding her in a warm embrace. "Why weeping, my heart?" he asked in an older brother's tone of teasing affection. "Surely your marriage has not treated you so ill?"

"No." She smiled at him through her tears. "No, of course not."

"That's good." Talorcan leveled a glance at me. "I know this is a marriage of state. But it is my hope that your husband will prove worthy of you, my sister. As I in turn will seek to be a worthy husband to Alais."

I bowed. "I am trying, your highness."

True and not true.

I hadn't been unkind, not since that first day of our journey. And I hadn't laid an ungentle hand on her since the night we talked, the night Mavros arranged for the Showing at Valerian House. Even in the throes of lovemaking, I'd been tender and considerate. I'd made her laugh playing the flute and singing silly songs, I'd listened to tales of her childhood. I'd even told her some of my own; innocuous tales of life at the Sanctuary of Elua.

I'd discovered that we liked one another, Dorelei and I. But I was fearful of giving free rein to my emotions. Fearful that all those emotions and longings I suppressed would spill forth, rendering me bitter and cruel.

Still, in my own way, I was trying.

And mayhap if I played at being the kind and gentle husband long enough, it would become true. Master Piero once told us that we might embody those qualities we desire to possess by embracing them, over and over, until the line between seeming and being is no more. I'd attempted that much on this venture.

Surely no one could ask for more.

EIGHTEEN

WE SPENT TWO DAYS IN Bryn Gorrydum before departing for Innisclan.

Phèdre had hoped that Hyacinthe might visit while we were in Bryn Gorrydum, but Talorcan shook his head when she voiced it. "No, my lady. I believe he will attend the nuptials, but Master Hyacinthe seldom leaves his Stormkeep. He bears a great responsibility."

Somewhat in his tone made her cock her head. "But all is well?"

"Oh, yes." He nodded. "He wards the Straits as ever."

"Who choose?" Brigitta made an impatient gesture. "What ship?"

Talorcan blinked at her. "My lady?"

"Who chooses which ships are granted passage?" Eamonn clarified helpfully. "The Cruarch or the Master of the Straits?"

"Ah." Talorcan frowned. "Well, 'tis a complicated matter. Master Hyacinthe has agreed to bar passage to no ship of Alba, nor"—he nodded in my direction—"Terre d'Ange, save at his extreme discretion. As for trade-ships from other nations, only those which the Cruarch has approved are permitted, pending Master Hyacinthe's agreement. 'Tis but a formality, as they are generally in accord. My lord Drustan often hears petitions when visiting the Queen. Thus far, Master Hyacinthe has been in agreement with my lord Drustan."

Eamonn translated for Brigitta. "Skaldia?" she asked.

"Including Skaldia, yes." The Cruarch's heir smiled at her. "I believe their suit was brought at the behest of others. 'Tis a recent development and a cautious one. But perhaps your charm will hasten the process."

This time Brigitta understood him well enough to color at the unlikely—to my mind—compliment. Phèdre still wore a thoughtful look. "What of the matter of a successor, your highness? Has . . ." She hesitated. ". . . *Master* Hyacinthe made any decision?"

"I don't believe so." Talorcan turned his gaze toward her. His dark eyes were unreadable. Sidonie wore a similar look in public, sometimes. Strange to think they were cousins, more closely related than she and I were. I pushed the thought away and wondered instead what manner of husband Talorcan would make for Alais. I had the sense she admired and respected him, but of a surety, there was no passion there. "You would know if he had, would you not? It is well known in Alba that Master Hyacinthe holds you in the highest regard."

"Well, he damnably well *ought* to," Joscelin muttered.

"We're friends, yes," Phèdre said. "But I don't believe he would inform me in such a matter without speaking to the Cruarch first. I wondered, that's all."

Talorcan shook his head. "Nothing is resolved."

The conversation turned to other matters. I thought about Hyacinthe, the Master of the Straits. In Night's Doorstep, Emile and others remembered him as he'd been when Phèdre first knew him: a merry Tsingano lad, quick with a laugh, with a knack for making a profit. It was hard to reconcile that image with the man I'd met aboard the Cruarch's flagship, who had eyes that looked like shadows crawling at the bottom of the sea and held the power to tame the waves in his hands. He was still young, but something ancient had looked out of him. I suppose facing the prospect of aging eternally would do that to a man.

Small wonder Hyacinthe held Phèdre in the highest regard. She'd freed him from the curse that had bound him to such a fate.

I wondered how old he must be now. Not so old, really. A little over forty, mayhap; he and Phèdre were near the same age. He was wed to Sibeal, Drustan's other sister. They had two young children, a girl and a boy. In accordance with the Cruithne's matrilineal line of succession, either one would have been eligible to be named as the Cruarch's heir. Alais had told me in utmost secrecy that her father had asked Hyacinthe if he were willing to allow either of his children to serve. Hyacinthe had told him flatly, no.

And one did not argue with the Master of the Straits.

Not even the Cruarch.

We departed Bryn Gorrydum in good order. If the city had proved larger and more sophisticated than one might expect, any notion that Alba was tame vanished within a half day's ride. At first we followed the course of the Fayn River westward. It was a broad, slow-moving river, suitable for barge traffic, and an old Tiberian road ran alongside it. Still, the city gave way rapidly to rolling countryside, dotted here and there with small croft-holdings. It was very green, a green so intense it smote the eye.

Around noon, Urist pointed to a stone marker along the roadside. It was old and worn, half covered in lichen, and I had to squint to make out the symbol on it, a spiral ending outward in a pointed arrow. *"Tais-gaidh,"* Urist said briefly. "Here we turn north."

"That means the path we follow is held freely in trust for all the folk of Alba," Eamonn whispered to me in his helpful way. "No man may bar another from travelling on *taisgaidh* land, and no man may do violence to another."

"I know what it means," I said. "I spent several hundred hours with the Daughter of the Grove learning such things. Would you care to know the fines levied against a man who bars another's passage? It varies depending on whether or not he was bringing cattle to market."

"Sorry." He grinned. "I forgot."

"It's not so much the fines as it is the heresy," Dorelei offered quietly. "The *taisgaidh* places are old, as old as the Cullach Gorrym. One does not violate the old ways unless one wishes to invoke a curse."

"Oh, aye," Eamonn agreed. "That, too."

I shaded my eyes with one hand as we turned northward. We'd left our fine carriages behind in Terre d'Ange, but the wagons bearing our stores and tribute for the Lady of the Dalriada creaked behind the plodding mules, wheels leaving damp ruts in the grass. The sky was a soft, luminous grey. Beneath it, unending greenness stretched in every direction, broken only by the occasional outthrust promontory of rock and the distant glimmer of an inland lake. I could discern no path, no further marker. "Well, there's somewhat the *ollamh* never mentioned. How does one avoid getting lost?"

Eamonn shrugged. "Practice."

If it was true, Urist must have had a good deal of practice. We found a second *taisgaidh* marker before nightfall. An odd business, a squat stone column set in the middle of nowhere atop a shallow rise. This one was covered with moss. Urist had to scrape at it with his fingernails to bare the symbol. He sighted along the direction the spiral arrow pointed and nodded in satisfaction. "We'll make camp here tonight."

It was the first time since we'd left the City of Elua that we'd made camp under the open skies; or at least that *I* had. In a way, it reminded me of happier times. We dismounted, staking the horses and mules, allowing them to graze on the abundant pasturage. As the sun dipped toward the horizon, several of the D'Angeline soldiers set themselves to erecting tents for their royal charges, while others spread out to gather firewood in a nearby copse. Armed with short bows, Urist's Cruithne set forth to shoot for the pot, bagging several hares, soon efficiently butchered.

A handful of campfires blossomed along the hillside.

From one, the familiar strains of a D'Angeline marching-song emanated. It had originated here in Alba, long ago, with a contingent of Admiral Rousse's men who dubbed themselves Phèdre's Boys.

"Man or woman, we don't care! Give us twins, we'll take the pair!"

"Name of Elua!" In the firelight, Phèdre looked dismayed and amused, and a good deal younger and more beautiful than she had any right to. Beneath a canopy of stars, we might have been anywhere. We might have been in Jebe-Barkal, making our way toward forgotten Saba. "Am I never to be free of it?"

"No." Joscelin smiled at her. "Not likely."

My heart surfaced, aching. I watched them, watched her raise her face to his. Watched him kiss her tenderly, his lips lingering on hers. Once upon a time, after Daršanga, it had seemed to me that if what was broken between them could be healed, all would be right with the world. It still seemed true to me; only it hurt too much to feel it, because I hadn't trusted myself to love that strongly. So I pushed the feelings away, looked away, letting my gaze fall on the tribute-wagons, silhouetted in the distance.

"What did you choose as a tribute-gift in the end?" I asked Eamonn. "I never heard."

"Books." He looked smug. "We mean to start an academy, Brigitta and I."

Brigitta nodded.

Eamonn's arm was slung around her neck, and she was curled against him, her long legs interwined with his, stretching toward the campfire. They looked as indolent and comfortable as a pair of basking leopards, the two of them. I smothered a pang of envy and glanced at my wife. "An academy filled with dangerous *books*," I said. "What do you think?"

" 'Tis a good thing, I think." Dorelei considered. "I know the *ollamhs'* concerns, but is knowledge not a gift in any form?"

"Spoken like one of Shemhazai's descendants!" Joscelin said in approval.

She flushed prettily. "Alba fears change, but not all change is bad. Brigitta has told me somewhat about the University of Tiberium. It would not be a bad thing, I think, if the young men of Alba sought honor in exchanging words and thoughts, and not raiding cattle and avenging blood-feuds."

"It hasn't stopped the Caerdicci," I observed.

"No, but it slowed them down," Eamonn said. "Without scholarship, there would be no agreement among the city-states, no Caerdicca Unitas."

We talked for a while longer before turning in for the night. I lay awake for some time, listening to the breeze rustle the walls of the oiled silk tent I shared with Dorelei. I thought about war, knowledge, and change, and all those things we used to discuss under Master Piero's guidance. Tiberium seemed long ago and far away, which wasn't entirely bad. At least here in Alba, I was freed from the suffocating coils and snares of intrigue that bound me, both in Tiberium and in Terre d'Ange.

The Unseen Guild had no foothold here.

No one cared that Melisande Shahrizai was my mother.

Life would be a good deal simpler. If I tried hard enough, I might even learn to like it. And mayhap with time and distance, the heartache would grow bearable; the boulder dwindle to a pebble.

In the way that happens when one lets one's thoughts drift, I fell asleep without knowing it until the sound awoke me. A huffing sound, deep and guttural, followed by a low, drawn-out groan. Something was moving around the outside the tent, something large.

I sat upright in my bedroll. Beside me, Dorelei was sound asleep. I eased my sword from its scabbard and got carefully to my feet. Another huff and snort, somewhere to the right of us. When I stooped and touched the ground with my fingertips, I could feel it tremble beneath the creature's heavy tread.

A bear. It had to be a bear.

My palms broke out in a cold sweat, rendering my grip on the sword-hilt slippery. I glanced at Dorelei in an agony of indecision. No time to wake her, no time to explain. I doubted a lone man could kill a full-grown bear with a sword, but at least I could draw it away. I could die an inept hero, and let the sentries explain to my loved ones over my mauled body how a *bear* had wandered undetected into the heart of our campsite.

If I thought about it for another instant, I'd lose my nerve. So I didn't. With my blood roaring in my ears and my heart thundering in my chest, I dashed through the tent-flap; darting left, then whirling right to face the bear, the sword braced in both hands, angled across my body.

There was nothing there.

Not a bear, not even a dog. Nothing. Only our tent standing beneath the stars, its walls rippling softly in the breeze. I sidled around it, crossing one foot carefully over the other, sword at the ready. The grass was cool, not yet dewy. There were no tracks, no prints left by anything larger than the soldiers who'd erected our tent. Nothing heavy enough to make the ground tremble had been here.

There was an odor, though. A rank, musky odor.

I circled the tent, my nostrils flaring. Was it real or was it the spectre of Daršanga that haunted me; the stench of fear and ordure, the coppery tang of blood, the decaying vegetable reek of the stagnant pool? I couldn't tell.

The stars were high and bright overhead. I could make out the whole of our campsite. There was nothing to see. No vast, shambling shadow moving among us. The horses and mules were dozing in their picket-lines. Our tents and wagons stood undisturbed. Men slept wrapped in bedrolls around the glowing embers of our campfires. Here and there around the outskirts, sentries were posted, gazing out into the quiet night.

Feeling like a fool, I lowered my sword. Even the odor had vanished. I must have dreamed of Daršanga without realizing it, somehow conflating my memories with tales of the Maghuin Dhonn. I'd done such a good job of burying my feelings, I wasn't even aware of my own nightmares anymore.

Well, at least I hadn't awakened the entire camp screaming at the top of my lungs, which was my usual response to haunted dreams. Although I daresay it wouldn't be much less embarrassing if one of the sentries took notice and came to ask why I was prowling around in my underdrawers and waving a sword.

I slipped quietly back into the tent. Dorelei was still sleeping. I sheathed my sword and lay down beside her, keeping my sword close. For a long time, I was too tense to sleep, my body buzzing with alarm. I made myself listen to my wife's slow, steady breathing, to the rustling of the tent walls, to the ordinary sounds of camp beyond. Bit by bit, my racing pulse ceased to thud and my tense muscles relaxed. With my right hand resting on the hilt of my sword, I slid slowly into sleep.

The last thing I heard was the sound of pipes and a woman's laughter.

Surely, another dream.

In the clear light of morning, it seemed all the more absurd. I contemplated mentioning it to Eamonn or Joscelin or even Urist, but when I took a surreptitious turn around the tent, peering at the grass to confirm that there were no inhuman tracks, I found nothing. Whatever I'd imagined, it was clearly the product of my sleep-addled mind. There had been no bear here. By daylight, it was obvious that I'd dreamed the entire thing.

Dorelei caught me at it. "Did you lose something?" she asked, puzzled.

"Only my wits." I picked a bright yellow sprig of buttercup and tucked it behind her ear, belatedly noticing the short hunting bow she carried and the quiver over her shoulder. "Were you planning to shoot someone?"

She smiled, flashing a dimple. "A grouse or two, mayhap. We've a bit of time before they strike camp, and a bird for the pot never goes amiss. Will you come?"

"Why not?" I agreed.

I knew Cruithne women were skilled with the bow, but this was the first time I'd witnessed aught save Alais attempting to shoot at targets. We made our way across the down to the hazel copse. Along the way, Dorelei bade me collect a number of good-size stones. I obeyed with cheerful perplexity. At the edge of the copse, she grew intent and focused, staring at the underbrush.

"There." She nocked an arrow and pointed with the tip. "Throw a stone."

I cocked my arm to throw, gazing at her for a moment. The bow described an elegant arc, her hands steady on it, upraised arms unwavering. Her face was rapt with concentration, lips parted. The yellow buttercup looked pretty against her black hair. I wondered if I could ever bring myself to have feelings for her.

"Imriel!" she whispered. "Now!"

I hurled the rock into the underbrush. A trio of grouse burst from the cover, wings rattling. Dorelei's bow sang, and one of the birds plummeted. She laughed aloud, girlish and delighted, and I found myself grinning. "Well done, my lady."

Dorelei curtsied in the D'Angeline manner. "Thank you, my lord."

We stood there, smiling at one another. Back at the campsite, a long blast sounded on Urist's battle-horn, alerting us that it was time to depart. I was almost sorry to hear it. "One grouse it is," I said lightly, retrieving the bird. It was warm and still twitching. I eased her arrow free and broke its ruffed neck with a quick twist, putting an end to its spasms. I wiped the arrow clean with a hank of grass and handed it to her. "Here you are."

"My thanks." Dorelei returned the arrow to her quiver. She glanced toward the camp, then back at me, hesitant. "It is . . . it *is* going to be better here in Alba, isn't it? You and me?"

I nodded. "Better, yes."

"Good." She flashed another dimpled smile, filled with relief. "I thought so, too."

We returned to camp without delay, delivering the grouse to Galan, the Cruithne warrior who had taken it upon himself to serve as chief cook for the royal contingent. He clucked his tongue approvingly, promising a fine luncheon of spit-roasted fowl. I caught Phèdre's gaze on me, wondering.

I felt guilty at it, and wasn't sure why.

And then Urist blew the summons, and we were off, riding across Alba.

NINETEEN

Such was the pattern of our journey.

By day we travelled the *taisgaidh* paths under Urist's expert guidance, and I marveled that such vast expanses of hospitable land remained uninhabited. Betimes we caught sight of distant farms and villages, and once we intercepted a raiding party of Tarbh Cró warriors who fixed us with hard stares, but declined to violate the unwritten rules that governed the old ways. For the most part, northern Alba was a green gem, unspoiled and untrammeled.

By night, we sat around the campfire and talked.

Those were my favorite times.

"What do you think, Lady Phèdre?" Dorelei asked one night, greatly daring. "*Should* Master Hyacinthe pass on his knowledge?"

Phèdre was quiet for a long time, gazing at the crackling embers. If Joscelin had an opinion, he didn't voice it, choosing instead to regard her in silence. "I don't know," she said at length. "I truly don't."

"All knowledge is worth having," I quoted. Joscelin smiled.

Phèdre didn't. "It's not the knowledge," she said slowly. "It's the *power*. 'Tis an unnatural thing for any mortal to wield. A dangerous thing."

"You did, love," Joscelin reminded her softly. "You spoke the Name of God."

"It was a gift, a gift given me for a purpose." She turned a troubled gaze on him. "An ancient wrong was redressed. 'Tis a different matter if one speaks of Hyacinthe choosing a successor so that Alba may continue to guard its shores."

"True." He stroked her hair. "Mayhap there are other wrongs to set right."

She smiled reluctantly. "I'd sooner there weren't."

"I think it should end," Eamonn said firmly. "Lady Phèdre is right, it is too much power for one person to wield. If a sovereign becomes a tyrant, the people may rise up and overthrow him. What would happen if the Master of the Straits chose his successor poorly? Who could stand against him?"

"Is it worth leaving Alba undefended?" Dorelei asked. "Surely, Master Hyacinthe would choose wisely in such a grave matter."

"And if he does not?" Brigitta asked, choosing her words with care. She was able to follow our conversations as long as we didn't go too swiftly, and preferred that we spoke Eiran or Cruithne to afford her the practice. "Or the next time, or the next? One day, Alba is maybe tyrant, bad tyrant. Like Tiberium." She shrugged. "Like Waldemar Selig tries. In Skaldi, he is a great man. You all make me think, maybe not. One day, it may be the same in Alba. Sea goes everywhere, rule all the seas. Everyone obeys."

It made me smile to imagine tiny Alba ruling the world. And yet mayhap it wasn't so strange. Tiberium was only a city, and yet its empire had encompassed the whole of the Caerdicci peninsula, all of Terre d'Ange, large tracts of Aragonia and Skaldia. It had even reached Alba's shores.

Not so strange at all, really.

"Well, he couldn't rule *all* the seas," Joscelin said logically. "Hyacinthe's power has limits, does it not? And he cannot be vigilant in all places all the time."

"A hundred leagues times three," Phèdre murmured. "And his sea-mirror is blind beyond the lands whose coasts border his demesne. Still . . ."

"Maybe he teach others," Brigitta suggested. "Masters take students."

"A plague of Hyacinthes," Joscelin mused.

No one laughed. Phèdre accorded Brigitta a look of deep respect. "You make very good points, my lady. Every day, I comprehend more and more why Prince Eamonn was willing to risk so much to win your hand."

Brigitta smiled shyly. "Old enemies, new friends."

The journey wasn't always easy. The *taisgaidh* paths led us along a pass through low mountains where the ground was covered with a loose scree that made our mounts and the wagon-mules lose their footing. Betimes the wagons got stuck and had to be pushed free. It rained a good deal more than I was used to. Twice, we risked losing our way in a mist so dense we could have ridden within three yards of a marker without seeing it. When that happened, Urist simply called a halt, and we waited for the mist to lift.

We were travelling without attendants, without many luxuries, having reckoned the burden of added baggage and personnel would outweigh the benefits. It hadn't surprised Eamonn that Dorelei found it no hardship; Alban royalty don't live pampered lives. Phèdre surprised him, though.

He said as much one afternoon when the drizzle had turned to a steady rain, heavy enough that we'd all donned our cloaks.

I laughed at him. "You've no idea, do you?"

Eamonn blinked, rain dripping from the hood of his cloak. "What do you mean?"

"In Jebe-Barkal during the rainy season," I said, "the rain falls so hard it's like standing under a bucket. The mire is so deep, betimes our pack-donkeys sank to their hocks. Everything rots. The horses get saddle-sores. And when it doesn't rain, there are blood-flies. They lay eggs in the open sores. You have to pick them out, or the wounds will grow and fester." I raised one hand, wriggling my fingers. "That was our job, Phèdre's and mine. We were the best at it because we had the smallest fingers."

"Truly?" Eamonn glanced dubiously at Phèdre, riding ahead of us.

"Truly," I assured him.

Other than rain, mist, and the occasional benign sighting of other travellers, our journey was uneventful. I had no more dreams of bears that woke me in the middle of the night and sent me plunging out of our tent, half naked, sword in hand. I had no dreams at all, not that

I remembered. But betimes when I hovered on the verge of sleep, I thought I heard the other thing: pipes, and a woman's laughter.

And yet when I wrenched myself back to wakefulness, there was nothing.

Only silence.

When I asked Dorelei if she'd heard anything peculiar in the night, she only gave me a worried, puzzled look and shook her head. And so I concluded it had to be my mind playing tricks on me. It made sense, I suppose. I'd been playing Hugues' flute, remembering the goat-pipes of my childhood. And a woman's laughter . . . ah, well. There was no mystery there, only another painful memory to bury.

Except that I'd never heard the tune the piper played before in my life.

And the laughter wasn't Sidonie's.

Well, and so. The human mind is a strange place, filled with endless vagaries. I was Elua's scion as well as Kushiel's, and I had transgressed against his sacred precept. I had turned my back on love, at least for the time. Somewhere deep inside in my heart, I felt guilt at it. Small wonder my mind was concocting phantoms. Since there was naught to be done about it, I endured it and hoped it would pass.

Still, it made my skin prickle.

On the tenth day of our journey, we reached the outskirts of the Dalriada's holdings. After the low mountains, the land was once more green and lush. Eamonn breathed deeply of the air, filling his lungs.

"Do you smell it?" he exulted. *"Home!"*

It smelled much the same to me as anywhere else in Alba, but I made no comment. I knew too well what it was like to return home after long absence and great travail.

We made camp that day in a meadow alongside a beech forest; earlier than was our wont, at Eamonn's insistence. He chose the site himself with great care, acting mysterious. When I asked him why, he laughed and went to speak with Urist without answering. I saw the dour Cruithne grin unexpectedly and nod, and Eamonn returned.

"Come and see," he said. "All of you."

Holding Brigitta's hand, he led us into the forest. The sun was still some distance above the horizon and the slanting light filtered greenly through the trees. It was an old, old wood with a high canopy, and little grew beneath it save dense moss covering the rocks and boulders that dotted the ground. Eamonn picked his way as though there were a discernible path, periodically glancing overhead. The second time he did, Phèdre pointed in the direction of his gaze, and I saw a faded hank of red thread tied to a branch.

Presently, we heard the faint trickling of water. It was a quiet sound, and it made me realize we'd all been walking silent and hushed. "There," Eamonn whispered, pointing. He smiled at Brigitta. "Brigid's Well. A sacred place belonging to your sacred namesake. You see it is true? We share long-ago roots."

Near the base of a large tree decorated with more red thread, a stone dolmen had been erected. It was shaggy with moss, and a dark aperture lay in its shadow. Water seeped out between the rocks around it, a dozen gleaming trickles gathering to form a streamlet that wandered a few yards before vanishing in the damp soil.

"What do I do?" Brigitta whispered back.

"Here." Eamonn went forward and knelt before the dolmen. He offered a prayer to the goddess Brigid and invoked her blessing on his wife and friends, then dipped one cupped hand into the aperture. It came out dripping. He beckoned to Brigitta. "Drink."

She knelt beside him, sipping from his broad, cupped palm. Her eyes brightened with surprise. "It's sweet!"

Eamonn grinned. "Like you, my heart." He drank the rest, then drew a crumbled oatcake from the pouch on his belt, setting it atop the dolmen. "Now the rest of you."

"We brought no offering," Phèdre protested.

"There is no need." He shook his head. "You are my guests in this land."

Joscelin approached the dolmen and knelt with his usual economical grace. He bowed his head, offering a silent prayer, then drew a cupped handful of water from the darkness. Phèdre joined him and they both drank, smiling at one another.

And then it was my turn.

I knelt before the dolmen and spoke a simple prayer the *ollamh* had taught me. "Good goddess, we thank you for your bounty and honor your ways," I murmured, dipping my hand into the hidden spring. The water was colder than I'd expected. And I'd expected it to have a mineral odor, but it didn't. It smelled clean and sweet, like berries. Dorelei came forward to kneel beside me, steadying my hand against her lips to drink from it. She, too, smiled at the water's taste.

I smiled back at her and drank.

Foulness filled my mouth, sharp and shocking. It tasted of leaf-mold and rot and berries, yes, but fermented berries turned rank and rancid. I nearly gagged. My head jerked back in shock, and I saw my own shocked reflection in Dorelei's eyes. I swallowed convulsively, fighting another impulse to gag.

"What is it?" she asked in alarm.

"Imri?" Eamonn echoed her, his joy giving way to concern.

I couldn't bring myself to spoil his pleasure. Whatever the matter was, clearly it was *me* and not Brigid's Well. The water had tasted sweet to everyone else. "Cold." I gritted the word out. "Sore tooth, that's all."

In the back of my mind, I heard an echo of a woman's laughter.

"Oh, aye." He relaxed. "We'll be at Innisclan tomorrow. My old nurse will make you a poultice for it."

"My thanks." I got to my feet. Out of the corner of my eye, I caught sight of a wiry clump of brownish hair caught on the bark of the giant beech. My thoughts flashed back to the warning lessons of my childhood in the mountains. *Bear sign*. I blinked. No. It was only a knot of red thread, tangled and faded, dangling from a branch.

A shiver ran over my skin.

Truly, I was losing my wits.

On the way back to camp, I wanted to spit over and over to get that taste out of my mouth. I didn't, though. I kept my mouth shut on it. In time it faded until it was merely cloying, and then somewhat that hovered betwixt unpleasant and tolerable. Dorelei shot me sidelong glances, wondering. Alone among our company, she'd seen my face when I drank. She didn't believe my tale of a toothache.

By the time we returned to camp, the sun was growing low. Around the campfire, they were calling for us to join them and dine. Dorelei hesitated when Eamonn and the others went forward.

"Imriel." She tilted her head. "What happened there at the spring?"

"I'm not sure." I touched her cheek. "Somewhat strange. A trick of sorts, mayhap. I don't want to ruin Eamonn's homecoming. I'll tell you about it when we're alone tonight, and you can give me your thoughts. All right?"

Dorelei nodded. "Of course."

No one else had noticed aught amiss. The mood was cheerful. At Eamonn's request, I played my flute after we'd all dined. As the sun sank below the horizon, I played the familiar songs we'd sung on our journey, finding I'd grown proficient at them. Dredging my memory, I essayed a lively, skirling tune I'd heard aboard the *Aeolia*, the ship that had borne me home to Terre d'Ange after the siege of Lucca.

It seemed fitting, and I don't think I acquitted myself too badly. I couldn't remember the words that Captain Oppius' sailors had sung, but it didn't matter. It was a merry tune, designed to set hands to clapping and feet to stamping.

The sound of our merriment drowned out the drumming of approaching hoofbeats. It wasn't until we heard shouts from the sentries that we realized we weren't alone. Joscelin was on his feet in a heartbeat, sword drawn, and Eamonn and I right behind him. Brigitta drew a wicked-looking dagger, and Dorelei retrieved her hunting bow. Only Phèdre remained calm and seated, cocking her head to listen to the exchange of hails.

"Friends, it seems," she observed.

It was a party of a dozen or so riders, their figures vague in the twilight. One of them detached from the rest, riding toward us. Eamonn squinted. "Mairead?" he called, then raised his voice to a bellow. *"Mairead!"*

There was a wordless whoop in reply. Horse and rider charged into our midst, scattering all of us. I caught an impression of a woman's face, a wild mane of ruddy-gold hair, firelight gleaming on the horse's flanks as it planted a rear hoof dangerously near our campfire.

"Eamonn!" The rider dismounted with careless aplomb, flinging both arms around his neck and kissing him. "You're home!"

"Mairead, girl!" Eamonn hugged her as though he meant to crack her ribs. "What are you doing here?"

The riderless horse was turning in excited circles, adding to the mayhem. Brigitta was scowling, fingering the hilt of her dagger. I caught the horse's reins and led it safely to one side. "Don't worry," I said to Brigitta. "I've a strong suspicion that's not an old lover."

Her scowl eased. "Sister?"

I nodded at the pair of them, tall and loud and exuberant. "What do *you* think?"

Indeed, so it proved. After the initial exchange of greetings, Eamonn called us over to introduce us to Mairead, the elder of his two younger sisters. She was tall and rangy, with an open, friendly face that bore a smattering of golden freckles and a grin to match Eamonn's.

I liked her immediately; I daresay all of us did. Even Brigitta smiled when Mairead embraced her with uninhibited warmth. "*You're* the one!" Mairead exclaimed. "Oh, sister! You've no idea how long we've been waiting to meet you!"

"One half a year, I think," Brigitta said, careful and precise.

"Is it only that long?" Mairead's brow wrinkled. "Oh, well, since Eamonn's letter arrived, I suppose. It seems like longer. We've been so worried, waiting and hoping all these months. And he left years before it." She thumped her brother's shoulder. "You were gone *so long*! I want to hear all about it. I want to hear all about Terre d'Ange and Tiberium and Skaldia . . . Skaldia! And all these people, your foster-family . . . oh, Dagda Mor, they're right out of the stories! And Lady Dorelei, you're very welcome among us . . . Eamonn, what are they all doing here? Oh, Mother's going to be so pleased. Well, I think, anyway."

Brigitta looked bemused, having lost the thread of her words long ago.

"Slow down." Eamonn laughed. "There's time. And it's hard for Brigitta to understand when you gabble."

Mairead thumped him again in indignation. "I don't gabble!"

"You do," he informed her.

"*You* do," she retorted. "You always did. Talk, talk, talk!"

After some bickering and discussion, Eamonn went with Mairead to greet the Dalriada who'd ridden with her and make them welcome at our camp tonight. They were friends of his from childhood, and we heard the roars and shouts drifting across the darkening meadow. A fleeting memory of Sidonie crossed my mind. *He's just so infernally loud!* I pushed the thought away, blowing a few idle notes on Hugues' flute.

"Well," I said lightly to Brigitta. "Now you've an idea what you're in for."

"Yes." She nodded. "I think I will like it."

Once they had matters settled, Eamonn and Mairead returned. Although it was growing late, we stayed awake for a time. Eamonn was reluctant to tell the tale of his Skaldic courtship of Brigitta, wanting to save it for Innisclan, but he told her about the tribute we bore for the Lady of the Dalriada, and how Queen Ysandre had wished to escort him home in honor.

In turn, Mairead told us that she had been leading a scouting-party.

"You?" Eamonn scoffed fondly.

She elbowed him. "I'm the oldest after Brennan and you, am I not? Brennan rode north, and I rode south. Some clan-holders have complained about calves being taken. There have been rumors of *bears*." She shook her head. "But we found no bear sign, only your campfires."

A shudder ran up my spine.

Bears.

Dorelei glanced at me. "Bears?" she asked cautiously. "Or . . . ?"

"The Old Ones?" Mairead grimaced. "I cannot say. I thought they had no cause to trouble the Dalriada. Mother has long maintained a truce with them. But perhaps we have given them cause. If we have, I do not know what it is. Or perhaps they're merely curious. Or hungry."

"Old Ones?" Phèdre murmured. Anyone who didn't know her would have thought her sleepy. "I don't know that name."

"The Old Ones, the Wise Ones." Mairead made a gesture intended to avert bad luck and nodded at Dorelei. "So we call them to avoid giving offense. Some of them play tricks if not given proper respect. How do the Cullach Gorrym call them?"

"We don't," Dorelei said in a tight voice. "If we must speak of them, we call them by name. But it is better if we do not speak of them at all."

Mairead eyed her. "The Dalriada believe otherwise."

I cleared my throat. "Kinadius called them bear-witches."

"Men fear things more than women," Brigitta observed, paying close attention to the conversation. "Like Lucius and the dead."

"Perhaps, but Lucius was right, my love," Eamonn said. "He had reason to fear the dead. Still, we have made our camp beside Brigid's Well, and I think no harm will come to us here." He yawned. "My friends, it grows late. Imri, why don't you give us a song to fill our heads with pleasant dreams as we take to our beds?"

I set the flute to my lips and played the first thing that came to mind. It wasn't until I was well into it that I realized it was the piper's tune, the one that plagued me. My fingers faltered briefly on the holes, but I kept going. It was a plaintive melody, and yet there was somewhat seductive about it, too. A yearning promise of ease, of bittersweet desire. Around the campfire, my listeners' faces softened, sinking into private reveries.

The sight filled me with unease, so much so that I stopped playing. Eamonn shook his head like a man waking from a nap and gave another mighty yawn. "Dagda Mor! You've gotten good on that thing. Well, bed it is. Come, Mairead, you can share with us."

I wasn't tired, not at all.

"I'm sorry, Imriel." In the tent Dorelei and I shared, she was heavy-lidded and yawning, too. "I know I promised, but can we speak in the morning? We've been travelling for a long time, and I'm bone-weary."

"You weren't so tired last night," I reminded her.

"No." She smiled with remembered pleasure, the sort of smile that makes any woman look beautiful. "And I won't be at Innisclan, but tonight I am."

I gave up. "Sleep well, then."

"Mmm." Dorelei closed her eyes. "What was that song you played? It was lovely."

"I don't know," I said. "That's the thing. I keep hearing it in my dreams. That, and a woman's laughter. Only it's not in my *dreams*, exactly. It's that time just before you fall asleep, when you're not quite one or the other. That's why I asked if you'd heard aught peculiar. I wanted to tell you about it and what happened today at Brigid's Well, and to ask . . ." I hesitated. "Well, after what Mairead said, to ask what you know about the Maghuin Dhonn. Because I don't feel I'm in danger, not exactly, but I don't feel safe, either. Someone or something is playing tricks on me."

A faint snore escaped Dorelei's parted lips.

I sighed.

Wide awake and lonely, I sat cross-legged on my bedroll, twisting Sidonie's ring around my finger. I was alone in a strange land, and although it was a beautiful land, it seemed not to want me here. I missed my home, and oh, gods! I missed Sidonie. I wished I could talk to her. I wished she was here or I was there.

I wished I could lose myself in her.

For the first time in many days, I lowered the rigid guards I'd erected around my thoughts and let myself think of her.

Ah, Elua! It hurt, but it felt so good, too. I chose a memory of our lovemaking; only one. They were like perfect pearls on a strand, precious and far too few. I pushed away the strangeness and the nagging sense of fear and sank into my memories with a vast sense of comfort and indulgence, playing them over in my mind. Every kiss, every gasp, every thrust was etched there. Sunlight in her hair, the sheen of sweat, the honey-sweet taste of her mouth. It drove everything else away, until I was taut with desire.

Nothing else mattered.

I propped myself on one elbow, stroking my throbbing phallus with my other hand. *Is this what you want?* Another memory; too many, too fast. I was spending them too quickly. I couldn't stop, though. Faster and faster. Sidonie, wrists straining. Begging. Shuddering over and over as I took her relentlessly, driving her to new heights, plunging to new depths. I stroked myself harder, my testes rising and tightening at the memory.

It came fast and hard. I rolled to one side and hissed between my teeth, my seed spurting onto the ground.

And then it was over. I flopped onto my back and lay panting. Turning my head, I could make out Dorelei's profile in the dim light of the low-burning campfire that filtered through the tent walls. Sleeping, peaceful and oblivious.

I felt better and worse, all at once. And I felt tired. I'd opened the floodgates and other memories sought to crowd me, tender and importunate and hurtful. I was too tired to fight them, to tired to wrestle them into submission. Instead I fled, seeking refuge in sleep, eased by my body's languor.

This time, I didn't hear the pipes.

Only the woman's laughter.

TWENTY

IN THE MORNING, a handful of Mairead's riders departed for In-
isclan to give warning of our impending arrival. Unencumbered
by wagons, they were likely to arrive some hours before us. The young
Dalriadan warriors were a loud, merry lot. They'd stayed up late, drinking and boasting with the Cruithne and the D'Angelines, and seemed
none the worse for wear. I was glad relations seemed amicable among
all parties, and I envied them.

My own head felt thick, as though I'd drunk too much wine. Too
much emotion, like as not. The boulder of my buried heart shifted and
groaned, disturbed from its place of rest far, far beneath the surface of
my life.

"Shall we talk now?" Dorelei asked me, clear-eyed and well rested.
"I'm sorry I couldn't stay awake."

I made myself smile at her. "It can wait. I can't think straight with
all this lot around. My head's a muddle."

She smiled back at me, dimples flashing. "They are a bit loud."

No one else was melancholy. It was a fine day, bright and clear,
with nary a cloud in sight. All of last night's concerns were forgotten.
No one spoke of Wise Ones, Old Ones, bear-witches, or the Maghuin
Dhonn.

And in the bright light of day, that was fine with me.

We made good time, following the tracks of the Dalriada. Before long, we came upon rutted paths and the wagons travelled more
smoothly. There were low stone fences marking pastures, and cattle
watched us with incurious eyes. The mules pricked their ears, the Bas-

tard pranced beneath me. We sang as we rode. I played Hugues' flute, although not *that* song.

The air took on a tang of salt. Gulls circled with raucous cries.

From atop a grassy rise, we beheld the land spread below. Innisclan, the vast hall and scattered outlying holdings, the mill and the smithy, the grazing cattle. And beyond, the sea, grey and shining in the afternoon sunlight.

Phèdre reached for Joscelin's hand. "Oh, love! 'Tis the same!"

"So it is." He smiled at her. "Do you remember . . . ?"

She flushed. "All too well."

The whole of Innisclan turned out to meet us. I would have known Eamonn's mother anywhere. The Lady Grainne of the Dalriada was tall and imposing. Strands of grey dimmed the fire of her red-gold hair and there were lines on her strong face, but her eyes crinkled like her son's when she smiled.

Eamonn greeted his mother with a sweeping bow, then straightened to receive her embrace, grinning with delight. He introduced Brigitta to her. After that, there was a good deal of exuberant shouting and hugging as various siblings came forward, and then at last, the rest of us were presented.

As Ysandre's delegate, Phèdre made a graceful speech regarding the tribute we'd brought. The Lady Grainne listened to it with a look of amusement.

"Books!" Her grey-green eyes crinkled. "You always do bring interesting gifts, Phèdre nó Delaunay."

Phèdre smiled. "This was Eamonn's choice."

"We mean to start an academy," he told his mother. "Brigitta and I."

She raised red-gold brows. "Very interesting."

While the Lady's eldest son Brennan took charge of the tribute-wagons and oversaw the unloading and storage of their cargo and accommodations for our escort, we were ushered into the hall of Innisclan, where a welcoming feast was being laid on the great table. It was a vast space, most of it given over to the hall. As honored guests, we were accorded private chambers; small stone cells scarce large enough to hold a narrow bed.

"It's *tiny*," I whispered to Dorelei.

"Hush." She pressed a finger to my lips. "This isn't Terre d'Ange."

As soon as we'd had a chance to wash our hands and faces and change our travel-stained attire, we were summoned to eat. It was a lengthy affair, and a noisy one, too. The Lady's children talked over one another, eager to hear of Eamonn's doings and share their own. During the course of the meal, I managed to sort them out. Brennan was the oldest, his mother's heir. After Eamonn and Mairead came another sister, Caolinn, and then Conor, the youngest at some fifteen years.

Save for Conor, they were all cut from the same cloth, tall and red-headed. He was the quiet, odd one of the lot, with thick black hair and dark, thoughtful eyes out of which he kept stealing covert, fascinated glances at Phèdre. I remembered Eamonn telling me that, except for his sisters, none of them had the same father. As for those fathers, none were in evidence.

Seeing his siblings all together, I could understand better why the Lady Grainne had been sanguine about permitting her second-oldest to wander the earth, footloose and unfettered. There did seem to be an awful lot of them.

Once the meal was finished and the storytelling began, they fell silent, though. Everyone sat rapt while Eamonn related the tale of his courtship of Brigitta. Partway through, Conor rose quietly to retrieve a lap-harp. He held it throughout the telling, head bowed, fingers moving over the strings without touching them.

When it was over, Caolinn sighed. "That's so romantic!"

"Why?" Mairead shrugged. "He did a lot of chores, that's all. There's naught romantic in chopping wood and hauling water."

"For love's sake? Of course there is." Her sister turned to Conor. "You think so, don't you?"

Head still bowed, he nodded. "I do."

"Will you make a song about it, little brother?" Brennan asked with a smile. "He's very good, you know," he said to the rest of us. "He can play any tune he's ever heard, perfect to the note. One of the old bards born anew, like as not."

Conor's averted cheek flushed. "Go on!"

"Will you play for us, Conor?" Phèdre asked. "I'd love to hear you."

His flush deepened, but he nodded again and began to play an Eiran ballad, singing in a low voice.

He *was* good; good enough to play in any salon in Terre d'Ange. Although he sat hunched over his harp, his thin fingers plucked at the strings with graceful precision and the harp's tone rang out pure and sweet. Gradually, as he played, he sat straighter in the chair. His voice was rough with adolescence, but it held true.

"That was lovely," Phèdre said when he finished, smiling at him. "Thank you."

Conor turned beet-red.

"My musical child," Grainne said fondly. "A gift of his father's."

"You should play together." Under the table, Eamonn nudged my foot. "Imri's been practicing on the flute this whole way. He's not bad. Go on, go fetch your flute."

"Later, mayhap," I demurred. "You lot must be weary of it."

"I'm not." Conor looked directly at me for the first time. "I'd like it very much, Prince Imriel."

"All right." I raised my brows. "Will you promise to call me *Imriel*, Prince Conor?"

He smiled and flushed yet again. "I will."

Elua, I remembered that age! Awkwardness and embarrassment at every turn. Colts' Years, Joscelin said they called it in the Cassiline Brotherhood.

I fetched Hugues' flute and put on a solemn face. "Now, this is a D'Angeline song for very special occasions. On our journey, we translated it into Eiran to honor all of you. I'll play the first verse, and mayhap my lady wife will do the honor of singing for us?" I glanced sidelong at Dorelei, who looked bemused.

As soon as I blew the first few notes, she laughed. I played the song about the little brown goat and Dorelei sang along. Everyone laughed, hearing the verses. Conor grinned, his dark eyes sparkling. At the second verse, he joined us, playing a merry, lively accompaniment. His fingers danced over the strings, embellishing the simple child's melody in ways I'd never imagined.

"Very nice!" Eamonn applauded.

"You see it's true," Brennan said smugly. "He only needed hear it once."

"Indeed." I lowered the flute, then paused. "Conor, if I played a tune for you, could you tell me if you'd heard it before?"

He nodded. "Yes, of course."

I'd only played the opening measure of the mysterious piper's tune that haunted my nights when Conor turned ashen-pale.

"No!" he said violently. "'Tis no tune I've ever heard."

"Conor!" his mother said in surprise. "That's no call to be rude."

"Sorry." He mumbled the apology, then rose abruptly and set his lap-harp on the table. "I've got to be gone. Sorry."

I watched him leave, his narrow shoulders hunched and taut. "Did I offend him somehow, my lady?"

"No." Grainne sighed. "He's a broody lad, my youngest. He's been prone to odd fits these last few years. Pay him no heed, he'll come around."

Eamonn nudged me again. "Mayhap *you* could talk to him, Imri. You know a thing or two about brooding."

"I'll do that," I said, ignoring the jibe.

After Conor's precipitous departure, the conversation turned to bears. Unlike his sister, Brennan's scouting party had encountered bear signs; tracks that led from a crofter's pasture into the edge of the forest. There, in the soft loam, they simply ended.

"Made my hair stand on end, it did." Brennan rubbed the back of his neck, remembering. "It's *them*, sure enough."

"What do the Wise Ones want with us?" Eamonn asked, puzzled.

"You're the one toting cart-loads of wisdom this way," his older brother retorted. "Mayhap they don't like its flavor."

Eamonn looked at his mother. "Do you think it's true?"

"I don't know." Grainne's face was troubled. "The Dalriada have enjoyed a long truce with the Old Ones." She glanced involuntarily toward the door. "If they are wroth for this cause or some other, I hope they would speak openly to me."

"You mean you truly do deal with them?" Dorelei asked, startled.

"I do," the Lady of the Dalriada said firmly. "There are two sides to every story, young Cruithne. Even theirs. And if the Old Ones hunger,

I do not begrudge them a few cattle. Much that was theirs has been lost to them."

"So you don't reckon them malevolent?" I asked.

"Malevolent?" Grainne gave me a curious look. "No. Capricious, yes, but not malevolent." She shook her head. "But this is a joyous occasion. Let us speak of more pleasant matters. Tell me," she asked Eamonn with a smile. "How did you find your father? Is he well?"

Thus, the moment passed.

I wanted to hear more about the Maghuin Dhonn and mayhap discuss my own experiences, but the Lady Grainne had made her wishes clear, and I reckoned it could wait. I was beginning to think she might be the best person to discuss this with, since she seemed to know more about the Maghuin Dhonn than anyone else had thus far admitted. And if it was bear-witches haunting me, whatever it was they wanted, they'd made no move to reveal themselves during our long journey across Alba. Now that we were ensconced in the hall of Innisclan itself, I doubted that would change.

In that, I was mistaken.

That night, Dorelei and I made love in the narrow bed we shared in our tiny chamber, forgetting all notion of serious conversation. There had been *uisghe* served by the end of the evening, and we were both a little drunk and ardent, laughing over the contortions required to keep from falling off the bed. It was sweet and foolish and pleasant, and I fell asleep afterward untouched by melancholy, with no piper's tune or woman's laughter echoing in my dreams.

I did dream, though.

I dreamed of making love to Sidonie.

It was a vivid, piercing dream, more intense by far than the memories I'd indulged in the other night. I could feel her, taste her, hear her voice in my ear. It shocked me into unwelcome wakefulness, groaning with regret and unfulfilled desire as the strands of the dream slipped through the fingers of my awareness. My rigid phallus ached, and so did my heart.

Pipes, and a woman's laughter.

"Come here."

The words tied a knot around my will and drew me. At times I'd felt what it was like to stand outside myself and see into another person; to see the good and bad in them, the fault-lines on their soul. I had seen how cruelty could be used, and chosen not to use it. Now it was as though I stood outside myself and watched *me*, helpless and dismayed.

Without the slightest intent of doing so, I rose in silence, donning my clothes. I left my sword-belt where it lay. The piper's tune beckoned, filled with yearning and promise. I glanced at Dorelei, sleeping peacefully. I left our bedchamber.

The great hall of Innisclan was quiet and mostly empty. A few of the Lady's men were sleeping there; guards, drunk on *uisghe*. I passed them by. My feet moved with no conscious volition. I didn't want to go wherever I was going. I just . . . did.

In a distant part of my awareness, with every step, I felt certain I would stop. I meant to stop. And when I didn't, the distant part of me thought I would open my mouth and cry out for help. One shout would wake the household. One shout would bring Joscelin from the bedchamber he shared with Phèdre, sword at the ready.

And I just . . . didn't.

Instead, I kept walking. I didn't want to, but I did. As though I moved in a waking dream, I followed the summons, followed the tug on my heart, followed the piper's tune. Somewhere inside, I was shivering with fear, but I couldn't stop. I unbarred the door and walked into the night. There was a full moon, small and distant, silvering the Alban landscape. And there, beneath it, was a small, distant figure.

A woman.

I walked toward her. She stood beside one of the low stone fences. I saw moonlight glint on the silver pipe she lowered from her lips as I drew near. Whatever charm bound me, it eased somewhat as the melody faded. I took a sharp breath and came back to myself, smelling loam and musk and fermented berries, feeling fear give way to anger.

"Lady." The word emerged, harsh and raw. "Who are you?"

The woman peered at me. She was small and dark, with coarse black hair and pale, pale eyes. Her cheekbones were high and broad and there were marks on her face; woad tattoos. A pair of claws bracketed her eyes. "You may call me Morwen."

"Morwen." I clenched my fists. "What do you want of me?"

"I'm not sure yet." She studied me. "You were careless, you know."

I shook my head. "You speak in riddles."

"Often, yes." Morwen smiled. With one hand, she stroked a leather bag that hung about her neck on a thong. A bolt of desire shot through me, so acute it weakened my knees. She regarded me with amusement. "We were curious and a bit afraid. Your marriage is a portent of change. I've been following you. Have you not heard me? And then you dreamed of love and spilled your seed on *taisgaidh* soil for anyone to find." She reached into the leather bag and withdrew an object; a crude mannekin formed of soil and clay. She showed it to me, then replaced it in the bag. "That was careless."

I gritted my teeth. "What have you done, lady?"

"Oh, I've bound you with your own desires." A frown creased her brow. "I mean no harm by it. We are not sure, any of us, what is the best course. Not even Berlik. We cannot untangle the threads to see past the gates into the future, not yet. But this, at least, I have done."

She stroked the leather bag.

I groaned.

"Will you make love to me?" Morwen inquired. "You want to, don't you?"

"No." I glared at her. "Not *you*."

She laughed. It was the laughter that had haunted my dreams. Not Sidonie's; not the laughter that had turned my world upside down. But her fingers stroked the leather bag that contained my seed mixed with Alban soil, and all I could do was groan.

"I could *make* you want me," Morwen said. "Mayhap that would change things."

I bowed my head. *"Duzhmata,"* I whispered. *"Duzhûshta, duzhvarshta."*

Ill thought, ill words, ill deeds.

The shackles of desire loosened, held at bay by the spectre of Daršanga. It seemed the lesson of Bryony House had not been useless after all. Breathing raggedly, I glanced at Morwen. Her lips were parted in surprise.

"Interesting," she said mildly. "D'Angeline magic?"

I gave a bitter laugh. "Hardly. Why are you doing this?"

Morwen tilted her head. "Curiosity." She took a step closer to me, peering at my face once more with those odd, moon-pale eyes held between raking tattooed claws. "We are a very old people, D'Angeline, and you are a very young one. Your coming may be a tide we cannot stop; or it may not. We have held Alba for a long, long time."

"The Maghuin Dhonn?" I said. "Not for centuries, I hear."

She reached up to stroke my cheek with one hand, tightening her grasp on the leather bag with the other when I sought to jerk away from her touch. Her fingers smelled of musk and berries. "Oh, yes. We hold the secret heart of Alba. All those places sacred to the Cruithne, to the Dalriada; ours, first."

"Until you sacrificed your *diadh-anam*," I hazarded.

"That is a lie." Her fingers curved. I felt the prick of heavy claws against my skin, and then they withdrew. Morwen stood. "Are you brave?" she wondered. "Or merely foolhardy?"

I closed my eyes. "Tired, mostly."

"Poor boy." She laughed and stroked the leather bag, and a rill of unwelcome desire ran through me. "You shouldn't *want* so badly. These bonds are of your own making. I merely tied the knot."

Behind my closed eyes, I evoked another memory. Sidonie, standing in a shaft of sunlight in Amarante's bedchamber. Her unguarded smile when she turned to see me; her laughter when I bowed and greeted her as the Sun Princess. My heart, expanding with unexpected joy. "You should be wary about tangling with D'Angelines in matters of love, lady," I said to Morwen, opening my eyes. "Blessed Elua does not like it."

"This is not his place," she said simply.

"True," I said. "But I am his scion, and Kushiel's, too."

We regarded one another. "I will go now." Morwen tapped the leather bag. "You will not be harmed, not here on the Lady Grainne's holdings. But I think that Alba, old Alba, does not want you here. If if you are wise, you will go. Go back to your Terre d'Ange and your Elua and your love."

"Lady, I would like nothing better," I said grimly.

She shrugged. "So, go."

As I opened my mouth to reply, a cloud passed over the moon. Shadows moved like fog and the pale glint of Morwen's eyes winked out. Something large and heavy moved in the darkness, snuffling, its tread heavy enough to make the earth tremble. My skin prickled all over and I shook myself like a horse freed from the harness, all vestiges of desire gone.

The cloud passed.

Nothing was there.

I swore, long and hard. And then I made my way back to the hall. When a dim figure stepped out of the shadow of the doorway, I grabbed unthinking for the hilt of my absent sword, then set myself to fight unarmed, every muscle tensed and ready.

"Prince Imriel!" A low boy's voice. "It's only me."

"Conor." I lowered my clenched fists. "Ah, yes. The lad who'd never heard the tune I played."

He shivered, although it wasn't cold. "You saw her, didn't you?"

"I did." I eyed him wryly. "Is the lady a friend of yours?"

"No!" Conor wrapped his arms around himself. His voice dropped to a whisper. "One of them was, once. He taught me . . . he taught me a song or two. Charms." His voice grew almost inaudible. "He said he was my father."

"Your *father*!"

"Shhh!" He sounded miserable. "Please!"

"Name of Elua!" I raked a hand through my hair. "Is that a bad thing? To have one of the . . . Old Ones . . . for a father?"

"No. Yes." His voice cracked. "I don't know. It's scary."

"Now that, I can believe." I glanced involuntarily over my shoulder. "Conor, listen. I've just had a very . . . strange . . . and unpleasant encounter. Right now, I think we should both go back inside, bar the door, and set one of those sleeping guards on it; and mayhap on me, for that matter. In the morning, I would like to have a long talk with your lady mother. And if you haven't, mayhap you should. Does that sound wise?"

He nodded. "Yes."

"Good." Putting a hand on his shoulder, I steered him toward the door. "Let's go."

TWENTY-ONE

I AWOKE WITH THE STRONG sense of being watched and opened my eyes to find Conor perched on the foot of my narrow bed. I grabbed my sword at my bedside and had it half drawn before I recognized him. The action sent him scrambling away from me in alarm.

"Elua!" I said in disgust. "You shouldn't startle a man like that."

"I'm sorry." In the doorway, Conor hunched his narrow shoulders. "I didn't think you'd sleep so late."

"Neither did I." After my encounter with Morwen, I hadn't thought I'd sleep at all. I had, though. I'd laid down beside Dorelei and fallen into a black pit of exhaustion. I glanced around and saw my wife was nowhere in sight. I didn't hear much noise from the hall, either. "Where is everyone?"

"Gone to look at a site to start a library. They're inspecting a lot of the books and moving them. Lady Phèdre was not happy when Brennan said he put some of them in an empty dovecote." He looked warily at me from beneath the thick fringe of his coarse black hair. "Can we talk to my mother now? You promised."

I didn't think I'd made any promises, and I certainly hadn't intended to involve myself in *his* discussion with Grainne. What was between them was a private matter. I opened my mouth to say so, and saw the hunger beneath the wariness in his dark eyes. Betimes, 'tis easier to share a burden with a stranger than a loved one. And if there was anyone who knew about unwelcome parentage, it was me. I sighed and began dragging my clothes on. "Yes, all right."

The hall of Innisclan was quiet and mostly empty. In the kitchen, a cheerful cook's assistant gave me bread and honey soaked in cow's milk to break my fast. Bear-witches or no, I'd spent too much time on short rations during the siege of Lucca to go hungry willingly. I ate it standing, my fingers dripping, mindful of Conor's impatient gaze.

"All right, all right!" I licked my fingers clean. "Let's go."

The Lady Grainne granted our joint request for a private audience with bemusement. She led us into her private quarters, which included a small salon. At her invitation, I took a seat on a wooden chair covered with sheepskin dyed scarlet. Conor, standing, fidgeted.

"Do you want me to start?" I asked him.

"Yes, please," he mumbled.

Taking a deep breath, I told her the whole of the story. The pipes, the laughter, the bear-sound outside the tent. Brigid's Well, the charmed tune. Morwen's summons and the binding she'd laid on me.

At that, the Lady of the Dalriada stirred. "With what did she bind you?"

"Desire." I met her gaze squarely. "Seed spilled on *taisgaidh* soil. She had a mannekin molded of dirt and clay."

She nodded. "I see."

I related what Conor had told me; or began to. I hadn't gotten far before he interrupted.

"You said he was a *bard*!" he shouted at his mother, his voice cracking. "A wandering *bard*!"

"That he is." Grainne's tone was grave. "I did not lie."

"Why didn't you *tell* me?"

"Ah, lad!" She smiled sadly. "I'm sorry. I thought you'd ask when the time came. Surely, you always knew you were different, just as Eamonn did. I didn't reckon on your father visiting you. I should have. They do like to play sly tricks, the Old Ones."

"Last night was no mere trick," I said briefly.

"No. No, it wasn't." The Lady Grainne rose and paced the room. "It concerns me."

"You!" I raised my brows.

"Do they mean to harm Prince Imriel?" Conor asked, sounding ill. "*Can* they?"

She didn't answer right away. "It is no secret that the Old Ones spoke against his marriage to Dorelei mab Breidaia. Still, it is done, and I do not think they will break their long truce with the Dalriada. But I do not like this business of the binding charm, either." Her grey-green gaze touched on me. "That was careless of you."

"Name of Elua!" I spread my hands. "How was I to know? Fine. What now, my lady? I'm not minded to abandon Dorelei, turn tail, and flee to Terre d'Ange on a bear-witch's threat, but I'll not be at this Morwen's beck and call, either, wondering if I'm about to be lured into ambush. And I'm asking you, because you seem to be the only person in Alba with any experience in dealing with the Old Ones." I glanced at Conor. "Indeed, rather more than I reckoned."

"Ah, well." Surprisingly, Grainne smiled. "Love and desire are curious things, are they not? Still, I am not the only one. And this magic lies beyond my purview."

"Aodhan would know," Conor murmured.

"Have you spoken to him?" his mother asked.

He nodded without meeting her eyes. "I told him about the . . . the man who taught me the charmed songs. He said unless I wished to study the Path of the Grove, it would be dangerous to use them."

"This Aodhan is an *ollamh*?" I asked.

"He is," Grainne said thoughtfully. "But he is of the Dalriada, and he has dealt with the Old Ones for many long years. Understand," she added, "in Eire, the Old Ones befriended us. And unlike the Cruithne, we never quarrelled with them, neither there nor here in Alba. They taught us many things about herb-lore and the sacred places, aye, and magic, too."

"Shapeshifting?" I asked.

"The old tales say so." Conor shivered. "I asked Aodhan about it. He said it was true. He said it is wild magic, and we lost it when we began to tame places. Nothing is to be had for nothing."

I frowned. "I see."

"Well, no one ever tamed the Old Ones," Grainne said. "And old Aodhan is none too tame himself. If anyone will know the wisest course, he will. Will you take Imriel to see him?" she asked Conor.

He straightened his shoulders. "I will.

The Lady Grainne consented to make excuses to the others for us, and it was agreed that the matter would not be discussed until we had the *ollamh*'s counsel. I reckoned there was no merit in it. At best, it would only sow concern; at worst, I feared Joscelin's reaction. When it came to my safety, he was unyielding. I wouldn't put it past him to organize our D'Angeline guards into a war party and ride forth to confront the Old Ones. And while there was a part of me that would like to do that very thing, the truth was, I was a Prince of Alba by right of marriage now, and I had to be mindful of Alban law, which unfortunately made no provision for being enchanted against one's will.

It was, however, clear that breaking a host's truce of long standing was a violation of the laws of hospitality. I had been ensorceled and embarrassed, but I was unharmed. I did not have cause to bring a blood-feud to Grainne's doorstep. She had the right to claim insult from Morwen, but I doubted she'd have much luck with that.

It was a piece of irony. Firdha had crammed my head with ten thousand bits of law and lore, none of which applied. I hoped I'd have more luck with this Aodhan.

"Shouldn't we arrange for an escort?" I asked Conor as he led me to the stable. Our company had set up an encampment in an open field not far from the hall. I could see our men, Cruithne and D'Angeline alike, bored and idle, dicing and gossiping.

He shook his head. "Aodhan won't show himself if we do."

"I see," I said, although I didn't.

He gave me a considering look. "It's safe, you know."

"I'm glad you think so," I said wryly.

We caught sight of the others as we rode forth from Innisclan, or at least the men. Eamonn and his bright-headed brother Brennan, pacing off a possible building site with Joscelin's keen Siovalese assistance. Eamonn, seeing me riding beside Conor, lifted one hand in salute. I waved. No one thought it odd. After all, I'd promised to have a word with the lad.

"How far is it to Aodhan's?" I asked Conor.

"Oh, only an hour or so," he said. "Or mayhap two."

At least it was a pleasant ride. For most of it, we rode along a ridge that paralleled the sea, picking our way amidst the occasional boulder. It was a fine day, sunlight sparkling on the water, a light breeze lifting wavelets. I glanced often at the empty water and thought about how the Master of the Straits warded Alba's coast, and what it might mean if he ceased to do so.

Along the way, I sought to draw out Conor. "Are you wroth with your mother?"

He hunched his shoulders. "No," he said in a voice that meant *Yes*.

"I would be," I said. "Do you know, something very like happened to me."

He looked at me warily. "Truly?"

So I told him, then, how I had come to find out who I was. How I'd thought myself an orphan and been raised in the Sanctuary of Elua, how I'd been stolen from it. How I'd been rescued from a terrible place, and how I had learned, from the inadvertent words of a soldier, that I was the son of Benedicte de la Courcel and Melisande Shahrizai.

"What did you do?" Conor asked, wide-eyed.

I shrugged. "Sulked."

He colored. "No, *really*."

"It's true," I said. "I was angry at Phèdre for not having told me."

Conor rode in silence for a while, thinking. "Well, but it's not the same, is it?" he said at length. "She's not your mother."

"No, she's not," I agreed. A memory; her wrist in my grasp, a leap in her pulse. Kushiel's Chosen. I ignored it. "But it's a little bit the same, Conor. And I forgave her because I knew she loved me." I leaned over in the saddle and nudged him. "It could be worse, you know. Better one of the Old Ones than the realm's greatest traitor."

He sneaked a sidelong glance at me. "You think?"

"Oh, yes," I said. "I do."

At a place where a narrow stream emptied into the sea, we departed from the high ridge and turned inland. We followed the stream's course as it burbled over mossy rocks and miniature falls. The underbrush grew thick and dense, until we were forced to dismount and hobble the Bastard and Conor's shaggy pony, continuing on foot. At one point, we entered a thicket of blackberries so dense it forced us to crawl.

"Are you sure about this?" I asked, swatting at bracken.

He held a finger to his lips. "Shhh!"

I hushed and listened, pitching my ears to hear intently as

Phèdre had taught me. Somewhere, there was humming; a man's voice, deep and resonant. Conor clambered to his feet, thorns plucking at his woolen tunic. "Master Aodhan!" he called. "It's me, Conor! I've brought a friend, at my mother's request. Is that all right?"

The humming broke, then resumed.

"I'm thinking it's fine." I squirmed out from under the brambly canes. "Come on."

At a place where the stream widened and deepened enough to pool and eddy, we found the *ollamh* of the Dalriada engrossed in fishing. Aodhan was perched on a moss-covered rock, casting his line carefully on the waters. At first glance, he was an unprepossessing figure: a nut-brown man with a bald pate and a white beard knotted in tangled braids.

"What will you, my sons?" he called.

I bowed. "We come seeking your wisdom, Son of the Grove."

"Wisdom!" He snorted. "Better you'd come for fish. Today's a lucky day, it seems." As if to illustrate, he began winding in his line, a fine speckled trout thrashing on the hook. "Well, come on down, then."

Conor and I descended the embankment while the *ollamh* freed his trout from the hook. He placed it in a partially submerged willow creel and tied the lid shut, then rose to greet us.

"Conor, lad!" He gripped the boy's shoulders with sturdy, weathered hands and grinned at him. "Finally got up the courage to speak to your mother, did you?"

The boy blinked. "How did you know?"

"Ah, it's written on your face, lad. At your age, everything is." The *ollamh* turned to me. "And you wear your heritage stamped on yours. The D'Angeline prince, is it?"

"Imriel de la Courcel." I accorded him another bow. "Well met, Son of the Grove."

Another snort. "I'm a hermit, not a court bard. Call me Aodhan."

I smiled. "Imriel."

"Well met, then." Aodhan shook my hand. His felt as tough as old leather. He searched my face, his deep-set hazel eyes small and bright beneath bushy white brows. "You've scarce arrived among the Dalriada, young Imriel. What trouble have you gotten into that concerns the Lady Grainne enough to send you to seek out an old hermit's advice?"

"One of the Old Ones placed a binding on him," Conor informed him.

"Indeed!" The bushy eyebrows shot up. "Well, lads. Give me a hand with these fish, and I'll tell you what I can."

Aodhan plucked the creel from the water and began trudging alongside the steam. For all his age—I'd guess him to be at least seventy—he moved with alacrity. Beneath the hem of his plain, rough-spun brown tunic, the calves of his bare legs were knotted like oak.

We followed him to his home, if one could call it that. The *ollamh* lived in a cave, albeit a dry and cozy one, fragrant with the odor of dozens of herb bundles that hung drying from the walls. They were everywhere, tied with leather thongs to outcroppings and promontories.

In front of the cave, the ground had been swept clean and leveled. A slender wisp of smoke arose from the ashes of a neatly laid firepit.

"I expect you remember how to clean a fish." Aodhan handed Conor the dripping creel. "Mayhap you can give your fair D'Angeline friend a lesson while I stoke the fire."

"I know how to clean a fish," I said.

"Indeed!" His eyes twinkled. "This is a day of surprises."

There were five trout in the creel. Conor and I ventured a few yards downstream and made quick work of gutting and cleaning them. By the time we finished, Aodhan had a skillet heating over a brisk fire.

"Nice work, lads." He popped the fish into the skillet, where they began to sputter and sizzle. "So, tell me about this binding." For the second time that day, I related the story. Like the Lady Grainne, the *ollamh* asked what Morwen had bound me with. When I told him, he snorted. "That was careless."

I rolled my eyes. "Yes, so I'm told."

"Ah, but how were you to know, eh? Still, a young man like yourself, newly wed . . . you're meant to be getting heirs on your bride, lad, not spilling your seed on barren soil!" Aodhan studied me, then turned his attention to the fish, reaching out to flip them with his bare fingers, heedless of the heat. Bits of fish-skin stuck to the hot skillet. "Desire," he mused. "Harboring a secret one, are you?"

I didn't answer.

Aodhan nodded to himself. "That'll give the binding power, all right."

"Can it be broken?" Conor asked.

"No." The *ollamh* prodded at the nearest fish with one horny thumbnail, testing its doneness. "Not without the mannekin, I fear." He glanced up at me. "You might bargain for it, or her Ladyship might. The Old Ones do love a bargain."

"Such as . . . ?" I asked.

"Well, there's *uisghe*." Aodhan grinned. "They're partial to strong spirits, they are. Or you could give them what they want and go home, which is a bargain they're more like to accept."

I watched him pluck the fish deftly from the skillet and pile them on a wooden platter. "Is that your counsel?"

"Don't know just yet." He proffered the platter. "Tell me why you're here, lad." Freeing one hand, he rapped his knuckles on the hard-packed earth. "Here in Alba."

"The succession—" I began.

"No, no!" Aodhan waved his free hand dismissively. "I know all about the politics. Even hermits have ears. Why are *you* here?"

I took a piece of fish from the platter, juggling it from hand to hand. It was hot. Conor and the *ollamh* began to eat, picking flaky white flesh from the bones. "Because I believed it was the right thing to do," I said slowly. "Because I'd given my word. Because I thought mayhap dedicating my life to ensuring a peaceful succession for Alba and Terre d'Ange was a way to atone for my mother's sins." I glanced at Conor. "It's a long story."

"Could you learn to love it here?" Aodhan pointed. "And mind, eat your fish, lad. 'Tis best when it's hot."

I obeyed, thinking. "Yes," I said at length, swallowing. "Alba's very beautiful."

"You D'Angelines and your beauty." Aodhan snorted, but I thought he was pleased with my answer nonetheless. He shoved another hunk of fish into his mouth, his braided beard waggling as he chewed. "Will you stay?"

I met his shrewd gaze. "I don't know."

"Well." He nodded. "An honest answer. Eat, and I'll give you mine." He reached out and tapped a startled Conor in the center of his forehead. "And *you* mind, lad! Everything you hear today is under the *ollamh's* seal of discretion. Breach it, and you'll be sorry."

"Yes, Master Aodhan," he murmured.

We finished eating and washed our hands in the cool stream. Aodhan cleared his throat. "Here's my thinking, young Imriel. You seem to have the makings of a good man in you, and Alba owes you a chance to prove it; aye, even old Alba. There's naught I can do to break the binding, but there are protections I can lay over you if you're willing."

"Will I be safe, then?" I asked.

"Safe!" Another snort. "Nothing's *safe*. But it will render the binding harmless so long as the protections are maintained. The rest is up to you." He studied me. "Mind you, it comes at a price, and that's whatever this great passion is with which the witch bound you."

My heart gave a sudden leap of anguish. "Forever?"

"No, lad." There was a note of sympathy in the *ollamh's* voice. "Only for so long as you wear my charm. I cannot change your heart. Underneath, you'll be the same. But whatever desire drove you to spill the seed that's in the witch's keeping . . ." He shrugged. "Waking or sleeping, you'll no longer feel it."

"And this Morwen won't be able to summon me with it?" I asked.

Aodhan nodded. "Even so."

I twisted Sidonie's ring on my finger, then made myself stop, pushing away all thoughts of her. Mayhap it would be for the best. I took a deep breath and gathered my courage. "All right. If you're willing, I'd be grateful."

He wiped his damp hands on his tunic. "Let's be about it, then."

After our homely luncheon, it was strange to see Aodhan perform a formal ritual. He ducked into his cave several times, emerging with an array of items. The skillet was banished from the vicinity of the fire, which was stoked anew with branches of rowan and birch. He cast a handful of herbs on the flames, and a pungent smoke arose, smelling of camphor.

"Pennyroyal," Aodhan said briefly. "Take off your boots and stand over there, lad."

Once again, I obeyed.

I stood barefoot on the hard-packed earth while Aodhan drew a circle around me with a broom made of hazel twigs, then fetched a pouch full of salt and retraced his steps in the opposite direction, sprinkling salt along the circle. Sunlight filtered through the trees that lined the stream, shining on his bald brown pate. I felt foolish, but Conor watched with grave eyes.

The *ollamh* began to chant.

"The charm of Brigid ward thee; the charm of Danu save thee; the charm of Manannan shield thee; the charm of Aengus defend thee."

His voice was deep and rolling and musical, and there was power in it. Any feeling of foolishness vanished. I felt the air shiver against my skin. The sunlight grew brighter and the tree-cast shadows darker and sharper. Aodhan circled me; once, twice, three times.

"To guard thee from thy back," he intoned, tying a length of red yarn first around my right wrist, then around my left. *"To preserve thee from thy front. From the crown of thy head and forehead."* He stooped, tying a length of yarn around my right ankle. *"To the very sole of thy foot."* He secured the last piece of yarn around my left ankle.

I stood without moving as he rose and knotted a leather thong around my neck.

"From all who seek to bind thee, be thou protected!"

His final words tolled like bell. Aodhan clapped his hands together, the sound so loud I jumped a little.

And I felt . . . different. Not bad, not good. A little numb. There was a quick pang of loss, but it was distant and far away. Somewhat had changed, somewhat had shifted. It was as though a thick wall had sprung to life inside me; dividing me against myself, protecting me from myself. Behind it, I felt calm and peaceful.

He grinned at me. "Well, that's that, young Imriel. How do you feel?"

"All right," I said. "I'm not sure. Is that bad?"

"No, no." He shook his head. "Mind, you'll have to keep it up. If any of the threads fray, they'll need to be replaced by an *ollamh*. I reckon even a court bard can manage one of the old spells." He tapped whatever it was that hung at my throat, strung on the leather thong. "That's a croonie-stone. Don't take it off."

"All right." I fingered it. A smooth stone, a hole in the center. Once again, a seal of protection hung around my neck; this one wrought by nature. At least this time I knew it was there, and why. "Is there aught else I should know?"

"Well, you might consider bargaining with the Old Ones. It's always worth a try." Aodhan took up the hazel-twig broom and busied himself with sweeping away the traces of his circle. He snorted. "And you might have a greater care where you spill your seed. Now get out of my way, will you?"

I moved. "How can I repay you for this, my lord?"

Aodhan glanced at me, then at Conor, sitting quiet and watchful. "The lad knows."

I remembered what Conor had said about the Path of the Grove. "You want him to study with you."

"The old ways, aye." Aodhan swept briskly. "It's in his blood."

I looked from one to the other, marking a similarity in their brown skin, in the angle of their broad, high cheekbones, that transcended the disparity of age. Not Cruithne, not Dalriada. Other. I'd seen it last night by moonlight. "And yours?"

He smiled and didn't answer. "Go on, now! You've bothered me long enough."

We went.

TWENTY-TWO

A T DINNER THAT NIGHT, I steeled myself and told the tale for a third time.

If I could have avoided it, I would have. But there was no way of explaining the lengths of red yarn knotted around my wrists, the pierced, sea-polished stone hanging at my throat. So I told it, leaving out the bit about the mannekin and spilled seed, and any mention of Conor's parentage. We'd agreed, he and I, to keep one another's secrets.

"Dagda Mor, Imri!" Eamonn exclaimed. "How do you manage to find trouble wherever you go?"

I smiled grimly. "Just lucky, I reckon."

Joscelin looked thunderous. "This is not acceptable," he said quietly to Grainne, his tone all the more fearsome for its calm. "What do you mean to do about it?"

"*Joscelin.*" His name emerged more sharply than I'd intended. I sighed. "I'm sorry. But I am not . . . without blame . . . in the matter. And Alban law is clear. As I am unharmed, there is little recourse." I raised my hands, displaying my yarn fetters. "Her Ladyship has provided good counsel nonetheless."

"If anything happens to you—" he began.

"It won't." Conor, flushing, spoke up. "Master Aodhan is very wise."

"Still," Phèdre murmured. "I am troubled." Her dark gaze rested on me, seeing things no one else saw. The scarlet mote of Kushiel's Dart floated on her left iris, a promise of things that never would be. It didn't seem to bother me as it used to. "What will you, love?"

I set my jaw. "I'll not flee, if that's what you mean."

Beneath the table, Dorelei's hand groped for mine, finding it and clutching hard. I squeezed back, stealing a glance at her lowered profile.

"You are content, then?" Phèdre asked softly. "To let matters stand?"

"I am, for the most part." I took a deep breath. "The *ollamh* said Alba owed me a chance to prove I was a good man. I mean to take it." I turned to Grainne. "My lady, Aodhan also said that the Old Ones love a bargain. How might such a thing be accomplished?"

"Chance and luck, usually," the Lady of the Dalriada said wryly. "Encounters with the Old Ones are subject to their whims. Still, Morwen has insulted my hospitality, and I am nothing loath to bargain on such a basis."

"How do we reach them?" I asked. "I don't suppose they've fixed lodgings."

She looked at Conor and didn't answer.

Conor looked at the table. "He taught me a song to summon him if I had need," he whispered. "The harpist."

"What harpist?" Mairead asked.

His skinny throat worked. "A . . . a man I met. One of them."

"One of the Old Ones!" His sister punched his shoulder. "Why didn't you tell us?"

Brennan gave his mother an odd look. "I remember a harpist."

"So do I." Eamonn frowned. "At least, I think I do."

"Should I summon him?" Conor asked the Lady, lifting his head.

"The choice is yours," Grainne said gently.

He sat for a time without moving, then rose from the dinner table and fetched his harp. Without a word, Conor unbarred the door to the hall and walked out into the soft blue twilight. A moment later, we heard the first notes arising; a wild, mischievous flurry that softened into a plaintive, teasing air. The Lady's other children stared at one another, openmouthed.

"His father was one of *them*?" Eamonn asked, dumbstruck.

"Ah, well." Grainne smiled. "And who are you to stare, my wandering son, with your Skaldic bride? He's like to keep the old ways, even as you bring the new. 'Tis a fine balance."

"Eamonn." Brigitta laid a hand on his arm, a look of profound bewilderment on her face. "Will you explain all of this to me later? Slowly? In Caerdicci?"

"I'll try," he said, sounding none too sure.

Outside the hall, the music continued. I got up from the table and stood outside the door to listen. One by one, the others followed. We all stood together, watching and listening.

Conor was a solitary figure, vague in the dim light. He looked small and lonely, head bowed over the harp he held. But his fingers danced on the strings, and the notes rang out, clear and carrying, over the distant green hills. The last note fell with a sustained, dying echo. When he turned around and walked back to us, his dark eyes were shining.

"How did you know?" he asked his mother.

"Oh, he tried to teach me, too." She smiled again. "Only I never learned to play the harp. We'll see what happens, shall we?"

After that, it seemed there was little to say; or mayhap what there was to say was too big for words. We made for a quiet and thoughtful lot. As the evening wore on, it became apparent that Conor's father was not going to manifest immediately. Joscelin excused himself early, and Phèdre went with him.

I knew he was unhappy with what had transpired, and I didn't blame him. I was none too pleased with it myself. Still, I thought I'd done the best I could, under the circumstances. Morwen was right, Blessed Elua had no place here; not yet, anyway. But mayhap if I could come to love Alba, that would change.

In bed that night, Dorelei examined the charms of protection the *ollamh* had placed on me; the red yarn, the croonie-stone.

"My D'Angeline prince," she murmured. "Who would have thought?"

"You've been quiet through all this," I observed.

She toyed with the croonie-stone. "It scares me."

"What part of it?" I asked gently.

"All of it." Dorelei raised her eyes to mine. "Tell me, was she beautiful?"

"Morwen?" I shook my head. "No."

"And yet she bound you so easily." She wound a lock of my hair around her fingers. "They *are* dangerous, you know. The Maghuin Dhonn. They're wild and unpredictable, and one can never be sure what they want. It's funny." She gave a faint smile. "If I lost you to . . . your D'Angeline, whoever she is . . . at least I'd understand. You love her. This, this is just malice."

"Dorelei." I caught her hand and laid it flat on my chest. "Look at me, wrapped all around in the *ollamh*'s charms. I'm not going anywhere."

"I'm glad," she said simply. "Imriel, when this is over, can we leave? I like Eamonn very much, truly, and all his family. But I miss my own."

"Shall we return to Bryn Gorrydum?" I asked. "Or take up residence at Clunderry?"

"We don't have to do either, yet." Dorelei laid her head on my shoulder, and I shifted to accommodate her weight, sliding my arm around her. "We could go to Master Hyacinthe's Stormkeep with Phèdre and Joscelin."

I stroked her hair. "Well, it's like to be the safest place in all of Alba, that's for sure."

"True." She smiled drowsily against my shoulder. "And mayhap my aunt Sibeal will know why my dreams have been silent since we wed."

To that, I had no reply.

I held her close with one arm and continued stroking her hair, humming softly, until I felt her body slacken in sleep, her breathing deepening. And somewhere along the way, I fell asleep myself; a deep, dreamless sleep, unhaunted by the sound of pipes or a woman's laughter.

On the morrow, the day dawned bright and clear, and seemingly free of harpists. I arose feeling more refreshed by my night's sleep than I'd felt in ages. Before I dressed, I sat on the edge of the bed, feeling for the croonie-stone at my throat and checking my wrists and ankles, making sure the bits of red yarn were securely knotted.

Dorelei watched me with a dimpled smile. "You're like a parcel I can't unwrap."

"Consider it mere adornment," I suggested.

Her smile deepened. "All right."

We made love, laughing and hushing one another when the sounds from the great hall intruded. Innisclan was not built for privacy. I thought about what Aodhan had said, and understood for the first time that learning to love Alba and learning to love Dorelei were one and the same.

I didn't think of Sidonie.

For the first time, she seemed far, far away. On the far side of the Straits that divided our lands, on the far side of the charms of protection that bound me. I had given myself over to Alba, and Aodhan rendered me proof against my own innermost desire. Even the dark surge of Kushiel's bloodline seemed far away, tied to my feelings for Sidonie.

"That was nice," Dorelei murmured.

I made a sound of agreement deep in my throat.

"Do you think we made a child?" She rolled over in the narrow bed, lacing my fingers in hers and laying my hand on her belly. "I'd like to."

"Would you?" I squirmed downward to plant a kiss on the soft brown flesh below her navel. "Well, then. I reckon we should keep trying."

"*Imriel . . .*" She breathed my name.

I spread her thighs and plied her with my tongue until she shuddered and writhed and tugged at my hair. She tasted of the sea and smelled of fresh-baked bread. I slithered up her body, my wrists and ankles bound with red yarn. I entered her, the croonie-stone hanging between us as I hovered above her on propped arms.

"Now," Dorelei whispered. "Now!"

I arched my back and spent my seed in her, obedient.

Her face was soft with pleasure. "That was nice," she said, echoing her own words.

"Indeed." I kissed my wife. "We should get up. I promised Eamonn I'd make an offering at his uncle's burial mound."

The household of Innisclan was still in a subdued mood, digesting the news of Conor's paternity and waiting in an apprehensive hush to see what would come of his summons. At Dorelei's suggestion, we paid a visit to the encampment where our men were idling to warn Urist that one of the Maghuin Dhonn might be approaching.

He spat on the ground and made a gesture to avert evil. "By the Boar! What did you go and do *that* for?"

"There'll be no trouble on the Lady's grounds," I said firmly. "Not from this quarter."

Urist eyed me dourly, jerking his chin toward the bindings of red yarn around my wrists. "There already has been by the look of you."

"Just promise me you'll offer no offense," Dorelei pleaded.

He folded his arms. "I do. Unless he gives cause."

With that, we had to be content. Afterward, we visited the mound where Eamonn's uncle was buried. It was a simple grass-covered dome ringed round the base with a wall of stones. I was surprised to find there were no markers, nothing more elaborate.

"Why would it be needful?" Eamonn asked. "We know where he is."

We climbed the gentle slope to the apex, where his uncle's head was entombed, facing toward the east where he'd fought the battle in which he died, far away across the Straits. Bringing forth a silver flask, Eamonn poured a libation of *uisghe* onto the ground. He handed it around and we all followed suit. Dorelei looked grave as a priestess, the amber liquid sparkling as she poured. Brigitta closed her eyes when her turn came, her lips moving in a silent prayer. It must be passing strange for her, I thought. For all any of us knew, it was one of her own kinsman had slain him.

When it was done, Eamonn sighed. "Rest easy in the Fair Lands, Uncle! May your spirit guard and protect us."

"Do you think he is pleased?" Brigitta asked.

"I do." Eamonn smiled at her. "If I could not bring him the heads of his enemies, at least I've conquered Skaldia in a different way."

Brigitta made to strike him with her open palm and he dodged, laughing. They chased one another down the side of the burial mound. Below, in the open meadow, Eamonn caught her about the waist and bore her to the ground. Brigitta landed atop him. She thumped his chest with the heel of his hand, then kissed him. They made a pretty picture, entwined amid the buttercup and clover blossoming in the meadow. I felt a pang of envy, but it was distant and muted.

"What are you thinking?" Dorelei asked curiously.

"I'm thinking his uncle wouldn't have minded," I said, taking her hand. "And that peace is a good deal more pleasant than war."

The balance of the day passed uneventfully. Joscelin was engaged in helping Eamonn draft plans for his academy, but I spoke to Phèdre about accompanying them to visit Hyacinthe, explaining Dorelei's longing to see her own family, and she agreed readily.

"Poor child, I don't blame her. This must not be easy on her." Phèdre studied me. "What of you?"

I shrugged. "I'm fine."

"You seem . . ." She drew her brows together in consternation, at a rare loss for words. "I don't know, love. You're taking this very calmly."

I thought about it. "Do you remember what Joscelin said after we left Saba? When I was upset because you looked the way you did in Daršanga?" Phèdre shook her head. "It was later that night, when you thought I was asleep. You asked if it bothered him. He said you walking around with the Name of God in your head was just one more damned thing to get used to."

"Elua!" She gave a startled laugh. "I'd forgotten that."

"Well, that's how I feel." I touched the croonie-stone. "The Maghuin Dhonn, this . . . it's just all one more damned thing to get used to." I glanced toward the east, toward the distant Straits and faraway Terre d'Ange. "In a way, they may have done me a favor. You see, whatever it is that the *ollamh* did, I'm protected from my own desires." I lowered my voice. "Or at least my feelings for Sidonie."

Phèdre was silent for a long moment. "I'm not so sure that's a good thing."

"No?" I shrugged again. "Neither am I. But at the moment, I don't have a great deal of choice. So if a curse turns out to carry an unexpected blessing, I may as well enjoy it."

We might have spoken further, but at that moment Mairead and Caolinn appeared. Like Joscelin, I'd kept up the practice of telling the hours on our journey, much to the bemusement of our Alban escort. The Lady's children had heard tales of our peculiar discipline and the Cassiline fighting-style and had come to beg me to importune Joscelin for a joint demonstration.

So I went to fetch him and he agreed, albeit with grumbling. Before supper was served, we put on a good show for them in the yard before the hall, in large part because Joscelin began to press me a good deal harder than was his wont. Having left our wood practice-blades in Terre d'Ange, we were sparring with real steel, his daggers against my sword. We'd done it before, but Joscelin was usually more careful.

"Are you angry at me?" I asked, using the sword's reach to keep him at bay.

Joscelin sidled around, forcing me to turn so that the light of the lowering sun was in my eyes. "Angry, yes. At you, no."

I squinted at his dark silhouette. "What would you have me do?"

He took an unexpected step, feinting low with his left-hand dagger. I parried awkwardly and cursed as his right-hand dagger descended, trapping my blade with the quillon. His left-hand dagger rose to prick the underside of my chin. "I'd have you be *careful*!"

A smattering of cheers and applause arose. Joscelin stepped back and gave his Cassiline bow. I sighed and sheathed my sword.

"Well done, indeed!" a strange, melodious voice said. "An art worthy of song."

I turned slowly, the hair on the back of my neck prickling.

"Dagda Mor!" someone whispered.

The harpist stood on the far side of the yard, arms spread to show he bore no weapons, only his harp slung over his back in a leather case. He was a tall, rangy figure with strong, striking features, coarse black hair streaked with iron-grey.

"My lord Ferghus," Grainne emerged from the hall and inclined her head in greeting. "Be welcome to Innisclan."

"Lady Grainne." He smiled easily, showing white teeth. "My thanks."

Everyone in the yard was very quiet as the harpist Ferghus approached. Joscelin watched him warily, crossed daggers at the ready. Conor was there, his eyes wide with wonder and fearful apprehension. The harpist paused, laying a lean brown hand on his head.

"Well played, lad," he said.

"Thank you," Conor whispered.

Joscelin shifted when Ferghus drew near, blocking me. The harpist gave another easy smile, showing his empty palms. I touched Joscelin's arm and stepped out from behind him.

"So you're the one would be a Prince of Alba," the harpist said.

I offered my hand. "Imriel."

He took it. "Ferghus."

At close range, he didn't look dangerous; but he didn't look *safe*, either. There was a hint of something wild glinting in his black eyes, slanting the planes of his cheekbones. Like Morwen, the scent of forest loam and fermented berries clung to him. Untamed places, I thought. And though his jerkin and breeches were of roughspun brown cloth, he carried himself like a king.

"Will you dine with us, my lord?" Grainne asked calmly. "There's a matter I wish to discuss with you."

"Shall I sing for my supper?" he asked. "As in days of old?"

Her red-gold brows rose slightly. "If you wish."

Unexpectedly, Ferghus roared with laughter. "Ah, Grainne, Grainne! I've missed you, lass." He stepped toward her, touched her cheek with affection. "Too long, it's been." Something caught his eye. "Ah, and who's this?"

Grainne introduced Phèdre.

The harpist looked at her for a long, long moment. I couldn't see his face, but hers was unreadable. Joscelin and I exchanged a glance. In silent accord, we moved closer. But Ferghus offered no threat, only took a long breath.

"And so the harbingers of change are upon us once more," he said lightly. "With dancing blades and beauty to put the stars to shame. Twenty years ago, we failed to take heed, and the world turned upside down in your wake. What now, I wonder?"

"Is he always like this?" Phèdre asked Grainne.

The Lady of the Dalriada smiled. "More or less, yes."

The harpist loosed another unexpected peal of laughter. "Oh, indeed! Well played, fair lady, well played." He bowed to Grainne. "And to you, my lady, I accept your offer of hospitality. I would dine in your hall this evening."

So it was that Innisclan hosted a master bard of the Maghuin Dhonn. It was a strange, constrained meal. To be fair, Ferghus was an exemplary guest. He ate and drank with gusto, complimenting the fare. There was nothing obvious about him that was extraordinary. He didn't even have the woad facial markings that Morwen bore and that rendered the Cruithne exotic to a D'Angeline eye. And yet strangeness clung to him like a cloak. He brought a tang of wild places into the stone halls of Innisclan with him.

He was as different in his own way as *we* were.

D'Angelines.

The realization struck me at the table, as I glanced at Ferghus, at Phèdre and Joscelin. They, too, looked out of place there. I supposed I did, too.

"What a thing, eh?" The harpist caught my eye. "Earth's Oldest and Youngest dining at the same table."

"So you claim, my lord," Dorelei murmured.

"Little sister of the Cullach Gorrym." His unblinking gaze fell on her. "Our blood flows in *your* veins, too." He splayed three fingers, touching his cheek below his right eye. "Where do you think your mother's line gets its gift?"

Dorelei turned pale, the woad dots that marked her own cheek standing out in contrast. "If it is true, it is also true that we never used it for ill."

"Will you give insult in the Lady's own household?" Ferghus smiled his easy smile. "Ah, now! That's no way to bargain for your prince's freedom. Tell me, lass, do you love him? The pretty lad with the sea-blue eyes and another's name written on his heart?"

Her pallor turned to a violent flush.

"Ferghus . . ." Grainne began.

"You spoke of insult, my lord?" I interrupted, keeping my voice as light as his. "Then I do believe we are at quits, for you have just given insult to my lady wife." I smiled at him. "But mayhap we can mend our differences over a cup of *uisghe*, for there is the matter of another insult yet to be discussed."

He tapped the table with lean, restless fingers. "Morwen, is it?"

"You know perfectly well it is," Grainne said to him.

Ferghus eyed her sidelong. "Fetch the *uisghe*, then. I've a fancy to play a tune first."

She nodded at Conor and Caolinn, who ran to fetch a jug of *uisghe* and a tray of earthenware cups. Brennan poured while Ferghus removed his harp from its case and checked the tuning with loving care. The harp looked old, the wood smooth and polished through long handling. It was a simple, unadorned instrument, but the sweeping lines were wrought with exquisite beauty.

The harpist tossed back his cup of *uisghe*, so quickly my throat burned in sympathy. He closed his eyes and smacked his lips, then held his cup out to be refilled. He drank half of that, then settled the harp on his lap.

"Listen," he said to us, and began to play.

To describe perfection is an impossible thing. Ferghus played the harp the way a swallow takes wing, effortless and graceful. The first notes brought tears to my eyes. His playing was so beautiful, it made me want to laugh and weep all at once. My heart ached within my breast, pierced by the sheer loveliness of it.

And then he began to sing.

He sang well, although no better than any number of musicians I'd heard in the Queen's salon. It was his harping that uplifted the song and made it soar. It was so beautiful, it was hard to concentrate on the verses he sang. It was some long minutes before I realized I recognized the tale he was telling, or at least some version of it.

It was a story of the Maghuin Dhonn, and how they had suffered under the yoke of Tiberium. How they had tried to accommodate them, to assimilate them, as they had accommodated the folk of the Cullach Gorrym, the Tarbh Cró, the Eidlach Òr, and the Fhalair Bàn.

How they had failed.

How their people had sickened and died as the army of Tiberium occupied the land, taming it with stone roads, bringing strange diseases from faraway places. How they had dwindled and fled to the wild places, the last bastion left to them.

How they had prayed to their untamed gods and goddesses and to the Maghuin Dhonn herself, their *diadh-anam*, the lodestone of their existence. How the greatest magician among them, mighty Donnchadh, fasted and prayed. How he had drunk the sacred broth and gone alone to the Place of the Gates, and beheld a vision of the future.

How mighty Donnchadh had seen how it might be averted through great sacrifice, and how he had transformed himself into a living incarnation of the Maghuin Dhonn, the mighty Brown Bear. How he had suffered himself to be sold into captivity and tormented for sport, until in his wrath he tore loose the stakes that bound him, and slew the Tiberian Governor of Alba.

How he had lost his humanity and saved his people

The song ended, the last notes fading into a profound silence. Ferghus sat with head bowed, his cheek leaned against the uppermost curve of his harp. I thought about his song, weighing it against the account of the Tiberian historian Caledonius, and the tale Drustan mab Necthana had told me about a bear-cub raised on human flesh by a maddened magician of the Maghuin Dhonn.

I did not know where the truth lay.

"My lord, you play most beautifully." It was Phèdre's voice that broke the silence. Ferghus lifted his head and gazed at her. "And yet I am confused by your story."

"How so?" he asked.

Phèdre rested her chin on her fist, contemplating him with lustrous eyes. "'Twas Cinhil Ru of the Cruithne who united the tribes of Alba and drove the Tiberians from your soil. How is it, then, that the Maghuin Dhonn claim the credit?"

"Magic is a deep thing, lady, and the ways of gods are mysterious." Ferghus stroked the gleaming wood of his harp. "Cinhil Ru rallied the Four Folk of Alba by telling them false tales about bears fed on the flesh of babes. He told them the Maghuin Dhonn had gone mad, that the same fate would befall all of them if they did not stand together. And so they did." He showed his white teeth in a smile. "And afterward, once the Tiberians were gone, there came the Master of the Straits. For many, many years, Alba was protected."

"Now that, surely, had naught to do with the Maghuin Dhonn," I said.

He turned his smile on me. It looked friendly, but the appearance was belied by the restless glitter of his eyes. "Who can say? All things are bound to one another, though the bindings are hidden to the eye. I am a skilled bard, but a poor magician."

"Speaking of bindings . . ." I tapped the croonie-stone.

"Ah, yes." Ferghus set down his harp with care and drank the rest of the *uisghe* in his cup. "'Twas wrought in fairness, Morwen's binding, on *taisgaidh* ground. Yet you claim insult for the lad's carelessness?" he asked Grainne.

"I do," she said. "It matters not where the charm was wrought. He was summoned against his will while he was a guest in my household. Will you have the world claim the Lady of the Dalriada cannot protect an honored guest in her own hall?" Grainne shook her head. "Indeed, I claim insult. But I am willing to forgive it in exchange for the mannekin trinket."

Ferghus looked longingly at the *uisghe* jug. "Is that the whole of your offer?"

"Would you have me sweeten it?" She laughed. "Fine, take the jug."

"I will." He reached across the table, snatching it agilely and setting it before him, then rose. After replacing his harp in its leather case, he slung the case over his shoulder. "I will take your offer to Morwen, and to Berlik, too. He will want a say in the matter." His voice changed. "Tell me, Grainne. What if they refuse? Will you break our long truce?"

His words hung in the air. Everyone looked to Grainne, who frowned. "So long as the lad is unharmed, I will not break our truce," she said slowly. "But so long as he is bound, the Old Ones will be unwelcome in my holdings."

"Ah, lady!" Ferghus' gaze lingered on Conor. "'Tis a hard answer."

Grainne nodded. "'Tis a hard question."

"So be it." The harpist plucked the *uisghe* jug from the table. "I'll return ere too many days have passed."

With that, he took his leave.

TWENTY-THREE

In the days following the harpist's visit, we spoke of little else.

I tried not to engage in the speculation, for I could see it troubled Conor, and I felt for the boy. He took to absenting himself to pay long visits to the *ollamh* Aodhan, which I thought was to the good. The *ollamh* had a foot in both worlds, and he would give the boy good counsel.

For my part, I was curious about the disparity between the history Drustan had related and the harpist's tale. I asked Dorelei for her thoughts, but she was reluctant to discuss it.

"Can you not leave it be, Imriel?" she pleaded. "You've been told it's ill luck to speak of them. Do you not believe it yet?"

I ran a finger beneath the strand of red yarn tied around my left wrist. "I only want to know the truth."

"Your *wants* are dangerous things," Dorelei muttered.

I gave her a hard look. "You've had no cause to complain of them lately."

It was the first time we'd quarrelled; or come near to it, anyway. Like Conor, I decided it would be best if I absented myself for a time. I saddled the Bastard and rode to the seashore, where I spent the better part of an afternoon reading the book of love letters Sidonie had given me.

Aside from pity for the plight of Remuel L'Oragen and Claire LeDoux of Namarre, I found myself unmoved. It was an unnerving sensation. I sat on a boulder and stared at the sunlight sparkling on the waves, trying to recapture the feelings I'd struggled so hard to suppress.

I couldn't do it.

They were still there. Of that, I was sure. Aodhan hadn't lied. I could sense them, in the same way I'd been aware of my own helpless will the night Morwen had summoned me. But I could no longer feel them.

I'd thought myself glad of it until I'd tried. Now I was no longer sure. I tugged at the croonie-stone, wondering what would happen if I removed it. And then I thought about that night. *Come here*, Morwen had said, and I'd gone, obedient as a lamb to slaughter.

"Blessed Elua," I murmured. "What will you?"

There was no answer, save from the Bastard, hobbled nearby. He lifted his speckled head and snorted, gazing at me with incurious eyes. So I sighed, untied his hobbles, and rode back to Innisclan.

By the time I arrived, I'd nearly forgotten the harsh words Dorelei and I had exchanged. Seeing her, I remembered and made an apology. She accepted it with a smile and tendered an apology of her own, and the matter was forgotten.

So instead I spoke to Phèdre regarding the Maghuin Dhonn, asking her which version of their history she believed true, Drustan's or Ferghus'.

"Like as not, the truth lies somewhere in between." She was quiet for a moment. "Do you believe the tales of shapeshifting?"

I thought about Morwen. "Mayhap."

"Caledonius wrote that when they skinned the bear, they found a human body beneath its pelt," Phèdre observed. "I don't know, love. It may be that what Ferghus said was true, that it was powerful magic at work. And it may be that Drustan said was true, and the Maghuin Dhonn succumbed to madness nonetheless." She smiled, but it didn't reach her eyes. "One truth does not discount the other."

"No," I agreed. "It doesn't."

We were both silent then, remembering Daršanga, where dark magics were at work and madness held sway. Where I had been enslaved through a quirk of unhappy fate. Where Phèdre and Joscelin had rescued me, and averted a great evil.

"All things are bound to one another," Phèdre mused. "Though the bindings be hidden to the eye. 'Tis an interesting notion."

"The harpist was an interesting fellow," I said wryly.

She laughed. "Grainne thinks so."

"The Lady Grainne has . . . interesting . . . tastes." I eyed her. "You haven't . . . ?"

"No, no." Phèdre looked amused. "That was a long time ago. She was merely curious, I think."

"What of Hyacinthe?" I asked.

"Hyacinthe." Her expression warmed when she said his name. "I'll tell you one thing. I'll be glad when we're safe under his aegis."

It wasn't exactly an answer, but it wasn't exactly my concern, either. Once, not long ago, it would have bothered me. Now the sharp edges of my jealousy seemed worn away. Some of it, I thought, was maturity. I'd grown and changed a great deal in the past year, and I'd even learned somewhat of what it meant to be in love.

But some of it wasn't. Some of it was due to the muting of my own desire.

Later, I tested the notion, forcing myself to envision somewhat that should have tormented me: Maslin de Lombelon in Sidonie's bed.

It gave me a distant pang. Somewhere, on the far side of the *ollamh's* protections, I knew it hurt. I knew it provoked irrational jealousy, bitter and hateful. But I didn't feel it, except as a vague irritation; a response, mayhap, to somewhat I'd read in a book or heard in a friend's tale. To be honest, I was in two minds as to whether I *wanted* to feel it. Mayhap what I'd said was true and this curse was an unexpected blessing after all. To be sure, it made my life with Dorelei easier to bear. We'd exchanged words, yes, but even that wasn't entirely a bad thing. It was a sign that the relationship between us was growing real. We were no longer walking on eggshells around one another, fearful of giving offense.

And Sidonie . . .

Ah, Elua! We hadn't been sure, either of us, that our feelings would last. Mayhap it was for the best if mine withered and died, smothered under a blanket of Alban sorcery. Mayhap my feelings for Dorelei would grow into the kind of passion for which I yearned.

So I told myself, anyway.

In the meanwhile, we continued to enjoy the hospitality of the Lady of the Dalriada, awaiting a response from the Old Ones. Several days passed. Eamonn and Joscelin were engaged in plans for the academy and library—like all Siovalese, Joscelin had a keen interest in architecture. Our bored escort of D'Angeline and Cruithne soldiers were pressed into service, digging trenches to lay the foundations for the library. Phèdre and Brigitta were content to explore the treasure trove of books we'd brought, having conceived an unlikely friendship on the course of our journey here.

And I, I spent a good deal of time with Dorelei.

By day, we rode for pleasure and for sport, hunting and shooting for the pot. She taught me to use the Cruithne short bow and we made a game of it, trying to outdo one another. Betimes, some of the Lady's children accompanied us; at other times, we ventured out alone. We grew easy with one another.

By night, we spun out our evenings with long meals in the hall of Innisclan, telling stories or playing music afterward. The Lady's clan was a high-spirited lot, and if there was any strangeness in the way they treated Conor, it soon passed. The protection the *ollamh* had placed on me held. When we retired to bed, there were no pipes, no laughter, no mysterious tug on my will. Indeed, save for the yarn fetters and the croonie-stone, my life held a semblance of normalcy.

And then the Maghuin Dhonn returned.

As with the harpist's visit, they appeared as the sun was growing low in the west, shortly after we'd sat down to dine. This time, we were alerted by shouts from our escort's encampment, sending us hurrying outside into the yard to see what transpired.

There were three of them. They came from the north, pacing unhurriedly over the green hills, their long shadows pointing eastward toward Terre d'Ange. I felt my heart stir within me as they drew near, filled with a mix of hope and uncertainty.

Urist's men turned out, wary and watchful, forming a double cordon through which the Maghuin Dhonn must pass. The Old Ones ignored them. I could smell their scent on the evening breeze, musk and loam and berries. The air felt dense and heavy with it.

Two of them, I knew; the harpist Ferghus and the woman Morwen. I didn't know the third. A man, a big man, half a head taller than the harpist. Like Morwen, he had eyes as pale as mist, framed by raking woad claws. Berlik, I guessed; both had mentioned the name. Although the evening was warm, he wore a bearskin robe, rendering him even bulkier.

In the yard, Grainne stepped forward, Brennan at her side. The rest of us arrayed ourselves cautiously. Dorelei moved closer to me, and Joscelin's hands rested on his dagger-hilts.

"Lady." The big man greeted Grainne. His voice was deep and husky. I couldn't place his age, but he had the most somber, sorrow-laden face I'd ever seen.

Grainne inclined her head. "My lord Berlik."

"I have heard your offer," he slowly. "For six days, I have fasted and prayed. Some glimpses of what will be have been afforded me. Others have been denied." Berlik turned his head and his strange, pale gaze rested on me, palpable as a touch. The woad-marked flesh below his eyes sagged with weariness. He turned back to Grainne. "The trinket belongs to Morwen, and she will not be swayed. The offer is refused."

Someone drew a sharp breath. I swallowed hard against a intense surge of disappointment, mingled with a tinge of treacherous relief. Glancing at the woman Morwen, I saw no triumph in her face, only a strange, careful gravity. The leather bag that had hung around her throat before was missing.

"Do you deny the insult?" Grainne asked.

"I do not." Berlik shook his head, stirring shaggy black locks. "I bear an offer in turn. Do you forgive the insult, I will swear that no member of the Maghuin Dhonn will harm so much as a hair on the lad's head, anywhere on the length and breadth of Alba's soil."

Grainne was silent a moment. "By what oath?"

"By stone and sea and sky," he murmured, "and all that they encompass. By the sacred troth that binds me to my *diadh-anam*."

"And the Maghuin Dhonn have so consented?" she asked the other two.

"We have, Grainne," Ferghus said. All the lightness had fled his voice. "Not a hair on his head, not a scratch on his skin. Not by any means."

"I don't understand." Grainne took a step closer to them, searching their faces, and Morwen's last of all. "Why? If you mean Imriel no harm, why not surrender the trinket?"

"I cannot." Morwen looked small and diminutive before the Lady of the Dalriada, but she raised her chin to meet the Lady's eyes, steady and uncowed. "It is *he* who means us harm. This may be our sole protection against it."

"What?" I raised my voice in protest, pricked by the comment. "I intend nothing of the kind! Or at least I damnably well wouldn't if you'd leave me be."

Morwen fixed me with her moon-pale gaze. "You do not know what will come to pass."

"This is absurd," Joscelin said flatly. "Lady, I do not mean to gainsay your rule, but—"

"Ah, no!" The harpist Ferghus raised a warning hand. "Do not think it, warrior. We are three and unarmed, but we are not powerless." There was an edge to his easy smile. "You would buy our lives at certain cost. Meanwhile, the trinket lies elsewhere, hidden. You do not know who will claim it if we fall. Be wise, and accept our oath."

"Prince Imriel," Grainne said. "What will you?"

Dorelei's fingers dug into my elbow, but there was no guidance in her grip, only fear. I frowned and looked at Berlik. He stood patient and unmoving, his massive head bowed a little. I pried Dorelei's fingers loose from my arm and walked forward to confront him. Beneath his shadow, the scent of loam and berries was stronger, mingled with the rank odor of his bearskin robe. I had to crane my neck to see his sad, heavy face.

"What she said is a lie," I said to him.

"No." There was sorrow in his pale, shadowed eyes. "It may or not be many things, but it is not a lie."

"A riddle?" I asked.

Berlik shrugged. "Truth is a riddle."

I touched my sword-hilt. "Your kinswoman has somewhat I might claim as my own. What if I offered challege for it? Would you answer for her?"

His voice dropped to a low rumble, so low no one else could hear it. "Look down."

I glanced down. The sleeves of his bearskin robe ended in shaggy paws, fierce black claws protruding slightly. Berlik's vast shoulders shifted. The claws flexed and curved. I looked back up at him.

"You do not wish to do that," he said in the same low voice.

"Nor do I wish to be bound, my lord," I said.

"Things are not always what they seem." Raising one hand—if that was what it was—Berlik touched the croonie-stone at my throat. A single claw clicked against polished stone. "Accept our oath. You may be grateful for it."

There was no lie in his eyes, only sadness. Or madness? I couldn't tell. Strangely, I almost found myself drawn to him, or at least wishing to speak further with him. But he said nothing else, only watched me silently.

I sighed, stepping back from him. "So be it."

Grainne nodded. "Then swear, my lord Berlik."

The bearskin robe rippled as he raised his hands; a man's hands, large, but ordinary. At breast-height, he clasped his left hand into a fist, folding the other atop it. "By stone and sea and sky, and all that they encompass, I swear this. By the sacred troth that binds me to my *diadh-anam*, I swear this. Across the length and breadth of Alba, no man nor woman of the Maghuin Dhonn shall harm this man Imriel; not a hair on his head, not a scratch on his skin."

The words hung like thunder in the air. Somewhere in the distance, a flock of birds took flight, wheeling across the bloody sky. Cattle lowed uneasily.

Berlik inclined his head. "Do we have your forgiveness, Lady?"

"You do," Grainne said. "So long as your oath holds."

"I will not be forsworn." He smiled, awful and grim. " 'Twould be a dreadful fate."

I wondered what he meant. I wished he would stay and speak further with me. Unlike the others, I sensed no mischief in him. I wanted to know why he looked so sad and weary, what burden bowed his shoulders. I wanted to know why they believed I meant to harm them. It seemed unreasonable. If I bore them ill will, surely, they must see it was due to their own actions. It was all so very strange, I wasn't even sure what I felt. If we could only talk in a reasoned way, mayhap all this could be resolved.

But instead, there came low notes drawn from a harp's strings; a sweet, yearning air. The tune Morwen had played on the pipes, the charmed tune that had haunted my dreams, was even more poignant in the harpist's hands. I'd not even seen him remove his harp from its case, but there it was, braced beneath his chin, his lean brown fingers moving over the strings.

A strange, hushed peace settled over everyone present; the Lady and her children, Phèdre and Joscelin. Even Dorelei, even Brigitta; even Urist and the Cruithne and D'Angelines under his command, who stood aside, letting the Maghuin Dhonn pass.

I watched them go.

The music touched me; the charm didn't.

At the last moment, Morwen turned and gave me a long, impenetrable look. *Tell me, was she beautiful?* No, I'd said to Dorelei; I'd thought I meant it. Now I wasn't sure. There was beauty there, unfamiliar and wild.

I lifted one hand, gripping the croonie-stone.

Morwen smiled and passed.

And then they were gone, three figures moving into the deepening twilight. As they crested the distant rise, one remained upright. The harpist, still playing, the notes fading. Two figures dropped. One large and one small. Four-footed, shambling. My skin crawled. The fear I hadn't felt in their presence came home to roost.

"It's all right." A hand slid into mine. Conor, squeezing hard. "I think it is."

I squeezed back. "I hope you're right."

"So do I, Prince Imriel," he murmured. "So do I."

TWENTY-FOUR

WE DEPARTED FROM INNISCLAN two days later.

It was a bittersweet leavetaking. Our time spent with the Lady of the Dalriada and her children had been pleasant, but it had been strange and unnerving, too. Like Phèdre, I would be grateful for the security Hyacinthe's mantle of power afforded.

We said our farewells. Eamonn and Brigitta would be attending the Alban wedding ceremony held for Dorelei and me in Bryn Gorrydum in a little over a month's time, so that, at least, was a casual parting. Conor was hoping his mother would allow him to come, and promised to play his harp at our wedding if she permitted it.

As for the others, they sent us on our way with fond regrets, and mayhap the slightest bit of relief. I daresay Innisclan would be calmer for our departure.

Once again, we set forth on the *taisgaidh* paths under Urist's expert guidance, retracing our steps across the green isle of Alba.

If our outbound journey had been lighthearted, this one was more somber. Our encounter with the Old Ones had everyone uneasy. Oddly enough, I was the least disturbed of the lot of us. The Maghuin Dhonn had sworn an oath not to harm me. Whatever else was true, I was certain Berlik meant his oath with absolute sincerity.

My nights were free of haunting incidents.

My days were free of thoughts of Sidonie.

I left the *ollamh*'s protections in place, checking every morning and evening to ensure that the red yarn was still tied securely around my ankles and wrists, the croonie-stone hanging around my neck. Berlik's oath may have been sincere, but my will was still subject to Morwen's ensorceled charm. I had no desire to be lured out of my tent in the middle of the night, filled with heartache and desire. Of a surety, she could do great damage to my relationship with Dorelei without harming a hair on my head.

I liked Dorelei. At least I'd allowed myself to learn that much. I liked her a great deal. She was quiet and thoughtful, but she liked to laugh, too. She was an easy person to be with, and exactly the person in private she seemed in public, steady and unchanging. There was no malice in her, and a good deal of kindness.

Did I love her? No. There was none of the obsessive passion I'd felt for Sidonie, soaring, searing, and absurd. I never felt my heart swell within my breast at the thought of her, never felt her name stitching an endless pattern through my thoughts. With the *ollamh*'s bindings on me, I wasn't sure I *could* feel that way for anyone. But I wasn't miserable, either; racked with longing, struggling against the adamant shackles of unwanted love.

Anyway, all that seemed like a dream, now.

And it might be that love would grow between us yet, Dorelei and I. It wouldn't be the same. It would be a gentler thing, an easy fondness growing slowly into somewhat deeper. As Amarante had said, love wasn't always a raging tempest. It could be a safe harbor, too.

As we crossed Alba, I began to think mayhap that wouldn't be so bad. Every safe harbor I'd known had been stolen from me. My childhood home, my very sense of identity, my scholar's retreat in Tiberium. Even Phèdre and Joscelin's love had become a place fraught with dark undercurrents when I'd grown from a boy to a young man. There were worse things in the world than finding a lasting peace as Imriel, Prince of Alba, husband of Dorelei. Paradoxically, the very binding placed upon me had freed me to find that peace.

Things are not always what they seem, Berlik had said.

Truth was a riddle.

We arrived at the Stormkeep on a hot, sweltering day. Although it was only a day's ride from Bryn Gorrydum, it was an isolated place, perched on a high crag overlooking the sea. It had been a Tarbh Cró holding, once, but Drustan had granted it to Hyacinthe and Sibeal some years ago.

"Not the most welcoming place, is it?" Joscelin observed, gazing up at it.

"No," Phèdre murmured. "He found a taste for solitude."

It had always been hard for me to reconcile the high-spirited, half-breed Tsingano lad of their memory with the man I'd met. But for ten long years, Hyacinthe had labored under a *geas*, apprenticed to the old Master of the Straits, studying the secrets of wind and wave written in pages of the lost Book of Raziel. When the old Master had died, his power and his curse had passed to Hyacinthe, binding him to an isle in the midst of the Straits; binding him to a life of eternal aging.

Phèdre had freed him from the curse, or I daresay he'd still be there. But there was no way to remove the burden of power, to restore the years of carefree youth he'd lost.

"Have you met him?" I asked Dorelei.

"Oh, yes." She nodded. "He's . . . imposing."

The approach to the castle was a winding path up the crag. There had been defensive fortifications once, but the ditches were crumbling and silted and the drawbridges hadn't been raised for years. A man who could call thunderbolts down on his enemies had little fear of attack.

"Should we bring our escort or have them make camp here?" I asked Joscelin, uncertain what protocol dictated. "Is Hyacinthe even expecting us?"

"Phèdre sent a message," Joscelin said absently, shading his eyes and staring at the Stormkeep. He let out a laugh and pointed. "I'd say he is."

I squinted. There were banners fluttering from three corners of the keep's single turret. Two were familiar: the Black Boar of the Cullach Gorrym and the lily and stars of Terre d'Ange. The third, I'd seen only once: a black field with a ragged crimson circle, pierced by a barbed golden dart. Kushiel's Dart. It had flown from Admiral Rousse's flagship when we'd sailed to rescue Hyacinthe.

"Damned Tsingano," Joscelin said softly. He and Phèdre exchanged a long, private glance, then he shook himself. "Let them make camp here. I doubt the keep's big enough to accommodate them."

So it was that the four of us mounted the pathway alone, our horses picking their way along the winding path. At the top, we found the portcullis raised and the tall doors to the Stormkeep's inner courtyard standing open.

We were expected.

They were there, waiting for us. A pair of Cruithne stable-lads waited to take our mounts. And beyond them was the Master of the Straits and his family.

Hyacinthe.

It had been some seven years since I'd seen him. I'd been no more than a boy when it had all happened, but seeing him brought it all back. The wind-driven ship, the maelstrom. The bright figure emerging from it, awful and wonderful. Phèdre, standing on the waters, speaking the Name of God.

"Hyacinthe." She said his name through tears, dismounting.

I watched them embrace, a lump in my throat. He didn't look all that much older; nor did she. But they'd known one another for a long, long time. I saw his face when he released her, saw the flicker of anguish and regret that came and went so swiftly I might have imagined it.

"Cassiline." Hyacinthe approached, hand extended.

"Tsingano." One corner of Joscelin's mouth quirked. He clasped Hyacinthe's hand. "Good to see you."

"And you." Hyacinthe moved to hold Dorelei's reins as she dismounted. "Welcome, my lady Dorelei," he said courteously. "Your aunt has been very much looking forward to this visit, as have I."

"Thank you, Master Hyacinthe," she whispered.

He tilted his head. "Please, go greet her."

I watched her go, exchanging happy greetings with the Lady Sibeal, Drustan's sister, who appeared to have two smallish children clinging to her skirts. Joscelin went to Phèdre's side. She hugged him briefly, hiding her face against his neck. The Bastard sat motionless beneath me, prick-eared and interested.

"So." Hyacinthe took hold of the Bastard's bridle. "Imriel de la Courcel."

I dismounted with alacrity and bowed, keeping a wary eye on the

Bastard, who continued to behave himself. "My thanks, Master Hyacinthe, for your hospitality."

Hyacinthe looked at me without speaking. Dark eyes; Tsingano eyes. As dark as the Cruithne. Only things shifted and changed in their depths, like shadows moving over the ocean's floor. There was power enough behind those eyes to scatter the Maghuin Dhonn to the four winds. "I would not have Phèdre nó Delaunay's foster-son stand on ceremony with me," he said at length.

I put out my hand. "Imriel, then."

He clasped it. "Hyacinthe."

Thus, our welcome at the Stormkeep. Dorelei reintroduced me to her aunt, the Lady Sibeal, whom I'd also met as a child. She embraced me with unreserved warmth as a member of the family. We all met their two children. Galanna, the girl, was six; the boy Donal was four. At first they were shy of us, but it passed quickly. Once it did, we discovered they were both prone to chatter.

For all its isolation, there was a surprising degree of warmth and informality within the keep's walls. There was no garrison, but they maintained a small household staff, a mix of Alban folk who cooked and cleaned, and tended to the stables and the extensive gardens that supplied much of the Stormkeep's provender. They were respectful of their imposing master and seemed genuinely fond of Sibeal and the children. Hyacinthe showed us the place, as gracious as any regional lord playing host to old friends; except that his holdings included a locked room at the top of the tower, which contained an ancient leather case bound with bronze straps, in which resided pages torn from the Book of Raziel.

"This is where you study?" Phèdre asked, gazing out the high windows.

"I come here to think." Hyacinthe watched her. "There's naught left to study."

She glanced at the case. "You've committed it all to memory?"

He nodded. "All of it, yes."

"The *ollamhs* would approve," I observed.

Hyacinthe laughed. "So Sibeal says. Come, I'll show you the sea-mirror."

He led us to the rear of the keep, where a small, windswept terrace extended to the edge of the cliff. A narrow stair led down to the sea, waves crashing against the rocks. There was a pillar at each corner of the terrace, and in the center, a broad, shallow bronze basin sitting on a tripod, filled with seawater.

Joscelin took a deep breath. "It's been a long time since I saw that."

"'Tis not the same vessel," Hyacinthe said. "This one was wrought of ore smelted on Alban soil. Still, it serves the same purpose. Is there aught you would see, Cassiline?"

"No." Joscelin shook his head. "I saw enough the last time."

"Phèdre?" Hyacinthe asked.

She smiled. "All I desire to see is here. Let the children choose."

Hyacinthe turned to us. "What will you?"

"Can it show my mother?" Dorelei asked.

"Of course." He inclined his head and swept one arm over the basin. The water within it rippled in a manner that owed nothing to the wind, then went still. When it did, it reflected not sky, but a scene unfamiliar to me: a room filled with afternoon light, three Cruithne women sitting and conversing, their hands busy with embroidery-work. I leaned over the basin and stared, fascinated.

"That's your mother?" I pointed to the one with a look of Dorelei and Sibeal, careful not to disturb the surface of the water.

"It is." Her voice was warm. "And that's Kinada beside her, Kinadius' mother, and her daughter, Kerys. She's a friend of mine. They're in the parlor of Clunderry Castle."

It looked to be a pleasant place; a safe harbor. Nice.

"What will you see, Imriel?" Hyacinthe asked.

I shrugged. "I can't think of anything."

"Imri!" Dorelei nudged me. "What of Alais?"

"All right, yes," I agreed. "May I see Alais?"

"You may." Hyacinthe made no second pass over the basin, but the water rippled and the images on its surface blurred and changed.

It was another scene of domesticity, this one set in a place I knew well. The room had been the royal nursery once; it had been converted into a study, and Alais and I had spent many hours there under the *ollamh* Firdha's tutelage.

Alais was there.

So was Sidonie.

My heart gave an odd, constricted leap. From the look of it, they were quarrelling. I watched Alais fold her arms, scowling. Although I couldn't make out her face as well, Sidonie looked perturbed. I was aware, at a great distance, of a desire to make her laugh, to smooth the troubled look from her brow. Her lips moved; Alais shook her head, then glanced sharply away. I saw her mouth tighten. Maslin de Lombelon entered the room. He made a stiff bow to Alais, then offered his arm to Sidonie.

I fought the urge to clutch the croonie-stone.

She didn't take his arm, not right away. The perturbed look gave way to puzzlement. Her head turned, as though someone distant had called her name. For a moment, it seemed Sidonie gazed directly out of the sea-mirror at me.

My heart thudded in my breast. The red yarn around my wrists and ankles seemed suddenly tight and binding.

And then Maslin must have spoken, although his back was to the sea-mirror, for Sidonie's expression changed to her usual one of composure, and her lips moved in reply. She moved past Alais to take Maslin's arm and they left the room together. Alais flung herself into a chair, glaring after them. The wolfhound Celeste padded over and laid her hairy chin on Alais' knee, begging to have her ears scratched.

The image faded. The water became water, reflecting only sky.

"Siblings." Dorelei smiled. "Talorcan and I used to fight when we were younger. You wouldn't think it, but we did. What do you suppose they were quarrelling about?"

"I don't know," I murmured. "Maslin, mayhap. Alais doesn't like him."

"Sidonie does," she said. "So I heard, while she was away at Naamah's shrine."

"Yes." I gathered myself and turned to our host. "My thanks, my lord. That was most interesting."

"You're welcome." Hyacinthe looked at me for a moment, dark and grave. His sea-shifting eyes had gone still. I remembered that he had another gift; a Tsingano gift. The *dromonde*, the gift of sight. It was what had drawn him to Sibeal, to a daughter of Necthana's line. I wondered what he saw, and found myself afraid to know. But whatever it was, it passed. "You must be weary and hungry from your journey," he said. "Let me show you to your chambers ere we dine."

After Innisclan, the chambers seemed spacious. We refreshed ourselves and joined our hosts for dinner. It was a pleasant meal, due in large part to the children, who were permitted to attend during the early portion of the evening. In them, I could see a bright shadow of the man their father had once been, merry and irreverent.

"You're *pretty*," Galanna informed Phèdre, clambering down from her chair and flouncing her skirts. "Do you like my dress?"

"Very much, my lady." Phèdre smiled. " 'Tis as lovely as you are."

She tossed her silken black hair. "I know."

Joscelin grinned at Hyacinthe. "There's D'Angeline blood in that one."

"Oh, do you reckon, Cassiline?" Hyacinthe shifted the burden on his lap; the boy Donal, who'd ensconced himself there. It was an image I'd never thought to see; the Master of the Straits as rueful father. Donal leaned forward, intent on grabbing a serving-spoon from a dish of baked pears. "No, no, let it be."

"They're a bother, aren't they?" Sibeal said fondly, rising to pluck Donal from Hyacinthe's grasp. "Forgive us for inflicting them on you. Anyway, 'tis time they were a-bed. Let's find Nurse, shall we?"

A chorus of howls ensued.

"Here, I'll take him." Dorelei reached out her arms. "Just for a moment."

"As you will." Sibeal transferred him gladly. The boy settled into Dorelei's lap with a sigh of victorious contentment, and began telling her a long, rambling tale about chasing a frog in the garden that morning.

I watched them together. Dorelei smiled, bending her head to listen to her young cousin. He had a round, impish face, his father's black curls, and a pair of protruding ears. If we had children, they'd be close kin.

"We wanted to give their lives a semblance of normalcy." Hyacinthe was watching them, too. "And I wanted them to have the things I never had."

"Like a father?" Phèdre asked softly. "It seems you're a good one."

"He indulges them terribly," Sibeal said, smiling at him.

Hyacinthe smiled back at her. "That's because I can always lock myself in the tower and leave you to deal with them."

The children were permitted to linger for a few more minutes, and then Sibeal exterted her maternal will and declared an end to it. The nurse, a befreckled young Tarbh Cró woman who clearly doted on the children, was summoned and led them away. I laughed at the production they made of it, with downcast heads and dragging feet, futile pleas trailing behind them.

After their departure, we spoke of more serious matters, telling them what had transpired with the Maghuin Dhonn. I expected Sibeal to be reluctant to hear them discussed, but she didn't seem as troubled by the Old Ones as Dorelei and the Cruithne in general. I suppose being wed to a man who could command the seas to rise and fall had that effect.

Hyacinthe was interested. "Drustan's asked me to keep an eye on them," he said. "'Tis a funny business, though. I can't always see them. Not all of them."

"In the sea-mirror, you mean?" Joscelin frowned.

He nodded. "Betimes I can't find them, even though I know where they ought to be."

"Mayhap it's because betimes they're not human," I murmured.

"I've wondered about that," Hyacinthe said. "And I've wondered, too, about their stories of coming to Alba long, long ago, when the Straits were still covered with ice. If it's true, their magic is old, as old as what's written in the Book of Raziel, only different."

Dorelei shivered beside me.

"Can you speak the *dromonde* to learn the truth?" Phèdre asked, curious.

"Not without one of the Maghuin Dhonn before me." Hyacinthe shook his head. "And mayhap not even then. The *dromonde* looks backward as well as forward, but I do not think I can see past the origins of the Tsingani."

There was a good deal more conversation about them, but it was speculation and came to naught in the end. When all was said and done, neither Hyacinthe nor Sibeal knew any more about them than we did. Still, the evening wore on and grew late in the process, until Sibeal declared it was time for the adults to be abed, too.

"We've not even spoken of your affairs," Phèdre said to Hyacinthe. "Have you made any decisions?"

"Yes." He glanced at his wife, then back to Phèdre. "But we'll speak of it on the morrow." Hyacinthe grinned, and for the first time, there was a merry glint in his black eyes, mortal and ordinary. "I may have one last task for Anafiel Delaunay's pupil and her Perfect Companion."

TWENTY-FIVE

O N THE MORROW, I found myself abandoned.

Hyacinthe, Phèdre, and Joscelin closeted themselves in his tower to discuss whatever mysterious task it was for which the Master of the Straits might seek the assistance of Kushiel's Chosen and a Cassiline warrior-priest. Dorelei besought the counsel of her aunt in the matter of her dreams, which had been silent for longer than was their wont.

And I, who was neither a god's chosen, a warrior without parallel, nor a visionary dreamer, was left to my own devices.

Oh, I had a task of my own to accomplish; one small measure of responsibility. Hyacinthe had offered to extend the Stormkeep's hospitality to a half dozen of our men, which was as far as the keep's resources could stretch. The rest would be dismissed with generous pay to await us in Bryn Gorrydum, which would be better than the idle tedium of the encampment.

The unused garrison quarters were being cleaned and aired that morning. I rode down to the base of the crag to consult with Urist.

He polled the men, asking for volunteers. I wasn't surprised when the D'Angelines elected to a man to depart for Bryn Gorrydum.

"No offense, your highness," one of them said cheerfully, "but I've heard tell there's a pleasure-house in the city where a few of Naamah's Servants have elected to serve." He nudged the fellow next to him. "You'll do in a pinch, but I fancy somewhat prettier. Cleaner, too."

"Buggering perverts," Urist remarked without heat.

"Painted prude," the D'Angeline retorted cheerfully. "Your highness, will you tell Lady Phèdre and Messire Joscelin that it's been an honor to ride with them, bear-witches and all?"

I smiled. "I will."

To no one's surprise, the six who elected to stay were Urist's men, members of the *ollamh* Firdha's former honor guard. They drew lots for it, grumbling and arguing, while the others taunted them with exaggerated tales of the pleasures they were forgoing. Urist watched the proceedings with a wry, competent gaze that put me in mind of Gallus Tadius. It made me strangely nostalgic for my days as a member of the Red Scourge in Lucca.

There are worse things than being a soldier; one among many, a cog in a wheel. Gallus Tadius taught us to do our jobs, and he taught us well. As much as I'd hated the drilling, I'd come to take pride in it, too. By the time Lucca's wall fell, we'd all known what to do. Gallus Tadius gave us orders. We followed them.

There was a simplicity in it.

I missed that, even if I hadn't been terribly good at it.

I'd slept poorly the last night. I didn't dream of Sidonie—indeed, if I dreamed at all, I do not remember—but my thoughts kept returning to her, blurred and incomplete. Ever since I'd seen her in Hyacinthe's sea-mirror, I'd felt myself chafing at my bindings. They felt tight and bothersome, and I was frustrated by my inability to truly *feel* my own emotions. I knew it worried Phèdre. Blessed Elua bade us to love as we willed. Was I violating his precept in protecting myself from the Maghuin Dhonn? Did it matter that I was doing my best to learn to love Dorelei? I didn't know.

After I'd distributed a generous purse among the men, Cruithne and D'Angeline alike, I left them to the work of striking the camp. I let the Bastard stretch his legs along the high cliffs overlooking the sea, giving him his head. Like me beneath my charmed bonds, he'd chafed at the slow, measured pace of caravan travel.

The Bastard ran for the sheer joy of running, plunging and snorting, exuberance bursting beneath his speckled hide. Clouds of seagulls swirled overhead at our approach, soaring with raucous cries. I laughed at the sight, thinking of Master Piero and the pigeons. I let the Bastard run until the Stormkeep was small in the distance behind us and his hide was darkening with sweat.

And then I slowed him to a walk and turned him, and we began to make our slow way back, picking a path amidst the boulders and out-croppings. I didn't feel any wiser, but at least I felt a good deal calmer.

"Imriel."

The Bastard spooked at Morwen's voice, shying violently. I clung to his barrel with my thighs, ripping my sword from its sheath. "Name of Elua! What do you want of me?"

Morwen sat perched on a boulder, knees drawn up beneath the hem of her roughspun brown dress, arms wrapped around them. Her feet were bare, dirty brown toes clinging to the rock. "You don't need to be afraid," she said. "Berlik swore for all of us. I mean you no harm."

I cursed and wrestled the Bastard to a standstill. "Then why are you here?"

The leather bag hung around her throat once more. She touched it, and I became accutely aware of my bindings. "Your desire summoned me."

"Not of my will," I said shortly.

Her pale eyes blinked between woad claws. "Nonetheless."

"Morwen . . ." I sighed. "I'm weary of games and riddles. I ask again, what do you want of me? Did you come to bid me go home again?"

"No." She cocked her head, considering. "'Tis too late for that, I think. The future is woven of many threads, but the skein is tangled and knotted. Some have already been cut, others are fraying. More than one pattern emerges. We do not know how to unravel this riddle."

"You might try simply living your life and letting me live mine," I said wryly. "That's how we ordinary folk do it."

Morwen shook her head. "The stakes are too high."

The croonie-stone around my neck felt heavy. My wrists itched, hot and tingling. I dismounted, dropping the Bastard's reins, and walked toward Morwen, my sword in my right hand. Her body quivered, but she made no effort to flee. I could smell her scent, rank and earthy. "What," I said through gritted teeth. "Do. You. *Want*?"

"You made an offering to the land. But you didn't, not really. It was meant for another, far, far away. And your wife is not enough, will never be enough. That much, we have seen. But the future keeps changing." Her chin rose, wide, pale eyes fixed on my face. She grasped the leather bag containing the mannekin charm with one hand, and splayed the other over her belly. "I want your child."

I lunged at her, grabbing for the leather bag.

I missed.

Elua! I was fast, but Morwen was faster. She dodged and I stumbled over the empty boulder, falling hard on my left side, mindful of my sword. My wrists and ankles burned, and the croonie-stone felt like a millstone. By the time I got to my feet, she was running, a small brown figure fleeing over the green landscape.

Like a fool, I gave chase, but she ran faster than any mortal woman ought to be able to run, and her figure dwindled before me. I collected my wits and turned back to find the Bastard, but by then he was skittish and unwilling to be caught.

It took me long minutes to calm him, fearful all the while that he'd bolt and step on one of his trailing reins and break his stupid speckled neck. By the time I succeeded, Morwen was long gone. Even the itching of my bonds was fading. I rode in the direction she'd gone and spent the better part of an hour searching to no avail. Disgruntled, I turned back for the Stormkeep.

There, I found everyone in good spirits; or at least the Cruithne were. Phèdre and Joscelin were still in the tower, and Hyacinthe was watching the sea-mirror. But the Lady Sibeal and Dorelei were entertaining Urist and his handful of men at the long table in the great hall, laughing and chatting animatedly.

"Imriel!" Dorelei glanced up as I entered. She was sitting beside Kinadius and she looked happy. He rose with alacrity, offering me his chair. "We were just speaking of you. Will you not get your warrior's markings ere we're wed?"

I dropped into the chair beside her. "You wish me to get my face tattooed?"

Kinadius snickered. Dorelei gave me a dimpled smile. "I think you'd look very handsome with a proper warrior's marks. Kinadius says you're owed them for the battle you and Eamonn fought."

I eyed her, uncertain whether or not she was teasing. "Eamonn didn't feel the need."

"It's not a Dalriadan custom," Urist said.

"Nor is a D'Angeline custom." I forced myself to smile. "We tattoo our backsides like civilized folk." At that, they laughed. "Tell me," I said, thinking of the markings Morwen and Berlik bore. "Why do you do it?"

They glanced at one another. Kinadius shrugged. "It's a mark of honor. It puts fear into one's enemies, knowing you've killed good men before them." He tapped the warrior's crescent and spear in the center of his brow. "That's for the first. Like I told you, it's your due, unless you were merely boasting."

"You mustn't pay them any heed," Sibeal said kindly to me. "Warriors think the sun rises and sets on their feats, and wear their prowess on their faces that everyone might know it. But you'll note I made no such request of my lord Hyacinthe."

"What of you?" I asked, curious.

"Did the Daughter of the Grove not tell you?" Dorelei asked.

I shook my head. "I know what it means, but not why."

"Those who dream true dreams are marked, that others might know it and heed their words when they speak." The happiness in Dorelei's face ebbed away, leaving something troubled behind. "Or so it should be."

I wondered if her talk with her aunt regarding her dreams had gone badly. I'd thought to tell Dorelei about my encounter with Morwen immediately upon my return, but now I thought better of it. She was preoccupied; and among the myriad things of which I was sick unto death, like riddles and games, mysterious interfering strangers, and people wanting me dead because of somewhat that happened before I was born, was having my personal tribulations the topic of endless, fruitless discussion. Morwen had neither harmed nor threatened me, and what she had said had no bearing on anyone but Dorelei and me. Later, in private, we would talk.

"Ah, I see," I said gently. "It seems I've a lot to learn yet about being a proper Pict."

Her smile returned. "Are you saying you'll you do it, then?"

"This?" I smiled back at her. "Not likely."

That night around the dinner table, an atmosphere of hushed, secretive excitement prevailed. Whatever it was Phèdre, Joscelin, and Hyacinthe were about, they weren't minded to tell anyone, and it made them cryptic and awkward. The children were oblivious to it; Urist and his men were dining in the garrison quarters. Lady Sibeal looked tranquil and undisturbed, and I guessed she knew. That left Dorelei and me to exchange confused looks.

When Galanna and Donal were packed off to bed under the nurse's auspices, I asked pointedly, "Would you all prefer that we follow them?"

They exchanged non-confused looks.

"Forgive us." Hyacinthe inclined his head. "We will let the matter rest."

"Hyacinthe . . ." Phèdre murmured.

He raised his brows. "Would you have them burdened with it?"

"No." Dorelei rose from the table with unexpected vigor. "I'll not speak for Imriel, but whatever *it* is, I've no interest in being burdened with it. And so, I'll bid you good night."

I rose, torn, as she left the hall.

Sibeal gazed after her niece with quiet concern. The others looked at me. Figures out of legend, all three of them. Phèdre nó Delaunay, Kushiel's Chosen, with her dart-stricken gaze and the Name of God in her thoughts. Joscelin Verreuil, her Perfect Companion, the Queen's Champion. Hyacinthe, the Prince of Travellers, Master of the Straits.

"Imriel, if you wish—" Joscelin began.

"No," I said slowly. "Like Dorelei, I don't need another burden to carry. If you decide I do, then I'll listen. Right now, I think it best if I go talk to my wife."

No one spoke against it. I took my leave and made my way to the chamber that Dorelei and I shared. As I passed the corridor leading to the garrison, I could hear the sound of Urist's men bantering over their cups. Once again, I envied the simplicity of their lives.

But I'd failed at being a simple soldier, too. I hadn't been boasting, I'd acquitted myself well enough during the siege of Lucca, and none of my comrades had cause to complain of me. Still, my fellow soldiers hadn't loved me, either. I didn't have the knack of easy camaraderie that Eamonn did. And in the end, simplicity had evaded me. The Duke of Valpetra had sought me out, bent on vengeance because I'd cut off his hand. I'd survived only because Canis, my mother's willing tool, had given his life for mine.

It seemed like a long time ago.

I found Dorelei gazing out the room's single window, shutters open onto the summer breeze. The window looked inland, and twilight was falling over the green plains. She turned and gave me a swift, half-hearted smile. "I'm sorry. I didn't mean to be rude."

"You weren't." I sat on the bed.

"Do you know what they're about?" she asked.

"No." I smiled wryly. "Oh, I could hazard a guess, which I daresay is why they're not bothering to hide it. It's somewhat to do with the Book of Raziel. Phèdre and Hyacinthe have written back and forth to one another for years on the matter."

"I didn't know they used to be lovers." Dorelei's voice was nearly inaudible.

"Long ago." There was only a single oil lamp burning low, and the room was growing dark. I found a pair of tallow candles and lit them. "Did your aunt Sibeal tell you? Is she troubled by it?"

"Yes, and no." She watched the candle flames grow, casting shadows. "She said she always knew, that it didn't matter. That what is between them is strong and good, and enough for the both of them. That if he were to betray her, it would never be under their own roof." Her mouth twisted ruefully. "And that love is a complicated business."

"What of your dreams?" I asked. "Did she know why they've gone silent?"

Dorelei sat on the bed beside me. "Because of you."

"Me!" I was startled.

"Not at first." She took my hand. "At first it was likely because I was far from home, and . . . scared. And then, mayhap, because of *them*." Her lips thinned. "That music you heard, the charmed song. *They* may have interfered."

"And now?" I asked.

She traced the threads of red yarn around my wrist. "We see only glimpses, you know. Riddles. Our own fates, or those we love. Those to whom our lives are bound." She was silent a moment. "I saw my father's death when I was eight years old. I didn't understand the dream until it happened."

"I'm sorry," I said quietly. I knew her father had been killed in a rockslide when she was a child, and she'd always spoken fondly of him. I hadn't known she'd foreseen his death.

"Thank you." Dorelei squeezed my hand. "The thing is, my life is bound to yours now. And you're bound against charms."

"Harmful ones." I hesitated. "*Their* magic."

"It may be it's all of a piece." Her voice dropped again. "I told her what he said, that harpist. That our gift came from their blood. She said it might be true."

"Well, of a surety, they're obsessed with trying to unravel the future." I took a deep breath and told Dorelei what had transpired with Morwen that day. She listened to me without interrupting, grave and concerned, until I got to the part where I tried to grab the leather bag.

A disbelieving giggle burst from her. She clapped one hand over her mouth and stared at me. "You didn't!"

"I did," I said.

Dorelei's eyes were wide as saucers. "What did she do?"

"Ran." I grinned. "Ran like a rabbit. I wasn't anywhere close to catching her."

"Are you jesting?" she asked dubiously.

I shook my head. "I wouldn't. Not about this, I promise. But why would she say she wanted me to get her with child? It makes no sense. A month ago, she wanted me to leave Alba and return to Terre d'Ange."

"A lot may change in a month," Dorelei murmured.

It was my turn to stare. I opened and closed my mouth several times, no doubt looking as dumbstruck as I felt. "Are you . . . ?" I cleared my throat and gestured with my free hand in the vicinity of her belly. The words emerged in a whisper. "With *child*?"

"Well, what did you think we were about!" she said tartly. She let go my hand and sighed. "I don't know for sure, Imriel; not yet. But I think so, yes."

"But that's . . . that's wonderful!" I blinked. "Isn't it?"

"Is it?" Dorelei looked steadily at me. "Nothing's really changed, has it? Not beneath these." She reached out to pluck at the red yarn. "If it had, these wouldn't be needful."

"I don't know." I thought about my glimpse of Sidonie in the sea-mirror, my encounter with Morwen. The way the bindings had itched and chafed, the croonie-stone had grown heavy. "Probably not." I returned her even gaze. "I'm doing my best, and I think 'tis fair to say we've grown fond of one another, but it may never change, Dorelei. I'll not make any false promises. What of you? Would you claim to love me?" She made no reply. "When I returned today, you were happy, there with your aunt and Urist's men. Kinadius leapt up like a scalded cat when I entered the hall. He'd hoped to court you one day, you know."

Dorelei flushed. "What are you saying?"

I spread my hands. "Only that he's the sort of man could make you happy, and I'm not."

"A proper Pict, you mean?" She smiled sadly. "It doesn't matter, Imriel. Neither you or I entered this marriage thinking to find love and happiness."

"No, but one can hope," I said.

"One can." She rose and went to gaze out the window again. "And one can recognize the moment when hope turns to folly, too. But it's not only that. It's all become so complicated. We agreed to a marriage of state. You didn't agree to having your heart's desire locked away behind an *ollamh*'s charms. I didn't agree to have my dreams silenced. Mayhap these are signs that should be heeded."

"What will you?" I asked simply.

Her slender shoulders rose and fell. "You know, I've thought about it from time to time. The sky wouldn't crack and fall if we were to part. My brother is the Cruarch's heir, yes, but he needn't worry about naming an heir of his own for years and years. The Cruarch may have conceived this solution, but 'tis Terre d'Ange pushed for it."

The answer took me by surprise. I'd no idea she'd thought seriously about ending our marriage. Since I didn't know what to say to it, I only addressed her latter comment. "Believe me, I know," I said. "I felt the pushing."

"So fearful of protecting their interests!" Dorelei laughed, but there was no humor in it. "Our nations are allies and both of us profit by it. Why should that change, no matter who rules? Tell me truly, Imriel, what do they think a child of ours would guarantee? Unquestioning fealty?"

"I don't know." My chest felt tight. "My lady, I never claimed to agree with my countrymen. Despite Blessed Elua's teaching, they place far too much significance on his bloodlines."

"And yet you agreed to this," she mused. When I didn't answer, she laughed again, short and humorless. "Do you know what the worst thing is?"

"No," I murmured.

Dorelei turned to face me. "I actually do love you." There were tears on her brown cheeks. "Not . . ." She made an impatient gesture. "I don't know, not like it is in the ballads. It's stupid and it hurts. You're insufferably self-absorbed, and you make me miserable."

"I'm not—" I began.

"Oh, you *are*!" She laughed bitterly, dashing at her tears. "And then you do your best to be kind and charming, and you look at me, truly look at me with those stupid blue eyes, and smile, and my heart turns upside down, and I *hate* it, and I hate you for it."

"That would be love," I said quietly.

"Now you know." Dorelei sniffled and wiped her nose. Her voice hardened. "So what will *you*, Imriel de la Courcel?"

I sat on the edge of the bed, elbows propped on my knees. "You spoke of parting. Is that your wish?"

"I don't know." She sounded weary. "Betimes, I think it would be better for both of us. You'd be free. I'd be able to dream freely again. Mayhap all this strangeness that's been attendant on our marriage would end. I'd like that, very much. It frightens me to have the . . . Old Ones . . . meddling in our lives. And I . . . this would pass, I think, in time."

"What of the child?" I asked.

"What would you have me say?" Dorelei smiled ruefully. "It would hardly be the first child in Alba raised without a blood-father. There would be no lack of men at Clunderry willing to play the role. You'd acknowledge him, I hope. Or her. I've not been with anyone else."

"Of course!" I glanced up at her, stung.

"So." Dorelei shrugged. "Mayhap we should cancel the Alban nuptials. You'll have to tell me what's needful to recant the vows we swore in Terre d'Ange."

My head ached. I felt a sense of loss, keen and piercing; the first true emotion I'd felt since Aodhan placed his protective charms on me. *What if there's a child?* Sidonie had asked. I'd made some careless reply, assuming it would make little difference. I thought about my mother's letters, filled with an unexpected depth of maternal passion, and about the way Hyacinthe devoted himself to his children, having grown up fatherless. And I thought about Dorelei calling me self-absorbed, too.

And Morwen. Morwen had said the future had changed. I wondered if she'd known.

"I'd rather not." I swallowed. "If . . . if there is a child, I'd rather it were born knowing I cared enough to wed you, to stay with you. To be a father to my daughter or son, at least long enough to see him draw his first breath, laugh his first laugh. But . . ." I took a deep breath, trying to ease the tightness in my chest. "Not at the cost of your happiness, Dorelei. I'll abide by whatever you wish."

"You mean it?" she asked.

I nodded. "If my staying will make you miserable, I'll go."

She considered me. "And if you stay, what happens later? To us?"

"I don't know," I said honestly. "If we find that our lives together don't contain enough happiness to sustain us, so be it. At least we will always know we tried, and so will our child. If he becomes Talorcan's heir, he'll have the full mantle of legitimacy." I hesitated. "'Tis your choice, truly. Do you think you could endure my presence a while longer? Even if it meant the loss of your dreams?"

Dorelei laughed, but this time there was no bitterness in it, only sorrow. "Oh, I think I could manage it."

"Good." The ache of emptiness retreated a little. I smiled at her. "You're sure?"

"I think so, yes." She sighed and left the window, coming to sit beside me. "You know, this wasn't the discussion I'd planned on having, but I'm glad we did. 'Tis time and more we were fully honest with one another, and this time I'm more to blame than you. We did promise to be friends to one another."

"Many a marriage of state is built on worse," I agreed.

"True."

Her admission of love hung between us. I hadn't known she felt that way, hadn't even suspected. For as much attention as I'd been paying her, it was my own feelings, or lack thereof, I'd been obsessing over. Self-absorbed, indeed.

I cleared my throat. "Shall I see if there's another guest chamber available?"

"Well, I didn't mean we had to take it *that* far," Dorelei said quickly, then flushed. We both laughed, although she stopped first, turning somber once more. "We should wait a while, though. I'll know for a surety in a couple of weeks. If I'm right, then there's no harm in making love. The damage is done, as it were. But if I'm wrong . . ." She fell silent.

"What if you are?" I asked. "If you're not with child, what then?"

The strength of women is different from the strength of men, deep and enduring. Dorelei looked at me, her eyes dark and solemn. She touched the red yarn bound around my wrist. "Imriel, I don't know what the Old Ones want, and I don't care. You're not meant to live this way and neither am I. If I'm not with child, then I think it would be for the best if you boarded the first ship to Terre d'Ange. Don't you?"

"Yes." There was a vast relief at saying the words. "I do."

She smiled sadly. "Good."

TWENTY-SIX

OUR RELATIONSHIP CHANGED for the better after that night. Dorelei's honesty had been as bracing as being doused with a bucket of cold water. I'd been working so hard to convince myself that things might be fine between us, if only I tried hard enough. If only I pretended to be what I thought I should. And bound behind charms, I'd done a better job of fooling myself than I had her.

It was a blessed relief to have it in the open between us. I stopped trying so hard to be pleasant and charming, and discovered she liked me well enough as myself. I worried less about being attentive, and more about actually paying attention to what she thought and felt.

We grew easier with one another, truly easier. If Dorelei's feelings for me troubled her, we spoke of it. And if my bindings chafed, I acknowledged it.

Oddly enough, they didn't, though. Not as they had.

I spoke to Phèdre about what Dorelei and I had decided, alone and in private. She was Queen Ysandre's confidante, and I thought it best to tell her first. She heard me out in thoughtful silence. "Are you upset?" I asked when I'd finished.

"Upset? Elua, no!" Phèdre laughed in wonderment. "I'm still trying to get my thoughts to encompass you with a child of your own."

The words drew an unexpected grin from me. "No, but about the other thing. Dissolving the marriage if she's not with child."

"No." She glanced involuntarily toward the east, toward Terre d'Ange. "No, Ysandre will be, and I daresay Drustan, but for my part, I'd be relieved. Even if you are safe from harm, I don't like the idea of you wrapped round with an *ollamh*'s charms, your own nature divided against itself. 'Tis contrary to Elua's precept. And surely, they'll have to acknowledge the matter is troubling. Neither of you can be blamed for the choice."

"You'd stand by us, then?" I asked.

"Of course." Phèdre sounded surprised. She hesitated. "What do you mean to do afterward, Imri?"

We hadn't spoken of Sidonie since leaving the City of Elua. "I've no idea," I said truthfully. "Nothing rash, I promise." I raised my brows. "Mayhap I could accompany you and Joscelin on whatever it is you're about."

"Oh, that." She smiled at me. "So you do want to know, then?"

I thought about it. "Not really, no."

Phèdre laughed and kissed my cheek. "Fairly spoken."

In some part of me, I knew all of this would come to naught. *'Tis too late for that*, Morwen had said when I'd spoken of returning to Terre d'Ange. *A lot can happen in a month*, Dorelei had said when I'd told her. There was a line drawn between those two things, taut and inevitable. Even I, dumbstruck and shocked to my callow core at the notion of impending fatherhood, had seen it without prompting.

But we waited until we knew for a surety.

In its own way, it was a pleasant time. Although I reported my encounter with Morwen to the others, there were no further sightings of the Maghuin Dhonn. The Lady Sibeal ran her household with a firm, gentle hand. Phèdre, Joscelin, and Hyacinthe continued to engage in their private intrigue, which involved long conferences in the tower, maps, and hushed, esoteric arguments. Awe gave way to a measure of familiarity. Day by day, the Master of the Straits began to seem more human, more mortal. The heavy mantle of responsibility that weighed on him seemed lighter in their company.

Meanwhile, Urist and his men alleviated the tedium with hunting and shooting for the pot, and Dorelei and I often rode with them, vying with one another for sport as we'd done at Innisclan.

I felt myself suspended between one thing and another; the known and the unknown. What would come, would come, and there was naught I could do about it. In truth, I couldn't have said what I truly wanted.

Betimes, freedom beckoned. There was no denying it.

But at other times, I found myself gazing at Dorelei, filled with an inexplicable tenderness. Ah, Elua! The notion that we had begotten *life* between us . . .

It is an old mystery; the oldest mystery.

I prayed to Blessed Elua, and my prayers were simple. *Love as thou wilt*, he bade us. But he failed to elaborate on all the myriad forms of love that existed. And so I prayed, simply, that whatever happened, I acted in love.

"You're sure?" I asked Dorelei when she told me.

"Yes, I'm sure!" She swatted at my hands as I raised her skirts, laughing helplessly as I held her down on our bed and pinned my ear against the soft brown skin of her belly. "Imriel, let be. 'Tis too early. There's naught to hear."

"How do you know?" I lifted my head. "Have you done this before?"

"No." Her fingers knotted in my hair, her face softening. "Come here."

I went.

Sibeal sent for a wise-woman, an herb-witch who'd attended her own birthings. It was women's business, that, and I wasn't privy to it. She was a nut-brown woman, wizened and bent. Later, Dorelei told me she'd poked and prodded, testing her insides with surprisingly gentle fingers, smelling them afterward, her broad nostrils flaring.

At the time, I knew only what the wise-woman reported.

"Oh, aye!" She gave us a gap-toothed grin, her head bobbing. "The lass is with child."

I knew; I'd known all the while.

It made me tender, it made me solicitous, it made me a little bit mad. I couldn't get past the notion of it. I forgot, altogether, about the bindings on me. During the days, I was content. At night, I made love to Dorelei, crooning to the child in her belly.

"Which one of us do you *want*?" she asked me once, tartly.

At that, I sat back on my heels. "Would you have me lie, my lady, and say the child has naught to do with it?"

"No." Her dark eyes filled with tears. "May the gods help me, I'll take what I may have of you. After all, it doesn't matter now, does it?"

"I'm sorry," I whispered. "I grew up without the benefit of parents to love me. I'll not have our child do the same."

"I know," Dorelei whispered in reply.

Somewhere, somehow, we'd come to understand one another, Dorelei and I.

During those days, my bonds, like Hyacinthe's responsibilities, rested more lightly on me. Oh, I checked them daily, but there was naught to threaten them. I bore them easily. Betimes, I was glad of them. Without the ache of desire plaguing me, I was able to take genuine joy in moments of ordinary happiness.

It came almost as a surprise when the day arrived for us to depart for Bryn Gorrydum, but summer was fleeting and Hyacinthe had watched the Cruarch's flagship cross the Straits in his sea-mirror. It was time. Only a month ago, I would have faced the prospect of repeating my nuptial vows with a vague, half-felt dread, masked by steel resolve and false courtesy. Now I was calm.

So it was that we all set forth, riding in the company of the Master of the Straits and his lady wife. The children, who had grown fond of us, howled bitterly at being left behind. I watched Dorelei embrace them in farewell and promise to visit, a tender ache in my breast. I wondered if the child we'd made together, their young kinsman-to-be, would emerge stamped with the inexplicable trait of some unknown ancestor, like Donal and his protruding ears.

The thought of my impending fatherhood still overwhelmed me with unfamiliar emotion.

In ways I'd never guessed, it seemed I was truly my mother's son.

Although the city was only a day's ride away, we elected to make camp a half league or so beyond its outskirts that evening. Urist sent Kinadius to fetch the rest of our escort to accompany us on the morrow, that we might enter the city in splendor befitting the Master of the Straits, a Princess of Alba, and assorted D'Angeline royalty.

"How long has it been since you camped a-field?" Joscelin asked Hyacinthe as we lounged around the campfire that night.

"Not as long as you might think, Cassiline." Hyacinthe sounded amused, and far younger than he had when we'd first arrived. "I do leave the Stormkeep at times to wander about. I do it quietly, that's all."

He'd appeared at Montrève once when I was a boy, not long after Phèdre had rescued him. I'd not been on hand to witness his arrival, but I still remembered watching him leave; a dim figure on a grey horse, vanishing into the dawn mists. I wondered what it felt like to command the elements, to reconcile that self with the Tsingano lad who'd told fortunes for coin in Night's Doorstep. My own struggles seemed small and insignificant beside his fate.

In the morning, the full complement of our men arrived, and we rode the rest of the way to Bryn Gorrydum.

If our initial reception had been a trifle cool, this one made up for it. Whatever reservations Albans might have about Dorelei's and my marriage, they held the Master of the Straits in high esteem. The Cruarch himself met us at the city's edge, accompanied by an honor guard. On Drustan's right was his heir Talorcan, and on his left . . .

"Imri!"

Alais' voice was filled with lilting joy. If she'd been at all wroth with me for her suspicions regarding Sidonie, she'd forgotten it. Indeed, she looked happier than I'd ever seen her. Her face was alight with it, her violet eyes sparkling.

I smiled with genuine pleasure. "Hello, villain. 'Tis good to see you."

We rode in procession through the city to the fortress. Alais chattered with boundless enthusiasm the whole while, telling me every detail of their journey across Terre d'Ange and the Straits and their arrival in Bryn Gorrydum. She barely spoke of home, and I didn't ask.

I'd been right about one thing I'd told her some time ago—the Albans loved her. There was no tribute the way there would have been in the City of Elua, no cheering and throwing of flower petals, but I could see it in the faces of folk lining the streets as we passed. They smiled at the sight of her, warm and indulgent, taking pride and pleasure in her obvious delight at being here in Alba.

I felt a little of that warmth spill over onto me, and I was glad of it.

When we reached Bryn Gorrydum's stony grey fortress, we found it full to the rafters. Our Alban nuptials would be a far smaller affair than the wedding in Terre d'Ange, but the Palace could house nigh unto a hundred peers without straining, and the City of Elua was vast. A small handful here in Bryn Gorrydum felt like many, many more. After the peaceful isolation of the Stormkeep, I felt ill at ease being confined with so many folk.

With her father's blessing, Alais took it upon herself to show us to our quarters, while Talorcan tended to Phèdre and Joscelin, and Drustan himself to Hyacinthe and Sibeal. There was a welcoming feast already under way in the great hall. As Alais escorted us through the narrow corridors to our rooms, the roar of it seemed to echo everywhere.

"'Tis enough to make me miss Innisclan," Dorelei whispered.

"I know," I whispered back. "Me, too."

I'd hoped for a chance to have a quiet word with Drustan, to tell him about the Maghuin Dhonn and all that had transpired since we left Terre d'Ange, but it was not to be, at least not that day. Our nuptials wouldn't take place until two days hence, but it seemed the celebrating had already begun in earnest, and we were expected to make an immediate appearance.

"Hurry, won't you?" Alais pleaded. "*Everyone's* here, and they're all waiting!"

"Everyone?" Dorelei cocked an amused brow at her.

"Everyone!" Alais repeated.

In Terre d'Ange, the fête wouldn't have properly begun until the guests of honor arrived, but this was nothing at all like a D'Angeline affair. For the first time, I truly felt the vast chasm that existed between life in Alba and home. Our initial arrival in Bryn Gorrydum had been quiet and uneventful, and the differences hadn't struck me as hard in Innisclan or Stormkeep, where we'd been the guests of old friends.

But this; this was an affair of state. It was raucous and informal, and if there was a protocol, I couldn't determine it. And if everyone was indeed awaiting us, there wasn't much evidence of it. From what I could see, they were already having a fine time.

The hall was crowded and sweltering in the late-summer heat. There was a long trestle table piled high with food. The sight of an enormous roast, glistening with fatty juices, made my stomach a bit queasy.

There were people standing and milling around the table, laughing, jesting, eating, and drinking. Dark Cruithne, and the more fair, ruddy folk of the Tarbh Cró and the Eidlach Òr. Most of the men clustered around the table, while the women, of whom there were far fewer, seemed to be at the far end of the hall. There were children and dogs underfoot. Servants shoved their way through the throng, bearing platters of food and pitchers of drink.

"There's Eamonn!" Alais pointed across the hall, where his bright head was visible. "He and Brigitta arrived yesterday, and his younger brother, too!"

"Has my mother not arrived?" Dorelei asked.

"Oh, yes! I'm supposed to take you to her." Alais took Dorelei's hand and plunged into the crowd, leading her across the hall.

I began to follow, but I didn't get far before I was waylaid. Phèdre and Joscelin were yet to make an appearance, and my D'Angeline features stood out like a beacon.

"You're the young prince!" A stalwart blond fellow with impressive drooping mustaches clapped a hand on my shoulder. "Gwynek of Brea."

"Imriel de la Courcel," I offered.

"Welcome!" He grinned beneath his mustaches. "Peder, come greet the young prince! And by all that's holy, bring the lad a drink."

A taller version of Gwynek came over to introduce himself, thrusting a goblet of mead into my hand. By the time I'd won my way free, I'd met a dozen clan-lords of the Eidlach Òr and the Tarbh Cró, all of whom were deemed important or influential enough to be invited to attend our nuptials.

They were friendly, but there was a testing edge to their friendliness; even with each other. Travelling the *taisgaidh* ways, quiet and undisturbed—save for Morwen's mischief—Alba had seemed a peaceful place. Now I remembered Drustan saying there was always feuding among the clans. It was easier to believe here. I could well imagine these men drinking together under the same roof in cheerful brotherhood, and going home to plot raids on one another.

I met a few of the Cruithne clan-lords, too. They were more somber and less effusive, gauging me with dark eyes. More than once, I caught lingering gazes studying my bare, unmarked face, wondering if this untried warrior was worthy of being made an honorary member of the Cullach Gorrym.

It was Eamonn who came to my rescue, shouldering his way through the crowd. "What a crush!" He gave me a lopsided grin, suggesting he'd had more than a few cups of mead. "It's worse than that riot in Tiberium, eh?"

"Or suppertime at Innisclan," I muttered.

He laughed. "Come on. You've got family to meet."

With Eamonn's aid, I made my way to the far side of the hall. It was quieter there, with chairs set about for the women, who were conversing far more peaceably than the menfolk.

Dorelei was seated beside her mother, holding her hand and smiling. The Lady Breidaia glanced up at our arrival, her eyes shining. Indeed, all of the women were beaming, including Alais, who looked fit to wriggle right out of her skin. Even Brigitta was smiling, and Conor, seated among the women with his harp on his lap, was grinning wide enough to split his face. I guessed Dorelei had told them our news.

I bowed deeply to Breidaia. "Well met, my lady. 'Tis an honor."

Someone giggled. "Such manners!"

"Imriel is always polite," Dorelei observed. "Except when he's not."

Ignoring her daughter, Lady Breidaia rose and placed a gentle kiss on my cheek. She had a calm, warm presence, and I liked her immediately. "Welcome to the family, Imriel," she said softly. "We're so very pleased."

Alais let out a squeak. "Oh, Imri! Aren't you excited?"

I felt myself grin as foolishly as Conor. "I am, actually."

"Why?" Eamonn looked perplexed. "I mean, you *are* already wed, aren't you?"

"Not that," Brigitta said with affectionate scorn. "They're having a child."

"Dagda Mor!" Eamonn stared at me. "You are?" I nodded, and he glanced over at Brigitta with a grin of his own. "Well, we'd best busy ourselves, hadn't we?"

At that moment, Drustan and the others entered. Those who were seated rose, and a silent hush of respect fell over the hall. Some of it was for the Cruarch of Alba, but I daresay a good deal of it was for the Master of the Straits.

And, too, for Phèdre and Joscelin.

After all, they were the ones had freed him.

Save for the bustling servants, clearing empty platters and bringing laden ones in turn, the hall was still. Drustan stood for a moment, surveying it. "My lords and ladies," he said in his steady, commanding voice. "We are gathered to celebrate the nuptials of my sister's daughter, Dorelei mab Breidaia of the Cullach Gorrym, to Imriel nó Montrève de la Courcel of Terre d'Ange. In their honor, I pledge that for three days of the new moon, from sunrise to sunrise, this table will never stand empty. Will you join us at it?"

There were shouts and cheers, and a scuffle for seats on the long benches that lined the table, which I daresay would have been less muted if not for Hyacinthe's presence. A few places of honor for the Cruarch's family and guests were reserved at the head of the table; the rest appeared to be claimed at will.

How does one measure the length of a meal without beginning or end? We sat for hours. It was simple, hearty fare, but there was so much of it I wanted to groan. I washed it down with mead until my head was swimming and my tongue felt coated with the sweetness of fermented honey.

The Albans ate and drank ceaselessly, loud and clamorous. Many of them eschewed utensils, making do with belt knives and hands, slipping tidbits to the dogs lounging under the table. I caught Alais doing the same, having brought the wolfhound Celeste with her. Celeste looked guilty; Alais looked delighted. Somewhere I could hear Eamonn's voice raised in argument. It made me laugh, despite the fact that my head was ringing.

"Welcome to Alba, Prince Imriel." Dorelei gave me a dimpled smile.

At the head of the table, Drustan leaned forward, his eyes crinkling with amusement. "We do have more . . . civilized . . . affairs," he offered in a low tone. "But I thought it best if this was held in the truest Alban tradition."

"Boundless hospitality?" I asked, remembering Firdha's teaching.

He nodded. "Indeed."

"I think it's lovely," Phèdre said in seemingly perfect sincerity.

Joscelin glanced sidelong at her. "You would say that."

"I think," Hyacinthe murmured, "that I would only endure this for *your* foster-son's sake, Phèdre nó Delaunay."

I spread my hands. "Please, my lord! I beg you, don't suffer on my account."

It *was* lovely, though; in a noisy, clattering, sweltering, overstuffed way. Whether the folk seated at the table were enemies or rivals outside the hall's confines, all were friends and comrades within it. Such was the blessing of the Cruarch's boundless hospitality. When everyone had eaten and drunk their fill, a good many of the platters were cleared, and fewer full ones were brought. I felt I could breathe easier. Outside, the sun must have set, for some of the contained heat in the hall began to dissipate.

Pitchers of cool water went round, followed by jugs of *uisghe*.

Conor mac Grainne tuned his harp and began to play. For the second time that night, everyone fell silent; this time, to listen.

In the short time since I'd last seen him, his playing had grown stronger and deeper. Before, I'd thought he was good enough to play in any D'Angeline salon. Now I thought he was better than any harpist I'd heard, save for his father. There was no magic in it; no charm. Only skill and beauty.

Conor didn't sing tonight, but on the third tune he played, Breidaia lifted her voice unexpectedly, clear and sweet. On the second verse, Sibeal joined her; and on the third, Dorelei, shy and faltering at first, settling into clarity. Their three voices rose and fell in intricate, intertwining harmonies, weaving a song like threads on the loom of Conor's harping.

When it ended, he placed his hand on the strings of his harp, stilling them.

"Elua!" Phèdre's eyes were bright with tears. "I've not heard the like since . . ."

". . . Since the night Moiread died," Hyacinthe finished.

"It is fitting," Drustan said quietly. Moiread had been his youngest sister, slain in the battle for Bryn Gorrydum; Eamonn's sister Mairead was her Eiran namesake. "It is fitting that we remember past sorrows, even as we celebrate present joys. My mother would have been pleased. I would that she had lived to see this day." He nodded toward the middle of the table, where Conor was seated. "Truly, you may claim a bard's boon of me for this night's playing, young prince of the Dalriada. May I ask one of you?"

"Of course, my lord." A heated flush reddened Conor's cheeks.

Drustan smiled gently. "Give us another tune, lad. A merry tune, that we might end this night in gladness."

Conor took a deep breath. "Of course, my lord!"

He played a merry tune, his thin brown fingers dancing over the strings, plucking and teasing, picking out a melody that goaded one's heart to lift and one's feet to dance, infectious and mirthful. A good many folk did rise to dance, including Phèdre, laughing, who hauled a protesting Joscelin to his feet. On and on, Conor played, his melody scaling new heights with every change of verse.

"Will you?" I asked Dorelei.

"Will *you*?" She flashed her dimpled smile.

So it was that we danced in the hall of Bryn Gorrydum, on the first eve of our Alban nuptials, amid strangers and loved ones alike. And when Conor at last ended his song, we were breathless and laughing, the both of us.

"The babe . . . ?" I asked, belatedly anxious.

"The babe is fine." Dorelei took my hand and placed it on her belly. She smiled into my eyes. "I, however, find myself growing weary."

Glancing around the hall, I realized that a number of folk had departed. Hyacinthe and Sibeal were gone; and the Lady Breidaia, too. Joscelin was coaxing Phèdre up the stair, the two of them engaged in some private banter. Others were, it seemed, prepared to spend the night in merriment, making the most of the Cruarch's hospitality.

"To bed?" I whispered.

Dorelei's dimples deepened. "Aye."

"Imri!" Alais, flushed and sweating, intercepted us mid-escape. She'd been dancing, too, with Talorcan. "I forgot. I've a letter for you, from Mavros."

"Mavros!" His name seemed like somewhat from a dream I'd forgotten. I glanced at Dorelei, eager to be alone with her, and saw my own desire reflected in her eyes. "Ah, well. Surely it can wait until morning?"

"I suppose." Alais was noncommittal. "'Tis your business. He's your cousin."

"Tomorrow, then." I mounted the stair, tugging at Dorelei's willing hand as she ascended with me. "Tomorrow."

TWENTY-SEVEN

THERE WAS NO TIME to read Mavros' letter, on the morrow or the next day. There was simply too much to be done. After a sleepy-eyed Alais delivered it to me as promised, I tucked it away in my things. After the wedding, I thought, I would read it. Until then, 'twas easier not to think of home.

And to be sure, there was more serious business afoot.

For one thing, we had a long, private conference with Drustan and told him about the Maghuin Dhonn. Although he seemed somewhat distracted, he was troubled by the news.

"I'd almost rather hear they're trying to stir trouble among the Tarbh Cró again," he muttered. "At least it's easier to understand." Drustan sighed. "Clunderry has a strong garrison, but I'll ask Urist to select another twenty men and take command of it. He's got a good head on his shoulders, I trust him as much as anyone I've fought with. And you'll have the Lady Firdha in residence, too. Alais will be continuing her studies with her."

"Can she—?" I gestured at my fetters of red yarn, remembering the dismissive way Aodhan had spoken of court bards.

"Yes, yes, of course," Drustan said absently. "Whatever's needful."

"Are you certain?" I asked. "She was unwilling to speak of the Maghuin Dhonn."

Drustan shrugged. "*Ollamhs* can be overly superstitious. I'll talk to her."

"Is everything all right, my lord?" Dorelei asked. "We didn't wish to disturb you on the eve of our nuptials, but we thought you should know."

"Yes, of course." The Cruarch of Alba heaved another sigh. "'Tis a hard piece of news Stormkeep's master gave me today, that's all. Although I imagine the responsibility will fall to your generation in the end."

"He's chosen not to train a successor, hasn't he?" I asked.

"I thought you knew," Drustan said wryly. "No mind, you'd have to be told sooner or later. I'll ask you to keep it silent for now. His decision won't be a popular one, and I'd rather not have it linked in people's minds with your wedding. I've not decided what to do about it."

"Of course, my lord," I promised, and Dorelei nodded.

"Mayhap he can be swayed," Drustan mused. "Or at least pursuaded not to destroy the Book of Raziel's pages."

"What?" I was startled.

"Oh, yes." His dark eyes were somber. "Master Hyacinthe is concerned that the knowledge is too dangerous, and he is minded to see it pass forever from this earth with him." He shook his head. "I do not know the answer. It is a grave matter, and I would sooner discuss it at length. I would be willing to take the Book into my own safekeeping rather than see it destroyed."

"You couldn't use it, you know." I frowned. "'Tis writ in an alphabet no one can read."

"I know." Drustan looked steadily at me. "But it is a powerful tool of protection. Alba's curse has become Alba's blessing. I would not discard such a gift out of hand. It may be that one day someone could decipher it." He smiled a little. "Your own heir, mayhap."

Dorelei and I exchanged a glance. "I'm not so sure I'd want that," she murmured.

Nor was I.

I thought about the way Hyacinthe sought so assiduously to protect his own children from the burdens of power, and I thought about how he'd changed over the course of our stay at the Stormkeep, seeming to grow younger and easier in his skin. I'd attributed it to Phèdre and Joscelin's presence; old friends who had known him long before he was the Master of the Straits. Doubtless that was part of it.

But part of it may have been the sheer relief of having the thing done, the decision made. He would carry his burden until the end of his days, but there it *would* end. For good or for ill, no one would carry it afterward.

At least if he truly meant to destroy it.

I had my doubts. I didn't know Hyacinthe well enough to guess at his thoughts, not really. But I knew Phèdre and Joscelin better than I knew anyone on the face of the earth, and it wasn't in either of their nature to do such a thing gladly. Phèdre had dedicated years of her life to the pursuit of arcane wisdom, and Joscelin was a scion of Shemhazai, whose credo was *All Knowledge Is Worth Having.* Whatever it was they'd been plotting over the past weeks, I was willing to bet it wasn't destroying the pages of the Book of Raziel.

I was also wise enough to keep my mouth shut on the thought.

After our meeting with Drustan, Dorelei and I were separated in accordance with Alban tradition, which had been explained to me that morning along with a great many other details. Since there were fewer of them—most of the clan-lords didn't travel with their wives—the women were sequestered in a private salon, while the men occupied the great hall.

"What do the women do there?" I asked Eamonn.

He grinned. "Talk frankly about bedchamber secrets. They're all very excited about having Phèdre among them."

"I don't doubt it." I laughed. "And what do we do?"

"Eat, drink, brag about women, and get into fights," he said cheerfully. "Like as not, you'll get at least one challenge tonight."

"Lovely," I said.

He was right, of course.

The eating and drinking commenced immediately; in truth, it had never really ended, thanks to the Cruarch's boundless hospitality. If I'd thought last night was raucous, it was nothing to this one. Hyacinthe was not in attendance, for which I didn't blame him. Drustan presided over the early proceedings, then offered a toast in my honor and turned the affair over to Talorcan, retiring.

Once he'd left, the bragging began.

It took a more stylized form than I'd anticipated, beginning with verses of praise offered to one's absent lady-love, each man standing to declaim his own. As the night wore on and the *uisghe* circulated, the poems grew increasingly ribald and the bragging more pronounced. Conor mac Grainne, the youngest one present, listened with mortified delight, while his older brother teased him for squirming.

When his turn came, Eamonn rose. "Brigitta's eyes are blue as hare-bells," he said with pride. "Her hair is wind-tossed flax. The curve of her arse makes strong men weep, and her tongue is as sharp as her dagger."

I glanced at Joscelin and cleared my throat. "You don't have to stay."

He looked amused. "Oh, I know."

When my own turn came, I didn't have it my heart to be ribald. After all, my wife's brother was present. I rose, feeling Talorcan's gaze resting on me. "Dorelei's heart is like a hidden well," I said, feeling awkward. "Deep and without fathom. And I am a shallow bucket, who only dreams of plumbing its depths."

The ensuing cheers seemed earnest. I flushed and sat down.

Joscelin raised his brows. "Where did that come from?"

"Oh." I wiped my sweating palms on my knees. "We've been talking a lot, she and I."

"My lord Joscelin!" Eamonn called. "Will you not honor your lady?"

To my surprise, Joscelin rose. "Phèdre—" he began, then halted. Sitting below him, I watched him smile to himself, quiet and private. "Phèdre yields with a willow's grace," he said softly. "And endures with the strength of mountains. Without her, life would be calm; and yet would lack all meaning."

There was a little silence then.

"That's beautiful." My friend from the preceeding night, Gwynek of Brea, leaned forward and thumped his cup on the table in a surfeit of maudlin drunkenness. "Beautiful!"

Joscelin nodded. "My thanks, my lord."

The mood he'd instilled lasted all of a few moments before veering back toward ribaldry and boasting, which led directly to the fighting. It began good-naturedly enough with bouts of arm-wrestling, brawny clan-lords planting their elbows on the table and straining against one another. Harmless enough, I thought.

But then an argument broke out between two contestants; one of the Tarbh Cró and one of Talorcan's men, who accused him of cheating. The Cruithne folk of the Cullach Gorrym, I'd noted, tended to grow more volatile with drink. It wasn't long before they were on their feet, shoving one another. Someone began shouting, "Staves! Staves!" and other voices took up the cry until Talorcan smiled and gave his assent.

In short order, a pair of ashwood quarterstaves were produced, and the two commenced to batter at one another with considerable ferocity. Everyone shouted, cheering them on. When the Tarbh Cró went down with a glancing blow to the temple, eyes rolling back in his head, I winced; but his fellows merely laughed and dragged his limp body off the floor.

The Cruithne, whose name was Brude, grinned and spun his staff. "Anyone else?"

"I'll have a go!" my friend Gwynek called.

And so it went. Brude defeated Gwynek and another clan-lord before losing a bout that cost him bruised ribs and a broken, bleeding nose. He accepted defeat with good grace, sitting down to tilt his head and pinch his nose, while solicitous fellows poured *uisghe* down his throat.

"Has anyone ever died doing this?" I muttered to Eamonn.

"Oh, yes," he said, watching Brude's vanquisher take on a new opponent. "Many times."

It was one of the Tarbh Cró who emerged as the best of the lot; a seasoned fighter named Goraidh. He had a weather-beaten face and reddish hair faded with silver, but he was strong and skilled and quick on his feet. With a sense of rueful inevitability, I watched him level his staff and point at me.

"Let's see what the young prince is made of!" he cried.

And of course, a roar of agreement ensued. Cups were pounded on the table, my name was shouted. I sighed and rose, hoping to emerge alive and intact. I'd a little experience with the quarterstaff—Hugues had taught me the rudiments—but not much. What a piece of irony it would be if I survived slave-traders, mad rulers, a murderous kins-woman, and sorcerous bear-witches, only to be brained on the eve of my wedding.

"Imri." Joscelin beckoned. "Watch how he cocks his head. I don't think he sees well out of his right eye."

"Is that all the advice you've got for me?" I said glumly.

"Mind your footwork," he offered. "And try not to get killed."

It was the Tarbh Cró, under the leadership of Maelcon the Usurper, who had slain Drustan's uncle, the old Cruarch, and driven Drustan into exile among the Dalriada. That fact did not escape my attention as I took the proffered staff in both hands and faced Goraidh.

He bared yellowing teeth in a battle-grin. "Shall we dance?"

I shrugged. "As you wish."

Goraidh came at me, flicking a quick, testing blow with the left end of his staff. I parried it easily. With an agile twist of his wrists, he re-versed the staff and swung low at my legs, forcing me to skip backward. Some of the watchers jeered.

Goraidh laughed. "Stand and fight, lad!"

I sidled to the left, watching his head turn. Joscelin was right. "Not likely! I want to keep my face pretty for my wife on our wedding night."

That drew a good laugh; even Goraidh chuckled. He was still turn-ing to face me, cocking his head to get a fix on me with his good left eye, when I circled farther to his left, deft and sliding, and jabbed him hard in the kidney.

Mind your footwork.

Goraidh grunted. I spun back the other way and caught him wrong-footed and unready. His mouth gaped as I swung at his unprotected head.

At the last instant, I pulled the blow short and settled for a solid tap. "Will you do my wife a kindness and concede?"

I wasn't sure, for a moment, how he'd react. His blue-grey eyes nar-rowed and he tightened his grip on the staff. I settled into a defensive stance, smiling and watchful.

For a mercy, Goraidh decided to roar with laughter. "All right, lad! Since the lady likes your pretty face so well, I'll leave it be." Lowering his staff, he reached out to tousle my hair with rough familiarity. "You're a slippery devil, but you're all right."

Thus passed the eve of my second wedding. My bout with Goraidh garnered respect and friendliness, which manifested itself in the form of a great deal of *uisghe*. At some point, I recall Talorcan placing an ancient steel-plated leather helmet with a boar's tusks protruding from the cheekplates on my head and proclaiming me an honorary brother among the Cullach Gorrym. This required that I toast each man present. The last thing I recall, before the hall began to slide sideways in my vision, was someone asking plaintively, "Are you *sure* we can't give him his warrior's mark?"

In the morning, I awoke with a roiling belly and an aching head. There was no mirror in the guest chamber, and Dorelei was still sequestered with the women. I felt at my forehead, unable to determine whether the pain there was the aftereffects of drink, or a fresh tattoo. When Joscelin came to fetch me, he caught me peering at the flat side of my dagger, trying to get a glimpse of my reflection.

"Did they . . . ?" I gesturing at my brow.

"No, I wouldn't let them." He grinned. "Talorcan insisted on challenging me to a bout over it."

I squinted at Joscelin. "How is he?"

He laughed. "Sore."

The wedding itself took place in a park in the center of the city; a place held in trust for the folk of Alba, *taisgaidh* land left to grow wild and undisturbed. Anyone who wished was free to attend, and by exchanging our vows there, Dorelei and I offered a symbolic pledge that our union was made for the sake of Alba itself.

'Twas all very, very different from our D'Angeline nuptials. By the time we arrived in our separate parties, male and female, my head was clearing. Dorelei and I smiled at one another. She wore a simple saffron kirtle and a wreath of yellow celandine on her black hair. I was clad in the old Alban style in a pair of dark breeches, bare-chested, wearing naught but a red cloak over my shoulders.

There were two *ollamhs* presiding; Firdha and a man named Colum. They stood erect and unsmiling, both of them holding gilded oak branches. Beyond them, in a circle, were all the invited guests. The women looked fresh and lovely; I noted that the men looked rather worse for the wear, and Talorcan was sporting a sling on his right arm. Beyond the invited guests were the commonfolk who had chosen to attend, of whom there were quite a few. I was pleased to find that the mood seemed one of festive curiosity.

The ceremony began with a lengthy invocation of Alba's deities, great and small, belonging to all the Four Folk; gods and goddesses of the moon and sun; of fire and healing, smithcraft and cattle; horses, wells, springs and rivers; of battle and poetry; of wild things, growing things, of abundance and plenty. On and on the list went—Lug, Saolas, Nerthus, Macha, Brigid, Aengus, Bel, Manannan, Hengest, Danu, Crom, Aine, Cailleach . . .

I knew the names, or most of them. Religion in Alba was at once complex and simple, a mixture of deities, ancestors, and earth spirits. There were no temples, only sacred places. Of those, there were thousands. I had to own, though I understood the lore, I didn't yet grasp the faith in my flesh and bones. But mayhap it would come in time. For our child's sake, I would try.

After the deities, the *ollamhs* invoked the blessing of the *diadh-anams*, the guiding spirits of the Four Folk; the Black Boar, the Red Bull, the Golden Stag, and the White Horse. The sun was hot overhead, and I felt sweat trickle along my brow. It was the only thing, I thought, that these two wedding ceremonies had in common.

It seemed like a very long time ago that I'd stood beside Dorelei in the Palace gardens, sweltering and heartsick in my high-collared doublet.

When the *ollamhs* had done with their invocations, they beckoned. Dorelei and I came forward and presented ourselves to them, bowing deeply. "Dorelei mab Breidaia, Imriel de la Courcel. Shall you plight your troth to one another?" Firdha asked.

"Daughter of the Grove, for a year and a day, we shall," Dorelei answered firmly. There was a little murmur among the onlookers at her words, not necessarily disapproving. We had discussed this at length, she and I. Albans practiced two forms of marriage; one binding, one less so. If, after a year and a day, we chose to part, the matter would be ended, at least as far as Alba was concerned.

Firdha nodded. "So be it. Join your hands."

We faced one another. I crossed my wrists, clasping Dorelei's hands in mine. We stood and smiled at one another as first Firdha, then Colum, twined our wrists together with red yarn, adding to the layers that already bound mine, invoking another lengthy series of blessings for health, happiness, and fertility.

The *ollamh* Colum tapped my shoulder with his golden oak branch. "Speak your vows."

"By stone and sea and sky, and all that they encompass, for a year and a day, I pledge myself to you, and you alone," I said softly.

Dorelei's hands tightened on mine, slippery with sweat. Her dark eyes were raised to meet my gaze. The first time we'd wed, I'd been the one felt the sting of sacrifice.

This time, it was she.

For so long as our lives were bound together, for so long as I was bound by Aodhan's charms, her dreams would be silent. What that meant to Dorelei, I couldn't even begin to imagine. I was humbled by it. "By stone and sea and sky, and all that they encompass . . ." Her throat moved as she swallowed. "I pledge myself to you, and you alone."

There were cheers then, surprisingly hearty. The *ollamhs* invoked a final blessing, and then Dorelei and I walked around the circle together, side by side, our wrists still conjoined. When we reached Drustan, we found the Cruarch smiling.

"Rejoice, daughter of my sister," he said to Dorelei; and to me, placing a thick gold torc around my nearly bare neck, "Be welcome, Prince of Alba."

More cheers.

I felt humbled by them and bowed my head. "I will try to be worthy, my lord."

Drustan's eyes glinted. "I know."

When we had completed the circle, we returned to the center. The *ollamhs* unbound our wrists and presented us with the lengths of red yarn; Firdha's to Dorelei, Colum's to me. They were luck-charms now, meant to be saved for the birth of our first child. With these threads, we would tie off the birth-cord that bound mother to babe, preparing it to be severed.

"Ward them well," Firdha said.

Dorelei and I glanced at one another. "We will," I promised.

So we were wed a second time, and the second was better than the first; far better. As I glanced around the circle of folk who surrounded us, I saw only love and good wishes. No one had wept at our D'Angeline nuptials, but now I saw Phèdre's eyes bright with tears; and many others, too. Alais was weeping openly, as was Dorelei's mother, Breidaia. Eamonn and Brigitta had clasped hands, gazing at one another and remembering their own nuptials in besieged Lucca. Even Joscelin's stoic look appeared a bit put-on, and I caught sight of the Master of the Straits grinning at him.

"What happens now?" I whispered to Dorelei.

She smiled, dimpled. "More eating and drinking. What else?"

There was a special horse-litter waiting to carry us back to the fortress for the third and final day of celebration. It was a open affair with a low railing, draped with fine-combed red wool and strewn with cushions, slung fore and aft between a pair of perfectly matched white horses; a gift, I learned later, from the Lady of the Dalriada.

Once our procession was under way, many of the watching commonfolk approached to touch the hanging drapery and partake in the blessings the *ollamhs* had invoked for us. Despite the lead rider's best efforts to set a slow, even pace, the litter lurched and swayed somewhat fierce. Dorelei and I laughed breathlessly and clutched at one another, fearful of being pitched overboard.

Some distance from the edge of the park, it stopped.

I didn't know why, not at first. I only knew a tense hush fell over the procession. The commonfolk around us vanished, melting away unobtrusively.

And then I saw the Maghuin Dhonn.

Berlik in his bearskin robe, I knew; and Morwen and Ferghus. There were a score of others with them, men and women alike. Aside from Berlik and Morwen with their mist-colored eyes, they were all as dark as the Cruithne, only marked with a strange, wild air and a different angle to the planes of their faces. They stood quiet and motionless in their roughspun clothes, watching and waiting. None of them appeared armed, although Ferghus had his harp over his shoulder. I didn't see the leather bag around Morwen's neck, and guessed it was hidden away once more.

Drustan rode forward, his face impassive. "You are not welcome here."

"It is *taisgaidh* land, Cruarch." Berlik's voice was as I remembered, like something emerging from the deep, hollow places of the earth. "Will you profane the old ways?"

Drustan ignored the question. "What do you want?"

Berlik's pale, somber gaze rested on Dorelei and me. I felt her shiver violently at my side. "Not all of the *diadh-anams* of Alba have been invoked this day. We come to offer the blessing of the Maghuin Dhonn upon this union. Do you refuse it?"

I was silent, not knowing how to answer.

"We do." Dorelei's voice was unexpectedly forceful. "There is a shadow on you, my lord; on all of you. I wish no part of it."

Berlik inclined his head slightly. "There is darkness in all of us, lady; even in the heart of Alba. It is not wise to ignore it."

"Is that a threat?" Drustan asked sharply.

The Maghuin Dhonn looked steadily at him. "No, Cruarch. It is a truth."

Although the skies were clear, somewhere in the distance there was an ominous rumble of thunder. Hyacinthe, seated atop a bay gelding, was still and silent, but there was no trace of the merry Tsingano lad about him now; only the Master of the Straits. The mantle of power clung to him as clearly as Berlik's bearskin robe, and infinitely more dangerous.

The weary lines etched on Berlik's face deepened.

"So," he said to Hyacinthe. "You too, magician?" Hyacinthe made no answer. Berlik sighed. "We are few," he said, addressing his words to all of us. "We are ancient, and we are few. The old blood runs true in very few of us, now. But we have been Alba's caretakers for a long, long time. The future narrows. Much that we have preserved lies in jeopardy. Remember that we made this offer."

With that, Berlik bowed, his robe rippling around him, then turned and began walking westward across the park. All of his folk followed, wordless. Only the harpist Ferghus sent a parting glance in our direction, and that was at his son Conor, riding at Eamonn's side. Conor averted his eyes, not meeting his father's gaze. Outside of Innisclan, no one knew his paternity.

"Talorcan." Drustan beckoned. "Take as many men as you can muster and follow them. Once they leave sacred ground, ensure they depart the city."

"Aye, my lord." Talorcan hesitated. "Do you wish us to engage them?"

Drustan gave a hard smile. "If they give you just cause, yes. But I will not defile the wedding day of my sister's daughter by breaking the rule of law."

Talorcan made him a left-handed salute. "Aye, my lord."

Thus we were a far smaller party that returned to Bryn Gorrydum's fortress, and the mood was chastened and somber. Although the Cruarch's table of endless bounty was groaning and laden again, for once, no one had the heart to tackle it properly. Instead, there was a good deal of muttered speculation about what *they* wanted.

I wondered, too.

Elua help me, I believed Berlik's offer had been sincere; as sincere as his oath. I only wished it wasn't all cloaked in mystery and portent. I intended Alba no ill; indeed, I'd grown fond of the land. If the Maghuin Dhonn beheld some dire future approaching in which I inadvertently did great harm, I wished they'd simply *tell* me. Mayhap there was somewhat to be done about it.

It wasn't long before Talorcan and his men returned, empty-handed and grumbling. The Maghuin Dhonn had proceeded beyond the borders of the city and vanished into *taisgaidh* land; truly vanishing, leaving no tracks.

"I wish this hadn't happened today," Dorelei murmured unhappily.

"So do I, love." My gaze fell on Conor, quiet and withdrawn. No doubt he was troubled, too, albeit for different reasons. I snapped my fingers. "Conor! Conor mac Grainne, did you not promise to play at my wedding?"

The boy raised his head. "You're sure?"

"I am," I said. "Charm us, lad."

His eyes widened at my choice of words, but he reached for his harp and began to play. At first his fingers faltered on the strings, but slowly they gained in steadiness. A tune emerged, sweet and stately and compelling.

Whether or not there was magic in it, I couldn't have said; not for a surety. If there was, I was bound against it. But I watched while everyone gathered fell silent to listen, smiling dreamily, and I thought there was. Conor played like a man trying to scale a mountain or lift a heavy boulder, his eyes closed in concentration, his coarse black hair plastered to his damp brow. But slowly, slowly, the mood in the great hall of Bryn Gorrydum shifted.

When he finally ceased, there were cheers.

"To my brother!" Eamonn shouted, getting to his feet. "The finest harpist in seven generations of the Dalriada!" He hoisted a goblet of mead. "To Imri, the best friend a man could ask for, and to Dorelei, who nonetheless deserves better!"

Laughter.

Cheers.

It wasn't perfect, not quite. I daresay nothing ever is. But it salvaged the day. Worries over the Maghuin Dhonn were set aside in favor of celebration. There was eating and drinking; there were innumerable toasts. There were harmless quarrels and arguments, and jests about my pretty face, which Dorelei endured, blushing. Conor played quietly throughout the evening, his dark eyes closed, spiky lashes splayed on his broad cheekbones, stitching together a melody that interwove past and present and future alike.

Along the way, day gave way to night, and night wore on into the small hours of morning. One by one, celebrants peeled away, staggering off to their chambers. Some, like Hyacinthe and Sibeal and Drustan, departed early. Others stayed longer.

When Phèdre and Joscelin bade us good night, she cupped my face in her hands, gazing up at me. She seemed so small to me now, and vulnerable; the scarlet mote of Kushiel's Dart floating on her dark iris. Once, it would have disturbed me to my core. Now it didn't.

I daresay she knew. She always knew.

"You seem . . . happy, love." She smiled ruefully. "Despite everything."

"I am," I said honestly. "Despite everything, I am."

Joscelin cleared his throat and nodded at Dorelei, slumped over the table and sleeping peaceably, her head pillowed on one arm. His summer-blue eyes glinted. "You might want to look to your lady wife."

"I will," I promised.

Once they had gone, I tried to wake Dorelei, who murmured in protest. So I scooped her into my arms. She nestled her warm brown cheek against my bare chest as I mounted the stairs, ignoring the ribald jests from below.

"Imriel," she whispered. "I do love you."

"I know." I kissed her brow. "So do I."

"You don't." One hand scrabbled at my chest, then fell limp, dangling. "Not really."

"I do," I avowed. "As best I can, and a bit more beside."

Our bedchamber was decorated with shriveled flower petals and the lamps were burning low. I laid Dorelei gently on our nuptial bed and eased her out of her kirtle. She heaved a great sigh, curling onto her side, one hand resting on her lower belly. It had begun to evince a bulge, only the tiniest bit. I drew the blankets over her and laid down beside her.

And there I lay.

And lay.

I was awake; I was wide awake. I listened to Dorelei's soft, rhythmic breathing. I listened to the sounds of the fortress settling into slumber. The last of the straggling celebrants quieting; the last of the Cruarch's servants clearing the detritus of our nuptials.

At last I gave up and rose.

I pulled on my breeches and retrieved Mavros' letter, padding barefoot and bare-chested down to the great hall, where the torches yet smoldered. A good many Albans were strewn about, snoring hard.

I cracked open the seal of House Shahrizai and read.

Mavros had penned a brief letter, lighthearted and typical, filled with snippets of idle gossip. It was only a cover, an excuse to send a letter from Sidonie, written in Caerdicci for discretion's sake. I'd known,

I suppose; or at least suspected. I just hadn't allowed myself to think on it.

I skimmed her opening words and felt nothing.

No; not true.

I felt, for the first time in weeks, my bindings itch and constrict. Somewhere, I was aware of a vague, distant pain, but it was as if it belonged to someone else. I scratched my wrists and my ankles, shifting the letter that the torchlight might fall more fully on it. I read Sidonie's opening words again.

The croonie-stone around my neck felt hot and heavy, entangled with the golden torc. I ran one finger beneath the leather thong to free it, sweating. It came free so easily; so easily. Almost without thinking, I ducked my chin and yanked. The leather thong stretched. I hauled it over my head, scraping my cheeks and ears.

I didn't feel any different, only mildly shocked at my own impulsive actions and aware that my heart was beating faster. I held the polished croonie-stone in my hand, staring at it. Already, it felt cooler and lighter. I strained my ears, listening for the sound of pipes, for Morwen's laughter. There was nothing. The Maghuin Dhonn had left the city, had gone far away. At the moment, I was safe.

Surely, I thought, for a few minutes, there was no harm in this.

I read the beginning of Sidonie's letter for a third time.

Dear Imriel,

You may laugh if you like, but I have wasted several costly sheets of paper trying to find the words to write to you in a manner befitting the correspondence of Remuel L'Oragen and Claire LeDoux. Like as not, I would still be trying if Amarante had not finally observed with some asperity that I have never been given to poetic sentimentality, and there is no reason to suppose that would change just because I miss you. I do believe I was beginning to irk her, which is no small feat.

So if you are expecting a paean celebrating everything from the drowning-pools of your eyes to the sinewed arches of your feet, lingering over the veinèd glory of love's throbbing scepter, you will be disappointed.

But I do miss you, and it is an ache that never goes away. Life continues, day by day. I pretend to be someone I am not, wearing my self like a mask, stretched over the aching void that is your absence in my life. I miss you. Waking, sleeping, eating, riding, talking, breathing; I miss you. It is a simple, constant fact of my existence. The fact that I hate and resent it makes not the slightest difference at all.

I miss you.

It struck me like a punch to the belly. There in the Cruarch's hall, surrounded by slumbering Albans, my throat constricted and I caught my breath in a gasp that was half laugh, half sob. The dam of my heart had cracked, and the torrent of emotion threatened to drown me. Love, desire, tenderness, humor; even the sweet mercy of gentle cruelty. It was all there, all bound up in an inextricable knot. All alive and immediate and insistent, and wonderfully, horribly poignant.

And ah, Elua! For the first time I *knew* beyond question that I wanted to spend the rest of my life with Sidonie de la Courcel.

I sat there for a long time, reading and rereading her letter in its entirety, the croonie-stone in my hand, laughing quietly to myself, tears in my eyes. I could have read it over for hours. All too vividly, I could picture Sidonie writing it; the expression on her face, hovering between self-mockery and earnestness. She wrote quickly and neatly, each letter of each word formed with swift, exacting precision. For no reason at all, that fact made my heart swell and ache.

I loved her.

And upstairs, my twice-wed wife was sleeping, our child growing inside her.

And I loved her, too.

I hadn't lied to Dorelei. It wasn't the same, it wasn't anywhere near the same. And yet even now I felt it. I read Sidonie's letter for the dozenth time, lingering over it. And then I bowed my head and prayed to Blessed Elua, holding the leather thong on which the croonie-stone was strung in both hands. Swiftly, fearful that hesitation would weaken my resolve, I forced it over my head.

Stone clinked against gold, settling against my throat.

My feelings dimmed.

My bonds itched and burned.

Elbows propped on the Cruarch's table, I rested my head in my hands and breathed slowly, willing everything to subside.

And slowly, slowly, it did.

It was still there, walled away. Nothing had changed. Nothing would change. Until the day I died, by whatever unfathomable forces govern the mortal heart, I would adore my cool, haughty, funny, passionate, surprising cousin Sidonie beyond all reason.

But I was a husband, too, and soon to be a father. And I had sworn a vow this very day; a vow I'd meant. For a year and a day, I'd pledged myself. I'd sworn it by the same oath that the Maghuin Dhonn had sworn to do me no harm. Blessed Elua might forgive me for breaking it for love's sake; I was not certain the myriad gods and goddesses, and Alba herself, would do the same.

I folded away the letter and went upstairs to lie awake in my nuptial bed.

TWENTY-EIGHT

ALL THROUGHOUT THE following day, guests departed amid a flurry of well-wishes.

Hyacinthe and Sibeal were among the first to leave. "My gift to you is a promise to Phèdre and Joscelin," the Master of the Straits said to me. "Inasmuch as I may, I will keep watch over Clunderry in the sea-mirror; and the Maghuin Dhonn, too. If I see aught amiss, I will send swift word to you and Drustan alike."

"My thanks, my lord. It is a great kindness." Feeling awkward, I touched the croonie-stone at my throat, remembering the day he'd shown us the sea-mirror and the way he'd looked at me afterward. "Master Hyacinthe . . . may I ask you a question?"

He smiled a little. "You may."

"Did you ever speak the *dromonde* for me?" I asked.

Hyacinthe didn't answer right away. He looked thoughtfully at me, shadows shifting like slow currents in his dark eyes. "I saw somewhat, once," he said at length. "A glimpse."

I cleared my throat. "Was it harmful to Alba? Or Dorelei?"

"No," he said, slow and puzzled. "You were alone, and it was snowing. You were kneeling beneath a tree, holding a sword."

It was Dorelei's dream, the only one she'd had of me. I remembered her telling me, back in Terre d'Ange, as I'd slid into a drunken slumber. A shiver brushed my spine. "Thank you."

He smiled wryly. "For what it's worth, you're welcome. As Phèdre might well tell you, the *dromonde* can be a vague business, muddled as a dream and filled with odd portents. It may mean somewhat altogether different than it seems. But have a care this winter nonetheless. Sibeal's counting on you and Dorelei to visit next summer, babe in tow."

I smiled back at him. "I will and we shall."

We bade farewell to Eamonn and Brigitta that day; and to Conor, although I didn't see him at first. It was Dorelei who nudged me and nodded. In a quiet corner of the hall, Conor and Alais were deep in conversation, oblivious to aught else.

I raised my brows at Eamonn. "What do you know about *that*?"

Eamonn grimaced. "Not a blessed thing. Dagda Mor! He knows she's betrothed to Prince Talorcan." He whistled sharply. Conor's head came up, his brown cheeks flushed. "Sorry, my lady," Eamonn said to Dorelei. "I'm sure the lad meant no harm by it."

"Ah, well." She watched the two of them make their way toward us. "They're young."

Fifteen, I thought. In Terre d'Ange, that was too young to play the Game of Courtship in earnest, too young for admission to the Night Court. Old enough for other games, though. Alais' violet eyes were sparkling in a way they seldom did at home. At sixteen, she was pledged to wed Talorcan in a ceremony that would doubtless make our nuptial celebration look miserly. There would be no Game of Courtship for her. Alais and Talorcan seemed to like and respect one another, but I'd seen naught else between them. I remembered what she'd said when I asked if she'd consented to the betrothal. *I couldn't think of a reason not to.* I wondered if she fancied she might find one in Conor mac Grainne, son of the Lady of the Dalriada and a harpist of the Maghuin Dhonn.

"Why are you looking at me like that, Imri?" Alais asked.

"No reason," I said. "Yet."

Like as not, it was only harmless flirting. Still, Elua, what a mess that would be! For some perverse reason, the thought made me grin. Alais narrowed her eyes at me. "Whatever it is, it's not funny."

"You're probably right about that," I agreed.

Amid fond farewells and further promises of visits, they took their leave; and once the Dalriadans had left, there were dozens of clan-lords who must be thanked for their attendance and whatever gifts they'd brought.

All in all, 'twas a long, wearying day of courtesy.

I was glad Phèdre and Joscelin weren't leaving today, although the matter was problematic in its own way.

Two days hence, Dorelei and I, along with her mother and Alais, would leave to take up residence at Clunderry. It was Joscelin's initial desire to accompany us there to see to the skill of the estate's garrison and the security of its borders he had done in Montrève. Urist, appointed by Drustan to accomplish that very task, had taken it amiss. The Cruarch had stayed out of the matter thus far, and so had Phèdre, although I daresay she would have been glad to go to Clunderry with us. It was my first test of statecraft as a Prince of Alba, and fortunately, I'd had enough wits to consult Dorelei on the matter.

"Truly?" She had hesitated. "Imriel, it is not only Urist who would take it amiss. In the eyes of Alba, it is we who saved Terre d'Ange in her hour of need. It would not sit well to have a D'Angeline presume to teach us."

Together, we had made our decision, and I was glad I'd heeded her counsel. That night, over a blessedly quiet meal, we discussed the matter. I'd thought Joscelin would be angry, but he surprised me, merely smiling ruefully.

"You've a point," he said. "I wouldn't have tolerated it at Montrève."

"You're welcome to come, of course," Dorelei added.

Phèdre fixed her with one of those deep looks. "I remember how it was when I first inherited Montrève," she mused. "They're a stiff-necked folk, the Siovalese." Joscelin snorted, which she ignored. "No matter what I might have done, no matter that I was my lord Delaunay's legal heir. They were none too pleased to have the estate given over to a City-born courtesan. The wisest thing I did to earn their trust was to stay away a good deal of the time until they realized I didn't intend to alter the nature of Montrève."

"You think it best if you don't come with us," I said, realization dawning.

"What do you think?" Phèdre glanced around the table.

It was all family there that night; Drustan presiding, Talorcan, Breidaia, and Dorelei, and then Alais, Phèdre, and Joscelin. Strange to think, they *were* all my family, bound by ties of blood, fosterage, and marriage. The Cruithne glanced at one another, and it was my wife's mother who answered.

"I think it is in your heart to do otherwise," Breidaia said to Phèdre, her voice gentle with compassion. "But I think what you say is wise. Let the folk learn to love the children on their own merits, in their own time. Then, when a pair of D'Angeline heroes out of legend grace Clunderry's threshold—in the spring, mayhap, when the babe is due . . ." She smiled, her cheeks dimpling like her daughter's. ". . . your presence will be received as a blessing."

"Why wouldn't it be *now*?" Alais asked, bewildered.

"Because people can be foolish," Drustan said. "And fearful of heroes not their own."

So it was decided. We would depart for Clunderry, and Phèdre and Joscelin would return to Terre d'Ange. Or at least I thought so; I still wasn't entirely certain what they'd concocted with Hyacinthe.

On our last day together, I scavenged an hour's brief privacy and attempted to write a reply to Sidonie. That much, at least, I owed her. It wasn't the hardest letter I'd ever written—that, I'd written to Phèdre and Joscelin in Lucca, when I thought there was a good chance I'd not survive the siege—but it was awful in its own way.

I'd run a fearful risk once; I didn't dare remove any of the *ollamh* Aodhan's protections. And so I struggled with pen and ink and guilt, scratching at my itchy bindings, trying to find access to my own charm-bound feelings and give voice to them. It was as hard as chewing on rocks, and what I wrote was an absolute muddle.

Dear Sidonie,

There is so much I would say to you, and so much I cannot, for reasons that would take far too long to explain. I have stumbled afoul of strange magics here. Ask Phèdre or Joscelin; they will tell you what I mean.

You will hear this, so I will say you were right; a child changes things. I cannot make any grand promises and I cannot, in fairness, ask you to await me. What is in my heart has not changed; and yet it has grown to encompass things I did not imagine. If you seize some other chance for happiness, I will understand; even if it is Maslin, although the thought makes me ill, or it should. I cannot feel what I feel.

I sound like an idiot. I'm sorry.

You would be better off without me. I love you, though. Right now, I don't know how to make all of this work. But I swear to Blessed Elua, if I can find a way to be with you, I will. It may not be the way we would choose, but things aren't always.

None of this is making any sense. Just . . . ask P&J to explain. I will come when I can, although it will not be for a year, at the least. If you find it in yourself to save a place in your heart for me, I will be glad. If you do not, I will understand. Either way, I love and miss you. Nothing will change that, ever.

It was so dreadful, I nearly destroyed it. But there was no time to draft another, and the thought of leaving her forsaken with no reply at all filled me with an ache of remorse so vivid I could feel it through the charms that bound me. So I sealed it and penned a swift response to Mavros, which was equally oblique but not nearly as tortured, then sealed them both together in a packet.

I managed to catch Joscelin alone in the guest-chamber he shared with Phèdre, sorting methodically through their things and packing their trunks. I gave him the packet. "Will you see this is delivered to Mavros?"

Joscelin weighed it in his hand. "Mavros."

My face felt warm. I scratched my left wrist. "I promised that you and Phèdre could explain . . ." I plucked at the yarn. "This."

"To Mavros?" Joscelin eyed me. "Imri, come with me."

I followed him through the castle, up the southeastern tower to the top of the fortress. There were guards posted in the tower chambers, but the parapet was unmanned. Joscelin leaned against a crenellation and folded his arms, the sea breeze tugging at the braided cable of his blond hair.

"All right." I faced him. "There's a letter for Sidonie as well. Mavros will see she gets it. I would be grateful if you explained to her, too. I tried, but it's a mess."

"You still fancy you love her?" he asked.

"No." I shook my head. "I'm sure of it."

"And Sidonie?" he asked. "Does she feel the same?" I nodded. Joscelin sighed. "I hoped this would pass, Imri. I truly did."

"Do you think I didn't?" I asked. "Do you think *she* didn't?"

"No." His mouth twisted humorlessly. "What of Dorelei? The hidden well whose depths you dream of plumbing? The other night, you told Phèdre you were happy. Was that a lie to set our minds at ease?"

"No. No, it wasn't." I searched for the words. "Joscelin, I *am* happy . . . but the me that's happy isn't entirely real. And Dorelei knows it as well as I do. Whatever's best for the both of us, and for the babe, we'll decide it together."

Joscelin tilted his chin, his blue gaze searching the summer sky as if to find answers written in the scudding clouds. "You do have a knack for finding the most difficult paths, love," he murmured. "I swear to Elua, I've half a mind to snatch you from Alba and . . ." His voice trailed off.

"Take me on a journey to hide the pages of the Book of Raziel where no one in living memory might find them?" I suggested.

His brows shot up. "What makes you think *that*?"

I laughed. "Don't worry, I've said naught of it, nor will I. And as far as the letter goes . . ." I spread my hands. "Sidonie may well decide I've lost my wits altogether, and I wouldn't blame her for it. Mayhap it would be for the best."

"Do you believe that?" Joscelin asked.

"No," I said.

There atop the windswept fortress of Bryn Gorrydum, we regarded one another. "'Tis strange," Joscelin said softly. "I thought it was hard when you left for Tiberium, but 'tis harder to leave you than it was to let you go, Imri. When a year and a day have passed, and you've a child of your own, you may find you feel the same way."

"I know." I swallowed. "I've made no promises I cannot keep and I have no false expectations. You'll see the letter delivered, though?"

"I will." Joscelin pried himself upright. "With assurances that you've not lost your wits." He hesitated. "Imriel, of all the women in the world, why Sidonie?"

I thought about it. "You know, I remember Eamonn telling me that Brigitta made him feel he wanted to be a better man. And you, you told me you began to fall in love with Phèdre when you were enslaved in Skaldia, when her courage put you to shame."

Joscelin nodded. "I understand."

"No, you don't." I smiled wryly. "I feel that way all the time, Joscelin. I feel that way about Dorelei, about Phèdre—I feel that way about *you*. Eamonn, Drustan, Grainne . . . Name of Elua, I spend far too much of my life feeling that way, and when I don't, it's because I feel like I'd like to kill someone, like Barquiel L'Envers. With Sidonie . . ." I shrugged. "I don't. I just feel like myself, truly myself. And that it's a fine thing to be. And I think she feels the same way. I don't know why; truly, I don't. I only know it's true."

He looked at me for a long moment. "I think I do begin to understand."

"Good," I said. "Mayhap you can explain it to me one day."

So it was done, and I felt at once glad and guilty. The packet of letters was hidden away in Joscelin and Phèdre's trunks. They would leave, bearing it—and Elua only knew what else—far from Alba's shores.

And I would stay.

We spent our last night together, there in the fortress of Bryn Gorrydum. With the boisterous clan-lords gone, it seemed a gentler, more pleasant place. 'Twas a place, I thought, that could use more of a woman's presence. I watched Drustan grow warmer and more relaxed with so many of the women of his family in attendance. I'd not given much thought to the plight of Drustan mab Necthana, the Cruarch of Alba. For some eight or nine months of the year, depending on the weather, he and Ysandre were parted. If he took lovers here in Alba, 'twas done discreetly, for I never heard of it. Of a surety, Drustan had no official consort or lover.

Nor did Ysandre.

They'd chosen that, the two of them. Chosen a life of abnegation to cement the alliance betwixt our nations, chosen to let no rumor dilute it.

I wondered if it was worth the cost.

On the morrow, we parted ways, saying our farewells in the courtyard. And whether it was because I was the one staying and not the one leaving, or because the charms that bound me blunted my emotions, for me this parting was easier than it had been when I'd gone to Tiberium.

"Look at you," Phèdre murmured, touching the torc around my neck. "A proper Alban prince."

"I'm trying," I said.

"I know." She gazed at me, eyes bright with unshed tears. "I'm proud of you. Take care of yourself, love. And your family."

"I'll do my best," I promised.

"Mind your footwork," Joscelin said. "And try not to get killed."

I laughed. "I will."

Accompanied by the D'Angeline honor guard that had escorted us to Innisclan and back, they departed for the harbor, where the Cruarch's own flagship would carry them to Terre d'Ange. As I watched them ride through the gates of the courtyard, I felt, for the first time, a hollow sense of abandonment.

"Are you all right, Imri?" Dorelei, standing beside me, slid her hand into mine.

"Yes." I took a deep breath and smiled at her. "You've never called me that before."

"I'm sorry. It's Alais' doing." She smiled back at me. "I won't if you don't like it."

I squeezed her hand. "I like it."

Our party wasn't a large one, but we were laden with all the tribute gifts from our wedding, and it took a while to get the wagons loaded and the journey under way. At last it was done, and we said our farewells to Drustan and Talorcan; a far less arduous affair, since Clunderry was a mere three days' ride from Bryn Gorrydum.

And then we were off.

Another journey, another destination. Alba was a beautiful land, but I was growing weary of traversing it; and weary, too, of being a guest in someone else's manor. I would be glad to stay in one place for a while and call it home.

For two days, we followed one of the old Tiberian roads, departing on the third day to continue on a smaller road of hard-packed dirt. Dorelei described Clunderry to Alais and me as we rode. It was her childhood home, and her face lit up when she spoke of it.

By all rights, the estate should have belonged to the Lady Breidaia; and so it had for many years. It was by her own request that it had been deeded to Dorelei and me. Breidaia had never aspired to land and titles, and she had administered Clunderry alone for the long years since her husband's death. She was eager to lay down the burden and assume an honorary role with no responsibilities save pottering in her gardens and watching the many grandchildren she hoped we would bear her thrive.

I was glad, since it made Dorelei happy.

We arrived on the morning of the fourth day. Everything was much as Dorelei had described it. The sparkling little Brithyll River wound through the fields, widening at one point to form a small, weedy lake. Clunderry Castle perched on a low rise not far from the lake, sturdy and squat, looking more welcoming than imposing. Outlying buildings with thatched roofs dotted the landscape, and farther upstream sat the mill, its sails turning lazily.

The fields to the south and east were given over to growing crops—wheat, barley, and hay, for the most part, and a small apple orchard. To the north, the same low stone fences we'd seen everywhere in Alba meandered over the hills, where scores of cattle grazed.

Beyond, westward, it was all *taisgaidh* land, wild and wooded. There were elaborate laws regarding hunting and foraging rights on sacred ground, all of which Dorelei and I were expected to know and administer.

And there on the verge of the wood was the *ollamh*'s stone hut, where Firdha would take up residence, continuing to tutor Alais. There were elaborate protocols involved in seeing to an *ollamh*'s every need, too.

Somewhere in the woods beyond, I knew, there were other places, sacred places. The oak grove where Dorelei had slept under the *ollamh*'s tutelage, learning to read the secrets of her dreams. The ring of standing stones, where, she whispered, it was rumored the Maghuin Dhonn had once offered blood sacrifices in exchange for dark magic. These things, too, were under the aegis of our protection. We were responsible for seeing that the ancient laws governing the *taisgaidh* ways were upheld and none of the sacred places were profaned.

We drew rein for a moment, gazing at Clunderry.

"I love it!" Alais said fervently, provoking a grin from dour Urist. "It's so pretty!"

Dorelei glanced at me. "What do you think?"

"I think we're home," I said.

TWENTY-NINE

THE FOLK OF CLUNDERRY received us with reactions ranging from joy to wariness.

Most of the wariness, I must own, was directed at me. The dark Cruithne-stamped features that had marked Alais as alien in Terre d'Ange stood her in good stead here, and her exuberance was infectious.

And most of the joy was evoked by the return of Dorelei, who was well liked by the household there. Her friend Kerys—Kinadius' sister—was one of the first to greet her, racing into the courtyard to fling her arms around Dorelei's neck.

"Oh, I've missed you!" she said impulsively, then turned. "Is this *him*?"

Dorelei nodded. "Imriel, this is my friend Kerys."

I had dismounted and was holding the Bastard's reins, wary of turning him over to a stable-lad without warning. I bowed. "Well met, my lady."

"Oh." Kerys' eyes grew wide as she gazed at me, and her hands rose involuntarily to cover her mouth. "Oh!" She bobbed a curtsy. "Oh!"

"Don't worry." Dorelei smiled wryly. "You'll grow accustomed to him."

She was right, but it took time.

During the first weeks that we esconced ourselves at Clunderry, I nearly wished I *had* gotten my first warrior's mark, if only to blend better. It wasn't the first time I'd been the only full-blooded D'Angeline present in a foreign land, but of a surety, it was the only time I'd been set in a position of authority over a folk not my own.

And unfortunately, it wasn't just my features that set me apart. Terre d'Ange maintained a presence in Alba's cities, but few of my countrymen ventured into the rural areas. As a result, most of the ordinary folk of Clunderry knew D'Angelines only by reputation and rumor. They eyed me askance, waiting for me to display signs of the infamous D'Angeline licentiousness, wondering if I would begin a campaign of seduction and cut a swath through the willing lasses—and mayhap a few of the lads—of the estate.

Ironically enough, it reminded me of my own reaction when my Shahrizai cousins had summered at Montrève, bringing their smoldering Kusheline glamour with them. I'd been in a state of anticipation, half dreading and half hoping to catch Mavros in some thrilling, unspeakable act.

And so, like my kinsmen, I made it a point to conduct myself with perfect propriety. Of a surety, 'twas easy enough; I'd pledged myself to Dorelei in an oath I meant to keep, and all my darker desires were bound and muted. But the cause for that set me apart, too. The story of the Maghuin Dhonn's ensorcelment circulated; folks looked at the red yarn around my wrists and the croonie-stone at my throat and murmured. Even my morning practice of the forms of the Cassiline discipline, which I'd kept up diligently and refused to relinquish, drew stares and giggles.

But slowly, slowly, it changed.

I daresay it would have been more awkward if it hadn't been for Alais. Kinadius and several of the younger Cruithne under Urist's command had appointed themselves her honor guard. For several hours of the day, Alais studied with the *ollamh* Firdha, learning the myriad symbols and their meanings that might be found in dreams, and a good bit of herb-lore, too. When she was free, Alais explored every inch of Clunderry Castle and the immediate surroundings, accompanied by her honor guard and her ever-present wolfhound; and where she went, people were charmed. As they grew fond of the Cruarch's half-breed daughter, they warmed to the idea of a half-breed heir to Clunderry.

And slowly, to me.

Lady Breidaia's presence helped, too. Dorelei was close to her mother and I'd no doubt confided in her. I saw them talking together in the salon, heads bowed toward one another. Betimes I saw Dorelei's mother gaze at us with a trace of sorrow in her dark eyes, and I felt guilty that I didn't love her daughter as she deserved. But Breidaia was a warm and wise soul, and she saw clearly that I was doing my best and honored me for it.

Remembering Montrève and how the old Siovalese lords made it a point to labor side by side with their holders, I was determined to spend time acquainting myself with the various tasks involved in running the estate.

One of the first things I did was to consult with Urist regarding the security measures he'd taken. Clunderry was a sizable holding, some three thousand hectares, and it was impossible to maintain a constant patrol on its borders. But we spent two days riding the length and breadth of the estate, following the patrol routes he'd established, and he pointed out the places where he'd thought it best to establish permanent sentry posts. Somewhat to my surprise, he considered the estate of Briclaedh to the north one of the greatest threats.

"What about . . ." I hesitated. ". . . the Old Ones?"

Urist looked at me out of the corner of his eye. "If those ones come, they'll travel the *taisgaidh* ways, Prince Imriel. 'Tis a hard thing to post sentries in the forest. We'll keep watch on the verges, but we'd be better served by poachers and foragers in its depths. I've put out word that there's a reward for anyone who spots aught amiss in the woods." He coughed into his fist. "And, mayhap, forgiveness of any fine they might have incurred."

"All right." I thought about it. "Wise enough. But why Briclaedh?"

"Ah, well." Urist grinned. "Ask your lady wife."

My ramble with Urist aside, days and evenings at Clunderry were beginning to settle into a calm rhythm. In the mornings, Dorelei and I consulted with the castle steward, discussing important matters such as the day's menu and the necessity of repairing a leaking roof in the stables. The steward was a quiet, competent fellow named Murghan, who had lost his sword-arm in battle in his younger days. One-armed or no, he'd once been a formidable warrior and he was admired more than pitied. It was well known that he'd shared the Lady Breidaia's bed for many years since her husband's death, but he made no presumptions because of it, and I thought well enough of him.

In the afternoon, three times a week, the reeve of Clunderry made his report to us. His job, for which we paid him an annual stipend, was to supervise the daily workings of the estate and adjudicate minor disputes. At every meeting, he provided us with a litany of Clunderry's progress and problems. The reeve, Trevedic, was a young man, earnest and eager. He'd learned his job at his father's knee, and he was anxious to make a good name for himself. We reviewed his decisions, and any more complicated claims for which we might be expected to hold audience.

Beyond these responsibilities, our time was our own. While I explored the workings of Clunderry, Dorelei spent a good deal of time in the pleasant, sunlit salon I'd seen in Hyacinthe's sea-mirror, where the women of the household gathered to spin and sew and converse. Although it was early yet, the babe she carried made her fatigued and betimes queasy, which the older women assured us, laughing, was normal.

In the evenings, we gathered in the great hall to dine. The atmosphere was warm and relaxed, and more often than not, we were joined by other members of the household; the steward Murghan; Kinada, who served as a lady-in-waiting to the Lady Breidaia, her daughter Kerys and son Kinadius.

"So," I said the evening I'd returned from my excursion with Urist. "Unless I am mistaken, I recall that Leodan mab Nonna of Briclaedh attended our nuptials and presented us with a silver salt cellar. Tell me. Why does Urist want to post a guard to the north?"

The Lady Breidaia rolled her eyes. Kinadius winked at Dorelei.

"Oh, well." Dorelei colored slightly. "He did make an offer for my hand before our betrothal was announced. I refused at the Cruarch's behest."

"And . . . ?" I asked.

"Well, he's nearly honor-bound to make a raid, isn't he?" Kinadius asked cheerfully. "He's abided by the Cruarch's will and shown good faith. Now he's obliged to test your mettle, and like as not he will before the weather turns." He tapped his woad-marked brow. "He can claim insult because you're not a fit warrior."

"Name of Elua!" I laughed in disbelief. "Are you jesting?"

"He's not, I fear," Breidaia said calmly. " 'Tis how young men earn their marks in peacetime."

"And clan-lords increase their herds," Kinadius added.

"By raiding cattle they don't need from friendly estates?" I asked.

"Well, yes," he said.

"That's foolish," Alais observed.

Kinadius grinned at her. "You're allowed to think that. You're a girl."

Alais wrinkled her nose at him. I pushed away an inadvertent memory of Sidonie that seeped through my bindings, scratching my wrists and thinking. I was sick and tired of being bound by all manner of strictures and unable to act. "But I've a right to my first warrior's mark, Kinadius, you said so yourself. I chose not to receive it because it's not a D'Angeline custom."

"Aye, and you didn't want to mar your pretty face." He eyed me. "So?"

"So," I said slowly, "if Leodan mab Nonna claims I'm not a proper warrior, then he's calling me a liar. And as such, he's given insult, hasn't he?"

"What are you plotting?" Dorelei asked suspiciously.

I shrugged. "What if we claim insult and raid Briclaedh first?"

There was a little silence around the table, then Kinadius let out an excited whoop. "I'd say you're beginning to think like a Prince of Alba," Dorelei said, a mixture of pride and rue in her voice.

It was a pointless undertaking, an exercise in the enduring folly of mankind and, most especially, the violent futility of masculine pride. And in one fell swoop, it endeared me to the folk of Clunderry in a manner that months and months of sober behavior, hard work, and courtesy wouldn't have accomplished.

Urist, seasoned, sensible Urist, loved the notion. It surprised me a little.

"Ah, how not!" The Cruithne commander jabbed at me with his forefinger. "Do you think I'm not a man, lad? Do you think I don't want to serve a lord I can be proud of? Aye, and the men I command, too?"

"No, of course not," I said.

He fixed me with a hard gaze. "Afraid, are you? Having second thoughts?"

"Afraid, no." I frowned. "Second thoughts, yes."

We were sitting in his garrison-chamber, a tiny cell scarce large enough to hold a bed, a chest for his belongings, and a pair of chairs. "Listen, lad." Urist laid his hands on his knees and faced me squarely. "I've an idea you're loath to make enemies. But 'tis a friendly skirmish, nothing more. You're not going to incur a blood-feud over a cattle-raid. Showing your mettle before anyone dares test it is the best idea you've had since you set foot on Alban soil."

"And if Briclaedh retaliates?" I asked.

"They might." He shrugged. "If they do, they'll seek to reclaim what's theirs, no more, and consider the score settled. You'll still come out of it with the upper hand. Do you see?"

"I suppose," I said reluctantly.

Urist transferred one hand to my left knee and squeezed hard. "Good lad!"

Thus it was that my first real act as a Prince of Alba, a role I'd agreed to play for the purpose of fostering peace and prosperity, was to stage a cattle-raid on my nearest neighbor.

Once the matter was decided, plans were implemented swiftly lest word leak to Briclaedh, only a day and a half away. Urist chose a raiding party of thirty men, a mix of veterans and green lads. He informed me cheerfully that if I wanted to garner any measure of respect, I would have to lead them myself, to be the first into battle and the last to retreat.

I tried to imagine explaining my actions to everyone at home and failed miserably. There was a good reason, I thought, that Drustan downplayed Alba's dangers. It wasn't that they were so terribly dire, but that the culture was unfathomable to a D'Angeline mind. To be sure, Terre d'Ange had known periods of strife, but any quarrels that had played out on a large scale had been driven by ambition, greed, or grievous insult, not some manufactured slight of honor.

This seemed unnervingly like . . . sport.

I spoke to Alais about it, reckoning she was the only one who would understand. She listened gravely to my concerns.

"It is stupid," she said when I'd finished. "Any *girl* could tell you as much."

"Do you think I should put a halt to it?" I asked.

"I don't think you can, Imri," Alais said simply. "This isn't Terre d'Ange."

I sighed. "I don't suppose you've had any helpful dreams."

"No." Her brows furrowed. "I'm beginning to learn to understand them better, or at least I would if I had them, but I don't."

"My fault?" I asked.

Alais nodded. "Firdha says I'm too close to you, that all of us are. As long as you're bound like this . . ." She pointed at my wrists. "It's like there's a fire in the hearth, but a great stone is blocking the chimney. All we can see is smoke."

"I'm sorry, love," I said. "I'd take them off if I dared."

She shuddered. "Don't."

I didn't; indeed, I had Firdha check my bonds. Although the strands of red yarn were beginning to fade and fray, they were holding sturdy. She allowed grudgingly that Aodhan had done good work and she was reluctant to tamper with it unless it was needful.

All was in readiness. The night before our departure, after we retired to our bedchamber, Dorelei presented me with a gift.

"Close your eyes," she whispered. "And hold out your hands."

I obeyed, mystified, and felt her slide somewhat heavy over first one hand, then the other, careful not to snag the yarn tied around my wrists. I felt the familiar weight of a pair of vambraces settle into place, the inner leather soft against my skin. Her deft fingers did the buckles.

"You can look now."

I opened my eyes. The vambraces gleamed in the lamplight. The steel plates were riveted to the outer layer of hard-boiled leather. Silver plate overlay the steel, etched with the image of the Black Boar of the Cullach Gorrym, bristling and fierce, in the bold, flowing lines of the Cruithne style. I ran my fingertips over the surface, tracing the curve of his tusk. It was skillfully done, too smooth and shallow to hold the point of a blade.

"Do you like them?" Dorelei asked shyly.

"They're wonderful," I said honestly.

"They were meant to be finished earlier." She took my right hand, turning it over and kissing my knuckles. "But mayhap they'll help keep you safe."

I cupped her cheek. "Thank you."

"Oh, well." She gave her dimpled smile. "I've watched you and Joscelin spar. He said you've never had a pair of your own. A proper pair."

"No." I shook my head. "I found a pair in Lucca, an old rusted pair. They saved my life. But I never . . ." I thought about it. "I don't know. I suppose it would have felt presumptuous. After all, I'm not a Cassiline."

"I don't care about that." Dorelei leaned forward and kissed my lips, taking my other hand and placing it on her belly. "I just want you to come home to me, that's all."

I kissed her back. "I will."

That night, I gained a measure of insight regarding why men wage war for foolish causes. For all that women's wisdom runs deeper, they are tender and ardent on the eve of sending their men into battle. With the spectre of bloodshed hanging over us, Dorelei and I made love that night, and it had a poignancy I'd never felt before.

And in the morning, I went forth to raid cattle.

THIRTY

WE LAY ON OUR BELLIES in the hazel copse, gazing down into the valley.

The slanting rays of the setting sun warmed the grey stone of Briclaedh Castle. It was smaller than Clunderry, but the pasturage that surrounded it was richer.

"Leodan of Briclaedh must have two hundred head of cattle," Kinadius said admiringly. "How many do we try for?"

Urist glanced at me, his eyes like polished stones.

"Twenty," I said. "Settle for no less than ten."

Urist grunted his approval.

It was, I thought, one of the most unforgivably idiotic ventures I'd ever undertaken; and that was saying somewhat. There were far easier ways to acquire ten head of cattle. The glow of Dorelei's ardor had faded on the first day's ride. Now I was merely hot and sticky with sweat, and I had hazel twigs tangled in my hair.

But I was in command of this folly. And so I narrowed my eyes and studied the lay of the land. It would have been a simpler business in the late autumn, when the cattle were herded into pastures abutting the keep, close to the byres and hay-barns. Now they were still spread out far and wide, gleaning the hillsides.

"How many of Leodan's men are like to respond?" I asked Urist.

"On short notice?" He shrugged. "A score."

I lifted my gaze to the keep's towers. "Sentries on duty?"

"Of course." Urist's teeth gleamed. "But 'tis a half-moon tonight."

I shaded my eyes and gazed southward. "All right, then. A pair of men on each of the first two gates; one to open and close, one to guard his back. A dozen to drive the cattle and ride herd on them. I'm not doing this for naught."

"That leaves . . ." Urist counted on his fingers. "Fourteen to fight?"

I bared my own teeth in a smile. "Afraid, are you?"

"No," he said stubbornly.

"Good." I clapped his shoulder. "Let's regroup and await nightfall."

Like Clunderry, Briclaedh's estates lay alongside *taisgaidh* land. We'd made our camp in a clearing that afternoon. We'd had a devil of a time making our way through the thick undergrowth and getting there unseen, but under Urist's guidance, we'd managed it. The woods felt stifling and oppressive, and the horses were restless and stamping. Still, no one came. Unlike Clunderry, it seemed Briclaedh's folk weren't eager to venture into the sacred places; or mayhap it was simply that Briclaedh's garrison commander hadn't thought to post a reward for sighting strangers the way Urist had.

I gave the men my orders. There was no quarrelling; they merely nodded, and the dozen assigned as cattle drovers began cutting hazel switches.

Dusk came early in the dense woods. We led the horses in a single file to the verge of the copse, wincing at every crackling step. There, we waited for the twilight to fade over the valley.

It was a clear night. The waxing half-moon hung over the eastern horizon, growing brighter as the sky darkened, an array of stars emerging. Warm squares of golden light marked the windows of Briclaedh Castle and its outlying buildings. Across the gentle, rolling hills, cattle settled for the evening, legs tucked beneath them, dark, dim lumps under the night sky.

"Ready?" I asked in a low voice.

There were murmurs of assent.

"Let's go, then."

We moved out from the shadows of the copse, riding slow and fanning out across the hill as we descended into the valley. There was no fence on the *taisgaidh* side of Briclaedh, and it was my hope that we were far enough from the castle sentries to pass undetected into the pasturage.

It worked, too. I sent the two teams of gatekeepers riding hastily toward the south, searching for gates rendered near-invisible by darkness. The rest of us waited, horses milling, while cattle lifted their heads and gazed at us with incurious eyes. I checked the Bastard's reins to be sure they were knotted together, a trick Urist had taught me.

In the distance, a torch kindled; then another, nearer.

The gatekeepers were in place.

I nodded to the drovers. "Go."

There is no quiet way to stage a cattle-raid. The drovers spread out across the hills and began yelling and shouting, swinging their hazel switches. Cattle bawled and lowed, lumbering to their feet in their awkward way, hindquarters first. The drovers shouted back and forth to one another, rounding up as many head of cattle as they could find and driving them toward the first gate in a massive, pounding press of confusion, all of which went on for far too long.

"Fun, eh?" Urist grinned.

I pointed toward the castle. "Here they come."

Dark figures came pelting over the fields. Urist had guessed wrongly. There were no more than a dozen mounted warriors, clinging bareback to saddleless horses; but there were dozens more following on foot, a swift-moving stream only a few moments behind. My heart began to pound in my chest.

"Take the riders!" I shouted. "Take the riders, and head for the gates!"

And then they were on us, and we clashed.

Within a heartbeat, the melee was a complete mess. Briclaedh's men were whooping, uttering wild war-cries; so were Clunderry's. Tattooed Cruithne faces were everywhere, and in the faint light I was hard put to tell friend from foe. 'Twas a stroke of dubious luck that my unmarked face made me a clear target. I didn't have to worry about striking a blow against one of Clunderry's men; I was surrounded by Briclaedh's. Dropping the Bastard's knotted reins, I guided him with my knees, turning in a tight circle and laying about me on both sides, sword in my right hand.

"D'Angeline!" Leodan mab Nonna came alongside me; I knew him by his thick brows, which met over his nose. We locked swords, swaying. "What the hell are you doing?"

"Claiming insult," I grunted. "Not a proper warrior, am I?"

In the moonlight, I saw him smile fiercely. "Ah, well."

Wind whistled on my other side. Trusting to training, good hearing, and blind luck, I swung my left arm in an arc and felt a blow glance off my vambrace.

"Don't kill him!" Leodan shouted in alarm. "Hostage, hostage!"

I dug my heels into the Bastard's sides and he plunged free. Somewhere in the midst of pandemonium, I swear I heard Urist snicker. Half of Leodan's men were injured or unhorsed; the other half were pursuing Clunderry's fleeing riders. Urist was among them; I must have imagined the snicker. The first wave of Briclaedh's foot-racing warriors arrived, panting, to find me alone and abandoned.

Leodan mab Nonna raised his heavy brows. "Take him."

Once more, I turned the Bastard in a circle, swearing with fury. There were too many of them, and now that I knew they meant to take me alive, I was loathe to strike killing blows. I flailed at the Cruithne with the flat of my blade while they ducked and dodged, tattooed faces grinned up at me, tattooed hands reaching to grab at my legs, my sword-belt, my left arm, dragging me from the saddle.

The Bastard squealed. I kicked my feet free of the stirrups and let them take me. I landed on my back atop two men and used the unexpected momentum to tear free of their grip, somersaulting backward and coming up in a crouch, sword at the ready, facing a semicircle of unmounted men.

"Nice trick." Leodan glanced away, distracted. "The horse, lads, the horse! I want that spotted horse, too."

They all looked, and so did I. Unlike Urist and his men, the Bastard hadn't deserted me. He stood with legs splayed and ears flat, snaking his neck and snapping at the Briclaedh warrior who was attempting to grab his bridle.

"Oh, the hell you do!" I growled.

Without thinking, I shoved my sword into its scabbard, turned my back on my assailants, and charged the fellow attempting to catch the

Bastard. I tackled him around the waist and brought him down with a thud. We rolled around in the mire of the cow pasture, grappling with one another. I'd learned to wrestle in Siovale. I came up on top and punched him hard in the mouth, feeling his teeth break the skin of my knuckles. He gaped at me, bloody-mouthed.

Most of Leodan's men were hooting and laughing, jeering at their comrade, paying scant heed to me. The rest were chasing the Bastard, arms spread wide, trying to form a circle to enclose him. He evaded them with short dashes, snorting with alarm.

D'Angelines may be vain, but even we admit that the Tsingani are the best horse-breeders and -trainers in the world; and the Bastard was Tsingani-bred and -trained. He might be a bastard, but he was *my* Bastard. I got to my feet, stuck two fingers smeared with cow-dung in my mouth, and whistled sharply.

The Bastard's ears pricked.

"Oh, hell," Leodan muttered.

Bursting past his would-be captors, the Bastard came at a canter. He barely slowed for me, but it was enough. I reached up to grab the pommel, swinging myself astride by main force. Leodan's men were scattered, unmounted and unprepared. I settled myself in the saddle and turned the Bastard's head toward the south, grinning at the lord of Briclaedh. "My thanks for the cattle."

He roared; I didn't wait to hear what.

I clapped my heels to the Bastard's flanks, and his gait moved smoothly from a canter to a full-out gallop. Together, we raced across the dark pasture.

There was an abandoned torch burning at the first gate, the butt-end wedged in a crevice in the cobbled stone fence. The gate itself stood open, and we passed through it without slowing. It seemed like a great deal of time had passed, too much time, but midway across the second pasture, I caught up with the others.

Our drovers were anxiously herding cattle through the second gate, while Urist and his warriors held Leodan's remaining outnumbered horsemen in an uneasy standoff.

I slowed the Bastard to a walk. "Hello, lads."

Someone whooped.

Urist gave me a wary smile. "You're here."

"No thanks to you." I eyed him. "Let's get these cattle home, shall we?"

He made a fist, pressing it to his brow, then his heart. "Aye, my lord."

I should have been angry—I *was* angry—but at the same time, I understood. This was Alba. I'd needed to prove myself to my allies as surely as my enemies. I gazed at Urist and saw him, truly saw him. He was a proud man, and he needed to serve a lord he could admire. Drustan was one such; even serving the *ollamh* Firdha had been an honor, albeit one he hadn't sought. He was no fool—he'd known Leodan of Briclaedh wouldn't want to kill me and risk the wrath of Terre d'Ange. Still, he'd been willing to take the chance of humiliating me.

I could call him on it and earn his resentment.

Or I could accept the jest and keep his respect.

I chose the latter.

After all, we'd prevailed; and if no one had earned his warrior's mark in the process, no one had died, either. That pleased me. So we sent Leodan's last men packing—I daresay they were glad enough of the excuse—and hustled Briclaedh's cattle through the second gate, closing it behind us.

Urist didn't think there would be further pursuit, or at least not that night. We were armed and moving swiftly in the near-dark. If Leodan meant to retaliate, he would wait. But as a precaution, I ordered Kinadius and a sensible veteran named Timor to lag behind and keep watch. The rest of us hurried onward, herding our reluctant charges. By daybreak, we'd have crossed Clunderry's northern border.

Despite the foolishness of it all, I had to own, I felt good. My blood was singing in my veins; I felt more alive than I had in weeks. At Kinadius' prompting, I told the story of how I'd foiled Leodan's attempts to take me hostage, giving all the credit to the Bastard. I forgave their role in it and enjoyed their laughter and admiration, listening idly as they began to invent poems to describe the night's adventure.

I wondered what Sidonie would make of it.

Like as not, she'd think it was ridiculous; and she would be right, of course. Still, I thought, she was a woman. She would give me a warrior's welcome. I could nearly see her face, torn between disparagement and desire. Desire would win, of course. Ah, Elua! I dreamed about it as we rode, letting the Bastard dawdle, letting the others set the pace. Coming to her bedchamber, rank with sweat and besmirched with mire and cow-dung.

It wouldn't matter. It wouldn't.

Sidonie might laugh; she would laugh. The thought of it made my heart soar. But if I pressed her, if I laid my filthy hands on her and undid her stays, laying her bare, her black eyes would turn soft and blurred. My fingers would leave marks on her creamy skin. Her mouth would seek mine, begging wordlessly, her thighs would open . . .

"Imriel."

Morwen's voice roused me from my waking dream.

I was in the woods.

Alone.

Icewater trickled down my spine. "What?" I whispered. "What is it?"

Moonlight scarce penetrated the dense foliage. I could make out Morwen's pale eyes, the shape of her hand lifting as she clutched the leather bag at her throat. "You summoned me."

"No," I croaked. "No, I didn't."

"You did." Her fingers tightened. I groaned. "Dismount."

I obeyed helplessly. The Bastard eyed me wonderingly as I sank to my knees. Morwen approached, as grave as a priestess. She took my left hand in hers and undid the buckles on my vambrace. "See?"

The red yarn had gotten tangled in the straps. It must have snapped when Leodan's men dragged me from the saddle.

I closed my eyes. "No."

"I can give you what you want, Imriel." Morwen moved closer, crouching, showing me the leather bag. The scent of her, rank and overripe, surrounded me. "You sought to make a bargain. I am offering one." With her other hand, she reached out to stroke my groin. "Give me a child."

The mingling of disgust and acute desire was excruciating, and in a horrible way, far too close to the waking fantasy I'd conceived. I tried to ward her off, but my arms seemed to weigh two hundred pounds apiece. I couldn't even lift them. "Why?" I whispered.

"I've seen her." Morwen's pupils dilated, black circles rimmed by pale grey. "I've seen our daughter, Imriel. A child of two worlds, a child of two folk. She will walk the old ways and the new and preserve the balance between them. She will be a magician, a powerful magician." Her fingers fumbled at my breeches, picking at the laces. She drew a sharp breath. "Mayhap even powerful enough to unlock the secrets of the Master of the Straits!"

Bile rose in my throat as her hand closed around the shaft of my phallus. *Love's throbbing scepter.*

"I swore an oath!" I said in anguish. "For a year and a day, I pledged myself to Dorelei, and Dorelei alone. By stone and sea and sky, and all that they encompass. Alba's ancient oath; *your* oath, Morwen! Would you have me break it?"

She paused. "In your heart, you are already forsworn."

I gritted my teeth. "I do not consent to this."

Morwen smiled, her hand moving on my phallus. "This says otherwise."

I struggled for memories of Daršanga, but they were too far away; and my memories of Sidonie were too close. Desire burned, caustic and harsh. My body seemed to belong to someone else. Morwen reached out with one hand and pushed my chest. I toppled onto my back, helpless. My spine arched, hips thrusting. My fingers scrabbled at the forest loam. Morwen began to crawl up the length of my body, hitching her skirts with one hand, the other clutching the leather bag that held the mannekin.

"I will give this to you when we are done," she said. "It is a small price to pay for your freedom. And Alba's future is at stake."

I felt her moist nether-lips slide along the length of my phallus and hissed through my teeth. Her smell filled my nostrils. The worst of it was, appalled and disgusted as I was, I wanted her. It was as though all the brightness and glory I'd ever found in desire was held in that vile bag, and all that was dark and disturbing surged forth to meet it. I wanted her to free me, I wanted to turn her over in the dark forest and rut like a beast, taking her from behind and shoving her face into the loam.

No.

"Blessed Elua be my witness," I whispered. "I do not consent to this. Mighty Kushiel, hear your scion. This is blasphemy, and I will avenge it."

Morwen hesitated. "Your gods are not here."

"Imriel!"

It was Kinadius' voice. Branches crackled in the offing, broken by tramping feet. A horse whickered; the Bastard raised his head and replied. A grimace of fury contorted Morwen's face, the tattooed clawmarks writhing. She squeezed the leather bag so hard, I thought my testes would burst, and I couldn't tell whether it was with pleasure or pain. Tears trickled from the corners of my eyes.

I laughed through my tears. "No, but one of my men is."

Morwen let go the bag and leapt off me with unnerving swiftness, her hands forming rigid claws. I got stiffly to my feet and read her shadowed face.

"Don't do it," I said, drawing my sword. "I swear to Elua, if you think to attack him in any form, I will defend him to the death. And if you think you can get past me without doing me grievous harm, you're sore mistaken. Are *you* so eager to be forsworn, Morwen?"

She made a guttural sound deep in her throat. For a long moment, we stared at one another. There was fury in her gaze, but there was despair, too; a kind of desperate madness. The crashing, cracking sound of Kinadius blundering through the woods grew closer.

Morwen fled.

Deeper into the woods, deeper into *taisgaidh* land. She vanished in the darkness, with scarce a sound to mark her passage. I sighed and sheathed my sword, and set about tying my breeches before Kinadius found me. I felt the dull ache of thwarted desire, bone-deep and awful, thudding futilely in my groin.

"My lord!" Kinadius stumbled out of the trees. "What in Lug's name are you *doing*?"

I picked up the vambrace Morwen had removed, showing him the tangled yarn. "Bear-witch."

His eyes showed the whites. "Where?"

"Gone, for now," I said wearily. "Let's go. I've need of the *ollamh*'s services."

We made our way back to the verge of the woods where Kinadius had tethered his mount. I had no recollection of having entered them, but the Bastard and I had left a trampled path. I was lucky Urist had noticed my absence, lucky he'd led a dozen men back to search for me, lucky that Kinadius, bringing up the rearguard, had spotted our trail.

Or mayhap 'twas more than luck.

Betimes the gods answer our prayers in a sideways manner.

One by one, we caught up with the other searchers. Kinadius told them in a single hushed word what had happened. *Bear-witch*. I got heartily sick of hearing it.

"What did she want?" one of them finally asked.

I gestured at my crotch. "What every woman wants. Didn't get it, though."

There was a shocked pause, and then Urist roared with laughter and the others did, too. Men are always apt to laugh when fearful. It helped, though. By the time we caught up with the drovers and the fourteen head of cattle we'd stolen from Leodan of Briclaedh, the men of Clunderry had grown easy with me once more. They decided it was a grand jest that their D'Angeline lord—a man who'd proved he could take a jest himself—had such a pretty face it could render even a bear-witch lovestruck.

I smiled wryly and didn't disabuse them of the notion, although I wished it were that simple.

Although we were all wary and on edge, the balance of our journey was uneventful. Leodan launched no pursuit, and Morwen attempted no further gambit. We crossed into Clunderry as the sky was turning grey, and Urist declared a rest. The men slept in shifts, an hour at a time, while others kept watch over the weary cattle.

I didn't sleep.

"My lord, I swear to you, I'll stand watch over you myself," Urist said fervently. I daresay he felt guilty, and well he should. "I'll not let anything befall you."

"It's all right," I said. "I'm not tired, that's all."

True and not true.

I was tired; I was bone-tired. I was bruised and battered, my cut knuckles stung, and I stank of cow-dung. The dull ache of desire hadn't faded, and Morwen's scent lingered in my nostrils.

But I was myself.

And despite everything, the air in my lungs tasted fresher; my vision seemed clearer and brighter. My unfettered heart sloughed off the shackles of Alban magic and sang, as pure and clear a tune as Ferghus drew from his harp-strings. Like a prisoner granted an unexpected day's leave, I meant to enjoy every moment of it. I watched the sun rise in the east. I watched each blade of grass cast its own sharp-edged shadow. I watched the men of Clunderry snore in their bedrolls. I watched the cattle chewing their cuds, slow and meditative.

I thought about Sidonie.

I thought about Dorelei, too.

And I offered prayers of thanks and hope to Blessed Elua and his Companions, and all the myriad deities of Alba.

I hoped someone was listening.

THIRTY-ONE

"*F*ROM ALL WHO SEEK *to bind thee, be thou protected*!"

Firdha clapped her hands sharply. I blinked, sitting cross-legged on the floor of her stone hut. Without leaving the circle of salt she'd inscribed around me, I raised my wrists and examined the fresh bindings of bright red yarn, peered at my ankles.

"How do you feel?" Firdha inquired.

'Twas strange to think how I'd lost so much and felt it so little when Aodhan worked his charm on me. I'd made a good job of burying my heart. The loss had seemed distant and removed.

This time, it was different.

I'd let myself feel, and I felt it go. A deep loss, severing me from myelf. I felt it; felt the world lose brightness and fade. Like a stone blocking a chimney, Alais had said; to me, it felt more like a sodden blanket flung over a bright-burning hearth. Once again, I was divided against myself for my own protection. Tears sprang to my eyes, born of a pain I could no longer feel. "Fine," I said softly. "I feel fine. My thanks, Daughter of the Grove."

Firdha nodded brusquely and began to sweep away the salt with a hazel-twig broom. "Go, then."

I went.

Alais had watched the ritual with a pupil's grave interest, but she left the *ollamh*'s hut with me, taking my hand and squeezing it. "I'm sorry, Imri," she said. "Did it hurt?"

"Thanks, love." I summoned a weary smile. "No, not exactly."

"That's good." For a moment, I thought Alais would say more, but she didn't.

The rest of Clunderry was in high spirits following the cattle-raid. Urist had decided it would be for the best if my misadventure along the way was kept quiet, and his men had agreed. They would double their watch along the *taisgaidh* border and increase the reward for sightings, but in truth, there wasn't a great deal else to be done.

I told Dorelei, of course.

She'd suspected somewhat was amiss. I'd gone directly to Firdha's hut upon returning, without even pausing to bathe. No one else in the household thought it odd, but they didn't know D'Angelines the way she did. I told her about it immediately afterward, soaking in the tub while she scrubbed gently at my myriad bruises.

"I wondered," Dorelei murmured when I'd finished. "I had a dream last night."

"A true dream?" I asked.

"No." She smiled wistfully. "No, I dreamed it was spring. My belly was huge, and I could feel the babe moving. I was fat and lazy and happy. You kept trying to feed me honeycomb, you said it would make her sweet-tempered."

I laughed. "Her?"

"In the dream, I was sure of it. But it wasn't a true dream. It was nice, though." Dorelei examined me. "What's this in your hair?"

"Cow-dung," I said. "Dorelei, how do you know when a dream is a true dream?"

"Close your eyes." She poured a ewer of warm water over my head and began lathering my hair with a ball of soap. "You don't, not always. It takes practice. There's a way of paying attention in dreams, of listening for the small, still voice that says, 'Heed this.' Even then, you don't always remember or understand."

"Do you think that's what the Maghuin Dhonn do?" I asked.

Her hands stopped moving. "No," she said at length. "No, even if our gift does stem from the same roots, I think whatever it is they do is darker and more dangerous. Dunk your head, Imri."

I obeyed and came up streaming water. "Why?"

Dorelei regarded me, troubled. "If what they say is true, then they see far further and far more than the simple glimpses our dreams afford us. They see possibilities, things that may or may not come to pass, and they seek to alter the outcome. I don't know, Imriel. Even mere glimpses are difficult to bear. Too much knowledge may be a dangerous thing, enough to drive a person to madness. When you first encountered her, you said Morwen wanted you to leave Alba. Now this business of a child, a magician child . . ." She shuddered. "It sounds terrible."

"Don't worry," I said grimly. "I've no intention of giving her a second chance."

"I know." She took my hand and kissed the inside of my wrist below the soaked yarn binding. "But I wish you didn't have to live this way."

I caressed her face. "It's not all bad, you know."

"I do." Her dimples showed briefly. "Are you sufficiently clean?"

I got to my feet, dripping, and spread my arms. "What do you think?"

Dorelei laughed. It wasn't the laugh that had turned my world upside down and hollowed out a space in my heart no one else could fill; but it was *her* laugh, sweet and merry, ending in an endearing giggle.

And Elua help me, I had grown to love her.

It might not be enough, but what was there was good.

I climbed out of the tub and scooped her into my arms, hoisting her effortlessly. "I'd best do this while I can, hadn't I?" I teased.

"Mmm." Dorelei twined her arms around my neck and kissed me. "Will you still love me when I'm fat and lazy and happy?"

"All the more," I promised, carrying her toward the bedchamber.

"Will you bring me honeycomb?" she asked.

"Every day," I said. "Didn't I tell you? I'm very good at climbing trees."

Somewhere, there was a distant echo of loss. Trees. Sidonie's thigh flung over mine as we lay on our sides facing one another, still conjoined, her dark eyes limpid with pleasure; the aftermath of the most glorious, wondrous, terrifying intimacy I'd known.

I didn't think you liked climbing trees.

I don't.

I pushed the thought away and deposited Dorelei on our bed. She laughed breathlessly, reaching for me. I made love to her, tender and slow. I felt as though I were trying to hold all of Alba in my arms, trying to make love to the land itself.

For all the shadows that hung over it, for all that I ached somewhere behind my bindings, that night marked the beginning of the best times I spent at Clunderry, and they were among the best times of my life.

I'd won acceptance.

And I'd done it on my own merits; by conceiving of the cattle-raid, by venturing forth to lead it. By prevailing against the odds to win my freedom, by accepting the jest. There was a feast that night, and when Dorelei and I descended, hand in hand, to take part in it, the ensuing cheers were loud and sincere. Her face glowed, and I daresay mine did, too. For the first time, I truly felt we'd made a home here.

After the raid, Urist doubled the watch on our northern border, but there was no immediate retaliation forthcoming. Leodan of Briclaedh decided discretion was the wiser part of valor and sent a rider under a banner of truce with a polite message requesting the return of his cattle. We provided his man with generous hospitality and sent him back with a polite message of refusal.

"That's all right, then," Urist said in satisfaction. "He'll not try anything until after the harvest season. Too much to be done."

And indeed, there was. The long summer was drawing to an end. Although the days were still warm, they were growing shorter and there was a chill to the night air. The hay had already been gathered, and every day the crofters were afield, swinging their long sickles and felling the wheat. It was bundled into sheaves and brought to the threshing barn, where it was beaten with flails. Afterward, the grain was winnowed from the straw and chaff, then carefully weighed under the reeve's supervision. Each crofter retained a portion, while the lion's share belonged to Dorelei and me.

It was arduous work, and in the weeks that followed, I took part in all of it. I wasn't trying to curry favor with the crofters; it was a Siovalese tradition and I was genuinely curious about how they lived. Clunderry's wealth, such as it was, was built on their sweat and labor.

And too, I had an idea that some D'Angeline innovation might lighten their burden. Trevedic the reeve laughed as I stood outside the mill, sketching the shape of its sails, but it seemed slow and inefficient to me. And surely, I thought, there was a better way to thresh the grain in the first place. I'd tried my hand at that, too, and it was backbreaking work.

"You look like a peasant," Dorelei informed me when I returned to the castle stripped to the waist, dust and chaff plastered to my sweating skin.

I grinned at her. "Do you like it?"

She eyed me. "I'm not sure."

I began writing a long letter to Joscelin, detailing the workings of the estate and asking his counsel on Siovalese engineering. I wished I'd paid attention the day he'd taken me to see Tibault de Toluard's hypocaust system for germinating early seeds, not to mention the inner workings of Montrève. I did know somewhat about it, but we'd never stayed there through harvest season—that was when we returned to the City.

The work didn't end with the harvest. Summer turned to autumn. The cattle were driven into the mown fields to graze on the stubble, and the bull was penned to stand stud to the cows. Fallow fields were plowed and harrowed in preparation for spring; winter crops of barley and oats were sown. The apple harvest was gathered and pressed into cider. Beech and oak trees dropped their nuts, and the pigs were driven into the woods to forage.

I liked it; I liked all of it, even the hard work. It kept my mind from wandering and gave me no time to brood. For the first time in many years—mayhap since I was a child tending goats at the Sanctuary—I felt truly useful.

And there were no signs of the Maghuin Dhonn.

It wouldn't last, of course. I had no illusions on that score. But while it did, I meant to relish every moment of the respite. As hard as I worked, I kept a sharp eye on my bindings, mindful that none were loosened or frayed. The croonie-stone never left my neck.

There were two things I did that autumn that made me proud.

For the first, I asked around and learned that there was a crofter on the estate of Sionnachan, some leagues to the south, who was renowned for his honey. I sent a message to Golven of Sionnachan asking permission to consult with the fellow. Mayhap it was because I was wed to the

Cruarch's niece, or mayhap it was because I sweetened the request with a gift—a fine sword-belt with a gilded buckle of D'Angeline workmanship—but Lord Golven sent the beekeeper himself in reply.

Milcis the beekeeper was a gentle soul, with a shock of white hair and bright black eyes. I liked him very much. When I told him why I wanted to keep bees at Clunderry, he beamed with approval.

"You're a good husband, my lord," he said. "Never mind the child! Trust me, when a woman's breeding, there's naught like good honey to sweeten her mood."

Together, we paced the estate. Milcis showed me the best place to set up an apiary, betwixt the apple orchard and the woods. He taught the village thatcher how to construct bee-skeps out of straw, and consulted with the master of the orchard on the best way to capture swarming honeybees come spring.

"Can we not hope for an earlier harvest?" I asked anxiously. "The child's due in the spring."

Milcis laughed. "Ah, no, my lord! Like breeding women, bees keep their own season. But never fear, it will make her milk run sweet, and she'll be grateful for it. When the babe begins to teeth and grow fretful, put a little on its gums and she'll bless you for a wonder." When I frowned, he regarded me warmly. "Your first, is it?" I nodded, and he placed a gentle hand on my shoulder. "I've a goodly bit of honeycomb laid by for the winter. Do you know, 'tis the one food that never spoils? Never fear, my lord. I'll see right by your lady wife."

"My thanks," I said earnestly. "And I'll see right by you, my lord beekeeper."

I tried to keep it a surprise, but Dorelei learned what I'd done from one of our reeve's reports. After Trevedic had left, she shook her head in amazement. "Bee-skeps, Imriel?"

I smiled at her. "I did promise."

"You did." Dorelei sat on my lap. The swell of her belly was visible now, even beneath clothing; slight, but pronounced. She sank her hands into my hair, gathering it in her fists. "Why do you have to be so *nice*?"

"I'm trying not to be insufferably self-absorbed," I said. "Would you rather I didn't?"

"No." She kissed me, then released my hair and smoothed it. "You're doing a good job of it."

"With your permission, there is one selfish thing I'd like to do." I tilted my head, regarding her. "I'd like to build a small shrine to Blessed Elua."

"I suppose it's fitting," Dorelei said slowly. "Our child should know her full heritage."

"Or his," I reminded her.

"Or his," she agreed.

That was my second deed. With Dorelei's blessing, I sent a messenger to the Temple of Blessed Elua and his Companions in Bryn Gorrydum town, bearing a letter with my request and a generous offer of compensation. A swift affirmative reply returned, with a promise of an effigy and a priest to perform the dedication to follow.

It would be a simple affair. Clunderry had little in the way of decorative gardens, where such a shrine would be housed on a D'Angeline estate. Here, the primary purpose of the castle's gardens was to provide foodstuff; herbs, carrots, onions, lettuce, sorrel, leeks, parsnips, and the like. There was a market held once a week a couple of hours ride to the east, where excess crops were sold and traded, but by and large, Alban estates were far more self-sufficient than D'Angeline ones. Outside the cities, they had to be. Alba simply hadn't yet attained the same level of commerce and trade that Terre d'Ange had.

But the Lady Breidaia had a small flower garden which she maintained for pleasure, growing roses, columbine, and lavender, and there was a place near the little lake where lilies grew wild. After consulting with Alais, who was pleased by the notion, it was there I decided to set the shrine. Urist's lads lent a hand. We built a small arbor to house the effigy, and Breidaia generously donated plants from her garden.

I did most of the work of transplanting them myself, reckoning it ought to be done with reverence, and it gave me a profound sense of satisfaction. The rosebushes were barren, the lavender dry and desiccated, and the columbine looked nearly dead, but their roots were healthy and thriving. Come summer, the arbor would be glorious.

A week after the work on the arbor was completed, Elua's priest arrived; or priestess, rather. It was a bright, crisp day, and all of Clunderry paused to watch her arrival as she entered the estate, accompanied by two acolytes and a horse-drawn wagon.

After so long among the Cruithne, it came as a bit of a shock. I'd not seen another D'Angeline face save Alais' for weeks on end, and she could nearly pass as Cruithne. And, too, the priestess was young. I hadn't expected that.

I greeted her in the courtyard, bowing. "My lady priestess, I am Imriel of Clunderry. Be welcome here."

"Imriel of Clunderry, is it?" A smile touched her lips. One of the acolytes scrambled out of the wagon and held her reins as she dismounted. "Well met, your highness. I am Nehailah Ansout."

She took my hand and I gave her the kiss of greeting without thinking. Her lips were soft and cool. Beneath the blue robes of her office, Sister Nehailah Ansout was tall and slender. Despite the day's chill, her feet were bare. Her bright blonde hair fell down her back in a long, thick braid and her hazel eyes were flecked with green and gold.

My bindings began to itch.

"Where is your lady wife?" the priestess asked.

I cleared my throat and tried not to scratch at my wrists. "Awaiting you within, my lady. She is with child, and we thought it best if she didn't wait in the cold air."

"I see." Her hazel gaze roamed over me, taking in the golden torc and croonie-stone around my throat, the red yarn at my wrists. "You have indeed become a Prince of Alba, your highness."

I fought the urge to check my fingernails for dirt. "I've been trying."

She introduced her acolytes, Denis and Michelet. They were a pair of fresh-faced lads, and I daresay neither was a day over eighteen. Together, they lifted the effigy, swaddled in crimson silk, out of the wagon and carried it inside. It was a small piece, standing waist-high, but heavy with it.

I escorted Sister Nehailah. Her bare feet made no sound on the flagstones, but her long braid swayed as she walked. Out of the corner of my eye, I caught sight of Kinadius gaping and shook my head at him.

In the great hall, Dorelei was waiting, along with her mother and

Alais. Her eyes widened a little at the sight of the priestess, but she greeted her graciously.

It felt odd to have D'Angelines at Clunderry. We held a small feast in their honor that night. On the morrow, the effigy would be placed and the shrine would be dedicated, and Sister Nehailah and her acolytes would take their leave, but for a brief space of time, a piece of Terre d'Ange had entered Clunderry.

It made me yearn for home.

It was a longing that owed naught to desire; although there was that, too. It was somewhat deeper, somewhat bred in the bone. A simple thing, a yearning for the sights and sounds and scents of home, to be surrounded by people who didn't look askance at my unmarked face, who thought and worshipped as I did.

I watched Alais that night, trying to gauge if she felt as I did. I didn't think so. She and Kerys giggled and flirted with the young acolytes; especially Michelet, who had unruly blond curls, a turned-up nose, and blue eyes yet to acquire a priest's detached calm. And I caught Dorelei watching me when she thought I wouldn't notice.

Dorelei retired early that evening, and I rose to accompany her.

"Stay." She touched my hand. "I'm sure you'd rather."

"Prince Imriel." Sister Nehailah stood. It was dark enough that the torches and candles were lit, and the flickering light played over her robes and turned her braid into molten gold. Her face was calm and grave. "If it's no trouble, your highness, I would beg a word with you."

I glanced at Dorelei.

"I wouldn't refuse a request from an *ollamh*," my wife observed. "Stay."

I kissed her cheek. "I'll be along soon."

Like Bryn Gorrydum, Clunderry wasn't built for privacy; and at any rate, I'd no intention of closeting myself with Nehailah Ansout. I beckoned her to the far end of the table.

"What is it, my lady?" I asked.

Sister Nehailah folded her hands in her lap and studied me. Young though she was, of a surety, she'd acquired a priestess' detached look. "I have heard about this." Although she spoke the Alban tongue flawlessly, she'd switched to D'Angeline. She nodded at my bound wrists.

"I do not fully grasp Alban magic, but it is my understanding that you are protected against your own desires. It troubles me."

I scratched my bindings. "Believe me, it troubles me, too."

"Is there aught that might be done?" she asked.

I turned my hands outward. "You know why I wear them?"

"I do." The priestess frowned. "I bespoke the Cruarch when the tale reached my ears. Lord Drustan is generous and open in his support of our temple, fledgling though it is. It is his hope that D'Angeline visitors and his own kin may feel at home in Alba."

"Well, then." I shrugged. "You know it is Alban magic that binds and threatens me, and Alban magic that binds and protects me. If there is aught Blessed Elua can do about it, you'd know it better than I, my lady."

She shook her head. "I have no magic to offer."

"So." I ran one finger beneath the yarn. "The bindings stay."

"In defiance of Blessed Elua's precept?" Sister Nehailah asked softly.

"Not entirely." I met her gaze squarely. "I do love my wife, my lady."

Something in her expression shifted. "I hear a deeper truth behind the words you are *not* saying, Prince Imriel. There is another you love and desire."

I looked away. "My lady, I spoke true. And Dorelei carries our child, a child who may one day become heir to Alba. I've prayed for guidance, but Blessed Elua has been silent. Mayhap with the shrine, that will change. Or mayhap Dorelei and I will be left to muddle through this as best we may. If you have advice, I'd be pleased to hear it."

"I wish I did." She was silent for a moment, then gave me a wry smile; more woman than priestess. "There aren't many in Elua's priesthood willing to take a posting to Alba. I thought I would benefit from the opportunity. Still, you might be better served by someone with more experience. I will write to my own teacher, Brother Louvel. Mayhap his wisdom will prove a better guide."

"My thanks," I said. "I appreciate it."

"I do have one thing for you." Sister Nehailah withdrew a sealed letter from the folds of her robe and handed it to me. "This was delivered to Bryn Gorrydum the day before I left. The Cruarch bade me deliver it to you."

My hand trembled as I took the letter. "Thank you."

Another long look. "You are welcome," Sister Nehailah said. "I will pray to Blessed Elua on your behalf. But it is in my heart that even he cannot protect us from ourselves, and that, Prince Imriel, is the crux of the matter."

With that, she took her leave of me. I sighed, turning the letter over and over in my hands. I recognized the insignia of House Shahrizai on the wax seal and Mavros' handwriting, firm and jaunty, addressing the letter to me. At the opposite end of the table, Alais and Kerys were still flirting with the acolytes. Kinadius had joined them, looking disgruntled and jealous. It made me smile ruefully, but they'd come to no harm through it. I was glad my young cousin was finding a way to play the Game of Courtship after all.

I cracked the seal and opened the letter.

Mavros had written a full page. I put it aside. The other letter was a single line written on a piece of foolscap.

Imriel,
Come when you can, with or without your wits.
S.

That was all, but it was enough to make my throat tighten. No one else in the world could make me want to laugh and cry all at once with a single sentence. With a pang, I pushed the bit of scrap into the nearest candle-flame. It caught at once, flaring and singeing my fingertips. I dropped it onto the flagstones, smearing the ashes with the heel of my boot.

"Is everything all right, my lord?"

It was the steward, Murghan. I'd not even noticed him approach, quiet and efficient as he was. There was compassion and concern in his dark gaze.

"Fine." I rose. "I'm off to join Lady Dorelei. You'll see to it that our guests want for naught?"

He nodded. "I will."

I bade a good evening to the acolytes and Clunderry's household. Alais' violet eyes were sparkling vividly, and she was flushed with high spirits. I wanted to ruffle her black curls the way I had when she was a girl, but I kissed her cheek instead.

"Have fun, love," I said to her.

I left them laughing and happy and went to join Dorelei, who was still awake. She looked at me with an unspoken question in her face.

"It was nothing," I said to her. "Sister Nehailah wanted to speak to me about these." I indicated the bindings. "She's going to write to the priest who taught her to see if there's aught to be done."

Dorelei's face eased. "That's good, then."

"Yes." I blew out the lamp and lay in the darkness, haunted by the priestess' words.

It is in my heart that even he cannot protect us from ourselves . . .

THIRTY-TWO

I N   T H E   M O R N I N G , the effigy was placed and the shrine was dedicated.

As proud as I'd been of the arbor, I had to own, it looked a bit forlorn in its autumnal bleakness. Still, when the statue of Blessed Elua was set into place and unveiled, I felt a sense of peace settle over me.

It was done in the old style, crude and simple, yet somehow more powerful for it. A more elaborate effigy would have mocked its surroundings. With the reedy lake at his back, Elua smiled serenely in the direction of the castle, his arms outstretched.

"Blessed Elua be with us, here and everywhere." Sister Nehailah uncorked a flagon of oil and anointed the effigy. A scent of roses arose. "May your Companions watch over us and guide us. May you hold us in your hand and keep us safe. May we ever walk in your footsteps and follow your precept."

Watchers murmured curiously to one another. The *ollamh* Firdha was present. I glanced at her once, but her face was unreadable.

When her prayers were complete, Sister Nehailah spread her arms, echoing the effigy's stance. "In the name of Blessed Elua, I dedicate this shrine to his worship, and the worship of his Companions."

The air seemed to brighten. I took a deep breath, smelling roses.

"That was nice," Dorelei said, sounding surprised.

"What were you expecting?" I grinned at her. "An orgy?"

"I wasn't sure," she admitted.

So it was done, and I felt better for it. Sister Nehailah and her acolytes departed, but a piece of Terre d'Ange stayed behind. And while I found no guidance at Elua's shrine, I did find it easier to pray there, and my mind was always calmer afterward.

Betimes, Alais went with me, though not as often as I did. As autumn dwindled toward winter, the weather turned cold and the breeze over the lake was bone-chilling.

"Do you ever miss it?" I asked her one day. "Home?"

"Sometimes." Alais knelt beside me, shivering a little despite her thick woolen cloak. "But I do love it here, Imri." Her voice dropped. "More than home. And I'm happy here with you and Dorelei and Aunt Breidaia, and Firdha, and everyone." She watched Celeste nosing around the dry, brittle reeds at the lake's edge. "I miss my mother, mostly. And Sidonie. We didn't part well."

My heart contracted painfully. I touched the croonie-stone at my throat. "Why?"

Alais looked sidelong at me. "You saw us in the sea-mirror. Dorelei told me."

"I didn't want you to think I was spying." I smiled, but Alais didn't smile in answer. "Maslin of Lombelon?"

She nodded. "I never liked him, you know. He treated you badly, and he never had the slightest interest in me. I think he's false and ambitious, and he masks it with rudeness. Sidonie thinks he's blunt and honest. We quarrelled about it."

My bindings itched. Somewhere, on the far side of the *ollamh*'s charms, bitter jealousy stirred. I gazed at Blessed Elua's face, rubbing my palms on my thighs until it passed. "He may be ambitious, Alais; and of a surety, he's proud and arrogant. Still, I don't think he'd play Sidonie false."

The words surprised me, a little, but they were true. Alais frowned. "Mayhap. I don't know. Anyway, I don't think he makes her happy."

"Does she make him happy?" I asked.

"Not really, no." Alais gave her reply without looking at me.

"Alais . . ." I touched her arm.

"You know, I understand it all a little bit better, now." She fixed her gaze on the wolfhound. "It's different here in Alba, at least for me. I see why people play the game for fun. It *is* fun, though I imagine it can be dangerous, too. I wish . . ." Her voice trailed off.

"What do you wish, love?" I asked.

Alais did look at me, then. Her nose was red with cold, but her eyes were direct and unwavering. "I wish I had more time before wedding Talorcan."

I took a deep breath. "Then you should have it."

"How?" she asked.

"We'll talk to your father." I shifted to sit on my heels, warming my bare feet. "Alais, sixteen is young to wed. The sky won't fall if your nuptials are postponed for a year." She watched me with uncertainty and hope. "Besides," I added, "you came to Alba to spend this year studying with the *ollamh*, right?" Alais nodded. I plucked at the red yarn around my left wrist. "Well, you've hardly had a chance."

"Actually, I've learned a great deal," she said.

"In theory," I pointed out. "But you're not dreaming, are you?"

"No," she said slowly. "Do you think Father might listen?"

"I do," I said. "And I think there's merit in waiting to sort out this business with the Old Ones before wedding another member of House Courcel into the ranks of Alban's succession. I'm quite sure your mother would agree on that score."

"Will you talk to Father?" Alais asked. "He's more like to heed you."

"I will," I promised.

She smiled, but there was an edge to it. "You know, there's not much I'd change about Alba, Imri. I love it here, I truly do. But I would change the laws of succession."

"And rule as Alba's Queen?" I asked.

Alais' chin rose. "One day, yes."

I didn't laugh. I looked gravely at her. Everything it seemed the Maghuin Dhonn had tried to bind me to or trick from me was already present. Alais loved Alba; Alais carried within herself the balance between the old ways and the new.

"Alba could suffer worse fates, love," I said.

I kept my word to her and sent a message to Drustan mab Necthana requesting an audience with him. To my surprise, he sent a prompt reply informing me of his intention to visit Clunderry to attend the Feast of the Dead.

I had to own, the celebration was one I faced with a certain apprehension.

'Twas the time of year when all of Alba held that the veil between the living and the dead was at its thinnest, as the days grew shorter and shorter, edging toward the Longest Night. Almost everyone at Clunderry had some tale of encountering a departed spirit during the Feast of the Dead, but none of them had ever seen a living man possessed by a dead one.

I had.

Still, it was important that I take part in it. Firdha informed me of this in no uncertain terms. "You got your shrine, Prince Imriel," she said. "Give Alba's dead their due."

"Does the shrine displease you, Daughter of the Grove?" I asked politely.

"Me?" Her black eyes gleamed. "No."

I paused. "The Old Ones?"

The *ollamh* shrugged. "Give the dead their due."

So Clunderry prepared to honor the dead and receive the Cruarch. Drustan's visit was an honor, but it would strain our hospitality. Together, Dorelei and I consulted with the steward and fretted over our stores. I think mayhap the Lady Breidaia took pity on us and had a word with the steward Murghan, for after days of being polite and deferential, he advised us outright to cull the herd and slaughter several of the older cattle in preparation.

"What about the pigs?" I asked.

"Oh, no!" Murghan looked shocked. "That's not done until *after* the Feast of the Dead."

I smacked my brow. "Right. Cattle it is."

Between one thing and another, we managed to get everything in readiness for the Cruarch's arrival. Urist's men doubled up in the garrison and slept two to a pallet, grumbling and complaining.

Urist took a sanguine view. "At least I can pull my lads off the northern border for the feast. No chance Leodan will try to surprise us with the Cruarch in residence."

"Would he profane the holiday thusly?" I asked.

"No." Urist bared his teeth in a fierce smile. "But he might try it the day after when everyone's sated and careless. *I* would."

Drustan arrived on a cold, blustery day with an escort of fifty men. Clunderry was crammed full to overflowing, but no one seemed to mind. The Cruarch had brought half a dozen casks of *uisghe* with him as a gift. Two were breached the first night; one in the garrison to be shared among the men, and one in the great hall to be shared by the household.

It felt strange to entertain the Cruarch in my own home and preside over such a large gathering. But in truth, the first night went relatively smoothly. Drustan was a gracious guest, at home and at ease among family. And although Dorelei and Breidaia were disappointed, I was glad to note that Talorcan hadn't accompanied him. Drustan had bidden him to host the Feast of the Dead at Bryn Gorrydum, reckoning it was good practice.

"Besides," he said to me after the plates had been cleared that evening, "the celebration grows a bit wild. Folk lose the sense of it there in the city. I prefer to honor the dead in the old way, amid the standing stones and the oak grove. You've seen to it that the paths are clear?"

"Oh, yes," I said. "Firdha made sure of it."

"Good." Drustan nodded. "You've done a good job here, Imriel. Better than I would have reckoned."

"I'm trying, my lord," I said.

"I've noted." He eyed me. "So what was it you wished to discuss?"

I told him, quietly, why I thought it would be wise to postpone Alais' and Talorcan's wedding for at least a year. Drustan listened to me, watching Alais as he did. She was entertaining several of the minor lordlings who had ridden with him, sparing Dorelei some of the burden of serving as hostess to the merry mob. She managed it with a maturity and aplomb that she'd never evinced in Terre d'Ange. I daresay Sidonie would have been proud of her sister.

My Alais was growing up.

"You've a point," Drustan said when I finished. "I'd as soon see the matter settled and done, but . . ." He shook his head. "Mayhap we acted in haste the first time." His voice dropped. "I never reckoned the Maghuin Dhonn would do such a thing."

"Nor I," I murmured. "I didn't know it *could* be done."

"I've word from Sister Nehailah," Drustan said unexpectedly. "She's heard from her mentor."

"So soon?" I asked in surprise. "How?"

He grinned. "I was curious myself, so I badgered the secret from her. It seems some of the temples use doves to carry messages over great distances. She's promised to teach me more."

I thought about all the doves roosting in the cypress trees outside Naamah's Temple and smiled. "Clever. Did her teacher have any counsel?"

"Of a sort, yes." Drustan's face grew sober. "'Tis his opinion that since the talisman that binds you was wrought of Alban clay and soil, 'tis only on Alba's soil that you are bound."

"And free of it elsewhere?" I asked softly.

The Cruarch of Alba nodded. "Yes."

I blew out my breath and glanced at Dorelei. She looked happy, her face soft with contentment. Her cheeks had grown rounder as the babe grew within her; or mayhap it was the result of Milcis' fine honey. She caught my eye and smiled, dimples showing deeply.

"A hard choice," Drustan said with genuine sympathy.

"Truly." I squared my shoulders. "My lord, I'm not going anywhere until the babe's born. I've promised her that much. We will talk, though."

"Imriel . . ." Drustan hesitated. "If you would hear my counsel, I would say that if there is sufficient love present, a marriage may endure on a quarter-measure of time. Of a surety, I ought to know." He patted my shoulder. "Think on it, and I will think on your words tonight. I must needs consult with Talorcan before I give any answer, and with my own lady wife, too." He laughed. "Mayhap Sister Nehailah will permit me the use of her doves."

That night as we lay abed, before blowing out the lamp, I told Dorelei about the priestess' message and what the Cruarch had said.

She listened gravely, her dark eyes luminous. "So he proposes a marriage like his own?"

"I think so, yes."

"It wouldn't be, though. Not really." Dorelei toyed with the red yarn around my wrist. "You'd have to consent to be bound here in Alba. Every time you came, you'd have to give up your freedom."

"I know," I said. "And you your dreams."

"Could you do such a thing?" she asked.

"I think so." I stroked her hair, black and shining, straight as fine-combed silk. "In truth? I don't know, love. We never know what we're capable of doing until we're called upon to do it. I'd try, though. What of you? Could you endure it?"

Dorelei smiled ruefully, her face averted. "Oh, yes."

"Well, then." I shrugged.

She looked up at me. "What about *her*?"

It had been a long time since we'd spoken of it. I didn't answer right away, realizing I'd not thought it through. *What if there's a child?* Sidonie had told me she would hate knowing there was such a large part of me she couldn't share. But that was true, regardless; and she already knew it. *Come when you can, with or without your wits.* Would Sidonie be content with three-quarters of my life? Would she be willing to take me as a consort while I continued to be wed to my Alban wife? To bear her own heirs out of wedlock? It would be a tremendous sacrifice to ask of her. And I didn't even want to begin to think about how Queen Ysandre and the D'Angeline peerage would react. Mayhap it would be better all around if Dorelei and I let our vows lapse when the year and a day had passed.

And yet . . .

"I don't know," I said softly. "Truly, Dorelei, I don't. But I do know we've made a life together here, and a child between us, and I can't walk away from that altogether. Not now, not ever."

"I'm glad," she whispered.

THIRTY-THREE

O N T H E D A Y O F T H E Feast of the Dead, we fasted.

Oh, to be sure, the kitchens were hard at work all day long; in Clunderry Castle and in every crofter's thatched hut. They turned out tarts and pies, all manner of puddings and oatcakes by the score, while soups simmered, roasts sizzled in their own juices, and capons grew crisp-skinned and tender. But none of it was meant to be eaten, not yet.

Outside the castle walls, the foundation for a great bonfire was laid with care, a tall cone reaching toward the steely grey sky. Despite the cold weather and the hunger, everyone was in good spirits.

Although I understood the protocol of the celebration, I had no idea what to expect. I'd felt the presence of the dead unleashed among the living in Lucca and it hadn't been pleasant. The prospect of courting them deliberately had me nervous and on edge. I couldn't help thinking about the way Gallus Tadius had taken possession of Lucius. Dorelei assured it me it was nothing like what I'd witnessed in Lucca. Betimes the dead appeared to one, but often they didn't. She claimed to have seen a spirit once; the spirit of her aunt Moiread, who had died in the battle of Bryn Gorrydum.

"How did you know it was her?" I asked.

"I didn't," she said. "She looked a lot like my mother, only younger, and there was a brightness about her. And she was carrying a bow. She smiled at me. When I told my parents about it, they said it was her."

"What did it mean?"

Dorelei shrugged. "'Twas a sign that she was happy in the underworld. That she died well, with courage and honor, and that her death had been properly avenged."

"What about the unhappy dead?" I asked.

"They're not happy," Dorelei said. "And they don't smile."

When the invisible sun began to sink below the western horizon, all the lamps, torches, and candles in Clunderry were extinguished and the cooking fires were banked. A portion of all the food prepared that day was carried outside the castle walls and set on a long trestle table erected for the purpose. We bundled ourselves into warm clothing and thick woolen cloaks and gathered outside around the looming pile of brush and firewood, taking up unlit torches prepared for the occasion.

Darkness seemed to rise upward from the cold, barren ground. The *ollamh* Firdha lifted her hands and invoked the gods of death and the underworld, inviting them to open their gates that the dead might visit the living and be honored. She invoked the gods of fire and light to illuminate their paths and welcome them with brightness and warmth, and invoked the *diadh-anam* of the Cullach Gorrym to guide us.

When the *ollamh*'s invocation was finished, Alais presented her with a flint striker. The Daughter of the Grove knelt and kindled the fire, the sparks bright and vivid against the gloaming.

It caught quickly, pitch-soaked twists of straw roaring to life. Within minutes, the bonfire was a roaring blaze, a tower of flame licking at the sky. Drustan stepped forward to light the first torch, and cheers echoed throughout Clunderry.

The procession began.

Firdha led it, flanked by a pair of the Cruarch's men, holding their torches high to light her way. One by one, we all came forward, dipping our torches into the bonfire, then proceeding past the trestle table, where we retrieved an item of food. I picked up a small mincemeat pie. The smell made my empty stomach rumble.

The procession crossed a stretch of darkened field, heading toward the *taisgaidh* woods. As I had promised Drustan, the paths had been cleared, although I'd not travelled them myself. I'd not ventured into the woods since the night of the cattle-raid.

As Firdha entered the darker shadow of the trees, I turned back to glance behind me. We were at the forefront of the procession. It snaked behind us, hundreds of people long, torches flickering all the way across Clunderry. The sight made me shiver with a mix of awe and apprehension.

"Are you all right?" Dorelei asked.

"Fine." I smiled at her. "Hungry."

The woods were dense, but the path was wide and clear. It had to be, else we'd set fire to the place. Even so, it made me nervous. Dry branches reached down toward us like brittle fingers, eager to touch the crackling flames.

The Cruithne do this every year, I reminded myself.

I set my fear aside and concentrated on the dead, trying to honor them in my memory. To be sure, I had enough of them. I thought about all who had died in Daršanga, all the victims and martyrs and valiant fighters. *Remember this.* I thought about my comrades in Lucca, and the soldiers I'd killed with my own hand, praying for their forgiveness. I thought about Gilot, who had died a hero after all; and Canis, who'd given his life for mine.

I thought about Dorelei's dead; my family, now. Her grandmother, her father, her young aunt. I prayed that they would smile upon her.

We entered the oak grove. They were ancient trees with vast, spreading crowns and gnarled trunks, twisting roots thicker than a strong man's arm emerging from the soil. My skin prickled and my bindings itched. This was a sacred place.

In the center of the grove, Firdha pointed. One of the men escorting her knelt and planted his torch in the soil, then rose and kindled a second torch from it. Firdha raised her hands and gave another invocation.

"Mothers and fathers, brothers and sisters, husbands and wives, sons and daughters, feast and be welcome among us this night!"

There, we left our offerings of food, a steady pile growing around the burning torch. And then the *ollamh* led us onward, the path twisting and winding as it led out of the grove and deeper into the woods.

How long we walked, I could not say. I never grew tired and the time passed as if in a dream; it could have been hours or merely minutes. At last the woods opened onto a clearing and the ring of standing stones was before us.

I'd heard tell there were larger ones elsewhere in Alba, and I daresay it was true; but this was large enough. There were nine stones, all standing on end, all solid granite, and none less than half again as tall as I was. I touched one as we entered, following Firdha. It was rough and cool to the touch.

"Here." Firdha pointed to a half-buried boulder that marked the center. Her other escort knelt and planted his torch beside it. Drustan mab Necthana beckoned into the torch-streaked darkness behind us, and two of his men came forward, carrying a cask of *uisghe* between them. They placed it atop the boulder, and Drustan pulled out the cork bung.

Uisghe flowed, pouring over stone and seeping into the earth. I could smell the tang of it.

There was another odor, too; darker and deeper. It was mixed in with the scent of loam and night and fermented grain. Blood. Old blood.

Firdha raised her face to the dark sky and opened her arms. "Crom, Cailleach, Macha, Balor! We bring tribute and thanks! May Alba's dead rest gentle in your keeping, and receive the honor of the living this night!"

I shuddered.

Nothing happened, though. Firdha lowered her arms and led the procession around the interior of the circle of stones. Well and so, I thought as we completed the circle and the procession began to double back on itself; that is that. What did you expect, Imriel? This is Alba, where you've no dead of your own.

The horse beside me tossed its head and snorted in agreement.

Name of Elua! I nearly jumped out of my skin.

"What is it?" Dorelei asked quietly.

I pointed at the horse and rider pacing alongside us on the path, pale and spectral, as though they were wrought out of mist. I could see torch-bearing figures walking on the other side of the path clear through them, still proceeding toward the standing stones. "There. Him. Them. Do you see?"

"No." She shook her head. "Who is it?"

I lifted my gaze to meet the rider's eyes. I knew him; I knew his face. He was D'Angeline. An old man, grave and sorrowful. His face was wrinkled, but I knew it. I knew the strong, firm line of his brows, the angle of his jaw visible beneath the sagging skin. I'd seen it in the Hall of Portraits in the Palace in the City of Elua. I'd seen it in the mirror.

"Father?" I whispered.

The rider lifted one hand; whether in acknowledgment, benediction, or apology, I could not say. Mayhap it was all three. I'd thought Berlik of the Maghuin Dhonn had the saddest face I'd ever seen on a man. I was wrong. My father's face was sadder. I reached out to him unthinking, and he vanished. There was only the path and the woods and the long, winding line of processionists passing us in the opposite direction.

"Oh!" I blinked. "Dorelei, he's gone."

"It's all right." She took my arm and pressed it against her warm, living flesh. "They can't stay long, Imriel. They never do." She smiled up at me. "Mayhap he wanted to behold his grandchild in the womb."

You will wonder about your father . . .

My father had spent his life in exile for the sake of political gain, and hated it. Bitterness had poisoned him. He had come to despise his own half-Caerdicci children. My mother had known it. She had exploited it. And I had followed in his footsteps in a way, though I'd never thought on it. But it wasn't the same, not at all. Although I missed Terre d'Ange, I'd learned to love Alba. I'd learned to love my wife, who had taught me to be a better person. Would my father love this half-Cruithne grandchild of his?

I hoped so. I hoped death had brought wisdom to him.

"Mayhap," I said to Dorelei. "I hope so."

Still, I wished he hadn't looked so sad.

Upon our return to Clunderry, the great bonfire was burning much, much lower. The fires were rekindled in the hearths, the oven-embers uncovered, the lamps and torches and candles were relit, and at last we feasted. Hungry though I was, I hovered over Dorelei first to ensure that the long walk hadn't overtaxed her and she ate well. I'd tried to persuade her not to take part in the ritual, but she'd pointed out that she was perfectly fit, and there were women among the crofters further along in their pregnancies than she was walking in the procession.

We stayed awake until the small hours of the night, sharing memories of our dead, and tales of those glimpsed along the paths, our tongues loosened by *uisghe* and the strangeness of the night.

I learned a great deal about the members of my household that night, and I daresay they could say the same of me. D'Angeline politics were distant and of little interest to most Albans, especially here in the countryside. The history of my parentage came as somewhat of a novelty to them.

"I'd a brother was a traitor," Urist offered unexpectedly. "Remember, my lord?"

Drustan nodded quietly. "I do."

"What happened?" I asked.

"He chose to side with Maelcon the Usurper." Urist gazed into the depths of his cup. "I killed him myself in the battle of Bryn Gorrydum. He'd been sore wounded, but I finished the job. I pray for his forgiveness every day." He looked up. "I saw him on the paths, once. I think he wanted me to know he understood."

"Mayhap he wanted *your* forgiveness," I said.

"Do you think that's what your father sought?" Urist asked shrewdly.

"I don't know." I frowned. "Mayhap."

The memory stayed with me for many days, long after Drustan and his men had departed. The enormity of my mother's crimes had always overshadowed my father's; he'd never even been convicted of treason, having died before he could stand trial. And my mother's living presence had always overshadowed his absence. Even having vanished, she remained a presence in my life. I'd felt it at the Palace, and I'd felt it in Caerdicca Unitas, where her man Canis had saved my life. Here in Alba, beyond the reach of the long arm of the Unseen Guild, 'twas the first time I'd truly felt free of it.

But my father . . . I'd never given him much consideration.

As the weeks passed and late autumn gave way to winter in Clunderry, I found myself thinking a great deal about the past, looking for clues to the future. My father's children from his first marriage, Thérèse and Marie-Celeste, had turned their back on their D'Angeline heritage and flung themselves into marriage and intrigue in La Serenissima. I hoped that wouldn't happen with Dorelei's and my child.

Still, I thought, if it did, I would try to bear it with grace and understanding. I wouldn't disdain him—or her—for the choice. I hoped our child would embrace both sides of its heritage, but I'd not shove any false notions of D'Angeline superiority down its throat.

I wondered if my father had done that with his half-Caerdicci children, making them feel inadequate. I suspected mayhap it was so. To be sure, Alais and Sidonie had experienced a measure of the same prejudice from many of the realm's peers. Sidonie was capable of meeting it with withering contempt, but Alais . . . it had hurt her.

And even Sidonie . . .

I remembered the first time we'd made love. I'd told her, afterward, that I liked her black eyes, the way they didn't match the rest of her. I remembered what she'd said. *You don't mind?*

And so I meditated on my father's spectral visit and resolved, over the course of the winter, to take it as a warning and learn from his mistakes. If Dorelei's and my child emerged with jet-black hair and eyes, toast-brown skin, dimpled cheeks, and a predilection for poetry, cattle-raids, and *uisghe*, I'd love it not a whit less.

I told her that one night as we lay in bed. I was rubbing flaxseed oil on her belly, which had acquired an impressive rondeur.

"I never thought you wouldn't," Dorelei said in surprise.

"No?" I smoothed more oil over her taut skin, watching it gleam. Dorelei said she could feel the babe moving, but I couldn't, not yet. Another month, the older women assured me. "I worry, that's all."

"You shouldn't." She smiled at me. "You may be insufferably self-absorbed, but you *do* have a good heart, Imriel."

I hoped it was true. I'd wondered before in my life what manner of person I'd have become if I'd grown up as the goatherding orphan I'd believed I was. But I'd never thought to wonder what I'd be like if I'd grown to manhood as the son of Melisande Shahrizai and Benedicte de la Courcel, shaped by my mother's machinations and my father's bitterness.

Very different, I suspected.

Ambitious.

Arrogant.

Mayhap ruthless.

No one, I thought, was all good or all bad. I'd learned that in Lucca. And if I had goodness in me that hadn't been destroyed by Daršanga— the stunted tree reaching for sunlight—almost all of it was owed to Phèdre and Joscelin's influence in my life. I owed them so much I could never repay. But mayhap I could do it by giving my own child what they had given me; deep, abiding, unconditional love.

Impending fatherhood made me thoughtful and reflective, and no doubt a great deal of it was due to my own troubled heritage. But in truth, there wasn't much else to do. The harvest was gathered, and we'd slaughtered the pigs after the Feast of the Dead. The meat was salted and curing. The cattle hovered close to their byres, rendering a raid unlikely.

There were no sightings of the Maghuin Dhonn; none at all.

Mayhap, I thought, that like the Brown Bear that was their *diadh-anam*, the Old Ones slept through the winter.

To be sure, this was the time of year when everyone stayed indoors and gathered around the hearth to stay warm, telling tales and making music to amuse themselves. It should have been dull, but it wasn't. Wrapped in my bindings, I was content with the slow, measured pace of life, rendered miraculous by the growing life in Dorelei's womb.

It felt strange not to celebrate the Longest Night, though.

It didn't pass unmarked in Alba, but their rituals were different. They do not celebrate the night itself, but the following day, bidding farewell to the old year and ushering in the new with the Day of Misrule, when all is rendered topsy-turvy and the lords and ladies dance attendance on their servants.

I was privy to all the plans, and I fully intended to play my role. But on the Longest Night itself, I found myself uneasy, itching and restless. It didn't help that Alais entertained the household with an interminable, detailed description of how the Longest Night was celebrated in Terre d'Ange; all the sparkling *joie*, sumptuous glamour, and elegant, intricate costumes. It was the first time I'd heard her speak of home with such fond animation, and the Cruithne listened in fascination, begging for further tales of glittering excess.

"Do you remember Eamonn and his hammer, Imri?" she asked. "When he was the Skaldic thunder-god?"

"Oh, yes," I said. "I remember."

"You were a scandal that year, Eamonn and House Montrève!" Alais laughed. "But Sidonie topped you last year, didn't she?"

"Your sister?" Kinadius asked.

Alais nodded. "She came as the Sun Princess. 'Tis hard to explain."

My throat tightened. Of a sudden, it felt as though the red yarn around my wrists and ankles was cutting my circulation. I rose, my hands and feet feeling hot and uncomfortable. Dorelei's head rose at my abrupt movement. I took a deep breath. "You know, Alais, it *is* the Longest Night. Someone should keep Elua's vigil."

I didn't wait for her response. I sketched a brief bow in Dorelei's direction, not meeting her eyes, and blundered for the door, borrowing a cloak as I exited the castle, the gate opened by a startled guardsman.

Outside, it was cold.

A light snow had fallen, and it was cold enough that it creaked beneath my boots. I trudged toward the frozen lake and Elua's shrine. The sky was clear and the stars were bright overhead. I could see my breath rising in plumes of frost. Clunderry looked peaceful and prosperous beneath the winter sky, slats of warm light glowing through the shuttered windows of every cottage.

Near the edge of the lake, I paused to remove my boots. Leaving melted footprints in my wake, I approached the shrine. Beneath the barren arbor, the effigy of Blessed Elua smiled serenely under a cap of snow.

I bowed and kissed his feet, then stepped and knelt, bowing my head. The croonie-stone was heavy around my neck.

A year; only a year.

A year ago tonight, I had danced with Sidonie and kissed her behind the hollow mountain in the ballroom, had sat atop a table in Cereus House and watched the revelries, had ridden barefoot and rag-clad through the streets of the City to watch the dawn come at the Temple of Elua. A year ago tonight, it had all begun in earnest. It seemed like much, much longer; and it seemed like yesterday.

I wanted to pray, but I didn't have any words. Only memories so strong and vivid they strained at my bindings. I rested my hands on the ground before me, cooling them, and heard the sound of snow crunching behind me. I recognized the footsteps, steady and deliberate. Phèdre had taught me to listen for such things.

"Urist?" I called.

He grunted. "How'd you know?"

I didn't answer his question. "It's all right, I don't need a minder."

Urist leaned against a tree. "I disagree."

He was right, of course; I didn't like it, but I couldn't argue against it. And so Urist stayed while I knelt and kept Blessed Elua's vigil, melted snow soaking the knees of my breeches. At some point, one of the others came to relieve him—Budoc, I thought. And then, later, Kinadius. He was restless, shifting and coughing and blowing on his fingers. I finally turned to raise my brows at him.

"Sorry, my lord," he apologized. " 'Tis cold."

"It's almost over," I said.

Kinadius managed to contain himself then. I stayed and watched until the sun rose. There was no horologist to announce its arrival. Somewhere in the middle of the night, a heavy bank of clouds had covered the sky, and dawn broke grey and sullen.

Still, it was dawn.

I got to my feet, gazing toward the east. In Terre d'Ange, the revelers would be stumbling toward their beds. I wondered, briefly, who would be sharing Sidonie's, and pushed the thought away. It wasn't as hard as it might have been. I was stiff and very, very cold.

"Is it finished, my lord?" Kinadius asked. I nodded. "Let's get you back, then."

There was no temple vestibule, warmed with braziers, in which to thaw. My hands and feet were too cold to draw on my boots. I leaned on Kinadius and hobbled back to the castle. He glanced behind us once, shaking his head at the dark, melting tracks my bare feet left in the snow.

"Just like the story of your Elua, isn't it?" he said. "Do you reckon flowers will bloom where you tread?"

"Not likely." I smiled. "I'm surprised you know of it."

He smiled back at me. "Oh, I learned a few things in the City."

The castle was just beginning to stir when we returned. There wasn't any water heated for a bath yet, so I simply shucked my damp clothes and crawled into bed beside Dorelei. Although I was careful not to touch her, I'd begun to shiver violently and it woke her. She rolled over to regard me, her head pillowed on one arm.

She knew.

She didn't say anything, but I could see it in her eyes. Dorelei was no fool, and she'd come to know me. She'd seen the change in me when Alais had spoken of Sidonie. She'd never wanted to know to whom my innermost heart was given. Now she did. I opened my mouth to speak, and she covered my lips with her free hand.

"Don't," she murmured. "Let me keep what's mine." Taking her hand away, she leaned over to kiss my cold lips, then smoothed the hair from my brow. "Go to sleep. I'll wake you in a few hours."

Betimes there is a mercy in things left unspoken.

I obeyed, and slept.

THIRTY-FOUR

THE DAY OF MISRULE was a riotous affair, and tired though I was, I enjoyed it. I was young and I'd gotten used to going short of sleep in Lucca. My body hadn't lost the knack of it.

And too, it gave Dorelei and me reason not to dwell on the unspoken.

Lots were drawn among the most junior members of the household to determine who would be the Lord or Lady of Misrule, and the honor fell to a scullery lad, a lowly cook's apprentice named Hoel. He was crowned with a wreath of dead oak leaves and given a wooden spoon for a scepter, and for the course of the day, his word was law. His first act was to order the Cruarch's last cask of *uisghe* breached, which met with great approval. His second was to declare that all the men should dress in women's attire, and the women in men's.

To be sure, this provoked hilarity; and rightfully so. Dorelei stared at me, clad in her green kirtle, and burst into helpless laughter. It fell to my knees and left my shins bare, and even with the stays unlaced, it strained tight across my shoulders.

"Oh, Imri!" She gasped. "You'll split the seams."

"I'll buy you a new gown," I promised. "A dozen."

One of my shirts fit over her belly easily enough, but we had to scout around to borrow a pair of drawstring breeches from a stout fellow named Lonn, one of the members of the original garrison. The pants had to be rolled at the ankle many times to keep her from tripping, and pinned to keep them in place.

"You look like a little girl dressed in her father's clothes," I observed. "A very fat little girl."

Dorelei swatted at me. "You carry the babe, then! You're dressed for it."

Throughout the day, the peers of Clunderry waited hand and foot on the commonfolk; or at least pretended to. In truth, all the actual preparations had been completed the day before, and Hoel issued outrageous demands, which were met with pranks.

"You!" He snapped his fingers at me. "Scullery lad! I have heard of this drink you call *joie*. Bring me a cup!"

I bowed. "At once, my lord."

In the kitchen, Alais and Kerys rummaged through the pantry cupboards, unstoppering bottles and smelling the contents between giggles. They were both clad in clothes borrowed from Kinadius and looked quite charming, although they were making a fearsome mess.

"Ooh!" Kerys jerked her head back. "Here, my lord. Bitter verjuice."

"Perfect," I said.

I served it to Hoel, who took a sip and spat it out. "You call this *joie*?"

"Oh, yes, my lord," I said solemnly. "Distilled in the Camaeline Mountains, as cold as ice and burning like fire. Is it not sweet to the tongue?"

So it went throughout the Day of Misrule, culminating at last in a long, drunken feast. After pretending to serve scorched cuts of meat and an uncooked mess of pottage, we relented and brought forth the meal of salt beef stew that had simmered in the kettle overnight, trenchers of bread, cold capons, pickles and sausages, all of which we'd already sampled in the kitchens.

When it was done, Hoel bade us entertain his "court." Until I die, I will never forget the sight of tattooed Urist, the veteran warrior, declaiming a love poem in a saffron kirtle. Still, Alais and I had conspired beforehand, and we won the biggest laugh when I played a slow quadrille on Hugues' flute and Alais danced slowly with an unhappy-looking Celeste, the wolfhound's paws on her shoulders.

Thus did Clunderry celebrate the year reborn.

Afterward, once the mayhem was over and the mess was cleared, life settled into the same quiet, wintry pace. The sun may have returned, but it would be a long time before the land felt its full warmth. Still, there'd been somewhat purgative about the Day of Misrule. All things considered, I would prefer to celebrate the Longest Night in the D'Angeline manner, but I could see the merit in the Alban tradition. I could think of a number of D'Angeline peers who would benefit from setting aside their dignity for a day and reveling in sheer absurdity.

Days wore on to weeks, one much like another.

I marked the passing of time by the slow, steady rise of Dorelei's belly; and by other changes in her body. Her breasts grew fuller and fuller, and they were passing tender. Her navel protruded under the rising pressure, and there was a faint, dark line on her skin, reaching down from her navel toward toward her pubis.

It was mayhap a week after the Day of Misrule that I felt the babe move myself for the first time; a slight flutter against my palm as I massaged flaxseed oil into her tight skin.

"Oh," I said, startled. "Oh!"

Dorelei laughed. "You felt it, then?"

"I did." I marveled at it. "I really did. Elua! Do you not find it passing strange to think there's a little *person* in there?"

"Very much so," she agreed.

Betimes we made love, carefully. It was most comfortable for her to ride astraddle of me, rocking slowly, her burgeoning belly resting on my abdomen. Those were the times I was glad of my bindings. I felt filled with infinite patience, infinite tenderness. I liked to watch Dorelei take her pleasure, her face flushed, black hair clinging to skin damp with sweat. In those moments, I felt my heart full to bursting, and she seemed very beautiful to me.

We spoke of the future, at least in terms of Alba.

We didn't speak of Sidonie.

Not directly, at least. Dorelei made me promise, one night after we'd made love—one of the last times before the discomfort began to outweigh the pleasure—that I would return to Terre d'Ange by the summer's end. Not long ago, I'd have leapt at the offer; now, since I'd felt the babe move, it seemed harder to promise.

"What if you need me here?" I asked.

"I don't." Her gaze was direct. "Imriel, if you wanted to stay of your own will, nothing would make me happier. But . . ." She lifted the croonie-stone from my throat. "Your will's not entirely your own, is it?"

"No," I admitted softly.

Dorelei smiled sadly. "When you come back, I'll know it is."

"I will," I said. "I promise."

"I believe you. I'll always believe you." She let go the croonie-stone and twined a lock of my hair around her fingers. "I hope the babe has your hair," she mused. "Look how it curls. I always wanted mine to do that. Though if I had to choose, I'd like her to have your eyes."

"Or him," I reminded her.

"Or him." Her dimples flashed. "A pretty lad with sea-blue eyes . . ."

She fell silent. It was there, then, between us. I remembered where I'd heard the phrase. Ferghus, the harpist. *Tell me, lass, do you love him? The pretty lad with the sea-blue eyes and another's name carved on his heart?*

"Dorelei . . ." I whispered.

She shuddered. "It's going to be terribly complicated, isn't it? When you go home?"

I nodded slowly. It was.

"Will you promise to take care of yourself?" Dorelei asked. She laughed and sniffled all at once. "I don't want to lose you altogether."

"You won't," I promised. "Never."

For ten days in late winter, it snowed steadily, until the snow was hip-deep in places. I put Urist's garrison to work shoveling paths between the cow-byres and the barns where the dried hay was stored, working alongside them myself. It helped break the monotony, and the physical labor felt good. We were all growing lax for lack of exercise.

I kept up the discipline of my Cassiline training, though. The folk of Clunderry no longer stared and giggled, reckoning it merely a harmless eccentricity on my part. A couple of the younger guards—Kinadius and Uven—had grown intrigued and asked me to teach them. I did my best, but I didn't have Joscelin's patience, and 'tis a discipline best learned young. Still, we whittled practice-blades out of wood, and betimes held mock bouts in the hall. It helped pass the time and it kept me sharp.

After the heavy snow, the weather changed. Winter eased its grip. The days began to grow longer and milder and the deep drifts of fluffy snow dwindled into heavy, sodden masses. Children and young people were given license to race around outdoors, flinging snowballs at one another before the snow vanished altogether.

Spring was on its way.

With the harbingers of spring came an unexpected visit from Prince Talorcan. He appeared unannounced at the gates of Clunderry, accompanied by a score of men.

I offered him a fulsome welcome. Most of Clunderry was delighted to see him, especially the Lady Breidaia and Dorelei, happy to have their son and brother visiting. To be sure, Talorcan was a pleasant fellow, well-mannered and reserved. The only time I'd seem behave in a manner that was less than circumspect was the night before my nuptials, when he'd presided over the quarterstaff bouts and placed the antique boar-helmet on my head, and to be honest, I'd been too drunk to remember it well.

But although he greeted his mother with genuine fondness and exclaimed over his sister's enormous belly, I doubted this was a visit of mere courtesy. Alais and I exchanged glances, wondering.

"How long till the babe comes?" Talorcan asked. "You look ready to burst!"

"I feel like it," Dorelei said. "But Cluna says another month."

He smiled. "Good old Cluna's attending you?"

She nodded. "Of course."

It had been a point of contention between us. Cluna and her mother and her mother's mother before her had served as midwife to most of Clunderry, and there was a good deal of dissent over whether or not she was named for the estate, or the estate took its name from her line. Of a surety, her family had been here a very long time, and Cluna was one of the few women the *ollamh* Firdha considered a friend. Still, she was growing elderly—she'd attended the births of Dorelei and Talorcan—and she was trained as a wise-woman, not a proper chirurgeon. As soon as the weather broke, I'd wanted to send to Terre d'Ange for a chirurgeon, but the women of Clunderry had laughed at me. Dorelei had the final say, and that was an argument I'd lost.

We put up Talorcan's men in the garrison and entertained him throughout the day, making small talk over the evening meal. It wasn't until after dinner that he got down to business. Dorelei excused herself early, and I daresay mayhap Lady Breidaia sent round a discreet word, for the rest of the household followed her lead, leaving Alais and me alone with the Cruarch's heir.

Talorcan sat across from us, folding his hands on the table. He was not, I thought, entirely pleased with the way matters had developed. I wished I wasn't bound. I couldn't read him as clearly as I might otherwise.

"It is Prince Imriel who made the proposal," he said to Alais. "And yet he would not have done so without your consent; or indeed, at your request. Before I give my answer, I would like to hear the reason from your lips, my lady. Why do you wish to postpone our wedding?"

"*Your* answer, my lord?" I asked politely.

Talorcan shot me a look. "I come as the Cruarch's mouthpiece, of course." He smiled disarmingly then. "I'm a man shunned, Imriel! Give me leave to ask why."

"I'm not shunning you, my lord." Alais frowned. "It's not our custom to wed so young in Terre d'Ange. I agreed to it because settling the matter was supposed to foster continued peace and prosperity between Alba and Terre d'Ange, like Imriel's marriage to your sister."

"And so it has done," Talorcan noted.

"Yes, and stirred unrest in Alba!" Alais said tartly. "My lord, my kinsman is bound twofold by Alban magic. I watched his face when the Daughter of the Grove restored his broken bindings. It changed. A brightness went out of it, blown out like a candle-flame."

"You're afraid," he said softly.

"Yes." Alais met his gaze steadily. "Yes, I am. And the gift of my birthright is blind and useless. I came to Alba to learn what it meant to be a daughter of Necthana's line. I wish time to do this. Is a year's grace so much to ask?"

"No." Talorcan sighed. "No, it is not."

"So the Cruarch accedes?" I asked.

"He does." Talorcan's mouth quirked. "And I am given to understand that her majesty Queen Ysandre privately insists upon it until such time as she may be assured the Maghuin Dhonn are not a threat to her daughter. However . . ." He paused. "It is Lord Drustan's plan that the news be released quietly. At the same time, even more quietly, the news will be released that Master Hyacinthe will not train a successor."

Alais cocked her head. "Why?"

"Politics," I murmured.

Talorcan inclined his head. "Master Hyacinthe may be of Tsingani blood, but he is D'Angeline by birth. It may be that some in Alba will perceive the postponing of our wedding as an unfavorable response to his decision. Those who have concerns over Terre d'Ange's influence in Alba will welcome it as such."

"As opposed to the insistence of the Queen of Terre d'Ange?" Alais inquired.

"Yes," he said.

We all sat in silence for a moment. I didn't like it, but I understood it; and in the end, it was Alais' choice. If she aspired to rule Alba one day, either on her own or at Talorcan's side—who knew my young cousin harbored such ambition?—she was getting her first real taste of Alban statecraft.

"All right," she said at length. "I'll say naught to counter the notion." She gave the Cruarch's heir a sudden, dazzling smile. "Thank you, Talorcan."

I couldn't be sure, but I thought he flushed beneath his warrior's markings. "You're welcome, Alais. I'm sorry. I didn't know you were so scared."

So the matter was decided. Having delivered the Cruarch's answer, Talorcan departed with promises to return the following month after the babe's birth, although not before giving me a most welcome gift—a letter from Phèdre.

It was old, having been written during the early months of autumn and sent . . . well, I wasn't entirely sure from whence it had been sent. Of a surety, it had spent long months on the road. According to the letter, Phèdre and Joscelin had elected to travel to Illyria to pay a visit to an old friend, and mayhap conduct some business on behalf of the Queen there.

There was indeed an old friend in Illyria—Kazan Atrabiades, Commander of the Illyrian Merchant Fleet and former pirate. However, I sincerely doubted that Joscelin harbored any deep desire to visit with him. Kazan Atrabiades had been Phèdre's rescuer, once; and her lover, too. With the aid of the Ban of Illyria, Kazan had smuggled her into La Serenissima in time to prevent the assassination of Queen Ysandre. It was Joscelin who had done the actual preventing, but without Kazan, neither of them would have been there.

That was another of the many stories whose details I'd learned from Gilot.

Strange to think, if it hadn't been for an Illyrian pirate I'd never met, my mother's scheme might well have succeeded. I'd been a babe of six months' age; neither Sidonie or Alais had been born. At that time, my aging father was still Ysandre's heir.

And I . . .

I might be the King of Terre d'Ange by now.

The thought made me shudder.

It made me think, too, about what Dorelei had said of the Maghuin Dhonn; how it might drive one mad to know too much, to see too many possible futures. I was glad my life was free of such burdensome gifts. Merely surviving without doing harm seemed chore enough.

At any rate, I didn't believe the letter; or at least not wholly. They might have gone to Illyria, but I suspected it was a starting point and not an end. Wherever they were, I suspected, very strongly, it had to do with my theory about whatever they'd been plotting at Stormkeep and the pages of the lost Book of Raziel.

That suspicion, I kept to myself.

If you've need of aught, Phèdre had written, *speak to Ti-Philippe. He knows Montrève's business. Take the best of care of yourself and Dorelei and the babe-to-come. May Blessed Elua hold and keep you until our swift return.*

Well and so, I thought; Ti-Philippe knows. That was good. He'd been Phèdre's man since before I was born. Cheerful and irreverent as he was, he was loyal to the bone, and I thought he'd sooner die than divulge her secrets.

It saddened me a bit to think that they wouldn't be here to attend the birth. It made me feel older, too. I was a man grown, and soon to be a father. It was heartening to know they trusted me to handle it without their assistance. Still, it would have been a comfort to have them here.

Especially after Urist's discovery.

'Twas a few days after Talorcan had departed. Urist begged a word of me without saying why. His face was grim as he led me across the fields, past the *ollamh*'s stone hut and into the woods. Pale green leaves were budding on the beech trees, the oaks were beginning to bear fuzzy catkins and new undergrowth was sprouting through the loam. For a time, we followed the trail that led to the oak grove and the standing stones, and then Urist turned toward the south. He moved silently in the woods, and I did my best to follow his lead.

"There." He pointed.

It was an oak tree, flakes of dry bark rubbed off to expose the pale, reddish new layer beneath. I looked closely. There was coarse brown hair snagged in the rough grooves.

"Bear sign," I murmured.

Urist nodded. "There's another one, too, with claw marks. Do you want to see it?"

"One's enough," I said. "How did you find it?"

"Marec the Thatcher spotted it," he said. "Hunting squirrels, I reckon. I didn't ask." He shrugged. "Could be natural."

"And it could be one of *them*," I said. "Post extra sentries on the woods' edge, and give Marec the reward you promised. Tell him you'll double it if he spots an actual bear. Preferably of the ordinary den-dwelling, cub-rearing sort."

Urist gave another nod. "And if it's not?"

I checked my bindings. They were firm. "Let's hope it is."

THIRTY-FIVE

I WAS LOATH TO TELL Dorelei about the bear sign. She was so near to her term with the babe, I hated to trouble her; and in truth, she'd grown unwontedly moody and irritable in recent days. I didn't blame her. She did indeed look ready to burst, her feet were swollen, and her back ached somewhat fierce.

I did, though. I'd had a bellyful of keeping secrets from people I cared about in Tiberium, and I reckoned I owed her honesty.

And in the end, it didn't matter.

When Morwen of the Maghuin Dhonn appeared, she did it openly.

It was late in the afternoon, and I was sitting in the sunlit salon with Dorelei, keeping her company while her mother and the other women embroidered and chattered. Work around Clunderry had resumed after the long, idle months of winter—the cattle had been driven to the farther pastures, and fields were being plowed and manured in preparation for next month's sowing—but I'd decided to forgo working alongside my people in favor of spending time with my wife.

We were trying to settle on a name for the babe. We'd agreed it should bear an Alban name, but Dorelei thought it should be a name not wholly unfamiliar to the D'Angeline tongue, and I agreed.

"By all rights, if it's a boy, it should be named after your father," Breidaia observed.

Dorelei and I exchanged a glance. "I loved him and miss him, Mother, but Gartnach doesn't fall smoothly from D'Angeline lips," she said. "Anyway, what if it's a girl?"

It was at that moment we heard the clamor; running feet and a horn blowing. Kinadius burst into the salon, wild-eyed. "Bear-witch!"

I leapt to my feet. "Where?"

He pointed in the general direction of the woods. "She just . . . she just walked right out of the woods. That woman, the one with the pale eyes." His throat worked as he swallowed. "Urist is there, dozens of us with weapons drawn, and the *ollamh*, and . . . and Lady Alais." He licked his lips. "She wants to speak to you, my lord."

"Alais?" I asked stupidly.

Kinadius shook his head. "The bear-witch," he whispered. "Says she's come to offer a bargain."

I drew a sharp breath. Dorelei levered herself to her feet with difficulty. Her face had turned white, but it was set and determined. "I'm going with you."

"The hell you are," I said.

Her eyes flashed. "The hell I *am*!"

"Fine." I turned to Kinadius. "Get the rest of the garrison."

He obeyed without a word. It was an imposing delegation that turned out to confront Morwen. If I hadn't been in a grim mind-set, I might have felt foolish. Morwen stood calmly at the edge of the woods, a few feet behind the carved stone marker that indicated it was *taisgaidh* land. She appeared small and harmless, clad in a coarse brown dress, her feet bare and grimy, but her mist-pale eyes didn't blink between the tattooed claw marks on her face, and Urist and his lads held her at bay, hunting bows drawn. Firdha was there, looking disturbed, and Alais beside her. The wolfhound Celeste was growling softly deep in her throat.

Morwen ignored them all, ignored the scores of new arrivals, looking past them to meet my eyes. She inclined her head, ignoring Dorelei on my arm. "Prince Imriel."

"Morwen," I said. "What do you want?"

"You sought to make a bargain with the Maghuin Dhonn," she said. "I come to offer one. Will you hear it?"

Dorelei's fingers dug into my arm. "Speak your piece," I said tightly.

"It seems the future has chosen its course. I wish to show you a glimpse of what will come," Morwen said. "In exchange, I will give you the mannekin charm you covet. The Maghuin Dhonn will relinquish all claim on you."

My heart gave a fierce leap in my breast, but I schooled my features to stone. "Why?"

"You will understand when you see," she said.

"Why should we trust you?" Dorelei asked. Her brow was damp with sweat, but her voice was cool. "You've done us nothing but harm."

"Have I?" Morwen smiled slightly. "All throughout these endless winter months, you've had a husband who loves you to warm your bed, Dorelei mab Breidaia. Can you say of a surety it would have been so without Alban magic to tame his restless heart?"

"No," Dorelei said steadily. "But I would have welcomed the chance to try."

A flicker of uncertainty crossed Morwen's face. "It is too late."

"Too late for what?" I asked.

"Many things." The uncertainty vanished. "Knots are undone, the skein is unraveled. If naught changes, only one thread is certain. Will you see it and understand?"

I took a deep breath. "How?"

"Come with me tonight to the standing stones," Morwen said. "And by the light of the full moon, I will show you." I made no answer. "The oath of the Maghuin Dhonn stands, Prince Imriel. By all that is holy, I swear I will do you no harm. You may bring your men if you wish. They may not enter the ring, but they may stand outside it and watch." She read my face. "Once it begins, I will give you the charm. As soon as it ends, you may destroy it. You will be free. Free of all bindings, free of all claims. Free to welcome your son into the world as your own true self."

"This is a trick," Dorelei murmured.

"No," Morwen shifted her gaze and fixed her pale eyes on her. "No trick, little sister. You will be free, too; you and your kinswomen. Free to dream, free to see past the fog that clouds your vision. It is the gift of your bloodline, of blood we share. You hunger for it, do you not?"

Dorelei swallowed. "Not enough to trust you."

The bear-witch shrugged. "Then you will hunger all your life, all of you, for visions that will not come. Imriel is bound to us, and you are bound to him."

"Only on Alban soil," I noted.

"Our magic?" Morwen inclined her head. "That is true. But what binds Dorelei mab Breidaia and her kin are ties of love and blood."

"There are worse things," I said.

"Than love and blood?" She smiled. "To be sure. But these are gifts meant to be given freely. If they are not, love may be poisoned, and blood may turn bitter as gall. Such is the heritage that runs in your veins. Is that what you wish, Imriel de la Courcel?"

I thought about the terrible sorrow in my father's face and turned to Firdha. "Daughter of the Grove, what is your counsel?"

The *ollamh* looked stricken. Still, when I called upon her, she squared her shoulders and approached Morwen. She held the gilded oak branch of her office so tightly her knuckles whitened. Urist jerked his head, and the men of the garrison spread out. I beckoned to Alais, who hurried to my side, her fingers locked around Celeste's collar.

"Where is the talisman?" Firdha asked.

"It is near," Morwen said calmly. "But you will not find it."

"Give it unto my keeping, and I will hold it," Firdha said. "I swear it by the grove."

Morwen considered; or pretended to. "No," she said at length. "Not until he has seen. That is the bargain I offer." She tilted her head. "The price of freedom is knowledge, lady. You ought to know its worth. If Imriel accepts this bargain, he will understand why we made it, and we will be at quits for all time. But I cannot change the terms."

Firdha studied her for a long, long time. Morwen bore her scrutiny in silence. At last the *ollamh* turned to address me. "Prince Imriel, the choice is yours. But if it is your wish to do this thing, I tell you this. I would not trust in the oath her people have sworn. I would bind her by an oath uttered in her own words, in the ring of standing stones itself. An oath that no harm come to you, nor to any member of your household, with the direst of consequences. With your permission, I would administer it myself."

"Would you swear such an oath?" I asked Morwen.

Her chin rose. "I will."

She wasn't lying, or at least there were no tell-tales. Beyond that, I couldn't read her. Frustration, yearning, and foreboding warred in me.

Beside me, Dorelei was shaking her head, but her face was troubled and unsure. I glanced up at the sun. "I must confer with my wife," I said to Morwen. "I'll return at sundown to give you my answer."

The bear-witch nodded. "So be it."

With that, she turned her back fearlessly on Urist's men with their drawn bows, melting into the forest. Urist glanced at me, and I shook my head at him. "Let her go, but post a guard on the woods."

No one spoke on the walk back to the castle.

I wished I knew what to do.

As the news spread through Clunderry, Dorelei and I retreated to our bedchamber to talk in private. I propped pillows on the bed so she could recline in comfort, then sat on the end with her feet in my lap, rubbing them. Neither of us knew what to say.

"I don't like it," Dorelei finally said. "And I *don't* trust her."

"Nor do I," I murmured.

"Good." She hesitated. "Still . . ."

"What if it's genuine?" I asked.

Dorelei nodded. "I've thought . . . betimes I've thought about the blessing they offered. At our wedding. I've wondered if we were right to refuse it. If *I* was right. I made that choice, and I'm not sure it was the right one. This choice is yours."

"But you don't think I should dare take her bargain," I said.

"I don't *know*!" Her voice broke. "No, I don't, but . . . what comes next, Imriel? That's the thing. Every time I hope mayhap they'll leave us in peace, they come back. Charms, tricks, oaths, seductions . . ." She drew a long, shaking breath. "What if this truly did put an end to it?"

"Wouldn't that be nice?" I said wistfully.

"Yes." Dorelei was trembling. "Hold me, will you?"

I set her feet down gently and shifted to the head of the bed to enfold Dorelei in my arms from behind. She leaned back against me, resting her head on my shoulder. I laid my right hand on her straining belly and felt the babe kick. "Oof!"

She made an effort to smile. "That was a strong one."

"Little Gartnach is restless," I said.

That made her laugh. "You know, I did have a thought. Isn't it odd how things occur to you at the strangest times? My father's mother died in childbirth, and he grew up bearing his father's name. Gartnach mab Aniel."

"Aniel," I mused.

"It nearly sounds D'Angeline, doesn't it?" she said.

"Anael is one of Blessed Elua's Companions," I said. "And Phèdre's lord and mentor was named Anafiel Delaunay."

Dorelei folded her fingers over mine. "So he'd be named for both our families."

"And if it's a girl?" I asked. "Anielle?"

"Anielle." She tasted the word. "It's not an Alban name, but it almost could be. And it could be D'Angeline, too. It's pretty, don't you think?"

"I do," I said.

"Aniel, Anielle." A smile curved her brown cheek. "I like it."

I tried to peer around her to see her dimples. "It could be twins, you know."

"It feels like it." Dorelei twisted awkwardly in my arms. "Imri . . . I do want you to be free. I want it more than anything for you. For us. For the babe. Whatever the future holds, I'd have you face it as a free man."

"And you, too." I stroked her face. "The bear-witch was right about that. You're bound as surely as I am, only in a different way."

"Love and blood, and the fog that clouds my vision." She smiled wryly. "'Tis true. It's like a great dark cloud hanging over me, Imriel. I'd breathe easier if I were free of it. To dream once more, to face the woods without fear . . . mayhap it's worth the risk."

We regarded one another.

"Firdha would administer the oath," I said softly.

"And Urist and his men would be there to keep watch," Dorelei said.

"So." I tightened my arms around her. "Is it decided?"

"Yes." She swallowed. "Are you frightened of what you might see?"

I shook my head. "All knowledge is worth having."

So it was decided, right or wrong; and I felt better for having the decision made. Dorelei and I descended into the great hall together and informed our household of the decision. Everyone nodded gravely.

I pulled Urist aside to discuss the matter of an escort. We settled on three dozen men under his command, enough to encompass the ring of stones. It would leave the garrison short-handed, but Urist reckoned it was worth the risk.

"I fear the Old Ones more than a cattle-raid," he said grimly.

We had an early supper, keeping a wary eye on the lowering sun. I didn't eat much. I felt strange and lightheaded, drunk on the prospect of freedom. Ah, Elua! To face each new day without the eternal litany of checking my bindings, to be free of the damp, smothering blanket that lay over my soul, to be *myself* . . .

It would be glorious.

The sun was hanging low over the western woods when the *ollamh* Firdha cleared her throat and declared it was growing late. Urist had assembled his men. They were all ready, swords at their belts, hunting bows slung over their shoulders. I took arm, too. Dorelei insisted on doing it herself. Alais helped, kneeling to buckle my old rhinoceros-hide sword-belt around my waist.

"Be careful, Imri," she whispered.

"I will, villain." I kissed her cheek when she rose. "I'll be back before you know it."

Alais sniffled. "Don't call me that!"

I extended my arms, and Dorelei slid the vambraces over my forearms, one after the other, taking care not to tangle my yarn bindings. "May all the gods of Alba and the *diadh-anam* of the Cullach Gorrym be with you," she murmured, buckling them in place. She looked up at me, her eyes bright with tears. "Oh, Imri! Come home safe and free."

I hugged her, feeling the swell of her belly pressed between us. "I will, love," I promised. "I promise." I stooped, then, and kissed her belly. "Both of you."

Dorelei laughed through her tears. "Keep your promise, Imriel de la Courcel!"

I straightened and smiled at her, bent to kiss her lips. "I always do."

She clung to me for a moment, then let me go.

"'Tis time," Urist said quietly.

I nodded. "Let's go."

THIRTY-SIX

MORWEN WAS WAITING at the edge of the woods. She took in the sight of Firdha and Urist and his men with a faint smile. "Ready, are you?"

"Yes," I said briefly.

She tilted her head. "Then come."

We followed her into the woods in a procession echoing the Feast of the Dead, with a handful of Urist's men carrying torches. Morwen led it, swift and silent on her bare feet, needing no torch to light her way. The paths were still fairly clear, not yet overgrown. We passed through the oak grove, where she stooped and placed her hands on the earth, murmuring a prayer.

I wished I'd taken the time to visit Elua's shrine.

On and on we walked. Torchlight made the trees seem to shift and writhe. I found my ears straining at every sound. My nerves were strung taut as harp-strings and my bindings itched ferociously. By the time we reached the clearing, the moon had risen above the treeline. It was full and round as a coin, drenching the glade in silvery light. The standing stones seemed majestic and peaceful, casting stark black-on-dark shadows on the grass.

"Two things." Morwen faced me. "Before we begin, your men must extinguish their torches. And you may not enter the stone circle wearing steel."

I frowned. "Why not?"

"Because that is the way the magic works," she said patiently.

"Let me hear you recite the Daughter of the Grove's oath," I said.

There was no trace of a smile on her face, no hint of mockery. "As you wish."

Firdha led Morwen into the center of the standing stones, there beside the half-buried boulder where she had offered the *uisghe*. They spoke together, their voices low and indistinct, and then, to my surprise, Morwen bowed to the *ollamh*, who raised the golden branch of her office. The bear-witch stooped, touching earth, touching stone, then rose, lifting her empty palms to the sky.

"I, Morwen of the Maghuin Dhonn, do swear this oath," she said, her voice clear and carrying. "No harm will befall Imriel de la Courcel of Clunderry this night, nor any member of his household, nor any person dear to him. I swear it by stone and sea and sky, by all the gods of Alba, and by the *diadh-anam* of the Maghuin Dhonn. If I lie, let my magic be broken and my life be forfeit. Let every man and woman's hand be raised against me, let my name be gall on their lips. Let the gods and the *diadh-anam* forsake me, and let the land itself despise my footfall. Let my spirit wander for ten thousand years without solace."

The earth seemed to shudder beneath the soles of my boots. A slight breeze made the torches ripple, and I saw Urist nod with grim satisfaction. It was a powerful oath.

Morwen lowered her arms. "It is done."

"It is," Firdha said.

They returned slowly to the outer edge of the stone circle. The *ollamh*'s face was grave. Morwen's brown skin looked more pale than usual, the claw tattoos standing out like dark slashes around her eyes. "Does it suffice?" she asked me.

I clenched my hot, itching hands into fists. "Let us do this thing, lady."

So it began.

I unsheathed my sword and drew my daggers from their scabbards, giving my weapons into Urist's keeping. I unbuckled the vambraces with their chased images of the Black Boar that Dorelei had placed on my arms with loving care. I checked the bindings beneath them.

"Take off your boots," Morwen said softly. "Your feet must touch the earth."

I obeyed. "Thus do we worship Elua, too."

"Truly?" Her brows furrowed. "I did not know."

"Mayhap there is much we might learn of one another," I said. "Is that all?"

"Yes." She reached out her hand. "Come with me."

I took her hand and went.

The grass was cool beneath my feet, damp with dew. Morwen's touch was light and careful, though it almost seemed her fingers trembled. Urist and his lads spread out to position themselves around the perimeter of the standing stones, torches bobbing like fireflies. Firdha stayed behind. She, too, would keep watch in her own way. When Urist's men were in place, he gave a signal and the torches were snuffed.

Beside the center boulder, Morwen let go my hand and bowed her head. "Here."

"What must I do?" I asked.

"Wait." Beneath the stars and the bright moon, she stooped for a third time, digging her fingers into the earth surrounding the boulder, an object too large and heavy for five strong men to move. There was a scraping sound. Her shape changed, surging and rippling. I heard her groan. The boulder shifted in its deep mooring, and my mouth went dry.

It *rose*. A solid slab of stone, lichen-stained and half buried. Morwen's hand—or something like it—shot out and reached into the hollow beneath the boulder, snatching at a hidden bundle and removing it.

The boulder settled back into place.

Morwen laughed, low and sad. She straightened and covered her eyes. Fingers or claws? I blinked, unsure. Fingers. She lowered them. "Sit," she said. "Sit and be welcome."

I sat. Morwen sat opposite me and placed her bundle atop the boulder, unrolling it. There was a wineskin, a stoppered jar, a wooden cup, a leather bag, and a knife of chipped stone. She unplugged the wineskin and poured a measure of dark liquid into the wooden cup, showing it to me. "I will drink first."

I watched her drink, watched the muscles of her throat move. When she had finished, she poured a second measure and handed me the cup. I sniffed at it. It smelled earthy and bitter and foul. "What is it?"

"Mushroom tea." Her pale gaze held steady. "A gift of the earth, Imriel."

I lifted the cup toward the stars. "Blessed Elua, hold and keep me," I said, and drank. It tasted like it smelled. I gagged, but I managed to swallow it, setting down the wooden cup.

"Well done." Morwen unstoppered the jar and daubed unguent on her fingers, closing her eyes and smearing it onto her closed lids. She blinked a few times. "Lean forward and close your eyes."

I obeyed. Her fingertips felt cool. I kept my eyes closed as she smeared unguent on my lids, trying not to flinch at her touch. I could smell the ointment, sharp and herbal. I could smell *her*, loam and fermented berries. I could taste the mushroom tea on my tongue, acrid and bitter, drying the tissues of my mouth.

"It begins." Morwen reached across the boulder to grasp my right hand. "Here." She placed the leather bag in my palm. "As I promised."

I stared at it, gaping. When I closed my fingers on it, I could feel the shape of the mannekin charm it contained. My blood pounded in my veins, in my wrists and ankles and temples. My entire body throbbed.

"And here," she added, picking up the stone knife.

Fast; so fast! Before I could react, the stone blade snicked forth, the tip sliding beneath the yarn bindings around my right wrist and severing them. My heart expanded within my breast and freedom rushed in upon me, swift and almost sickening. I drew a deep breath, reeling where I sat. "Ah, no!" I whispered. "Elua!"

"Did you think you would be able to see, bound as you were?" Morwen asked in a hard voice. "Don't worry, I will make the offering." She turned her left hand palm-up on the boulder. The stone knife snicked again, chip-edged and keen, opening a cut on her wrist; and then she did the same to her other hand. Her hands reached for mine, slippery with blood. "Put the mannekin aside and hold hard to me. If nothing else, you *will* see. And you will understand."

I did as she said.

For a long time, nothing happened. Morwen closed her eyes and breathed slowly. Her face was calm and serene beneath the claw-marks, despite the steady seep of blood from her wrists. I tried to emulate her, but my body was shivering with an uncomfortable mixture of excitement and nausea. My belly clenched on the mushroom tea, and I thought for a time I might vomit.

Slowly, slowly, it passed. The shivering stopped. My body began to feel warm and heavy. I relaxed, bit by bit, feeling stored tension ease from my neck and shoulders. Morwen opened her eyes and smiled at me.

"You see?" she said. "A gift of the earth, nothing more."

I laughed. "We're allowed to speak?"

"Oh, a little," she said. For some reason, it made us both laugh. I sat, holding her hands across the boulder, and thought about how much better things would have been if we'd spoken honestly and openly from the beginning. If the Cruithne had spoken frankly about the Maghuin Dhonn, their powers and their claims, instead of shunning them out of superstition. If the Maghuin Dhonn had approached me and spoken frankly of their concerns, instead of trying to trick and bind me.

I tried to tell Morwen this, but the words emerged in a muddle and I was overly conscious of the way my voice echoed within my own skull.

"Hush," Morwen said. Her pupils had grown enormous. "Just watch for a time."

So I did.

It seemed the night had grown brighter; or mayhap my vision was altered. Everything seemed very sharp-edged and clear; the stones, the blades of grass, the slow, spreading puddle of blood trickling over the edges of the boulder. I could see near and far all at once; a branch on a distant tree and a twig caught in Morwen's hair. It was exhilarating, but it was unnerving, too. I tried looking at the sky overhead. At first the black velvet spaces between the stars were calming; then I thought about the night sky's infinite depth, and it made me dizzy.

"Think of a pleasant time," Morwen said.

I thought about Sidonie.

Elua knows, I didn't mean to. It seemed wrong, there in one of Alba's sacred places, with Dorelei's kiss still lingering on my lips. But I couldn't help it. I was free of my bindings. The moment Morwen spoke, my thoughts leapt to Sidonie, as swift and straight as an arrow from the bow. Sidonie in a shaft of sunlight, smiling. Tangled in bedsheets.

Propped against the door of the bedchamber in Naamah's Temple, her legs around my waist. Glancing at me with stricken eyes when it was announced the Cruarch's flagship had been spotted. Throwing rose petals at my wedding, her face a mask.

Golden hair, spread on a pillow.

A golden cord, knotted.

A knot of gold on my finger.

Images crowded me, changing and mutating. I shook my head, trying to dispel them. My heart ached, and I had to struggle to draw breath.

"Let her go," Morwen said unexpectedly. "Look to the stones."

As though her words had given me permission, I was able to break the chain of my thoughts. I breathed slowly and deeply, gazing at the standing stones. They seemed immensely tall and powerful. When I blinked, I thought I could see runes and markings carved on them; whorls and spirals and crosses. Although I couldn't read them, it seemed they whispered a story to me. And then it seemed the stones were moving in a slow, endless dance.

Morsen drew a long, shuddering breath. "Now you see."

The moving runes made pictures.

The stones were telling a story.

A boy. There was a boy. I saw the stamp of House Shahrizai on his face; in his dark blue eyes, the full curve of his lips. And Cruithne blood, too. Images flickered. Clunderry, and Dorelei. Laughter. Dorelei lying motionless in a bed, and old Cluna drawing a sheet over her face. Me, and the boy clinging to me. Me, setting him down gently and prying loose his grip.

The boy, with Alais. Tending the shrine of Elua.

The boy, older, flushed with anger, shouting at Urist.

And then he was gone. The dance faltered and the world lurched.

"What?" I whispered. "What happened to him?"

"He left Alba." Morwen's voice was low. "Wait."

The dance resumed, and the boy was back. My son; a young man, now. Shrewd and beautiful, with calculating eyes and a charming, indolent smile that masked ambition and complicated desires. I remembered somewhat Phèdre had said about my mother. *In a roomful of people, she shone.*

So did my son.

I watched him grow to full adulthood. I watched him plot and scheme. I watched him smile to himself as quarrels broke out across Alba. I watched quarrels escalate into war. I watched him acquit himself well in a losing battle. I watched him crowned Cruarch in a hasty ceremony when Talorcan was slain.

I watched him appoint D'Angelines to office.

I watched him lead an army composed of as many D'Angelines as Albans sweep across the land, crushing all resistance. He was a fearless leader, and a ruthless one. I watched him turn women and children from their homes and torch their houses. I watched him kill a wounded man begging for mercy.

I watched him ride in a victorious procession.

I watched him issue decrees.

I watched D'Angeline architects swarm over Bryn Gorrydum. I watched as the last of the Maghuin Dhonn were hunted like animals. And I watched as all across Alba, my son ordered the oak groves burned, the standing stones lashed round with chains and dragged down by teams of oxen.

I watched until I could no longer bear it.

"Make it stop." I raised my voice. *"Make it stop!"*

Morwen released my hands with limp, sticky fingers. The visions faded, although the world was still strange and pulsing. I felt sick and disoriented.

"Your son is a monster, Imriel," Morwen said quietly.

"You don't know it's true!" My voice was thick.

"I do." She sat quiet and still, her hands resting atop the boulder in a puddle of her own blood. A lot of blood. "There were other visions around you, before; a confusion of them. At first you departed and he wasn't there. Then there was our daughter to balance him. But one by one, they all went away. This is all that's left."

"Why?" I whispered.

"I don't know." She sounded sad. "It seems his mother lost a second child before term and died. What happened to you, I cannot say, save that you never set foot on Alban soil again. And it seems your son conceived a powerful hatred of the Maghuin Dhonn."

A mad laugh bubbled out of me. "And why do you think that might be, woman!" I shouted at her. "Name of Elua! You've done naught but plague and torment me since I came to Alba! Elua!" I ran my hands over my face, forgetting they were sticky with her blood. "Did you ever think," I said bitterly, "that mayhap if you hadn't meddled in our lives in the first place, none of this would come to pass?"

"Yes." Morwen gave me a terrible smile. "I did."

I stared at her in horror. Somewhere, there were horns sounding. The air between us pulsed, filled with twisting runes and symbols. I waved my hand before me, trying to make them vanish. I couldn't see right, couldn't think right. But I was free and unbound and I could see one thing. A fault-line on her soul, a deep and awful secret.

Horns.

Clunderry.

"You lied," I said simply.

She lifted her hands feebly. Blood ran down her forearms. A lot of blood. The stone knife had cut deeper than I reckoned. "The Maghuin Dhonn have kept their oath," Morwen said. "You are unharmed. It is only I that am forsworn. I am a sacrifice."

After that, I went mad.

There are large parts of that terrible night I do not remember.

I remember stumbling from the stone circle, barefoot and blood-streaked, shouting for Urist. I do not remember putting on my sword-belt, although I did. I remember bits and pieces of racing through the darkling woods, thinking that the very trees despised me.

I remember seeing the castle gate open.

I remember screaming.

And the bear.

And Dorelei.

I didn't see her until later. And I didn't understand until later that the castle gate was open because Leodan of Briclaedh had staged his retaliatory cattle-raid that night, having received word that Clunderry's garrison would be short-handed the night of the full moon, and no one had remembered to close it when the garrison raced out in response.

The bear . . .

For a time, Kinadius and a handful of men who had managed to double back held it at bay in the courtyard, shooting at it with hunting bows, but it was hard to aim in the moonlight and it takes a lot to kill a bear. A big bear, as big as Berlik of the Maghuin Dhonn was for a man. It burst through their line just as we arrived, killing Uven, roaring toward the castle gate.

I remember Urist behind me shouting, "Spread out!"

I ran straight for the bear, racing through the open gate, holding my sword point-outward in a two-handed grip. Fast; faster than I'd ever run. I screamed. The bear roared. I could smell it, rank and musky. Fermented berries. It swatted at me, knocking the blade from my hand and sending me tumbling. Kinadius and his men shot arrows at it from behind. It roared. I picked myself up, picked up my sword. I heard my own voice shouting, "Close the gate!"

I stood in front of the gate.

The bear charged me. It was like a wave, like a great dark wave breaking over me. I swung my blade, aiming for its eyes. Its sad, pale eyes; Berlik's eyes. It rose up then; blotting out the stars. It roared. Red maw, white teeth. Black claws. I stepped inside its guard, jabbing for its guts.

It struck before my blow landed.

I didn't feel the wounds, not right away. Just the blow; a vast, inconceivable impact. I lay on my back, staring at the moon and stars, wetness spreading over my chest. If I could have laughed, I would have. "Forsworn," I whispered. "All of you."

Blackness.

The next time I opened my eyes, I was in the great hall. There were a great many people around, talking and weeping. Some of them were hovering over me, asking me things. I was on a table. I turned my head. There was another table. Dorelei lay on it. Her head was turned toward me at an unnatural angle. Her eyes were empty and open. There was a cloak draped over her, over the swollen mound of her belly. It was sodden with blood.

I wept.

Blackness.

THIRTY-SEVEN

WHERE DO WE GO when we vanish deep inside ourselves? I do not know, but I went there for a long, long time. Alais told me later that they weren't sure if I would live or die. If anyone had asked me my preference in the matter, I'm not sure which I would have chosen. I was very badly injured and out of my mind with horror, grief, and guilt.

I recall almost nothing of the days following the attack. Most of the time, I was unconscious; when I wasn't, Alais said I raved and babbled about moving stones and blood and the Maghuin Dhonn.

And my son, the boy who became a monster.

There is a mercy in madness and forgetting.

I don't think I could have borne those days.

I had a few vague memories. Lady Breidaia, weeping as though her heart would break. Talorcan, shouting in fury. Drustan. Later, I learned that Hyacinthe had kept his promise. He'd caught a glimpse of Morwen and Berlik in his sea-mirror and sent a pair of swift couriers.

Too late.

The Maghuin Dhonn had struck more swiftly.

I remember Firdha speaking ritual words, and a sense of terrible loss. And I remember a jolting wagon and a great deal of pain. Someone cursing at the Bastard. Sweating and shivering. Anxious faces. Alais, placing a cool, damp cloth on my brow, begging me not to die.

For a long time, nothing more.

When at last I came to myself, I was in a strange place. It was bright with sunlight and there was birdsong. I was lying in a bed with cool, clean sheets. My mouth was parched and my eyelids felt heavy and crusted. When I cracked them open and squinted, I could make out a small figure with black curls sitting in a figure and reading a book.

A rush of indescribable relief washed over me. A dream, I thought; a fever-dream. I'd been sick, as sick as I'd been after the first time I'd kept Elua's vigil with Joscelin on the Longest Night. I was sick, and Ysandre had ordered me brought to the Palace.

I tried to laugh and made a croaking sound.

"Imri?" Alais' head lifted. *"Imri?"* She dropped her book and hurried to kneel at my bedside. I tried to sit up and discovered I couldn't. My entire torso was swaddled in thick bandages and it hurt unbearably. I rested my head on the pillow and gazed at Alais, watching her violet eyes fill with tears.

No dream. It was real, all real.

"Can you hear me?" Alais asked softly. "Imri, do you understand?"

"Ye—" The word stuck. I tried to moisten my stiff, dry tongue. "Yes."

"Oh gods!" she breathed. "Elua be praised! Here." She cradled my head and put a clay cup to my lips. It felt cool and soothing, and that first sip of water was better than the best thing I'd ever tasted. Alais gave me several more sips, then rose. "I'll get the chirurgeon."

"Where am I?" I whispered.

"Bryn Gorrydum," she said. "The Temple of Elua and his Companions."

She hurried out and returned shortly with the chirurgeon, a young man named Girard, sworn to Eisheth's service. He placed a hand on my brow, lifted my lids to peer at my eyes, and bade me stick out my tongue. "The fever's broken," he confirmed. "How do you feel, your highness?"

I tried to answer and began to cry.

"It's all right, my lord." Girard stroked my hand. "There's healing in tears."

"Not enough tears," I choked. "Not for this."

"No," he said softly. The chirurgeon had sea-grey eyes, warm with compassion. "I don't imagine there are. But weep them anyway, my lord, and try to stay with us for the sake of the living." He rose. "I'll send word to the Cruarch. And I'll send for broth and a tincture of opium for the pain."

I shook my head. "No opium."

Girard paused. "As you wish, my lord."

I rested my head on the pillow, exhausted. Alais returned to kneel beside me. For a long time, neither of us spoke. "Promise me you won't die, Imri," she said at length, her voice sounding small and lost. "I don't want to lose you, too."

"Oh, Alais." I couldn't. "It *hurts*."

"I know." Her eyes welled again She laid her hand on mine. "Please?"

"I'll try." I glanced over and saw that there was red yarn tied around my wrist. My right wrist. I remembered the stone knife. Freedom. Firdha, and a sense of loss. "Alais, why am I bound again?"

She dashed away tears. "For safety."

"But the mannekin . . ." I stopped. I had no memory of what had become of the leather bag containing it. I'd put it in my lap when Morwen bade me take her hands. "Lost?" Alais nodded somberly. "Ah, Elua!" A bitter laugh escaped me. It felt like something stretched and tore in my chest, but I welcomed the pain. "Surely, I must be cursed!"

"Don't say that, Imri," Alais begged. "Don't!"

I closed my eyes. "Tell me what else I've missed."

Bit by bit, she did. An acolyte arrived with a steaming bowl of beef broth. Because it hurt too much to lift my arms, Alais fed it to me with a spoon and told me that I'd been unconscious or raving for ten days. The bear had wounded me badly, laying me open from shoulder to hip. At Clunderry, the wounds had begun to fester and I'd developed a raging fever. It was Drustan—I'd remembered aright, he and Talorcan and an armed escort had arrived on the heels of the horror, alarmed by Hyacinthe's message—who had made the decision to have me moved to the temple in Bryn Gorrydum, which had recently been joined by a young priest of Eisheth trained as a chirurgeon.

I laughed bitterly and wept when I heard it. "I told her. I *told* her she needed a proper chirurgeon to attend her!"

"Dorelei?" Alais asked softly, dabbing at my tears with a kerchief.

I nodded. "She died," I whispered. "In the future I saw. Carrying a child, another child. And I left, and never came back. I left our son."

Alais frowned. "Why?"

I turned my head away. "I don't know. What else?"

She told me that Dorelei was dead, which I knew. In a toneless voice, she told me that the bear had broken Dorelei's neck with a single swipe before savaging her belly. That the babe was dead, too. And that Talorcan had gone nearly as mad as I had, driven by rage at the murder of his sister and his sister's child. That he had ordered Morwen's lifeless body retrieved from the stone circle so it could be buried beneath Dorelei's feet. That he had sworn an oath of vengeance, and half the men of Clunderry had sworn it with him. They'd ridden out in pursuit of Berlik and his folk. All across Alba, the Maghuin Dhonn were hunted. Even the Lady of the Dalriada had pledged her assistance, and Eamonn had taken up the hunt himself. I thought about his brother Conor and shuddered.

"Have they found them?" I asked.

Alais hesitated. "Some. Not the magician."

I stared at the ceiling. "Send for your father. I need to speak with him."

The Cruarch of Alba came to visit me on the morrow.

I'd slept through the night, albeit fitfully. The pain kept me awake. In the morning, the Eisandine chirurgeon Girard came to examine my wounds. A pair of acolytes gently propped me half upright as he unwound the bandages. I'd an idea they'd done it before, though I remembered naught of it. Girard unwound long lengths of clean linen, then carefully peeled away a layer of cotton padding.

I looked down at myself and hissed through my teeth.

Four raking, parallel gouges ran the length of my torso, angling from my right shoulder to my left hip. Around the furrows, my flesh was raised and swollen and inflamed; tending toward pink in a few places, reddish in others, seeping a yellowish, crusty matter.

"You should have seen it three days ago, your highness," Girard said calmly. "Believe it or not, it's beginning to knit. 'Tis a mercy no vitals were pierced."

He bathed my wounds with an infusion of lavender; a scent of home, a scent that brought new tears to my eyes. And then he applied a poultice of comfrey and agrimony, and rebandaged my injuries with gentle hands.

Thus did I receive Drustan mab Necthana.

A day's lucidity and a diet of beef broth had restored a measure of strength to me. I was able to receive him sitting, propped on pillows. As he entered my bedchamber, it struck me for the first time; Drustan looked *old*, his face worn with sorrow beneath its tattoos. "I'm so glad you're alive, Imriel," he said in a direct, earnest tone.

Whatever words I'd meant to say caught in my throat. The loss of Dorelei and our son struck me anew, and my eyes burned with tears. "Forgive me, my lord."

He pulled over the room's single chair. "There is no need. I failed you."

"No." I took a deep, experimental breath, pressing my hand to my chest. Nothing fell out, so I tried another. "We all did. We all failed one another."

"I don't understand," Drustan said quietly.

"Doesn't matter." I shook my head. "Just . . . don't punish them all, my lord. All of the Maghuin Dhonn." His eyes widened. "They saw what they saw. I saw it, too. I saw my son, my lord; *our* son. Dorelei's and mine. Aniel. We would have named him Aniel." I drew another ragged breath. "Something happened. He grew up wrong. Bitter, angry. He would have done very bad things."

Drustan regarded me in silence for a moment. "And for that, you *forgive* them?"

His voice was low and deadly. I wanted to shout or cry, I didn't know which. *"No!"* I found the strength to raise my arms, to press the heels of my hands against my eyes. I rocked, trying to blot out the visions. Burning groves, toppling stones. People, hunted, eyes stretched wide with terror. "Don't kill them all, my lord. Don't. They are forsworn, their strength is broken. I don't think most of them knew."

"The magicians did," he said.

"Yes." I lifted my face from my hands. "And one is dead, and the other . . . yes. His name is Berlik." Something cold and hard settled into place inside me. "As I am Kushiel's scion, my lord, let mighty

Kushiel bear witness. I swear to you, I will see Kushiel's justice done. I claim Berlik's death for myself. If Talorcan finds him, I beg leave to wield the blade that kills him. If Talorcan cannot find him, I will. I will not rest until he is dead."

"And yet you plead clemency for the others?" he asked.

"For the innocent ones, yes." My burst of strength had faded, leaving me unspeakably weary. "I am a traitor's son, my lord. Should I be slain for it?"

Drustan looked away. "I will think on your words."

"Thank you." I paused. "And Berlik?"

"Berlik." He smiled sourly. "The Master of the Straits cannot find the magician in his sea-mirror, and Talorcan has lost the bear's trail. How can one lose a bear's trail? Would that I'd sent Urist with him."

"The bear is not always a bear," I murmured. "But I would have thought Urist would insist on going."

"No." Drustan looked back at me. "Urist will be accompanying *you*, Imriel. By his own request and my order. Home, to Terre d'Ange. As soon as the chirurgeon pronounces you fit to travel."

"Oh, no." I shook my head. "I'm staying."

"You are not." His face was adamant. "Imriel de la Courcel, I will think on your words. And when Berlik is captured, I will think on your request. But you are still bound by the Maghuin Dhonn, and you will not be safe until you're no longer on Alban soil."

"My lord!" I protested. " 'Tis a matter of honor."

"Is it a matter of honor that no one around you is safe?" Drustan asked, his voice rising with helpless fury. "By the Boar, lad! Dorelei mab Breidaia is *dead* and your child with her. My sister is inconsolable. Who will be next? Alais?"

Sick with guilt, I didn't answer.

Drustan sighed. "I'm sorry. I don't blame you, Imriel. I blame myself. But you draw trouble like a flame draws the moth. I cannot afford the risk. You're going home. This is not a matter on which I will be swayed."

"As my lord wills," I murmured.

It hurt; and yet he was right. While that damned talisman was still out there and Berlik at large, I wasn't safe. I didn't give a damn for my own safety, but his words had hit hard. There were others to think of. Others who might suffer Dorelei's fate.

Drustan might not blame me for it, but I did.

The days that followed were difficult. I don't think I could have endured them if it hadn't been for Alais. Betimes it would have been all too easy to sink into the black oblivion of utter despair. In the long, dark hours of night I would lie on my sickbed and think about dying, and the thought seemed sweet to me. It wouldn't be hard. All I had to do was resolve to refuse all food and will myself to die. I'd seen women do it in Daršanga. There, in the midst of hell, they had seemed tranquil. I wanted that peace.

But then, in the mornings, Alais would come, cajoling and pleading.

"You promised," she said. "You promised to try!"

It wasn't until the fourth or fifth day that I noticed somewhat amiss. "Where's Celeste?" I asked her. "Does the temple not permit dogs?"

Alais went quiet. "Do you remember that time with the boar?"

"Ah, no." My heart ached anew. "Oh, Alais!"

She wiped her eyes. "She tried to protect us. To protect Dorelei."

"I'm so sorry," I whispered.

"We buried her beside Dorelei in a place of honor. Talorcan said she deserved it." Alais sniffled and tried to smile. "When you come back, someday, mayhap you can bring me a pup from Montrève. Not soon, but someday. I don't think Celeste would mind. I think she would want me to have one of her great-grand-nieces at my side."

"Of course." I blinked. "Surely, you're not staying?"

"I think I am." Her small face turned grave. "Not at Clunderry. Father won't allow it, and I'm not sure I could bear it. But he said I might continue my studies at Stormkeep, and live with Hyacinthe and Aunt Sibeal. Aunt Breidaia will be there, too. And Firdha agreed to it."

"Why?" I asked.

"I belong here," Alais said simply. "And I want to learn." She looked down at her lap, knotting her fingers. "Do you remember I told you I had a nightmare about a bear, once? And I thought it wasn't a true dream?" I nodded. "Well, I think mayhap I was wrong." Her fingers worked. "It might have made a difference. I don't know."

"There was nothing you could have done, love," I said gently. "And trying to meddle with the future is a bad idea. Dorelei thought it drove the Maghuin Dhonn a little bit mad, and I believe she was right. That's what this was all about, you know."

Alais looked up, her eyes troubled. "Yes, but I can't help *having* the dreams, Imri. Or at least not without being someone I'm not, all bound up like you are. I don't think that's right, either. Surely there's a balance. Not to seek a greater gift than one was given, but to understand the small one and use it wisely. That's all. Do you think it so wrong?"

I thought about it. "Well, you did tell me about the man with two faces. It helped me remember Lucius was my friend, and that may have made a difference in Lucca."

"I had another true dream about you, once," Alais said softly. "Do you remember?"

"Did it involve a snowstorm and a barren tree?" I asked.

She shook her head. "I dreamed we were brother and sister, really and truly." I didn't say anything. Alais smiled sadly. "I thought it meant you were to wed Dorelei and I was to wed Talorcan. I think I may have been wrong about that. Firdha says one of the most dangerous things you can do is apply your own desires to a dream's meaning."

"Alais . . ." I murmured.

"It's all right." She drew her knees up beneath the skirt of her gown, wrapping her arms around them. "I don't know why I was so upset about it. You and Sidonie." She cocked her head, considering. "No, that's not true. I was jealous. You were always *mine*, Imri." I raised my brows, and Alais laughed. "Well, not like *that*! Like . . ."

"Like a brother?" I suggested.

Alais nodded. "I love Sidonie, I do. Not many people know her well. She's very . . . careful. But it can be hard to be her younger sister. Everything was always set, everything was certain for her. She's the Dauphine. She's the pretty one, the proper one, the one who never gets her clothing torn, or spills her food, or blurts out the wrong thing at the wrong time, or gets forgotten, or cares what anyone thinks."

I thought about linen ripping beneath my fingers and Sidonie's voice at my ear, gasping ragged entreaties, and despite the pang of guilt that came with it, I smiled for the first time since Dorelei's death. "That's not really true, you know."

"Well, it always felt like it." Alais smiled too, wistfully. "And then there was you, Imri. I was too young to remember the arguments, and anyway, I didn't care. I only knew you were brave and strong and kind, and a little bit wild and dangerous, but in a good way. Like a fierce, loyal dog that no one else can pet. And you'd had adventures; terrible adventures and wonderful adventures. And you weren't afraid of anything, but you always listened to me and treated me like a real person."

Her description startled me. "Is that how I seemed?"

"Oh, yes!" Alais' face glowed. "And everyone else except Phèdre and Joscelin was too stupid to see it; too stupid to see you, the real you. That made you *mine*."

"Oh, Alais!" My throat tightened. As though her words had dislodged a core of grief trapped deep in me, I started crying again; deep, racking sobs that made my chest ache.

Fearless, she'd said. Ah, Elua! I'd been anything but.

I wept for the child I'd been, masking terror that made me awaken thrashing and screaming in the night. I wept for the man I'd become, trying to be good and making a mess of it. I wept for Sidonie, who had reckoned the cost of our dalliance so much better than I, and yet had taken the rare risk of being careless.

I wept for love's terrible price.

I wept for Dorelei, who had been brave and strong and kind, and taught me to be the things I only pretended to be. Who had forced me to confront my own insufferable self-absorption with courage and honesty. I wept for her warm, brown skin that had smelled like fresh-baked bread, for the dimples that showed in her cheeks when she smiled, truly smiled.

And I wept for our son, who never had a chance.

It felt like being torn apart; and yet the chirurgeon Girard was right. There was healing in it. I was aware, distantly, of Alais' alarm. She went to fetch the chirurgeon, and I heard his gentle voice telling her not to worry, to let my grief run its course.

And in time it did.

When it passed, I was limp and exhausted and hollow. My chest and abdomen ached with a deep, burning pain, and I could tell my healing wounds had been opened anew. But I felt calmer, like the sky after a terrible storm has passed, discharging all its fury.

Alais was still there, watching me fearfully. "I'm sorry, Imri," she whispered. "I didn't mean to make you cry."

"It's not your fault." I dragged my forearm over my swollen eyes, then shifted and patted the bed. "Come here." She came over and curled up beside me. I ran my hand over her black curls. "Whatever happens, in my heart, you'll always be a sister to me, Alais. I couldn't ask for a better one."

She swallowed. "I'm so sorry about Dorelei. I miss her."

"So do I." I closed my eyes. "So do I, villain."

"You loved her after all, didn't you?" she asked. "In the end?"

"I did." I stroked her hair. "It was hard not to."

"But not like you love Sidonie?"

"No." I opened my eyes and met her solemn gaze. "No, that was different. I'm sorry if it was hurtful to you, Alais. I didn't intend it to be. Neither of us did."

"I think Sidonie must love you very much," she mused.

"Do you?" I asked.

Alais nodded. "I do. She's like that. She's very fierce, even though it doesn't show."

I couldn't help but smile. "Oh, I know."

She made a face. "It's a little strange to think about, Imri."

"Well, don't think about it," I suggested.

"But I might have to, mightn't I?" Alais considered me. "I'll do it if you promise to stop thinking about dying."

"Oh, you will, will you?" I tugged at one of her curls. "I'll be honest. It hurts, Alais, at least right now. It feels an awful lot like dishonoring Dorelei's memory."

"You smiled, though," she said shrewdly. "I saw it. Anyway, Dorelei wouldn't want you to die, Imri. She'd want you to go on living. And she would want you to be happy. I know."

"It's complicated." I shrugged. "We'll see."

Alais kissed my cheek, then clambered out of bed. "I have to go," she said. "It's getting late, and you should rest. I think Messire Girard wants to check your bandages, too." She stood for a moment, pursing her lips. "There's something else you should know."

I peered at her. "Oh?"

"Father got a message last night," she said. "Hyacinthe was watching in his sea-mirror. He saw a bear climb out of the water on the far side of the Straits, yesterday morning, in Azzalle. It lay on the shore for a long time. He thought it was odd."

A cold, satisfying rage rose in me. "Did he kill it?"

"No." She frowned. "He said that he couldn't be sure. He's seen other bears, dozens of them, and he's not going to start calling down the lightning to purge the earth of them." She shuddered. "We . . . we told him to look for a bear with pale eyes, but he couldn't tell. Do you think a bear could swim that far? Father didn't."

It was at least seven leagues across the Straits at the narrowest part. "I don't know," I said. "But if I were Berlik, I'd try."

"That's what I thought," Alais said.

THIRTY-EIGHT

ALAIS' WORDS GAVE ME a reason to live.
I wanted vengeance.

I'd known hatred before. In Daršanga, I'd hated to the depths of my young soul. I'd hated the mad Mahrkagir and his terrible Âka-Magi, and Jagun the Tatar warlord who had seared my flesh with a burning brand, marking me like cattle. I'd hated them with sick, help-less loathing, and I'd gloated over their deaths.

This was different.

It was a pure, clean, righteous fury, cleansing as fire. Life was dis-tilled to a simple purpose. I was a man, not a child. I was not helpless. I would heal and regain my strength. I would hunt down Berlik and kill him, and then I would bring his skull back to Clunderry to be buried at Dorelei's feet for all eternity.

It had seemed like a barbaric custom, once. Now I understood it.

I became a model patient. Since I would not be allowed to travel until the chirurgeon Girard said I was ready, I heeded every word of advice that he gave me. I suffered my bandages to be changed, my wounds bathed and salved. I ate everything I was given, drank every tonic. I slept when he told me to rest, my conscience soothed by the clarity of my purpose. When he allowed me to get up and walk about, I did. When he told me not to overexert myself, I didn't.

I resolved to make myself as cold and hard as a blade, keen and ruthless.

Alais came every day to keep me company. She told me how the hunt for Berlik was progressing. Mostly, it wasn't. There was no sign of him in Alba, and the Maghuin Dhonn who had been found professed a terrified innocence. She told me that Drustan had imprisoned several of them and put them several to hard questioning, but he hadn't killed anyone yet. She told me that Drustan had written to Bernadette de Trevalion to bid her spread word thoughout Azzalle to search for a bear with pale eyes, or a man with bear-claws tattooed on his face. I thought what a grim piece of irony it would be if the woman who'd tried to have me killed for the sake of stale vengeance became the agent of Kushiel's justice.

Days passed.

Bit by bit, my body healed.

It was Urist, of all people, who tempered my resolve. He paid me a visit, bringing with him my daggers and vambraces, which he had retrieved from the stone circle when Talorcan had ordered him to fetch Morwen's body. My throat tightened at the sight of the vambraces, remembering Dorelei buckling them on my arms that terrible night, but I didn't weep. I told him that once we were on D'Angeline soil, I meant to begin hunting for Berlik. I asked for his aid; for the sake of Dorelei, for the honor of Clunderry.

I thought he'd give it unstinting, but then, I thought he'd have ridden with Talorcan, too. Instead, Urist gave me a long look. "I'll do it on one condition. You're to return to the City of Elua first."

"And lose weeks?" I scowled. "Name of Elua! Why?"

"There's no proof that bear-witch bastard's crossed the Straits. And you're not going to be fit to ride for at least a month, anyway," he said. "I talked to that D'Angeline healer. He said he'll consent to allow you to travel in another day or two, so long as you do it as an invalid. Litter or carriage."

"That's not an answer," I observed.

"True." Urist sat upright in the bedchamber's single chair, hands on his knees, facing me. He'd sat just so the night we'd talked about the cattle-raid on Briclaedh, only he looked older and wearier. "My lord, your wife was a sweet lass. And no matter what anyone says, her blood's on both our hands, isn't it?"

It was a relief to hear someone acknowledge it. "Yes," I said. "It is."

"Guilt's a hard burden to bear," he mused. "Take it from a man who killed his own brother, traitor though he was. Believe me, I want vengeance for the lass as much as you do." He smiled ruefully beneath his worn, blurred warrior's tattoos. "When all's said and done, you weren't a bad husband to her, nor a bad lord to Clunderry, either. She loved you. She knew you, too; better than you knew her, I'll wager."

"I'll wager you're right," I murmured.

"I promised her I'd do this if anything happened to her before the babe was born," he said. "See you home."

My eyes stung. I tilted my head and gazed at the ceiling. "Why?"

Urist was silent a moment. "She said if I didn't, she feared you'd let guilt and anger eat out your heart. She said you'd understand."

I did and I didn't. Dorelei had known. She'd known about Sidonie; she'd known me. I didn't want to go. I didn't think I could bear to face that guilt, not yet. And yet, nor did I want to deny Dorelei's spirit her final wish. I drew a shaking breath. "And if I do . . . ?"

"I'll stand by you." Urist looked at me without blinking. "Honor your wife's last wish, lad, and I'll ride to the ends of the earth to get vengeance for her."

"Your word?" I asked.

He nodded. "My word."

I got to my feet and clasped his hand. "So be it."

Urist had spoken truly; that evening, Girard told me he thought I'd be fit to travel after another day's convalescence. He made me promise that I would continue to heed his advice, that I would confine myself to travelling by carriage or litter.

I agreed readily. By now, I could move my arms freely without pain and walk for short distances, but I couldn't even wear real clothing. I was forced to wear a loose-fitting shirt to cover my bandages, and a pair of baggy drawstring breeches that reminded me horribly of the breeches Dorelei had donned for the Day of Misrule, when she'd laughed so hard at the sight of me wearing her kirtle. I'd tried putting on my sword-belt, but my wounds were knitting, and the hard rhinocerous-hide chafed and dug into the tender flesh.

So it was decided. Drustan was notified and the arrangements were made.

I was going home.

On my last evening, I went to the temple proper. Sister Nehailah had visited me in my sickbed, of course. The first time, shortly after I'd emerged from darkness, she had simply offered her deepest condolences. The second time, she had spoken words intended to be consoling. I'd thanked her for her courtesy and told her I was in no fit mood to hear about the mysterious agencies of Elua's mercy.

Somehow, I felt different after talking with Urist.

The effigy of Elua was similar to the one installed at Clunderry. It was located in the central courtyard, an open area left to grow wild. I couldn't bring myself to kiss the effigy's feet, but I knelt in the grass and gazed at his face.

"If you wished to punish me for failing to heed your precept, my lord, I would that you had punished *me*," I murmured. "Dorelei was innocent."

There was no answer. I thought about what Sister Nehailah had said. *It is in my heart that even he cannot protect us from ourselves.*

It was true. In the end, that was the crux of the matter. Dorelei and our son had died because I was in love with someone else. Oh, there were other reasons, but I couldn't hide from that truth. If I hadn't loved Sidonie, there would have been no mannekin charm, no dark magic with which the Maghuin Dhonn could attempt to twist my fate and alter the future.

And yet, despite all of it, knowing it, Dorelei's last wish had been to send me back to Sidonie.

"Why did she do it?" I asked. *"Why?"*

There was no answer, but none was needed. In my heart, I knew. Dorelei had loved me. She'd loved me in that awful, glorious, maddening way I hadn't been able to love her. She had known me well enough to know that if aught happened to her, I would blame myself, punish myself. She had wanted, more than anything, for me to be free; and yes, to be happy.

How in the world that could come to pass, I couldn't imagine.

I rested my hands on my thighs and bowed my head. There were the strings of red yarn tied around my wrists; one faded and worn, one bright and new. During my convalescence, I'd barely even been aware of them. The croonie-stone around my neck weighed no more than a feather. I'd have borne them lightly, gladly, for the rest of my life if it would have brought Dorelei and our son back. If it would have undone that terrible, terrible night.

Nothing would, though.

Not even vengeance.

"I'll do my best, love," I whispered, touching the earth. Somewhere beneath Alba's soil my wife and unborn son rested. "'Tis a hard thing you ask of me. I *will* see you avenged, that I swear. But I'll try not to let it consume me altogether." I swallowed my tears. "Not to let it make me bitter and twisted."

I rose, feeling a little bit better. When I turned, I saw Sister Nehailah watching me. Dusk was falling, and her bright golden hair glowed. She didn't speak when I approached her, merely smiled with sorrow and compassion, touching my hand.

On the morrow, we set sail to cross the Straits.

It was a somber farewell. Not even a year ago, I'd arrived on Alban soil, a D'Angeline prince with a wife he didn't want, hiding my misery behind a smiling mask. I was leaving as a widowed Prince of Alba, and the heart that had weighed heavy as a stone last summer felt shattered and hollow.

Any other year, Drustan would have sailed with us, but this year he was delaying his visit to Terre d'Ange in order to stay abreast of the hunt for Berlik. He gave a packet of letters into Urist's keeping, then clasped my hand soberly. "I'll send word."

I nodded. "As will we."

His grip tightened on my hand. "You will always be family."

I wondered if the Cruarch of Alba would say that if he knew his niece's last request was to send me home to his daughter. My eyes burned and I had to choke back a mad laugh. "Thank you, my lord."

Alais was the hardest. She clung to me, hard enough to make my healing wounds ache. I ignored the pain and wrapped my arms around her, resting my chin on her curly head. "Elua bless and keep you, little sister," I whispered. "Be safe and well."

"Oh, Imri!" She pulled away and looked at me, tearstained. "You, too."

There wasn't anything else to say.

We boarded the Cruarch's flagship. Urist had recruited a score of men, all members of Clunderry's garrison, including Kinadius, who had left Talorcan's search to accompany us. We nodded at one another. He would take half the men and begin searching in Azzalle, asking questions, while the rest of us went on to the City of Elua.

The rowers set to on the oars and the ship eased into the harbor. Our royal escort stayed, watching. Drustan stood behind Alais, his hands on her shoulders. In the distance behind them rose the walls of Bryn Gorrydum, draped with black for mourning. I stood at the railing with one hand raised in farewell, watching them dwindle.

Watching Alba dwindle.

I did weep, then, for the first time in days. Silent tears, running down my cheeks, mingling with the salt spray of the ocean. After a time—a long time, I think—Urist came over and patted my shoulder awkwardly with a hard, callused hand. "Rest, my lord. The healer said so."

I had promised to obey.

I rested.

We sailed into Pointe des Soeurs the following morning. A month ago, my heart would have leapt at the sight of the shore of Terre d'Ange looming larger in my vision, the land stretching behind it. Now I felt numb.

Pointe des Soeurs had been a lonely fortress once. Like Bryn Gorrydum, it had grown a great deal. There was an escort awaiting us on the dock. I thought that they would be disappointed to learn that the Cruarch was not aboard, but I was wrong. Word had already been sent. During the long days I'd spent in my sickbed, there had been a great deal of correspondence back and forth across the Straits.

I knew that, of course, but all my thoughts had been focused on the hunt for Berlik. Somehow, I'd not given thought to the fact that all of Terre d'Ange knew of my loss. It made me feel vulnerable and exposed.

It didn't help matters that it was Bertran de Trevalion waiting to receive us. When I thought about it later, it made sense. Pointe des Soeurs lay within the duchy of Trevalion's holdings; he was a high-ranking young nobleman known to have been my friend.

No one knew, not even Bertran himself, that his mother had tried to have me killed.

On the dock, he greeted me with a sincere bow, sympathy written all over his open, earnest face. "Your highness, House Trevalion offers its profound condolences."

"Thank you, Bertran." I fought back a swell of grief. "That's kind."

He nodded. "I'm awfully sorry, Imri. Truly."

All the faces of the people around him were somber and grave. D'Angeline faces. I was home, and I felt like a stranger. I took more comfort in the presence of Urist and his men. Home. Clunderry had become a home. I wished I was there, watching Dorelei smile at the breakfast table while Kinadius teased his sister. The Cruithne were silent, and I daresay they felt the same way.

But we were here to seek vengeance.

The thought strengthened me.

I thanked Bertran again for his courtesy. The ascent to the fortress was steep, and he'd brought a litter chair with bearers to convey me. I felt like a fool sitting in it, and the Bastard, freed from the confines of the hold, eyed me skeptically; but I knew I couldn't ride and I wasn't sure I could make the climb on foot. When the bearers stepped forward to grasp the poles, Urist shook his head. "We will do it," he said in heavily accented D'Angeline. "He is the lord of Clunderry and we are his men."

Bertran looked startled. "As you wish."

We stayed in the fortress that night. For a mercy, Bertran had the good sense not to plague me with too much hospitality. He met with Urist, Kinadius, and me and told us in a straightforward manner that there had been no sightings of pale-eyed bears or tattooed magicians reported throughout Azzalle.

"You're sure he's here?" he asked.

Deep in my bones, I was. I was sure that the bear Hyacinthe had seen was Berlik. He was forsworn; his people were forsworn because of him. I'd seen the sorrow in his eyes. He would flee Alba. He would take himself as far, far away from his people as he could, carrying his curse and his darkness with him, trying to protect them.

"I'm sure he crossed the Straits," I said. "He left a trail. We'll find it."

Bertran shrugged. "I hope you do."

Before he retired for the night, he provided us with maps of Azzalle with markings that indicated where questions had been asked, where they hadn't. We pored over them, plotting a course of action.

Urist and I were the last two awake. Although I was tired and sore, I was reluctant to take to my bed. In a strange way, it felt like it would sever my last waking bond to Alba, and Dorelei. And so we sat, the two of us, drinking wine in front of the hearth, our feet propped on a low table.

"You've not cut them," Urist said unexpectedly.

I blinked. "Cut what?"

"The *ollamh*'s bindings." He nodded at my wrists. "You're on D'Angeline soil."

I'd forgotten. "Do you think I should?" My head was swimming a little from the wine. "I'm not sure it matters here. Do they still work? I don't even know what I feel anymore, Urist." I shook my head, trying to clear it. "Anyway, what if the priests are wrong? If Berlik has the charm, and he's here, I don't want to take any chances."

"Here." Urist sat upright and fished in a pouch at his belt, proffering an object.

I stared at it, the blood pounding in my veins.

The charm, a grimy little mannekin, lay in his hardened palm. It was a vile object, wrought of Alban dirt and clay and the essence of my desire, seed spilled carelessly on *taisghaidh* land. The cause of untold suffering.

"You had it all along," I said slowly.

"Oh, aye." Urist nodded. "'Twas there in the stone circle, where you left it, near the dead bear-witch." His black eyes held mine without wavering. "What was I to do, lad? I've never withheld a truth from Drustan. But I made the lass a promise, and I never had children of my own. I'm a warrior. I made her a warrior's promise. This seemed the surest way to be certain you were sent away from Alba."

"Damn you, Urist!" I knuckled my eyes. "How do we destroy it?"

"I asked the *ollamh*," he said steadily. "Like this." His hand clenched.

The mannekin crumbled. As simply as that, it was destroyed. Urist held his hand over his winecup, releasing a stream of grainy dirt that sank into the dark liquid and vanished. He handed me the cup. "Cast it on the fire."

"That's all?" I asked.

"That's all," he said.

I leaned forward. My wounds twinged. I jerked my hand. Wine and dirt and careless seed spattered. The fire flared and hissed. Smoke rose up the chimney.

"Throw the cup, too," Urist murmured.

I hurled it, hard. It burst into a dozen shards.

"Done." He plucked a knife from his belt. "Give me your hands. I'll cut the bindings."

"Urist." I hesitated. "Do you know *why* Dorelei asked this of you? I don't ask for myself, not this time."

He fixed me with his hard gaze. "She didn't say it in plain words, but I've an idea. You moped your way across this land at the outset, yearning for someone that wasn't her. I watched you, boy. You grieved the lass. She loved you despite it. And somehow, you managed to make yourself worthy of her. I wouldn't be here if you hadn't."

"I tried," I whispered.

Urist gave me a curt nod. "She knew." He took my left hand, lay-ing it palm-upward across his knees, wedging the point of his knife beneath the yarn. It was too soon, too sudden. I tried to withdraw my hand, struggling feebly. Name of Elua! I was weak.

"Urist!" I sharpened my voice. "She never told you *who*, did she?"

"Does it matter?" he asked.

"It will matter a great deal to the Cruarch of Alba and the Queen of Terre d'Ange." My voice broke. "A *great* deal, Urist."

His mouth gaped. It looked very red in his blue-whorled face. He stared at me without speaking for a long moment, then closed his mouth and licked his lips. "The royal heir? Drustan's eldest?"

I nodded. "I love her. That's . . . that's how the bear-witch was able to bind me. That's what these bindings are protecting me from." I swal-lowed. "My feelings for her. And when you cut the bindings, I'll feel it again. All of it."

He stared some more. "And Dorelei knew?"

"Yes." My eyes stung. "Dorelei knew."

Urist took a deep breath. "I gave her my oath. This girl, does she love you?"

"I think so," I said. "But Urist . . . trust me, Queen Ysandre will *not* be pleased about this. What you unleash in me could set the entire realm at odds."

"So you were good enough for the Cullach Gorrym, good enough to marry Dorelei mab Breidaia, good enough to beget Alba a successor, but not good enough for the Queen's daughter?" Urist's lips curled with scorn. The tip of his knife flicked upward. "Well, that's what I think of that, lad."

The red yarn parted and fell.

Something in my heart opened. There wasn't the vast, inrushing swell of emotion I'd felt in Bryn Gorrydum when I'd removed the croonie-stone and read Sidonie's letter, nor the creeping, insidious tide I'd felt when the binding had broken the night of the cattle-raid. It was subtle, a sense of relief and ease, as though someone had removed a heavy pack I'd been carrying so long, I'd forgotten I bore it.

Something wrong in the world was righted.

I was free.

I took the knife from Urist's hand and cut the binding on my other wrist, then removed my boots and cut the bindings from my ankles. I held the yarn in my hand, remembering. *You're like a parcel I can't unwrap*, Dorelei had said. *Consider it mere adornment*, I'd told her. We'd made love in our narrow bed in Innisclan, laughing and hushing one another. I wondered if that was the time we'd gotten our son. I threw the yarn on the fire, then untangled the croonie-stone's thong from my torc and pulled it over my head. I put it in the pocket of my baggy breeches to keep for remembrance.

It was done.

THIRTY-NINE

O N THE MORROW, we set out for the City of Elua.
        Bertran wanted to escort us himself, but the thought of travelling for days in his company made my head ache. I begged him instead to stay in Azzalle and give whatever aid he might to Kinadius and his men in their search for Berlik's trail, and at length, he agreed. He insisted I take a fine carriage belonging to House Trevalion, to which I acceded.

I hated travelling by carriage. It was fine for short excursions within the City, especially in winter, but in the warm spring weather, it was hot and stifling. D'Angeline roads are well laid, but no road is perfectly smooth, and I found myself jouncing on the carriage's stiff seats. At the end of the day, I was sore and aching.

I tried riding astride, but even when the Bastard behaved himself and paced sedately, I could feel the swaying motion of sitting upright in the saddle tugging at my healing wounds. One never thinks, until one is badly injured, about the myriad intricate ways in which the parts of one's body are connected.

It was frustrating, how slowly I healed. Girard had provided a store of salve and clean bandages. I couldn't even tend myself, but had to be helped, like an infant. It was a piece of luck that one of Urist's men, Cailan, was a wise-woman's son. He was a quiet, shy fellow with a gentle touch, although the others assured me he was a demon in battle. Every night, he unwound my bandages to wash my wounds and apply salve.

The first time he saw them, he gave a low whistle. "You're lucky to be alive, my lord."

"So I'm told," I said.

They *were* healing, if not fast enough to suit me. The redness was fading, and there was no more yellow matter, only thick scabs. But Berlik's claws had cut deep. It was infuriating, how weak it made me. A week into our journey, I began practicing the Cassiline forms, slowly and carefully. Tentative as I was, the first time I made it through telling all the hours, I was panting and my legs trembled with helpless exhaustion. Still, I kept trying.

Slowly, slowly, it grew easier.

We avoided cities and villages in favor of making camp in the open. Urist and his men preferred it, and it suited me fine. I still felt raw and exposed, my grief too intimate to share with anyone who didn't understand it. On the road, we got a lot of odd looks from fellow travellers wondering why a member of House Trevalion was travelling with an escort of Cruithne, but no one bothered us. At least that was one good thing about the carriage. I could remain anonymous.

None of us spoke much on the journey.

They were good men, the men Urist had recruited. Most were veterans who had fought alongside him in the battle of Bryn Gorrydum; it was the younger ones who had elected to stay with Kinadius and search for Berlik. These were taciturn fellows, filled with quiet purpose, and their presence was a comfort.

I thought a great deal, jouncing in my carriage, about the vision Morwen had showed me in the stone circle. I thought about my son, Dorelei's and my son, and wondered what had befallen him to turn him so thoroughly against Alba. Her death? *My* death? I'd left, and I'd never come back. Having come so close, so heartbreakingly close, to being a father, I couldn't imagine I would ever abandon a child of my own blood so thoroughly.

Mayhap I'd died.

Mayhap Barquiel L'Envers finally got his wish.

And yet, it was his D'Angeline heritage our son had embraced. I'd never reckoned on that. Somehow, I'd been so sure he would be Alban, through and through. But he'd left Alba, gone to Terre d'Ange for many years. Mayhap I'd sent for him before I died. I wondered what had happened. Had he fallen in love and been thwarted? Had some

D'Angeline peer deemed Melisande Shahrizai's half-breed grandson an unfit match? Had politics intervened? Had he seen his return to Alba to serve as Talorcan's heir as exile? Had it made him twisted and bitter?

Mayhap that was why my father's spirit had looked so very, very sad when he appeared to me at the Feast of the Dead. He was a man who'd grown bitter in exile. Mayhap he'd seen that the same fate would befall my son.

In the end, I would never know.

My unborn son was dead.

Dorelei was dead.

As we travelled across Terre d'Ange, those dreadful truths settled slowly into my bones. Gone. They were simply . . . gone. And nothing in the world I could do would bring them back. All I could do was offer them the solace of vengeance.

Without becoming a monster myself.

It was important, that. I wondered if it was one of the reasons Dorelei had extracted Urist's promise. If she had seen the potential in me. She had known me well enough to know I would dedicate myself to vengeance if anything happened to her. I wondered if she had sensed, dimly, her own fate hanging over her, shrouded behind my bindings and her silent dreams.

Or if she'd simply loved me that much, and truly wanted me to be happy. Dorelei hadn't been perfect. She had been too quick to dismiss all of the claims of the Maghuin Dhonn out of hand, too quick to reject their blessing. She'd been cranky toward the end, carrying our child. But on the balance, she'd been awfully *good*.

Slowly, slowly, my thoughts turned to Sidonie.

It hurt; Elua, it hurt! Alone in my carriage, I stared at the gold knot on my finger and clenched my fist. It felt awful and horrible and disloyal, and . . . ah, Elua! It felt like life and hope, a bright, shining thread wrapped around my heart, as hard and tight as the knots I'd tied around her wrists on her birthday. I'd been sheltered from my love for her for so long, but the closer I got, the more intense the yearning grew.

I missed her.

I wanted her.

I didn't deserve her.

A year. I gazed out the carriage window as we passed burgeoning fields of sunflowers and lavender. Could it truly be only a year ago that Sidonie had turned seventeen? Elua, but that was young! Still, she never seemed as young as she was, even as a girl. And now, her natal day must have passed. I'd missed it. I daresay I'd missed my own. I'd lost track of days. Weeks. Somewhere, I thought, I must have turned twenty years of age. And Sidonie would have turned eighteen, gaining her majority.

I wondered if it would matter.

I couldn't think about it for long. It hurt too much.

I didn't realize how close we were when we made camp the last night, and it came almost as a surprise to see the white walls of the City of Elua shining before us in the early morning light. My last homecoming had been joyous. This one wouldn't be. Outside the gates, Urist called a halt, ranging alongside the carriage. He leaned down in the saddle, peering into the window.

"What will you, my lord?" he asked. "Shall I alert the Palace?"

"No," I said. "No, I'd rather enter quietly."

There was no queue at the gate this time, no Tsingano lads idling, waiting for news. I watched Urist speak to a yawning guard, leaning on his spear. I watched the guard's eyes widen. He came over to the carriage window and bowed. "Forgive me, your highness. We didn't know when you were arriving. Shall I send word to her majesty?"

"Is my foster-mother in residence?" I asked. I knew there had been no word of their return by the time I left Alba, but I wasn't sure what had transpired while we were on the road.

He shook his head. "I'm afraid not. Lady Phèdre and Messire Verreuil are abroad."

"No, don't bother, then. I'll go directly to the Palace."

The guard nodded. "Very sorry for your loss, your highness."

My throat tightened. "Thank you."

I closed my eyes and leaned back against the cushions as we entered the City of Elua, listening to the sounds of the city waking. Domnach was driving the carriage, he had a light, steady hand on the reins, and our passage was smoother than usual on the well-tended streets. I felt strange and weightless, filled with emotions I couldn't begin to name. I listened to the calls of vendors as we passed the market, to the hoofbeats of my escort, to the murmur of Cruithne voices. A few people called out inquiries as we passed, wondering at the sight of the Bastard and his distinctive markings, following the carriage on a lead-line.

The ostler at the Palace knew him. "That's Prince Imriel's horse. His highness isn't . . . ?"

"Dead?" Urist asked bluntly. "No."

Domnach leapt down from the driver's seat and opened the door for me. I got out slowly, dreading the sight of the pitying, wondering stares.

"Prince Imriel." The footman on duty had come into the courtyard. He greeted me with a bow. "Welcome home, your highness. I am sorry it is during a time of grief." Servants of the Palace are known for their composure and exquisite manners, but his brows rose a little at the sight of me, clad in loose-fitting Alban garb, a gold torc around my throat. "How may I serve you, your highness? Are you . . . well?"

"I'm fine," I said wearily.

"For a man torn apart by a bear," Urist added.

The footman's brows twitched. "Yes . . . I, um. Yes. We heard. I'll send for the Queen's chirurgeon."

"Later," I said.

"Very good." He inclined his head. "I'll alert her majesty. Shall I tell her you're in your quarters?"

I stared at the open door of the Palace behind him, at the two Palace Guardsmen flanking it, upright and splendid in their Courcel blue livery, at the gleaming marble beyond. I hadn't been sure what I'd do when I arrived until this very moment. "If you like."

He blinked at me, uncomprehending. I walked past him, walked into the Palace. Urist and his men fell in behind me.

It was still quiet this early. We'd risen before the dawn; Urist liked to travel light and swift. There were servants moving efficiently from the kitchens to various quarters, carrying covered trays from beneath which the aroma of food seeped. They shot startled glances in our direction. There were a few very late, very drunk revelers in the Hall of

Games who didn't notice our passage. Most of the salons were empty. Our footsteps echoed in the marble halls.

At the foot of the sweeping staircase that led to the royal quarters, I put my hand on the polished mahogany railing and paused, gazing upward at the gilded fretting on the balcony above. She was up there.

Urist stood at my shoulder. "Not going to your own room, are you?"

"No." I turned to face him squarely. "Our paths part here for a day or so. The Master of Chambers should be about shortly to see you're given proper lodging, I'm sure the footman will have summoned him." I extended my hand. "I'll send word in short order regarding our return to Azzalle. Urist, I cannot thank you enough for your service."

He folded his arms, ignoring my hand. "Like to be trouble, is there?"

"I've no idea," I said honestly.

He shrugged. "Then we'll guard your back until you do."

I gazed at him. I could see the fault-line; the old, old guilt over his brother's death. I could see loyalty, pride, and stubbornness. Urist bore my scrutiny unflinching, and every man of Clunderry's garrison present stood behind him, silent and unmoving.

"All right." My eyes stung. "Thank you."

It seemed to take a long time to climb the wide marble staircase. I could feel the exertion straining my wounds; or mayhap it was my heart pounding in my breast as though to burst free of my ribcage. My chest ached. All the weight of the world it seemed I'd set down when my bindings were cut had returned, trebled.

Grief. Guilt. Longing.

There was a maidservant slipping through the door to Sidonie's chambers, carrying an empty tray. She paused to flirt with the guard on duty. I saw the guard's face change as he saw us approach, my Cruithne and I. He looked dumbstruck. He looked even more dumbstruck when I walked past him and knocked on the door.

"Prince . . . *Prince Imriel?*" he stammered. "You can't . . . her highness . . ."

Urist interposed himself between us.

I opened the door to Sidonie's chambers.

It struck me hard. Amarante was there in the salon, coming to answer my knock. The blood drained from her face. She took a sharp breath, shook her head, and pointed wordlessly.

I walked through the salon.

Sidonie was standing in her sunlit dressing chamber. Her honey-gold hair was coiled in a coronet, a few locks loose on her shoulders. Her gown was a pale gold satin brocade. The stays hadn't been laced yet, trailing down her back.

Our eyes met.

Hers filled with tears, black and shining.

Ah, Elua.

I walked to her in a daze. My legs gave way beneath me. I sank to my knees, pressing my face against her, wrapping my arms around her waist. Her arms enfolded me, holding me tight and hard, hands clasping my head. We stayed that way for a long, long time. There was noise in the hallway, voices. Cruithne and D'Angeline. I didn't care. Nothing else mattered.

"Oh, Imriel!" Sidonie's voice, breaking. "I am so, so sorry."

I lifted my face to gaze at her. "I know."

Tears, streaming down her cheeks. "I keep thinking . . . if we had been honest, if I'd been braver . . . It wouldn't have happened."

"I know," I whispered. "I do, too. But it's not your fault. You couldn't have known, no one could. We were trying to do the right thing, the sensible thing."

She touched my tear-damp face. "I wish we hadn't."

My heart swelled and ached all at once. This was love, in all its fierce, awful glory, tinged forever with sorrow and regret. "So do I. Oh gods, Sidonie! So do I."

The voices in the hallway hadn't gone away; they'd grown closer, or at least two of them had. One was Amarante's, sounding uncommonly harried. I knew the other one, too. A cool voice rising to a sharp, irritated note, unaccustomed to being thwarted.

Sidonie raised her head and breathed a single word. "Mother."

"Name of Elua! One would think—" Ysandre de la Courcel halted in the doorway and beheld the scene confronting her. For a moment, her face was utterly blank with shock. "No. This is unacceptable."

Behind her, Amarante shook her head in a helpless gesture. I let my arms fall from Sidonie's waist. Sidonie released me slowly. I sank down to sit on my heels.

"No," Ysandre said simply, as though saying it would make it so. Bright spots of color rose to her cheeks. "Oh, no."

Sidonie held her ground, her face still and grave. "I would speak to you about this."

"No," Ysandre repeated. She turned to Amarante in a fury. "You . . . you are dismissed for conspiring to treason!" Amarante glanced at Sidonie. Ysandre pointed toward the door exiting the quarters, which was thronged with Cruithne. "Don't look to her. Go! Now!"

Amarante hesitated.

"Don't go," Sidonie said to her, and then to Ysandre, "Mother, I'm of age, and Amarante is sworn to my service, not yours. You've no right to dismiss her. And there is no treason here, only love, however ill-advised. We need to speak."

"Love!" Ysandre laughed bitterly. "That's a fine jest."

"Ysandre." I got to my feet with difficulty, pressing my bandaged torso. "I'm sorry. Elua knows, sorrier than I've ever been. We should have been honest. We should have been brave. Or mayhap just dared to be foolish." I smiled sadly. The Queen didn't smile back, but she was silent, listening. "My lady, the truth is, I have loved your daughter since she was sixteen years old. We weren't sure. We thought it might pass, both of us. We *hoped* it would pass. So we did what we thought was right and sensible. I'm sorry, I can't help that I love your daughter. I did my best not to." My voice cracked. "I did all you asked of me, Ysandre! My wife, our child . . . do you think I don't grieve for them?"

"And yet," Ysandre said coldly, "conveniently, they are gone."

My ears rang.

If Ysandre could have taken the words back, I think she would have. She had a temper and she'd spoken in haste. It didn't matter. A white-hot rage possessed me. I could have struck her; I wanted to strike her. Since I couldn't, I pushed past her in a state of perfect fury. Thanks be to all the gods of Alba and Terre d'Ange for Urist and his men. They fell in around me, insulating me. I strode down the corridor and descended the staircase in their midst, deaf to everything around me, striding through the main hall.

And then there was Maslin de Lombelon, blocking my way, his lips moving. I couldn't hear through the ringing in my ears. I shoved futilely at him, and we struggled for a moment. Urist stepped forward, laying a warning hand on his sword-hilt. Maslin grabbed my arm and pointed, his face filled with intense, complicated dislike.

"*Imriel!*"

I turned and saw Sidonie.

She walked toward me, steady and deliberate. Maslin released me in disgust. I could hear again, hear the murmurs of speculation rising. The Palace was awake, buzzing with gossip. People were hurrying to see. Footsteps, running; guards shouting. I waited, aware of the slow, steady pounding of my heart. There, before a watching audience, Sidonie put her arms around my neck and kissed me.

It was a gentle, tender kiss, but the intent was unmistakable. I heard the gasps of shock. The Cruithne moved to encompass us in a protective circle. I bowed my head and leaned my brow against Sidonie's, resting my hands on her waist. "You know I can't stay here."

"She didn't mean it," Sidonie said. "She was angry."

"It doesn't matter." I swallowed. "I have to leave, Sidonie. We're going back to Azzalle to hunt the man who killed Dorelei."

Her dark eyes searched mine. "Today?"

I hadn't meant to leave today. I'd meant to take at least a day to recover from the journey, to speak with Ti-Philippe. Mayhap a few days. In a day or two, I'd thought, I'd be fit to ride. It would make up for lost time, travelling without the carriage.

"Stay." Sidonie saw my hesitation. "Send for me."

"You'd come?" I asked.

She gave me a rueful smile. "Well, secrecy's not an issue anymore, is it?"

I didn't laugh. "I can't stay long."

"I don't care," she said.

"All right." I let her go, pulled away. "I have to go."

A considerable crowd had gathered. Freshly wakened peers, excitement chasing away their drowsiness. Servants abandoning their tasks, gossiping behind their hands. Guards, lots of guards. Queen Ysandre was moving through the throng, flanked by a dozen of them. Maslin de Lombelon appeared to have six or seven under his command.

I thought he might order them to block me, but he didn't. Instead, he gave a crisp order, and they stood aside. His face was stony as I passed. Urist and the Cruithne fell in behind me without a word. Together, we left the Palace.

In the courtyard, the ostlers scrambled to retrieve our barely stabled mounts and rehitch the carriage. I took a deep breath and stared at the sky.

"Whither now, my lord?" Urist asked.

"I'm not sure."

FORTY

I N T H E E N D, we went to the townhouse.

No one followed us through the streets of the City, but my back prickled and I could tell Urist was wary. I wished to heaven and hell that Phèdre and Joscelin were there. The Palace was buzzing like a hornets' nest, and I'd no idea what to do. I hoped Ti-Philippe would at least be able to tell me when they were likely to return.

Unfortunately, Ti-Philippe was gone.

"I'm so sorry, Imri," Hugues said as soon as the initial joyous furor over my return had faded. "He's gone after them, after Phèdre and Joscelin. He left to try and fetch them back as soon as we heard the news from Alba."

"Do you know where?" I asked.

"Not for sure." His face was troubled. "Illyria, that's what they said. But why would they be gone so long?"

"Philippe didn't tell you?"

He shook his head. "He said he'd sworn not to, even to me."

I sighed. "When were they planning to return?"

"Late summer, mayhap autumn—" There was a pounding at the front door, and Hugues rose to answer it. "One moment."

"Hugues!" I said sharply. "If it's the Palace Guards . . ." I paused. What would I do if Ysandre had decided to fetch me in chains for despoiling her daughter with my traitor's seed? Urist caught my eye and shrugged. "I don't know. Go see."

"What in the world have you done, Imri?" Hugues asked, perplexed.

I smiled grimly. "Oh, you'll hear."

It wasn't the Palace Guard.

It was Mavros; an unwontedly serious Mavros. I rose to greet him as he strode into the salon, his multitude of blue-black braids swinging. "I'd heard it was true. Here you are, alive, and causing all manner of trouble," he said, giving me a brief kiss and hard embrace that made me wince. "Elua be thanked."

"'Tis good to see you, too," I offered.

"Don't jest," he said briefly. "You're in trouble."

"What did he *do*?" Hugues repeated in a bewildered tone.

"Stole the Dauphine's heart, it seems." Mavros gave him a tight smile. "Suborned Alban troops to help him infiltrate her quarters for a tryst."

"Name of Elua!" I raked a hand through my hair. "That's a lie."

"Oh, I know." Mavros turned his tight smile on me. "I lent a hand with the heart-stealing, remember?" He jerked his chin at Urist. "But what in all the seven hells are *they* doing aiding you?"

"Honoring my wife's last wish," I said shortly.

His brows shot up. "What, her last wish was to send you into *Sidonie's* arms?"

"*Sidonie?*" Hugues echoed in disbelief.

I sat down on the couch.

"Yes." Urist folded his arms. His face was impassive. "It was."

Mavros stared at him. "Why on earth?"

"Because Dorelei loved me, Mavros." I buried my face in my hands. "Because she loved me, and she *knew* me." I lifted my head. "It doesn't matter. We're not here for long. Why did you come?"

He regarded me. "Well, I stuck my nose in at the Palace to gauge the mood, and if I were you, I'd get out of the City. The Queen is wroth, Sidonie is in disgrace with at least half the Court, and someone was seen riding for hell-for-leather in the direction of Barquiel L'Envers' estate in Namarre." He cleared his throat. "I'm not sure if my father will belt me or kiss me for it, but if you're minded to linger a day or so—and some sharp-eared folk said you were—I'd like to offer the hospitality of House Shahrizai, cousin. No one's using the hunting manor, and it lies beyond the City's walls."

I remembered. "You're sure?"

"You're family," Mavros said simply. "I'm sure."

It was a solid thing; as solid as the support of Urist and Clunderry's men. I rose to embrace him. "You're a good friend, Mavros," I said. "We'll not be there long."

His twilight-blue eyes gleamed. "You're going a-hunting larger prey?"

"Oh, yes." I nodded. "Kushiel's justice."

"May it come to pass." Mavros' hands rested on my shoulders. "I'm sorry, Imri. I don't pretend I knew Dorelei well. But what I knew, I admired."

The Cruithne murmured.

"She was worthy of your admiration," I said thickly. "Thank you."

"I'll send word to Duc Faragon," Mavros said. "Elua only knows what the advocacy of House Shahrizai will do, but in the absence of Lady Phèdre, we'll stand by you. I can attest that your motives, however insane, weren't driven by aught but passion."

"Can you get a message to Sidonie?" I asked. "Tell her where I've gone?"

"Like as not." Mavros pursed his lips. "Her personal guard seems to be quite loyal to her. Maslin de Lombelon's doing, I believe. He's her second in command, and bucking hard for the captaincy . . . or somewhat. Pity there's no time for gossip."

"Just tell her," I said.

We didn't waste any time departing the townhouse, although Eugènie wept at it, and Hugues wasn't happy. But I reckoned Mavros' advice was sound. If the Queen decided to act—or worse, L'Envers did—I didn't want Urist and his men to be trapped in the City. It had never occurred to me that I'd be accused of subverting their loyalty. I promised Hugues that I would send word when we departed for Azzalle, and dispatches along the way informing him of our progress. Beyond that, there wasn't much else I could do.

The manor house was only a half league outside the City, but it was private and isolated. There was a good meadow for hawking, and the rest was surrounded by woods. Although we weren't expected, there was a small household staff on duty at all times, maintaining the house in readiness lest some member of House Shahrizai decide on a whim to entertain a hunting party.

The steward was a slender, handsome man of middle years whose hair had gone grey at an early age. His name was Isembart, and he took my sudden arrival, accompanied by a handful of tattooed Cruithne, and the announcement that Mavros had granted me usage of the manor with immaculate aplomb. If there are any servants in Terre d'Ange better trained than those at the Palace, surely it's in House Shahrizai.

"Very good, your highness," Isembart said without batting a lash. "The master chamber awaits you, and I'll see Commander Urist and his men are given guest-rooms. May I order a bath drawn and a meal prepared?"

"Thank you, yes."

"Are there any other comforts I may see provided for you or your men?" he asked.

I wondered what that might entail. "No, thank you. But if the Dauphine Sidonie should arrive, please admit her immediately. Anyone else, delay and fetch me."

He bowed smoothly. "Of course, your highness."

At any other time, I might have laughed at Urist's wry reaction to the opulence of the hunting manor and the efforts of its household to pamper him. He stared blankly at the offer of a warm, scented bath and a massage, then elected to ignore the staff altogether, pretending he spoke no D'Angeline. Instead, he ordered a pair of men to double back and look for pursuit, another to stand sentry duty in the woods at the end of the drive, and the rest to search the house and grounds.

I had a bath, although I declined the massage.

It was the first proper bath I'd had since Berlik had attacked me. Girard hadn't wanted my injuries submerged, but I reckoned they'd healed enough. I soaked as long as I dared, luxuriating in the warmth and aroma, until the long half-healed scabs raking my torso grew soft. I patted them carefully dry with a towel. They bled in a few places, but only a little. Underneath the scabs, they were knitting cleanly.

When I was done, Urist came to report. He eyed me. "You look more yourself, my lord. In a manner of speaking."

"I feel it." I'd rummaged in the clothes-press in the master chamber—an elegant room hung about with tapestries of hunting scenes, a tall canopied bed, and a well-stocked flagellary—and found a pair of soft deerskin hunting breeches that sat low on the hips and were loose enough in the waist that they didn't chafe, as well as an oversized linen shirt with carved wooden buttons. I was wearing it open, leaving my chest bare. I'd been able to unwind the bandages myself, but I couldn't rewind them.

"Shall I fetch Cailan?" Urist asked.

I shook my head. "Let the wounds breathe. It will do them good. What did you find?"

"No pursuit," he said. "At least not yet. The lads scouted two or three escape routes toward the north through the woods if it comes to it. A good hunting armory. Longbows and boar-spears. Be good to take with us if your kinsmen won't mind."

"I'm sure they won't."

"There's a meal near ready." Urist sniffed the air. "Coneys and capons, all sorts of good things. Odd place, this." He cocked his head. "Do they bring prisoners here?"

"Prisoners?" I asked. "No. Why?"

"Well, there's a room . . ." His voice trailed off. He put his hands on his knees and fixed me with his direct gaze. "No mind. My lord, what do you plan to do?"

I took a deep, experimental breath, looking down at myself, watching my wounds strain. It didn't feel too bad. They were deepest over my chest and ribs, trailing off at the ends. The scabs were already flaking at my shoulder and hip, revealing pink new skin. "Give me another day. I ought to be able to sit a horse by then. We'll move faster for it."

Urist nodded. "Fair enough. What about the girl?"

I glanced up at him. "I don't know, Urist. I hope to see her before we leave. She may come, she may not. She may not be able to. She will if she can."

"And if there's pursuit?" he asked. "If your Queen wants to clap you in chains?"

I took another deep breath, prodding my healing flesh. "I don't think I've a choice. I wouldn't be able to keep up with you on a hard flight. As for you and your men, whether to submit or flee . . ." I spread my hands. "That's your choice. I'd sooner have you hunting Berlik than waiting for the Cruarch to sort this all out, or at least your part in it. But it could be dangerous."

Urist snorted. "Life's dangerous, lad."

"I tried to warn you," I said.

He shrugged. "When all's said and done, you've done naught wrong, nor have we. Queen Ysandre's got a name for being a fair and just ruler. She's angry, aye; like as not, angriest at all at her daughter. Betrayal comes harder when it's blood. 'Tis easier to blame you for it, and she may, but I doubt she'll do aught rash."

His words made me feel better. "You've a way of putting matters into perspective."

"You're young." Urist smiled slightly. "You'll learn the trick of it."

"I hope so," I said.

Sidonie didn't come that day, nor did anyone else. We spent the day making preparations to travel once more; sorting through out stores, tending to our mounts, sharpening our swords, restringing bows. In consultation with Urist, I drew up a list of goods we needed, and spoke to Isembart regarding sending a servant into the City to purchase them at market.

We would need money, too. Drustan had provided Urist with sufficient funds for our journey here, but not enough for prolonged travel. I hadn't thought about that in my precipitous flight from the City. I wrote out a letter of request drawing on the accounts of my own neglected estates, which Isembart readily agreed to have delivered to Hugues to present to my factor. One had the sense that if I'd asked for a cameleopard and a troupe of acrobats to entertain us on the morrow, he'd have promised it without hesitation.

Like as not, my time would have been better spent resting, but my nerves were strung too tight. Anger, guilt, longing, grief . . . my emotions were at war with one another. A part of me wished we'd simply left the City and kept going, ill-provisioned or no. A part wished I'd stayed at the Palace to face the storm of acrimony. A part wished the Queen *would* send someone to fetch me, to force matters to a head.

It wasn't until nightfall, when it was obvious that no one was coming, that I felt my tension ease. Isembart's staff prepared a sumptuous meal, the second of the day. Aside from Timor and Gilbrid, who were on sentry duty, we all dined together. The dining hall was ostensibly a rustic affair, with rough wooden beams crossing the high ceiling and a great hearth where a roaring fire would be laid in winter, but the meal was served on plates of gleaming white porcelain, so fine they were nearly translucent, and eaten with gilded utensils, their handles wrought in the interlocking key pattern that was the emblem of House Shahrizai.

It made me smile to see Urist and the others fumble with their forks and spoons, surreptitiously resorting to belt knives and bare hands. I didn't care. They were warriors, not courtiers. I set down my own spoon and picked up a steaming bowl of venison broth, putting it to my lips and slurping. Others followed suit with relieved alacrity, woad-stained hands gripping the delicate bowls gingerly.

It would have made Dorelei laugh.

I wished she were here to see it.

'Twas a melancholy thought, but there was sweetness in it, too. There had been good times between us, many of them. I might have lost sight of that if she hadn't extracted this promise from Urist. During the days of my convalescence, when I had thought only of vengeance, I'd hardened my purpose by remembering her death. Her open, unsee-ing eyes, head turned at an unnatural angle. Blood soaking the cloak that covered her. The knowledge that beneath it lay our son, so near to full term, slain in the womb.

I wouldn't forget. I would never forget.

But I would remember her alive, too. The delight in her dimpled smile, the way she'd laugh when I played the song about the little brown goat. Her shy pleasure when she had presented me with the vambraces she'd had made for me.

All those things, and a thousand others. And above all else, I would never forget that if I ever found happiness in my life, somewhere on the far side of vengeance, I would owe it all to Dorelei mab Breidaia, my wife.

FORTY-ONE

IN THE LATE MORNING of the following day, Sidonie came.

After the first day, I'd steeled myself against expecting her. In the midst of a dramatic moment, her promise had sounded well and good, but in the cold light of reason, I thought it unlikely that Ysandre would permit it. The Queen was a stubborn woman.

But then, so was her daughter.

Urist's sentries let them pass. I was in the armory, testing hunting bows, trying to gauge the measure of my slowly returning strength against the sort of draw required to slow down a charging bear. I didn't believe it when Isembart came to fetch me.

"Forgive me, my lord," he said politely. "I understood your orders were to admit the Dauphine. Mayhap I was mistaken."

"No," I said. "Elua, no!"

I hurried to the receiving salon, my heart racing. I felt unaccountably nervous. I hadn't been yesterday. Whatever I'd felt, it had been too incomprehensible and vast to admit mere nerves. Today it was different. And I still wasn't entirely sure it was true.

It was, though.

Sidonie was there, accompanied by a dozen guards. Palace Guards, clad in livery of Courcel blue, but there were vertical stripes of a paler blue on their doublets, too. Maslin de Lombelon, who was mercifully not present, had been wearing one yesterday. She was of age now. She had her own personal guard. Mavros had said they were loyal to her. They must be, I thought, to accompany her here.

An attendant was taking Sidonie's cloak when I entered the room.

It was rain-dappled, and there were drops of rain in her hair. She was wearing a gown of amber silk. And although she was looking away, she turned her head toward me when I entered, the way it had been between us for so long.

"You came," I said stupidly.

Her brows rose. "I keep my promises."

I wanted to laugh and cry all at once, to sweep her into my arms and cover her face with kisses. I couldn't, though. Today was different. It would have felt like a grave impropriety. And so we stood there, unsure how to proceed, while her guards and Urist and his men eyed one another.

"This is Captain Claude de Monluc," Sidonie said, breaking the silence. "My lord Claude, Prince Imriel de la Courcel."

A tall man with blond hair and keen, light blue eyes stepped forward and bowed, correct and exact. "Well met, your highness."

I put out my hand. "And you, my lord." Claude de Monluc hesitated only a heartbeat before clasping my hand. His grip was firm, and his expression gave away very little. "This is Urist mab Wrada," I said, introducing him. "Commander of the garrison of Clunderry. Urist, her highness Sidonie de la Courcel, Dauphine of Terre d'Ange."

Urist nodded, arms folded. His expression gave away absolutely nothing.

To my surprise, Sidonie crossed over to him and laid a hand on his arm. "I understand from Imriel's kinsman that you brought him here to honor his wife's last wish, my lord Urist," she said quietly. "Thank you. That must have been difficult."

His face softened. "Ah, well."

Sidonie turned to me. "We should talk."

I was glad one of us, at least, had a sense of propriety. "In my quarters," I said. "Urist, I leave you in charge."

Any other time, I would have given Sidonie my arm as a matter of simple courtesy. Even when we'd disliked one other, we'd observed Court protocol. Today I didn't. We walked side by side, not touching, conscious of the distance between us, conscious of the watching eyes of the men behind us; half of them still grieving Clunderry's loss, half of them weighing their loyalties and contemplating the Queen's displeasure.

It was a blessed relief to close the door to the master chamber behind us. Sidonie let out a long, shuddering sigh. I reached for her and she came into my arms. I enfolded her and she wrapped her arms around me, pressed her face to my chest. I rested my cheek against her hair, feeling the rain's dampness.

"What shall we talk about?" I murmured.

Her lips curved in a smile. "Anything. Nothing."

We stood without moving for a long time. It felt so good to hold her, I could have stood forever. It was Sidonie who moved first, lifting her head, exploring my chest lightly with her fingertips and feeling the bandages Cailan had rewound last night beneath my shirt. "How bad is it?"

"Bad," I said. "Getting better."

"May I see?" she asked. I nodded. Sidonie undid the wooden buttons on my shirt, one by one. She had a deft touch, quick and neat. She went slowly, though, unwinding the bandages. Tears rose to her eyes, rose and overflowed. When the last coil of the clean linen strip fell away, she gasped. "Name of Elua!"

"You should have seen it before," I said wryly.

"Don't jest." Sidonie shook her head. "The first news we heard, they weren't sure if you'd live or die, Imriel. I never thought one could die of sorrow, I truly didn't. But something broke inside me that day."

"I'm sorry," I whispered.

"Will you tell me about it?" she asked softly. "Phèdre and Joscelin did try to explain before they left, but I'm not sure I understand what happened. Any of it."

"Oh, gods." I winced. "That letter . . . I'm so sorry."

"I know." Sidonie searched my face. "I just want to understand."

I nodded. "I'll try."

We sat on the bed. I held her hands and began to talk. I told her all of it, without censoring any of the details. Things I hadn't told anyone. How hard it was to leave her, how I'd tried to make my heart into a stone and bury it. The ways the Maghuin Dhonn had haunted me. The flute song, the laughter, the fouled spring. The night I'd let myself think of her for the first time, spilling my seed on *taisgaidh* soil. Morwen, the charm. The bindings I'd consented to. Dorelei, carrying our child. Berlik's vow. How I hadn't grasped the enormity of what I'd lost until the night of my Alban nuptials, the night I'd taken off the croonie-stone to read her letter, laughing and weeping like a madman.

Once I began, I couldn't stop.

The words came and came. Clunderry, the cattle-raid, and Morwen again. The ever-changing future. The sight of my father's spectre during the Feast of the Dead. Spring and hope, and Dorelei great with child, and then that night, that terrible night. The visions I'd seen in the stone circle. Alba at war. The burning groves, the toppling stones. My son, the monster.

The horns of Clunderry.

The screaming.

Berlik.

My voice faltered, there. I couldn't speak of it, not yet. Of Dorelei lying on the table, her head turned too far, her eyes empty and open. Blood soaking into the cloak that covered her swollen belly. Not yet, mayhap not ever. It didn't matter. I'd said enough. I was wrung out, damp with sweat. Sidonie pulled away and buried her face in her hands, shuddering.

"It *was* us," she whispered. "That's how they bound you."

I didn't lie to her. "Yes."

"I wonder that you can bear the sight of me," she murmured, lifting her head.

"Sidonie." I gazed at her. All of the wondrous contradictions of her nature were written on her face. The dark Cruithne eyes, at odds with her fair coloring. The strong line of her brows, the same shape as my own, a legacy of House Courcel, countering the delicacy of her features. The sweet shape of her pink lips. I laughed with sorrow. "Ah, Elua! I didn't think I could bear it either, not yet. I wouldn't have come if Urist hadn't insisted. If Dorelei hadn't made him promise. And the truth is, she was right. Nothing's changed it, not time or distance or horror. I love you. I could look at you forever. And I do believe that for whatever unfathomable reasons, Blessed Elua wills it." I hesitated. "Unless you feel differently?"

"No." She shook her head, then reached up and drew my head down to kiss me. "No. Never." She kissed my lips, my throat, laying a trail of kisses toward my bare, ravaged torso. A shock of desire flared through me. "I love you."

Ah, gods! It felt like a benediction.

"Sidonie." My voice shook. "I swore an oath, I pledged myself to Dorelei and no other for a year and a day."

"'Tis a vow meant to be kept to the living." Her black eyes glittered with love and anguish. "How long will you stay here? A day? Two days? And how long will you be gone? Months? A year? I know you have to go. And Elua help me, I'll wait for you. For as long as it takes, I'll wait. I will." She dashed impatiently at her tears. "But do you believe the gods are so cruel as to deny us this one morsel of joy?"

"I don't know," I whispered.

"I do. And I'll not deny Blessed Elua's precept a second time." Sidonie looped her arms around my neck and began kissing me; a gentle rain of kisses, falling on my lips, my cheeks, my jawline, my eyelids, punctuating her kisses with murmured words. "Blessed Elua, hear your scion and grant us mercy, for we do but follow your precept. Gods of Alba, hear your scion and grant us forgiveness . . ."

That was as far as she got.

I was a man, mortal and in love. I took her face in my hands and kissed her, deep and devouring. And ah, Elua! It was so, so good.

I pulled her down on the bed, still kissing her. Sidonie clung to me, her body pressed against mine, making small noises deep in her throat. I unlaced her stays and got her out of her gown, kissing every inch of flesh I exposed. Her hands tugged impatiently at the laces on my breeches. I kicked off my boots, shimmied out of the breeches. My wounds burned, but I couldn't have cared less. I rolled down her stockings, kissed the arches of her feet, then worked my way upward, spreading her thighs.

When I tasted her, Sidonie cried aloud, her hips bucking. She buried both hands in my hair, tugging. "Please!" she gasped. "Inside me, all of you. Please!"

I crawled up the length of her body. Slippery. Somewhere, my gouges were cracked and bleeding. It didn't matter. Nothing mattered

but sliding my rigid, aching phallus inside her tight, wet warmth, hard
and deep, filling her to the hilt.

Why do we fit so well together?

Guilt and desire and yearning merged into one aching need.

Her heels, locked behind my buttocks. I growled, shoving her
thighs wider. Fitting myself deeper. Her hips rocked upward to meet
my thrust, nails digging into my back. Over and over, I drove into her,
riding desire like a wave. Everything I'd wanted, everything I'd been
denied. Our bodies were slippery with my blood. She bit my shoulder
to stifle her cries, biting and sucking at my flesh.

I wanted more and more and more, and all that I wanted, Sidonie
gave. She was the bright mirror and the dark all at once, reflecting all
of me, good and bad. We reflected one another. We fit.

It drove away the horror. It kept the memories at bay.

It was a promise of absolution.

I felt her climax, the helpless shudder and surge of her body. I rode
it hard, pushing her, pushing myself, until I could ride it no longer. I
flung my head back, my back arching, and spent myself in her in a long
spasm of white-hot pleasure.

And then collapsed on her, panting.

Sidonie freed one hand to stroke my face. I gazed into her black
eyes, soft and satiated now. Her golden hair was spread over the pillow
in tangles. The bright and the dark. She moved her head and kissed
my lips with infinite tenderness. "You're bleeding. I don't think that's
good."

"Probably not," I murmured.

She pushed gently at me. "Roll onto your back."

I obeyed, and watched her rise. She went to the washstand to fetch
a bowl, a ewer of water, and a clean cloth. From behind, her naked
body looked bright as a flame in the dim chamber. She came back to
kneel beside me on the bed. There was blood smeared on her breasts
and belly, sticky and drying. Sidonie ignored it, washing my wounds
with care.

"You're a good chirurgeon," I said softly.

She rinsed the cloth in a bowl of clean water and dabbed at my ribcage. "I'd like to lock you up for a month or so, and nurse you back to health."

I winced as the cloth caught the edge of a scab. "I'd have to punish you for being careless."

"Oh?" Sidonie smiled. "I can be *very* careless."

"You?" I smiled back at her. "Never."

"Only the once." She dropped the cloth in the bowl, then leaned down to kiss me before sitting back on her heels. "A very fateful once. Sit up. I need to put your bandages back on. I don't think it's bad, but you're still bleeding."

I let her rewind my bandages, and then I poured clean water in the bowl and made her kneel while I washed my drying blood from her, watching the pink-tinged water run over her creamy skin. "I was surprised that you came here," I said. "I was afraid to hope."

"Believe me, it wasn't easy." She smiled ruefully. "Mother threatened to have me confined to my quarters. And I threatened in turn to withdraw from the Palace altogether and take up residence on one of the estates that are a rightful part of my inheritance if she attempted to curtail my freedom. It makes a difference, having one's majority."

"I know," I said. "I ran all the way to Tiberium."

"And I ran to you." Sidonie gazed at me. "To snatch a morsel of joy."

My chest tightened. "I'd stay if I could," I said. "But I can't." The spectre of Dorelei's death rose between us. "I can't forgo Kushiel's justice. Not even for you, Sun Princess."

Her brows quirked. "Did I ask you to?"

"No," I said quietly. "You didn't."

"When will you—"

A knock at the door interrupted her. "My lord?" It was Urist's voice, muffled through the dense wood. "There's a D'Angeline lord demands to see you and the girl. Amaury Trente. Says he's the Queen's emissary. Small escort, four men. I don't think they've come to fight. Should I admit him?"

Sidonie and I glanced at one another. She sighed. "Go. I'll follow in a moment."

"Yes, show him to the salon," I called to Urist, who answered in the affirmative. I dragged on my breeches and boots, shrugged into the linen shirt and left it unbuttoned. There was fresh blood seeping through my bandages. I helped Sidonie find her scattered clothing, then kissed her and left her to comb out her thoroughly tangled hair while I went to see what Lord Amaury wanted.

He was seated in the receiving salon and got to his feet when I entered, offering a perfunctory bow and straightening with a speech already on his lips. It faltered at the sight of me. "Elua's Balls! You look like—"

"I know," I said curtly. "It was a bear, Lord Amaury. What do you want?"

His lips moved soundlessly for a second. "Where's Sidonie?"

"She'll be here in a moment." I sat down in a chair near his. "Well?"

Amaury Trente looked unhappy. I knew him. He was the Queen's man, a good one and loyal. He'd served as her Captain of the Guard for a time, and he'd headed up the company that had travelled all the way to Khebbel-im-Akkad to rescue me, although he'd stopped short of crossing into Drujan. Only Phèdre and Joscelin had dared cross that border. When they'd led me out, alive if not unscathed, Lord Amaury had been the first person to greet me as Imriel de la Courcel. The moment was etched in my memory. Until then, I hadn't known.

"I . . ." Lord Amaury swallowed. "I'm sorry for your misfortune, Imriel."

"Thank you." I didn't offer anything else. He took a seat and looked around at Urist and the silent Cruithne, then back at me. His gaze slid away from mine, fixed at a point on my uninjured left shoulder. He blinked. I glanced down involuntarily, twitched my unbuttoned shirt to cover what was unmistakably a large, vivid love-bite.

Amaury blushed, and blushed deeper as Sidonie entered, rising and bowing to hide it. "Your highness."

"Lord Amaury." Her voice was cool. "What is it my mother wishes?"

Amaury blinked at her, too. I didn't blame him. Sidonie looked collected and composed, her hair neatly coiled, and not at all as though she'd recently been writhing in bloodstained sheets, gnawing at my flesh in the transports of passion.

"Your mother . . ." he began, then paused. "May I sit?"

Sidonie inclined her head. "Of course."

We all sat. Amaury Trente cleared his throat. "Her majesty Queen Ysandre . . . Sidonie, your mother wishes you to put an end to this, quietly and with no further fanfare. Both of you. She . . . she sends me in good faith to ask what might so move you."

"I see." Sidonie cocked her head, gazing steadily at him. "Well, my lord, common sense has failed to do so, as has time and distance. And now, it seems, so has foul magic and grievous tragedy." There were lamps lit against the day's gloom, and her black eyes held their flickering light. "So tell me, my lord, what bribe does my mother think will prove effective?"

"A measure of greater autonomy?" Amaury suggested uncomfortably. "More responsibility? Or mayhap *less*? I don't know, Sidonie. I'm here to ask." When she didn't answer, he cleared his throat again. "What of you, Imriel?"

"Can her majesty turn back the hands of time and alter the past?" I glanced at Urist's implacable face. "I would take that offer, Lord Amaury. To have the past year of my life to live over, to change the course of the future. To see Dorelei restored to life, to see our child born, whole and hale, and raised with loving joy." I rubbed my eyes with the heel of one hand. "That, I would accept."

Lord Amaury's voice was low and miserable. " 'Tis easy to say."

"No," I said. "No, it's not."

He drew breath to make a reply, but whatever he might have said, it was lost in a sudden clamor rising outside the manor house. Hoofbeats, racing footsteps, the sound of a hunting horn raising an alarm.

All hell broke loose.

In the chaos that followed, it was difficult to discern the sequence of events. All I know for certain is that Barquiel L'Envers was the first to arrive, accompanied by a large contingent of armed men. He swept past Urist's sentries, dismounted, flung open the main door, and strode into the receiving salon like a bleak wind, his face lined with weariness and rigid with hatred, his cropped hair bristling. Later, I learned he'd ridden straight through the night to get here.

"Traitor-spawn!" L'Envers hissed, grabbing at the loose collar of my shirt and yanking. His violet eyes bulged, the whites shot through with red. "Seducing whore's son! Get your blade. I'm calling you out, *now*!"

"Barquiel!" Lord Amaury's voice, sharp. "Look at the lad, man! He's in no shape for this."

L'Envers didn't care. He shook me. Lacking the strength to break free of his grip, I didn't bother trying. Instead, I spat in his face.

He roared. There was a lot of roaring, a lot of shouting and shoving. Urist, interposing himself between us, holding a knife pointed at L'Envers' belly. Barquiel L'Envers letting go of me and cursing him for a tattooed Pictish savage. I backed away. Claude de Monluc, Sidonie's Captain of the Guard, was giving crisp orders, ushering her out of the salon. Others, arriving. Soldiers in the livery of the Royal Army. A scent of apples. Ghislain nó Trevalion.

Hugues, wide-eyed, clutching a satchel.

Mavros Shahrizai, my cousin, looking overwhelmed.

Maslin de Lombelon, his face pinched and tight, trying unexpectedly to reason with Barquiel L'Envers.

Too many people, too much mayhem. It spilled over into the great hall. It made my ears ring, reminding me of another night, filled with blood and madness. Ghislain's soldiers were confronting L'Envers' men; Ghislain was confronting Barquiel L'Envers himself. Urist and the men of Clunderry trying to ward me. Amaury Trente was pleading in vain for calm. Servants were scrambling to get out of the way. Everyone else was lost in the swirl. I didn't know how they'd all got there, what they wanted. I shook my head, filled with helpless rage.

A shattering sound.

A ewer of fine porcelain burst against the flagstones.

"Enough!" Sidonie's voice cut through the chaos like a knife, high and clear and utterly controlled. There were bright spots of color on her cheeks. I'd never seen her angry. She looked like her mother, only younger and more vibrant. Her guardsmen surrounded her warily. She whipped her head around. "Lord Amaury, has my mother disinherited me since this morning?"

Everyone grew very still.

"No, your highness," Amaury Trente said quietly.

"Then I believe I hold rank here." Sidonie surveyed the room. "My lords, I am not insensible of my duty. I am well aware of the ramifications of what I have done, and I am prepared to discuss them with my mother and anyone she deems necessary, as soon as she is willing to acknowledge that I am not a recalcitrant child bent on rebellion. Now is not the time, and here is not the place."

I wanted to cheer. I saw Urist give a fierce grin, his eyes glinting.

"Oh, *duty*, is it, child?" Barquiel L'Envers began contemptuously. "You don't begin to understand—"

"Yes, I do." Sidonie raised her voice. "My *duty*, Uncle, is not to you. It is not to secure the hold of House Courcel on the throne of Terre d'Ange, and it is not to advance the interests of my blood kin or those to whom they are indebted. It is to Terre d'Ange itself." She drew a deep breath, trembling a little. "It is to ensure the peace and prosperity that my mother has won for our nation continues. It is to honor our existing alliances, and seek out new allies. It is to safeguard our borders against all enemies. It is to ensure that the least among us may lead joyous and tranquil lives, secure in the knowledge that Blessed Elua's precept prevails here." Her chest rose and fell sharply. "*That*, my lords, is the vision of rulership my mother imparted to me. Would that she trusted me to honor it."

Eighteen years old, and save for a pair of chambermaids doing their best to make themselves invisible, the only woman in the hall; and she put the peers of the realm to shame. If I'd had any lingering doubts that I loved her, they would have vanished in that instant. Only Barquiel L'Envers was stubborn enough to persevere.

"You're a fool, girl." He pointed at me. "He's Melisande Shahrizai's son."

"I'm well aware of that." Sidonie's voice hardened. "Mayhap you forget, my lord, whence we come. My mother was raised under the shadow of being named a murderess' get, thanks to the intemperate actions of your own sister, who caused the death of my grandfather's first betrothed." Her gaze travelled around the room. "My lord Ghislain, you abjured the name Somerville after your father raised an army to seize the City. Your wife's mother and brother were executed for treason. No one rises to power with an unblemished heritage."

"Yes, but—" L'Envers began.

"But *what*?" The word cracked like a whip. "You have offered Imriel nothing but mistrust from the day he arrived. And yet despite it, he has given nothing but loyalty to House Courcel. If there has been any hint of treason about him, it is because you put it there yourself, my lord."

It was true, but no one had ever dared say it in public. Not even Ysandre. I felt a wave of gratitude wash over me. In the deafening silence that followed, Barquiel L'Envers turned purple with fury and humiliation. His fists knotted. Sidonie lifted her chin and stared defiantly at him, daring him to deny it. Only the quick pulse beating in the hollow of her throat gave any indication she was less than utterly fearless.

Elua, but I loved her.

L'Envers took a step toward her. Her guards shifted. Although he looked as though he tasted bile, Maslin de Lombelon stepped forward to confront his former patron, shaking his head. Ghislain nó Trevalion ordered everyone to stand down. My palms itched, and I wished I was armed.

What might have happened in that moment, I cannot say. Amidst the silence, there was a sound in the entry. It was a Cruithne warrior who broke the uneasy tableau, bursting into the hall. Deordivus; one of the young men who'd ridden with Kinadius. He was alone and travel-worn, spattered with mud, but there was a grin splitting his woad-stained face. Heedless of the gathered throng, he pushed his way through to me while D'Angeline peers stared, bemused, forgetting about L'Envers and his quarrel.

My heart beat hard in my breast, a steady drumbeat calling for justice.

"We found it." Deordivus' hands rose to grip my upper arms. His grimy fingers left marks on my sleeves. His grin widened. "We found the bear-witch's trail!"

FORTY-TWO

IT TOOK A WHILE for matters to settle after Deordivus' arrival, but they did. A great deal of the credit was due to Ghislain nó Trevalion, though I paid scant heed to what transpired. All I know is that he managed to get L'Envers and his entourage to quit the manor house, withdrawing his own men to ensure their departure.

Before he left, he paused to bid me farewell. "Good hunting, Prince Imriel."

I nodded, distracted. Mavros had procured maps from a study, and we were poring over them; Deordivus indicating the bridge where Berlik had been seen crossing from Azzalle into the Flatlands. A man, travelling in human form. I wondered if his shapechanging magic was leaving him as he travelled farther from Alban soil. "My thanks, Lord Ghislain."

Ghislain rested a heavy hand on my shoulder. "What her highness said is true, you know. I don't presume to gauge your intentions here, but I'm not hypocrite enough to pass judgment on you based on your mother's actions. I wanted you to know it."

I glanced up at him. Like his son Bertran, he had an open, honest face; but there was a shadow of knowledge behind his eyes that his son lacked. He knows, I thought. Bernadette must have confessed it to him. He knows that his wife sought to have me killed. "Thank you, my lord. I appreciate it."

His grip tightened briefly. "May Kushiel's justice prevail in mercy and wisdom."

With that, he left us.

Our plan was simple. Kinadius and his men were following Berlik's trail. Kinadius had sent Deordivus to bring the news to us and another fellow to Alba to alert Drustan and Talorcan. We would leave on the morrow. They would send word back to the Flatlander bridge-keeper that we might follow in their tracks.

It was only the leaving that was hard.

Sidonie waited while I conferred with Deordivus and Urist, speaking in low tones to Lord Amaury, Claude de Monluc, to Mavros, to a Hugues rendered suddenly shy and tongue-tied. Maslin de Lombelon was gone. I hadn't noticed him leave.

After a time, she approached the table where our maps were spread. I pushed my chair back and rose to greet her, acutely aware of my own neglect. Vengeance and love didn't make for good bedfellows. Or mayhap I was still insufferably self-absorbed.

"I'm sorry," I said awkwardly.

Sidonie shook her head. "Don't be. Shall I go?"

"Can you stay?" I asked.

"Until the morning?" She tilted her head, smiling slightly in the direction of Lord Amaury, who was sitting with his head bowed, tugging at his curly brown hair. "Oh yes, I think my mother's emissary is sufficiently abashed that there will be no trouble."

"I would like it," I said quietly. "I would like it very much. What you said today . . ." I paused, unable to find adequate words that sufficed to express the vast love and awe within me. "You were magnificent. Truly."

"Ah, well." There was no pride in her expression, only a deep, complicated sorrow. "I've had a long time to think about being brave, Imriel."

Urist grunted. "Better late than never, eh?"

Sidonie nodded. "Yes, my lord. I'm trying."

So it was decided.

I spoke to Hugues, who had come to deliver a satchel full of coin, courtesy of my factor. He was still wide-eyed, out of his element. I thanked him for his kindness and promised to send word at every opportunity. And I thanked him, too, for the gift he'd made me the last time I'd departed from Terre d'Ange.

"The flute?" Hugues blushed. "Oh, it was a silly gift."

"No, it wasn't." I shook my head, thinking about Dorelei's laughter. "It was perfect."

"Well, I'm glad you liked it." He embraced me carefully, mindful of my wounds. "Please come home safe, Imri. I don't want to be the last member of her ladyship's household to see you alive."

I swallowed hard. "I'll do my best."

Mavros, too, took his leave. He'd come out of loyalty when he'd gotten word of L'Envers' entourage heading for the manor house. "I don't know what I expected to do," he said wryly. "Serve as a witness, mayhap, if he killed you out of hand. Declare blood-feud on behalf of House Shahrizai."

"You're a good friend," I said. "Truly."

Mavros shrugged. "You do keep life interesting, cousin." He tugged aside the collar of my shirt, peering judiciously at the love-bite it covered. "Very impressive," he said to Sidonie, who merely raised her brows. "You're a bundle of surprises, your highness."

I swatted his hands away. "Yes, and you're incorrigible."

"So I'm told." He took my face in his hands, and I was moved to see that beneath the careless amusement, there were tears in his eyes. "Take care of yourself."

"I will," I said softly. "I'm coming home with that bastard's head in a bag, Mavros."

"Good." He nodded. "Good."

Lord Amaury was staying out of a morbid sense of obligation, although I daresay he was none too pleased about it. In the morning, he would escort Sidonie back to the Palace, along with his men and her personal guard. I might have felt sorry for him another time. As it was, I couldn't put a name to what I felt. I'd never had such powerful emotions warring in me.

It was Sidonie who took matters in hand. With quiet, assured competence she spoke to the steward Isembart. I saw him bow in acquiescence, and although his features were schooled to near-perfect inexpressiveness, I could sense the relief behind them.

"Very good, your highness," he murmured.

I was watching her out of the corner of my eye while Urist and I went over our preparations for departure on the morrow; the supplies that had been delivered, those we would need to procure on the road. Sidonie caught my eye and smiled, returning to the table where we were working, still spread with maps.

"This is where he was seen?" she asked, touching the map.

"Yes," I said. "Crossing a bridge."

She cocked her head. "If he bears north, he's bound for Skaldia."

I shivered involuntarily. "I know."

Sidonie spread her hand on the map. "So." For a moment, her shoulders slumped; then she straightened and regarded me. "When you've finished here, I'll be in the master chamber. Dinner will be served to Commander Urist, Lord Amaury, Captain de Monluc, and their men in the great hall."

I watched her walk away, back straight, coiled hair shining.

Urist watched me. "We're finished."

"We haven't—" I began.

"Strong-willed, that one." He jerked his chin in the direction Sidonie had gone. "Drustan's eldest. Go. There's nothing to be done here I can't handle."

I went.

She's like a house without a door. That was what Dorelei had said of Sidonie; the only thing she'd ever said about her. I understood what she meant. It wasn't true, though. I leaned in the doorway of the master bedchamber, watching Sidonie peruse the contents of the flagellary cupboard. She could be closed and careful, but on her own terms, she was utterly uninhibited. The contrast never failed to give me a thrill of shock and delight.

"See anything you like?" I asked.

She shot me an unreadable glance over her shoulder. "Oh, yes. But not today." She closed the cupboard doors. "I didn't expect you so soon."

"Urist dismissed me," I said.

"Urist." The master chamber had a generous hearth, with a pair of sumptuous chairs and a low table before it. A fire had been laid in the hearth, and there was a winejug and a platter of cheese and dates on the table. Sidonie poured wine into the goblets provided. They were wrought of the same fine white porcelain, so thin the red wine showed through in a faint blush. "He must have cared very much for Dorelei to honor her wishes in this."

"Yes." I took one of the goblets and sank into a chair. "More than I knew. But she was easy to love."

Sidonie gazed at me. "Why did she do it?"

"She loved me," I said softly. "Very much. More than I deserved. She wanted me to be happy. And I think she feared that if aught happened to her, I'd let myself be consumed with vengeance."

"Will you?" she asked in a low voice.

I turned the goblet in my hands, studying it. "No." I lifted my head and met her gaze. "No. Because along with my guilt and grief, I will carry with me a promise of hope. Of redemption. The memory of Elua's grace and mercy. The memory of you defying your mother and half of Terre d'Ange for my sake." I smiled a little. "Not to mention Barquiel L'Envers."

"That was long overdue," Sidonie murmured.

"Yes." I set down my goblet. "But I *will* have vengeance. Dorelei's blood demands it. And . . ." I caught my breath and looked away. "And our son's."

"Aniel," she whispered.

I nodded. I'd told her the name we'd chosen, Dorelei and I. "I would have loved him," I murmured, hearing my voice break. "No matter what. I don't believe the vision Morwen showed me. I can't. I won't. I wouldn't have let that happen, not while there was breath in my body. I would have found a way, some way . . ."

"You would," Sidonie said steadily.

I met her gaze again. "It doesn't frighten you?"

"No." Sidonie picked up her goblet and drained it. She'd walked out of this bedchamber without blushing to greet Lord Amaury, she'd set an entire roomful of peers on their ear without any sign of fear, and she hadn't twitched an eyelash when Mavros complimented her on my love-bite, but her color rose now, unexpected and girlish. "Imriel, will you please come home safely and marry me?"

"Yes," I said promptly.

She sighed. "Oh, good."

We both laughed then, feeling self-conscious at the enormity of the decision. What else was there to do? I felt Elua's mercy gather us as though in a vast net, letting the grief abate. Time. It was a small space of time, but it was ours. I reached out and caught one of her hands, tugging gently until Sidonie came to sit on my lap. She smelled like rain and wood-smoke and herself, honey-sweet with a tinge of salt. I loosed her hair from its neat coils, sinking my fingers into it and kissing her until a discreet knock sounded at the door. Sidonie raised her head, dark eyes vague with pleasure. "I sent for a bath before dinner."

"Send it away," I suggested, nuzzling her throat.

She wriggled. "Your bandages need to be soaked loose."

"Do they?" I asked, uninterested.

"Yes." Sidonie kissed me quick and hard, biting my lower lip, then slipped off my lap. I watched her open the door and incline her head graciously, admitting a series of impeccably polite servants bearing buckets of warm water to fill the bath, pouring scented oil into the steaming water.

It seemed to take forever.

She was right, of course. When the servants had finished at last, I let Sidonie undress me with grave deliberation. My once-clean bandages were stuck to my skin, caked with dried blood. I stepped into the bath and sank down, sighing as the warm water loosened the blood-stiffened linen. I rested my arms along the edges of the tub. "Are you going to leave me alone here?"

Sidonie eyed me. "No."

Water sloshed over the edges of the bathtub as she stripped and joined me. Servants of House Shahrizai came and went, setting forth an elaborate, intimate dinner on the low table before the hearth. Firelight danced over Sidonie's fair skin as she unwound my bandages. Beneath the water, our legs entwined. She frowned with concentration. A few thin threads of blood rose from my cracked scabs, tinting the water.

"So how dangerous is he?" she asked.

"Berlik?"

Sidonie nodded, still concentrating.

I rested my head against the tub's rim. "I don't know. He's travelling as a man now, and not a bear. I don't know how powerful his magic is, now that he's cursed by a broken vow and left Alba's soil." I paused. "For that matter, how dangerous is Barquiel L'Envers? You made an enemy of him today."

"Not as powerful as he thinks." Sidonie finished her task and dropped the sodden mass of blood-soaked bandages over the side of the tub. "Not anymore. I know you weren't happy with the decision Mother made, but his power has dwindled considerably since he lost command of the Royal Army. I'm not afraid of him."

"You turned Maslin de Lombelon against him," I said softly.

"No." She shook her head. "Maslin turned himself. I told him once when we were quarrelling what my uncle had done to you, seeking to frame you as a traitor. Maslin has a keen sense of honor."

"What happened between you?" I asked.

"Ah, well." Sidonie's mouth quirked. "It was a bad idea. I should have listened to Amarante. She warned me that it was too soon, that I was just trying to distract myself. That his feelings were strong. She was right." She was quiet for a moment. "Maslin tried to comfort me after we heard about what had happened. During that time when no one knew if you were going to live or die. It was kind. He was trying to be kind. And I suddenly couldn't stand having him anywhere near me. I'm not proud of that."

"I'm sorry," I said. "But he's still in your service?"

"Oh, yes." She gazed into the distance. I sensed there was a part of the story she wasn't willing to tell, knowing there was no love lost between Maslin and me. "He insisted. And I felt guilty enough that I assented. Maslin . . . you know, any man in my guard would be expected to risk his life to save mine. It's a simple fact, true of any royal guardsman. But I don't think any of them save Maslin would welcome the opportunity." A shadow crossed her face. "Anyway, I don't want to talk about him."

"Fair enough," I said. "How about this, then. Sidonie de la Courcel, do you actually think we could wed without tearing the realm apart?"

"Mmm." Her gaze returned, glinting with amusement and determination. "Well, I don't think it will be *easy*." She slid forward in the tub, wrapping her legs around my waist. "But if we don't try, we'll never know."

Her skin was wet and slippery from the oil, sliding deliciously against mine. The last discreet Shahrizai servant placed one last item on the table and withdrew, closing the door behind him with a click. I slid my hands down Sidonie's waist, worked them under her buttocks, and drew her toward me.

"Oh, no." Her eyes narrowed. "You're not going to exert yourself and start bleeding again. At least not until after dinner."

"It's no effort," I assured her.

"Nonetheless." She picked up a ball of soap. "I insist."

I let her bathe me, smiling at the simple pleasure she took in it. It reminded me of the pleasure I'd taken in rubbing Dorelei's belly with flaxseed oil when the babe had gotten so big. The memory hurt, but it was good, too. And strangely, it did nothing to lessen my arousal. When Sidonie finished, we both clambered out of the tub. She patted me dry with a thick towel, careful not to disturb the water-softened scabs.

"Leave it be for now," I said. "They need to dry. I've a salve to put on them later, it will keep the bandages from sticking."

"Oh, I've somewhat else in mind at the moment." Sidonie slid a dressing-robe over my shoulders; heavy black silk embroidered with the golden Shahrizai key pattern, thoughtfully provided. Her lips curved in a wicked smile. "Don't worry, it's no effort."

She led me over to the nearest chair, the robe hanging loose around me, then knelt between my knees when I sat. Her naked skin was moist and flushed from the bath, her hair spilling over her shoulders in damp coils.

At the first touch of her mouth on my taut phallus, I groaned and sank both hands into her hair. Sidonie made the *languisement* an act of worship, performed with lips and tongue; beautiful, wonderful, and maddening. The sounds she made, the murmurs of pleasure, set my entire body to quivering. I never wanted to it to end and I never wanted to stop watching her. And then she took the whole of my shaft into her mouth, cheek and throat muscles working, and uttered a deep, stifled moan, and my eyes nearly rolled back in my skull. I held her head hard, my hips jerking, as my body sought to turn itself inside out, sending spurt after spurt of seed down her throat.

"Name of Elua!" I sank back in exhaustion. "No effort?"

"A little, mayhap." Her voice was low and sensuous, hoarse from her exertions. Sidonie gathered herself and rose to straddle my lap, sitting on my knees. We regarded one another. "I love you," she said. "You're headed off Elua-knows-where, like as not into a hostile nation, pursuing a man who may or may not be able to turn himself into a bear, a bear that nearly killed you. Imriel, I understand why you have to do this. I do. But if you don't come back, if you don't survive this, I will spend the rest of my life with an aching hole in my heart, mourning you."

I wound a lock of her damp hair around my fingers. "And this helps?"

"Yes." Sidonie traced my lower lip. "If nothing else, I want to leave here with the memory of you inside me. Everywhere."

"Everywhere?" I asked.

She leaned forward and kissed me. "We'd better eat. You're going to need your strength."

The servants of the manor house had provided a prodigious feast. We uncovered platters to find roasted partridge with a quince sauce, rabbit stew, simmered leeks and mushroom tarts, an array of nuts and candied peels of orange and lemon.

To my surprise, once the food was revealed, I discovered I was ravenous.

Small wonder, I suppose.

Sidonie, clad in a robe that was the twin of mine, ate half as much as I did and spent the balance of the time watching me with a spark of laughter in her eyes. "You needn't stare," I observed, washing down a mouthful of partridge with a swig of cool white wine.

She smiled. "Your appetite amazes and impresses me."

I swallowed another bite and pointed my fork at her. "You're the cause."

"Oh, I know." Her smile deepened. "It's just . . . Elua! I don't want to let a moment pass unmarked. It seems so strange, after all the secrecy and hiding, to be here with you, like this. Even if it's only for one night. To have stood up to my mother, to have defied all those men today . . ."

She shook her head in wonderment. "You know, I never thought I'd do such a thing for the sake of love. I could never have imagined the need. Betimes I think the gods must have a peculiar sense of humor, to visit this on us. Don't you?"

"Yes." I put down my fork. "Sidonie, if it comes to it, what if your mother *does* threaten to disinherit you?" When she didn't answer, I pressed the issue. "Is it worth the cost?"

"Is it to you?" she asked.

"To spend my life with you?" I didn't hesitate. "Yes, of course. But it's not my birthright we're talking about."

Sidonie lifted her chin, gazing at the ceiling. "Blessed Elua cared naught for crowns or thrones," she mused. "It was your mother who said that, wasn't it? You told me so, once. Melisande Shahrizai may have done a great many bad things, but she was no fool." She looked back at me, her black eyes unfathomable. "If it comes to it, and I pray it doesn't, it would be *my* choice, my goatherd prince. Not yours. Mine."

Why it was those words that caught at my desire and aroused me beyond bearing, I couldn't say. There is no logic in love or desire.

It sufficed.

It sufficed to ignite a maelstrom in me.

I cleared the table with a sweep of one arm, sending dishes and platters clattering in a wholly unnecessary gesture. I stooped and picked up Sidonie, cradling her in my arms and carrying her to the bed, neatly remade by the manor house's servants. This time there were no clothes to be disposed of, only robes, easily shed. I laid her on her stomach. She turned her head and watched as I went to fetch a vial of scented oil from the corner where the bathtub stood.

"Everywhere?" I asked softly, spreading a glistening trail down her spine.

Sidonie nodded, wordless.

Creamy skin, young and tight. I worked the oil into it, lower and lower. I pulled her to her knees, spreading her buttocks with both hands. Braced on her elbows, she shuddered when I touched the tip of my tongue to the puckered rose of her anus. Shuddered harder when I slid one oiled finger into her, then two. With my other hand, I caressed Naamah's Pearl. Sidonie cried out, convulsing around my fingers.

"Do you want this?" I slid my fingers out of her and grasped my phallus, slickening it with oil. I positioned the swollen head at her rear entrance, prodding. "Do you?"

"Yes." She gasped. "Elua, yes!"

I eased it into her, slowly. We both caught our breath when the head of it breached the tight ring of muscles. Ah, gods! She was so tight it nearly hurt, but it was so good, too. Inch by inch, I sank into her, until I'd sunk to the hilt, my testes pressed against her swollen nether-lips. Her head was turned on the pillow, her profile clean and clear, her features suffused with unspeakable pleasure.

"So full," she whispered.

I withdrew a few inches, then thrust slowly back into her. She slid one hand between her thighs, rubbing. Faster. Her hips thrust backward to receive me, urging me onward. Faster, harder; full, deep strokes. I dug my fingers into her flesh hard enough to bruise, my breath ragged. The sensation when she climaxed was indescribable, sending me over the edge in an excruciating spasm of pleasure, buried deep inside her.

For a long moment, neither of us moved.

I rested my cheek on her back. "I don't want to leave you."

"I know," she said quietly.

It took a great effort to make myself move. My limbs felt heavy, my entire body languid with pleasure. I pulled away slowly, my softening phallus slipping from her. Sidonie sighed and rolled over. I lay down beside her.

She turned her head. "Did your wounds reopen?"

I glanced down at myself. "Not much."

"That's good." Sidonie closed her eyes. "I'll go fetch that salve. In a moment."

"It can wait." I pulled her closer to me, settling her head on my uninjured left shoulder. "Stay here a while."

"All right," she murmured.

Which of us fell asleep first, I couldn't say. I heard her slow, steady breathing deepen, felt her limbs growing lax. And then there was only darkness, warmth, and peace, the low crackle of the fire dying in the hearth, the smell of lovemaking and the rain-washed scent of her hair. I slept and dreamed of joy.

FORTY-THREE

THE KNOCK AT THE DOOR of the master chamber came before sunrise. Urist and I had agreed that we should leave at the day's first light. I donned my borrowed dressing-robe and opened the door to find Isembart bearing an oil lamp.

"Forgive me, your highness," he said. "Commander Urist said you wished to be awakened." He glanced past me into the wreckage of the darkened room; the cold bath, blood-sodden bandages beside it, the remains of our dinner strewn around the floor amid shards of broken crockery. And the heir to Terre d'Ange, naked and sublimely disheveled, sitting in a tangle of bedclothes. Isembart's expression never changed. "I'll send attendants."

"My thanks." I took the lamp from him, closed the door, and eyed Sidonie. "You might put some clothes on, you know."

She smiled sleepily. "He's a steward for the Shahrizai. I daresay he's seen worse."

"Do it for my sake, then," I suggested. "Or I'll never be able to bring myself to leave."

"Mmm." A hint of regret clouded her smile. "Don't tempt me."

There was a part of me that yearned to stay. To barricade the door and return to the bed with Sidonie. To make love until we were limp and exhausted, covered in sweat and drenched with love's juices. To tie her to the bedposts and fling open the doors of the flagellary. To explore every pleasure, the sharp and the sweet alike. To forget about the world that lay beyond these four walls and lose myself in her.

But there was the matter of vengeance.

I took a deep breath, feeling my scabbed bear-gouges stretch and crackle. I thought about Dorelei, laughing and alive, our son growing in her belly. All the lovemaking in the world wasn't enough to assuage the deep ache of that grief. Berlik had rent my heart as surely as my flesh, and it was a scar I'd carry to the end of my days. I thought about the bear-witch and his sad, sad face. Somewhere to the north, Kinadius and the others were following his trail. I had to join them. There would be no lasting peace for me until Berlik was dead, and his head buried at Dorelei's feet.

And if mighty Kushiel was merciful, I'd find the chance to kill him myself.

Sidonie slid into her dressing-robe and crossed the room. She touched my face, kissing me lightly. She was the eldest child of the Cruarch of Alba and the heir to the Queen of Terre d'Ange. I didn't need to speak to her of love, honor, and duty. "There's clean water in the ewer by the washbasin. Go wash, and I'll find that salve you mentioned."

I obeyed.

She did a good job of tying the bandages, better than the first time. She was a quick study. I watched her deft fingers at work and thought about what Alais had said about her. "We talked about you," I said. "Alais and I."

Sidonie gave me a quick glance. "Did you?"

"Yes." I smiled. "She came to visit me every day in the temple, after it happened. I don't think I could have endured it without her. She said betimes it was hard to be your sister, because you're always the proper one. But that you're fierce, too, only it doesn't show. I said I knew that." I watched her mouth quirk with amusement. "She said it was hard to think about, you and I. But she promised she would, if I promised to live."

"Blessed Alais," Sidonie murmured. "I miss her."

"Berlik killed her dog," I said.

"I know." Her hands went still for a moment. "Turn around, I need to knot this in the back."

I shifted. "Did you know Alais wants to rule Alba?"

"Oh, yes." Sidonie tied the final knot. "Or at least to rule as Talorcan's equal and see their children inherit. Imriel . . ." She sighed, sitting back on her heels. I turned to face her. "Will you please go kill this man, this cursed magician, so you can avenge your wife and your unborn child, and come home and marry me so we can spend the rest of our lives making love and discussing politics?"

Her eyes were bright with tears. I swallowed. "Yes."

"Good," she said.

While we spoke, attendants arrived and set the room in order; cleaning away the mess, kindling a new fire in the hearth, bringing boiled eggs, sausages, fresh-baked bread, and an assortment of fruits. They were swift and efficient, and once they had finished, there was nothing to do but dress and eat.

And leave.

Once we were under way, I thought, it would be all right. I would feel the drumbeat of my heart calling once more for justice, calling as it had yesterday when Deordivus arrived. There would be only the keen, insistent tug of vengeance, hard and cold. But right now, the memory of last night's intimacy was too close, and the thought of leaving brought a tightness to my throat that made it hard to eat.

We both dressed in silence. I watched Sidonie brush her hair, turning a glorious tangle of locks into a smooth, shining fall. "Will you be all right at Court?" I asked her.

"I'll manage." She wound her hair into coils, pinning it artfully. "My mother's temper will cool, and you're not without sympathizers, Imriel. After all, you *are* emerging as a figure of great and terrible romance." The words were wry, but the shadow of sorrow was still there. "It will help when Phèdre and Joscelin return," she added, pausing. "What in Elua's name are they doing, anyway? 'Tis an odd time for them to be gone."

I laughed. "Unless I'm mistaken, hiding the Book of Raziel."

Her hands froze. "Does anyone else know this?"

I shook my head. "No."

"That's a grave trust you've imparted to me," she said slowly.

"I know," I said.

Sidonie set down her hairpins with an inarticulate sound, came over and kissed me. I held her hard and kissed her back. "I hate this," she whispered against my mouth. "I hate it so much." She pulled away, pressing the heels of her hands to her eyes for an instant. "You should go. This is only going to get harder. Where's your sword-belt?"

I pointed.

She fetched it, knelt, and buckled it around my waist. I drew another deep breath, testing the pressure and pain. It was bearable. She'd found the vambraces, too; rose and slid them into place, fastening the buckles. My eyes burned. "Dorelei did this for me," I said hoarsely. "The night . . ."

"Don't say it." Sidonie touched my lips with two fingers. "She loved you. I love you."

"I have to go," I said.

She nodded. "Make it swift."

Urist had everything in readiness. We were travelling light for speed. No carriages, no wagons. Only our mounts and four pack-horses. They had assembled in the narrow courtyard, ready and waiting. A stable-boy was holding the Bastard's head. I slung my saddlebags over his haunches, lashing them in place. I wasn't carrying much, either. Salve, clean bandages. A change of clothing, borrowed from the closet of the master chamber. A woolen cloak. The satchel of coin Hugues had brought. His wooden flute. The polished croonie-stone. A golden torc around my throat, a golden ring knotted around one finger.

The dawning sky was grey, holding the promise of more rain. The Cruithne were mounted and waiting. Lord Amaury Trente was there. The Dauphine's Guard was there. I glanced at the Bastard. He blew hard through flared nostrils and tossed his speckled head, doubting whether or not I was ready to ride. I wondered, too. Urist watched me without comment. He didn't say what he was thinking, but I could guess. If I could ride a woman until my half-healed wounds burst their seams, I could ride a horse. No excuses.

I didn't offer any.

Time to go.

Lord Amaury said somewhat; I don't know what. It sounded as though he wished me well. I trusted it was so, nodded, and shook the hand he offered.

Sidonie.

Her guardsmen, headed by Captain de Monluc, stood behind her in tight, neat ranks. She looked small standing in front of them, the regal tilt of her chin belying the tears in her eyes. Neat and proper.

What a lie that was.

It felt like my heart would burst.

I didn't have any words left. There was too much to say, not enough time to say it. I enfolded her in my arms and held her close, held her hard enough to hurt, hard enough to defy all the forces of the world that sought to separate us. Sidonie clung to me, burying her face against my chest. I bowed my head over hers. I didn't want to let her go, not ever. Horses snorting, a shuffling of hooves.

"Go." Sidonie pushed me.

I went.

My eyes were blurred. I took the Bastard's reins, found the stirrup, and hoisted myself blindly astride. Settled myself in the saddle. I shook my head, blinking, trying to clear my eyes. "I love you," I said roughly.

Tears shone on her cheeks. "Just come home."

Urist blew his hunting horn; a clear, clarion call, piercing the leaden dawn. Unexpectedly, Amaury Trente saluted, pressing a closed fist to his heart. His brown eyes looked over-bright. After a second's hesitation, Claude de Monluc followed suit, and so did all his men; Sidonie's guards. Another time, it might almost have made me laugh. Now it made me want to weep. Urist glanced at me.

"Ride." I cleared my throat and repeated it more strongly. "Clunderry, *ride*!"

We rode.

We rode fast and hard, thundering down the entryway and turning onto the road. Deordivus took the lead, heading unerringly north. My wounds burned and ached. I concentrated on keeping my seat. The Bastard ran smoothly beneath me, stretching his legs. I gritted my teeth and settled into the pain, welcoming it. It was a fair price to pay for the pleasure I'd taken.

Behind us, the manor house dwindled.

I don't know how long or how far we rode in that first burst. Deordivus led, but Urist set the pace. Too fast for common sense, really, but he knew what he was about. He'd watched me, he gauged me. Trees and fields passed in a green blur. Urist didn't give the order to slow for a long time. Not until the wind of our passage had blown away the sharpest of the lingering remnants of yearning and desire that clung to me, until I was able to fix my mind on the distant horizon.

"Walk!" Urist called.

We slowed to a walk.

It must have been a long time; the other horses were blown, and the Bastard was sweating, reins damp with lather. I patted his neck, then felt at my torso. If I was bleeding, it wasn't bad.

Urist ranged alongside me. "All right, lad?"

I nodded.

"Doesn't come often, does it?" There was sympathy in his voice. "Passion like that."

I gazed at the grey sky. "Gods above, I hope not."

He laughed, reached over and patted my arm. "Remember who you owe it to. Hold hard, ride hard. Do it for *her*." Urist's voice hardened. "Our lass, our sweet lass, the one who loved you enough to free you."

"She was my wife, Urist." I held his gaze. "She would have been the mother of my son. Do you truly imagine I could ever forget what I owe her?"

"No," he said after a moment. "No, I don't."

After that, he left me to ride in silence, and the others did, too. I was grateful for it. It had been a hard parting, harder than anything I could have imagined. The first time, I'd felt numb and half-dead inside. Sidonie and I had been young and uncertain. It was all different now. There was no uncertainty and all my emotions were honed to a keen edge, aching and tender. For the first time in my life, I knew, beyond any shadow of doubt, exactly what I wanted. I knew, beyond any shadow of doubt, that I was wanted in turn. And I was riding in the opposite direction.

I didn't try to hide the pain from myself. I settled into it, letting the pain in my heart echo the soreness of my wounds. In time, both would diminish and grow more bearable. I knew that now. After Dorelei's death, I hadn't thought the enormity of that grief would ever grow less raw and overwhelming, that I'd ever wake to face a new day without feeling my heart scourged anew with a tide of anguish and helpless fury.

But bit by bit, I was learning to live with it. We live, we heal, we endure. We mourn the dead and treasure the living. We bear our scars.

Some of us more than others.

There was guilt, of course. There would always be guilt. If Sidonie and I had been more brave, if we'd had the courage to trust in our love, in Blessed Elua's precept, Dorelei wouldn't have died. The shadow of that knowledge would always lie over us. That, too, I would learn to bear. So long as there was brightness, I could accept the darkness.

As we rode, I became aware that we hadn't managed to outrace gossip. It had been two days since Sidonie walked up to me in full view of the watching Palace and kissed me; one day since she'd managed to silence Barquiel L'Envers in front of a considerable audience. D'Angelines love gossip, and the news had spread fast. Every traveller we passed glanced curiously at us, and there were covertly pointing fingers, wondering stares, hushed whispers.

But they had heard the other news, too.

News of Dorelei's terrible death, of magicians and bears and dire enchantments. Of the oath of vengeance I'd sworn, of the trail that had been found. Urist and his men rode grim-faced, surrounding me, countenances forbidding comment or question, and I was glad of it, since I'd no wish to speak to anyone. Still, it seemed to me that mayhap not all of the stares were condemning. In some, especially among the commonfolk, there was a measure of awe and sympathy.

It gave me hope. I cherished it, that hope.

We made camp that night near the edge of a forest in northern L'Agnace. I was stiff, my muscles unaccustomed to riding, but not as sore as I expected to be. The overcast sky had cleared before sunset, so we didn't bother with the tents. I lay wrapped in my bedroll, gazing at the stars. I went over in my mind the memory of every moment I'd spent with Sidonie in the past day. Every moment, great and small. I polished them like jewels, examining every facet.

And then I put them away, one by one, locking them away safely in my heart. Not buried, not denied. Safe. Hidden. Like as not, we had a long, dangerous journey ahead of us. I needed my wits. I couldn't afford to be distracted, mooning endlessly over my girl. And if there was anyone in the world who would understand, it was Sidonie, with her streak of cool pragmatism; Sidonie, who'd been careless only a fateful once.

I put away the memory of her farewell last of all.

Just come home.

I slept, and dreamed of vengeance.

FORTY-FOUR

IN THE DAYS THAT FOLLOWED, we rode northward and passed through L'Agnace and Namarre and into Azzalle. Our journey was uneventful. My wounds continued to heal, my stiffness abated, and we made good time. Several days after crossing the Azzallese border, we found the bridge across the Rhenus River, and left Terre d'Ange behind. When we paid the bridge-keeper the toll and asked after a message, we found our first indication that our quest through the Flatlands wasn't going to be met with generous assistance.

"I am to be paid for the message by the fine D'Angeline lord." The bridge-keeper's eyes glinted with avarice. "So they promise, the Picts."

"How much?" I asked.

The bridge-keeper sucked his teeth. "Gold ducat."

I glanced at Deordivus. "Is that true?"

He shrugged. "What did he say? I can't make out a cursed word."

It was true, the bridge-keeper had a thick accent. We had trade relations with the Flatlands, and along the border formed by the Rhenus River they spoke some D'Angeline, but farther inland they spoke a guttural dialect resembling Skaldic. The Flatlands weren't a proper nation, but a loose consortium of farms, villages, and small merchant-guilds. For years, they'd formed a buffer between Terre d'Ange and Skaldia, neither of us reckoning them worth a great deal of bother, except when the Skaldi sought to use them as one of the staging-points for invading Terre d'Ange. Phèdre and Joscelin had first met Ghislain nó Trevalion, then called Ghislain de Somerville, at one such battle.

I discussed the matter with Deordivus, and we determined that yes,

Kinadius had promised the bridge-keeper payment, but a lesser sum. I gave the man a coin worth twenty-five silver centimes. He pocketed it and pointed northeast: "A Tsingani company come through, maybe two, three days, carrying a message from Picts. You meet them in Zoellen town, on the Issel River, at the inn with crowned goose sign. Or maybe they leave message there."

"How far?" I asked.

He shrugged again. "Your horses? Maybe two, three days."

So it began.

We followed the road north. The terrain wasn't truly flat here, not yet. In truth, except for the quality of the road, it didn't look much different from Terre d'Ange. It was the people who looked different, earthy and solid, without the unmistakable stamp of Elua or his Companions on their features. Although I'd travelled a great deal in my young life, nearly every voyage from Terre d'Ange had begun with a sea crossing. The only one that hadn't was when the Carthaginian slave-traders had taken me into Aragonia, and I'd been drugged nearly insensible. It seemed strange to cross a river and find myself in a strange land.

As in Terre d'Ange, we got a lot of curious stares. How not? A lone D'Angeline travelling with a handful of tattooed Cruithne was out of place almost anywhere in the world. Still, no one troubled us.

By the second day, the landscape flattened. Despite its lack of variety, it was a pleasant land, laced with rivers, dotted with farms and villages. The weather was mostly clear and the summer sky seemed to hover low over the land, suffused with hazy golden light. It was a small territory, heavily domesticated, lacking the wild, untamed places the Maghuin Dhonn favored. Small wonder Berlik had chosen to travel as a man, if choice it was.

Somehow, I thought not. If he'd swum across the Straits in bear form, surely he could have forded the Rhenus. And there was enough unpopulated land along it that he could have managed the crossing unnoticed. No, he'd crossed the bridge as a man, on foot, out of necessity.

I was surprised to note that the farther north we went, the more travellers we encountered, including caravans with numerous wagons of goods. Many of them seemed bound for the western coast. Thinking about it, I remembered seeing Flatlander trade-ships in Bryn Gorry-dum's harbor.

"Oh, aye," Urist said when I asked him about it. "More trade than ever, every year." He didn't sound pleased about it. "Not just Flatland-ers. They've petitioned the Cruarch on the behalf of others. He's allow-ing a bit."

There had been a Skaldic dragon-ship in the harbor, too. A recent development and a cautious one, Talorcan had said. "The Skaldi?" I said. "Well, there's naught to smooth over old quarrels like mutual profit. Mayhap it will help if we need to cross their border."

Urist grunted. "Mayhap. Not deep inside Skaldia, I'll wager that much." He rode without comment for a few minutes, then added, "It's not just the Skaldi seeking trade, either."

"Who?" I asked.

"Northerners. Wild folk." He shrugged. "Names I've never heard before. Too many to recall, speaking all manner of odd tongues. Some Flatlanders brought a shipment of goods a while back, I heard. Furs, amber. New markets and such. We're that, all right."

"Interesting," I said.

"If you say so." Urist surveyed the landscape. "It's always the fellow in the middle takes the least risk and the biggest cut, isn't it? These Flatlanders aren't stupid."

"Well, they don't look like they engage in cattle-raids for fun," I said, and he laughed.

On the third day of our journey through the Flatlands, we followed the Issel River and reached the town of Zoellen, which lay nestled alongside its banks, just south of a second river, the Voorwijk, that ran east to west. It looked to have been a small market-town that had found itself at a crossroads during a time of burgeoning trade, and grown ac-cordingly. The narrow streets were laid out in a haphazard fashion, and we wasted a good deal of time wandering them on horseback until we found the inn the bridge-keeper had indicated, sporting a sign with a goose wearing a pointed crown.

Urist and I went inside.

After we had been outdoors, it was dark and close inside the inn. I was vaguely aware of a dim figure seated at a wooden table hopping down from a stool. "Gods and goddesses of Alba be thanked!" a voice said in Cruithne, somewhat drunkenly. "You're here."

I squinted and made out a youthful face, bearing a single warrior's mark on its brow. I knew him, he'd been one of Alais' favorites at Clunderry. "Selwin? Where are the others?"

"Hunting." His voice turned glum. "We lost the trail."

"Doubt it's at the bottom of a tankard of ale," Urist observed dryly.

Selwin drew himself up with drunken dignity. "Kinadius left me here to wait for you or Talorcan," he said. "And it's very, very tedious." He nodded at the innkeeper, who smiled pleasantly at us, and dropped his voice to a whisper. "Doesn't speak a word of Cruithne or D'Angeline. I don't know how I was supposed to leave a message if we *had* found the bear-witch's trail."

"No mind," I said. "Can you take us to Kinadius?"

He hiccoughed. "Aye, my lord."

Before we left, I settled his account with the innkeeper, a business conducted largely in pantomime. I spoke some Skaldic; bits and pieces Phèdre had taught me during the learning-games we'd played when I was younger, and some gleaned from Brigitta, when we'd played similar games on the journey to Alba. Still, it was far from my mother tongue, and I had a hard time making out the innkeeper's dialect. In the end, he wrote down the tally on a slate tablet with a piece of chalk. I withdrew a few D'Angeline coins from my purse, and we pushed them around the counter together until we'd come to an agreement.

"So," the innkeeper said cheerfully. *"Pelgrim?"*

I frowned. "Pelgrim?"

He pointed northeast. "Yeshua?"

I shook my head. *"Jäger.* Hunter. We're hunting . . ." I didn't know the word for murderer, or witch, or even bear. I spread my hands helplessly. The innkeeper blinked at me, good-natured and uncomprehending, blunt-cut blond hair falling over his broad, sweating brow. I sighed and thanked him, and we took our leave.

Selwin led us, weaving slightly, to a site a few hundred yards beyond the outskirts of Zoellen, where Kinadius had made camp. I brooded as we rode the short distance. I'd not put a great deal of thought into the difficulties posed by a lack of a common tongue until now.

Save for a few bedrolls and items of little value strewn about, the encampment was empty. Selwin assured us that Kinadius and the others would return well before nightfall to report, so we set about picketing the horses and making ourselves comfortable. While we worked, Selwin grew sober enough to relate the tale of their journey to date, how they'd ridden from the border to Zoellen, crisscrossing the land and asking questions, following the rumor of Berlik's passage.

"How are you managing to communicate?" I asked.

He fished in his pack and withdrew a piece of birch-bark. "Like this."

I studied the images on it, incised with the point of a hot knife. A crude bear, its eyes white and staring. A man's face, staring eyes bracketed by claw-marks. "Clever."

Selwin stowed the bark. "We ask, they point. No bears, but there were sightings of the magician, all right. At least until we got here."

Within the hour, the others began returning in groups of two and three. Their faces lit upon seeing us, but our arrival was the only good news the day brought. Berlik's trail remained cold.

Before the sun set, Kinadius gathered his men around a patch of hard-packed dirt where a crude map had been sketched, depicting a swathe of land south of the Voorwijk River. Comparing tales, they extended the map's boundaries, adding the territory covered that day. I was impressed by their innovation and thoroughness.

"It's no good, though." Kinadius shook his head. "We've gone over every inch of country within a day's ride."

"So what do we do?" I asked. "Backtrack to the last sighting?"

He sighed. "Or forge ahead and hope to get lucky. Betimes it works."

"But if it doesn't, we lose days," one of his men added. "It's happened."

Urist peered at the map. "Where was he last seen?"

Kinadius pointed to a spot in the dirt to the southwest of his crude map. "It was around here, I reckon. A little more than a day's ride. Some lad herding cattle saw him crossing a field near sunset. Thought he was going this way." He traced a line that angled more or less north-east in the direction of Zoellen town. "So we reckoned this was a good place to make camp and cast a net. No luck, though."

"You've not crossed the river to the north?" Urist asked.

"No." Kinadius tapped his drawing-stick on the map. "There are bridges here and here, and here to the west of the Issel. No bridge-keepers, but lots of people around on foot and in boats. We spent the whole first day covering those. No one saw him cross."

"Lots of people coming and going, aye," Urist observed. "Not staying in one place. How far ahead of us is he? Weeks? Months?"

"Hard to say." Kinadius shrugged. "At a guess, two or three weeks."

"And more if we backtrack." Urist scowled in thought. "I'm for trying our luck across the river." He glanced over at me. "Unless you disagree."

I shook my head. "You're the tracker."

Kinadius grinned. "It's good to have you back, Urist."

With our course decided, we turned our attention to dinner, which consisted of cold biscuits purchased in Zoellen, and peas and salt pork simmered over the fire in a large kettle. I swabbed the inside of my wooden trencher with a hunk of biscuit, sopping up the last bit of stew, listening with regret and amusement as Deordivus described the meal he'd eaten at the Shahrizai hunting manor to the envy of Kinadius and his companions.

"What passed there in the City, my lord?" Kinadius asked me curiously. "I know Urist made Dorelei a promise to see you home, but I never understood why." His voice softened when he spoke Dorelei's name. Still, despite his feelings for her, he'd never shown any jealousy or animosity toward me. I glanced at him. He was a handsome young man, with a direct gaze and clean, bold features beneath his warrior's markings. And clever, too. They would have made a good pair, I thought, and guilt stopped my tongue.

"By the Boar!" Deordivus said. "I'll tell you, it was a hell of a scene I walked—"

"That's enough, boy!" Urist raised his voice. "Politics are a hard business," he continued in a quieter tone. "For Alba's sake, Lady Dore-

lei wed a man she barely knew, a stranger. And although he loved another, Prince Imriel did the same for Terre d'Ange. The lass wanted
him to be happy, that's all."

"Oh." Kinadius blinked. "I see."

"I'm sorry," I said to him. "Truly sorry."

"Don't suppose you could help it." A muscle in his cheek twitched.
"Funny, I thought you'd come to care for Dorelei. Lug knows, she
thought the world of you."

I held his gaze. "I'm here, aren't I?"

"I suppose so," Kinadius said slowly. "So who is she?"

"Hah!" Urist gave a fierce, mirthless grin. "That's where it gets interesting. Would you rather I tell it?" he asked me, and I nodded.

It was better coming from Urist. He was one of them, Cruithne. He
put it to Kinadius and his men the way he'd put it to me the night he'd
given me the mannekin charm to destroy and cut my bindings. I was
in love with the Cruarch's eldest daughter, the heir to Terre d'Ange.
And Queen Ysandre reckoned I was good enough for Dorelei mab
Breidaia, good enough to breed an heir for Alba, but not good enough
for her own daughter. It stung their pride; and well it should. When
all was said and done, Urist was right. I sat and listened, staring into
the campfire.

When Urist had finished, the mood had eased. With Urist's indulgence, Deordivus told the tale of the scene he'd witnessed upon
his arrival at the manor house, relating it with relish. There were more
than a few chuckles. Kinadius came over to sit beside me, his shoulder
brushing mine. For a time, neither of us spoke.

"I'm sorry," he said presently. "I didn't mean to judge you."

"My thanks." I fiddled with a dry branch, breaking off bits and
tossing them into the campfire. "You were right. I did come to love
Dorelei. A great deal."

"We all did." Kinadius propped an elbow on his knee and rested
his chin on his fist, gazing into the crackling flames. "Remember the
Day of Misrule? I've known Dorelei since we were children, and I don't
think I'd ever seen her happier. I was, too. Gods and goddesses, I nearly
pissed myself laughing at the sight of you wearing her kirtle."

I smiled. "I remember."

"I didn't expect that from a D'Angeline," he mused. "Didn't expect you to be willing to make a fool of yourself. Didn't expect you to care for Clunderry's honor."

"Didn't expect much," I said wryly.

"I do now," Kinadius said. "We *are* going to catch this bastard, aren't we?"

I lifted my head and looked toward the northeast. Somewhere in the darkness beyond our campsite, Berlik's trail awaited us. Urist's decision was right. I could feel it, a stirring in my heart. The sound of bronze wings, rustling. North. The Maghuin Dhonn had come from the northeast, so long ago the Straits were covered with ice. "Yes," I said. "Oh, yes."

Kinadius laid a firm hand on my shoulder. "I'm glad you're here."

"So am I," I said.

FORTY-FIVE

W E BROKE CAMP on the morrow and rode east along the bank of the Voorwijk River.

I'd thought Urist would want to cross at the first opportunity, but I was wrong. He frowned at the busy, well-travelled stone bridge and shook his head. We passed it and rode onward. The second bridge was smaller, wrought of timber and not brick. Here we paused. Urist cocked his head, watching a heavily laden wagon cross the wooden bridge. His tattooed nostrils flared. "What's that stink?"

Kinadius pointed downriver. "A tannery."

"Huh." Urist shaded his eyes and stared. There were figures working on the far side of the river, turning hides with large wooden paddles. "Promising."

"Why would the bear-witch visit a tannery?" someone asked.

"He wouldn't," Kinadius said. "But I'll wager those fellows working are there every day. That's your thinking, isn't it?"

Urist shrugged. "Worth a try."

We crossed the bridge and made our way to the tannery. The stink of half-cured hides grew stronger the closer we got. It seemed to be a thriving little business. As we approached, a tall man came out to meet us in the yard, wiping his hands on an apron and eyeing us with open curiosity. He greeted us in the Flatlander dialect, sounding pleased and quite incomprehensible.

All the Cruithne looked at me.

"*Gud morgen,*" I said awkwardly. "*Wir jäger sind . . . wir sind jag ein mann.* A man, we're hunting a man." I beckoned to Kinadius. "Lend me your drawing, will you?"

I dismounted and showed it to the tanner, who nodded vigorously. *"Ja, ja!"* he said. *"Der Bär-Mann!"* then added a swift burst I couldn't understand. The tanner laughed and laid his hands on my shoulders. *"D'Angeline, ja?"*

"Ja," I said. *"D'Angeline."*

He turned and shouted toward the complex of buildings that made up the tannery. A woman emerged, hurring toward us. Like the tanner, she was of middle years, with a face that must have been pretty before work and care took their toll. The tanner said somewhat about her— his wife, he called her—in a proud voice. She beamed at me, clapping her hands together in obvious pleasure.

"A D'Angeline!" She bobbed a curtsy. "How we may help you, my lord? Fine leather? Maybe for boots? Or very fine, maybe for gloves?"

Her accent was thick, but her D'Angeline was more than passable. I smiled at her in relief. "Not today, my lady. We're searching for a man . . . or mayhap a bear." I showed her the drawing. "Have you seen him?"

Her eyes widened. "That one! Yes, he was here."

My heart lifted. *"Here?"*

"Yes, yes." She nodded. "A pelgrim, with the others."

I shook my head. "No, not a pilgrim. *This* man."

"This man, the bear-man." She took the drawing from me, tracing the incised claw-marks. "Yes, he was here." She turned to her husband and they exchanged a quick flurry of words. "Come," she said to me. "I show."

Urist and Kinadius dismounted to join me. The tanner and his wife led us into a warehouse filled with piles of cured hides in varying levels of quality. He rummaged in one and brought forth a luxuriant armload of fur, presenting it to me with a smile.

A bearskin robe.

I caught my breath, lightheaded and sick. Beneath the pervasive stench of the tannery, I could smell rank musk and sour berries, the scent of the Maghuin Dhonn. Urist and Kinadius exclaimed in Cruithne, the words suddenly as alien to my ear as Skaldic. My healing wounds burned. I shook my head, trying to clear it, and my knees nearly gave way beneath me.

It was Urist who led me out of the warehouse. In the yard, I sat beneath a linden tree and lowered my head, taking deep breaths until the worst of the dizziness passed. The tanner's wife pressed a cup of cool water into my unsteady hand, her face worried. I drank it and thanked her.

"I am sorry," she said. "He is your friend, this man?"

"Friend!" I laughed bitterly. "Elua, no!"

The tanner's wife frowned. "But he is Pict, like them."

"He killed my wife," I said shortly.

Her mouth hung open in shock. She turned to her husband. Another exchange, low and murmured. The tanner, the bearskin robe draped over one shoulder, looked troubled. "I do not think it is the same man," his wife said at length, a stubborn reluctance settling into her voice.

I leaned my head against the trunk of the tree. With careful hands, I undid the buttons on my shirt. Kinadius knelt beside me, grave as an acolyte, and undid the knots on my bandages, helped me unwind them and lay bare the gouges that angled across my torso, raking furrows of pink flesh and a patchwork of lingering scabs.

"His work," I said. "The bear-man's." The tanner's wife pressed the back of her hand to her lips. I held her shocked gaze. "Please, my lady. Will you help us find him?"

She nodded. "All right, yes."

While Kinadius rewound my bandages, the tanner's wife told us that Berlik had arrived at the tannery some days ago—three weeks, she thought, or mayhap a little more—in the company of a group of Yeshuite pilgrims. There had been a good many of them in recent years, seeking passage to the distant north; beyond Skaldia, where it was rumored they were building a kingdom. There had been ten or twelve of them, she thought. Two families, and Berlik. They had an ox-drawn wagon and two horses. They had stopped at the tannery to purchase leather and twine to repair a broken harness. Berlik had offered to trade his bearskin robe in exchange for this and other supplies. It was a good bargain.

"He seemed . . . sad and kind," the tanner's wife said, wondering. "So big, but gentle. There was a child with them—" She glanced at my face and fell silent.

"Did they say where they were bound?" I asked.

She shook her head. "They went east, along the Voorwijk. They didn't say where. But if they follow the pilgrims' route, they go to Maarten's Crossing to ask Adelmar of the Frisii for passage across Skaldia."

"Adelmar?" I asked.

Urist cleared his throat. Although he had difficulty with her accent, he recognized the name. "He's the one petitioned the Cruarch for trade rights," he said in his clumsy D'Angeline. "Holds the western border, I believe."

"Yes." The tanner's wife nodded. "A good man, a man of peace. A friend to pilgrims."

"I see." I felt slow and stupid. We were little more than three days' ride from the northern border of Terre d'Ange, and yet I knew less of my surroundings than Urist, who was a good deal farther from home. As always, I had a lot to learn. I rubbed my face. "Thank you, my lady. You've been a great help."

"I wish you well." The tanner's wife wrung her hands, restless. Strong hands, work-worn and thick-knuckled, yellowish from a lifetime of handling oak-tanned hides. I wondered at her fluent D'Angeline, at the pride in the tanner's voice when he spoke of her. There was a story there I'd never know. She gazed at me with deep concern. "But I think . . . I think this man, the bear-man you hunt . . . if he has truly done such a thing, I think he is sorry for it. There is great sorrow in him."

"There always was," I murmured. "But he did it anyway."

"That is a great pity," she said.

"Yes." I pushed myself to my feet, eyeing the bearskin robe her husband yet held. The sight of it no longer sickened me, but I detested its existence. "My lady, I wish to purchase that robe. I mistrust its magic, and you would be better off without it."

Urist nodded approvingly.

At least it was familiar ground for everyone. We haggled. In the end, I made them a good bargain; more than fair. They deserved it, the

tanner and his wife. We rode away from the tannery, following a course
eastward along the bank of the Voorwijk River, with Berlik's bearskin
robe stowed in our baggage, carried by an unnerved pack-horse.

I didn't blame the horse. The scent made me uneasy, too.

"What do you mean to do with it?" Urist asked as we rode.

"Destroy it," I said.

He smiled. "Good."

That evening, we made camp along the banks of the Voorwijk.
After picketing the Bastard, I sat down with Berlik's robe and set about
slicing it into strips, pausing periodically to hone my daggers. The fur
was dense and thick, rippling in my hands. A smell of musk clung to
my skin. I ignored it, working methodically. Strip, strip, strip. It was
hard work. Kinadius joined me, raising an inquiring brow. I nodded.
He beckoned. Others came, cutting the strips into smaller scraps. Urist
gave quiet orders, and several men set about gathering wood. A massive
bonfire was built, fire roaring heavenward. It was the largest fire I'd
seen since the Feast of the Dead.

When we had finished cutting it to shreds, we burned the bearskin
robe, piece by piece. Everyone took an armload of scraps. We fed them
into the fire, one by one. The fur sizzled and stank as it flared and
crisped, leaving bits of hide to curl and slowly char.

I didn't know if Berlik's robe held any enchantment, not for sure.
Morwen hadn't needed one, and I'd seen her body shift and change
in the darkness. I'd seen her pry loose a boulder that two strong men
wouldn't be able to lift. Mayhap the robe was meaningless, nothing
more than a badge of office, indicating his status as a magician of the
Maghuin Dhonn. Or mayhap it wasn't. If he'd crossed the Straits as
a bear, the robe had crossed with him somehow. And yet, if it was
charmed, why would Berlik have traded it for some leather goods and
supplies?

In the end, I didn't care. It was his, and there was a tremendous,
irrational satisfaction in destroying it. All of us felt it.

Once it was done, we let the fire burn down low, slowly collapsing
in on itself. It was too late to cook, so we ate cold rations that night.
Urist passed around a skin of *uisghe* he'd held in reserve, and we all had
a few swallows, watching the fire.

"One step closer," Kinadius murmured. "Feels like it, anyway."

Urist grunted. "But why pilgrims? Doesn't make sense." He slewed his gaze around at me. "Who are these pilgrims? Some sort of mad D'Angelines?"

"Yeshuites," I said. "And no, it doesn't make sense."

"What's a Yeshuite?" he asked.

At least what knowledge I possessed wasn't totally useless. I told them about the One God of the Habiru—the god whose angel Rahab had once bound the Master of the Straits—and how he had sent his son Yeshua ben Yosef to earth during the time of the Tiberian Empire. How the Habiru had hailed him as their savior, their *mashiach*. How the Tiberians had feared an uprising and convicted Yeshua, hanging him on a criminal's cross. How Blessed Elua was born of his blood, mingled with the tears of his beloved, Mary of Magdala, nurtured in the womb of the earth.

"But you said they weren't D'Angelines," Selwin said, bewildered.

"They're not," I said. "We share a point of origin, but little else." And so I explained how while Blessed Elua wandered the earth, causing rebellion in heaven, and came to be joined by his Companions and founded Terre d'Ange, the Habiru reckoned him misbegotten and followed their own course, revering Yeshua, and came to be known as the Yeshuites. Like the Tsingani, they had no fixed realm of their own. Unlike the Tsingani, they aspired to one. "There's a prophecy in their sacred books that says Yeshua will return to raise his people to greatness," I said. "And that they should make a place in the cold lands to await him."

"Reckon it's true?" Kinadius asked.

"I don't know." I propped my bedroll against the Bastard's saddle and reclined, easing my sore body. I thought about Morit and the scholars who had visited Terre d'Ange, spending so many hours in Phèdre's salon discussing these very matters. They came from distant Saba, where the lost Tribe of Dân maintained the old ways of the Habiru. They'd reckoned the entire notion madness, and of a surety there was great power and wisdom held in trust by their priests. But then, they knew little of Yeshua. "The wisest Yeshuite I know, a man named

Eleazar ben Enoch, said some passages suggest it's true, and others do not. The Yeshuites themselves are divided on the matter."

Urist snorted. "You see? That's the trouble with trusting to written words."

I smiled. "You have a point."

It was growing late. I closed my eyes and tried to remember what else Eleazar ben Enoch had said. He was a scholar and a mystic, a good man, gentle and kind. Phèdre admired him greatly. Something about believing that the *mashiach* spoke in parables, that the cold land was the empty places of the human heart. I didn't share his faith, but I could appreciate its beauty when he spoke of it.

All of that was true. And I could imagine it might be true of Berlik, too. I would be unwise to let my grief and hatred blind me. I couldn't imagine that he would ever forsake his own faith any more than I would, but he had struck me as a man who thought and felt deeply. I didn't believe he'd acted out of malice. I understood what the tanner and his wife had seen in him, and I was willing to believe he was filled with sorrow at what he perceived was the necessity of his actions.

It didn't matter. He had done it anyway. If the Maghun Dhonn had spoken openly of their visions, mayhap it all could have been different. Mayhap there was somewhat that could have been done. If I'd known they'd seen Dorelei's death in childbirth, I could have insisted that she be attended by a trained chirurgeon. Mayhap that alone would have been enough. But the Maghuin Dhonn hadn't trusted us with their truths. They'd simply tried to alter fate on their own. Berlik had slain Dorelei in cold blood, slain our unborn son in the womb. And for that, I would kill him. Kushiel's justice demanded it. The gods are merciful, but they are just, too. There was no repentance, no atonement that could ever suffice.

All of that was true, too. And I daresay in his heart of hearts, Berlik knew it. He was a murderer, and forsworn. There was no redemption for him, not in this life.

So what in Elua's name was he doing travelling with Yeshuite pilgrims?

FORTY-SIX

URIST CAME UP WITH a theory the following day.

We rode east along the Voorwijk River, stopping to make queries at farmsteads along the way. The drawing of Berlik elicited blank stares and shaking heads, but *pelgrims* got cheerful *ja, ja*s. Everyone had seen pilgrims passing. In fact, we saw a group ourselves, travelling with a canvas-covered wagon. Their olive-skinned features stood out among the fair Flatlanders, as distinctive as Tsingani or Cruithne.

"Cover," Urist said simply. "Disguise."

"He's a big man, Urist," Kinadius said doubtfully. "With tattoos."

Urist pointed at the wagon. "Aye, and the tanner's wife said the pilgrims had a wagon. Easy enough to hide a man in a wagon, even a big man."

"Why would they do such a thing?" Kinadius argued.

"Money?" Urist suggested. "He traded his robe to buy goods for them."

"There was a Yeshuite family hid Phèdre and Joscelin in a wagon, once," I said slowly. "They might do it out of kindness."

Domnach spat on the ground. "For that one?"

"They don't know what he's done," I said. "The tanner's wife liked him well enough."

"Aye, and he showed his face at the tannery," Kinadius observed. "Why? Makes no sense if he's trying to pass unnoticed."

"Mayhap he reckoned there was little risk," Urist said pragmatically. "Outside of leather merchants and folks in dire need, who in their right mind visits a tannery?"

There was no way of knowing for sure. By midday, when we'd failed to encounter any definitive sightings of Berlik, Urist and Kinadius conferred and called a halt. We made camp and split our forces, riding out in pairs. Doubling back, riding forward, casting a wider net toward the north. For all we knew, Berlik and the pilgrims had parted ways shortly after leaving the tannery.

I rode with Cailan, the wise-woman's son. The course we were assigned lay due north. We stopped and made inquiries at every farmstead and hamlet we encountered; asking at every mill, of every drover and goatherd. Over and over again, we showed the drawing of Berlik. *Der Bär-Mann*, I asked, remembering what the tanner had called him. Heads shook. I asked about *pelgrims*, too, to no avail. It seemed the tanner's wife was right on that score. The pilgrims' route lay east, heading toward Maarten's Crossing.

It was a tedious business, and it filled me with new admiration for Kinadius and his men, who had already put in so many long, tireless days. I hadn't reckoned until now what a truly daunting task it was, seeking a single man in a strange land. By the time Cailan gauged the angle of the sun and reckoned we'd best turn back, I was filled with relief.

There was a good stretch of empty meadow we'd crossed on our outward journey. I gave the Bastard his head there, letting him stretch his legs. Cailan's grey worked hard to keep the pace, sides laboring, hooves pounding. I took pity on him and slowed.

Cailan came alongside me, smiling. "You're feeling better."

I hadn't thought about it. "It still hurts, but it doesn't pull like it used to."

He nodded. "That's good."

Unfortunately, it was the best news of the day. We straggled back to the campsite in pairs, everyone tending to their own mounts. I led the Bastard to the river and let him drink his fill, walking him for a while before picketing him. There was good grazing here, and although we carried grain, we doled it out only as necessary. I checked his striped hooves, peering at them for stones. He snorted, snuffling my hair.

One by one, everyone reported.

Nothing.

No sightings of Berlik, not anywhere. No sightings of *pelgrims*, either, except along the eastern road. We sat around the campfire, discouraged, eating stewed peas and salt pork with stale biscuits.

"So!" Urist slapped his knee and glared at us. "We have a choice."

I listened to them argue. In the end, it was simple. If Berlik had stayed with the pilgrims, they were bound for Maarten's Crossing. We were travelling light. We could make up days riding there straightaway. And if we were wrong, we'd have to double back. All the way to the tannery to begin the process over again.

"What do *you* choose?" Urist asked me.

I spread my hands. "As I said the other day, you're the tracker. I'm willing to defer to your judgment, Urist."

"You know what I know." His face was implacable. "Either way, we gamble. This choice lies with the lord of Clunderry."

I tilted my chin, gazed at the emerging stars. Somewhere, mayhap not very far, the same stars looked down on the magician. I wondered if Berlik knew we were after him. I wondered if he'd already seen how it ended, there in the stone circle. I thought about the glimpse of the future that Dorelei had seen during the early days of our marriage. Hyacinthe had seen it, too. A snowstorm, a barren tree. Me, kneeling, sword in hand.

Weeping.

I wondered why.

"He's bound for a cold land," I said. "Mayhap the pilgrims' route suits his purposes as well as any. Let's try it."

Urist nodded. "So be it."

With the decision made, we turned in, wrapping ourselves in our bedrolls. Urist hadn't said it, but all of us knew he'd drive us hard on the morrow, and the next day and the next, as long as it took to reach Maarten's Crossing.

I slept soundly and rose early enough to perform my Cassiline exercises. Cailan was right, I was feeling better. I concentrated on ignoring the pain, and for the first time in weeks, the movements felt smooth and natural. Not effortless, not anywhere near it, but my body was remembering what it was like to be whole. When I finished telling the hours, I wasn't trembling. Urist eyed me without comment, then gave the order to break camp and saddle our mounts.

We rode to Maarten's Crossing.

It took five days, during which time the terrain grew wilder and less domesticated. Our road followed the Voorwijk, and it was still fairly well travelled by merchants, but to the north, we began to pass forests instead of farmsteads. It made me uneasy. I daresay all of us had the same thought. If Berlik was minded to part ways with the pilgrims, he could have done it anywhere. And once the magician plunged into the forests, there was little hope of finding him. The Maghuin Dhonn were at home in wild places, more so even than the Cruithne.

Although it was a futile task, Urist kept his eyes sharp as we rode, his gaze fixed along the roadside for any signs of a big man's tracks breaking away and heading north. If anyone could spot them, it would be Urist. He didn't, of course. If we'd been a day or two behind Berlik, he might have had a chance. Not after three weeks, not along a well-trodden road.

Still, he tried.

For my part, I prayed. The responsibility for the decision weighed heavily on me. I held rank here and I'd claimed this quest for my own. Urist had been right to push me into making the choice. But I couldn't help fearing I'd chosen wrong, couldn't help fearing we'd lost Berlik's trail. And I was acutely aware, the farther we rode, that we were headed for the border of Skaldia.

On the sixth day, we reached Maarten's Crossing. It was a big place, bigger than I'd reckoned. Once, I daresay it hadn't been much more than an outpost in the woods, but like Zoellen and Bryn Gorrydum and so many other places, it had grown a great deal in the last decade. Unlike other places, its growth appeared planned.

We'd thought to make camp on the outskirts, but the entire town was enclosed in a vast wooden palisade with guards posted at the gate.

Skaldi guards.

There were only two of them, but there was a gatehouse above the entrance, and I'd no doubt other guards were within shouting distance. Our company drew rein, eyeing the guards. They regarded us with sharp interest. Not hostile, but not welcoming, either. There was nothing to do but present ourselves.

"They might grant you a warmer welcome," I said to Urist. "Terre d'Ange isn't trading openly with Skaldia yet. There's a lot of bad blood lingering."

He grimaced. "It's not like we can hide your pretty face, lad! You should have listened to me and gotten your warrior's markings. Besides, I don't speak a word of Skaldic."

I sighed. "Right."

Urist deigned to accompany me. We dismounted and approached the guards on foot. Tall and strapping, the both of them, one blond and one ruddy-haired. They towered over wiry Urist, and stood a half-head taller than me. Small wonder Eamonn had been able to pass himself off as a Skaldi. The blond folded his arms across his chest and stared down at me.

"*D'Angeline,*" he said with distaste. "*Was wünschen Sie?*"

At least it was a familiar dialect. I explained in my mangled Skaldic that we were following the pilgrims, hunting for the bear-man. I showed them the drawing of Berlik. The blond laughed and bracketed his eyes with splayed fingers, then nodded and with one hand indicated a big man, a few inches taller than he was. A profound wave of relief swept over me.

"Is he here?" I asked. "*Ist hier?*"

They shook their heads and conferred, looking amused. The ruddy-haired one pointed at the sun and held up both hands, twice. Ten fingers, twice. Twenty days. He made a dismissive gesture and said something that clearly meant, *Go away, D'Angeline.*

"Adelmar," Urist said slowly and deliberately. "A-del-mar." He pointed at himself, then me, then the other Cruithne, making a sweeping gesture toward the west. "Alba. Cruarch. Adelmar."

The blond cast a dubious eye over us. "Cruarch?"

"Do you see this, you hulking idiots?" Urist said in a firm, reasonable tone. While I prayed silently that neither guard spoke a word of Cruithne, he tapped the golden torc around my neck. "Drustan mab Necthana, the Cruarch of Alba, gave this to him with his own hands. He's a Prince of Alba, and he's here on the Cruarch's business. And if your sodding Adelmar wants to continue enjoying trade rights with the Cruarch of Alba, believe me, he will see us."

I glanced at Urist. He gave a slight shrug.

And against all odds, it worked. After a good deal of rapid deliberation, the guards admitted us. The blond pointed in several different directions, giving me information I could only guess at. I thanked him graciously.

"What was that all about?" Urist asked.

"Damned if I know," I said.

Inside the palisade, I began to piece it together. There was a large cleared area where pilgrims and merchant caravans alike were encamped. Beyond lay the town proper, timber-built, laid out in a neat grid. It looked to be bustling, filled with Skaldi and Flatlanders and wealthier Yeshuite pilgrims. Many of the latter were wearing caps of bleached muslin embroidered with a flared crimson cross. Somewhere near the center, a great hall loomed. Adelmar, the guard had said, pointing toward it.

I explained what I thought the guard had meant. "We can camp freely or seek lodgings at an inn. The great hall, that's where we petition for an audience with Adelmar."

Urist shrugged. "Why waste time?"

I glanced around at our company. "We don't exactly look like a delegation from the Cruarch of Alba, Urist. We look like twenty-odd men who've been riding hard and living rough."

He snorted. "You just want a bath."

"It wouldn't hurt you, either," I retorted.

In the end, we decided that the bulk of our company would make camp, while five of us lodged at an inn. I picked Urist and Kinadius to accompany me, while the others drew straws for the privilege. A smug Deordivus drew one, while the other fell to one of the older veterans, a solid fellow named Brun. A good balance, I thought.

We left our mounts in the picket-line at the camp and entered Maarten's Crossing on foot. I felt pricklish and wary. Skaldi sauntered along the streets, longswords strapped to their backs, staring openly at us.

Get used to it, I told myself.

We were in Skaldia.

There was no trouble finding an inn. I picked the place at random, simply because the sign above the door—a proud rooster—reminded me of the Cockerel at home. It was run by a heavyset blonde Skaldi woman who took one look at me and beamed. "D'Angeline!" she cried, with considerable more enthusiasm than any of the men had showed.

"D'Angeline," I agreed, ignoring my companions' snickers.

I was just glad to be esconced peaceably. The proprietress, Halla, had no husband in evidence, but several tall daughters, ranging in age from some sixteen years to a few years older than me. They were fresh-faced and bright-eyed, eager and curious, and uncomfortably attentive. When I pantomimed filling a tub and bathing, they laughed and led me to a small room with a wooden tub, bringing buckets of cold, clean water.

"Baden?" one asked hopefully, holding a sponge.

"I'll manage," I assured them.

They lingered, watching me undress, oohing and ahhing at the sight of my wounds when I managed to get the bandages off. Since they didn't seem inclined to leave, I gave up on any attempt at modesty and asked them questions while I sat in the tub and scrubbed away the layers of grime that a dunk in the river never seemed to erase. I didn't learn much—none of the innkeeper's daughters had seen the bear-man—but my efforts to communicate amused them. There were worse ways to practice Skaldic, I suppose.

Once I'd finished, Urist and the others had a turn, albeit without the same level of solicitous attention. We rummaged through our packs to find our least filthy attire, although there wasn't much to choose from. Everything I owned smelled like horse. Well and so, I thought; if it doesn't trouble the innkeeper's daughters, I suppose it won't both Adelmar of the Frisii.

Clean and combed, we departed the inn and made our way to the great hall. I'd expected another confrontation, but to my surprise, the guards admitted us without any argument, pointing the way to a large antechamber filled with petitioners.

There we waited.

And waited.

There was a man in charge, a burly fellow with a heavy silver chain around his neck, trailed by an assistant carrying a scroll. He took our names on our arrival, giving us a long, hard look before bidding his assistant write them down. I made a point of repeating "Cruarch" and "Alba" several times, but it didn't appear to make an impression on him.

"Petty official," Urist said sourly. "He wants to make us sweat."

"Why don't we just go?" Deordivus asked. "We know the bear-witch was here. All we have to do is follow his trail like before."

I'd been watching while various petitioners were admitted beyond the antechamber, and others emerged. No one in the antechamber had one of those odd muslin caps, but a family of pilgrims were clutching them as they returned from their audience with Adelmar, chattering excitedly with one another. "Because this Adelmar can grant us passage across Skaldia to wherever it is they're bound," I said, nodding at them. "I think that's what the hats signify. I've a feeling we'd be a great deal less likely to get killed sporting those."

"We're not exactly pilgrims," Kinadius observed.

"No, but the Skaldi understand honor." I thought about Joscelin challenging Waldemar Selig to the holmgang outside the gates of Troyes-le-Mont. "It's worth a try."

Hours passed.

To my delight, I overheard another pilgrim family conversing in Habiru. I understood it better than I spoke it, but I'd learned a fair bit in Saba, and I hadn't lost it. I passed the time conversing with them and learned they were from a Flatlander town not far from Zoellen, and were bound for the northern kingdom.

"Vralia," the young husband said reverently. "So it is called after the new king."

"Vralia?" I tasted the word.

He nodded. "You know of it?"

I shook my head. "Tell me."

For the better part of an hour, he regaled me with tales of distant Vralia. It seemed for long years, the Yeshuite presence had merely been tolerated without making much impact on the fierce land, which was cold and harsh, and filled with quarrelsome tribes. The Yeshuites had built their settlements and defended them from raiding nomads. One of their leaders, a man named Micah ben Ximon, was a warrior of great renown. Stories of his prowess had been filtering through the Yeshuite community for years.

"It is said that he can best any swordsman with only a pair of daggers," the young Habiru man, whose name was Yoel, told me. "As was foretold. 'And he shall carve out the way before you, and his blades shall shine like a star in his hands.'"

My skin prickled. "Like so?" I crossed my forearms in the Cassiline manner.

Yoel's eyes widened. "You do know this tale!"

I laughed softly. "I know its beginning. Go on, my friend."

He told me how what power there was lay in the hands of the Vralings, ruling from the city of Vralgrad. How two brothers, Tadeuz and Fedor, had quarrelled over the throne some eight years ago. Fedor, the younger, had raised an army in rebellion, courting the wild Tatars and filling his ranks with them. He had been poised to overthrow Tadeuz, who sent in desperation for the renowned Yeshuite warrior, Micah ben Ximon.

"Ben Ximon told him, if you place your faith in Yeshua, I will lead your army to victory in his name," Yoel said. "And he did. It is said a great miracle took place that day." His face shone. "Now Tadeuz Vral rules in Yeshua's name. Truly, Yeshua's kingdom lives in the north!"

I kept my mouth shut on the thought that while he might rule in Yeshua's name, this Tadeuz Vral had seen fit to call his kingdom after his own name. "What happened to the rebel brother?"

"Imprisoned." Yoel smiled. "A Yeshuite king is a compassionate king."

I would have spoken longer with him, but the burly official summoned them. He then peered at his assistant's list, running a thick finger down the names written there. "Come tomorrow," he said to us in Skaldic. "Too late today."

I groaned. "It's very . . ." I couldn't think of the word for "important" or "urgent." I did my best to argue with him, but his expression hardened.

"Tomorrow!" he thundered.

The guards posted at the antechamber door began to take an uncomfortable interest in us. "Fine," I said reluctantly. "Tomorrow."

I broke the news to Urist and the others. Deordivus was angry, but Urist took it in stride. "We had a piece of luck at the tannery," he said philosophically. "And another one choosing to follow the pilgrims. Not every day's a lucky one."

"Let's hope tomorrow is," I said.

FORTY-SEVEN

ON THE MORROW we learned that Adelmar of the Frisii was a shrewd man.

We had to wait two hours that morning before we were summoned to an audience with him. For a ruler with the power to grant us safe passage through Skaldia, he wasn't a terribly prepossessing figure; middle years, average height, with thinning blond hair and sallow features. But he watched me coolly as I bowed and stammered through a greeting in my tortured Skaldic, and what he thought, I couldn't guess.

"Perhaps you would prefer to speak Caerdicci?" he asked in that tongue when I finished.

"Elua, yes!" I laughed, startled. "Thank you, my lord."

Adelmar smiled thinly. "Some of us *are* educated." He arched one brow. "I'll own, I'm curious. What brings one lone D'Angeline to our midst in the company of a group of Albans? You're either brave, foolhardy, or both."

I explained.

It took a while.

He listened without interrupting, studying my face. At one point, he glanced away to shuffle through some papers on a side table. When I faltered, he merely beckoned for me to continue. At last I finished. He propped his chin on one hand and regarded me. "I would very much like to believe you're a raving madman," he mused. "Unfortunately, I do remember this man of whom you speak, very clearly indeed. And my men have asked questions. It seems the women of Maarten's Crossing are filled with gossip about the young D'Angeline staying at Halla's inn. Terrible scars, it seems."

"I've not lied to you, my lord," I said.

"You should have," Adelmar said bluntly. "You should have told me you were pilgrims."

"Would you have believed me?" I asked.

His brown eyes glinted with amusement. "Not likely."

"Safe passage," I said. "That's all we ask. We're travelling swiftly. If he sticks to the pilgrims' route, we'll catch him within three weeks' time. A month, at most."

"It's not that simple." Adelmar rose to pace the room, hands clasped behind his back. "You're too young to remember the war, I suppose?"

"I was born after it ended," I said.

"I'll wager *he* remembers it." He paused in front of Urist, who favored him with an unblinking stare. "We might have faced one another on the battlefield, he and I, along the banks of the Rhenus. Neither of us much older than you are today, young prince. And do you know what I discovered?" he asked. I shook my head. "I don't have a taste for war," Adelmar said grimly. "Waldemar Selig was a great man, but he had a great man's impatience. I am a lesser man, but a patient one. After Skaldia's defeat, while my countrymen retreated to lick their wounds, I saw what the future might hold when Alba opened for trade. And I set about building a lesser empire than Selig envisioned, built on trade, and not glory."

I nodded. "So did many along the Caerdicci border."

"Yes," he said. "I studied among them. Unfortunately, my holdings here are isolated. We don't lie on the Caerdicci trade routes. So I looked east to Alba, and south to the Flatlands. And I looked north. Recently, the north looked back."

"Vralia?" I asked.

"An interesting man, Tadeuz Vral." Adelmar gave me another thin smile. "We held a meeting, he and I, along the southern border of his fledgling empire. He made me promises; promises of fur and amber and timber, promises of a vast, growing market for trade. And I made him a promise. I promised to grant safe passage through Skaldia for the

Yeshuite pilgrims with which he thinks to build a mighty kingdom in the north."

"Berlik's no pilgrim," I said.

"Can you gauge a man's heart so surely?" he asked. "He came to me as a pilgrim. Those with whom he was travelling spoke eloquently on his behalf. I saw no violence in him, only sorrow."

"He's not a Yeshuite!" I raised my voice. "Name of Elua, man! He's a magician of the Maghuin Dhonn. The people he was with—whoever they are, he's only just met them."

"A man's heart may change in a day," Adelmar said dryly. "Tadeuz Vral claims that his did. And he is a valuable ally."

"Are you refusing our request?" I asked.

He was silent for a moment. "I have no great wish to offend the Cruarch of Alba and the Queen of Terre d'Ange. If you were to return with a large delegation and a generous offering of thanks, enough to offset the ill will it would generate among my people and allow me to assuage Vralia's anger, I might be swayed. But, no. For the sake of one young D'Angeline prince's honor and a ragtag band of Albans, I can't afford to grant it."

"It would take weeks!" I protested. "We'd lose his trail altogether."

Adelmar shook his head. "I'm sorry."

I sighed. "Then we'll follow him without your blessing."

"And you'll die doing it," he said bluntly. "You don't have enough men, boy. I can keep the peace in Maarten's Crossing, and the Skaldi have no quarrel with the Yeshuites. You and your men, you're another matter. You'll be challenged before you've gone ten leagues. If you're lucky, you'll end up a slave in someone's steading. Take my advice. There may be things worth dying for, but revenge isn't one of them. Go home, find a pretty girl to warm your bed. Marry her, start anew." His mouth twisted. "A good-looking D'Angeline lad like you, I imagine you could take your pick."

"Not quite," I said. "My lord, will you forgive me if I take a moment to convey your words to my men?"

He waved a hand, then reached for a stack of papers. "Go ahead."

I told them, speaking in Cruithne, quick and low. Urist grunted at the bad news. "You sent a man to fetch Talorcan when you first found the trail, right?" he asked Kinadius, who nodded. "I imagine he'll bring a sizable delegation, all right."

"But no suitable bribe," I said. A second thought struck me. "Elua! Did we leave word for him after we decided to follow the pilgrims' route?"

In the excitement of the hunt, no, we hadn't.

"It's not too late," Urist said pragmatically. "We can send word back to Zoellen town. Send word to Queen Ysandre, too, asking for bribe money." His hard gaze rested on me. "Do you reckon she'll agree, or is she too angry at you for bedding her daughter?"

I raked a hand through my hair, tense and frustrated. "No. I don't know. It's what Drustan would want. I daresay she'll put aside her anger to honor his wishes. Urist, are you suggesting we wait here and let the trail grow cold?"

Adelmar set down his papers, cocking his head and watching us.

"Not all of us." Urist shrugged. "Send a couple of the young ones to fetch Talorcan and plead with the Queen. Imriel, Kinadius . . . you should wait here to meet them. The old guard and I will follow the bear-witch's trail into Skaldia, see how far we get." He glanced sidelong at Brun, his fellow veteran. "Like old times, eh?" Brun grinned and nodded slowly.

I thought about Dorelei's head turned on the table, her lifeless eyes. "I can't let you do it. Not without me."

"Why not?" Urist asked. "It's all we've ever known, lad. We're warriors, we're not afraid of a warrior's death. You're young. You've known grief, aye, but you've got a beautiful girl at home waiting for you." His gaze softened. "Don't throw your life away, lad."

I thought about Sidonie, too. The way she had touched Urist's arm and thanked him, the way she hadn't asked me not to go. The guilt that lay between us. I loved her, I loved her so much it hurt. But I knew, for a surety, that if I let Urist and his men ride into Skaldia to face death while I waited in safety for reinforcements at Maarten's Crossing, the guilt would eat me alive. "I can't do it, Urist. It's too much. Either we all stay, or I ride with you."

"I'm not staying," he said curtly.

"Then I'm going with you," I said.

We were deadlocked and stubborn, and we would have stayed that way a long time if Adelmar hadn't interrupted. "You seem to be quarrelling with your Alban commander," he observed in Caerdicci.

"Yes, my lord." I didn't bother explaining. "We will send for a delegation and a proper petition. But some of us will follow the magician's trail."

He pursed his lips, picked up a stack of papers and squared them, tapping them on the side table. I was silent, watching him wrestle with an inner decision. "What if I told you there was another way to find him?" he said at length. "A better way."

The gist of it was this: Adelmar of the Frisii knew where Berlik's pilgrims were bound in Vralia. He was a careful man and he kept careful records. He recorded the name, origin, and destination of every pilgrim to whom he granted safe passage. The families Berlik was travelling with hailed from a small village along the Rhenus, and they were headed for Kargad, another small village south of Vralgrad along the Ulsk River.

The pilgrims' route lay overland, northeast. But there was another way, a swifter way. Merchant ships were plying a route across the Eastern Sea, forging trade routes all the way from Vralgrad to the Skaldic port of Norstock.

"There's a Flatlander caravan bound for Norstock on the morrow," Adelmar said. "Carrying wool for a Vralian trade-ship. They've got a writ of safe passage and an escort of men loyal to me. I reckon I could allow one or two of you to ride with them as far as Norstock without causing too much trouble. One or two."

"What about passage to Vralgrad?" I asked.

Adelmar shook his head. "No business of mine. But Vralians are a curious folk. I reckon if you kept your mouth shut about hunting pilgrims, you'd find passage aboard their ship, all right. And if you happen to find yourself in Kargad before the pilgrims arrive, whatever you do there—and whatever happens to you afterward—well, it's no business of mine."

It was a risk, a major risk. "Can I give you our answer on the morrow?"

"I'll send word to the wool-merchant." Adelmar gave his thin smile.

"Ernst's his name. If you want to take my offer, find him in the camps before sunset. If not, I don't want to hear another word unless it's accompanied by a counter-offer. A very generous counter-offer."

I nodded. "Fair enough. Thank you, my lord."

With that, he dismissed us.

Betimes in life, there are no good choices. After our dismissal, I settled our account with the innkeeper Halla—much to the dismay of her daughters—and the four of us headed back to the camping ground to discuss the matter with the others.

For the most part, I listened and thought, while everyone else covered the same points, over and over. The surest course for catching Berlik was to follow his trail now. It was also the surest course for dying. Eamonn mac Grainne had managed to cross Skaldia only by passing himself off as Skaldi, and even at that, he'd gotten captured. If it hadn't been for Brigitta's determination, like as not he'd still be toiling as a carl, or dead. The surest course for surviving was to tarry and wait for aid from Alba and Terre d'Ange. And the course with the greatest uncertainty, but the greatest possible merit, was to take Adelmar's offer.

Berlik could part ways with the pilgrims anywhere, at any time. Berlik was unlikely to part ways with the pilgrims in Skaldia. He spoke Cruithne, he bore woad tattoos that could be mistaken for a warrior's markings. Only Adelmar's token kept him safe, and it meant he didn't dare linger in Skaldia, but must continue on to Vralia.

Berlik, everyone agreed, must look immensely silly in his muslin cap.

But it was also possible that Berlik *could* still turn himself into a bear. And without the aid of Skaldic countryfolk, a pale-eyed bear could survive undetected in the wilds of Skaldia for many, many years. Even with their aid—which could only be obtained if we tarried—he would be difficult to find. Talorcan had failed in Alba.

Which left Vralia.

One or two men.

I thought about Vralia. It was a mad venture. I knew next to nothing about the land. I didn't speak their tongue, whatever it was. Not a word of it. Except that I *did* speak some Habiru, and the land was increasingly full of them. And Micah ben Ximon, who served as

Tadeuz Vral's warlord, had been trained in the Cassiline fighting style by Joscelin Verreuil. Long ago, when I was yet a babe, and the Yeshuites in La Serenissima had been forbidden to carry swords. And from there, Micah ben Ximon had led his people to freedom and renown in a distant land. Impossible as it seemed, we might have an ally there in faraway Vralia.

It was a thin, shining thread of hope. There wasn't much time to make a choice. The sun was hanging low over the tree-tops. I fished in the purse at my belt until I found an old silver centime, one that bore the image of a youthful Ysandre de la Courcel. One that resembled her daughter. My hope.

"Tell me what to do, love," I murmured. "Should I chose hope or safety?"

I tossed the coin into the air. It spun, shining in the ruddy light. I caught it in my right hand and slapped it down on the back of my left. Lifted my hand, peered at it, and saw the Queen's young profile.

Hope.

I raised my voice. "I'm going to Vralia."

The Cruithne ceased their discussion and stared at me. "I'll go with you," Kinadius said after a brief pause.

Urist scratched his chin. "I reckon it's the prince's right to choose his companion."

I met Urist's steady gaze. He didn't ask, and he didn't offer. He didn't need to. He'd made a promise to Dorelei, and he'd sworn that if I honored her last wish, he'd ride to the ends of the earth to get vengeance for her. "Right," I said. "Urist, let's go find this Flatlander wool-merchant and tell him he's got two more men riding with him."

FORTY-EIGHT

WE LEFT MAARTEN'S CROSSING in good order. The wool-merchant Ernst wasn't delighted by our presence, but he was willing to defer to Adelmar's wishes. The Skaldi escort Adelmar had provided him weren't happy either, but he was right, they were loyal. They tolerated us.

Urist's remaing men drew lots for their assigments. Two to intercept Talorcan, two to ride to the City of Elua. The rest would wait in Maarten's Crossing; at least to the best of my knowledge. Once we left, I wasn't entirely sure that Cailan, Domnach, Brun, and the older men wouldn't follow Berlik's trail.

It didn't matter now. I'd chosen my course.

I made Kinadius swear on Dorelei's name that he would wait for Talorcan and the others. He wasn't happy about it, but he did it, and I thought he would keep his word. With reluctance, I begged another favor of him. I traded mounts with him and left the Bastard in his keeping. I hated to part with him, but if I'd understood the wool-merchant correctly, the Vralian ship was a small one, unable to carry horses. I didn't trust the Skaldi to return him safely, and Kinadius' gelding was a good deal less valuable.

"What if you don't come back, Imriel?" Kinadius asked.

I leaned my brow against the Bastard's warm, speckled hide. "Just take care of him."

Deordivus had once again drawn one of the short straws for Terre d'Ange. We weren't carrying paper and ink, and there was no time to write letters anyway. All I could do was entrust him with messages. For

Phèdre and Joscelin, wherever they might be. For Sidonie. For Alais, Mavros.

"Tell them I love them," I said.

"That's all?" he asked.

I thought about it. "It's all that matters." He nodded and turned away. "Wait." I worked the knotted gold ring from my finger. "Give this to Sidonie. Tell her it's a pledge." My eyes stung. "That I'll be back to claim it."

"Aye, my lord." Deordivus smiled a little. "That was a hell of a scene I walked into."

I laughed and rubbed my eyes. "Elua willing, I'll live to cause others."

So it was done.

There is little to relate of our journey to Norstock. It was only a day's ride overland, cutting across a peninsula through territory Adelmar held in reasonable security. Everyone was civil to us. There was no trouble. Norstock proved to be a small, bustling port. There was no trouble there, either. It wasn't just Skaldi; there were Flatlanders and other folk. Jutlanders and Götlanders, Ernst told us; northerners, folk who'd been isolated during the long years of hostility between Terre d'Ange and Skaldia, and the reign of the old Master of the Straits.

And Vralians.

They looked different from the other northerners, shaped from a different clay. By and large, they were darker than the fair northerners, black-haired or brown. It wasn't just that, though. The angle of their eyes was different, the way the skin stretched over their strong bones.

Our company located the Vralian ship in the harbor. It was small but sturdy, raised at stem and stern, with a flat bottom suited for a shallow draw. It sported a single square sail and only four sets of oar-locks to a side, and there was barely enough room in the hold to store the bales of wool. Ernst and the captain haggled, one of the ship's crew serving as interpreter. He spoke Skaldic with an accent so strange and thick, I despaired of understanding it. When they had finished their business, coins exchanged hands. I watched, trying to gauge their weight and value. Ernst pointed at Urist and me, saying something to the captain's interpreter.

We approached.

"Vralgrad?" the captain asked, raising strong brows over deep, penetrating eyes. Another face it was hard to read. His thick mustache didn't help.

"Vralgrad," I agreed, nodding firmly.

He said something to his interpreter, who said in Skaldic, "Why?"

That I understood, and I'd had a lot of time to think about my response. I drew my right-hand dagger from my belt and stooped to pluck the left one from my boot-sheath, then straightened to give the fluid Cassiline bow, my daggers crossed before me. "Micah ben Ximon."

It pleased them. The interpreter laughed. The captain smiled beneath his mustache. There was another exchange between them, and then the interpreter said somewhat I couldn't begin to comprehend, holding up several fingers. I glanced at Ernst, who looked away. Taking a guess, I made a show of rummaging in my purse to find a single gold ducat, showing only copper coins and a few silver. Some of the money we carried, I'd dispensed to Kinadius and the others. The rest was hidden in a pouch tied around Urist's waist. Best to be careful, I reckoned.

I held up the coin, pointing at Urist and myself, then the boat. The captain took it and studied it. After a moment, he pocketed it and nodded.

We had purchased passage to Vralia.

The captain beckoned. Urist and I bade farewell to the wool-merchant and Adelmar's Skaldi, charged with the task of seeing our mounts returned to Kinadius. By the gleam in their eyes, I was glad I'd left the Bastard behind. We fetched our packs and boarded the ship. The captain pointed to a spot where we'd be out of the way, then gave a few sharp orders. His crew set to at the oars. The ship lumbered awkwardly into the harbor until they got the wind at her back and raised the sail, which was marked with the same flared cross that adorned the pilgrims' caps. At that, the ship leapt forward and began forging a steady course up the coast.

We were off.

It was my understanding that the voyage to Vralgrad would take approximately two weeks. For the duration of the first week, we had good winds and fair weather. Standing at the railing, watching the coast fly past, I was elated and convinced that my choice had been a good one. As a further piece of luck, there was a Yeshuite man among the crew, a good-natured lad named Ravi. He was a year or so younger than me, but he'd been born in Vralia to one of the first families to settle there, long before it was a nation named after an ambitious ruler. He'd grown up speaking both Habiru and Rus, the common tongue of Vralia.

When he wasn't tending to his duties, Ravi and I spent long hours trading words back and forth; and when he was working, I assisted him, and we carried on our game. I was no sailor, but I'd spent a good deal of time aboard ships during my life, and I daresay I was more help than not. The captain, whose name was Iosef, watched us indulgently.

Urist, for the most part, napped. Still, we talked, and I knew that in his own taciturn way, he was pleased with the speed of our progress. The route overland was longer, and slower going. With each day that passed, we gained a day or more. If we'd guessed rightly that Berlik was bound for Vralia, of a surety, we'd reach it before him.

Then the weather changed.

It had been growing cooler all along. I wasn't sure whether that was due to our progress north or the change of seasons. I'd lost so many days during my long convalescence that spring and much of the summer had passed me by all unnoticed. And since we set out on Berlik's trail, time had been measured in the distance between us. After counting on my fingers and consulting with Ravi, I determined that it must be late summer yet in Terre d'Ange, or mayhap early autumn; the days growing shorter, but still warm and bright.

This far north, the weather was less predictable. The winds were strong and changeable. The sea grew choppy. Our progress slowed. Everyone grumbled.

I daresay there wasn't anything anyone could have done about the storm. I'd sailed on a good many ships, and Iosef was a decent captain. Not as good, mayhap, as Captain Oppius of the *Aeolia*, who'd dared a risky crossing to bring me home from Tiberium. We'd outlasted a fierce storm on that journey. And mayhap not as skilled as Eamonn's father, Admiral Quintilius Rousse, who had dared the ire of the old Master of the Straits more than once. But Iosef was a fair captain nonetheless.

There were other factors. His ship was smaller and less maneuverable. Despite its name, the Eastern Sea was mostly contained inland. It was more shallow, fraught with unexpected hazards. The storm struck in the small hours of the night, when no one could read the sky clearly to track its approach.

It struck with fury, sudden and abrupt, jolting me out of my restless sleep. There were neither bunks nor hammocks aboard the Vralian ship; only a narrow berth where everyone, including the captain, not serving on deck crowded and slept, the greasy odor of lanolin from the bales of wool drifting from the fore of the hold and filling our nostrils.

No lamps, either; not belowdeck. I awoke to pitching darkness and panic. Above us, there was thunder and the sound of running feet. Urist, next to me, grabbed my upper arm with hard fingers. I could barely make out the gleam of his eyes.

"This isn't good," he said grimly.

"No," I agreed.

Men scrambled past us, ascending the ladder. One dim figure scrambled back. I recognized Ravi's voice, babbling in Rus. Too fast for me to make it out.

"Habiru!" I shouted at him.

He said something else, then switched. "All hands! All hands to oars!"

"We're needed," I said shortly to Urist. "Let's go."

Much of that night lingers in my memory like a sea-drenched fever-dream. Half dressed and barefoot like the others, Urist and I got ourselves above deck. There was rain, pelting down like mad. Someone pointed, shouting. I saw a man fighting with the long shaft of an oar and tried to make my way toward him. The ship plunged and crashed. A wave washed over the railing. I staggered, slipped, got to my feet. Urist was ahead of me. I shoved him toward another bench, another lone oarsman. Lightning split the sky. I caught a glimpse of a figure in the rigging, trying desperately to loosen a knot.

I managed to reach the bench and take hold of the oar shaft, slippery and soaked with seawater and rain. The Vralian beside me gasped thanks. And then we both set our back to the task of battling the waves and keeping the ship upright.

It went on for hours, each one more miserable than the last. My arms ached; my healing scars strained as they hadn't for weeks. Time and again, waves crashed over us, nearly swamping the ship. I was drenched to the bone, cold and shivering. The wind was buffeting, changing directions. There was no way to run before it. Iosef's men managed to get the sail furled. It didn't matter. The sea had its way with us, sending us leagues off course.

It saved the last of its fury for dawn. I saw it; we all saw it. An island, looming in the grey light. Outlying rocks. A gathering wave, striking us sidelong. The ship canted on its side. I was lucky, I was on the lower end, digging my nails into the sodden wood of my oar shaft. The wave hurled us against the rocks, hard. There was a loud crack as our hull was breached.

I saw men tumble and fall.

I saw Urist flung from his bench, hurtling toward the railing.

I don't remember seeing his thigh-bone snap, and I don't remember grabbing him, keeping him from going overboard. I don't remember the captain shouting for everyone to abandon the ship, which like as not I wouldn't have understood anyway. Not in that panic. All I remember is Urist's face, ashen beneath his warrior's markings.

"I can't swim," he grated.

"I can," I said. "Enough for two."

The ship groaned and settled, creaking. Bilgewater rose around us. Men were babbling and shouting. Those who weren't wounded were already in the sea, swimming for the island's shore. The ship creaked and lurched lower. I slid my arms under Urist's, holding his face clear of the water, and gauged the distance.

"It was a damn good try." He grimaced. "Leave me."

I shook my head. "Not a chance."

Having struck its final blow, the storm's fury had abated; or at least, it had moved onward, passing over the sea. Still, it was a long, hard swim in cold, choppy water. I slid over the lower railing, now underwater, and hauled Urist over it. He cried aloud as his broken leg, unsupported, dragged in the water. His entire body jerked at the pain of it.

"I'm sorry!" I gasped raggedly, treading water. I got him in a headlock, wedging my forearm under his chin. "Just try to hold still. Please!"

Urist closed his eyes and nodded against my arm.

Elua knows how, but I got him ashore. I kept my death-grip on him, kept his face above water. Forced my aching, leaden limbs to keep reaching, fighting the cold water that sought to leach my strength. I wasn't hale, but at least I was whole. It came down, in the end, to counting each breath I drew and reckoning it a victory. My chest ached, but my lungs kept working. The island's rocky shore was strewn with bone-weary Vralian sailors. By the time we reached the shallows, I was too exhausted to stand. I towed Urist as far as I could, crawling over rough rocks, then sat with my hands laced under his armpits and scooted backward, dragging him inch by inch onto solid land.

"You're safe," I said in a raw voice.

Urist opened his eyes and grunted. "Look at that bitch. Still sitting there."

I followed his gaze. He was right. Out there in the grey drizzle, the ship, listing and half sunken, was hung up on the rocks. We might as well have stayed, clinging to the foredeck. I laughed helplessly. What else was there to do?

"How's your leg?" I asked Urist.

He rolled his eyes around at me. "Hurts like hell. Think I might puke. What do you expect?"

"Not much," I said wearily. "Not with my luck."

FORTY-NINE

THERE ARE SIZABLE ISLANDS in the Eastern Sea; populated islands, islands with ports large enough to warrant being regular stops on the trade routes.

Unfortunately, this wasn't one of them.

Once we'd dragged ourselves ashore, assessed the wounded and counted the missing—one of the ten crewmen hadn't reached the island—it didn't take long to determine that we were in a bad situation. No food, no fresh water, no shelter. No sign of habitation anywhere along the barren, stony shore or the pine forest behind it. No sign of the mainland coastline we'd been following. No sign of other ships on the vast grey expanse of the sea.

Aside from the man who'd gone missing, there was one in worse shape than Urist, a fellow named Kirill. He'd swum to shore unaided, then collapsed into unconsciousness. Someone said he'd taken a sharp thrust to the belly with an oar shaft. Other than that, the rest of us sported nothing worse than bruises and grazes.

Captain Iosef gave us time to catch our breath before he began issuing orders; pointing to the ship, to the forest. His voice was tired and cracked, and I was too weary to make out a word of what he said. Five of the most stalwart sailors plunged back into the surf and began swimming for the wreck. Two others began trudging toward the forest, carrying the unconscious Kirill with them. Iosef approached us, bringing Ravi to interpret.

I listened, then interpreted for Urist. "Says we're going to have to set and brace your leg if you don't want to lose it."

Urist didn't blink. "Just do it."

It was an ugly process. We slit his breeches to the hip, laying the leg bare. The snapped bone hadn't breached the skin, but it tented it obscenely.

"Don't look," I advised Urist. He didn't. Captain Iosef and I conferred through Ravi, who looked sick. Elua be thanked, Iosef had set broken bones before. I'd only seen it done. I straddled Urist's torso, squeezing it tight between my knees, and took a hard grip on his upper thigh, holding him still. I could feel the jolt run through him, his entire body straining as Iosef pulled carefully on the lower portion of the broken bone, easing it in place. Urist didn't scream, but he bit his lip hard enough to draw blood.

Iosef said somewhat cheerful. "Half done," Ravi translated.

We finished the job when Iosef's men returned from their excursions, using straight, sturdy branches to brace the from hip to ankle and lashing them in place with a long length of linen bandage salvaged from my pack.

"Done," Ravi said.

"Gods and goddesses, I could use a jug of *uisghe*," Urist said weakly.

Thus began our first day of being shipwrecked. We moved Urist farther up the rocky beach and set him beside poor Kirill, who still hadn't awoken. Two men set about building a makeshift shelter, and three others set out in search of fresh water, our most urgent need. The rest of us spent the day swimming back and forth to the wrecked ship, diving into the sunken hold and swimming in blind darkness, grasping whatever we could and hauling it out. The ship shuddered and quivered as we clambered over it, but it sank no further, held up by the rocks that breached its hull.

In the end, our tally looked a bit less hopeless. We'd salvaged a few parcels of hard biscuits wrapped in watertight oilskin and a pair of undamaged waterskins, and one of Iosef's men had found a spring-fed pond in the forest. A flint striker to kindle fire—that had been in my pack, a gift I'd received long ago in Jebe-Barkal. An axe, an adze, and other tools for repairing the ship, which proved useful for building a shelter. Several lengths of rope. Sodden blankets. One of the powerful hunting bows Urist and I had brought, though its string was likely spoiled by the saltwater and we hadn't found the quiver.

At least there was food and water. Iosef doled out a rock-hard biscuit apiece. I broke off chunks and held them in my mouth, waiting for the waterskin to be passed so I could soften them with a mouthful of water. I was too tired to chew.

I have never, ever in my life been as exhausted as I was by the end of the day. If there was any hidden blessing, it was that I was beyond caring what had become of our mission, at least in that moment. All I wanted to do was lay my head down and sleep. If Kushiel had appeared on that island in all his terrible glory and offered me Berlik's head on a flaming platter, I wouldn't have had the strength to take it.

Our shelter was a simple affair, a lean-to such as hunters might build to spend the night in the woods, built on a larger scale. We lashed layers of untrimmed green pine branches atop it to keep out the drizzle and spread pine mast over the stony soil, then packed ourselves beneath it, laying down in our damp clothing and sleeping the sleep of the dead.

At least I didn't dream.

Morning dawned bright and clear, but it brought two unpleasant revelations. Kirill had died in the night without ever waking. His belly was hard and distended, and I thought he must have been bleeding inside. On the heels of that discovery, we found a second body washed ashore; Pavel, the sailor who'd gone missing.

The ground was too hard to dig a proper grave; it had been difficult enough to sink poles for the shelter. Iosef shared out biscuits for our breakfast, and then we set about building a cairn some distance from our campsite.

It was hard work, but none of us begrudged it. It could have been any one of us lying in their places. With everyone save Urist lending a hand, we made short work of it, burying them under a vast mound of stone. When we had finished, we all gathered around and Iosef gave an invocation in Rus. I paid close attention and caught a few words I understood; death and peace and Yeshua.

It surprised me, a little. I hadn't thought of them as Yeshuites, except for Ravi. Of a surety, none of them were Habiru. I asked him about it later.

"Yes, of course," he said. "Didn't you see the cross on the sail? Tadeuz Vral only trusts the loyalty of men who have acknowledged Yeshua."

"I saw it," I said. "I thought it was Vral's insignia."

"In a way." He shrugged. "It is a sign that he rules in Yeshua's name."

I frowned. "Why not the *khai*?"

"You sound like my old Nonna." Ravi looked amused. "You know the *khai*?"

I sketched it in the hard-packed dirt. It was a character formed by combining the Habiru letters Khet and Yod to make *khai*. Living, the word meant; a symbol of the resurrection of Yeshua ben Yosef. All the Yeshuites I'd ever met in Terre d'Ange wore pendants with the symbol. Ti-Philippe had told Gilot that Joscelin had worn one for a long time. He would have been wearing it when he taught Micah ben Ximon how to fight in the Cassiline style.

"Ah, well." Ravi peered at my work. "Tadeuz Vral doesn't speak Habiru, let alone write it. He chose the cross to show his faith. To remind us of the cross that Yeshua died on," he added, seeing my perplexed look.

"Huh." I wasn't sure what I thought about that.

"It speaks to Vralians," Ravi said. "The *khai* doesn't."

He erased the character I'd drawn, murmuring a quick, reverent prayer in Habiru. And then we spoke no more of Vralia or Yeshua, for Captain Iosef summoned us all to confer over a midday biscuit.

I sat beside Urist and listened. I understood only one word in twenty, but one thing was clear; our captain was not a man given to despair. And neither, it seemed, were the Vralians. They listened and nodded as he spoke, pointing and offering suggestions.

What it came down to, I learned later from Ravi, was a realistic assessment of our situation. Our most pressing need was food, since the biscuits wouldn't last. There was an abundance of birdlife on the island, and fish in the sea. We needed to get the bow working as best we might and fashion arrows, and we needed to find the ship's fishing nets or fashion new ones.

Our second most pressing need was getting the hell off the island. Iosef thought we couldn't have been driven that far from the trade routes in a single night; that we might be near enough there was hope a distant ship might spot us. He proposed that we keep a lookout posted and build a signal pyre on the eastern shore.

He also thought there was also a good chance that he was wrong; that we could linger here for months without sighting a single ship. That our hope of salvation would pass us by in the night, unseen. That our pyre would go unremarked in the bright light of day. And if that happened, if we were still here come winter, no one liked our chances for survival.

To that end, Captain Iosef proposed we repair the ship.

"Is he serious?" I asked Ravi when he told me. "Can it be done?"

"Oh, he's serious." He gazed out at the listing, half-sunken ship. It lay almost a hundred yards from the shore, most of it deep water. The ship might be stable now, but there was a gaping hole in the hull, and it was filled with water. It was impossible to imagine we could shift it without having it sink like a stone. "And I have no idea. I hope he does."

Over the course of the next three weeks, we found out.

I know the precise duration of the time, because Urist kept track of it, marking each day with a slash on one corner-pole of our shelter. It would have driven him mad to lay idle all that time while we labored like oxen, but mercifully, Captain Iosef thought to put him to work. Urist spent long hours laboring over the hunting bow, unstringing it and rubbing the string with handful after handful of wool pried from a sunken bale, rinsed in fresh water and laid in the sun to dry, still greasy with lanolin; and after that, a mixture of pine rosin I gathered from the forest for him. It took two of us to restring it when he'd finished, but the string held when drawn.

Most of what we did those first days was salvage. The early going was rewarding. Everyone cheered when one of the fishnets was found, and for my part, I whooped with joy when a sailor named Yuri came up grinning, my sword-belt in hand. Dive by dive, piece by piece, we retrieved most of our belongings, exclaiming over boots, belts, and hunting knives. We found the second bow, and Urist went to work on that, too.

We whittled stakes for the nets and fished. The first day that we brought in a haul large enough to feed everyone was a glorious thing. Silvery herring, dozens of them, flopping on dry land. We spitted them on sharpened sticks and roasted them in the campfire, tearing them to pieces with our fingers, stuffing chunks in our mouths and spitting out bones. Elua, it was good!

"Look at you," Urist observed, propped by the fire. "A right savage."

I glanced around. It didn't take long for the trappings of civilization to fall away. All of us looked like wild men, unkempt and half-clad, huddled around the fire, chewing and smacking our lips. I shrugged. "I'm just trying to survive like everyone else here."

"You're good at it." Urist pulled his stick out of the fire, inspected his fish, and stuck it back into the flames. "Never would have expected that when I first met you."

"I'm full of surprises," I said wryly.

"Aye." He nodded. "That you are, my prince."

I raised my brows. "*Your* prince, am I?"

"As good as any, Imriel of Clunderry." Urist withdrew his stick and plucked the fish deftly from it, juggling it from hand to hand. "Saved my life, didn't you?"

I skewered another herring and began roasting it. "Not really. But I would have felt a right fool if I'd left you to die only to find you stuck there on the rocks, cursing my name."

He chuckled. "Aye, you would." He regarded his splinted leg, amusement fading. "Never thought I'd end up a cripple. Suppose it won't matter if we die here on this godforsaken island."

"It was a clean break," I said. "It may heal clean."

"So I can face death on my feet like a man?" he asked dourly.

"No." I watched my fish curl in the flames, the scales crisping. "I'm not giving in to despair, Urist. I've lived through too damned much to die here on this island. I can't bear to think about it, any of it. It will drive me mad. Captain Iosef thinks we can get this boat ashore and repair it. I have to believe it's true. So I'm not thinking about a damned thing except making that happen and keeping ourselves alive in the process."

"Stubborn bugger," Urist said, but there was warmth in his tone.

I pulled my fish out of the fire. "Damned right I am."

Between the fishing nets and the hunting bows—we managed to salvage the quivers, and Urist set his hand to making an additional stock of crude arrows—our sources of nourishment improved considerably. A good thing, too, because our work got harder. The fore of the ship's hold was packed with bales of wool, waterlogged and swollen. If we had any hope of raising the ship, we had to empty it.

We did, bale by bale. Teams of men, two and sometimes three, plunged into the dark hold, working in blind concert underwater to shift the cursed things. It was exhausting and unspeakably difficult. What I'd told Urist was true. I didn't let myself think about anything but the task before me. Betimes my chest ached, but the new scabs didn't split, so I ignored the pain and kept working. And slowly, bale by bale, we emptied the hold.

On Iosef's orders, we saved a few bales, towing them ashore on a raft of pine branches. The wool was spoiled, but I supposed if the weather turned cold before we succeeded in rescuing ourselves, we'd be glad of it. The rest, we tipped into the sea.

Then it came time to raise the ship.

It was a near-impossible task. We didn't have to raise it clean out of the water, Iosef said; just far enough to clear the damaged hull. By this time, I understood him well enough on my own. With Ravi's help, I'd picked up a bigger smattering of Rus, but much of it simply came from working with the Vralians, day in and day out. I didn't need to speak their tongue to understand them. Much of the time, we worked without words, all of us knowing what had to be done.

A good deal of preparation went into raising the ship. We stripped it of its sail and every bit of line. Ropes were spliced. Trees were felled, hacked into planks. A ramp of logs was laid at the shore. Pitch was gathered from the abundant pines and heated in the ship's lone cooking pot. The bales of wool we'd salvaged—cut loose from their bindings and dried in vast mounds—were towed back to the rocks. Iosef's plan came clear; he meant to use them to plug the hole before patching it.

If it was to be done, it would have to be done quickly. That much, we all understood. Once the hull was lifted clear of the jagged rock piercing it, only our strength would keep the ship from sliding into the depths, and that wouldn't last long.

The day we raised the ship, we carried Urist to the distant lookout post with its signal pyre that he might tend its fire. He grimaced at the pain, but didn't complain. All able hands were needed for the endeavor.

I saw very little of the actual effort. We'd found only one bucket, and Iosef had assigned me to bailing duty, reckoning I had the fastest hands of the lot. Men dove behind the stern, threading rope around it. Others drew the ropes taut, perched on awkward footholds on the rocks. The divers clambered out of the water and took up positions beneath the hull. I perched on the ladder descending into the submerged hold, waist-deep in water. Captain Iosef and a fellow named Ruslan who had experience as a carpenter stood at the ready with all our hard-won supplies.

Iosef gave the order. *"Go!"*

The divers strained to lift the hull free of the rocks. The rope-men hauled. The ship creaked and moaned. For a long moment, it didn't shift.

And then it did.

It came free with a lurch, sliding forward. The bottom scraped along the rocks, the prow nosed skyward. Water poured from the ragged hole in the hull. I was flung free of my perch on the ladder of the hatch. I trod water in the sinking waters of the hold, scooping water and flinging buckets of it over my head. A futile effort, mayhap, but every bucket less was less chance the ship would sink. Outside, I could hear men groaning under the strain of holding the ship in place, while Iosef and Ruslan worked frantically to pack the hole with wool to stem the tide of water and drill holes to peg the planks in place, slathering them with pitch.

The ship shuddered.

"It's going!" someone shouted.

It went, easing slowly backward into the water. Rocks, scraping. I kept bailing grimly. If it sank, I would swim. And we would be doomed.

It didn't sink.

With a hold full of water and a leaking patch, it wallowed. It wallowed so low the deck barely cleared the surface of the sea, but it didn't sink. We didn't dare try to board and row it ashore for fear the additional weight would submerge it for good, so I stayed in the hatch and kept bailing while everyone else plunged into the water, struggling to get hold of the ropes and begin the long, arduous process of towing it to shore.

It took the better part of a day, but we did it. By the time we got it into the shallows, the sun was hovering low on the horizon and we were too exhausted to attempt to roll the ship over the log ramp we'd built. My arms had gone completely numb. The patch had held, but it leaked like a sieve. The water in the hold was at the same level it had been when I'd begun.

Still, we'd done it.

At Captain Iosef's orders, I clambered out of the hold and hefted the anchor overboard, my arms shaking at the effort. He wedged it under a rocky outcropping to ensure the ship wasn't going anywhere. I climbed over the railing and dropped wearily into the shallows, splashing ashore to collapse on dry land. All of us sat in poses of utter exhaustion, contemplating our achievement.

As the day's last light faded, a lone figure hobbled down the shore, splinted leg swinging in an awkward arc. Urist had spent his day on futile lookout duty fashioning himself a pair of crutches from a couple of sturdy, forked branches he'd pillaged from the pyre. He stared at the ship for a long, wordless moment.

"I'll be damned," he said at length. "You did it."

FIFTY

It took another two weeks to get the ship repaired and seaworthy.

I lent a hand with all of the unskilled work; chopping wood, gathering pitch, fishing. I was a fair shot with a bow, but there were others who were better. Whenever we caught a sizable haul of fish, more than we could eat, we built slow-burning fires with green wood and smoked them on makeshift racks.

Captain Iosef was exacting in his repairs. Although the weather was growing cooler by the day, he wouldn't be rushed. Damaged planks were removed and new ones hewn to replace them. It was a mercy that the inner framework of the ship was intact. Slowly, slowly, it took shape, and I began to believe that we would leave the island.

I tended to my neglected weapons, polishing and whetting them. I began my days by practicing the Cassiline forms for the first time in long weeks.

The first time I did so, the Vralians stared in open astonishment. If anyone remembered the bow with which I'd greeted Captain Iosef so long ago in Norstock, I daresay they'd thought it was a mere homage to their hero. I ignored them, concentrating on telling the hours.

"Where did you learn that?" Ravi asked me that night around the campfire.

I smiled. "From the man who taught Micah ben Ximon."

He laughed. "No, really."

"It's true," I said. "Where did you think *he* learned it?"

"From an angel who appeared to him in a vision," he said seriously.

"No angel," I said. "Just a D'Angeline." I told him about the Cassiline Brotherhood and their training, and the story of how Joscelin had come to befriend the Yeshuite community of La Serenissima, teaching the art to a young Micah ben Ximon and others. How they had helped Joscelin and Phèdre thwart a plot to assassinate the Queen of Terre d'Ange during her visit there.

Ravi stared at me, wide-eyed. "And you know these people?"

I nodded. "I'm their foster-son."

In all the time we'd been together, working side by side, I'd told him very little about myself. Ravi whistled through his teeth. "I thought you were just . . . I don't know, an adventurer or a scout sent to explore."

"Oh yes, of course," I said, realizing he'd just handed me a vaguely plausible reason for our journey to Vralia. "That too."

"Do you report to the Queen of Terre d'Ange herself?" He sounded awed.

"I do." Elua knows, that was true. "And Urist is in the service of the Cruarch of Alba."

Ravi winced. "They'll not be impressed by our shipwreck. Will you tell them it doesn't happen often? It was a very bad storm."

I glanced over at the dim hulk of the ship, still visible in the fading light of day. "Ravi, if we get off this island and Urist and I return home in one piece, I promise you, I will tell them that the courage and strength of Vralia's men is without equal."

His young face beamed. "Well, that's true."

I felt guilty at lying to him; to all of them. We'd grown close during our travail in the wordless way that men do working together for a common cause. Still, what could I do? Urist and I were seeking to enter Vralia under false pretenses. If there was a dangerous task to be done here on the island, I would trust Ravi or Captain Iosef or any one of these men with my life. But I didn't dare tell them we were hunting a man who had entered Vralia as a Yeshuite pilgrim, intending to kill him.

Although it wasn't *we* anymore.

We hadn't talked about it yet, Urist and I, but I daresay both of us knew. He was lucky to have kept his leg, lucky it was a clean break, lucky it appeared to be healing. But a broken thigh-bone was a serious injury. It would take months to mend. Urist was able to hobble about on his crutches, but he couldn't put any weight on the leg, and there was no way he could ride.

I would be hunting Berlik alone.

At least I was hale. If nothing else, I had these weeks of hard labor to thank for it. Thinner than I had been, subsisting on a diet of fish and fowl, but with lean, hard muscle on my bones. The deep gouges Berlik's claws had rent into my flesh had healed, leaving angry red scars where they'd cut the deepest. Still, they were scars. Oftentimes they ached, and when I overexerted myself, I could feel them burn and tug, but they were scars.

On the thirty-first day of our ordeal, as reckoned by Urist's tally, Captain Iosef determined the ship was ready to be tested. Her hull was intact, her rigging restored. We rolled her down the ramp of pine logs into the deep water, setting our shoulders and heaving. She floated proudly. A handful of us stood ashore, watching as the others set to at the oars. Watching the sail unfurl.

They didn't go far, just far enough to test her seaworthiness. I shaded my eyes, watching the sail bob on the choppy waters, sporting its crimson cross. I thought about the pilgrims in Maarten's Crossing, sporting their muslin caps. Iosef ordered the ship brought back to shore, rolled up the pine ramp. He crawled into the hold, inspecting the seams. Measuring the bilge. He called for moss and more pine tar to caulk the seams. We scoured the forest for moss, gathered pitch in sticky handfuls.

Three days later, Iosef tested the ship again.

"She's ready," he said briefly upon returning. "We'll sail on the morrow."

Ruslan the carpenter had built a crude barrel. We tramped back and forth to the spring-fed pond, filling waterskins and our bucket, dumping their contents into the barrel. We packed the ship with our stores of smoked fish. As it transpired, the hardest part was getting Urist aboard the ship. In the end, we hoisted him in a cradle of rope, his splinted leg sticking out at a stiff angle. He cursed and swore as we wrestled him over the railing. I found an out-of-the-way place on the aft deck and tried to make him comfortable.

"You know I'm finished," Urist said to me, his jaw clenched. "I can't go on."

"I know," I said quietly.

His eyes glinted. "You'll not give up?"

"No." I sat cross-legged beside him. Captain Iosef gave an order. Men shoved; the ship lurched over the pine logs. Floated. Men shouted, scrambling to board the rope ladders. Set to at the oars, the ship turning. She presented her stern to the island. The sail was unfurled. It caught the wind, snapping. I watched the barren, inhospitable shore dwindle behind us and thought about Dorelei. Her dimpled smile, her lilting laugh. The son we might have raised together if she had lived. All those things Berlik had cut short, no matter how much it grieved him.

The way she had taught me to be a better person.

I'd spent a good portion of my life looking for those answers. I'd looked to heroes like Joscelin and Phèdre. I'd looked to wise men like Master Piero, the philosopher. In the end, I'd learned more about simple, common decency from my wife than anyone else. Dorelei had loved me. She had *known* me. She had shaken me from my youthful self-absorption. She had extorted promises to ensure my happiness. I owed her justice.

"No," I repeated to Urist. "I won't give up."

He grunted. "Good. Didn't think so."

By noon on the second day, we caught sight of the mainland, all of us cheering wildly. We were back on course. What a small distance it was, truly; little more than a day's sail, less if we'd had a stronger wind at our back. And yet it had been enough to render us utterly isolated.

On the following day, we put ashore at a small port-town called Yelek, situated on a jutting peninsula. I can only imagine the picture we made. Our ship was sound, but we looked like . . . well, as Urist had said, we looked like savages. All of us were burned brown by sun and wind, filthy and salt-crusted, our clothing frayed and tattered. There simply hadn't been enough fresh water on the island to bathe.

Yelek didn't have a bath-house, but it had a marketplace and a public well. While Captain Iosef explained our plight to the harbor-master, we stripped to the waist and dowsed one another with buckets of fresh water, shivering in the bright, chilly air. Women from the town eyed us and giggled, talking behind their hands.

"They're all looking at you," Ravi noted.

I dumped a bucket of water over my head, shaking it off like a dog. "And you."

"Oh, I think not." He smiled ruefully. "Between your face and . . ." Ravi cocked his head, glancing at my scarred torso. "What did happen to you, anyway?"

"Now you ask?" I said wryly.

He shrugged. "It seemed impolite."

I handed the bucket to the man beside me. "I was attacked by a bear."

"Some bear," Ravi murmured.

I gazed toward the north. "Yes," I said. "He was."

Those of us with money to spend bought warmer clothing in Yelek; ill-fitting woolen stuff sold by the vendors there. Urist and I were in good shape, the bulk of our monies having been tied in a pouch around his waist. The vendors looked askance at our D'Angeline coinage, but they weighed and accepted it, giving us change in Vralian currency. Copper coins, bearing the flared cross on one side and a sword on the other.

I bought a coarse woolen coat for Ravi, who had no money to spend, and for several of the other men in the same circumstances, embarrassed by their thanks. The weather was turning cold and the wind at sea cut to the bone; obtaining warmer gear was the main reason we'd put in at Yelek. I was glad I could help. I'd lost time in my quest for vengeance. Iosef and his men had lost a portion of their livelihood, the profits from this journey on which they had depended.

Which was more important?

I couldn't say.

Marginally cleaner and markedly warmer, we set sail from Yelek. Back to sea, back to following the coastline.

All the way to Vralgrad.

Unlike Yelek, Vralgrad didn't lie on the coast of the Eastern Sea, but leagues inland, straddling the Volkov River. It was a wide, slow, strong river. We beat a course upstream with sail and oars, passing many other small ships like ours. Ravi told me that there were a series of large rivers crossing Vralia, linked by smaller tributaries, that went as far as Ephesium. They had long been used as trade routes, although toward the east they were vulnerable to raiding Tatars, which was why Tadeuz Vral was looking to increase trade in the west.

That was a thought that made me uneasy. The Mahrkagir had courted the aid of several Tatar tribes. He'd promised me as a prize to the Kereyit Tatar warlord Jagun, who had a fondness for young boys. Jagun hadn't gotten his prize in the end, but he'd had a chance to toy with me. I bore the mark of his brand on my left buttock, a shiny, puckered scar. I still remembered the charred odor of my own flesh searing.

I put such thoughts aside as we sailed into Vralgrad. Although small and compact, it was an impressive city, far more so than I would have reckoned. The notion of a vast kingdom might be a new one, but the Vralings had ruled this particular region for a long time. According to Ravi, the city itself was over two hundred years old. It was encircled by a sturdy stone wall, and beneath the river there were heavy chains that could be lifted and stretched taut to keep enemy ships from entering.

The architecture was a curious mixture. The oldest buildings were square and squat, stone fortresses suitable for defense, but there was a good deal of newer timber-built construction. Here and there, one could see another style altogether, with high arches and pointed domes I guessed were due to an Ephesian influence.

We found a berth at the bustling quay. The wharf was filled with Vralians, mostly men, standing around in animated conversation; so animated, in fact, that our arrival elicited little interest. I glanced at Captain Iosef, frowning beneath his overgrown mustache.

"Not a lot of work being done here," Urist observed. "What's happening?"

I shook my head. "I don't know."

It wasn't long before we found out. The harbor-master ordered us not to leave the ship, but he was willing to share the news. In the small hours of the night, there had been an attack on the tower where Fedor Vral, the younger brother of Tadeuz, had been imprisoned for the better part of a year. Half a dozen guards had been slain. The attackers had succeeded in freeing Fedor and fled, taking the rebel prince with them.

No one, it seemed, was permitted to disembark. There was a handful of guards working their way down the wharf, interrogating new arrivals. They were an imposing lot, clad in heavy coats of white brocade worked with the flared cross in crimson, with wide sword-belts and tall black boots. We waited patiently until a pair of them boarded the ship. They took one look at Urist and me and began questioning Captain Iosef.

From Iosef's replies, I gathered that Ravi had passed on the story I'd told him; that we were scouts sent by the Cruarch of Alba and the Queen of Terre d'Ange. I heard Micah ben Ximon's name mentioned several times.

The guards responded by berating Captain Iosef for his carelessness in allowing such potentially valuable persons to be shipwrecked, a charge he denied with angry vehemence. I made an effort to intervene.

"Not his fault," I said in crude Rus. I made a motion with one hand to indicate waves pitching. "Good man. Bad storm, very bad."

The guards conferred, and one of them departed at a quick trot. The tallest offered me a crisp bow. "On behalf of Grand Prince Tadeuz Vral, I apologize," he said slowly and carefully. "We will escort you to the palace to meet with ben Ximon." He said something else I didn't quite understand.

"He's sent for a carriage for Urist," Ravi said helpfully.

I returned the guard's bow. *"Spasiba,"* I said. "Thank you."

It all happened very quickly. The carriage came in short order, the driver clad in crimson livery. Urist maneuvered cautiously down the loading plank on his crutches. The guards surrounded us respectfully, the tall one holding the carriage door open. We said awkward goodbyes to our shipmates, shaking hands all around.

"Come find me if you have a chance," Ravi said hopefully. "I'll be seeking cheap lodgings near the wharf until I ship out again. You can buy me a drink and tell me what Micah ben Ximon is like."

"I'll try," I said, knowing it wasn't likely.

It felt strange to leave them. We'd been working together and sharing close quarters for so many days, sleeping cheek by jowl beneath our shelter. I helped Urist into the carriage, then went round to get in the other side. The tall guard bowed again, opening that door for me. I thanked him as he closed it and gave an order to the driver.

And like that, we were off, bound for the palace.

Urist shifted his splinted leg with both hands, grunting. "So," he said. "Exactly what are we going to tell this Micah ben Ximon?"

I gazed out the window, watching as we passed a Yeshuite temple; a vast affair of white marble. It sported multiple towers, each topped with a gilded dome, and atop each dome, a spire with a golden cross. It looked new and ambitious, and unlike any other Yeshuite temple I'd ever seen.

"I don't know," I said. "I truly don't."

Fifty-one

As it transpired, we didn't have to tell Micah ben Ximon a great deal.

He already knew.

Urist and I were given fine quarters in the palace, with a sitting room and a pair of bedchambers. The tall guard, whose name was Havlik, assured me that word of our arrival would be sent to ben Ximon, who was understandably busy with the news of Fedor's escape. Doubtless he would see us soon. In the meantime, we were to rest after our ordeal. All our needs would be tended to.

Of a surety, that was true. We were given heavy robes and escorted to a bathing-chamber, where copper tubs were filled with water heated over a massive hearth. It felt unspeakably good to sink into warm water and scour myself clean. I pitied Urist, who had to settle for standing with one foot in a tub, his braced leg propped awkwardly outside it lest the splint grow sodden and warp as it dried, rubbing himself with a sponge and dripping onto the marble inlay.

By the time we returned to our quarters, there was a feast laid; meat jellies, roast goose, soft dumplings, and a boiled grain I didn't recognize. No wine, but there was beer. We ate until our bellies were groaning, while a steady stream of servants brought clothing for us to peruse. Once I'd finished eating and donned clean attire, I felt nearly human.

A Yeshuite chirurgeon came to examine Urist's leg. He poked and prodded, then complimented the job we'd done of splinting it and cautioned against removing the splint for at least another two weeks. I translated his comments for Urist, who grunted in disgust.

It was evening before Micah ben Ximon called on us.

In my mind, he was still the young man in the stories I'd heard. It was absurd, of course. I'd been a babe in swaddling clothes when Joscelin had taught Micah ben Ximon to fight with Cassiline daggers. The man who entered our quarters was nearing forty. He had the olive complexion of the Habiru, a neatly trimmed black beard, intense dark eyes, and the air of a man accustomed to being obeyed. How not? He was Tadeuz Vral's warlord.

"So," ben Ximon said without preamble, speaking Habiru. He must have learned from the chirurgeon that I spoke it. "I was told you know me. I think this is untrue."

It seemed the message had gotten garbled somewhere in translation. "Not you, my lord," I replied. "I know Joscelin Verreuil." I raised my brows. "Best known in Vral, it seems, as the *angel* who appeared to you in a vision?"

Ben Ximon gave a startled laugh. *"Joscelin?"* His expression shifted into a complicated look I couldn't decipher. "How?"

"He's my foster-father," I said simply. It wasn't true, strictly speaking, since Phèdre and Joscelin had never wed. But it was true enough.

Micah ben Ximon stared at me. When the guards had asked my name, I'd given it as Imriel nó Montrève. His lips moved, sounding it out. His eyes widened. "You're *her* son," he said slowly, switching unexpectedly to Caerdicci.

"Phèdre's?" I nodded. "Yes."

"No." His mouth twisted wryly. "Prince Benedicte's D'Angeline bride. I saw her unveiled in the Temple of Asherat that day. We didn't leave La Serenissima until six months after it happened. I spent half my life there. I remember her face. I remember the name of her babe, who went missing that day. You have emerged from a past I would forget, bearing both. And you are telling me lies."

Urist glanced from one of us to the other, trying to read our tones.

I sighed. "My lord, my full name is Imriel nó Montrève de la Courcel, and I have not lied to you. I was born to Melisande Shahrizai and Benedicte de la Courcel. I was adopted into the household of Phèdre nó Delaunay de Montrève and her consort, Joscelin Verreuil. It is a very, very long story. But it is a true one."

"Tell me," Micah ben Ximon said shortly.

I told him.

He was a good listener. He sat silent, staring at the ceiling, evincing no signs of impatience. When I had finished explaining how my mother had dispatched me to the Sanctuary of Elua, how I had been abducted by slave-traders and ended in Drujan, how Phèdre and Joscelin had rescued and adopted me, he let out a long, weary sigh. "So how is it, Prince Imriel de la Courcel, that you come to be in Vralia, seeking the life of a Yeshuite pilgrim?"

"I beg your pardon?" I asked, startled.

"Don't." Ben Ximon held out one hand, forestalling me. "If you've not lied to me yet, I pray you, do not start. It is clear that your tattooed companion hails from Alba. There was a skirmish on the southern border of Vralia some ten days ago, along the pilgrims' route. It seems a small party of Albans were hunting a pilgrim, asking questions. My men dispatched several of them and sent the rest packing. You are fortunate that I was able to keep the matter quiet. Tadeuz Vral has ties to Skaldia and hopes of trading with Alba. I did not want him to hear of it. I've posted a heavy guard along the border lest others follow."

I felt sick. "What has that to do with me?"

"I don't know." His dark gaze was steady. "Tell me."

I was silent for a long moment. "The man they were hunting killed my wife."

"I see." He looked away. "You are sure of this?"

"Yes," I said.

Micah ben Ximon rose and walked across the room, hands clasped behind his back. I explained to Urist in a low voice what we had discussed. Urist winced at the news of Alban deaths.

"It is a dangerous thing to bring a dream to life," ben Ximon said without turning around. "Here in Vralia, I have watched my deepest, dearest hopes take shape. And I am not entirely sure I like the shape they have taken."

"The cross and not the *khai*?" I asked.

"Yes." He turned to face me. "Your wife's killer would not be the first criminal to seek refuge in Vralia under the mantle of Yeshua's name. There have been others; Skaldi fleeing persecution for some petty crime. Tadeuz Vral possesses all the zeal of a true convert. He extends his protection to anyone willing to acknowledge his rule and the divine sovereignty of Yeshua ben Yosef."

"Including murderers?" I asked.

"Anyone," he said.

"This is a matter of justice." I held his gaze. "My lord, the man we seek is guilty. I daresay he would admit it himself if we found him. If nothing else, I ask only the right to escort him back to Alba where he might be tried for his crime."

Micah ben Ximon shook his head. "Vral will not allow it."

"Then I will seek justice on my own terms," I said.

His lips curved. "I would expect such persistence from Joscelin Verreuil's foster-son." He paused. "I'm sorry. You must have loved your wife very much."

My jaw tensed. "Not as much as she deserved."

"Ah." He nodded. "Vengeance and guilt. A powerful mix."

"She was carrying our child," I said. "Nearly full term. She was the niece of the Cruarch of Alba. If our son had lived, he would have been Alba's eventual heir."

Another complicated emotion crossed ben Ximon's face. "I'm sorry," he repeated. He returned to take his seat, steepling his fingers and thinking. "But even so, I cannot give you aid or sanction," he said slowly. "And if you are caught, I cannot promise protection. I can only advise you to be careful. Tadeuz Vral is distracted by his brother's escape. They have been at odds for some years now. If my men do not catch Fedor before he reaches a stronghold—and I doubt they will, since it is rumored there were Tatar tribesmen with swift mounts awaiting him outside the city walls—there may be once again be war in Vralia."

"Yeshua's victory proved short-lived," I observed.

"It's the damned Tatars," ben Ximon said.

It wasn't a sentiment with which I could disagree. "Why do they support Fedor Vral?"

"He admires them," he said. "Prince Fedor is willing to promise the khans eternal rights to vast tracts of grazing land. To keep them free of pilgrim settlements. To bribe the tribes to leave the eastern trade routes alone."

"And Tadeuz isn't?" I asked.

"No." Micah ben Ximon regarded me. "His head is full of prophecy. He believes that God has chosen him to be the rock on which a new kingdom is founded, and that I am his strong right hand, his sword to carve out a path for Yeshua's return. The first step is conquering or converting Fedor's loyalists and the Tatars. He will not treat with them in any other way."

"What do you believe?"

He shrugged. "Eight years ago, when Tadeuz Vral sent for me, my soul was on fire. I handed him a victory. I saw his heart change and the light of true faith shine from his face. I believed what he believed. Now . . ." He paused. "Already, the face of my people's faith is changing. In a generation's time, it may become unrecognizable. Perhaps it is Yeshua's will. I no longer know what I believe."

We spoke for a while longer, and I translated his words for Urist. In the end, it was agreed that we should stick to the tale I'd concocted. We were adventurers, sent to scout out the prospects in Vralia; Urist as one of the Cruarch's trusted commanders, and me as a young D'Angeline nobleman whose family had known Micah ben Ximon long ago. Ben Ximon was willing to vouch for us that far, at least.

Due to his injury, Urist would remain at the palace while I explored the land and verified with my own eyes the existence of the fabled river trade routes of Vralia.

And hunted for Berlik.

If I was caught, ben Ximon warned me, he would disavow any knowledge of my true purpose. He might be able to intervene with Tadeuz Vral and save me; or not. He made no promises. Vral was unpredictable.

"Fair enough," I said. "It's more than I expected." I paused. "Why?"

"You remind me of him," he said. "A little bit, anyway."

"Tadeuz Vral?"

"Joscelin." Micah ben Ximon smiled, a real smile. "Single-minded and stubborn as hell." His smile turned wistful, and for the first time

I could see the fierce, idealistic young man he must have been. "He taught me a great deal. I always hoped he would be proud of me if he knew what I'd done with it."

"I know the feeling," I murmured.

"And now I hope *I* may be proud of it." He rose. "The men who were killed, the Albans . . . my men challenged them, and they fought. I'm sorry. Were they companions of yours?"

"Yes." I relayed his words to Urist, who gave a curt nod of acknowledgment. I daresay the news made the same sick lump in his belly that it did in mine, but neither of us were in a position to do aught about it. "They took their chances."

"As will you." Ben Ximon tilted his head. "Is it worth the price?"

"We chose this freely," I said. "My wife didn't."

He sighed. "I wish you luck."

The meeting left me restless and impatient. My course was set. I knew where I was bound; the village of Kargad, along the Ulsk River, a tributary of the Volkov. That was where Adelmar had told me the pilgrims with whom Berlik was travelling were headed. I would find them and lie to them. Tell them I was sent by his kinswoman, Morwen. That, too, was true enough in its own way. It was her meddling that had set this long nightmare in motion.

And then I would find him, and kill him.

So long as he didn't kill me first.

Urist and I sorted through our baggage. I picked out the warmest and sturdiest of the clothing Tadeuz Vral's servants had brought. My sword-belt and blades, my flint striker. The better of the two hunting bows, and four steel-tipped arrows Urist had hoarded. My vambraces. The croonie-stone for remembrance. A blanket. A waterskin. Hugues' wooden flute. An assortment of D'Angeline and Vralian coinage.

"And this." Urist rummaged in his packs and handed me a leather drawstring bag, stiff with dried saltwater. "Here."

I eyed it. "What's this?"

"To carry his head," he said. "It was full of lime powder, but it dissolved in the shipwreck. I saved the bag."

I stowed it in my pack. "My thanks."

"Boil it down to the bone," Urist said. "Otherwise it will stink.

It's all right, the skull will be enough. The lime would have done as much."

"Good to know," I said.

"So who do you think was killed?" he asked.

"I wish I knew," I said softly.

"So do I." Amid the bounty the palace servants had provided us, there was a small stoppered jug of somewhat they called *starka*, a rye spirit flavored with fruits and spices. Urist found a pair of cups and poured for us. "They were men of honor," he said. "May their spirits rest easily. May all the gods and goddesses of Alba welcome them home."

We drank.

Urist set down his cup. "I don't like this," he said somberly. "Any of it. A zealous prince with a head full of odd beliefs, with no care for our honor. A strange place, a hostile place, and you all alone. That was never meant to be."

You were all alone, kneeling in a snowstorm, beneath a barren tree . . .

"I'm not so sure of that," I said.

"Still." Urist balled one hand into a fist and thumped the outside of his stiff, braced leg. "I would that I were going with you."

"So do I." I took another swig of *starka*. It burned. "Believe me, I do. Urist, if I get caught, promise me you'll do the same as Micah ben Ximon. Promise me you'll disavow all knowledge of my purpose here."

He grunted. "I'm done with making promises."

I refilled our cups. "Please?"

Urist gave me a long, dour look. "Just get the bastard's head, my prince."

FIFTY-TWO

BEFORE I DEPARTED VRALGRAD, I had an audience with the Grand Prince Tadeuz Vral.

I rather liked him.

I hadn't expected that.

The summons came in the morning. It was a hasty affair—he was, as Micah ben Ximon had indicated, primarily concerned with his brother's escape. But he had heard the news and made time to meet with me in his chambers while he broke his fast.

"Sit," he said when I was ushered into his presence. "Eat."

I sat.

Tadeuz Vral studied me curiously. I studied him back. He was clean-shaven, with the same rugged bones I'd come to associate with Vralians, the skin stretched taut over the cheeks. Brown hair, lively brown eyes. No older than Micah. He grinned at me. Strong, white teeth. "Terre d'Ange, eh?"

I nodded. "Yes, my lord."

He said somewhat in a rapid spate of Rus. I shook my head, perplexed. Prince Tadeuz Vral reached across the table and took my chin in his hand, slapping my cheek lightly with easy familiarity. I was so startled, I didn't have time to take offense at it. "Your people are born long ago from *angels*, eh? So Micah says. Very nice. You make believers."

"In Terre d'Ange?" I asked, bewildered.

"Here. Yeshua's blood, yes? The Rebbes say angels walk the earth and talk to chosen people. Very beautiful like you. Maybe God sent you, too. I pray it is so." He beckoned to an attendant, who stepped forward and opened a sizable purse. Vral took a careless handful of coins from it and bestowed them on me, then made a shooing gesture with both hands. "Go, go! Go explore. Is a bad time, with my brother. Come back. We talk."

I went.

I didn't know what to make of Tadeuz Vral. There had been a warmth there; somewhat human. I'd thought to find him more like the Mahrkagir. *He'd* had a head full of odd prophecies, all right. And they'd damn near come true. If it weren't for Phèdre, they would have. Angra Mainyu, and ten thousand years of darkness. This felt very different.

I took my leave of the palace and made my way to the wharf, my battered saddlebags slung over my shoulder, the hunting bow and four arrows lashed to the strap.

I was alone.

I was well and truly alone, for the first time . . . well, since Daršanga, really. There had been isolated moments in Tiberium, but they were only moments. It felt strange.

There was a small market at the wharf. I bought strips of salted beef, hard biscuits, and dried fruit for the journey; staples that wouldn't spoil. There was a vendor selling luck-charms; pendants with flared crosses. I noticed a number of sailors wearing them. I purchased one, an inexpensive affair of painted wood and cheap gilt. With a twinge of guilt, I strung it around my neck. The vendor nodded in approval. I glanced toward the city, where the spires of the temple were visible.

"Forgive me, Yeshua," I murmured. "I mean no blasphemy."

There was no reply, no sense of presence. I wondered what Yeshua ben Yosef, the Habiru prince who had been the One God's son incarnate on Earth, would have made of these new followers of his.

I found passage to the southeast with a handful of taciturn fur-traders led by a fellow named Jergens. It was a small ship, smaller than the one that had brought us to Vralgrad, but when I pointed and asked, "Kargad?" they beckoned me aboard. They had room, having sold their goods in the city, and I reckoned the rivers wouldn't be as dangerous as the sea.

We were three days on the Volkov before we reached the Ulsk tributary. When we first cleared the wharf, Jergens surreptitiously tossed somewhat over the side of the railing, muttering under his breath. He caught me watching him and glared.

"You not tell," he said, pointing to my cross pendant.

"Tell what?" I asked.

It took a while before he could make himself understood, and Jergens wasn't a talkative man, but there wasn't much else to do on a small ship. It had been an offering to the *vodyanoi*, the water-spirit of the Volkov; a piece of superstition banned by Tadeuz Vral. People were not punished for keeping the old faiths, at least not overtly, but it was discouraged. If it became known that Jergens and his fellows did, merchants in Vralgrad would be reluctant to buy their next shipment of furs.

I thought about that on our journey. Thought about the speed with which Vralia was changing, and the way Vralia was changing the face of Yeshuite faith. About Alba and the Maghuin Dhonn, and how they had feared the old ways would be lost. About the vision of my son, Dorelei's and my son, who would have brought about that very thing.

And I wondered for the first time . . . if I were Berlik, if I had seen that future stumbling toward inevitability, what would I have done?

It was a chilling notion.

Still, I thought, change is not always bad. Of a surety, Terre d'Ange had changed when Elua and his Companions made it their home. In a few short generations' time, they had set their stamp on us, permanently and irrevocably. On our hearts, our minds, in our very blood. We were D'Angeline.

But it hadn't happened at the point of a sword.

What I'd said to Sidonie—the words she had quoted back to me, my mother's words—was true. Blessed Elua cared naught for thrones or crowns. Those were mortal ambitions. Nor did he care for glory or power or the fulfillment of mysterious prophecies or, insofar as I knew, aught but love, desire, and the myriad pleasures with which life was filled. I understood that in a way I never had before.

I thought about Yeshua ben Yosef, too. I wished I knew more about him. I'd never read the books of his life, the Brit Khadasha. But I'd heard Eleazar ben Enokh speak of him. I didn't think that the Yeshua he worshipped, a god of forgiveness and compassion, wished to carve out a kingdom with steel and blood. Still, after a lifetime of study, even Eleazar could not say for certain what this passage or that passage had meant.

That was the problem, Urist had said, with trusting to the written word. There was a truth to his claim; but I wasn't sure trusting to the spoken word and the chain of memory, as the Cruithne did, was any more reliable. When it came to the Maghuin Dhonn, the truth was Drustan had told me was not the truth the harpist Ferghus had sung for us. We were human, mortal and fallible. We forgot, we made errors, argued ambiguities, and twisted meanings to suit our own ends.

And in so doing, mayhap we reshaped the gods themselves.

Now *that* was a thought made me shudder to the bone. I wondered if it were true, and if it were, what would happen when some deity bent out of true by mortal ambition returned to set the record straight.

I wished there was someone with whom I could discuss such matters—who knows, mayhap Jergens would have taken a surprising interest—but my Rus was too poor for such heady conversation. So I sat with my thoughts in silence, huddling in my thick woolen coat when the wind blew, gnawing on salt beef, stale biscuits, and dried figs, taking a turn at the oars when we were becalmed, until we reached Kargad.

It was a pleasant little village, situated on the bank of the Ulsk. Men in fishing boats trawling for eel or trout glanced curiously at us as we headed for the narrow wharf. Habiru faces, for the most part. This was a settlement, not a trading post.

My arrival was unceremonious. Jergens didn't even bother to secure the ship, merely drew abreast of the dock, hovering long enough that I could toss my pack ashore and leap across the gap. He gave me a brief wave of farewell, and that was that. For the fur-traders it was out oars and back to the river, eager to set their traps before the snow fell. When all was said and done, I supposed I was lucky to be travelling with such an incurious crew.

I shouldered my bags and set about finding Berlik's pilgrims.

It was, in truth, a good deal easier than I'd feared. Thanks to Adelmar of the Frisii, I knew I was looking for the families of Ethan of

Ommsmeer and his wife. There were several women haggling with fishermen over buckets of eels along the wharf. I took the simplest approach, and asked one of them, speaking in Habiru. I picked the prettiest of the lot, a young woman who'd been stealing glances at me since I arrived, a small toddler clinging to her skirts.

"Your pardon, my lady," I said politely. "Do you know the house of Ethan of Ommsmeer?"

She blushed. "I do."

I stooped, balancing my pack, and picked up her bucket. "Will you show me?" I asked. "I'll carry your . . ." I didn't know the Habiru word for "eels." ". . . your long fish."

Her blush deepened. "I will."

Elua knows what she thought of me. I'd not given much consideration to Tadeuz Vral's words; that my face, my heritage as a scion of Elua and Kushiel, would lend credence to the mythos of Yeshua. In Terre d'Ange, as in other civilized nations, our presence is taken for granted. I imagined most Yeshuite pilgrims would know this, coming as they did from other lands. We are, as Eamonn always teased me, a pretty folk. But by the way my guide looked at me, uncertain and daring, I guessed she was unsure of my origins.

She couldn't have been any older than Ravi. I wondered if she'd been born in Vralia. She led me through a narrow maze of streets, carrying the toddler.

"Here," she said outside a wooden stoop. "Ethan's home."

"My thanks." I inclined my head and hoisted the bucket. "And yours . . . ?"

"No, no!" She shifted her child, snatching the bucket. "It is not needed."

Well, and so. I watched her hurry away down the streets of Kargad, carrying her child and her bucket, then raised my fist and knocked on the wooden door.

The woman who answered my knock didn't look surprised to see me. A Habiru woman, although by virtue of her rounded cheeks and the stray locks of reddish-blonde hair escaping her kerchief, I daresay there was some Flatlander blood there, too. She stood silently in the doorway, regarding me.

"I'm looking for Berlik of Alba," I said humbly. "I bear a message for him."

"Ja." She studied me for a moment without saying anything further, then opened the door wider. "We have been expecting you. Come in."

It wasn't a response I'd been anticipating, but I kept my mouth shut on that fact and entered. The house was a tiny one-room affair, divided by a hearth in the center that was the sole source of heat and, at the moment, light. There were beds built into niches in the walls. A young boy sat on the upper bunk, swinging his legs and staring at me with wide, dark eyes.

"Go fetch your father, my heart," his mother said gently to him. "You know where he is? Working on the cow-byre with Uncle Nisi?" The boy nodded vigorously and scrambled down the ladder on short, sturdy legs, leaving the door ajar in his haste. His mother smiled after him, closing the door in his wake.

"A good-looking boy," I ventured.

"He takes after his father," she said. "But it was Berlik saved his life."

"Oh?" I kept my tone neutral.

"Ja." She pointed to the area beyond the hearth, where a table and chairs stood. "Please, sit. Ethan will be here soon. There is pottage if you are hungry, or I can make griddle-cakes."

The thought of hot food made my mouth water. "No thank you, my lady." I set down my pack and took a seat. "How did Berlik come to save your son's life?"

"You should eat. You have come a long way." She withdrew a bowl from a neat little cupboard and ladled a serving of pottage into it, setting it before me. "We were crossing a bridge over the Voorwijk when the harness broke. The cart tipped. A great deal happened at once, and we did not see that Adam had fallen into the river." She placed a tin spoon beside the bowl. "Berlik was travelling the road behind us. He saw. He plunged into the river and rescued him."

I took a bite of pottage. "That must have been terrifying."

"It was." She sat opposite me and offered nothing further. I ate in silence. The sound of my spoon scraping the bowl seemed loud.

"Thank you, my lady," I said, finishing. "How shall I call you?"

"Galia," she said briefly.

"Galia." I nodded. "I am Imriel."

"Im-ri-el." She said it slowly. "The eloquence of God."

There was a noise at the door; her husband entered, stooping low to cross the threshold, his son on his shoulders. A whiff of cow-dung entered with them. He swung the boy down and set him on his feet. I rose in acknowledgment. "So you have come," Ethan of Ommsmeer said gravely. "As Berlik said you would."

"What did he say?" I asked.

He didn't answer right away. "Will you sit and drink a cup of beer?"

I shrugged. "If it would please you."

He didn't answer that, either, but went to wash his hands at the basin. I wondered if he was stalling for time. Galia fetched a pair of porcelain cups, filling them from a small keg in the corner, then took the boy and went into the front portion of the house, sitting beside the hearth and sewing quietly. Ethan took the seat opposite me at the table, and I sat again.

"Berlik is a good man, I think," he said at length. "A good man who has done a bad thing."

"Did he tell you that?" I asked.

"In time." Ethan sipped his beer. "At first he did not speak our tongue, although he learned it swiftly. But I knew. I could see the shadow of guilt that haunted his eyes, strongest of all when he gazed at Adam."

"And yet you trusted him with your son," I said.

Ethan met my eyes. His were dark, like his son's; quiet and soulful, set in a worn, gentle face. "He saved Adam's life," he said. "He traded his robe to buy us goods we could scarce afford. Adam thought him wondrous. I persuaded him to stay, to travel with us, for the boy's sake. Yes. I trusted him."

"And in time, you spoke," I said.

"Yes." He looked down, turning the cup in his hands. Strong hands, laborer's hands, engrained with dirt that a single scrubbing wouldn't re-move. "He told me he had done a thing too terrible to speak of. That he must flee as far as he might, carrying its curse on his shoulders, carry-ing it far, far from his people." He glanced up at me. "And as he learned

our tongue, I spoke to him of Yeshua ben Yosef, who lived and died in
the flesh that he might take the sins of all mankind on his shoulders
and bear them for eternity. All men, even such a man as Berlik."

"All of this before Maarten's Crossing?" I asked wryly.

"No." Ethan smiled a little. "No, he learned fast, but not *so* fast.
But I could see that his heart was good. I persuaded him to take the
pilgrim's cap and spoke on his behalf."

I nodded. "I see."

"But through Skaldia, we spoke." Ethan tilted his head, gazing into
the past. "When we crossed into Vralia, I could feel it was different.
I could feel it in the soil, I could feel it singing in the marrow of my
bones. A change. A kingdom built in Yeshua's name, a kingdom on
earth. That night, I prayed for Berlik, and I persuaded him to kneel
and pray with me. I told him that whatever he had done, if he was willing to surrender his heart and his guilt into Yeshua's keeping, he would
find forgiveness here. Berlik wept."

I swirled my beer. "And is it all you hoped, Ethan? Yeshua's
kingdom?"

"All?" he said thoughtfully. "Not all, no. There is much that is different and strange. The first time I saw the soldiers of Tadeuz Vral,
wearing the cross upon which Yeshua died as a badge of war, I felt
strange to myself. But there is hope, too. For me, for my family. Perhaps for Berlik, too."

Another silence fell between us. I had thought to lie to this man
and his family. Now that I was here, I couldn't. They knew too much.
The cross pendant weighed heavy around my neck, tugging at my conscience. Heavy as the croonie-stone, straining against my own desires.
I sighed and removed it, laying it on the table. The fire in the hearth
crackled. The cheap gilding on the cross glinted dully, its colors muted.
I felt lighter without it.

"Where is he?" I asked simply.

"Berlik said you would come." Ethan gazed at the cross. "The avenging angel." The muscles in his lean throat worked as he swallowed. "I
know you're not, not really. We're Flatlanders, we know D'Angelines.
And yet, a thing may be true and not true. Have you not found it to
be so?"

"Yes," I said. "I have."

His eyes were bright with tears. "There is a place . . . we learned of it along the pilgrims' route. It lies east, toward the Narodin Mountains. Miroslas. A yeshiva of sorts, a quiet place, where men go to think and be silent. It is said that the Rebbe there is a very holy man. He contemplates ways in which the Children of Yisra-el and Vralia may serve Yeshua's purpose alike. That is where Berlik went when he parted ways with us, to think and be silent."

"Miroslas," I said quietly. "My thanks."

Ethan shook his head. "He told us, he told me, that I was to tell you where he went. You, and you alone. I promised. I wish I had not."

"I'm sorry," I said. The fire crackled. On the far side of the hearth, I could make out the figure of Galia, still and listening, her sewing unattended in her hands. Adam sat quiet in his bunk, occupied with some child's toy. "Why do you think he did it?"

"I think there is a part of him that wishes to die," he said.

It crossed my mind that I would gladly have obliged him in Alba, but I kept my mouth shut on that thought, too. "Can I reach Miroslas by river?"

"No." Ethan rubbed his eyes. "Over land."

"The tanner's wife said you had horses." I felt at my purse. "Will you sell me one?"

He gave a short laugh. "We sold them to buy this house, and they have already been sold again. No one in Kargad has a horse to spare. If you want to buy a horse, go to Tarkov. There is a road leading east. It is only three days' walk. I would offer you our hospitality, but . . ." He glanced at Galia and his voice faded. "I am sorry."

"Three days." I nodded and stood. "All right."

"Will you kill him?" Ethan asked in a low tone.

I hoisted my pack and shouldered it. "Berlik never told you what he did, did he?" Ethan shook his head again. I gazed past the hearth, watching Galia with her head bent over her sewing, the boy Adam playing in his bunk. "No, I didn't think so. If he had, you wouldn't ask me that question."

"Killing him won't change anything," he said.

"It will for me," I said.

FIFTY-THREE

ALONE AND ON FOOT, I made my way to Tarkov.

For the first day, the road Ethan had mentioned—which wasn't more than a faint path, really—followed the Ulsk River. There, at least, I had the solace of seeing other people. But the second day, it veered eastward, into dense pine forest.

I went the whole of the second day without seeing another living soul, walking and walking. My boots, my old pair rescued from the shipwreck, chafed my feet. My scars ached with the strain of carrying my saddlebags. I shifted them from shoulder to shoulder and kept walking. The air was cold, cold enough to see one's breath. At least the effort of walking kept me warm.

I made camp that night alone under the pine canopy. Wrapped in a blanket, I sat beside the brisk little fire I'd built. I ate salt beef and drank sparingly from my waterskin. Beyond the campfire, I could see a pair of bright eyes reflecting light. Badger? Fox? Lynx? I fumbled for a branch to throw at them. The eyes vanished.

It occurred to me that I could die out here.

I pushed the thought away.

I found Hugues' flute in my bags. A foolish thing to bring, mayhap; an indulgence. I hadn't played it since the night Dorelei died. I wasn't sure if it would play true after its immersion in saltwater. But my pack had been one of the first items salvaged. When I set the flute to my lips and blew, it rang out clear and true.

I played mindlessly, melodies without a tune, my thoughts wandering. Berlik, the savior of a small boy. Justice. Mercy. Repentance. Men of Alba, men of Clunderry, slain in the pursuit. Was it worth the price? My fingers wandered over the holes. The last time I'd played alone in a wilderness, I'd been a goatherd. Soft and low, I played the song that all the children of the sanctuary knew, the song about the little brown goat.

Dorelei, laughing.

Dorelei dead.

"Yes," I said aloud, setting down the flute. "It's worth it."

I rolled myself in my blanket and slept, waking in the morning stiff with cold. There was a layer of hoarfroast sparkling on the ground, and my fire had burned down to a few banked embers. I blew them to life, warmed my hands, ate a stale biscuit. And then I stashed my gear, shouldered my pack, and started walking again.

It wasn't until the morning of the fourth day that I reached Tarkov, limping and footsore, and beginning to worry about the lack of water I carried. It was a glorious thing to see the dense forest suddenly give way to open fields surrounding a town large and prosperous enough to warrant being surrounded by a wooden stockade.

I limped gratefully to the gate, thinking less about vengeance than a hot bath and a warm meal, hoping I might find both here. There was a guard at the gate; Vralian, not Habiru. He gave me a long, puzzled look, but when I offered him one of Tadeuz Vral's copper coins, he shrugged and admitted me.

"Food?" I asked, miming. After three days in the woods, I was uncertain of my Rus. "Bath?"

He laughed and pointed.

I found my way to an inn by following my nose, which led me first to a good many private homes. At last I found a rangy timber building where a fellow with a formidable beard served me brown bread smeared thickly with butter, sizzling sausages, and a sharp dish of stewed cabbage, all of which I ate while he watched.

"Where are you from?" he asked.

"Terre d'Ange," I said. The innkeeper shook his head. "Far, very far." I pointed to the ceiling. "Buy room? Bed? One night?"

"Da, da." He continued to watch me. "Why are you here?"

"Buy . . ." Elua help me, I didn't know the word for "horse" in

Rus. "Do you speak Habiru?" I asked, switching. He shook his head. I slapped my thighs, mimicking the sound of trotting hooves, blew air through my lips. "A horse," I finished in D'Angeline.

The innkeeper grinned into his beard. "*Lózhat?*" he suggested, setting his legs astraddle and miming a man riding.

"*Da,*" I said gratefully, filing the word in memory. "You know where?"

He gave me a lengthy reply, speaking slowly and carefully as if to a child. I tried to recall if Phèdre had ever had this much difficulty communicating in her travels. Somehow I didn't think so. She soaked up language like a sponge. When I was younger, I had, too. It seemed harder now.

At any rate, if I understood the innkeeper aright, Tarkov was in the midst of an autumn fair, with the last buying and selling of livestock before the snow fell. It was held in paddocks near the eastern verge of town.

When he was done, he showed me to my room, a long, narrow, windowless chamber lined with straw pallets. Several appeared to be claimed already. I set my pack down on an empty one. "Bath?" I asked hopefully.

The innkeeper shook his head. Another lengthy reply led me to understand that there was a public bath-house in Tarkov.

"I'll find it," I said.

The men's bath-house wasn't an elaborate affair like those in Tiberium. It was a squat, windowless affair with thick stone walls to keep in the heat, a true luxury in a cold clime. Inside, there was a chilly outer chamber in which to disrobe, and then an inner chamber that was much like the one in the palace at Vralgrad, except the tubs were made of wood.

I didn't care. The room was thick with steam. There were other men there, some soaking in tubs, others sitting naked on stone benches, relishing the steamy heat. Vralians, staring curiously at me. At my face. At my scars. I didn't care about that, either. I'd been stared at a lot in my life. I eased my aching body into the hot water, feeling stiff muscles unknot, blisters and raw patches on my feet and ankles stinging.

I lingered there until the water grew tepid, then dragged myself reluctantly from the tub. No fine linens here; only a length of coarse burlap. I scoured myself dry, then dressed hastily in the antechamber. More stares and low murmurs. I ignored them.

By the time I left the bath-house, I felt immeasureably better. The cold air seemed bracing. Dorelei would have laughed, I thought, remembering how she had known somewhat was amiss when I went straight to the *ollamh*'s without bathing after my bindings had broken during the cattle-raid. Afterward, when my bindings were restored, she'd washed the cow-dung from my hair and told me about her dream of me feeding her honeycomb. The memory made me smile.

And Sidonie at the hunting manor . . .

Elua.

I'd kept those memories locked away in my heart. I hadn't let myself think about her. My girl. I did now. Only for a moment. The look of grave concentration as she unwound my bandages. Her skin, slick with scented oil; then, and later. It made me shiver with desire and longing. I missed her. It hurt.

Just come home.

I sighed, put the memory away, and went to buy a horse.

There were a number of them available for purchase, as well as cattle and a strange breed of long-haired oxen in separate paddocks. I leaned on the railing and eyed the horses. Most of them looked to be farm stock, broad-backed and platter-hooved, suitable for the plow. There was a shaggy pony I considered, remembering how Phèdre had told me of the pony they'd had in Skaldia, that had fared better than its longer-legged brethren. But then there were several others, with fine heads and alert eyes, that tempted me. I lingered longer than I should, trying to decide which to choose and how much I was willing to pay.

I was still trying to decide when the Tatars struck.

There was a guard posted outside the eastern gate. I was near enough to hear him shout. Near enough that when his disembodied head sailed over the stockade, I flinched. Near enough to see the young Tatar who vaulted over the stockade, launching himself from the saddle. To see his ankle twist on landing, sending him to his knees. Near enough that he actually caught my sword-belt, hauling himself upright with a grimace, while I stood frozen with shock. He let go of me, hobbling to unlatch the gate. Tatars on horseback poured through the opening, some of them riding two to a horse.

It happened so fast.

I stared, gape-mouthed and paralyzed, as they opened the paddocks. Ignored the cattle, stole the horses. It was so swift. If it had been an Alban cattle-raid, it couldn't have been planned better. More guards came, pelting on foot. The Tatars wheeled, shooting arrows with short bows. The guards dodged. One of the Tatars extended his arm to the young man who'd opened the gates. The young man hopped on one foot, missed his grip. The Tatar rider shrugged, shouting somewhat in his own tongue.

And then, in a flurry of pounding hooves, they were gone.

The guards swarmed the injured Tatar, bearing him to the ground and seizing his weapons. I was still staring when a man pointed at me, shouting somewhat. Six or seven guards turned toward me.

"No." I put up my hands, palms outward. *"Nyet, nyet!"*

The man was still shouting. I recognized him from the bath-house. Other onlookers offered hostile comments in Rus. My mind was a blank. I couldn't understand a word they were saying. All I could think, with a dull, sick realization, is that they'd seen me loitering, seen the Tatar grab my belt and haul himself to his feet.

I shook my head. "I don't know him!"

The head guard pointed at my midsection and said somewhat.

"My sword-belt?" I asked, bewildered. "All right." I unbuckled it and handed it over. "Friend, *da*? *Druk.*"

He took the belt and pointed at my breeches.

I backed away. "Oh, no. No."

When they swarmed me, I panicked and fought. It was stupid. There were a half a dozen guards, and dozens of onlookers willing to help. I was unarmed. My vambraces were in my pack at the inn. I was lucky they didn't kill me out of hand. They wrestled me to the ground outside the paddock, punching and kicking. Someone shoved my face into the cold mire, someone else wrenched my arms behind my back. Someone sat on my legs. Hands tugged at me, undoing my breeches.

All the horror of Daršanga, all the hurt and humiliation I'd managed to carry more lightly, came crashing down on me. I struggled, my body convulsing. It didn't matter. There were too many of them, men jumping in to help. They pinned my arms, put a booted foot in the small of my back. Dragged my breeches down.

A hard finger jabbed at me.

At the scar branded on my left buttock, marking me as the property of Jagun of the Kereyit Tatar tribe.

I closed my eyes. "Blessed Elua have mercy on me."

They dragged me to my feet, filthy and besmirched, my breeches around my knees. There was a sword-point poking my back, another aimed at my breast. I stood without fighting, two men holding my arms.

"I am not Tatar," I said in Rus.

There was a woman wailing somewhere. The widow of the beheaded guardsman, I guessed. The guard captain thrust his face close to mine. "You help them."

"No," I said wearily. "Ask. Micah ben Ximon. Friend, *druk*."

A shadow of doubt crossed his face. "Ben Ximon?"

I nodded. "Go to Vralgrad. Ask."

He didn't say aught else, but he gestured with his sword to the men holding my arms. They let go, although the sword-point pressed against my spine didn't move. I showed my empty hands, then stooped carefully to pull up my breeches. He let me lace them. My fingers were trembling.

"Come," the captain said.

"Where?" I asked. He said a word I didn't know. I learned it soon enough: prison.

They walked us both, me and the Tatar, through town; the Tatar hobbling in silence. He looked worse for the wear, with a split lip and a thin trickle of blood running down his neck from a lump on his skull. I daresay I looked much the same. I could feel my right eye swelling closed from a blow I didn't remember taking.

Tarkov must have been a peaceable enough place most of the time. There was a single gaol cell attached to the guardhouse, which was located in the center of town. Squinting through my left eye, I caught a glimpse of other buildings there. A freshly whitewashed temple, sporting a cross atop a single spire. A modest manor, which I guessed belonged to the local governor, whoever he might be.

And then I saw no more, as they ushered us into the guardhouse. The main chamber looked like guardrooms everywhere, with gear and half-eaten food strewn about, evidence of abandoned dice games. Warm braziers with stools drawn up around them, bedrolls tucked into corners.

The single gaol cell had a heavy wooden door. It was set with one small window, high and barred with iron. The lead guard unlocked the door. Three men shoved the stumbling Tatar past it. Prodded at sword-point, I balked.

"I not with him!" I said in frustrated Rus. "Ask ben Ximon!"

"We will," the captain said dourly.

The sharp tip prodded harder. I whirled in anger, slapping at the flat of the blade with my palm, trapping it against the door-jamb. The guard's eyes widened. I hooked his left leg with my right and jerked, hitting him hard beneath the chin with the heel of my left palm. He staggered backward, letting go his hilt. I seized his trapped sword. Behind me, the Tatar hooted and clapped.

"Shut *up*!" I shouted at him, wielding the sword in a two-handed grip.

"Friend." The captain shouldered past the man I'd disarmed. He opened his own arms, although he still held his sword. So did the dozen men standing behind him. Like the innkeeper, he spoke slowly to me, choosing simple words. "You come, Tatars come. You help him. You have a Tatar mark. War comes again. What do we think? Maybe you help Fedor Vral." He shrugged. "Wait. We send to Vralgrad and ask ben Ximon. Maybe you go free."

I hissed through my teeth. "I do not want be here with *him*."

The captain glanced past me. "Scared?"

"I do not like Tatars!" I said fiercely.

He shrugged again. "He cannot hurt you. Wait, or try to kill us all."

Elua knows, I wanted to. And Elua knows, I couldn't. Mayhap Joscelin could have. I couldn't. I hesitated for a moment, then threw down the sword. It skittered over the flagstones. The guard I'd taken it from scurried after it.

"Good choice," the captain said dryly, gesturing.

I took a step backward. The heavy wooden door slammed shut. Someone turned the key in the latch. I leapt and caught the iron bars, fingers clinging, and pressed my face to the window. "Send to Vralgrad!" I shouted. "Ask ben Ximon!"

"We will," came the reply.

I let myself drop, breathing hard. Turned to take stock of my cell. There wasn't much. Four straw pallets. A chamberpot. A pitcher of water. And one young Tatar, slumped on a pallet. He looked ashen beneath his brown skin, but he was grinning at me. He said somewhat in his own tongue, brows raised expressively. With his hands, he mimed my own actions with the sword. Whatever he said, it sounded admiring.

"Shut up," I said to him in D'Angeline. "Just . . . shut up."

The Tatar laughed.

FIFTY-FOUR

T**HE** T**ATAR'S NAME WAS** Kebek, although I learned it later.
For the duration of the first day of our joint imprisonment, I
didn't speak to him except to tell him to shut up and leave me alone.
On the following day, when a pair of guards opened the door to our
cell and ushered him out, I hoped I'd seen the last of him. Mayhap he
wasn't the one who'd wielded the sword, but of a surety, he'd been part
of a raid that resulted in a man's death. I wouldn't have been surprised
if they'd executed him; and I wouldn't have been sorry, either. It was
his damn fault I was here.

Alas, they brought him back, bloodier and a bit more battered.

And then it was my turn.

The captain wasn't taking any chances. He sent a half a dozen guards
to escort me to an inner chamber of the guardhouse. My pack was there,
all the items in it removed and placed neatly on a wooden table.

"Yours?" he asked.

"Yes," I said. After a day of silence, I'd had time to collect my wits.
"Is there person speak Habiru?"

The captain arched one brow. "Habiru?"

"I speak," I said. "Better than Rus."

He conferred with the other guards. One of them left. We stood
in silence until he returned with a man in ornate robes and a richly
embroidered cap. The captain bowed to him with obvious respect.
The sight of him filled me with relief. If I could explain, surely they
would see that the idea I'd had anything to do with the Tatar raid was
absurd.

"This is the Rebbe," the captain said. "Tell him why you're here."

"Shalom, my lord," I said to the Rebbe. "This is a mistake, a misunderstanding. I've nothing to do with the Tatars, and I didn't help the man. I was standing in the wrong place at the wrong time, that's all."

The Rebbe didn't look particularly friendly. "Why *are* you here?"

"To buy a horse." I pointed to the purse on the table. "My lord, I've coins given me by Tadeuz Vral himself. I'm a kinsman of the Queen of Terre d'Ange, sent to explore Vralia. As I told the captain, send to Micah ben Ximon. He will tell you it is true." I hoped it was true. Ben Ximon had warned me he might not be able to protect me if I were caught, but I hardly thought these were the circumstances he had in mind.

The Rebbe translated my words for the captain, who shrugged and said, "Why does he have a Tatar mark?"

"I was a prisoner a long time ago," I replied in Habiru. "In Drujan. There were Tatars there. One of them did it to me."

The Rebbe translated. The captain looked incredulous. I didn't blame him. He said somewhat lengthy. The Rebbe nodded and turned back to me. "What has Prince Fedor promised your Queen?"

I blinked. "My Queen?"

"Surely, you do not think we are all so foolish." He frowned. "Why else would you come at such a time? You went to Vralgrad to spy for Fedor, to learn Micah ben Ximon's plans, then you go east toward Petrovik, where Fedor has retreated. You have arranged to meet his wild Tatars here. So, what has he promised your Queen?"

I laughed in disbelief. "My lord, I mean no offense, but I'm not sure Queen Ysandre knows Vralia exists as a nation. I'm *very* sure she doesn't know Fedor Vral exists."

"Ah." The Rebbe studied me. "If she does not know of Vralia, how could she send you to explore?"

I could have bitten my tongue off. "Rumors," I said. "Tadeuz Vral sent a shipment of furs and amber to the Cruarch of Alba with an offer of trade. I was travelling with a companion, the Cruarch's man. He was injured in a shipwreck. He is in Vralgrad."

"How convenient," the Rebbe observed.

I gritted my teeth. "Not really, no."

He spoke with the captain of the guard. The captain picked up my vambraces, pointing to the flowing, stylized lines of the Black Boar of the Cullach Gorrym worked on them. I hated seeing him handle them. "This is Tatar work," the Rebbe said.

"It's *Alban*," I said in exasperation. "It's the Cruarch's insignia!"

"It looks Tatar," he said.

I opened my mouth to reply, and thought about the Maghuin Dhonn, who claimed to have crossed the ice to Alba many centuries ago. I thought about the stamp of their features; the set of their eyes, the slant of their cheekbones. How they claimed to have interbred with the Cruithne and taught them. If any of it were true, I realized, it was indeed very possible that the Maghuin Dhonn and the Tatars were descended from some common stock.

"Ah," the Rebbe said, watching me. "You do not deny it."

"My wife had those made for me," I said softly. "Dorelei mab Breidaia, niece of the Cruarch of Alba."

Another exchange in Rus. The captain shook his head in frank disbelief. "Such an important person you become," the Rebbe said. "Minute by minute, the story grows. Now you are married to the Cruarch's niece?"

"I was," I said.

"Maybe." He folded his arms. "You are a cunning fighter. You speak Habiru. You come to Vralgrad, you win ben Ximon's ear. You were a Tatar prisoner, you know their ways. You are, I think, the perfect spy."

He was absolutely right.

I spread my hands. "But I'm *not*. My lord, if I were a spy, why would I let myself get caught so carelessly? I'd be on my way to join Fedor Vral, not stumbling into the middle of a Tatar horse-raid."

"I cannot say. Perhaps some misfortune befell you. If you're not a spy, then why are you here?" the Rebbe asked. There was an honest curiosity in his voice. "*Here*, in Tarkov, on foot. There is nothing to see, nothing to explore. Why?"

It was the one question I couldn't answer. The truth would be worse than a lie. There was no earthly reason for me to be here, except that I was hunting for the man who killed my wife; a Yeshuite pilgrim. "Send to Vralgrad," I repeated. "Micah ben Ximon will vouch for me."

"Maybe you lied to him, too," the Rebbe said.

"Ask him what we talked about!" I raised my voice. "I don't know or care a blessed thing about his plans. He didn't say, and I didn't ask."

He conferred with the captain. "If Micah ben Ximon orders it, you will be freed," the Rebbe said. "Because it is possible, you will not be put to the same hard questioning as your Tatar friend. Your things will be kept safe and you will be unharmed. But if ben Ximon does not order it . . ." He shrugged. "You would be wise to confess and tell all that you know. Yeshua is merciful. If you are willing to cooperate, perhaps Tadeuz Vral will allow your Queen to ransom her spy."

"He's not my friend!" I shouted. "And I don't *know* anything!"

"Pity for you," the Rebbe said. "I suggest you pray."

With that, our interview was concluded. I was led back to my cell. The heavy door clanged shut behind me, the key turning in the lock. I flung myself on one of the straw pallets. Every muscle in my body was knotted with fury. The Tatar bestirred himself and asked me somewhat in his own tongue.

"Shut up," I said to him. "This is all your fault."

He pointed to his split lip, then a fresh graze over his left brow, miming punches. Pointed at my face with an expression of concern.

"No." I prodded the puffy, tender flesh around my right eye socket. "This is from yesterday. They didn't hit me today."

He nodded, then screwed up his face and made a universal gesture of apology.

"You damn well ought to be sorry," I said. "I hope they hang you. What the hell are *you* doing in Tarkov? Shouldn't you be roaming the plains or holed up in Petrovik with Fedor Vral?"

The Tatar pointed to his own chest. "Kebek."

"I don't care," I said.

"Kebek," he repeated, his expression open and hopeful, gesturing at me to reciprocate. He was young, younger than me. There were a few bristles of black hair growing above his upper lip. All I'd seen when I first looked at him was Jagun's face. Now that I looked closer, I could see an echo of the Maghuin Dhonn; and even fainter, of the Cruithne. His brown skin had the same warm tone as Dorelei's. His black eyes . . .

I closed mine. "Leave me be."

He didn't, of course.

Over the days that followed, I learned a few things. Neither the captain or the guards would tell me anything, but I listened to them gossip. I understood enough Rus to gather that their ungentle questioning of Kebek had been utterly futile. He didn't speak a word of Rus or any other tongue but his own. Their speculation was that he and the other Tatars had been part of the group that had helped Fedor Vral escape. Either they had somehow been cut off from the main party, or they had arranged to meet me here in Tarkov.

More depressingly, I learned within a week that Micah ben Ximon was no longer in Vralgrad. He was on the march, leading Tadeuz Vral's army toward Petrovik, a walled city nestled in the Narodin Mountains, where Fedor Vral was prepared to hunker down for the winter.

Vralia was at war.

"I am sorry," the captain of the guard said. "There are Tarkovan men going to join ben Ximon. I will send word with them."

"Please do," I said shortly.

I didn't care about any of it. Didn't care about the quarrel between Tadeuz and Fedor, didn't care who had promised what to whom. I lay in my cell mulling over my options and doing my best to ignore Kebek.

Once again, there were no good choices. This wasn't civilized Caerdicca Unitas, where I could send a message to the D'Angeline ambassador and bring the might and wealth of Terre d'Ange to bear; and I wasn't exactly in Ysandre's good graces anyway. I thought long and hard about begging the captain to send to Tadeuz Vral himself. It might be that the Grand Prince would intervene. He had seemed well-disposed toward me and interested in Terre d'Ange. On the other hand, he might very well believe I *was* a spy. With Vralia at war, I daresay he'd choose to err on the side of caution. Elua knows, I would if I were him. Of a surety, he was unlikely to let me continue to wander unattended around Vralia.

I could tell the truth.

Having met Tadeuz Vral, I didn't think he was a man likely to punish me for somewhat I hadn't done. I could claim to have repented of my intentions. If I was lucky, he would simply forgive me and send me home. And Dorelei's death would go unavenged, all my efforts for naught. It was a galling thought. I wasn't willing to accept failure. Not yet.

In the end, I couldn't think of a single course that didn't involve abandoning my hunt for Berlik except waiting for Micah ben Xi-mon's aid, and praying like hell that he was willing to give it. If he wasn't . . . well. There was always the truth.

And failure.

So I waited. Another week passed, then two. The captain thought it was at least ten days' ride to Petrovik, mayhap longer.

The worst part of it was the tedium. I wonder that more men don't die of it in prison. We weren't treated badly. After the first day, they didn't bother to beat Kebek. They didn't seem inclined to kill him, either. We ate what the guards ate, twice a day. When the temperature dropped further, coldness seeping incessantly through the stone walls, they took pity on me and gave me the bedroll from my pack.

It wasn't as bad during the day when the braziers were stoked in the guardroom and one could move about, but at night, when the braziers burned low, the chill sank into one's bones. I spent half that first night wrapped in my blanket in a state of profound irritation, listening to the Tatar's teeth chatter in the darkness.

"Elua!" I said in disgust, giving up. "Fine. Come here."

He made a questioning sound.

I patted my pallet. "Come here, you horse-thieving Tatar idiot. I'll share the blanket."

He crawled over to me, dragging his own pallet. Crawled gratefully beneath the blanket, huddling against me. His entire body was rigid and trembling with cold. He smelled of unwashed flesh and a faint, lingering odor of horse. In the pitch black of our benighted cell, there was nothing about him to remind me of Jagun. He might have been any half-frozen young man lying beside me. It seemed to take forever before he warmed enough to relax, murmuring somewhat thankful in a sleepy voice.

"Shut up," I said to him, but I said it gently.

I daresay the tedium was worse for him. At least I was able to communicate with our gaolers, albeit in a limited fashion. I had the distraction of listening to the guards gossip outside our cell, which helped improve my understanding of Rus. And I practiced the Cassiline forms, telling the hours with empty hands while Kebek watched with a mixture of admiration and perplexity.

If nothing else, he was persistent. He asked me questions I couldn't begin to comprehend, illustrated with lively gestures. I wished he wouldn't, because any semblance of conversation between us provided fodder for the notion that I was a spy.

In truth, every now and then, I did catch a word I recognized. Elua knows, I'd heard enough of the Tatar tongue spoken in Daršanga, although I'd done my best to forget it. And after a time, much to Kebek's joy, I gave up on ignoring him. When he asked if I had a woman, I knew what he meant. When he asked it for the tenth or twentieth time, I gave up and answered.

"Yes," I said in D'Angeline. "Oh, yes." I nodded and pointed at him. "And you?"

Kebek's eyes lit up and he nodded vigorously. He shaped her in the air with his hands; plump and rounded, standing only so high. He mimed her ample buttocks with particular fervor. It made me laugh. He grinned and pointed back at me, raising his brows.

I thought about Sidonie and smiled, trying to shape her. Taller than Alais, not as tall as her mother. There was no single attribute that stood out, or at least not one I could depict with my hands. Just everything in perfect proportion, precise and exact.

Kebek looked unimpressed.

"It's the way it all fits together," I assured him. "Trust me."

He didn't look convinced. He said somewhat else, miming. Stirring a pot; eating. Smacking his lips, rubbing his belly. Pointing in inquiry.

"A good cook?" I laughed and shook my head. "Elua, I doubt it!"

He mimed sewing, and I shook my head. Many noblewomen embroidered as a pastime, but I didn't ever recall seeing Sidonie doing it. Kebek mimed hunting, drawing a bow. I shook my head at that, too. Dorelei had been good with a bow; better than I was. Sidonie? She rode to the hunt, of course, but I'd never seen her shoot. I wasn't sure she enjoyed it any more than she enjoyed climbing trees. And it was quite possible that she'd never even seen the inside of a kitchen.

Kebek clicked his tongue dismissively, then shrugged and turned both palms upward, raising his brows to ask what in the world I saw in this useless woman of dubious attractiveness who couldn't cook or sew or hunt.

If I could have spoken to him, what would I have said? That the woman I loved was the heir to a powerful nation? That she had spent her life at her mother's knee, learning about diplomacy and negotiation and making difficult decisions that would affect the lives of thousands of people? That she might, *might* be willing to throw it all away for love of me? That she had a sly sense of humor and a wicked knack for mimicry? A stubborn streak and the capacity for fierce loyalty? The courage to stand down Barquiel L'Envers and defy the entire Court to adhere to Blessed Elua's precept?

All of it was true.

And none of it really mattered. In the end, I didn't know why I loved her to the point of distraction. I knew only that I did.

I drew a circle around my heart with one finger. "I don't know, Kebek. I just do."

He nodded with all the sagacity of his sixteen or seventeen years. We sat in silence a moment, thinking about our women. Kebek brightened and nudged me. He gave me another inquiring look and made a lewd gesture recognized the world over.

"That?" I sighed and lay back on my pallet, folding my arms beneath my head. "Oh, my friend, you have no idea."

FIFTY-FIVE

IF I HAD KNOWN how long I'd be stuck in a stone cell in Tarkov with Kebek the Tatar, I might have kept track of the days. But expecting to be freed at a moment's notice, I didn't. As a result, a great many days passed.

How many, I couldn't say.

There was no word from Micah ben Ximon in Petrovik. When I asked the captain, he shrugged apologetically and promised soon, soon.

In the meantime, a feast-day arrived.

It had, I gathered, somewhat to do with the initial victory of Tadeuz Vral over his brother's forces. The Feast of One Hundred Martyrs, the guards called it. Apparently, it was celebrated all over Vralia since the battle; or at least those parts of Vralia that lay under the control of Tadeuz Vral. The mayor of Tarkov sent a cask of *starka* to his guards.

They got drunk.

I'd never met the mayor of Tarkov, on whose orders I was detained. Whoever he was, I reckoned he was a weak or disinterested fellow, trusting his captain of the guard to handle the matter. I never knew the captain's name, either. He wouldn't give it to me, reckoning I might be a spy. But one thing I did learn: Vralians loved their *starka*.

They began with toasts to each and every one of the One Hundred Martyrs, naming ten at a time and downing generous gulps of *starka*. Then came a rousing retelling of the battle in which the One Hundred had led their fateful charge, followed by maudlin tales of noble, grieving widows and fatherless children vowing vengeance. By the time the maudlin tales gave way to songs, they were all well and thoroughly inebriated. Kebek and I lounged on our pallets, wincing at the loud, off-key singing. It made for a late, noisy night, but at least they were keeping the braziers stoked.

And then one of the guards got the idea of rummaging through my belongings, which were held in the adjacent room, and fetching Hugues' flute.

He played it very badly, but it didn't stop the others from encouraging him, laughing and shouting. A slow tide of fury rose in me. I got to my feet, pacing restlessly. Kebek watched me curiously.

"That flute was a gift," I said grimly to him. "I played it for my wife. It made her laugh."

He shrugged, not understanding.

"Hey!" I caught the bars of the window and pulled myself up. The guards on duty glanced at me. "You sound like a sick cow," I said in Rus.

The flute-player flushed. The others laughed at him, making lowing sounds. "You think you can play better?" he asked.

"Than a sick cow?" I asked contemptuously. "Yes."

The guards conferred, laughing and scuffling. To my surprise, one took the cell key from the nail where it hung and came over to unlock the door. They hauled me into the guardroom, half a dozen drawing their swords, relocking the door behind me. I watched them warily, but they didn't seem inclined to violence, just drunken fun.

"So play, spy," said the guard who'd taken my flute. He handed it to me. "Yes! Play for the honor and glory of the One Hundred Martyrs."

I glared at him, put the flute to my lips, and blew.

It was hardly my finest hour—I was out of practice—but I daresay the Vralians didn't know it. I'd found solace in music during the journey to Innisclan, pining for my lost love. Later, I'd kept it up during the long winter months at Clunderry. I hadn't begun as a very good player, but I'd ended as a fair one.

I played a solemn, martial dirge that made the guards bow their heads and press their fists to their hearts, remembering the martyrs. When I finished, they slapped my back and pressed a cup of *starka* on me. I raised it. "To the One Hundred Martyrs," I said, draining it at a gulp. I could see Kebek's face hanging in the barred window of our cell, suffused with envy.

"More." Someone began clapping out a beat. "More!"

I played every tune I could remember, and a few I couldn't. It went on long into the night. The Vralian guards laughed and stamped and shouted, drinking *starka* and periodically offering new toasts to their favorite martyrs. And in the back of my mind, a plan took shape.

I played without thinking, trying desperately to remember. The green smell of the Alban countryside in summer. A full moon glinting on a silver pipe. Morwen. The tune had haunted me all the way across Alba. I'd played it the night I'd spilled my seed on *taisgaidh* soil, dreaming of Sidonie.

It was *us. That's how they bound you.*

"Is enough, I think," one of the guards slurred. He gestured at me with the point of his sword. "You give honor to the One Hundred. Thank you. Now we put you back."

"One more," I said. "For sleep with peace."

He nodded blearily, going to fetch the key to my cell. Others were already yawning. One was tipping the cask, pouring the last dregs of *starka* into his cup.

I whispered a prayer and played Morwen's tune.

I had to close my eyes, unable to look. I shut out the world, shut out my thoughts, focusing on the melody; poignant and bittersweet, filled with the promise of desire and the deep ache of loss. Note after note, soft and lingering. I played them without faltering, every breath a prayer. And when I had finished, I lowered the flute and opened my eyes.

The guards were snoring.

Every last one of them.

My heart began beating quickly. I stepped over a sleeping body and tested the door to the inner chamber where my things lay. It was unlocked. Beyond, the room was dark. I didn't think it was used by anyone but the captain, and that only during the day. I moved silently, willing my eyes to adjust. They didn't. I found my saddlebags by touch, fumbling in the darkness. There was the hunting bow, there my sword-belt. I stowed my flute and prayed everything else was there, retreating carefully back to the guardroom.

My bedroll.

It was locked in the cell with Kebek. It didn't matter, I thought; there were others. I could steal one of the guards' blankets.

But then there was Kebek.

I stood for a moment in a state of profound indecision, then cursed inwardly. The guard with the key was slumped against a wall, slumbering peaceably, exhaling *starka* fumes. The key dangled from his fingers. I eased it from his grasp. When his fingers twitched, I thought my heart would stop. If they caught me trying to escape with Kebek, I doubted even Micah ben Ximon could convince them I wasn't a spy. At best, Kebek was a horse-thieving Tatar, and I should leave him. But I'd spent the last few weeks of my life sharing a blanket with him, and I couldn't bring myself to do it. He wasn't much more than a boy, and somewhere, there was a short woman with plump, round buttocks wondering if her young lover was dead or alive.

I wondered if Tadeuz Vral would prove merciful and ask for ransom.

I wondered if Ysandre would pay it.

For once, luck was with me. The guard didn't wake. I unlocked the cell door. In the dim light of the low-burning braziers, I made out the form of Kebek, sleeping. I knelt beside him and put my hand over his mouth, then shook him awake.

His black eyes snapped open and his body tensed. It eased when he saw me. I took my hand away, placed a finger to my lips, then pointed to the open cell door. Kebek's eyes widened. He sat up and gave me a hard embrace, kissing me on both cheeks. I shook my head at him, stuffing my blanket into my pack.

Despite his incessant questioning in the cell, he did know how to be quiet when it mattered. Together, we stole out of the guardhouse, taking whatever useful items we could find; spare blankets, a thick coat someone had doffed during the celebration, a half-eaten loaf of bread.

Outside, it was *cold*. Late autumn, I reckoned, but far colder than it would have been in Terre d'Ange. I shivered and gazed at the stars high overhead. It was late. The town square was empty and quiet. There was a light dusting of snow on the ground.

We were free.

What now?

It was Kebek who found an answer. Lifting his head, he sniffed the cold air, the beckoned and pointed. There was a stable attached to the mayor's manor house. We raised our brows at one another and went to explore.

Our luck stayed with us. The stable was guarded by one stable-boy, slumbering in the straw, his body wrapped around a jug. I could smell the *starka* at twenty paces.

It was dangerous, but not, I thought, as dangerous as venturing out on foot would be. We'd be caught too quickly. The hardest part was finding gear in the tackroom. I was grateful for the blindfolded games I'd played with Phèdre when I was younger. I searched with my hands, moving without a sound. Things were more or less where one would expect to find them; bridles hung on pegs, saddles slung over supports. I found burlap sacks of grain, too, and took two of those.

It took me several trips, while Kebek led a pair of horses into the square. He was good with horses. We worked quickly, silently, and efficiently together. In a trice, the horses were saddled and bridled. It felt strange to sling my bags over the crupper and mount. I hadn't ridden astride for months.

Our last hurdle to clear was the gate. I knew it would be barred from within at night. I didn't know if it would be guarded. We rode through the sleeping city. The horses' heads bobbed sleepily. The sound of their hooves seemed unnaturally loud.

There was no guard posted at the gate.

"Blessed Elua be praised," I whispered. Kebek said somewhat fervent in agreement. I slipped from the saddle, lifted the heavy bar. The gate creaked open when I shoved it. I led my mount through, and Kebek followed. I pushed the gate closed, and hoped no one was planning to raid Tarkov that night. It wasn't their fault they'd taken me for a spy. Under the circumstances, I would have, too.

There was a dirt road stretching eastward before us. Kebek and I glanced at one another. He pointed at the road. I shrugged. Ethan of

Ommsmeer had said Miroslas lay to the east. Insofar as I knew, our paths were aligned, at least for now. I wasn't happy about it, but it was the only road available to us. I swung myself astride. Kebek dug his heels into his mount's flanks, clicking his tongue.

We rode throughout the night, under the starlight. There was no pursuit. No one in Tarkov knew we were gone yet. It was quiet and peaceful, and a little surreal. I was a fugitive in a strange land, riding beside a young Tatar man.

Kebek looked happy.

Elua, I should have left him there.

We rode through a wood, but it wasn't as dense as the one between Kargad and Tarkov. By dawn, we had emerged. There was a stream with a skin of ice on it. We broke the ice and watered our horses and ourselves. In the daylight, I could see that Kebek had chosen wisely. The horses we'd stolen were at once sturdy and elegant, with short legs and shapely heads, calm and quiet. They looked capable of going long distances.

"You're no Bastard," I said to mine. "But you'll do."

It was a league or so after we emerged from the woods that the road forked. One path, the more faint of the two, continued eastward. The other veered south. Kebek pointed to the latter, raising his brows.

I shrugged. "Miroslas?"

His mouth twisted. His folk were nomadic, but he was in the service of Fedor Vral and he knew the lay of the land. Reluctantly, he nodded toward the eastern road. I tapped my chest and pointed at it. He tapped his own chest and pointed toward the south, saying somewhat in his own tongue.

"So we part ways." I put my fists together, then separated them.

Kebek nodded sadly.

We divided our things. Whatever he'd had to begin with, it had been seized in Tarkov. I gave him the warm coat we'd stolen and one of the blankets. A sack of grain, half the half-eaten loaf of bread. A few coins I wasn't sure he'd be able to use. I didn't have a waterskin to spare, and I couldn't afford to give him my sword or the hunting bow. Kebek shrugged. I wrestled with my conscience and gave him one of my daggers, the one I wore in a boot-sheath. It hurt to part with it, but I didn't think much of his odds of survival crossing hostile territory without a single weapon. There wasn't much point to freeing him if he didn't stand a fighting chance of living.

"Treasure it," I said to him. "It was a gift, too." I smiled a little. "Try not to use it for bad things, will you? I don't care who wins this war, Fedor or Tadeuz, but don't kill anyone who isn't trying to kill you. Just . . . go home and make love to your girl." I shaped her figure in the air. "In the end, nothing else matters."

Kebek nodded, then grinned. "Shut up," he said, mimicking me in passable D'Angeline.

I laughed. "Fair enough." I put out my hand, but he ignored it, stepping forward to give me another hard embrace. I returned it. "Good luck."

He said somewhat else; much the same, I daresay. And then I mounted my stolen horse and he mounted his, and we rode our separate ways. I glanced back a few times, and caught Kebek doing the same, but it wasn't long before my path headed into another wood and he was out of sight.

I wondered if he would make it safely home to his plump-bottomed girl. As much as I'd thought I disliked Tatars, I'd come to harbor a sneaking fondness for Kebek. I hoped he'd survive.

And I very much hoped that freeing him didn't get *me* killed.

I needed to find Berlik and finish my quest. After that, I could tell the truth and suffer the consequences. It wouldn't matter then, the deed would be done. And if nothing else, it would lend credence to the truth of my story; and there was Urist to back me up, and the story of the slain Albans that Micah ben Ximon had kept quiet, too.

All I could do was hope and pray that Tadeuz Vral would understand that it was a matter of honor and justice. That he would prove merciful or greedy or ambitious, or some combination of the three. Enough to grant me clemency or at least a chance to be ransomed. If Ysandre wouldn't pay it—and Elua knows, she might still be angry enough to leave me to languish in Vralia—mayhap Drustan would. After all, it was his niece I was avenging. And if he wouldn't, there was Phèdre; she'd sell Montrève if she had to. She'd sell *herself* if it came to it, and I wasn't sure which would fetch the better price. She hadn't taken a patron in over ten years, but the offers still came. Some of them were staggering.

It wouldn't come to it, of course. I had a considerable income and estates of my own, despite the fact that I neglected them. I'd never cared about wealth or status. I'd gladly cede it all if it meant getting out of Vralia.

Because all I really wanted in the world was to go home and make love to my girl.

FIFTY-SIX

BY THE TIME I FOUND MIROSLAS, it was well and truly winter in Vralia. Even in Terre d'Ange, the frost must have been thick on the ground. Summer had passed and autumn had come and gone since I began my quest.

If it hadn't been for the war, I daresay my luck would have been worse. I bypassed the first village I enountered, but I couldn't afford to bypass the second. I'd been two days and the better part of three nights on the road, with naught to eat but a quarter-loaf of bread. If I chanced waiting for another, farther village and it proved more than a day's ride, I'd starve. As it was, hunger made a knot in my belly, and I was starting to feel dizzy. I'd pushed myself and my stolen mount, trying to stay well ahead of any pursuit.

Luck was still with me.

Unlike in Terre d'Ange, gossip in Vralia didn't spread swiftly from town to town. The distances were too vast, and the commonfolk had little cause to travel during the cold months. No one in the small farming village I entered had heard news of a D'Angeline spy in Tarkov. The village was a quarter empty, for many of the young men had gone to enlist in Micah ben Ximon's army. The people I did encounter were curious and kind, especially the women. There was no inn, but a generous widow put me up for the night. She fed me and let my horse shelter in her cow byre. When I left the next day, she gave me three loaves of bread, a wheel of cheese, and a fur hat and mittens that had belonged to her husband.

I paid her with Tadeuz Vral's coins, feeling guilty. I might not be a spy, but of a surety, I was deceiving everyone I encountered. It was a feeling that stayed with me during my journey. I tried to avoid inhabited places, but when the snow began to fall in earnest, I had little choice. And too, there was the small matter of getting lost, which happened several times when I took a wrong turn and cost myself days. If I had pursuers, all I could hope was that it confused them.

Miroslas wasn't easy to reach. It lay several days' ride past the nearest village. If I'd been on foot, I might have given up. There had been heavy snowfall, and the path—it wasn't even a proper road—was nearly invisible. If it hadn't been for the peaks of the Narodin Mountains visible toward the east, I would have gotten lost. I spent half my time making camp; trampling snow before I could built a fire, breaking off pine branches to build a makeshift pallet, rigging windbreaks for my stolen mount, melting snow in a small iron pot I'd purchased from a family weathy enough to have one to spare.

When I did find Miroslas at last, it seemed almost a mirage. A yeshiva of sorts, Ethan had called it, but it looked more like a castle hidden in the woods; except that there were no walls, no defenses. Only an open courtyard, where an elderly man was sweeping snow.

Somehow, it seemed disrespectful to ride. I dismounted and approached on foot, leading my horse. The man paused, leaning on his broom and watching. "Shalom, father," I said in Habiru. "I'm seeking—"

"So the avenging angel has arrived," he interrupted me.

I said nothing.

"It is the wise man who knows the value of silence," he observed. "It is our policy to welcome all travellers. Yeshua's mercy knows no bounds." He pointed. "You may stable your horse there, poor beast. When you have finished, come find me. I am Avraham ben David, the Rebbe of Miroslas."

I inclined my head. "Imriel nó Montrève de la Courcel."

"I know who you are," he said.

I led my horse to the stables. There were no other horses there, only goats. A young Vralian man was there, milking one of them. He gaped at me, but said nothing, only pointed to an empty stall. I found the hayrack and a bucket. The Vralian pointed to a tub of water, already beginning to ice over. I lugged an armload of hay into the stall and filled the bucket with water for my grateful mount, then unsaddled him and rubbed him down with a handful of straw, trying to think what in the world I would say to the Rebbe.

It was a quiet place, Miroslas. A place where men go to think and be quiet, Ethan had said. It was true. As I learned later, many of the men there had taken an oath to dwell in silence, contemplating the glories of Yeshua. When I entered through the unguarded main door, the sound of my boot-heels on the flagstones seemed very loud. A fellow of middle years, clad in plain black robes, approached me with a wondering look.

"Rebbe Avraham told me to find him," I said softly in Habiru. He shook his head, uncomprehending. I repeated myself in Rus.

His eyes lit. He touched my arm and beckoned. I thought he would lead me to the Rebbe, but instead, he led me down a long corridor to a dining hall filled with long, empty tables. There I sat while he served me a dish of meat dumplings so good I nearly groaned aloud. If it hadn't been for all the silence, I would have.

When I had finished, he touched my arm again, motioning for me to leave my pack and follow him. It was a good thing I'd had practice in unspoken communication with Kebek. I followed him down another long corridor. We passed other men in plain robes. All of them looked curiously at me. None of them spoke.

He led me to the temple proper. It held the Yeshuite accoutrements with which I was familiar: the *khai* symbol inlaid in mosaic on the floor, the ever-lit lamp of the Ur Tamid. The ark containing the sacred scrolls; a replica of that original ark described in the Tanakh. I hadn't read the Tanakh. But I knew where it was, that ark. It was in Saba, on an island called Kapporeth, in the midst of the Lake of Tears. I hadn't seen it with my own eyes, but I knew. I'd been there. It was where Phèdre had found the Name of God.

And there was one thing here that was not there.

A great cross of rough-hewn timbers, lashed together and bolted to the wall. The Rebbe lay prostrate before it, his arms spread wide. My guide touched my arm a final time, nodded, and departed. I waited.

After a long time, Rebbe Avraham rose. He sat on a wooden bench and beckoned to me. I joined him.

"What do you see?" he asked me.

"A cruel way to die," I said.

"You find it barbaric." He nodded. "When Tadeuz Vral seized upon it as a symbol, I did, too. And yet, he is right." He turned a deep gaze on me. "Yeshua ben Yosef *chose* this. To subject himself to every humility mortal flesh might bear, to offer up his suffering, to make atonement for all of mankind. On his own shoulders, he bore this cross to the place of his own death, bloodied by the lash, enduring the jeers and spittle of an ignorant populace filled with fear and hatred. Should we not be humbled by this?"

I thought about Phèdre and Daršanga. "Yes, of course."

"And yet you are not," the Rebbe said. "Not enough to accept his sacrifice with gratitude."

I spread my hands. "My lord . . . I am D'Angeline."

"D'Angeline," he mused. "What does that mean? Elua ben Yeshua was born of the blood of the *mashiach*. And yet he rejected his birthright when it was offered to him."

"Blessed Elua had more than one birthright, Father," I said. "The one he chose was love."

"Carnal love," he said. "Not divine love."

I shrugged. "We are mortal flesh, my lord. How can we separate the two?"

The Rebbe sighed. "Here in this place, I seek understanding. I seek to understand Yeshua's will; Adonai's will. I seek to reconcile the Yeshua-that-was, the gentle philosopher, with the Yeshua-who-comes, the warrior. To reconcile the long history and traditions of my people, the Children of Yisra-el, with this fierce new faith of Tadeuz Vral. But I do not think I will ever understand D'Angelines."

I smiled wryly. "Nor I Yeshuites."

He was silent for a long moment. "I know why you have come. And I would ask you to find it in your heart to leave."

"Do you know what he did?" I asked.

"Yes." Rebbe Avraham's face looked old and tired. "Yes, I do. Many of the men who come here seek solace in silence and thought. Berlik did, too. But not all who come vow themselves to silence. Berlik spoke to me. We spoke at great length. I know what he did."

"Then how can you ask?" I said.

"Because it is my duty," he said quietly. "Because I have seen the depth of grief in his heart at his own actions. Because Yeshua's death granted all men the right to repent and atone. Is your Elua, your god of love, so merciless?"

"No." I gazed at the cross. The blood stirred in my veins, whispered in my ears like the distant rustle of bronze wings. "But I am not here on Elua's business, Father. I am here on Kushiel's. And his mercy is just, but it is stern."

"God's punisher," the Rebbe said. "He who loved his charges too well."

"Yes."

Another silence passed between us. "If this is love at work, it is no kind I recognize. Berlik is not here." Rebbe Avraham ben David squared his shoulders. "I sent him away. I could not allow this to happen under my roof."

"Where?" I asked.

"Do you know," he said without answering, "he sought to extract a promise from me. That I would tell you, if you came. You and you alone." His wrinkled lips twisted. "I wouldn't give it. I didn't want to know."

"Where?" I repeated.

His voice rose and cracked. "I gave no promise!"

I said nothing.

"I don't know," the Rebbe said at length. "Truly. It is a sin for a man to kill himself, even though he use another man's hand to do it. Berlik . . . Berlik believed he could see the future. That certain things were foreordained. I will not abet his madness."

"Berlik *did* see the future," I said. "Too much of it. I know, I saw it, too. That's why he killed my wife and our unborn child, my lord. And if he had to do it again, he would, no matter how deeply it grieved him. Again and again."

"I do not believe that," he said.

"Then let him convince me," I said. "Berlik has a right to his wishes. Mayhap this quest is not what I believe it to be."

Rebbe Avraham lifted his gaze to the cross. His lips moved as he prayed in silence. I waited. Watched his shoulders slump in defeat. "Betimes there are no easy answers, are there?"

"Not always," I said. "No. We try to be *good*. But the way is seldom clear."

"Berlik spoke of continuing," he said heavily. "Of going northeast. Of crossing the mountains. Onward, always onward. I begged him not to risk it, not with winter coming. To wait for spring. Miroslas . . ." He paused. "We have a writ from Tadeuz Vral himself. This land that lies northward under the shadow of the mountains—a great deal of it is set aside for our usage. Leagues and leagues, for silence and contemplation. Berlik needed solitude. I begged him to avail himself of the quiet spaces Miroslas has to offer; in the woods, alone. To hide. I do not know if he heeded me. I know only that he left."

"How long ago did he leave?" I asked.

"Six weeks ago, perhaps," the Rebbe said. "Before the heavy snows fell. There has been no word of him since. I cannot say if he stayed or went. I have told you all I know."

I took a deep breath, feeling a new burden settle into place. "Thank you, Father."

The Rebbe rose. "Don't."

It was the last word he or anyone else spoke to me in Miroslas before I departed. In fact, it was the last word I was to hear spoken by any voice not my own for a long time.

I left Miroslas in the morning. Like the people I'd met elsewhere in Vralia, the silent priests and acolytes had been generous. I was given a chamber with a hard cot on which to sleep, a basin of water for washing. I was fed another meal of plain, hearty fare. My bags were packed with a sack of pottage grain and a heavy parcel of dried, salted meat I couldn't identify. When I went to the stable to retrieve my mount, I found another sack of coarse grain, large enough to last a long time.

The same young Vralian was there milking the goats. "Why?" I said aloud to him. "If the Rebbe disapproves, why aid me? Wouldn't it be better to let me wander in the wilderness without succor and let God's will decide?"

The Vralian didn't answer; I wasn't even sure what language I'd spoken in. But he looked at me with grave eyes and offered me a dipperful of warm goat's milk. I sighed and shook my head. I could guess how the Rebbe would have answered my question.

It is my duty.

As I had mine, more arduous and distasteful with each day that passed. I led my horse into the courtyard. It was a clear day. The courtyard hadn't been swept yet, and the sun was bright on the new-fallen snow. Beyond lay a vast tract of woods, dense and pathless. I stooped and touched the ground.

"Blessed Elua, Mighty Kushiel, hear your scion," I murmured. "I cannot search forever. If it is your will that I find him, let it be swift. And if it is your will that I spare him, I pray you make it known to me."

There was no answer, but then, there seldom was.

I rose and continued my quest.

FIFTY-SEVEN

I DIDN'T COUNT THE DAYS.

What was the point? I had no fixed destination. I rode back and forth across the cold, snowy land, seeking any sign of Berlik; any sign of human habitation. I measured the passage of time by my dwindling supplies. I gauged my position by keeping sight of a particular peak of the Narodin Mountains, hook-shaped and distinctive. There would come a time when I could simply search no more, and would have to seek civilization or starve.

The sun rose and fell.

I kept searching.

I ate as little as I dared, but I had to be careful. If I was too weary at the end of the day to make a proper campsite, I ran the risk of freezing. I could hunt if it came to it, but I was short of arrows and hunting wouldn't feed my mount.

He was a good horse, patient and willing. I doled out grain in handfuls. I could abandon him, I supposed, and continue on foot. I wasn't sure I had the skills for it. I wasn't sure I had the *heart* for it. It wasn't just the cruelty. It felt like I'd been alone for a long, long time. Without the company of one single living creature, I wasn't sure I could continue.

There was a certain peace to it, though. The Vralian wilderness was rugged and gorgeous. My nameless mount and I plodded through pine forests, breaking a trail through deep snow. We scrambled up rocky inclines, and I caught my breath at the splendor of the vistas revealed at the tops. Pine forest spread like an endless carpet, the temple of Miroslas long ago swallowed by it. The tall, jagged peaks of the Narodin Mountains in the background. Frozen lakes, windswept and serene.

There was a good deal of wildlife in the wilderness. I saw foxes and rabbits, their pelts turned a snowy white for winter. Other animals I couldn't name, low and quick, with dark, luxurious fur and bright, curious eyes. Twice, a herd of deer like no other deer I'd seen, tall and deep-chested, with splendid antlers.

No Berlik.

Days passed, one after the other. Sunny days, cloudy days. Betimes it snowed too hard to see, and we were forced to hunker down and wait until it passed. I grew skilled at building windbreaks and shelters dug into deep snow to hold my body warmth, and learned to carry my waterskin filled with snowmelt inside my clothing so it wouldn't freeze during the day. My stolen mount grew shaggy. We slogged through snow and clambered over rock. Uncounted days turned into weeks. I don't know how many leagues Miroslas' holdings encompassed, but they were immense. And aside from the wildlife, they were utterly uninhabited.

There was no sign of Berlik anywhere. There was no sign of anything human in this emptiness save me, and there were days when I wasn't too sure about myself.

The days grew shorter.

The nights grew longer, so long they began to seem endless.

I tried to keep the flame of hope alive in my breast; Elua knows, I did. But the place was simply too vast, the task too hard. The long hours of darkness, the eternal loneliness, took their toll. Bit by bit, the flame guttered.

My supplies were running low the second time we encountered the big deer; low enough that I reckoned I'd have to turn back within a day. The first time, I'd seen the herd at a distance. This time, we came upon them at close range. The herd weren't scared of us, but only watched us with mild gazes as though wondering what strange manner of deer this was with a second body sprouting from its back. My horse stood patiently as I took off my fur mittens and reached for the hunting bow. I nocked an arrow and drew, aiming at the nearest.

The deer watched me, brown ears pricked.

It was an easy kill. In this cold weather, the meat would freeze, so I wouldn't have to worry about it spoiling. I wouldn't even have to dry and smoke it. Now I could keep searching longer. Weeks, mayhap. It was a very big deer. Of course, my horse would starve. But mayhap if I turned it loose, it would find its way back to Miroslas. And I could continue alone, on foot, lugging my packs and pounds and pounds of frozen meat. Tramping through the Vralian wilderness and searching for Berlik, who might well be on the far side of the Narodin Mountains, a hundred leagues from here.

I couldn't do it.

The flame of hope was extinguished.

I lowered the bow. "Blessed Elua forgive me," I murmured. "I don't want a reason to keep going."

The deer walked calmly away toward the herd, its tufted tail flicking. I took a long, shuddering breath, releasing it in a sound that was half laugh, half sob. Tears stung my eyes, threatening to freeze on my cheeks. I swiped roughly at them with one hand, then stowed my hunting bow and put on my mittens, turning my mount's head.

"It's over," I said.

There is a certain peace that comes with accepting failure, too. It settled into me like a stone. I accepted it. Accepted the knowledge that I *had* failed.

I had given up.

There are people in this world whose wills are capable of exceeding the limits of mortal flesh. I wasn't one of them. I was lonely and hungry and tired, and so cold that I'd forgotten what it felt like to be truly warm. I had failed, and nothing in my life would ever be quite right again. But I simply didn't have the will to continue.

I made camp that night thinking about all the people I had disappointed. About Urist and the men of Clunderry. Drustan, Breidaia, Sibeal, Talorcan . . . all of those who had loved Dorelei. Alais, and ah, Elua! I was ashamed to face Sidonie, knowing that the shadow of Dorelei's death would always lay between us. I had tried to atone for our guilt and failed. And Phèdre and Joscelin . . . the thought of the compassion and understanding they would extend made me cringe inside.

They'd never given up. Never.

But even the mortification of that thought wasn't enough to force me to keep going. The prospect was like a blank wall, unscalable and daunting. I could trek through this trackless wilderness for months. If Berlik was hiding here, I could miss him by a matter of yards. Then spring would come, and he would move onward into even vaster territories. And it wasn't just the sheer difficulty of it. Every step of the journey had chipped away at my will, ever since I arrived in Vralia. Micah ben Ximon, Ethan of Ommsmeer, Rebbe Avraham, my own doubts . . . all of them had led me to question the merits and cost of this quest.

In the end, it wasn't why I'd chosen to give up.

It just made it easier.

"I'm sorry, love," I said aloud to Dorelei's spirit. "You deserved better. You always did deserve better from me. But I did my best."

She would have understood, I thought. *Truly* understood. Dorelei had never expected the sort of heroism from me that I expected from myself. That the examples of those I loved demanded. All she'd ever wanted from me was honesty and a measure of kindness. And in that, at least, I'd succeeded.

The thought comforted me as I lay down to sleep in my snow wallow, blankets wrapped around my clothing, the farmer's widow's fur hat snug on my head. I watched sparks drift upward from my campfire and listened to my horse snuffle and snort behind the windbreak a few yards away. In the morning, I would think about the rest of my life and how I would begin to live it. Tonight, I didn't.

I fell asleep and slept without dreaming.

I woke to panic.

Not mine; my horse's. Its hooves stamped dully on the packed snow as it let out a low whicker of alarm. I was on my feet before I realized I was awake, fumbling for my sword-hilt with one mittened hand. The fire was burning low, casting a very small circle of light. Somewhere out there in the darkness, somewhat large was moving. Somewhat large enough to make the snow creak and groan. There was a rank, musky smell.

"No," I said. "Oh, no."

A bear roared.

My horse trumpeted with sheer equine terror and bolted, breaking its tether. I shouted a curse and dropped my sword, scrambling for the hunting bow. Flung off my mittens and nocked an arrow, tracking the darkness. A vast shadow moved; fast, faster than I remembered. I shot at it and missed. And then it was moving, fleeing. It could have killed me, but it didn't. It fled. Branches snapped in its wake. I ran blindly after it, floundering in the snow and crashing through branches, trying to fit another arrow to the string.

Gone.

I stopped, panting. I'd lost him. I'd also lost my hat, and probably my horse. I wasn't sure I hadn't lost myself. I closed my eyes and willed myself to breathe slowly.

There were stars overhead, but no moon. In the woods, there wasn't enough light by which to see. Still, a fleeing bear leaves a considerable path. I turned around and began the long, tedious process of following it backward by feel.

I don't think I'd chased the bear for more than a few moments, but it seemed like hours before I saw the flickering light of my campfire. With no hat or mittens, I was truly freezing. My horse was gone. I was lucky the fire hadn't gone out. I donned my abandoned mittens, then built up the fire with stiff, trembling hands and huddled beside it. My lungs ached from the exertion. My scars ached from the cold, from the memory the sight of him evoked.

"Damn you, Berlik," I said aloud. "Why now?"

It was him. I didn't harbor any doubts. In the deep winter of Vralia, any ordinary bear would have been slumbering until spring. I don't know why I'd been so damnably sure his magic was broken. He'd broken the oath he'd sworn on the troth that bound him to his *diadhanam*. It didn't seem fair.

Then again, life seldom did. At least not mine.

I dozed a bit, waking periodically to stoke the campfire. Mostly I waited for sunrise. I kept the hunting bow across my lap, an arrow at the ready, because it would have been foolish not to. I didn't really think he'd be back, though. If Berlik had wanted me dead, he would have killed me while I slept. I didn't know what the hell he wanted.

In the morning, I went to find out.

He'd left a trail a blind man could follow. So had my horse, but I reckoned he was halfway to Miroslas by now. I hoped so. And if I followed him, I would lose Berlik's trail. I ate a breakfast of pottage. Scoured my kettle with snow, melted snow to refill my waterskin. I packed my bags, slung them over my shoulder, and began trudging after Berlik.

On that journey, I counted.

It took seven days. On the third day, I shot a hare. That was the best day. The first day was hard. I'd gotten spoiled, riding. Oh, there had been times when I'd have to go afoot, leading my horse up some tricky escarpment, but it hadn't been this endless, grueling trek. And my ears were cold, so cold I feared they'd freeze. I'd hoped to find my fur hat, but some animal had dragged it away during the night. I'd looked for the arrow I'd shot at Berlik, but I couldn't find that, either. When I made camp that evening, I cut a swath of cloth from one of my blankets and wound it around my head. It was good, because I could use it to muffle my face, too.

The fifth day was the worst.

That was the day it snowed. Not so hard that I couldn't see, but heavily; steadily. Big, white flakes, falling straight downward, drifting through the air. Adding another layer to the soft blanket of whiteness.

Obscuring Berlik's trail.

I managed to follow it throughout the day, but the impressions his massive paws had left were growing more shallow. The edges were soft and blurred. I could no longer make out the sharp gouges of his long claws; the claws that had laid open my flesh. That had slain my unborn son. I thought about the day I had met Berlik. I'd asked him what would happen if I challenged him for the mannekin trinket. Berlik had showed me his claws. *You do not wish to do that.* He'd tapped the croonie-stone around my neck and bade me accept his oath. Told me that I might be grateful for it one day.

"You were wrong about that," I said aloud.

I hated to make camp that evening, but his trail was growing too faint. There was no way I could follow it in darkness, not even by feel. With my dagger, I made a gash in the bark of a pine tree, indicating its direction. I tossed a few hunks of frozen hare into pot with a handful of grain. There hadn't been a lot of meat on the hare, and I was nearly out of grain. The arrow with which I'd shot the hare had gone clean through it and embedded itself in a tree trunk. When I'd tried to wrestle it loose, the shaft had snapped.

That left me with a hunting bow and two arrows. I'd watched Urist make arrows on the island where we were shipwrecked, carving points and hardening them in the fire. But there had been no end of birdlife there. We'd gathered feathers on the beach for fletching, then plucked better ones from the birds we shot. I didn't have that luxury here.

I tossed my lone dagger end over end, catching the hilt. Joscelin had taught me to throw, of course, and I was a passing fair shot at twenty paces. Mayhap good enough to bring down a hare. Mayhap not.

By my best guess, I wasn't more than three or four days' ride from Miroslas. I'd ridden for a long, long time, but I'd been crisscrossing the land, looking for Berlik. Still, on foot, it was another matter. It might take me weeks. And I might well miss it on my first pass. If I did, it could take days to find it or reach the village beyond.

I should have shot the deer.

Fat snowflakes fell, sizzling where they landed on the embers of my campfire. I sheathed my dagger and stirred the embers with a long stick, then laid a few sturdy branches on the fire. I watched the flames rise, licking at the dry wood. Snow fell, catching in my hair, gathering on my shoulders. Melting on my cheeks like tears. I watched the fire. Showers of sparks, snapping and rising. Golden flames. I thought about Sidonie standing in a shaft of sunlight, her golden hair backlit. Tangled on a pillow. Her eyes, black as a Tatar's, filled with tears.

Just come home.

"I'll try," I murmured. "Swear to Elua, I'll try, Sun Princess."

The silent snow continued falling.

I slept fitfully and woke to a world of pristine whiteness. Somewhere in the night, the snow had ceased. Tall pines stood shrouded in white, the dawn breaking over them. The world seemed hushed and sacred. I could understand why a god would seek to built a kingdom here.

There was no sign of Berlik's trail.

It was gone, gone so thoroughly it might never have existed. I shrugged off my snow-covered blankets. I built the fire back up from its embers and boiled the last of my grain, eating it methodically with my fingers. Melted snow and refilled my waterskin. After a few errors, I found the tree I'd marked and brushed off the snow covering my mark. It pointed deeper into the forest, all of which was covered in a dense blanket of snow.

Trees and snow, nothing else.

I sighed, shouldered my pack, and began trudging.

FIFTY-EIGHT

T HERE WERE NO TRACKS, but there was bear sign.
As a boy in the mountains of Siovale, I'd been taught to
look for it. Patches on trees where the bark had been rubbed smooth.
Clumps of coarse hair. I'd never seen any near the sanctuary, but I'd
been taught to look.

I looked.

It was hard. Snow covered everything. But here and there, I found
it. From what I could determine, Berlik had been travelling in a
straight line. I followed in the direction I'd marked, looking for broken
branches. Looking for tufts of hair poking through their coating of
snow.

Whenever I found one, I made a fresh mark. When I didn't, I back-
tracked along my own trail to the last mark, adjusted my angle, and
tried anew.

I didn't find him on the sixth day. I did find a fox, which I tried to
kill by throwing my dagger at it. It dodged effortlessly the moment my
arm came forward. By the time I retrieved my dagger, it was gone. My
empty stomach growled. When I saw one of the other animals digging
beneath a tree, one of the ones I couldn't put a name to, I dropped my
mittens and nocked an arrow. The creature scurried, a dark, anxious
blur moving over the snow. I swung the bow wildly in an effort to track
it, shot, and missed.

I lost that arrow, too.

It wasn't that I was careless or unobservant. There was just so *much*
forest, so much snow. It could swallow up a castle without noticing. A

man was nothing; an arrow, less. I tramped around searching for the better part of an hour before giving up. The quest I had abandoned compelled me.

On the evening of the sixth day, I made camp and melted snow for my dinner. I drank as much as I could hold, and more. Water was good, water was life. I'd learned that in the desert when I travelled to Meroë with Phèdre and Joscelin.

I could live for days on water.

I could die on it, too.

It was snowing when I awoke on the seventh day. Not hard; almost idly, as though the snow were an afterthought. I felt a little weak, but clearheaded. I drank deep of snowmelt, then broke camp and struck out once more. It was another day like the others, filled with searching and backtracking.

Except that I found him.

If Miroslas had seemed like a mirage, I have no words to describe my reaction upon finding Berlik's cabin. It was small, very small. It stood in a tiny glade I could easily have missed. When I found it, I stood for a time and simply stared, my mouth agape. There were gaps between the rough-hewn logs of which it was composed. He must have built it himself.

I set down my pack and took up the hunting bow. Elua, it seemed like a long time since I'd borrowed it from the Shahrizai lodge. I nocked my last arrow and trudged across the glade. Around the cabin, the snow was packed hard, gouged by bear-claws and boot-heels alike.

I kicked the door open.

It wasn't much of a door, not really. It hung on leather hinges, sagging a little. Inside, the cabin was empty. No Berlik. Only strips of salted meat, hanging from the rafter poles to cure. There was a crude stone hearth in the center of the room, but the hearth was cold. A pallet of pine-boughs in the corner, covered in blankets and furs. On one wall, there was a cross; a pair of branches tied together with dried sinew. I surveyed it all, breathing hard.

Empty.

My heart ached. I was so tired.

There had been a tree outside. An oak tree, a barren tree. Dry branches reaching toward a stark, snowy sky. It nudged at my memory. There had been a tree in Dorelei's vision. I went outside. Trudged toward the tree, arrow nocked.

I would have seen him before if I'd looked more closely, but I'd been fixed on the cabin. He was sitting beneath the tree, still and motionless, watching me. A man, not a bear. There was an axe not far away from him, embedded in a stump, but his hands were empty, resting quietly atop his knees. As I approached, he stirred.

I aimed at his heart. "Don't move."

He did, though, rising to his feet. "I will not harm you."

My fingers trembled on the bowstring. "I've heard *that* before."

"This time it is true," he said in his deep voice. "I ask only that you kill me like a man, not a beast. Put down the bow."

"Damn you!" I shouted at him. "*Why*? Why here, why now? If you wanted to die, I'd have been glad to oblige you in Alba! *Why*?"

"So many questions." Berlik tilted his head and gazed at the sky. "It's beautiful here, don't you think? Wilder than Alba." He looked back at me. "When first I fled," he mused, "there was no thought behind it, only horror at what I had done. It seemed to me that perhaps if I fled far enough, I could carry it away from my people."

"And did you?" I asked.

"No," he said. "Not all of it. Only my death, freely offered, can make atonement. And only at your hands, for it was to you I swore the oath I broke." He was silent for a moment. "I would not have believed redemption was possible were it not for the Yeshuites. I broke an oath I swore on my *diadh-anam*. When I met them, I was a broken man."

"And Yeshua healed you?" I asked coldly.

"Yes." Berlik smiled. "He made me believe that the gods themselves are capable of forgiveness. That mayhap the Brown Bear of the Maghuin Dhonn herself would forgive me for breaking my oath to save our people."

My throat tightened. "Then why seek death?"

"Because it is the price," he said simply. "I am not a child of Yeshua ben Yosef. His sacrifice cannot pay the price for me."

My arms were beginning to shake with the effort of holding the bow drawn. Berlik watched me without comment. I sighed and lowered the bow, although I kept the arrow nocked. "And yet you hung Yeshua's cross on your wall."

"Yes." Berlik nodded. "To remind me." He was silent for a moment. "I do not know if it is presumptuous to call a god a friend, but if there is any god who would not mind, it is Yeshua ben Yosef. When Ethan first spoke of him, I thought it was a terrible thing to worship a god who let himself fall so low, who let himself be mocked and struck and hung to die like a criminal. But I came to see it. I came to see that he is the one god who understands what it is to fall low. That when every other face is turned away from you, he is the friend who is there, not only for the innocent, but for the guilty, too. For the thieves and murderers and oath-breakers alike, Yeshua is there."

I wanted to weep. "It doesn't change anything."

"It changed my heart," Berlik said. "And that is not a small thing." There was another heavy pause. "I prayed," he said. "I left a trail for you to follow, and I prayed that if you found me, the *diadh-anam* would accept my sacrifice as atonement, and not punish all of her people for my failure. When my magic returned to me, here in the woods, I knew it was so."

"Did you have to make it so hard?" I asked wearily.

"Would you have come here with a humble heart if I had not?" he asked.

"Probably not," I said. "Would it have mattered?"

"It does to me," Berlik said gravely. "It is my death. And I would have you understand what it is you are here to do. You could not do that with a heart filled with nothing but anguish and hatred."

I gave a short, bitter laugh. "So now I am here to do your bidding."

"We were never enemies, Imriel de la Courcel," he said. "If I had the chance to live my life a second time, I would do many things differently. I would not be so proud in seeking to force the future into a shape of my liking. I would place greater trust in the providence of our ancient *diadh-anam*, and less in my own gifts. I would have forced Morwen to give back the mannekin." He smiled sadly. "You told her it was not wise to cross D'Angelines in matters of love, that your Elua disliked it. I did not think his will could prevail on Alban soil. There were so many threads, so many futures. We were frightened. She thought that if we could control you, if we could bind you with your own desire, we could alter our fate."

I remembered the sorrow in his face. "You knew she was wrong."

"I feared it," he said softly. "I was not sure. Enough to offer my oath and pray you took it in friendship and trust. Not enough to gainsay her. There was one path, one future . . . the child of both worlds, your child and hers, that could have brought a time of glory to Alba. That path, you refused. And in the end, Morwen was not wholly wrong. She, too, paid a terrible price."

It was growing late in the day. The light was dimming, the trees casting long shadows. I was tired and cold and hungry. " 'Tis all well and good to admit to mistakes and say there might have been a better way," I said. "Elua knows, I've made enough mistakes of my own. But you'd do it again if you had to, wouldn't you? Kill Dorelei and our son?"

"For my people?" Berlik asked. "Yes. We are few. The Maghuin Dhonn will continue to diminish, to mingle and blend with the other folk of Alba. In time, we may become a memory. But we will not be stamped from the face of the earth, all our sacred places destroyed, our magic broken and our lore forgotten. And it may be that we have a role yet to play." He gazed at me with his pale, somber eyes. "You would have done the same. I pray you never have to make such a choice."

I was silent.

Berlik sighed. "It grows late. Shall we be done with it?"

I swallowed. "I suppose."

He knelt heavily in the snow. Even kneeling, he was a big man. He bowed his head and murmured a prayer, too low for me to hear, then raised his head and gazed up at me, snow falling on his face, catching in his shaggy black hair. "Let me die like a man. Please."

I put down the hunting bow and drew my sword.

"Thank you." Berlik smiled, genuine and startling. Somehow he looked humble despite it. There were tears in his pale eyes. He searched my face. "I'm so sorry. I promise you, it was swift. She felt no pain, only a moment's fear."

I nodded. "I'll try to do the same."

"My avenging angel," he said. "Thank you."

I nodded again, unable to speak. Berlik bowed his head. His coarse locks parted, revealing the nape of his neck. My blood beat hard in my veins and hammered in my ears like the sound of bronze wings clashing. I raised my sword high overhead in a two-handed grip. I was Kushiel's scion, here to administer his justice. For the sake of Dorelei, her life cut short too soon. For the sake of our unborn child. For the sake of the love I hoped to deserve.

For the sake of us all.

I was here to accept Berlik's sacrifice and to atone for my own sins. We had both transgressed against the wills of our gods. This was our moment of redemption. The gods had brought us here for a purpose.

And I understood for the first time what it meant that the One God's punisher had loved his charges too well.

"I'm sorry," I whispered.

I brought the sword down hard, hard enough to shear through bone. Berlik's neck gaped and his head lolled. His body slumped. Crimson blood spurted, vivid against the white snow. I raised the sword again and struck a second blow, severing his head from his body. It rolled free. I could see his face. His eyes, framed by the woad claw-marks, were closed.

He looked peaceful.

Blood seeped steadily into the snow from the trunk of his neck, the flow slowing as his heart ceased to drive it. More snow fell from above, flakes drifting aimlessly. A light wind sprang up, stirring the snow on the ground, making it swirl around us. Not a storm, just a breeze. It was pretty, really; or at least it should have been.

Berlik was right. It was beautiful here.

Beneath the shadow of a barren oak tree, I fell to my knees and wept as though my heart were breaking.

FIFTY-NINE

I BUILT A FUNERAL PYRE for him.

I didn't know what else to do. I kept his head, shoving it into Urist's leather sack. I couldn't bring myself to boil it down to the skull. I could barely bring myself to look at it. I hung it outside in the trees where scavengers couldn't get it, and let it freeze.

His body, I burned.

It took the better part of a day to gather sufficient wood for the pyre, but at least I had shelter and an ample supply of food. Berlik must have brought down one of those big deer. There was meat enough to last for weeks, and none of it spoiled. Even without the salt, it was cold enough to freeze in the cabin.

I built the pyre with dry branches and deadfalls, and dragged his frozen, headless body atop it. I lit it with the flint striker given to me long ago, and watched Berlik burn. His limbs twisted. The branches snapped and crackled.

"I'm sorry," I whispered again.

I slept on his pallet of pine-boughs, beneath the furs he'd gathered. I stuffed my bags with strips of salted meat. I wondered if Rebbe Avraham had given him the sack of salt I found in the cabin. I wondered what the Rebbe would make of my killing him. Of the fact that it was at Berlik's request.

I didn't care, much.

Not really.

After I burned Berlik's body, I studied the peaks of the Narodin Mountains. There was the one, hook-shaped and memorable. So long as I kept it over my left shoulder, I thought, I could chart a course back to civilization. I might miss Miroslas, but I had enough supplies now to reach the village beyond.

I set out the next day. Elua knows, I could have used a day of rest, but the thought of lingering there was unbearable. My purpose was finished. All I wanted was to go home. And I was afraid that if I thought about the effort it would take to get there, I'd lie down in exhaustion and die.

So I went.

When I was training under Gallus Tadius' command in Lucca, some of the men complained about how hard he made us work. He told us that in the old days Tiberian foot-soldiers were expected to carry loads of sixty or seventy pounds, and that we should be grateful we had it so easy. I hadn't thought so at the time, but in hindsight, the long, grueling days of drilling seemed like a pleasure-jaunt. The only thing I dared abandon was the hunting bow, reckoning that with one arrow, it wasn't likely to save my life. Between the salted meat, the kettle I needed to melt snow, my blankets and arms and the bag containing Berlik's frozen head, which I lashed to my belt, I was carrying a load worthy of a Tiberian foot-soldier. And I was doing it in deep snow, without the benefit of a proper pack.

Once again, my days dwindled into an endless blur of trudging, frozen and footsore, through good weather and bad. Making camp, breaking camp. Boiling strips of frozen meat and gnawing on it, drinking the weak broth for its warmth. Shivering through the endless nights, struggling through the all-too-fleeting hours of daylight. I didn't count the days. Once again, there was no point. On horseback, I might have been able to gauge the distance to within a day or so, having a rough idea of how far I'd travelled. On foot, I couldn't begin to guess with any degree of accuracy; and the days were so much shorter than they had been when I'd left Miroslas. I'd been at this for a long time.

I kept going.

My progress varied from day to day. Some days, I made good time, at least while there was daylight. On others, I chose my course unwisely and found myself floundering in waist-deep snow, my thighs aching as I forced my legs to move, the saddlebags slipping from my shoulders as I tried to use my arms to break a path. There had been times before when I'd had to break a path for my mount, but I hadn't been carrying sixty pounds of gear.

I did stop, once. Just stopped. I leaned back, resting my weight against the snowdrift in which I was mired, and closed my eyes. I thought about what a profound relief it had been to give up the first time. Although the sun never seemed to reach its apex anymore, it was a bright day. The slanting sun beat against my face, turning the private darkness behind my eyelids to red brightness. After my exertions in the snow, I almost felt warm. It wouldn't last. It would go quickly if I never moved again. Freezing wasn't supposed to be a terrible way to die.

Just come home.

I'd sent that damned ring back to Sidonie. She hadn't asked me to make any promises I couldn't keep, and I'd done it anyway. *Tell her it's a pledge,* I'd said to Deordivus. That I would be back to claim it.

Brightness, a dazzle like diamonds.

I keep my promises.

I pried my eyes open, squinted at the sun, and kept moving, flailing and struggling through the deep snow.

Most of the time, I simply trudged without thinking, my exhausted body working like a pack-horse. I was too tired to think, too tired for prayer. Later, if I survived, I would think about my encounter with Berlik. I would ponder what it all meant, whether what I'd done had been right or wrong. Whether there *was* a right or wrong in this matter, or only a long series of tragic events that hadn't needed to occur.

Later.

Like the priests of Miroslas, I did without speech. I hadn't spoken aloud since I burned Berlik's body. Before, I had. I'd talked to my horse until it bolted and left me stranded on foot; all the better with which to approach killing Berlik with a humble heart, I supposed. Even then, I'd been wont to speak aloud. Betimes to utter an involuntary curse; at others, for the solace of hearing a human voice, even if it was my own.

Now I wore silence like a shroud, and there was comfort in it. Why, I couldn't have said. Berlik's death had made a silent, still place in my heart, where the only words spoken were *I'm sorry.* My last words to the man whose sacrifice I'd accepted. Berlik, to whom I'd administered

Kushiel's justice. The words echoed in my heart. I couldn't bear to hear any others.

And then everything changed.

I was so accustomed to silence and solitude that when I first heard men's raised voices arguing in Rus, I didn't understand what it meant. There was no one there. I felt bewildered, like a man who couldn't read being asked to decipher a page of writing. I paused on the rocky incline up which I was trudging, which had the virtue of being windswept and almost clear of snow, and wondered if I'd gone mad.

It slowly dawned on me that the men were on the other side of the incline, which was why I couldn't see them yet. I was downwind, and their voices carried in the quiet wilderness. By the sound of it, they were growing closer, and swiftly enough that I guessed they were mounted.

I was in the open, and there wasn't anywhere to run; although I don't know that I would have if there had been. I wasn't scared. No one knew I was out here except the Rebbe of Miroslas, and he was the one who had told me where to search. It must be, I thought, that my horse made it back safely to the last warm stable he remembered. That Rebbe Avraham had been compelled by a Yeshuite sense of duty to send someone to search for me despite his dislike of my mission, reckoning I might be half frozen and dying in the wilderness.

A spark of gratitude warmed me; and in its wake, a sense of relief that abruptly weakened my knees. Elua, I'd been out here a long time! Surely the weeks had turned to months. I'd no false illusions of pride, not after what I'd endured. I'd gladly be rescued.

I managed to keep my feet and watched three men on horseback clear the crest of the incline some forty yards away. They paused, staring. I felt a grin split my wind-burned face and raised one hand in greeting.

All three of them drew their swords.

And one of them shouted in D'Angeline, his voice clear and carrying. "Imriel, *run!*"

I didn't.

I stood, gaping like an idiot, while the lead rider kicked his mount to a gallop and bore down on me. Atop the crest, the other two were circling each other, blades flickering and flashing. The oncoming rider leaned down from the saddle, sword in hand, his face grim and furious. I knew it, although I couldn't put a name to it. He was one of the guards from Tarkov.

At the last minute, I dropped my packs and ducked under his blow. "I'm not a spy!" I shouted at him. "I can explain! *Wait*!"

Or at least, that's what I tried to say. What emerged from my mouth was a dry, croaking sound. And it might have been in D'Angeline or Cruithne. I wasn't even sure. I swallowed frantically, backing away as he wheeled his horse, putting up my mittened hands in a gesture of surrender.

"Wait!" I got the word out in Rus.

He didn't wait.

I cursed with steady fluency in any number of tongues as he bore down on me for a second time, the dam of my long silence broken. I shook off my mittens and drew my sword. He gave me a fierce battle-grin as he brought his sword down in a stroke meant to split my skull from above.

I daresay he didn't expect me to parry it, at least not as strongly as I did. But the Cassiline fighting style is based on spheres of defense, and there is more than one series of forms designed to defend against a mounted enemy or an enemy on higher ground.

I used them all.

"Stop!" I shouted at him. *"Talk to me!"*

He didn't. He panicked, heeling his mount and jerking its head, seeking to circle around and make another pass at me. His mount stumbled, going to its knees, and threw him. Atop the crest, the D'Angeline who'd shouted a warning and the other man were still battering at one another.

"Wait," I said softly in Rus, approaching the fallen guard. "Listen."

He scrambled to his feet, shook his head, and charged me, sword extended.

I didn't mean to kill him. I didn't *want* to kill him. But I had been trained, very well, to defend my own life. At such times, it is the only thing that matters. I sidestepped his charge and angled my blade low, cutting him deep across the thighs.

He grunted and fell.

"I'm *sorry*," I said in anguish. "Damn you! Why wouldn't you listen?"

"*Imriel!*"

Another clear, carrying shout. I raised my head. Now the second Vralian rider was coming, howling in fury, the D'Angeline hot in pursuit. Fair hair streamed under the D'Angeline's fur hat, a hat much like the one I'd lost. I hoped it was Joscelin, except it didn't sound like Joscelin. And if it was, I couldn't imagine he'd have let his man get away. Not with my safety at stake.

The Vralian guard at my feet writhed, clutching his wounds. There was blood, a great deal of blood, gushing between his fingers. I'd cut one of the big veins. He wouldn't live, this one. Not in this wilderness.

And the other meant to kill me.

"Blessed Elua forgive me," I murmured, plucking my dagger from its sheath. I'd had time to think, this time. I wasn't standing gape-mouthed and stupid. I tossed the dagger in the air, catching it by its tip. I watched him loom large in my vision. He wasn't a fox or some quick-moving forest animal to dodge when my arm came forward, laughing at me with parted jaws before vanishing into the deep cover of the forest. Just a man, misguided. Nor more innocent or guilty than the rest of us.

Angry that I'd killed his comrade.

I didn't blame him for that. I was, too. But I didn't want to die.

His face was set in a rictus of fury. I recognized him, too. He was the one who had attempted to play my flute. The one I'd mocked. He rode a swift, surefooted mount. The D'Angeline pounding behind him was laboring to keep pace.

"I'm sorry," I whispered, and threw.

The dagger took him in the throat, the hilt protruding. He rocked back in the saddle, gurgling. Slumped, fell heavily to the ground. His mount cantered to a halt and began snuffling the stony ground. I walked over to him. There was blood trickling from the corners of his mouth.

He gestured to his throat.

I nodded and set my hand to the hilt. "Yeshua's mercy on you."

Everyone dies alone and no one wants to. Mayhap it is the one way, in the end, in which all of us are alike, no matter what our faith. I knelt beside the Tarkovan guard and plucked the dagger from his throat. His back arched, his body rigid as a bow. Blood and air bubbled from the wound. His hand scrabbled for mine. I held it, hard. I bowed my head, my trailing hair growing sticky with his blood.

"I'm sorry," I whispered.

He didn't answer.

He was dead.

I got to my feet. There was the D'Angeline on horseback, pulling up hard. I didn't acknowledge him yet. I couldn't. I walked over to the other Vralian, the man I'd struck with my sword. I was right, I'd hit one of the big veins. He lay in a pool of blood, already freezing into crystals at the outer edges, his open eyes staring at the blank sky. I knelt beside him, closing his eyelids tenderly.

"I'm sorry," I said. "I wish you'd listened."

He didn't answer either, of course.

"Imriel." A D'Angeline voice said my name. It sounded tight and strange.

I looked up into the face of Maslin de Lombelon.

SIXTY

WHEN I SAW MASLIN'S FACE, somewhere in the back of my mind, a part of me wondered if I truly *had* lost my wits. But it seemed whatever wits I yet possessed functioned without any conscious awareness on my part, for when I opened my mouth, what came out was "Are there others?"

Maslin stared blankly at me. "What?"

"Others!" I shouted. "Other guards!"

"Others?" He shook his head. "No, no others."

"Elua be thanked." It was my turn to stare. It *was* Maslin's face beneath the fur hat. No matter how hard I stared, it didn't change. "What in the seven hells are you doing here?"

"Rescuing you." His mouth twisted as he glanced at the scene. Two Vralian guards dead, both slain by my hand. "Or at least that was the idea."

"Why in the world—" I stopped. "Never mind. I'm too tired to talk. Lend me a hand."

He dismounted without comment. Together, we managed to calm and secure the two Vralian horses. I found my mittens and donned them; found my packs and slung them over the crupper of one of the horses. It wasn't until I bent down to take one of the corpses beneath its arms that Maslin stared again in frank disbelief. "What in the seven hells are *you* doing?"

"Take his legs." I pointed with my chin. "We can make camp over there on the verge of the woods. It's as good a place as any to built a pyre."

"A pyre?" He kept staring. "Are you out of your mind?"

"It's possible," I said. "But these men aren't guilty of anything except believing, for fairly good reason, that I was a spy. And they treated me well enough, until I escaped. I didn't want to kill them. At the least, they deserve better than being left for carrion." I struggled to hoist the Vralian's body. "I'll do it myself if you won't help."

Maslin shook his head and cursed under his breath, but he helped. Together, we got the bodies of both Vralians slung facedown over the saddles of their horses, limbs dangling. The smell of blood made the horses nervous, but they were well trained and didn't spook.

"You *are* mad," Maslin muttered.

I shrugged.

It wasn't far to the edge of the pine woods. We led the horses without speaking. It was early enough that I reckoned we could get the pyre built before nightfall and still have time to make camp. One of the Vralians had a hand-axe in his bags, which made the task immeasurably easier. I'd have taken Berlik's axe if I'd thought I could carry it. We cut and dragged dead branches, building the pyre some distance upwind from the campsite, out in the open where there was no chance of the fire spreading.

For all the long-standing animosity between us, Maslin and I worked well enough together, and everything went so much more swiftly with two people. He shot me frequent curious looks, but he respected my silence. I couldn't help but be glad he was there, whatever the reason.

When the camp was in order and the pyre built, we laid the bodies on it. I bowed my head and murmured a prayer in Rus, then lit the pyre. It took a while to catch, but once it did, it burned fierce and hot.

"Gods above, that's awful," Maslin murmured, watching the bodies twist.

"I know," I said. It was my second pyre in too little time.

"You're right, though. Better than being left for scavengers." He watched the flames. "Have you killed a lot of men?"

"No." I shook my head. "Not many."

"I heard you did in Lucca," he said. "That you killed a score of men, and the enemy commander stalked you through the streets and you killed him in single combat."

"He stalked me through the streets," I said. "And a man I barely knew died taking a spear meant for me. And then my friend Lucius gave an order, and his men shot the Duke of Valpetra full of arrows. That's how he died."

"That's not what I heard," Maslin said.

I shrugged. "It's true, though."

Maslin fell silent for a long moment. The fire crackled. "I thought that when the time came, I could take them both," he said. "I really did. And I think I could have, on foot. I'm good with a sword, you know. Very good. Even though I learned late, it came easily to me. But I never really learned to fight on horseback all that well."

"Nor did I." I put a mittened hand on his shoulder. "Maslin, if you hadn't been there, I *would* have died. They wouldn't listen. And I couldn't have handled them both. Not at once, not on foot."

"I'm not so sure of that," he said.

I squeezed his shoulder. "I am. Believe me, if I've learned nothing else on this journey, it's my own limits." I jerked my head toward the campsite. "Come on, let the pyre burn. There's naught else to be done here."

We walked back together, leaving the pyre burning lower behind us, a lonely beacon illuminating the twilight. Cold snow crunched and squeaked under our boots. The horses watched us with incurious eyes, sheltered by the windbreak we'd built together. I wondered if they would miss their masters. If they knew what had transpired.

Travel was easier with horses, but it was more work, too. Maslin and I tended to them. The Vralians had better gear and an extra kettle. We packed both of them with snow, melting it on our campfire and filling the clever, collapsible leather buckets they'd brought, suitable for holding water or grain. I wished I'd had such a thing. Before it bolted, my mount and I had shared the same pot.

Once we'd fed and watered the horses, we fed ourselves. The Vralians had better food, too; or at least more of it. Maslin watched me shovel pottage and scraps of salted meat into my mouth straight from the pot, using my fingers. He had a wooden bowl and spoon.

"You look half starved," he said.

I swallowed a mouthful of food. "I am."

"Did you get what you came for?" he asked.

I nodded at the leather sack hanging from a nearby branch. I'd hung it when we first made camp, the same as I'd done every night. "Yes."

Maslin gazed at it with sick fascination. "Is that . . . ?"

"It's his head." I put the kettle aside, my appetite gone. "Berlik's head. The man who killed my wife and son."

"Didn't you have it . . . ?" He gestured toward his midriff.

"Tied to my sword-belt?" I asked grimly. "Yes. What else would you have me do? It wouldn't fit anywhere else. Urist told me to boil it down to the skull, but I haven't been able to bring myself to do it yet. So I've just been carrying it, at least until I can bring it home to Clunderry to bury at Dorelei's feet. Don't worry, it's frozen through."

"Name of Elua!" Maslin shuddered. "It's a barbaric culture, isn't it? How . . ." His voice dropped. "How did you do it? Was it a fair fight?"

"No." I rubbed my eyes with the heels of my hands. "It's a long story, and I don't want to tell it tonight. Later, mayhap. Maslin, what are you doing here?"

"Ah," he said. "That."

"Yes," I said. "*That.*"

He picked at his bowl, scraping it clean with his wooden spoon. Then, at last, he put it to one side, sighing. It was funny. Maslin was older than me, at least by a few years. When I'd first seen him, working in the pear orchards of Lombelon, I'd envied him. His age, his surety of place. Now he seemed so much younger than I remembered him, and I felt a great deal older.

"Here." He rummaged among the Vralian's packs and brought out a wineskin. "*Starka.* Do you know it? It's sort of dreadful, but it gets better."

I took a swig and felt it burn all the way down, then handed it to Maslin.

"My thanks." He tipped it, swallowed, and gasped. "It was Sidonie."

"Oh?" I said mildly.

Maslin eyed me sidelong. "You do know about us?"

"A little." I retrieved the skin. "She didn't want to talk about you to me."

He looked grateful. "Nor you to me."

"Small wonder." I took another mouthful. "We're not the best of friends, you and I. Which makes me wonder why you're here."

"Not out of any fondness for you, to be sure. Sidonie and I quarrelled." Maslin took the wineskin back when I offered it, but he didn't drink, only held it. His mouth twisted again, wry and self-deprecating. "I was on duty when your Alban messengers came from Skaldia with the news that you'd been refused passage. That you and Urist were attempting another route while everyone else was awaiting support from the Cruarch and Queen Ysandre in Maarten's Crossing." He did drink, then, long and deep, tilting the bag and pouring *starka* into his open mouth. "And I, like an idiot, said somewhat awful. I told Sidonie that if you loved her, truly loved her, you'd never have left her in such a manner."

"Sidonie understood it," I murmured.

"Apparently." Maslin took another swig, then passed me the wineskin. "Didn't stop me. I told her it was obvious I cared more for her than you did. That I'd never have left her. And she gave me one of those looks . . . you know those looks, Imriel? And said if I *really* loved her more than you did, I'd prove it by going to help you."

I tried not to smile. "You reckon it will work?"

"You know, appearances to the contrary, I'm not a *complete* idiot." Maslin took the skin back and regarded it before drinking. "It doesn't matter, does it? It doesn't matter what I feel, or what she thinks about it. There hasn't been anything between us since you were nearly killed in Alba. It's you she loves, not me."

I didn't say anything.

Maslin smiled wryly. "It's been a long journey. I've had a lot of time to think."

"Why did you do it, then?" I asked. "If you knew it didn't matter whether you proved yourself to her or not?"

"I think I needed to prove it to myself." He passed the wineskin. "That I truly loved her."

"Did you?" I asked.

He looked at me sidelong. "You do, don't you? Love her?"

"Unfortunately," I said. Maslin narrowed his eyes in suspicion. I sighed. "Yes. Absurdly, horribly, gloriously, yes, I do. Maslin, this journey has been hell in more ways than I can name. A few days ago, I was so damn tired, when I got stuck in a snowdrift, I was ready to give up and die. And the only reason I didn't, the only thing that made me keep moving . . . Elua, it wasn't the thought that it would break Phèdre and Joscelin's hearts, which it would, and I owe them the sort of debt no one could repay in a dozen lifetimes. No. It was because I promised Sidonie I'd come back to her. So, yes. I love her."

"I thought I did," he said softly. "I truly did." He gazed past me at the distant glow of the pyre, little more than embers. "Sidonie said once that I didn't love her so much as I did the idea of her. Of us."

"The beautiful princess and her heroic Captain of the Guard?" I asked.

"Don't laugh." Maslin took back the wineskin. "You never felt that way?"

"Not about Sidonie," I said. "Mayhap we knew each other too well. And for the first five years of our acquaintance, she looked at me like I was dirt on the bottom of her shoe."

He smiled a little. "You do know the look I mean, then."

I laughed. "Oh, yes. And I know what it is to yearn to be a hero, too," I added more gently. "Name of Elua, Maslin! Remember who raised me."

"I never thought about it that way." He rubbed one hand on his knees. "Only about how cursed lucky you were." I raised my brows. "Oh, I know, I know. They rescued you out of slavery. But that just always seemed like something from a poet's tale."

"It wasn't," I said. "Believe me, I'd rather spend the rest of my life wandering the Vralian wilderness on foot than another day in Daršanga."

He drank, and passed the skin. "That bad?"

I drank. "Yes."

"Oh." He shook his head when I offered the wineskin and sat for a moment, arms wrapped around his knees, looking out at the night.

In the flickering light of our campfire, he looked so unsure and vulnerable, it touched my heart with tenderness. "Is that why you did it, Imriel? Came here? To be a hero?"

"No," I said even more gently than before. I could see the fault-lines in him, the same ones I'd seen when he was a proud lad of sixteen. I could see how they'd shifted and changed on this journey, beginning to heal. And I could see that while an unkind word would crack them open, honesty and compassion would bring greater healing to him. For the first time, I understood that Kushiel's gifts held mercy, too. "No, I came here because I loved my wife, too, Maslin. Not the way I love Sidonie, but as much as I could. Dorelei was a good person. And for many reasons, I needed to avenge her, or at least I thought I did. In the end . . ." My voice trailed off. I didn't know how to speak of it yet. I'd spoken more tonight than I had in months. "I don't know."

"A long story," he said.

"Let's get some sleep," I said. "I'm tired and a little drunk. We've got plenty of long days of talking ahead of us. Mayhap you can tell me on the morrow how in Blessed Elua's name you managed to find me out here."

Maslin laughed. "It wasn't easy."

"I believe it," I said.

We rolled ourselves in blankets and retired to our respective snow wallows. It felt strange having him there. It would have felt strange having *anyone* there. I'd grown accustomed to the solitude. But of all the people I might have expected to find me in the midst of the Vralian wilderness, Maslin de Lombelon ranked very, very low on the list.

Unless, of course, he meant to kill me. After all, no one would ever know. It was only the two of us, alone in the wilderness. If he left my bones for the scavengers, like as not, they'd never be found. And in her grief, Sidonie might just turn to the one person she believed had done his best to aid me.

"You don't, do you?" I asked drowsily.

"What?"

"Plan on killing me in my sleep?" I yawned. "Because if you do, I'd just as soon you get it over with tonight."

There was a pause. "No," he said in a dreamy voice. "But I would have liked to save you from mortal danger, and force you to spend the rest of your life knowing that every beat of your heart, every breath you drew, every moment of happiness you enjoyed, you owed to me."

I smiled. "That's a touching sentiment."

"You asked," Maslin said.

SIXTY-ONE

WE MADE BETTER TIME on horseback.

After the endless days of trudging, it was like heaven. We even had a spare mount to carry our gear. I didn't have to worry about slogging through the snow, shifting my pack from shoulder to shoulder, Berlik's frozen head banging against my legs.

It was such a relief, I didn't even mind the cold.

On the first day, Maslin told me how he had come to find me. He had arrived in Maarten's Crossing some three weeks after Urist and I had left, spoken to Kinadius, and resolved to follow our route. But Adelmar of the Frisii had refused to grant him passage to Norstock; had refused, indeed, to grant any further aid to any Albans or D'Angelines until a sufficient bribe arrived. Maslin offered his services as a mercenary to any number of merchants travelling to Norstock, all of which had refused him, wisely discerning that a D'Angeline guard was more likely to draw trouble than prevent it in Skaldia.

"Believe me," I said. "The wool-merchant was none too happy to have us, either."

"I wasted days," Maslin said glumly. "Lots of them."

In the end, he'd given up and struck out on his own. By the time he departed, Talorcan had arrived with a contingent of Alban warriors; and so had some bribe from Queen Ysandre. Maslin didn't know the details, but whatever it was, it was enough to convince Adelmar to grant passage through Skaldia to Talorcan and his men, following Berlik's trail along the pilgrims' route.

"Why didn't you go with them?" I asked, curious.

Maslin shrugged. "I'd heard the sea route was faster. And I was looking for you, not your wife's killer."

He'd made the short trip to Norstock without event, but his luck had failed him there. Unable to communicate in Skaldic or Rus, he'd managed to book passage to Vralgrad aboard a northbound ship; but he'd not understood its purpose nor its course. The ship had stopped at every single trading-post along the coast of the Eastern Sea, sometimes lingering there for days. The journey Maslin had thought would take two weeks took well over a month.

And he had arrived to find Vralia at war.

"It's funny," he said. "Once I realized the ship was stopping at every damned port between Norstock and Vralgrad, I reckoned that was it. I might as well enjoy the adventure, because there wasn't any other point to it. Then I got to Vralgrad, and no one could have cared less about anything but the war. Except for Urist. I'd managed to learn a few words of Rus aboard the ship. He heard I was asking after you and sent for me."

"How is he?" I asked. "Is he well?"

"Fine." Maslin shot me a glance. "A guest of the palace. Walking, with a stick. Worried. I thought you would both have been long gone. But he told me you were shipwrecked, and he got hurt. And he told me you'd heard the Alban forces got turned back at the border, and that you'd managed to get yourself imprisoned as a spy. Apparently, someone from Tarkov came to question him." His mouth twisted. "Urist told me you saved his life."

"Not really," I said honestly.

He shrugged again. "It's what he said."

"Did he have word of Talorcan's party?" I asked.

"No," Maslin said. "And if any came later, I didn't stay to hear. I set out after you."

It couldn't have been long after the captain of the guard in Tarkov had sent an emissary to Vralgrad that Maslin had arrived; but it had taken him a long time to find the village, having somehow thought it lay downriver along the Volkhov, and not inland. I had a hard time piecing it all together. In the end, it didn't matter. Maslin had reached

Tarkov the day after I'd fled it. And they had seized him, reckoning him a second spy.

"So I lied," he said simply. "The captain of the guard found a fellow who spoke Caerdicci to translate. Some scholar. I *do* speak Caerdicci, you know. I told them you were a renegade, acting against the Queen's wishes. And that I was here to bring you to justice on her behalf. They wanted to find you, enough to send a couple of men. I promised to aid them."

"So they let you join their quest?" I asked.

Maslin nodded. "They did. We got a long way off course and ended up weeks behind you. They were sure you were headed for Petrovik with the Tatar." He paused. "Why did you free him, anyway? That was stupid."

"I know," I said shortly. "Did they find him?"

He shook his head. "I don't think so. He must have been canny in the early going. They finally found enough people who'd spotted him, and not you. That's when we turned back. He didn't matter the way you did. Just a boy, I heard. Not a spy, not like you. They were awfully mad about that. We went back, and we went east instead of south." His lips curled. "It didn't take long. The second village we encountered, they knew of you. Knew you'd asked directions for Miroslas. There was some woman who'd aided you."

I glanced down at my mittened hands on the reins, smiling crookedly. "The widow."

"Was she?" Maslin asked. "I only ever understood one word in five."

"She was," I said.

"Oh." He was silent for a moment. Our mounts jogged together, side by side, in a slow trot. Gusts of frost rose from their nostrils. The third horse, the pack-horse, trailed behind us. "Well, after that, they didn't bother with the hunt. We went straight to Miroslas."

"And the Rebbe sent you after me?" I asked softly.

"Is that what he's called?" Maslin shrugged. "I don't know. There was a fellow, an old fellow, with quite a beard. The Tarkovans talked to him. I don't know what they told him. All I gathered was that you had been there, and there was a horse, some horse, that had turned up without notice. We followed its tracks until it snowed. After that, it was all guesswork and the two of them arguing. The rest, you know."

I plied him for news from home, of course, but he didn't know much. He'd left shortly after Deordivus had arrived with our news. It was strange to think how long ago that had been. It was still late summer in Terre d'Ange when he'd departed. Maslin's journey had been almost as long as mine had, albeit less fraught with peril.

There had been no sign of Phèdre and Joscelin, which was what I most longed to know. As for the rest, although Ysandre had agreed to bribing Adelmar, that was solely out of respect for Drustan, and had naught to do with any thawing of her feelings toward me. Relations between the Queen and her heir, Maslin reported, were strained.

"You do have a few adherents," he said. "Even in Phèdre's absence."

"Such as?" I asked.

"Some of the younger gentry," he said. "Ones who don't remember your mother. House Shahrizai. House Mereliot." He smiled wryly. "And there's a rumor among the Palace Guard that Lord Amaury Trente told her majesty she was being stubborn. Of course, you have your detractors, too."

"L'Envers," I said.

Maslin nodded. "He's not alone, Imriel. There are good many peers of the realm convinced this is all a part of Melisande Shahrizai's grand scheme."

"I'm not surprised," I said. "Are you one of them?"

He didn't answer for a long time. "No," he said finally. "There was a time when I would have been. Barquiel L'Envers was my patron when I first arrived at Court, you know. He does *not* like you. And he's very convincing."

"Sidonie told you what he did to me," I murmured. He gave me a wary glance. I raised one hand in a peaceable gesture. "It's one of the only things she told me. I wondered why you were trying to reason with him when he was raging at me."

"Yes." Maslin's lips thinned. "It was when I was pestering Sidonie about you. She never denied your relationship, she just refused to talk about it. It made me crazy. I reminded her about what you'd done. That conspiracy Bertran de Trevalion uncovered. She got angry and informed me exactly who was behind it, and what her majesty had done about it. I'd always wondered why his grace stepped down as Royal Commander."

"Now you know," I said mildly.

He almost smiled. "Yes, well, now *everyone* knows, after that scene at the Shahrizai lodge. Anyway, it forced me to admit to myself that if I'd misjudged him, mayhap I had you, too." He paused. "Funny. In the beginning, L'Envers was convinced it was Alais you were planning to court one day. That you'd been laying the groundwork since she was a child."

"Alais!" I was appalled. "She's like a sister to me."

"Oh, and Sidonie isn't?" Maslin raised his brows.

"No." I shook my head. "No, it was always different with us."

"Dirt on the bottom of her shoe," he said, remembering. "So what changed?"

"I don't know." I fidgeted with the reins. I felt self-conscious talking about her with Maslin. "Some of it was gradual. We grew up. I began to realize that some of the things that annoyed me about her, like her infernal composure, I actually admired. Then there was a day when everything just . . . changed. I couldn't even say why, exactly. It was like up was down, the grass was blue and the sky was green."

"I knew." He rode without looking at me. "No one believed me, not even L'Envers; at least not until that day we caught you leaving the orchard. Do you remember? It was before you left for Tiberium. But I knew."

"I believe you," I said.

"No one else watched her the way I did." Maslin's nostrils flared. For the first time since he'd found me, the old accusing note crept into his tone, familiar and unpleasant. "I saw it. You were the first thing she'd look for when she'd enter a room. It wasn't obvious, but I noticed. And if you were there, you were always looking right back at her."

"Maslin." I drew rein and waited until he halted and looked reluctantly at me. "Listen to me. Neither Sidonie or I intended for this to happen. We thought . . . Elua, I don't know. That it would run its course like a fever, mayhap. That's why I went through with my marriage to Dorelei and went to Alba. But it didn't pass. And I'm sorry. I'm sorry if you were hurt in the process. I'm sorry it wasn't you. Believe me, the last person on earth I wanted to fall in love with is the one person that would convince half of Terre d'Ange I have designs on the throne. But I can't help it, not without defying the precept of Blessed Elua himself. All right?"

He looked away and nodded. "All right."

"You're not going to challenge me to a duel like you did Raul L'Envers y Aragon, are you?" I asked. "I heard you beat him rather badly."

"No." A corner of his mouth lifted. "And I didn't challenge him. He did."

"All right." I touched my sword-hilt. "If you change your mind, I'm willing to oblige you. But I'd very much like to go home first. There are people I love there, and I have a debt of honor to pay to Dorelei mab Breidaia."

"I understand," he said.

I nodded. "Good."

It didn't exactly clear the air between us, but it helped. We rode for a time without speaking, the silence broken only by the muffled sound of the horses' hooves and the creaking of our gear. When our path was blocked by a deep drift, Maslin dismounted without a word to break a path. I offered no protest. I could still feel a deep exhaustion in every bone of my body. I watched him work, steady and efficient. We led the horses through the path he'd broken. When he remounted, his face was bright and flushed with the effort.

"Damned snow, eh?" he gasped.

"Tell me." I glanced at the hook-shaped mountain peak and pointed. "I think we want to bear a little south."

"Whatever you say." Maslin took off his fur hat, wiping his brow with his sleeve. He shook out his hair, pale and lank. "Elua! I could use a bath."

"That's what got me into trouble," I said. He gave me an inquiring look. "In Tarkov. They spotted my brand at the baths. And then the Tatars raided the horse-fair. That's why they thought I was a spy."

Maslin looked perplexed. "Brand?"

"A souvenir of Daršanga, where I was enslaved." I gestured beyond the mountain. "It's . . . I don't know where, exactly. Farther east and south, abutting the Tatar lands. The ruler there, the Mahrkagir, he was courting the Tatar warlords to aid him in a grand conquest. He gave me to one of them as a plaything. Among other things, Jagun took it on himself to brand my arse with a red-hot iron."

I don't know why I told him. I'd never told anyone who hadn't asked. There were quite a few people who *had* asked that I'd never told. Casual lovers; and some not so casual. Claudia Fulvia, for example. I'd told her only a partial truth, not the whole story. In fact, I'd never told anyone except Eamonn and Sidonie exactly how and where I got that scar; and once, in a spate of ire, the Queen's chirurgeon. I'd never even told Dorelei.

Maslin stared at me, his mouth agape. The ruddy color drained from his face. He closed his mouth with an audible click. "That's terrible."

I shrugged. "You know what else is terrible? Right now, for a hot bath, I'd almost chance being dubbed a spy again."

He gave a startled laugh. "I begin to think my long envy is misplaced."

We made the best use of the daylight we could, veering a bit southward and slogging through the endless pine forest. That night, we made camp in a glade so dense we didn't even need to built a windbreak. It had begun to snow again, more heavy flakes spiraling down from the dark heavens. Maslin brought out the *starka* again and we passed it back and forth between us, sitting beside the campfire.

"We were awful together," he said presently. "Sidonie and I."

"Why?" I asked.

"Oh, a lot of it was my fault." He tilted the wineskin to drink, then smiled at it as though it held a secret. "It's funny, because I thought we'd be so good together. And you know, we are, as friends and confidantes. She's good at ignoring the petty intrigue and gossip of the Court. All those idiots muttering about her being a Cruithne half-breed, diluting Elua's sacred bloodline. Dealing with it, dismissing it without seeming to. I could always see her impatience, though, even though she hid it well. It was part of what I loved about her."

"She doesn't suffer fools gladly," I murmured.

"No," Maslin agreed. "So why did I become one in her bed?"

I didn't have an answer. "I don't think she's proud of the way she treated you."

He sighed and lay back on the snow, folding his arms behind his head. "It's not as though she's blameless. I know. But the truth is, I was an ass. Far, far too much of the time. I just . . ." He scrunched his shoulders. "I was jealous of you. And I don't know, I wanted her to *need* me in a way that she didn't. Is that so wrong?"

"Not everything is a matter of right or wrong," I said.

"I suppose so." Maslin gazed at the dark sky, snow falling gently on his face. "My mother always said that my father liked being with her because he was a complicated man and she was a simple woman. He never told her any of his plans, she was innocent. She said it nearly broke her heart."

"At least you had the solace of knowing he did the right thing at the end," I offered.

"And died a hero." His tone was wry. He sat up, shaking off the snow. "Did you ever meet her?"

"Your mother?" I asked.

"Yours," he said.

"Twice." I took a swig of *starka*. "The first time, I was eight years old. Brother Selbert, the head priest at the Sanctuary where I was raised, took me to see her. I didn't know who she was. He told me she had been a friend of my parents. I thought she was wonderful. She was the most beautiful lady I'd ever seen, so kind to me, and her voice was like honey. I could have sat at her feet and listened to her for hours. The second time . . ." I took another swig. "I wanted to spit in her face."

"I think I would have," Maslin said.

"You know, she's still out there." I waved one arm. "Somewhere. That man who took a spear for me in Lucca, she sent him to watch over me. He told me so, and then he died and took her secrets with him." I contemplated the wineskin and took one more gulp before passing it to Maslin. "If there's one good thing about being stuck out here in the wilderness, it's that I've finally outrun her reach."

"True," Maslin said. "But you're going back."

"Not to her," I said.

He shrugged. "As you say, she's still out there."

SIXTY-TWO

SEVERAL DAYS LATER, we reached Miroslas.

The evening before we arrived, Maslin did me a kindness for which I truly will remain grateful to him. The days had grown so short that we were forced to spend many long hours idling around our campsites, unable to travel in darkness. Still, we made good progress during the daylight hours, and I knew we were getting closer.

After wrestling with the issue in my mind, I was resolved to stop there if we came upon it. If we missed it, I would press onward. But I felt somehow that I owed the Rebbe honesty. I would aim for Miroslas and let fate decide.

Maslin didn't agree, but he didn't argue the matter. After all, when all was said and done, he wasn't guilty of anything but trying to protect me, knowing full well that I was innocent of espionage. I was the one who had killed both the Tarkovan guards.

And Berlik.

During the lengthy nights, I told Maslin, bit by bit, what had passed between us. There were parts of the tale that confused him, but when I spoke of the difficulty of killing Berlik, he was more understanding than I would have reckoned.

"Nothing's ever as simple as it seems, is it?" he said.

"Not in my experience," I said.

"Imriel . . ." He hesitated, then nodded at the bag containing Berlik's head, tied to a tree-branch. "I understand better why you're reluctant to do what Urist recommended. But you've got to do somewhat about it."

I shuddered. "I know, I know."

Maslin was silent a moment. "I'll do it."

"It's my duty," I said.

"I know." He rose decisively and began packing one of our pots with snow. "But . . . name of Elua, man! Haven't you seen enough horror? I might not have come here for good and honorable reasons, but I'm here. At least let me make it meaningful."

I opened my mouth to protest, then closed it. "Thank you."

It was a long, ugly job. It took the better part of an hour to get a full kettle of snowmelt boiling. I made myself look when Maslin fetched the bag and removed Berlik's head. It was frozen solid as a rock, and it had frozen so swiftly that it was perfectly preserved. His bloodless skin was as pale as frost, save for the woad markings. His eyes were closed. He still looked peaceful. In a way, Berlik looked happier in death than I'd ever seen him in life.

"Kushiel's mercy on you," I whispered.

Maslin jerked his head. "Now go away."

I went some distance from the campfire and sat under a tree. I didn't watch as he lowered the head into the boiling water. I'd fetched Hugues' flute from my pack. I played it with my eyes closed, low and quiet. I thought about the harpist Ferghus, who had walked out of the gloaming to sing for his supper at Innisclan, summoned by his half-breed son Conor. I tried to remember the song he had played for us, the story of a magician of the Maghuin Dhonn and how he had sacrificed himself to save his people from Tiberium's conquest. I did my best to play it, until my fingers grew too cold to feel the flute's holes and I had to cease and don my mittens.

It took a good deal longer than that, of course.

Hours.

I had to return to the fire to warm myself. "You play well," Maslin murmured. "I didn't know."

I hugged my knees, shivering. "I practiced a lot in the past year. Dorelei liked it."

He gave me a curious glance, eyes reflecting firelight. "You really did care for her."

"Very much," I said. "You would have liked her, Maslin. She wasn't simple, but she was uncomplicated. She deserved better from me. She taught me a lot. And if there was any way I could undo this and give her back her life, I would. No matter what the price."

"I knew her a little from Court." He watched the kettle. "She had a nice laugh."

My throat tightened. "She did."

A log in the fire shifted. The kettle lurched. A little water spilled, hissing onto the embers. The aroma emanating from the simmering pot smelled like stew. The bile rose past the lump in my throat, choking me.

"Go," Maslin said, pointing.

Once more, I went.

I know what he did that night; what had to be done. Once Berlik's head had thawed and his flesh softened, Maslin had to fish it from the pot. Carve the flesh from the bone, remove the scalp and its coarse, shaggy hair. Prod within the nasal cavities with a sharpened stick, trying to loosen the brains housed within. All that I'd avoided, he did. Once he went to vomit, walking away from the campfire, returning and wiping his mouth. Twice he set the head aside and dumped the contents of the pot some distance from our site to begin anew, melting fresh snow.

It was a long night, longer than most.

In the end, it didn't smell like stew. It didn't smell like much of anything except hot iron and scorched water. When it reached that point, I returned permanently from my vigil beneath the tree and slept restlessly beside the campfire.

By daybreak, the water in the pot had boiled away and there was nothing left of Berlik's skull but clean bone, eyeless and grinning as it never had alive. Maslin, who looked bleary-eyed, had done a good job. I told him so and thanked him again.

"It was easier for me," he said in a tired voice. "I never knew him."

When we struck camp that morning, we returned Berlik's skull to the leather bag and left the cooking-pot behind. It was a lucky thing we had a spare, since I wasn't sure I could have borne using it again. I laid it on its side, thinking that mayhap some woodland creature would someday use it for a nesting place. It was the sort of thing, I thought, that would have pleased Berlik. I didn't know how I knew that, but I did.

Maslin watched me with bemusement. "You're a very odd young man, Imriel de la Courcel."

"I've been accused of worse," I said.

He laughed. "True."

We rode in companionable silence that day. After the first few hours, the horses began pricking their ears and quickening their pace. They had a better sense of direction than I did, and like my long-bolted mount, Miroslas was the last warm stable they remembered. I kept an eye on the mountain-peak, but I gave my mount its head. When the shadows began to grow long, a suggestion of blue dusk arising beneath the trees, we took a chance and pushed onward a little longer.

We reached Mirsolas a bit before nightfall.

The sight of it was as unexpected as the first time, a hidden gem tucked away in the woods. Indeed, with the warm glow of lamplight shining from its windows, casting squares of yellow on the heavy snow, it looked more welcoming than I could have imagined.

"You're sure about this?" Maslin asked. He was shivering a little and his tone suggested he hoped very much that I was. It was late to retreat and make camp.

"I'm sure," I said.

We must have been spotted, for one of the silent brothers was there to receive us at the door. He looked to be Habiru, and he inclined his head when I greeted him in that tongue, although he made no reply.

At his gesture, Maslin and I stabled our grateful mounts, helping ourselves to feed and water. To my pleasure, I discovered that the horse I'd stolen in Tarkov had indeed returned safely as Maslin had said, though it looked shaggy and thin yet. There was another horse stabled there tonight, just as shaggy but well-fed. I was curious about it and wondered to whom it belonged. I didn't have the impression the priests here kept mounts for their own usage, nor that they had many visitors; at least not at this time of year.

"I've no idea," Maslin said crossly when I speculated aloud. "Elua! Does your mind never stop chewing over every last little question?"

I smiled. "Far more often than Phèdre would like, believe me."

Inside, it wasn't long before we learned the answer, or at least a portion of it. We'd arrived at the regular dinner hour when all the brethren of Miroslas were served. The silent guide showed us to a chamber where we might leave our gear, then escorted us to the hall. There was no sign of the Rebbe, but the long tables that had been empty when I'd first dined there were filled with rows and rows of men of all ages, Vralian and Habiru alike. The only thing they shared in common were their sober black robes and their silence, although it was a charged silence, and our presence rendered it all the more so.

There was one fellow who was different. We were seated beside him at the end of one table. He wore some sort of soldier's livery; a heavy red tunic over black breeches and boots. There was a flared cross in black worked on the breast of his tunic, over his heart. He was hunched over a steaming bowl of meat dumplings, but he glanced up when we sat, his blue-grey eyes widening with an undefinable emotion.

"It is a sign," he murmured in Rus.

"Of what, my lord?" I asked quietly.

Our Habiru escort placed one finger against his lips and shook his head, motioning us to silence. His face looked troubled. I wondered why. Was it us or the rider?

Once Maslin and I had finished eating—which took a good long while, the dumplings were as good as I remembered and I was twice as ravenous—our escort rose and beckoned to us. We followed him. The soldier watched us go, his gaze unblinking.

Rebbe Avraham ben David was awaiting us in his private chamber. It was a spare, simple room. There was a cot, a rug on the floor and a fire in the hearth, with a trio of plain wooden chairs arrayed before it. There were no adornments. He rose when we entered. He looked older than he had . . . when? Six weeks ago? Two months? I wasn't sure.

I bowed. "Shalom, Father."

Maslin bowed, too, but said nothing.

"Is it done?" the Rebbe asked me in Habiru.

"Yes." I faced him without flinching.

He sighed. "By both of you?"

"No," I said. "I was alone."

"Sit." The Rebbe pointed to the chairs. We sat. "How was it done?"

I glanced at Maslin. "My lord, is there any other tongue in which we might converse? One my companion might share?"

Rebbe Avraham smiled wryly. "I think not, child. I was a younger man in the Flatlands, and I speak the low tongue, Skaldic and Habiru, and I have learned Rus. Your companion was silent here before. Let him be silent now. How was it done?"

"As Berlik wished," I said. "I sent him to his gods."

"Ah." He was silent a moment. "I had hoped the solace he found in Yeshua's mercy might guide him."

"It did," I said. "It guided him to the center of his own heart. Father, Berlik cherished what he learned in Vralia. He kept Yeshua's cross on his wall to remind him. He said . . ." I cleared my throat. "He hoped it was not importunate to consider a god a friend, and that if there was any god who would not mind, it was Yeshua ben Yosef, who is there for all the lost and broken people of the world. But Berlik was a leader of the Maghuin Dhonn, and a great magician. For the sake of his people, he made a bargain with their god to let his death pay the cost of their broken oath. And he believed it was answered." I paused. "If there is a kernel of truth to what his people believe, they are old, my lord. Very old. They speak of following their *diadh-anam*, the Brown Bear, from beyond Vralia to Alba when the world was covered in ice."

"And you believe this?" he asked.

"I believe what I have seen," I said. "I do not know what it means."

"I wish he had chosen otherwise. For Vralia's sake. For the sake of *my* people. We have need of men like him to shape the future of our faith. We are not all vowed to silence. Even in this quiet place, there were murmurs about him while he was here. There was such a depth to him, such a sorrow. Before he left, there were some here who began to speculate that he was one of the sainted ones, god-touched." He fixed me with a deep gaze. "And that a dark angel and a bright angel came to struggle for his soul."

I looked sideways at Maslin, his pale hair bright in the firelight.

"A fanciful tale." Rebbe Avraham snorted. "One can *smell* that you are mortal, and in need of a bath. Still, here you are." He looked thoughtful. "Which is which, I wonder?"

"Neither," I said. "Why did you send the Tarkovans after me?"

"I feared you were dead," he said. "They said you were a spy. I did not believe it, but I did not believe you should kill Berlik, either. Nor did I believe your silent companion sought your life. I hoped, somehow, it all might be averted. In the end, I consigned it to Adonai's will."

I sighed. "Well, then, it seems it was Adonai's will that two Tarkovan guards guilty of no crime save being too cursed stubborn and pig-headed to put down their swords and *listen* for one moment should die at my hand."

He bowed his head. "Dire news. I am sorry."

"You should be," I said. "You sent them."

"I bear responsibility for my choice, as you do for yours." Avraham ben David lifted his head. "If you had acknowledged the truth of your quest in Tarkov, they would not have believed you a spy and sought your life. Child, I am sorry, but I face larger choices than those which concern you. A great victory has been won in Yeshua's name."

"Fedor Vral?" I asked.

"The winter siege broke his followers' will," he said. "Lean and hungry, they opened the gates of Petrovik to Micah ben Ximon. Prince Fedor managed to flee beyond the mountains with a handful of Tatars, but his cause is all but lost. Ben Ximon did not even deem it worth the cost of pursuing him, not in winter. Thousands of his followers have deserted him." His old eyes were bright with strong emotion. "They are willing to acknowledge Yeshua as a portion of the terms of their surrender, and I do not know whether to rejoice or weep. Words spoken under duress do not suffice to change men's hearts. Grand Prince Tadeuz Vral sends a messenger asking me to come to Vralgrad to counsel him, and I do not know whether to stay or go."

I was silent, abashed.

While I had been engaged in my single-minded, solitary pursuit, a war had been waged and won. The fate of a nation had hung in the balance and shifted.

"Who is the Yeshua ben Yosef who holds sway in Vralia?" the Rebbe mused. "The friend who is there for the lost and lonely soul, or the warrior whose banner led Tadeuz Vral to this second victory? I do not know. And I am afraid."

"I understand," I said humbly. "I would help if I could."

"Perhaps you have." He drew a deep breath and gazed around the room. "You remind me that my choices affect lives. It is not enough to trust to Adonai's will. Our minds, our tongues, our hands are his tools. I will think on it, and pray." He nodded. "I thank you for coming to bring me this news yourself. Not all men would have done so."

"You cared for him," I said. "I wanted you to know that in the end, his death was peaceful. It wasn't what you wanted for him, but he was glad."

"And the Tarkovans?" the Rebbe asked. I didn't answer. His wise old gaze sharpened. "For the sake of the guilt we both bear, I'll make you a bargain, lad. Go to Tarkov to made amends. Tell them what befell their sons, brothers, and husbands. Tell them you have confessed it to me, and I have absolved you of all guilt and laid my blessing upon you, bidding you to spread the word among men that it is better to be filled with compassion than suspicion, and remind them that in the end, in Yeshua's kingdom, all men are brothers. That your coming is a sign all must be mindful of this, always and forever."

"Thus do we shape the world, Father?" I asked.

"Thus do we try," he said. "It should not strain your faith."

"No," I said. "Blessed Elua would not object."

"Blessed Elua," the Rebbe murmured, and shook his head. "You may go."

I rose, and Maslin rose with me, stifling a yawn. No doubt he'd been bored out of his wits, and him already half dead for lack of sleep. Together, we departed Avraham ben David's presence; the two of us, the bright and the dark.

SIXTY-THREE

OUR CHAMBER WAS COLD and the cots were hard. After the wilderness, it felt heavenly. Maslin and I didn't speak that night, only lay down and slept the sleep of the dead. By long force of habit, we woke before daybreak, and departed shortly thereafter.

As before, no one bade us farewell. This time, though, quite a few turned out to watch us go, including Tadeuz Vral's messenger, his scarlet livery a bright splash of color against all the somber black robes. It was a strange feeling.

"So what's that all about?" Maslin asked me.

I told him what the messenger had said upon seeing us, that our presence was a sign. And I told him about my conversation with the Rebbe. Maslin smiled a little at the notion of the pair of us as bright and dark angels, but what he said surprised me.

"Mayhap our coming *is* a sign, Imriel. Who knows? The gods use mortals to their own purposes."

"A sign of what?" I asked. "The messenger didn't say."

"Well, the Rebbe certainly had his ideas on how to interpret it." He glanced sidelong at me. "Surely you're not going to do it, are you?"

"Go to Tarkov?" I thought about it. "Yes."

"Why?" Maslin stared at me in disbelief. "They might well throw you back in gaol, you know."

"I don't think so," I said. "Not with Rebbe Avraham's blessing on me." I thought about it more as we rode. "I withheld the truth to pursue my own quest. I could have waited for word from Micah ben Ximon. Elua, if I'd waited long enough, you'd have come, and you might have told a different tale." I grinned at him. "My bright angel come to save me. Mayhap the pair of us could have convinced them."

Maslin snorted. "Not likely."

I shrugged. "Well, it's on the way."

"For the spawn of a pair of traitors, you have a perversely stubborn sense of honor," he observed.

"My thanks," I said wryly. We rode for a while without talking. "My father had a sense of honor," I said after a while. "Or so I'm told. It was just that it was misguided. That's how my mother was able to exploit him. He truly believed Terre d'Ange needed a pure-blooded D'Angeline heir."

Maslin shot me a look. "Do you?"

"Elua, no!" I dropped the reins to spread my arms. "Maslin, look at me. Do you think I'd be *here*, avenging my Cruithne wife, if that's what I held paramount?"

His lips twitched. "Not likely, no." His voice changed. "Do you ever wish you could have known him? Your father? Just to know what he was truly like?"

I picked up the reins. "I saw him once."

"Your *father*?" He frowned. "I thought he died when you were a babe."

"He did." I told him about the Feast of the Dead and how I had seen the spirit of my father riding beside me, old and sad. Sadder than anyone I'd ever seen, even Berlik. How I'd hoped, then, that he had gained wisdom and come to bless his half-Cruithne grandson in the womb. How I'd wondered later if he had known what was to come, and grieved at it. Maslin listened as I talked, his lips parted in wonder.

"I'd like to see my father," he mused. "I wonder how he'd look at me."

"With pride, regret, and sorrow," I said. "Pride at what you've done. Regret at the fact he wasn't there to share it, never had a chance to acknowledge you as his child. Sorrow at the burden his legacy laid upon you."

Maslin shot me another look, wary. "You're serious?"

"I am," I said.

He fell silent for a time, his mouth a hard line. "Gods above, Imriel," he said at last in disgust. "You know, the last thing on earth I wanted was to *like* you."

I laughed.

"It's not funny!"

"It is," I said softly. "Ah, Maslin! There was a time when I wanted, so badly, for you to like me. You were older. You seemed so sure of yourself. And there was no one else I'd ever met who might understand, at least a little, what it was like to be a traitor's son. To struggle with that burden, to need to prove it to oneself, over and over. All I ever wanted was your friendship."

"Is that why you gave me Lombelon?" he asked.

"No." I shook my head. "No, that was different. I thought it was right, that's all. That it should belong to you. Phèdre warned me that you might not be grateful. That you might come to hate me for it in the end."

"I did," Maslin said candidly.

"I noticed," I said.

We both laughed. Maslin grinned at me. "I'll always hate you a little bit."

"Only a little?" I asked.

"A bitter little husk of hatred," he said cheerfully. "Shoved into the deepest, narrowest corner of self-loathing in my heart, where I will continue to envy and despise you. For the fact that Ysandre de la Courcel searched the ends of the earth to acknowledge you as her kinsman, while my own paternity went unacknowledged and forgotten. For the fact that Phèdre nó Delaunay loved you enough to make you her foster-son, while I remained the gardener's daughter's bastard. For the fact that Joscelin Verreuil, the Queen's Champion, taught you to wield a sword while I was wielding pruning shears. For the fact that you rubbed these things in my face, whether or not you meant to. And, in the end, for the fact that Sidonie loves *you* and not me."

"Fair enough," I said. "What about the rest?"

"The rest of my heart?" Maslin asked.

I nodded.

He leaned over in the saddle and took my shoulder in a hard grip; one that lay somewhere between affection and violence. "I've a feeling I missed an opportunity somewhere. I'd count you a friend if you'd still have me."

"I would," I said. "Gladly."

Maslin released me. "Well, then."

Unlikely as it was, from that moment onward, I began to think of Maslin as a friend, albeit a prickly one. We worked together easily and rode together in tolerable companionship. The going was a good deal easier. We were travelling a road instead of breaking a path through endless wilderness. To be sure, it wasn't much of a road, but the snowfall was light enough that we could still make out the trail forged by Tadeuz Vral's messenger.

I was concerned about the reception we'd find when we reached the first village. Gordhoz was a midsized town; smaller than Tarkov, but larger than many of the little farming communities where I'd found hospitality. Maslin didn't know what sort of stories the Tarkovan guards had spread, here or elsewhere. But I reckoned we'd have to confront the issue sooner or later, so we sought out the village's single inn, which did a fair business offering food and lodging to pilgrims bound for Miroslas. I'd stayed there myself, as had Maslin and the Tarkovans.

"Ah." The innkeeper stood in the doorway and regarded us impassively. He was a barrel-shaped fellow with a mustache that reminded me of Captain Iosef, and he spoke in Rus. "The spy and his hunter."

"No spy, sir," I said. "It was a mistake."

He shrugged. "If you were a spy, you were a bad one. The war is won. You have money?"

I jingled my purse. "We do."

He opened the door wider. "Come in."

Betimes it is a blessing to be reminded that the world does not revolve around one's problems, and this moment was one such. Maslin and I stayed there a full day, reveling in luxury. The innkeeper had a pretty young wife who served us beer and stew, and blushed every time she met either of our eyes. I smiled at her more than I ought, just because it was so good to see a woman's face again.

"One crook of a finger and she's yours," Maslin observed.

I smiled. "Let's not buy trouble."

Instead, for a fee, the innkeeper's wife laundered our filthy clothing and blankets, lending us old shirts and breeches, patched but clean, that must have belonged to her husband. While our own things dried on racks before the fire, we dashed through the cold, snowy streets to the public bath-house.

It was much like the one in Tarkov where my troubles had begun; except this time I was careful not to allow anyone to see Jagun's brand. The other scars, I couldn't hide.

"Name of Elua!" In the room where we stripped down, Maslin actually paled at the sight of me. "That bastard nearly tore you in half."

"I know." My teeth were chattering. "Come on."

He kept stealing glances at me in the bathing-room, where we luxuriated in the heat and steam, scrubbing away weeks of stale sweat and unspeakable grime. We'd scoured ourselves with icy water from the basin in Miroslas, shivering in the cold chamber, but it had been a hasty, patchwork job completed in near-darkness. I hadn't seen my own naked body for a long, long time. It seemed almost a stranger's, ivory-pale from lack of sunlight, worn down to bone and sinew and lean, ropy muscle. No artist would ask me to sit for her now. The scars hadn't faded as much as I'd thought they might. They were still angry red furrows, slashing across my torso.

I caught Maslin's eye. "Still envious?"

"It's dwindling rapidly," he admitted. "I saw you in bandages that day at the Shahrizai lodge, I knew it was bad. Not that bad. Does it still hurt?"

I prodded scarred flesh. "It's tender deep down."

Maslin shook his head. "And you wept when you killed the creature who did that to you. That, my friend, I cannot begin to understand."

"I'm not sure I do, either," I murmured.

We left the village of Gordhoz the following day, clean and well-fed, our stores replenished. The innkeeper's wife looked sad to see us go. The innkeeper didn't.

Our journey to Tarkov was blessedly, blissfully uneventful. The Tarkovan guards had asked after me in Gordhoz to confirm I'd passed through on my way to Miroslas, but either they hadn't bothered elsewhere, or they'd taken a more direct route and missed the villages and farmsteads where I'd found shelter. Recalling the number of times I'd gotten lost, I suspected the latter.

The temperature remained bitterly cold, but the snow had tapered off. Many days it was bright, so bright that the sunlight on the snow was nearly blinding. Maslin and I rode with our eyes half-shut, the skies overhead a deep, vivid blue. In its own harsh, rugged way, Vralia truly was a beautiful country.

Both of us noticed that the days were growing longer. We tried to guess when the Longest Night, which was long indeed in Vralia, had passed, and where we had been. I thought it might have been the night before I'd killed Berlik. Maslin thought it was later, mayhap the night he'd tended to Berlik's head. Berlik's skull, jouncing in its leather bag, tied to our spare horse's packs, offered no opinion.

We talked about our favorite memories of the Longest Night; or at least some of them. He told me how it was celebrated at Lombelon, and how much he had loved it as a child. The year before I'd met him, he'd played the role of the Sun Prince in their modest pageant; that was his favorite year. I told him about maintaining Elua's vigil with Joscelin when I was fourteen, and how infernally sick I'd gotten afterward, how it was one of the only times I'd ever seen Phèdre angry at Joscelin. Maslin laughed when I admitted that I far preferred attending the fête with Eamonn in tow. He told me that the worst time he'd had on the Longest Night was two years ago, when he'd been sent to serve with the Unforgiven in Camlach after beating Raul L'Envers y Aragon badly in their duel.

Two years ago.

I didn't tell him that was my favorite Longest Night of all. I kept the memory to myself, savoring it. Sidonie, all in gold. She'd taken my hand, tugging, and we'd darted behind the musicians' mountain. There in the darkness, I'd pinned her against the false mountainside, my heart beating so hard I could feel it thudding in my chest. Her gilded sun-mask scraping my face as I kissed her for the first time. As she kissed me back, so hungrily it made my knees weak. Even now, the memory fired my blood. After the temple, I'd ridden home barefoot through the snow, clad in rags, and never even felt the cold.

Two years ago. Elua.

"What are you smiling at?" Maslin asked, curious.

"Nothing," I said softly.

He looked dubious, but he didn't press. Mayhap he sensed it was somewhat he didn't truly wish to know.

As we neared Tarkov, we began to see groups of soldiers on the road, returning home in jubilation. They looked splendid, clad in scarlet coats and fur hats. Many of them sang as they rode, hymns of praise to Yeshua. Songs of war. Always, someone carried a banner. Yeshua's cross waved above them, crimson on white. They had no knowledge of any tale of D'Angeline spies; or D'Angelines at all. One group hailed us with shouts, inviting us to share *starka* with them. Since there was no polite way to decline, we accepted.

"You see!" one of them shouted, clapping Maslin on the back. "Who are these beautiful strangers, eh? Perhaps it is true. Yeshua so favors us, he sends his angels to walk among us as mortal men!" He winked. "You tell Mighty Yeshua we gave you hospitality!"

Maslin looked startled.

"Just look grave and knowing," I advised him.

He did his best.

I could see why the Vralians thought as they did. Maslin *was* beautiful. That, I'd never denied. The Skaldi had called his father Kilberhaar; Silver Hair. In the sunlight, his pale blond hair almost glittered. Like me, Maslin had lost weight during our long travail. The bones of his face were stark and prominent, striking in an unearthly way. There was beauty there, but it was fearsome, too. I suppose I must have looked much the same.

We spent a day with the soldiers, then parted ways.

A day later, we reached Tarkov.

There were soldiers there, too; quite a few, coming and going through the southern gate, talking with the guards. It was hard to tell, but beyond the wooden stockade it seemed as though somewhat of significance was passing there. We drew rein at a distance and watched.

"Your mind's set on this?" Maslin asked with a frown.

"It is," I said. "But . . ."

We'd been travelling together for some time, long enough to know one another's thoughts. Maslin shaded his eyes, surveying the countryside surrounding Tarkov. In summer, it would be fertile farmland, but it was desolate now. To the north of the town, the pine forest that lay between Tarkov and Kargad rolled over the land like a dark carpet.

"I'll go wide and circle around." Maslin pointed. "That's our route, yes? I'll make camp a half day's ride to the north and wait for you in the forest."

I nodded. "You'll take Berlik's skull?"

He grimaced. "If I must, yes."

I put out one mittened hand. "If I'm not there by midday tomorrow, leave without me. Once you reach Kargad, you can take the Ulsk upriver to Vralgrad. I'll follow when I can. Whatever it is, I daresay I'll get it sorted out in time. But in case I don't . . ." I shrugged. "See his damned skull back to Clunderry, will you?"

Maslin clasped my hand. "Stubborn ass. Yes, of course."

I grinned at him. "My thanks."

I watched him depart from the road, leading our pack-horse. The leather bag containing Berlik's skull bounced and jostled. It was stupid. I'd worked so hard for that dubious, grisly prize to risk ceding it to another. But in the end, it didn't matter who brought it back to Clunderry. Once it was buried beneath Dorelei's feet, her spirit would rest easier. I believed that to be true. However much I'd come to understand Berlik, he had murdered her, horribly and violently. Her and our son.

But I had to go on living.

And the Rebbe had given me a charge. I wanted to go home. I wanted nothing more. I wanted to go home to the people who loved me. I wanted to feel Joscelin's strong presence keeping every danger at bay. I wanted to let myself be a child again for a few moments, to sit at Phèdre's feet, lean my head against her knee, and feel her stroke away my fears. I wanted to hear Hugues and Ti-Philippe bicker.

And I wanted to get on with the business of being a man, too.

Most of all, I wanted to fall into Sidonie's bed and never get out of it.

And I didn't ever want to tell her, yes, I killed two men whose only crime was being too stupid to listen, and I burned their bodies in the woods, and their bones and ashes lie there still, while those who loved them wonder what ever become of them. There was guilt enough between us. If there was atonement to be made, I would make it.

So I went to Tarkov.

SIXTY-FOUR

I DIDN'T EVEN MAKE IT to the gate before I was seized.

Four soldiers saw my approach and rode me down in a hurry, surrounding me. They stared at my face, then exchanged glances with one another. I dropped the reins and raised my empty, mittened hands, leaving my sword-hilt untouched.

"Peace," I said in Rus. "I am here in peace."

One pointed to me. "Are you Imriel de la Courcel?" he asked in Habiru.

"Yes," I said. "I am."

His face was grimly exultant. "Come with us."

I went without protest. Having committed myself to this course, I had no choice. I wasn't sure if I was a prisoner or a guest. They didn't disarm me, but they didn't give me time to speak, either. They hustled me through the gate and down the streets toward the town square. Outside the guardhouse, we dismounted and two of them ushered me inside.

The outer guardroom was packed with guards and soldiers alike. Some spectacle transpired in the next room, the captain's study, but I couldn't see what passed therein. The guards were thronged before the open door, their backs presenting a solid mass of humanity. Beyond them, I could hear the captain's voice shouting in Rus.

"Ask her, my lord! If he is innocent, *why did he free the Tatar*?"

"The captain asks, if he is innocent, why did he free the Tatar, my lady?" a vaguely familiar voice repeated in Habiru.

My soldier escorts shoved futilely at their comrades and the Tarko-van guards, pounding on backs and muttering urgently in low tones.

"Name of Elua! My lord Micah, I've no idea. Probably because he has a soft heart." It was a woman's voice, exasperated, speaking Habiru with a D'Angeline accent, and I would have known it anywhere in the world. I felt my heart crack open and soar, and an impossible grin spread across my face. "I let all the prisoners in La Dolorosa free, and I've *no* idea what they'd done."

"Yes, but—" Micah ben Ximon began.

The guards in front of us began shifting reluctantly. Someone pushed me from behind. The guards gave way. I stumbled through the open doorway of the captain's study and caught a glimpse of its occupants. No one noticed me yet.

"You know perfectly well he's not a spy," Phèdre said. There was a flush of anger on her cheekbones. Her eyes were bright with it. Every man in the room was staring at her in rapt fascination. Joscelin stood beside her, arms folded. Her voice turned calm and reasonable, with somewhat implacable behind its sweetness. "I don't care what your role in this was, my lord. You could have spared *one man* from the battlefront to send word that you vouched for him. Because I swear to Blessed Elua, if this idiot's men have killed him—"

It was Ti-Philippe who saw me first. His jaw dropped. He stared. His mouth worked, but only a squeak emerged. He grabbed Hugues' arm and pointed.

"*Imri?*" Hugues whispered, dumfounded.

It was enough to cut Phèdre's speech short. Her head whipped round. For a moment, I don't think she dared believe her eyes. I couldn't stop grinning. I watched her take a sharp breath, hands rising involuntarily to cover her mouth. Beside her, Joscelin found his voice and loosed a victorious shout of laughter.

And then we were all laughing and crying at the same time. One of the soldiers behind me gave me another shove and I stumbled forward to be hugged and pounded. Phèdre took my face in her hands and said my name over and over, kissing me.

"Stop." I pulled away, laughing. "Stop! What in Elua's name are you doing here?"

"Looking for you," Joscelin said softly. "Did you think we wouldn't?"

"No, I . . ." I took off my mittens and wiped my eyes. "I didn't know. Oh gods, it's good to see you. But there's somewhat I have to do here. I'm sorry. Give me a moment." I took a deep breath and turned to face the Tarkovan captain. "My lord," I said to him in Rus, "I am sorry I was not honest. I am not a spy. I was hunting the man who killed my wife. He fled here. I was afraid he was a pilgrim and you would stop me if you knew."

The captain's face looked hard and set. "Was he?"

"No," I said honestly. "In the end, no."

The captain looked at Micah ben Ximon. "You knew this?"

"I knew this," ben Ximon said. "I will answer to Tadeuz Vral for it."

"And my men?" The captain's mouth hardened.

"Dead." I squared my shoulders. "I'm sorry. I tried to tell them. They would not listen. We fought. I have told this to Rebbe Avraham ben David of Miroslas. He sent me here . . ." My Rus was inadequate, so I glanced at Micah ben Ximon and switched to Habiru. "To make atonement." I repeated the Rebbe's words. "'Tell them you have confessed it to me, and I have absolved you of all guilt and laid my blessing upon you, bidding you to spread the word among men that it is better to be filled with compassion than suspicion, and remind them that in the end, in Yeshua's kingdom, all men are brothers. That your coming is a sign all must be mindful of this, always and forever.'"

Micah ben Ximon translated the Rebbe's injunction into Rus, his voice growing soft toward the end.

For a long moment, no one spoke, including the D'Angelines present. At last the captain sighed. He made an unfamiliar gesture, touching his fingertips to his brow, chest, and shoulders. "As Yeshua wills," he said. "The Rebbe of Miroslas is said to be a great and wise man. I will abide."

A profound sense of relief filled me. "Thank you, lord captain. Truly, I am sorry."

"Why *did* you free the Tatar?" he asked.

I spread my hands. "It was wrong. But he was not much more than a boy. We shared a prison, a blanket. I felt bad."

"A soft heart," he said. "Is that the Rebbe's lesson?"

"Perhaps it is," Micah said unexpectedly. "Perhaps that boy will grow to a man and a leader of men, and he will be the one to extend the olive branch of peace, because a stranger did him a kindness once." His gaze rested briefly on Joscelin, who had once done him a kindness. "Or perhaps not. We cannot always know the outcomes of our actions."

"I know that," the captain said. "Still, two good men are dead."

"I will make recompense to their families and make good on any losses," Micah said. "What Phèdre nó Delaunay said is true. If I had spared one man from the siege to answer your query, they would not have died. No one is blameless here."

"You had more important concerns," the captain said shortly.

Micah ben Ximon tilted his head. "So I thought," he said. "And yet I am reminded, nations may rise and fall on a chance encounter. And old debts demand no less honor than new ones." He gave the Cassiline bow, crisp and correct, but without the effortless fluidity of Joscelin's. "On the morrow, I will take these people to Vralgrad."

The captain grunted. "Please do, my lord."

So it was done. We filed out of the guardhouse with an appropriate air of solemnity. My heart was so full, I didn't know what I felt. They'd come to find me. Of course they had. They'd been on the other side of the world, and I'd nearly gotten killed, then vanished into the wilderness. Still, it was like a dream, seeing them here. As strange as Maslin's appearance in the wilderness had been, this was no less unexpected, and a good deal more joyous.

I stopped in my tracks. "Maslin."

Joscelin raised his brows. "*Maslin*? What of him?"

"He came for me, too," I said. "Sidonie sent him. Not a-purpose, I don't think." I shook my head. "It's a long story. But he found me. I owe him my life, really, although he doesn't think so." I pointed north. "He's waiting for me, or at least he will be. We should send word."

"I'll fetch him," Hugues offered.

I grimaced. "I'm not sure if *fetching* is such a good idea. Maslin wasn't exactly honest with the captain, either. His involvement in this whole business didn't arise. I daresay the captain thinks I killed him along with the others. It might be best to keep it that way."

Ti-Philippe grinned. "What in Elua's name have you been up to, Imri?"

"Too much," I said.

"Oh, gods above," Phèdre said in a small voice. She covered her face with both hands. "We should never have left you alone in Alba with that curse hanging over you. And Dorelei, poor, sweet girl. Hyacinthe promised to keep watch. I thought if anyone could keep you safe, it would be him."

"He did try. And there wasn't anything you could have done," I said gently. "It wouldn't have changed anything."

She shuddered and lowered her hands. "You can't know that. Not for a surety."

"It doesn't matter," I said. "It's over."

We lodged that night in the manor of the mayor of Tarkov, who had gladly accepted the honor of turning his home over to the heroic warlord Micah ben Ximon. I never did meet the mayor, who had already taken lodgings at an inn where he might boast of his illustrious guests. Hugues and Ti-Philippe elected to go in search of Maslin together and await us wherever he'd made camp. I suspect they were being discreet, allowing us time alone together as a family. It made me smile, picturing the shock on Maslin's face when they found him. Out of the same tact, Micah ben Ximon retired early.

We didn't.

I wanted to hear their story first. Mine was too big. They didn't press. It was the sort of thing they understood. I daresay they didn't care, as long as I was alive to tell it. It was Joscelin who told theirs; Phèdre couldn't bear to. Ti-Philippe had set out after them as soon as the news from Alba had come. Acting without thinking, he'd gone immediately, while my life still hung in the balance. He'd found them in Kriti, completing their mysterious mission. Whatever it was, they concluded it in haste and departed immediately. For the entire duration of the long journey back to Terre d'Ange, they hadn't known whether I was alive or dead.

"I'm so sorry," I said. I'd been saying this a lot lately.

"Well, we found out as soon as we made harbor in Marsilikos." Joscelin smiled slightly. "Alive, and overturning the Court."

"Is Ysandre still furious?" I asked.

"Mm-hmm." He glanced at Phèdre. "We didn't stay long enough to attempt to reason with her. Not after weeks of not knowing, then hearing you'd set out on your own with Urist to some unknown land."

Their sea passage home from Kriti had been infuriatingly slow, plagued by bad winds. By the time they travelled to Maarten's Crossing, it was well into autumn. There had been no word yet of the fate of Talorcan's party, but Adelmar of the Frisii was growing anxious about his decision to allow them passage, fearful that his greed in accepting Ysandre and Drustan's bribes would cost him Tadeuz Vral's goodwill. He knew perfectly well who Phèdre and Joscelin were, and he adamantly refused to grant passage to them, and moreover, had sent orders to Norstock not to allow any D'Angeline or Alban passengers until further notice. Phèdre's solution was ingenious.

"We made our own pilgrim caps," Joscelin said. "Let Adelmar think we were leaving, then doubled back through the wood and caught the pilgrims' route further north."

I laughed. "You *sewed* for me?"

"No." Phèdre flushed. "Ti-Philippe did." I laughed harder. Her eyes sparkled. I think she was beginning to believe I actually was alive and well, sitting and talking with her. "I tried, I did. But I've never been handy with a needle."

Miraculously enough, it had actually worked. There were still stories told in Skaldia about the D'Angeline pair who had outwitted Waldemar Selig and ultimately caused his downfall; but no Skaldi in his or her right mind would imagine that they'd travel boldface the length of the land, passing themselves off as pilgrims under false names.

It was a long, long journey, rendered worse by encountering Talorcan and his men early at the outset. They'd arrived at the Vralian border to find the pilgrims' passage heavily guarded, alerted by the handful of Urist's veterans who'd made the attempt earlier. Largely outnumbered and unable to convince or bribe the Vralian border guard to grant them passage, Talorcan's company had been forced to turn back and they'd had trouble with the Skaldi on their return route. They were still seething from their defeat and had not the slightest idea what had become of Urist and me.

"So that's what happened to them," I murmured. "Talorcan must have been frustrated as hell."

"Yes." Phèdre nodded. "It was disheartening. Still, we kept going."

It was strange to think about all of us on our separate quests at the same time, struggling with mishaps, misfortune, and misunderstanding. Halfway through Skaldia, winter had struck with a vengeance. Ti-Philippe had gotten desperately sick, a relapse of the ague he'd suffered after swimming in the canals of La Serenissima. It must have been, I thought, around the time that I was beginning to search the endless holdings of Miroslas, while Maslin's Tarkovan companions were realizing that they'd ridden the wrong direction in pursuit of me.

Ti-Philippe had recovered, but his illness had slowed their progress. Although he begged them to leave him, they hadn't dared. Not in Skaldia. By the time they reached Vralia, the siege in Petrovik had ended and the country was abuzz with Micah ben Ximon's name.

"So we went in search of him," Joscelin said. "We found him a few days ago on the road from Petrovik bound for Vralgrad."

"And learned you'd been imprisoned as a spy, and he couldn't be bothered to spare a man to free you!" Phèdre's voice crackled with rare anger.

"Well, he *was* in the midst of a war," I said philosophically.

"He thought you were safe enough where you were," Joscelin said. "And that mayhap a few months in a gaol cell would cool your ardor for vengeance."

"It did, in a way," I said.

"Did you . . . ?" His voice trailed off.

"Yes." I rubbed my eyes. I'd forgotten, they wouldn't have understood all of what transpired in the guardhouse. I'd been speaking Rus when I spoke of Berlik. I hadn't done so badly after all, if I'd mastered—well, not mastered, but learned a bit of it—a tongue that Phèdre didn't know. "It wasn't what I thought it would be in the end. Not at all. But it's done. Maslin has his head," I added.

Joscelin stared. "His head."

"Well, his skull." I cleared my throat. "To bury under Dorelei's feet so her spirit will rest easily. We had to boil it. It was supposed to be preserved in lime, but that was spoiled in the shipwreck. Urist said it would be all right this way."

"His head," he repeated.

"It's an Alban custom," Phèdre murmured. "Remember Grainne?" And then, quite unexpectedly, she burst into tears.

"I'm sorry!" I said in alarm. "Please don't cry. I shouldn't have said anything about the head." I knelt beside her chair and put my arms around her. "I'm here, I'm all right. Everything is, or it will be."

"I know." She drew a shuddering breath. "Oh, Blessed Elua! Lucca was bad enough, but at least I knew Denise Fleurais at the embassy was doing everything humanly possible to get you out of there. This . . . Imriel, if you'd died out here, all alone, or in Alba . . . I just, I just don't know what I would have done."

"But he didn't, love," Joscelin said gently. "Look at him! We came all this way, and he didn't even need rescuing."

"You look at him!" she cried. "He looks five years older and worn down to the bone. He lost a wife and a child and nearly got killed, and we weren't there for him!"

"I know," Joscelin said, stroking her hair. "Believe me, I know."

I let Phèdre go and sat quietly on the floor, my arms around my knees. I didn't know what to say. I'd never seen her so thoroughly unstrung before, not even during the worst of Daršanga. It was unnerving. "You did rescue me," I said at length. "You rescued me ten years ago, and you rescue me every day of my life. Every skill I used to survive, the two of you taught me. Everything I know of hope and persistence in the face of despair, I learned from you. You taught me to love, and that love is reason enough and more to keep living."

Phèdre wiped her eyes. "We should have been there."

"I'm not a child," I said softly. "You can't protect me from the whole world, Phèdre."

"I can try," she said.

I smiled. "Do I really look five years older?"

"You look like hell," Joscelin said. "And by the way, what shipwreck?"

I opened my mouth to reply. "No," Phèdre said. The old, familiar strength surfaced in her expression; stubborn, surprising, and resilient.

The knowledge that she hadn't been there when it happened would always tear her up inside. But she would face this, as she had faced everything else. "Start at the beginning."

So I did.

I hadn't told anyone but Sidonie the whole story of what had happened that terrible night in Clunderry. I told it to Phèdre and Joscelin. It was easier. I'd had a longer time to live with it. I told it without faltering. I didn't dwell on the details, but I didn't censor them, either. And then I told the rest. Urist's promise to Dorelei. The upset I'd caused in the City of Elua. The pursuit, the pilgrims, the shipwreck. Tarkov, and Kebek the Tatar. Miroslas, and the long hunt that followed. It went quicker than I would have reckoned. There wasn't that much to tell, really. Days of labor on the barren island, days of tedium in a gaol cell, days and days of snow and cold, and then the end, and how it happened. It was the things I couldn't put into words that mattered the most.

They listened to those, too.

When I finished, Phèdre sighed. "I swear to Elua," she murmured. "I'd like to lock you up in a safe place and never let you leave."

"Sidonie said somewhat like that." I paused. "Did you see her?"

"We did." She didn't quite smile, but almost. "You held out a long time before asking."

I felt myself blush, and laughed. "You came a long way. I didn't want to appear insufferably self-absorbed."

"She's well," Joscelin said. "Terrified for you, engaged in a silent contest of wills with her mother, but well."

"Was there any message?" I asked hopefully.

"Just come home," Phèdre said.

SIXTY-FIVE

ON THE FOLLOWING DAY, we caught up with Maslin, Hugues, and Ti-Philippe west of Tarkov. Micah ben Ximon and the large contingent of soldiers with him accompanied us. Maslin still wore a stunned expression at the turn of events. I didn't blame him. I felt it, too.

Our plan was to continue on to Vralgrad. We didn't have a great deal of choice in the matter, since Micah was insistent on it. If luck was with us, Tadeuz Vral would be merciful and forgive me for the deaths of Berlik and the Tarkovan guards. In hindsight it was fortunate that Talorcan and his men had turned back in frustration rather than trying to give battle against the Vralian border guard. That, Tadeuz Vral would be unlikely to forgive. And thanks to Micah ben Ximon's discretion, he didn't know about the first attempt.

Mayhap since Micah had won a second war for him, it would render his mood charitable. Micah thought that the Rebbe's intervention might make the difference in the end; that, and the fact that Berlik had not chosen to accept the Yeshuite faith. I hoped so. Whatever transpired, we were like to be trapped there for a while until the spring thaw made a sea voyage possible. Our only other choice would be to attempt a passage overland through Skaldia. Somehow, I doubted the pilgrim-hat ploy would work as well in the opposite direction.

Riding from Tarkov to Kargad took only a day. It was strange to remember how long that journey had seemed when I'd made it before, alone and on foot. It hadn't even begun to snow at that point. Since then, I'd endured so much worse.

We passed through Kargad without stopping and continued along the banks of the frozen Ulsk River. I thought about Ethan of Ommsmeer and his family, but I made no attempt to contact them. I didn't think he would welcome the knowledge of what I had done.

I wondered what story might one day find its way to his ears; the hard truth, or the wishful fantasy concocted by the priests and acolytes of Miroslas? It would be a piece of irony indeed if Berlik of the Maghuin Dhonn became a Yeshuite icon in his death.

All along the Ulsk, and then later, the Volkov, people hailed Micah ben Ximon and his men as conquering heroes. I had supposed that the frozen waterways would be abandoned in winter, but I was wrong. Vralians are hearty and ingenious folk. There were a number of traders travelling over the frozen rivers in horse-drawn sleighs.

Ben Ximon acknowledged the cheers somberly. From what I could gather, he'd led an effective siege, marshaling his army and blockading Petrovik before its inhabitants were able to stock sufficient supplies to make it through the long winter without venturing outside its walls. There were women and children there. Some, I heard, were so weak they could barely walk by the time the surrender came. Some had likely died of sicknesses they would have survived otherwise.

Micah ben Ximon didn't look as though he felt himself a hero.

For our part, we drew the sort of wondering stares that D'Angelines in distant, isolated lands do; and mayhap that, too, would work itself into the tale.

"Did you know most Vralians believe an angel appeared to Micah ben Ximon in a dream and taught him to fight?" I asked Joscelin.

"So he said." He gave a half-smile. "And there I was, expecting to be hailed as his mentor. He asked for my silence on the matter, which is one of the reasons he agreed to aid us in securing your freedom. Unnecessary though it proved, I gave my word. You'll not see me draw my daggers in Vralia. I'll rely on my sword if I must."

"Does it trouble you?" I asked.

Joscelin shook his head. "Not especially. I don't condone the lie, but it doesn't sound as though he started it himself. He just never refuted it, nor did anyone else who knew. Anyway, it's his business."

I didn't tell him that I'd told the Yeshuite sailor Ravi that the myth was untrue, that I'd practiced the Cassiline forms in front of him and the crew. Still, my practicing on a shipwrecked shore—or behind the locked door of a gaol cell with only Kebek for an audience—wasn't quite the same as Joscelin revealing himself in all his prowess before Micah ben Ximon's men. I wondered if that particular truth would seep out, or if Ravi and the others would keep their silence and let the myth endure. When all was said and done, I doubted Joscelin would care either way. He had never been one to care about appearances or heroics or receiving accolades for his deeds. I daresay keeping Phèdre in one piece had kept him too busy; and then later, protecting me, too.

Maslin was quiet and withdrawn around him at first; around all of them. As he'd said, he wasn't a complete fool. For most of our acquaintance, he'd behaved very badly toward me, and having half of Montrève's household present reminded him of it. For a time, I wasn't sure if the tentative friendship we'd forged would endure, or vanish as Maslin sank back into envy and bitterness. But I hadn't reckoned on Phèdre, who had noticed the change between us and Maslin's withdrawal alike.

"You look so much like your father," she said to him one evening, when we were lodged in a small, smoky inn in a town whose name I can't recall. "I remember the first time I saw him."

"Oh?" It was all Maslin said, but there was hunger in it.

"It was at the Longest Night fête at Cereus House," she said. "I was shy of my tenth birthday, but the Dowayne permitted me to attend, as I'd be a part of my lord Delaunay's household the following year and no longer eligible."

That was the infamous fête at which Baudoin de Trevalion appeared as the Sun Prince, already plotting treason; and yet Phèdre managed to tell the story without a hint of censure, painting a vivid portrait of the affair—the madcap prince and his glittering entourage, Maslin's father Isidore d'Aiglemort foremost among them. She told other tales, too, and although all of us knew the shadow that would fall over d'Aiglemort's story in the end, somehow, she made it bearable and brought to life a time when Maslin's father was young and vibrant, the heroic leader of the Allies of Camlach and a darling of Terre d'Ange. If Maslin could have eaten her words with a spoon, I daresay he would have.

No one said aught to gainsay it. There was that which came after, yes. But in the end, Isidore d'Aiglemort gave his life to save his people.

I watched Maslin become easier in our presence that night. It was a kindness she was offering him, and he'd grown enough to accept it with grace and be grateful for it. I was glad for him.

It was another cold, bright day when we reached Vralgrad. The city threw open its gates to welcome its returning hero. Micah ben Ximon's bannermen carried their staves high. Yeshua's cross fluttered brilliantly under the hard blue sky, scarlet on white. In Terre d'Ange, Queen Ysandre would have been there herself to receive her royal commander, but there was only a company of royal guardsmen in their white and red brocade coats. Grand Prince Tadeuz Vral was in the temple, giving thanks to God and Yeshua ben Yosef for his victory. The streets were thronged with ordinary citizens clad in heavy winter attire, their breath rising in frosty gusts as they cheered and shouted.

They cheered us, too. After all, we were there with him.

It all felt very odd. I'd sooner have entered quietly with our small D'Angeline company. For good or ill, great events were stirring in Vralia, and they'd naught to do with us. I didn't even know what I thought about it. I'd liked Tadeuz Vral, which I hadn't expected. But then, I'd come to be fond of Kebek the Tatar, too. It didn't seem unreasonable to me that whoever ruled Vralia might come to some accommodation with the Tatars that didn't involve conquering them or forcing them to accept the Yeshuite faith. I might have liked Fedor Vral if I'd met him, too, but I hadn't. Vralia was a nation in the throes of transformation, and all it had been to me was the backdrop against which my own personal quest had played out.

And yet if Joscelin hadn't taught a young Yeshuite living in La Serenissima and forbidden to bear a sword how to fight in the Cassiline style, mayhap none of this would have come to pass.

Truly, the ways of the gods were mysterious and unknowable.

I was grateful when Micah ben Ximon headed for the great temple and dispatched us to the palace with a pair of royal guardsmen and a promise of hospitality. Grateful for the hospitality, grateful for the relative quietude. And most grateful of all to see Urist.

Tadeuz Vral had been generous. I daresay it was a lucky thing that the rumors from Tarkov had never reached his ears, or he might have rescinded his generosity. But they hadn't, and he hadn't. Urist was still esconced at the palace. He retained the same chamber that had been given us when we first arrived, although I found out later that he spent most of his time among the palace guards, dicing and following news of the war, picking up bits and pieces of Rus and teaching them to curse in Cruithne.

It must have worked well enough, for someone sent word to him. We had only just arrived in the great entry hall with its inlaid tile floor when he came limping out from a corridor, leaning on a walking-stick, a vast grin splitting his tattooed face. I was so glad to see him, gladder than I'd reckoned. When all was said and done, he was the only one who *had* been there at Clunderry when it happened. It made a difference, sharing the memory.

For a moment, we just stood there. I was carrying the battered leather bag with Berlik's skull, not daring trust it to any of the palace servants. Urist's dark eyes gleamed. "You did it."

"I did," I said.

He gave a nod. "Thought you would." He clapped me on the shoulder with gruff affection. "On to Clunderry, eh?"

"My lord Urist—" Phèdre began in protest.

He cut her off. "Let him be a man, my lady, and do a man's duty."

"Clunderry," I murmured. For the first time in a while, I thought about Dorelei lying slain. Her sightless eyes, her savaged belly covered with a blood-soaked cloak. I glanced at Phèdre's troubled face. "Urist is right. I need to see it through. Let's just hope Tadeuz Vral is inclined to let me go."

"He'd best be," Joscelin said grimly.

Whatever else might have been true, the Grand Prince of Vralia wasn't inclined to grant us an audience that day; nor the following day, either. We were in the same state of limbo I'd felt in Tarkov; neither guests nor prisoners. We were given lodging and hospitality, but we were attended by guards at all times. When we were within our chambers, they waited outside the door. When we ventured out, they accompanied us.

On the fourth day, there was a buzz of excitement in the palace. I asked one of our guards what it was about and learned that the famous Rebbe Avraham ben David had arrived from Miroslas to serve as the High Counselor to the Grand Prince. There was a train of refugees making its way from Petrovik on foot, a thousand strong. They had pledged to vow themselves to the Yeshuite faith, and the Rebbe's first act would be to preside over the ceremony.

On the fifth day, Micah ben Ximon came for us.

"He will see you," he said briefly. "All of you. I would counsel you not to lie. I have not spoken of what happened at the border, as you were not involved. Otherwise, I have told him the entire truth insofar as I know it."

"Are you in disfavor?" I asked.

His face was hard and set. "Not in any way his lordship can afford to show after the victory I won for him. But he is not pleased."

Unlike our previous encounter, this was a formal audience. It took place in the throne room, a vast, vaulted space with checkered marble floors that gleamed in the wintry light pouring through the narrow windows. Tadeuz Vral was seated in his throne, and beside him stood Rebbe Avraham. The Rebbe looked grave and thoughtful. The Grand Prince looked grim. He was clad in heavy brocade robes trimmed with ermine, and atop his head he wore a conical gold crown studded with gems, also trimmed with fur. His expression didn't change much as we approached, except that his eyes widened at the sight of Phèdre.

"So," he said to me. "You are back."

"Yes, my lord," I said. "To plead clemency."

Tadeuz Vral gave a sharp bark of laughter. "You accepted my friendship and my coin, and lied to my face! 'Behold,'" he quoted. "'He travaileth with iniquity, and hath conceived mischief, and brought forth falsehood. His mischief shall return upon his own head, and his violent dealing shall come down upon his own pate.' Is it not so written?" he demanded, turning to the Rebbe.

"It is," Rebbe Avraham said quietly.

"You see?" Prince Tadeuz said to me. "'God judgeth the righteous, and God is angry with the wicked every day.' You have slain three men under the mantle of my rulership. Why should I grant you clemency?"

I glanced at the others with me; at Urist, who had gauged my merits and found me worthy of loyalty, who had come to love Dorelei as a daughter, though he'd never said so in as many words. At Maslin, who had come in anger and envy, only to begin learning how to love. At Ti-Philippe and Hugues, stalwart, insistent, and loyal to the marrow. At Joscelin and Phèdre, the bedrock on which my existence rested. There were faint worry-lines etched between Phèdre's brows, but she held her tongue, trusting me to answer for myself. My heart ached with fondness.

"As this is your kingdom, I must answer to you, my lord," I said to Tadeuz Vral. "But I am Elua's child. I will not answer to your God."

His face flushed. "Well, it is against *my* law to slay a pilgrim!"

"Nor was he," I said steadily. "Not at the end."

"And yet you hunted him believing it to be so," Tadeuz Vral said. "Would it have mattered if it were true?"

There were a great many things I might have said.

In the end, I spoke only the truth. "I don't know."

"An honest answer." The Grand Prince seemed somewhat mollified. He propped his chin on one hand and contemplated us. "You are a small problem, but a vexing one. Micah tells me that the truth is more dangerous than the lie; that you are persons of some import, and perhaps I would be better served by discretion than righteousness." He paused. "I find it hard to believe that persons of true significance and power would travel in such a manner, but Micah has lived beyond Vralia's borders, while I know nothing else. And I do not wish to make an enemy of Terre d'Ange and Alba."

"Nor do we wish it," I said.

"What is your counsel?" he asked Rebbe Avraham.

"It is as I told you. I have spoken with the young man," the Rebbe said. "He did but defend himself agains the Tarkovans and I have absolved him of that crime. As for Berlik, I believe he speaks the truth. No one could have found that man in the wilderness if he did not wish to be found. He found the death he desired."

Tadeuz Vral frowned. "That is a sin."

"Not yours nor mine, my lord." Rebbe Avraham was speaking to Vral, but out of the corner of his eye he was watching Phèdre. He'd been doing so for a while. "Did you have aught to say, my lady?" he asked, switching to Habiru.

"Not yet." Phèdre answered in Rus, slow and careful. After all, she'd had a good ten days since Tarkov to improve her skills. "I listen." She tilted her head. A shaft of wintry sunlight fell across her face. The scarlet mote in her left eye floated, bright and vivid. She was Phèdre nó Delaunay de Montrève, and she held the Name of God in her thoughts. Beside her, Joscelin shifted, fighting the urge to cross his arms and rest his hands on his dagger-hilts. Phèdre gave the Rebbe a disarming smile. "If there is need to speak of . . ." She switched to Habiru, her vocabulary failing her. ". . . to speak of *ransom*, I will negotiate on Queen Ysandre's behalf, of course. Imriel is her kinsman and my foster-son."

"Rebbe Avraham!" Tadeuz Vral said irritably. "Rus, if you please."

"Indeed." The Rebbe inclined his head to Phèdre, then faced his lord. "If you would have my counsel, it is this. Berlik of Alba came to Vralia bearing his sin. Let them depart and take it with them."

"That's all?" Vral sounded disappointed.

Rebbe Avraham shrugged. "It is what is best for Vralia."

"You know, I wanted to *like* you," Tadeuz Vral said to me. "I wish you hadn't proved to be false." I felt an unexpected pang of guilt. He took off his crown and rubbed his brow. "So be it. Outside this room, we will not speak of what transpired here. You will remain as our guests. You will bear witness to the oath-taking of a thousand new Yeshuites. When the ice breaks, you will go." His voice turned fierce. "And you will tell your people, your Queen and your Cruarch, that Yeshua's kingdom reigns in the north!"

I bowed; everyone else followed suit. "As my lord wills."

With that, Tadeuz Vral left us. I translated what had passed for the others, speaking in D'Angeline. And now it was my turn to watch out of the corner of my eye as Rebbe Avraham descended from the dais and approached Phèdre.

"Shalom, Father," she said softly.

"Child." He reached out to touch her cheek. I reckoned Rebbe Avraham was old enough to call anyone "child" if he wished. "Even here in the north, the Children of Yisra-el pass tales from mouth to ear. Pilgrims come bearing them. Some years ago, one came to my ears. I have heard the tale of how the angel known as *Pride* was defeated when a D'Angeline woman spoke the Name of God, and the Master of the Straits was freed. I spent my youth in the Flatlands. I know his power. And I see knowledge that does not belong there in your eyes."

Phèdre said nothing.

"You did not tell me," the Rebbe said to me.

"Would it have mattered?" I asked, echoing Tadeuz Vral.

The Rebbe smiled. "I suppose not."

"Did you expect me to invoke the aid of the Master of the Straits and threaten to bring heaven's wrath down on Vralia if Prince Tadeuz had sought retribution against Imriel?" Phèdre asked mildly.

"I thought it was possible." His voice was grave. "You have named the young man your son. I do not discount the ferocity of a mother's love."

"Ah, well." She favored him with another sweet, disarming smile. "I would have negotiated first."

SIXTY-SIX

DURING THE TIME we spent in Vralgrad, waiting for the ice to break, I thought about love and ferocity.

I'd known, of course; I'd always known how much Phèdre loved me, and Joscelin, too; or at least I had for a long time. It hadn't really been *me* they'd come for in Daršanga. It had been an idea of me. A child; Melisande's child, but still a child, undeserving of his fate. By the time we'd reached Saba together, that had changed. We had become, however unlikely, a family. When Phèdre offered her life for mine on the temple threshold, she'd known exactly what she was doing and why.

I thought I had, but I hadn't, not really.

I hadn't grasped it wholly.

Women are wiser than men in such matters. I thought about Dorelei and our lost child; the son who would have become a monstrosity in Alba. I wondered if I would have loved him so much I would have done anything for him. Forgiven him any crime. The possibility, I thought, existed.

And I thought about Sidonie.

Alais was right, there was fierceness in her, however well hidden in public. And in me. I wanted her. I loved her. I knew that beyond any shadow of doubt. The thought of her losing her as I'd lost Dorelei made my blood run cold in my veins. And the thought of one day making a *child* together with her . . .

Ah, Elua!

It was terrifying.

When I thought about it, I understood why Phèdre had fallen apart at finding me safe. I thought about what Melisande had written to me, my blood mother. How she would have humbled herself and begged, paid any price to undo what was done to me.

You will wonder if I loved you. The answer is yes; a thousand times, yes.

I hadn't wholly believed it when I read it. Enough to hurt, enough to reveal an ache within myself that I'd denied existed. But then, I hadn't known how deep and fine love could truly cut. The love one feels as a child is altogether different. It may be fierce and overwhelming, but it lacks the acute awareness that comes with adulthood; the knowledge of choice and responsibility. Those things bear a keen edge.

Our days were mostly idle, waiting for the fête, if one might term it so, during which the captured rebels would be dedicated in Yeshua's name. The mood in Vralgrad was merry despite the interminable cold. Tadeuz Vral kept his word. If there were stories that circulated around our presence here, they were only that; stories. No one spoke the truth. Many of the older folk of Habiru descent were immigrants. They knew of D'Angelines, but did not question our presence, reckoning it was politics. The Vralians made up their own tales, reckoning our presence was a sign from God, a blessing upon Tadeuz Vral's victory. For that, I was grateful.

I went with Joscelin and Ti-Philippe to the wharf. I did my best to translate while they asked better questions than I would have conceived. We learned there were traders willing to carry our small party by sleigh to the mouth of the Volkov where it met the shores of the Eastern Sea. The trade-ships weren't sailing yet, but there were seal-hunters willing to dare the ice floes. For a sufficient price, we might find a hunting-ship to carry us southward as far as Norstock.

In the meanwhile, we got to know the court of Tadeuz Vral. It wasn't a court as D'Angelines would reckon it—there was no Hall of Games, no theatre, barely even a music salon—but it was growing lively. Nobles from other cities loyal to Grand Prince Tadeuz were pouring into the palace. Vralings, they called them; they were all related distantly by blood. Vralstag, Vralsturm . . . there were a dozen variants. Many of the lesser princes with daughters of marriageable age brought them.

As it happened, Tadeuz Vral was unwed. And while he didn't seem minded to make a choice anytime soon, he clearly enjoyed entertaining the prospect.

Without vanity, I daresay I might have had my pick of them. The unwed girls flirted with the men among us; and so did some of their mothers. Yeshua's edicts regarding celibacy and fidelity had not yet overridden simple human desire. Once or twice, I might have been tempted at another time, under different circumstances. Some of the Vralian women were quite lovely, forthright and direct, with straight, clean limbs and high-cheeked features. But in the end, I kept myself apart.

Maslin didn't.

He embarked on a covert affair with a young woman named Kata-lena, whose parents would have throttled her if they'd known she was jeopardizing her chances for a marriage with the Grand Prince. From what I could gather on meeting her, she seemed a tempestuous girl, given to displays of high emotion. Maslin seemed pleased with himself to the point of smugness.

"Don't you endanger our position here," I warned him. "And don't mislead her, either. It's unfair."

"Oh, I won't," he said airily. "Katya's heard both sides of the story. She reckons at worst she's a diplomat's mistress."

"You're not a diplomat," I pointed out to him.

"I might be." Maslin looked pensive. "I do believe I've come to like it here. Do you suppose Tadeuz Vral would let me stay for a time?"

"Not if he knows you're making love to his prospective bride," I said.

Maslin made a dismissive gesture. "He doesn't. And he won't. Katya's not a fool. She'd throw me over to marry him if it came to it, but it might not." He cocked his head. "You know, there are half a dozen girls trying to throw themselves at you. Have you not noticed?"

I shrugged. "I'm not interested."

"Why?" He looked genuinely curious. "Are you keeping chaste?"

I hadn't thought about it in those terms. "Mayhap."

"I didn't think you were such a Cassiline." Maslin grinned. "I hope you're not expecting Sidonie to return the favor. Because I will tell you in all honesty, my friend, I strongly doubt it."

A memory struck me; Sidonie sitting upright in our borrowed bed and shaking out her love-tangled locks, smiling sidelong at me, amused at my slowness to perceive what should have been obvious. *Anyway, Amarante doesn't sleep here very often.* No apology, no hint of self-consciousness. She had leaned down to kiss me, the tips of her breasts brushing my chest, her sun-shot hair falling around my face.

Elua knows why, but that was the first time I'd felt truly at peace with myself and who I was. Who we were, Sidonie and I, apart and together.

It was the first time I'd told her I loved her.

"That makes you smile?" Maslin observed wryly.

"In its own way," I said.

"Gods above," he said in wonderment. "You *do* love her."

I laughed.

Of a surety, it was true; I hadn't gone so long without love since I'd been sixteen years old and and gave my virginity to an adept of Balm House. But I hadn't been keeping chaste a-purpose. Some of it was due to a desire to honor Dorelei's memory. It hadn't been a year since her death. She'd extracted a promise from Urist and sent me to Sidonie's side for love's sake. Anything else would feel like a betrayal. And in truth, I didn't *want* anyone else. Not here, not now. Elua knows, that might change one day. It wasn't that I was immune to the promptings of desire; far from it. But I wanted more.

And whatever Maslin might say, I didn't think Sidonie was engaging in dalliance, either. I knew my girl. If she was engaged in a contest of wills with her mother, there was no way she was going to provide Ysandre any fodder with which to question the depth and seriousness of her feelings for me. There was Amarante, of course; but that was different. Amarante had been with her for a long time, longer than I had. And without impulsive anger firing her blood, I daresay even Ysandre would be circumspect about speaking ill of the daughter of the High Priestess of Naamah. I hoped so, anyway.

Elua, I wanted to go home.

The pilgrims came on foot, trickling into Vralgrad, straining the city to bursting. They didn't look overjoyed to be there. They looked sullen, tired, and defeated. I pitied them, although I had to own, I was grateful when the date for their oath-taking drew nigh.

It was a grand show of pageantry. Tadeuz Vral was no fool. He meant to dazzle them, as well as us, with a show of might and majesty; both his and Yeshua's.

The ceremony was held in the new temple, the one with the gilded domes and spires. We were given what was ostensibly a place of honor in the wings at the foot of the dais, alongside the lesser princes of the realm and their families.

The temple itself was vast and splendid, most notable on the interior for its frescoes. They were so new the colors fairly sang, bright and vivid. The style was simple and direct, but rendered with strong lines and flat expanses of color. On the side wall to the right were images from the life of Yeshua ben Yosef as depicted in the Brit Khadasha, and on the left, images of noble soldiers I guessed were meant to represent the Hundred Martyrs, along with a few others I didn't recognize.

Largest of all was the image of Yeshua on the wall behind the altar itself.

As in Miroslav, there was a cross hanging there, although this one was gilded and shone brightly in the filtered winter light. Above it, his feet nearly resting atop the vertical beam, was Yeshua. He dwarfed the instrument of his mortal death and loomed above us, his head stretching toward the vaulted ceiling. In one hand, he held a book. In the other, he held a naked sword. He had a neatly trimmed beard and hot, staring eyes. His expression was stern and challenging.

He did not look like a god one might call a friend.

Atop the dais, Rebbe Avraham stood waiting. His simple black robes were gone, replaced by stiff garments glittering with gems and gold stitching. His face was solemn and unreadable. There were a pair of priests flanking him, only slightly less ornately attired. One looked to be Habiru; the other, Vralian. Grand Prince Tadeuz Vral stood a step below him, still elevated above the masses. He was dressed in a plain soldier's livery, except it was adorned with a heavy, gem-encrusted sash of gilded leather from which an ornamental scabbard hung. His chin was raised, and beneath his fur-trimmed crown his strong-boned face was as stern as Yeshua's.

Somewhere in a distant tower, a resonant horn blew.

The doors at the far end of the temple opened. The two priests flanking the Rebbe began to sing a hymn of praise; first in Habiru, then in Rus, one echoing the other. A company of Vralian soldiers strode into the temple, led by Micah ben Ximon, who stopped to stand below Tadeuz Vral. At ben Ximon's signal, his men divided and formed an aisle.

The pilgrims entered in a long line.

All of them, whatever their stature, had been given a crude garment of undyed sackcloth to wear over their attire. I watched them enter; watched expressions of surly rebellion give way to careful neutrality in the presence of Tadeuz Vral. When the first reached the dais and sank to his knees, the cantors ceased to sing. A living, breathing silence fell over the temple. Rebbe Avraham ben David stood very still, his grey head bowed.

He had doubts; I knew he did. He had spoken of them to me. And I knew, too, that he had spoken with Phèdre after our audience with Prince Tadeuz, yearning to hear the tale of the woman who had been given the Name of God in distant Saba by a priest of the Lost Tribe of the Habiru. I glanced at her. She was watching the Rebbe, her eyes dark and somber. When he lifted his head with gathering resolve, she looked away. Joscelin, who knew her best, slid his arm around her waist.

"We are gathered here today to give praise to Adonai and his son Yeshua for the victory they have granted us," the Rebbe said in a strong, firm voice. "And to welcome our new brothers and sisters into the fold of true faith."

So it began.

One by one, each of the pilgrims approached the altar. Each knelt and swore faith, repeated the words Avraham ben David gave them. Each bowed his or her head to Tadeuz Vral and pledged loyalty, kissing the point of his extended sword.

It went on for a long, long time. There were a thousand pilgrims. When each was done, the Vralian soldiers directed them wordlessly to kneel in the temple, awaiting the finish. I didn't envy them. I grew restless from standing for so long, my feet aching. It must have been worse to kneel on the cold marble floor. Still, they did it.

They were the defeated; they had no choice.

The others must have grown weary, too. Of a surety, the Vralian nobility grew bored and tempted to whisper among themselves. I caught Micah ben Ximon shifting, and one of the priests yawned a few times. But the Rebbe's voice never faltered. One by one, he accepted their oaths, treating each with as much solemnity as though it was the first. As for Tadeuz Vral, he stood straight-backed and tall, holding his sword extended. It never wavered. His face was suffused with a complex mixture of humility and rapture.

I nearly envied him.

It must be a glorious thing, I thought, to be so *sure*. Sure of one's rightness and rectitude; sure of one's place in the world. It was not so different in a way than what I had first envied in Maslin. And yet it was, for others' lives hung in the balance. I thought about the fur-trader Jergens making an offering to the *vodyanoi*, fearful and furtive. Should such things pass from the world to serve one god's glory? Could faith be compelled at the point of a sword?

I thought of the vision Morwen had shown me.

Homes torched, people dragged from them. The Maghuin Dhonn hunted like animals, eyes stretched wide with terror, their magics failing. The oak groves ablaze, teams of oxen dragging down the stone circles. Stone, ancient stone, crashing and falling. D'Angeline architects swarming. A world broken and remade in a new image.

My son's face.

There were no sureties in this world.

There in the temple, I stooped and touched the floor, spreading my fingers against the cool marble. Somewhere far beneath it, there was soil and living earth. "Blessed Elua hold me in your hand," I murmured. "May your wisdom ever guide me."

I felt it, then. A surge of assurance, beating like wings in my heart. Not Kushiel, but Elua; Blessed Elua. I was his scion, too. His mantle descended on me as I straightened. I felt so many things; regret, sorrow, hope. There was such beauty in the world, but there was such cruelty, too. Such folly and madness. I did not understand the whole of what had passed between Berlik and me, and I did not pretend to understand all of what passed here today. But for the sake of Vralia and its people, I prayed that love and compassion would temper ambition and the urge for glory.

The feeling stayed with me throughout the interminable ceremony. A pull at my heart, a steady tug, beckoning me homeward. Blessed Elua's assurance, a promise of love. I had failed to honor his precept; failed to trust in the truth of my own heart. I would not do so again. It was enough. I had to believe.

The last pilgrim gave her oath. She was an elderly woman with bad knees made worse by the long journey, and she struggled to rise after kissing the tip of Tadeuz Vral's blade. He sheathed his sword and extended his hand to her, helping her to her feet. I couldn't see her face, but the look on Vral's was almost tender. The crowd murmured with approval. A soldier escorted her to kneel once more among the ranks of pilgrims, assisting her with care.

"Today, you are born anew into the true faith," Rebbe Avraham said, his voice sounding tired at last. "From this day forth, you are Yeshuites and loyal citizens of Vralia. Cast off the garments of your penitence."

A thousand supplicants struggled to remove the sackcloth they wore over their clothing, kneeling and clutching the rough garments.

"Rise," the Rebbe said. "Go forth and rejoice in the mercy of Yeshua ben Yosef and Tadeuz Vral."

With varying degrees of difficulty, they rose.

Some looked relieved; many merely looked exhausted. Here and there, I saw flickers of brooding defiance. The patient cantors lifted their voices in song, the sound of it filling the temple. I glanced at Phèdre. Her head was cocked slightly and she wore a look I knew; distant and troubled, like a soldier hearing the strains of a faraway battle. But when I caught her eye, she merely shook her head, and her expression turned smooth.

It was done.

The new-made Yeshuites shuffled forth from the temple, directed by Vral's soldiers. We watched and waited. I thought Vral might speak to us, but he didn't. When the last pilgrim had departed, he gave a brusque nod to the rest of us, D'Angelines and Vralian nobility alike. We filed out of the temple. The sun, which had been high when we entered, sat low on the horizon, bathing the snowy city of Vralgrad in soft amber light.

In the middle of the street, Ti-Philippe yawned, his jaw cracking. "Well, that's that, then," he said. "On to Alba?"

The steady tug at my heart gave me a twinge of sorrow. I was only mortal. There was a part of me that wanted to give Berlik's skull into Urist's keeping and go *home*. Home to Terre d'Ange, where the soil was blessed by Elua's blood and seed. Home to Sidonie, whom I loved. But I couldn't, not yet.

"On to Alba," I agreed.

SIXTY-SEVEN

MASLIN STAYED.

It surprised me, more than a little. I hadn't thought he was serious; and even if I had, I wouldn't have supposed Tadeuz Vral would agree to it. He was unaware of Maslin's role in our escapade, but we were all tarred to some extent with the brush of my falsehood.

Still, Maslin managed to convince Vral that he would be in truth that which I had pretended; a young D'Angeline nobleman adventurer, come to explore the length and breadth of this budding nation and its trade routes to the east before reporting back to his Queen. His Rus had improved tremendously since he'd taken Katalena to his bed.

Phèdre thought Ysandre would welcome Maslin's initiative, and she knew the Queen better than most. Of a surety, Sidonie would be willing to release him from her service. She'd kept him on at his own insistence. Still, I found myself worried on his behalf.

"You're sure?" I asked him.

His mouth twisted, wry and familiar. "I'm sure. After all, I've already covered a good portion of the damned country. This is somewhat *I* can do, Imriel. Somewhat that's all my own. Leave me to do it, will you?"

"What will you live on?" I persisted.

Maslin jingled a purse at his belt. "I've some funds yet. And Prince Tadeuz has promised his patronage if I prove a true advocate. So have a few of the lesser lords."

"Stay out of Tarkov," I advised him. "They won't have forgotten you."

"I will." We were drinking *starka* in the quarters I shared with Urist; Maslin had been lodged there, too. He tipped the jug, refilling our cups. "Tell Sidonie . . ." His voice trailed off. "I don't know what to tell her."

Urist snorted. "You might try the truth."

Maslin glanced at him. "Is he always this way?"

I smiled. "Yes."

He sighed. "Tell her I'm sorry. That I didn't mean to be an ass. And that I forgive her for goading me. I deserved it." Our eyes met. The silence and companionship of the wilderness lay between us. Maslin's mouth twisted further. "Tell her we became friends, Imriel de la Courcel."

"I will," I promised.

It was overcast and snowing the day that we left. We'd made arrangements to hire sleighs, donating our mounts to Micah ben Ximon as reparation for the monies he'd paid to the families of the Tarkovan guards. It seemed only fair, and my own mount had been stolen from Tarkov in the first place. There was no ceremony, no further audience with ben Ximon, with Tadeuz Vral, with Rebbe Avraham. By their own decree, our role in their drama was finished. There was only our small company of D'Angelines and one Alban, making our way on foot to the wharf of Vralgrad where a pair of sleighs awaited us on the frozen Volkov River. And there was only Maslin, huddled in a long, padded coat, to bid us farewell.

"Be kind to Katalena," I murmured, embracing him. "Remember, you're a diplomat now."

"I will." Maslin grinned. "Anyway, she dotes on me."

I cuffed him. "Don't be an ass."

What Phèdre said to him, I could not hear and cannot guess. I had already boarded the sleigh I would share with Urist and Hugues. Whatever it was, it brought tears to his eyes and brought him to his knees, his mittened hands clasped between hers. She bent her head and kissed him lightly, then climbed into her sleigh and settled into the seat between Joscelin and Ti-Philippe. They tucked fur blankets around themselves for warmth, and Maslin got to his feet.

The shaggy sleigh-horses shook their heads, bells on their headstalls jingling. Our drivers cracked their whips, calling out cheerful words of encouragement. The sleighs moved forward, runners creaking over ice and snow.

We were off.

I turned in the sleigh, craning my neck to catch sight of Maslin. For a time, I saw him there on the wharf, one arm raised in farewell. And then the veil of snow grew too thick to pierce, and I saw no more. I turned my gaze forward.

We were two days on the frozen Volkov, making our way to the sea. We lodged overnight in a town along the way, a stopping-point for merchants and traders. It was quiet during the winter months—except for the seal-hunters, there was little sea trade—and the few other guests at the inn were men with rough-hewn Vralian faces, laughing and talking animatedly among themselves. I thought about Captain Iosef, whose fortitude and determination had gotten us off the barren isle. I'd never had a chance to thank him properly.

And then there was Ravi, my helpful translator and teacher. He'd asked me to stand him a drink if I had the chance. I'd never even made an effort to find him. I hoped he was well, and that he'd found another ship on which to earn back his lost wages.

I hoped they were all well.

'Tis strange how many leavetakings one life can hold.

On the following day, the snow had ceased and the journey was almost pleasant, snugged as we were under heavy blankets of fur, the wind of our passage bringing color to our cheeks. We reached Pradanat, the outpost at the mouth of the Volkov, and lodged there.

In the clear light of day, the notion of hiring a seal-hunting ship lost a good deal of its appeal. Joscelin, Ti-Philippe, and I walked to the harbor; or at least what *had* been the harbor during warmer months. There was a ledge of ice extending for a good hundred yards from the shoreline into the Eastern Sea. Beyond, the open water looked grey and cold, glinting dully in the sunlight and dotted with ice floes.

There were seal-hunters who plied it, that much was true. They used small boats with shallow draughts, wide keels, and square sails, open to the elements. There wasn't even a hold. We watched as one was launched, dragged across the solid ice by a pair of sturdy ponies.

"Where do the hunters sleep?" I asked an amiable-looking Vralian fellow.

"Under the sails." He pointed. "See? At night, they haul the boat onto the biggest ice they can find, then *phfft*!" He grinned, showing a sizable gap between his front teeth. "Take down the sails, stretch them across the boat. Makes a nice warm tent."

I translated for Joscelin and Ti-Philippe.

"I think mayhap Phèdre should see this for herself," Joscelin said doubtfully.

He went back to fetch her while Ti-Philippe and I queried our new friend, whose name was Lasko, about the possibility of hiring a hunting-ship to ferry us to Norstock. He grew excited about the prospect.

"My cousin has a boat," he offered eagerly. "A most excellent boat! He will do it, I am sure. The hunting has been bad this winter. Too warm."

"There's always a cousin," Ti-Philippe commented when I translated. "And what in the seven hells does he mean too *warm*?"

I laughed. "Apparently, this is what passes for a mild winter in Vralia."

Lasko's mouth hung open at the sight of Phèdre approaching with Joscelin, Hugues, and Urist. I didn't blame him. It was hard to imagine anyone looked as utterly, spectacularly out of place as Phèdre nó Delaunay de Montrève on a snow-covered Vralian shore amidst a group of seal-hunters.

"Oh, my cousin will surely do this thing!" Lasko said fervently.

"Slowly, friend." I laid a hand on his arm. "The lady is dear to us all. Any man to lay a hand on her would surely lose it." I nodded at Joscelin. "Any one of us would guarantee it. But your cousin might want to note that *that* fellow happens to be one of the greatest living swordsmen in the world."

"I meant no insult." He sounded affronted, but his expression turned circumspect. "Still, I will mention this fact to my cousin."

Although we'd made no commitment, he went off to fetch his cousin. The others joined us. We watched as another boat was dragged across the ice and launched. The seal-hunters were hardy, wind-burned men, indistinguishable from one another in their heavy sealskin garments. Phèdre watched without comment.

"We'd have to sleep in the boat," Ti-Philippe informed her. "Under the sails. All of us."

"I heard." Phèdre glanced at me. "How long will we have to wait for a proper ship?"

I shrugged. "Until the ice breaks? From what I gather, it could be as little as a month or as much as three or four. They say it's a mild winter, but there's no telling how long it will last."

"Ah, well." She looked amused and rueful. "Given your experience, there's no guarantee that a proper ship would be any safer, just more comfortable. But this can't be worse than slogging through the wet season in Jebe-Barkal, can it?"

"I wouldn't be so sure," Joscelin murmured. "But it seems we'll find out."

So it was decided.

We met with Lasko's cousin, Skovik. To my relief, he seemed a steady fellow with calm eyes and a drooping mustache that reminded me in a reassuring fashion of Captain Iosef, although he was considerably younger. Before we even began to haggle over the fee, he spoke to us in a straightforward, honest manner.

"This journey can be made," he said. "But you must understand it is dangerous. It is why only seasoned hunters sail in the winter. You are not seasoned hunters. On the boat, you must do exactly as I tell you, always. You must agree to this, or I cannot take you. Not for any price."

Once we had agreed, which we did, then came the haggling. We had pooled our monies, all of us, and we had enough to meet Skovik's price with a bit to spare for the next leg of our journey. I served as translator, while Ti-Philippe drove the hardest bargain. We settled on a fee and agreed to meet on the morrow.

Whether or not that journey was more miserable than slogging through the rainy season in Jebe-Barkal was wholly a matter of opinion. When all was said and done, I didn't think it was. But unlike Joscelin, I'd never been prone to seasickness. And I'd been spent my childhood in the mountains of Siovale. I didn't mind the cold as much as Phèdre did.

And it *was* cold, no matter what the Vralians said.

Out on the open sea, there was no respite from it. We felt the wind cutting us before the boat was even launched, trudging across the broad expanse of ice while ponies dragged the boat alongside us.

Some yards from the edge, the ponies were unhitched. There were only two men serving as Skovik's crew; we would have to make up for the rest. The boat wasn't large enough to carry more. We took hold of the boat on its stern and sides and pushed, sliding it over the ice, which I prayed would hold us.

The ice held firm beneath our feet. The Vralian seal-hunters had a great deal of experience in gauging such matters. I grunted and pushed, the worn soles of my boots sliding. The boat grated over the ice and slid into the frigid water with a splash. Skovik's men grabbed barbed pikes and hooked the boat's railing with a practiced movement, securing it. It bobbed in the sea, looking little larger than a child's toy.

Skovik clambered aboard and beckoned. "Come."

Joscelin went first, stepping deftly over the railing and into the boat, steadied by Skovik's hand on his arm. The boat dipped and wallowed under Joscelin's weight and his face took on a greenish tinge almost immediately. He swallowed and stood with one foot on the railing, hoisting Phèdre aboard by main force. She was shivering, no longer amused. The rest of us followed. Urist, who still needed a walking-stick and had a difficult time navigating the ice, was the hardest, but between the three of us, Hugues, Ti-Philippe, and I managed to wrestle him aboard, as well as all of our baggage.

I went last. We stowed our gear as best we could and arrayed ourselves along the narrow benches at Skovik's directive, ensuring the boat's balance; and then he gave an order to his men, and they stepped aboard with careless ease, using their barbed pikes to shove off.

A narrow strip of grey water opened between our boat and the shore. Skovik gave an order. His men obeyed with alacrity, raising the square sails. They caught the wind and bellied. The expanse of water between us and the icy shore grew wider. Skovik took the rudder. He glanced at the sky and gave a hard, fierce grin.

"Seems your gods are with you!" he shouted. "Wind's blowing from the north!"

"Blessed Elua be thanked." Huddling in the prow, Phèdre wrapped her arms around herself and sought to sink deeper into her fur-lined coat. "I think."

It was by far and away the most perilous sea crossing I'd ever made. The wind stayed brisk and true, and our little boat ran easily before it. But the ice floes were a constant danger. Some of them were quite massive, looming above the grey water. Those were the ones on which we made camp at night, searching until we found an incline shallow enough to permit us to drag the boat atop the solid ice.

Sleeping was cramped and uncomfortable. Once the sails were stretched across the boat and lashed into place, our body heat warmed the trapped air, but it soon grew to smell stale and rank. Our meals consisted of salt cod, hard biscuits, and *starka*, which we drank in sparing amounts.

There was no way to carry water without it freezing solid, and nothing with which to build a fire on the floes. Skovik showed us how to scrape ice and pack our waterskins with it, wearing them under our clothing so the ice would slowly melt over the course of the day or night. Between that and the *starka*, it was enough to keep us from growing parched. I'd thought the melted floe-ice would be salty and unfit to drink, but strangely, it was only a bit brackish. When I dipped my hand into the sea and tasted the open water, it was bitter. Why that should be true, I cannot say, but it was.

The worst danger was the smaller floes, the ones that lurked at the surface of the water, barely visible. They didn't look like much, but they were larger beneath than above. With a strong wind at our back, if we struck one, it might breach the hull.

And if *that* happened, we were all dead. I was a strong swimmer, but I had no illusions on that front. The winter sea was deadly cold. If we were pitched into it, we'd freeze and drown in a matter of minutes.

On the first day, Skovik posted one of his men, an experienced spotter, in the prow. By the second day, he realized that Phèdre had grown as adept as a Vralian sailor at spotting dangerous floes and let her take over the task. She had a keen eye, trained to observe since childhood, and the patience not to be distracted. More than once, we were saved from a collision by her warning.

There were a few close calls nonetheless. With sufficient notice and a good wind, Skovik was able to avoid most of them, but when we came up hard and fast on a wallowing chunk of ice, we had to take to oars, rowing frantically to help change the boat's course, while his men balanced perilously, shoving at the ice with their barbed pikes.

Those were terrifying moments, the grey water rushing past our hull, the boat lurching precariously as Skovik's fellows leaned on their pikes. The first time it happened, I thought for sure we were doomed. Wood scraped along the ice, groaning. I was on the side nearest the floe, so close I couldn't even put oar to water. The pikemen shoved and grunted. Seawater sloshed over the railing, soaking our feet.

And then we were past it, sailing onward. The floe spun lazily behind us, barely visible, awaiting its next unwitting victim.

"By Lug the warrior and the Black Boar himself," Urist said with heartfelt feeling. "I swear, if I get my feet on Alban soil, I'm never leaving again."

We all felt it. But there were times when it was glorious, too, in a stark way. The nights were grueling and unpleasant, but the days could be lovely. Our luck with the weather held. We sailed through a world of empty sky, grey water, and ice. Farther north, we saw seals from time to time, although not often. They were comical creatures, ungainly on the ice, but graceful in the water, with dark, plaintive eyes and whiskered faces. Skovik and his men eyed them with regret, but with nine people in the boat, there was no room to take on additional stores if they'd gone hunting. I wasn't terribly sorry.

Later, as we went farther south, the ice ledge began to retreat and there were fewer floes and more birdlife. Great flocks of gulls and terns wheeled overhead, and we saw ducks and geese taking wing from the water.

"Spring's coming," Skovik observed.

It seemed hard to fathom. I'd lost all track of time. It felt to me as though it had been winter forever and would always be winter. He was right, though. By midway through the second week, we'd travelled far enough that the cutting wind no longer bit quite as deep. The ice ledge shrank farther; fifty yards instead of a hundred, betimes less. We were able to sail close enough to the coast that folk in the towns there waved to us as we passed.

And then one day we approached a port we didn't pass.

"Norstock," Skovik said briefly.

I wouldn't have recognized it from the sea. The harbor where Urist and I had booked passage with Captain Iosef was still frozen solid. We trimmed our sails, gliding gently until we bumped up against the ledge. Skovik's men reached out with their barbed pikes, securing the boat. They prodded the ice, testing, then dared scramble over the side, one holding the boat in place, the other grinning as he stamped on the ice with his sealskin boots, making sure it would hold.

Skovik tossed a pair of lines ashore, while Ti-Philippe struck the sails and lashed them. As the only experienced sailor among the lot of us, he'd been a valuable companion on this journey. One by one, we disembarked. We'd gotten fairly good at it by now, although I was concerned about the thickness of the ice ledge. Joscelin and I made sure Phèdre and Urist were well away before we attempted to haul the boat atop the ice.

A good job we did, too. When we hauled on the lines, the boat's prow rose out of the water and lurched onto the ledge. The ice crumbled beneath it.

"Back, back, back!" Skovik shouted.

It needed no translation. Half terrified and half laughing, we scrambled backward, digging in our heels and falling over one another, tugging on the lines, chased by the receding edge of ice. For a time, the boat forged a channel of open water. At last the ice grew thick enough to support its weight, and it slid atop the ledge with casual ease, resting there. We hauled it a few more yards until we were sure it was safe.

I flopped down on my back. "Name of Elua!"

"So." Skovik's face appeared above me. "Here you are."

"Here we are," I agreed wearily.

He smiled beneath his mustaches. "We go now to find brave men to sail north to Vralgrad with us and hunt along the way."

I got to my feet and extended my hand. "Safe travels to you."

He clasped it. "And to you."

I appreciated the sentiment. We'd made it safely to Norstock, for which I was grateful, but it meant we were back on Skaldic soil. I thought we stood a good chance of finding safe passage to the Flatlander border—Maslin had managed it alone, and the area seemed open to trade and well under Adelmar's control. Still, we were on foot, with a good deal of baggage. Somehow, I doubted we were going to find eager assistance in gaining transportation back to Maarten's Crossing.

And I doubted Adelmar of the Frisii would be glad to see us when we did.

SIXTY-EIGHT

I WAS WRONG.

It didn't take long to discover it. Skovik and his men headed into town, but it took us a while to get our gear unloaded and sorted. We'd barely finished and begun trudging across the ice ledge toward the town when the harbor-master of Norstock came out to meet us, a pair of armed guards at his side.

All of us dropped our packs and tensed.

"Don't." Phèdre shook her head when Joscelin's hand rose to reach for his sword-hilt. "They'd have brought more men if they meant violence."

She was right.

The harbor-master was a tall fellow in his late fifties or so. He had a deep scar that sliced his cheek and dented the bridge of his nose, and he looked to have seen his share of battles. But his grey eyes were calm and his manner was unthreatening. When he addressed us in Skaldic, Phèdre stepped forward and replied fluently in the same tongue. I watched her expression shift to one of bemusement as they spoke. He gestured in my direction several times. I tried to make out what they were saying, but after long months in Vralia, I couldn't summon the wits to follow in my rudimentary Skaldic.

"He says they've kept an eye out for you, Imriel," Phèdre said. "On Adelmar's orders." She sounded puzzled. "It seems he's had a change of heart. He's offering assistance."

"Why?" I asked.

She put the question to the harbor-master, who gave a brief reply and a shrug. "Orders," Phèdre reported. "He doesn't know why."

"Could be a trick," Joscelin observed.

"What would be the point?" Phèdre spread her hands. "He's got a whole town at his back. There's no need to trick us."

It was no trick. The harbor-master gave all of us a curt bow, then gestured to his men. They approached to assist us with our packs, making careful gestures to indicate that this was goodwill and not thievery.

"Huh." Urist leaned on his walking-stick. "Passing odd."

"Mayhap Queen Ysandre pressured him," I suggested.

"To help *you*?" Urist's gaze slewed around at me. "Not likely, lad. My money's on Drustan. Don't know how he took the news you're bedding his daughter, but at least it's his niece you're avenging."

I hefted the sack with Berlik's skull. "There is that."

The harbor-master, whose name was Ortwin, was as good as his word. He and his men led us to an inn, one of the only ones still open during the winter months. We weren't exactly welcome—the innkeeper looked unhappy at our presence—but no one offered any threat. We kept to ourselves and passed an uneasy night there, and woke on the morrow to find that Ortwin had assembled a company to escort us to Maarten's Crossing, with guards and mounts and pack-horses.

I asked Phèdre to thank him for his kindness, since she'd be able to express it far more eloquently than I would. She did. The harbor-master made a long speech in reply. At one point he nodded toward Joscelin, sitting impassively atop his loaned mount, the hilt of his sword jutting over his shoulder. At another point, he touched his own scarred cheek. Phèdre listened gravely to his words. She leaned down in the saddle to clasp his hand, speaking a few quiet words in Skaldic.

"What was that all about?" Hugues asked when we departed.

"Forgiveness." She glanced at Joscelin. "He knew who we were."

Joscelin raised his brows. "And forgave us?"

"He said he'd known peace and war, and peace was better," she murmured.

"Can't argue with that," Ti-Philippe offered.

Even so, it all seemed somewhat too good to be true. We rode warily, keeping a sharp eye on our escort. There were six of them and six of us, but the Skaldi might reckon the odds uneven, since our numbers included Phèdre, who was no warrior, and Urist, who was injured. They would be wrong, of course. Urist was uncomfortable riding astride, but an aching leg didn't render him less dangerous. And then there was Joscelin, who might well have taken on the entire company by himself.

But no.

There was no trouble. We crossed the narrow peninsula in good time. Ortwin's escort delivered us to the gates of Maarten's Crossing before the sun had set, and the guards posted outside the wooden stockade fence admitted us without a challenge.

Urist grunted. "That's a change."

The area where we'd made our camp was deserted save for a few fur-traders, who shot us dour looks. I wondered if it meant that Talorcan and his Cruithne, and Kinadius and the last of Clunderry's men, had given up and gone home. But when we made our way to the inn where a few of us had lodged—Halla's place, with the sign of the rooster—we found it wasn't so.

There were only two of them; Kinadius and Brun, who was one of Urist's veterans. Kinadius was there alone when we arrived, chatting with one of the innkeeper's daughters while she stirred a pot over the fire, his back to the door. I watched her eyes widen as we entered, and she fell silent. He turned out of curiosity and simply stared, open-mouthed and blinking.

"Prince Imriel?" he said cautiously. "My lord Urist? Is that you, or have I gone mad?"

"Close your mouth, lad," Urist said. "You look daft."

"Did you . . ." Kinadius blinked at me. Sudden tears brightened his eyes. "Is it done?"

I nodded and touched the bag. "It's done."

He closed his eyes and whispered a prayer. "Thank you."

After that came the usual chaos attendant on such reunions, with a hasty rush of news exchanged, everyone talking over one another, while at the same time we endeavored to arrange for lodgings. Phèdre took over that part, speaking quietly to a dazzled—and rather delighted-looking—Halla. As I had noted before, the women of

Skaldia didn't bear the same deep-seated hostility toward D'Angelines as the men did. I suppose women everywhere understand the folly of war better than men, since they are less likely to be blinded by the desire for glory in battle.

Between one thing and another, the six of us were soon situated at Halla's, downing bowls of stew and tankards of ale while her indefatigable daughters heated bathwater for us. Brun emerged from the room he shared with Kinadius, greeting us with taciturn pleasure.

While we ate, we learned that Prince Talorcan had indeed withdrawn in bitter disgust. After being ousted from Vralia and forced to retreat backward through Skaldia, he'd found himself unwelcome in Maarten's Crossing.

"It was a bad journey," Kinadius said. "Adelmar had given us a token of safepassage, but it didn't work so well when the Skaldi saw us in retreat. Those northern tribes are fierce. We got in a few skirmishes. Lost a few men."

"Any of ours?" Urist asked.

"Cailan," Brun said briefly. "Took two of theirs with him."

The wise-woman's son who had bound my wounds. They'd always said he was a fierce fighter despite his gentle touch. I felt a deep pang of sorrow and regret.

"Adelmar heard the tales. It didn't happen in territory under his control, but he wasn't willing to let Talorcan stay, not with a big company of warriors." Kinadius shrugged. "Talorcan was in no fit mood to make an argument Adelmar would hear."

"Foul-tempered," Brun agreed.

Kinadius gazed into his tankard. "Mmm. Said some things I daresay he regrets."

"To Adelmar?" I asked.

"No." He shook his head. "About you lot. After we saw your company on the way, my lady," he said to Phèdre. "That was a cunning trick you pulled." Phèdre made no comment. Kinadius took a gulp of ale. "Anyway, he said since it was a D'Angeline got his sister killed, it seemed the gods had decreed it was up to D'Angelines to avenge her." He gave me a direct look. "No one in Clunderry thinks that, my lord."

"He's right, though," I said quietly. "In a way."

"Aye, and he's wrong, too. I was there," Kinadius said. "I saw the bastard's claws dripping red with Dorelei's blood. I saw him kill Uven. Saw him lay you open like he was gutting a fish, Imriel. Guilt's one thing. We all share a measure of it, don't we, my lord?" he asked Urist. "All of Clunderry's garrison."

"We do," Urist said, kneading his aching leg.

"Well, blame's another matter," Kinadius said. "And I know damned well who's to blame for Dorelei's death. And if Talorcan thinks he's any more distraught over our failure to avenge her than I am, he's wrong." He flushed, but continued doggedly. "But I knew you'd do the right thing, Imriel. You and Urist."

I met his eyes. "My thanks."

"I didn't do anything but break my damn leg," Urist said wryly.

"So." Kinadius blew out his breath. "No one from Clunderry wanted to desert you. We wanted to stay in case you sent for us, in case you needed us. I met with Lord Adelmar and convinced him to let me stay with a single companion. Best I could do. We drew straws and Brun got the honor."

"Lucky," Brun agreed.

"I'm glad you did." I clapped Kinadius on the shoulder. "But I'm curious. Seems Adelmar's had a change of heart. He sent word to Norstock that we were to be given aid. Given what you've told me, it makes less sense than ever. Any idea why?"

Kinadius shook his head. "None in the world."

I should have guessed, I suppose; but it seemed like I'd been at the farthest reaches of the earth for a long, long time. Over the course of a personal, very private quest, I'd grown unaccustomed to thinking in terms of intrigue and the far-flung web of connections that bound me. That would have to change, of course. The moment I set foot on Terre d'Ange, I'd be immersed in politics whether I liked it or not. Still, here and now, it seemed very far away. The silence and isolation of the Vralian wilderness had sunk deep into my being.

They wanted to hear the story, of course. I told it in such a way as would satisfy them. The long, arduous quest. Berlik's penitent end, his head bowed for the sword. Blood on the snow. I didn't tell them I had fallen to my knees and wept.

By the time I'd finished, a message had come from the great hall. Our arrival had been noted. Adelmar of the Frisii summoned three of us to audience in the morning; Phèdre, Joscelin, and me.

"What do you think?" I asked Phèdre.

She had been quiet for most of the evening; all of them had, letting Alba's concerns take precedence. "I think we don't have a great deal of choice," she said. "Adelmar may be angry at the trick we played him, but I don't think he's fool enough to make an issue of it. He's an ambitious man, and we at least managed to pass through Skaldia without reprisal. And you've done naught but follow his suggestion." Phèdre rose, stooping to kiss my brow. "I think we'll find out on the morrow, so we might as well get a good night's sleep."

She was right, of course.

After our sojourn with Skovik and his men, it was still a great luxury to fill our bellies with hot food, bathe with warm water, and sink onto a straw pallet instead of sleeping in the bottom of a boat, covered with canvas. I slept without dreaming, and on the morrow, we presented ourselves at the great hall.

It was all very, very different from my first experience there. For one thing, there were no pilgrims awaiting audience. I daresay the Habiru had sense enough to wait until spring to travel through Skaldia. For another, the petty official who had made us wait before bowed obsequiously and ushered us immediately into Adelmar's presence.

He wasn't alone.

As before, Adelmar received us in his study. This time, it had been tidied. There were chairs set forth around a round table, and a jug and winecups set on it. The couple with him rose as we entered. He was a portly, prosperous-looking fellow; fair-skinned like the Skaldi; but with dark hair caught back at the nape of his neck with gilded clasp, and a neatly trimmed beard. His wife was a plain woman of middle years, unprepossessing, but there was a gentle shrewdness to her face. Both of them wore expensive, well-made attire. To my eye, it looked more fitting to wealthy merchants in Tiberium than travellers in Skaldia.

"Prince Imriel de la Courcel," Adelmar said smoothly in Caerdicci. "We are pleased to see you well." He wagged his forefinger at Phèdre and Joscelin. "Your ladyship, my lord, I fear you have played me a naughty trick. And yet I will forgive you, since no harm came of it."

"I'm sorry, my lord Adelmar," Phèdre apologized. "The matter was urgent."

Joscelin merely shrugged.

"So I perceive, now." Adelmar smiled. "You were a mother bereft and fearful. 'Tis my fault I did not recognize it as such, and not a threat to Skaldia. You must understand, your reputation precedes you."

Phèdre raised her brows. "Oh?"

"Oh, indeed." He made a gesture of dismissal. "'Tis of no mind. Please, meet my guests; Ditmarus of the Manni, and his wife Ermegart. Over the course of several long winter nights, they have heard your strange tale, and were anxious to meet you."

We exchanged greetings. I glanced down at Ditmarus' hand when he clasped mine. He wore rings on every finger. On his middle finger, there was a signet ring. It bore the impress of a lamp. It was a familiar image.

"I see," I said slowly. "Well met, my lord."

Ditmarus' grip tightened briefly. "Among the Manni, we seek to accomplish much the same as Adelmar seeks here for the sake of Skaldia." His Caerdicci was polished and impeccable. He gave me a bland smile. "Trade and prosperity. So much better than war, don't you think?"

"Of course," I said politely.

Phèdre tilted her head. "Do the Manni seek trade with the Frisii? I would not have thought the trade routes made it easy. Your lands lie to the south and share a border with Caerdicca Unitas, is it not so?"

"Oh, yes." Ditmarus turned his bland smile on her. "Still, Skaldia is Skaldia."

"We heard reports of the empire Lord Adelmar was building in the west, and a new empire arising in the north." Ermegart smiled at Adelmar with friendly interest. "We were . . . curious."

"There are ways in which we might aid one another," Ditmarus added.

Joscelin rolled his eyes.

I wished I could, too.

What exactly their mission was, I could not say. I daresay there was an element of truth to it all. A new vision of Skaldia had arisen from the wreckage of Waldemar Selig's dreams. Ditmarus and Ermegart belonged to the same tribe that had spawned Eamonn's wife Brigitta, and there was a certain hard-eyed pragmatism there. Adelmar had consolidated his hold on a considerable chunk of southwestern Skaldia. He'd made alliances with the Flatlands, with Vralia; even tentative overtures to Alba. It made sense that they would investigate.

But then, there was the ring.

And that, too, made sense. Of course. The Unseen Guild maintained a strong presence in Caerdicca Unitas. My mother had had ties to the Skaldi, and I wouldn't be surprised to find she had maintained them. I made polite conversation with Ditmarus and Ermegart. I allowed as how free and open trade between Terre d'Ange and Skaldia might benefit both our nations. On the point of my own influence, I demurred.

"You are a Prince of the Blood and a member of Parliament, are you not?" Ditmarus hesitated delicately. "And it is said you court the royal heir . . ."

"Said by whom?" I asked.

He shrugged. "It is rumored."

I did my best to mimic Phèdre's disarming smile. "Ah, well! I am D'Angeline, my lord. Matters of love are sacred, and not to be sullied by politics."

Ditmarus chuckled indulgently. "Ah, the romantic idealism of youth! Revel in it while it lasts, young highness. We do not mean to press or pry." He took Ermegart's hand. "Love's maturity has its pleasures, too. Such as working together for the common good of one's people. For *all* people." His expression turned grave. "There are those of us who believe Skaldia has much for which to atone. When we learned of your plight from Lord Adelmar, we urged him to extend a hand in friendship should the opportunity arise."

"My thanks," I said obligingly, adding to Adelmar, "We are all most grateful for your generous aid."

He gave another dismissive wave. "'Twas naught. I pray her majesty Queen Ysandre will accept it in the spirit of kindness." Adelmar's voice took on a note of asperity. "Although I would be appreciative if his majesty the Cruarch will forbear to make any further requests to send Alban troops into Skaldia."

"I'm sure the matter won't arise again," I murmured.

Adelmar studied me. "You got your man?"

"I did," I said.

His gaze narrowed. "And how do matters stand with Tadeuz Vral?"

"His highness was understanding." It was true, after a fashion. "He put down a rebellion by his brother, Prince Fedor, with great success. We were privileged to witness the conversion of a thousand new Yeshuites."

"Vralia!" Ermegart clasped her hands together. Her eyes sparkled with what appeared to be genuine excitement. "It sounds so exciting, doesn't it?" she said to her husband. "Perhaps we'll go there when the ice breaks."

Ditmarus stroked his beard, smiling. "Perhaps."

I didn't doubt it. In hindsight, the only surprise was that the Unseen Guild didn't maintain a presence there already, since there was clearly a history of trade between Ephesium and Vralia. But then, that had been disrupted by the rebellion of the Tatars under Fedor Vral's leadership for some years. And it might be that the interests of the Guild in Ephesium did not accord with members of the Guild in Skaldia or Caerdicca Unitas.

It would be a piece of irony, I thought, if it was my own personal quest that had brought the pilgrims' passage through Skaldia to the attention of the Unseen Guild, and not the steady emigration of the Yeshuites. But then, the Yeshuites were an unwelcome minority in many lands, a dispossessed people. Even in Terre d'Ange, they had been tolerated rather than embraced. I doubted the Guild had paid much heed to the slow Yeshuite trickle, finding them too small, powerless, and widely dispersed a folk to be of much use.

Of a surety, that was changing in Vralia.

We sat for a while longer, sipping wine and exchanging pleasantries. I couldn't help wondering about Ditmarus and Ermegart. He wouldn't have worn the ring if he hadn't meant for me to recognize him—or them, I suspected her, too—as Guild. They knew I was aware of its meaning. If there had been any doubt, I'd erased it myself by wearing a replica of Canis' medallion at the Longest Night when the Ephesian embassador was present. Was it a warning? A reminder of their reach? A renewed invitation? A subtle message from my mother?

"I'm curious, my lord," I said to Ditmarus. "What piece of news sent you to Maarten's Crossing in the depths of winter?"

"Ha!" He chuckled and cupped his ear. "I'm a merchant, young highness, and I keep my ear to the ground. Perhaps I heard there was news brewing in the north and opportunity on its heels. Perhaps I was merely lucky. I'll not give away my trade secrets without your most solemn oath, understand?"

"I believe I do," I said.

He smiled. "I thought you might."

The audience came to an end. Ditmarus and Ermegart bade us a cordial farewell. We did the same, and thanked Adelmar once more for his assistance, promising to speak well of his generosity to Queen Ysandre. I wondered if he'd been recruited as a member of the Guild. I couldn't imagine him consenting to be trained by them; but mayhap they made exceptions for sitting regents. To be sure, he was well-situated to make himself useful. Or mayhap during their time here, they had recruited a spy in his household. Or several spies.

In the end, I had no way of knowing.

Not without giving myself to the Guild.

We emerged from the audience into the cold, bright day. It had been dim inside Adelmar's great hall, which was sturdily constructed, but an unsophisticated and poorly lit piece of architecture. Skaldia had a long way to go before it reached the level of civilized comfort we enjoyed in Terre d'Ange. Even in isolated Vralia, where a handful of ambitious princes had managed to establish a rule of law over the course of generations, they had made greater strides. When all was said and done, I was glad that there were folk like Adelmar of the

Frisii willing to pursue such a goal through trade and alliance, rather than warfare.

"Well," Phèdre observed. "*That* was interesting."

I glanced at her. "You saw his ring?"

"Name of Elua!" Joscelin said wryly. "*I* saw his ring." He yawned and shook himself to alertness. "Enough talking. Onward to Alba."

SIXTY-NINE

THE BALANCE OF OUR JOURNEY was unremarkable.

To my mind, the best part of it was being reunited with the Bastard. I'd been almost afraid to ask; but no, Kinadius had kept him safe and found a place to stable him upon returning from their abortive excursion to Vralia.

"He's a headstrong, ill-tempered bugger," he said, watching our reunion, which consisted of delight on my part and wariness on the Bastard's. "I'll miss him."

Outfitting the rest of our company took some doing. Brun had also retained a mount, but the rest were lacking. Unfortunately, Adelmar's generosity in escorting us from Norstock and granting us safe passage from Maarten's Crossing didn't extend to the loan of mounts and pack-horses, and without pressure from him, the Skaldi weren't eager to bargain with us. In the end, we had to beg and barter with a handful of Flatlander traders wintering here, spending far too much coin on horses that wouldn't have drawn a single bid at a Tsingani horse-fair.

It left us with barely enough funds to cross the Flatlands, and not nearly enough to buy passage across the Straits when we arrived there.

"There's this," I said when we discussed the matter, tugging at the collar of my Vralian coat to reveal the golden torc around my throat. It was the one possession my gaolers in Tarkov hadn't taken from me; although I suppose it wouldn't have mattered, since I'd stolen all the rest back. Still, I'd not taken it off since Drustan gave it to me on the day I wedded Dorelei in Alba. "It ought to be worth enough."

"Don't even think it!" Urist's voice, unexpectedly fierce. "It marks you as a Prince of Alba and the lord of Clunderry. If you've managed to keep it this long, you're not giving it away, not now."

I opened my mouth to reply, but Kinadius, and even Brun, were nodding in accord.

"We'll find another way," Phèdre said to them. "Don't worry."

Joscelin eyed her. "You're not planning to . . . ?"

"No, of course not." She smiled ruefully. "And any mind, I'd like to think my asking price would be far in excess of passage across the Straits for a mere eight folk and their train. But then, mayhap that's vanity speaking, ignorant of the ravages of time and travel."

"No." Kinadius flushed. "It's not, my lady."

She smiled at him, and his flush deepened. "Well, we'll find a way. We can always sell the horses, if we can find a buyer. It would be a good deal wiser than paying cargo fees for them."

"Not the Bastard," I said in alarm.

Phèdre laughed. "No, love. Not the Bastard."

We set forth on our journey, and for all of Adelmar of the Frisii's forbearance, it was a blessed relief to know that we'd crossed from Skaldia into the Flatlands. Once we passed that point, I daresay all of us breathed easier for it. We followed the pilgrims' route along the banks of the Voorwijk, as we had done at the outset, passing the town of Zoellen and continuing westward. This time, there would be no turning south toward Terre d'Ange. Still, I felt a tug at my heart each time we passed a crossroads.

"You're sure?" Phèdre asked, noticing.

The leather bag containing Berlik's skull hung from my saddle. "I'm sure."

I thought about Phèdre and Joscelin as we travelled together. As unlikely a pair as they were, they had been together for a long time. It had been over twenty years since they fled Skaldia with a wild tale of treachery and impending invasion on their lips. Still, age sat lightly on them, as it does on many D'Angelines. A gift, mayhap, of Blessed Elua and his Companions. Betimes, when she was merry and glad—when we spotted the first crocuses peeking through the melting snow—Phèdre scarce looked old enough to be anyone's foster-mother, her face bright and fresh. At other times, I could see the weight of wisdom and experience on her;

beauty of a different kind, deeper and richer. And Joscelin. . . . Joscelin was Joscelin. Aside from the fact that the faint lines bracketing his mouth and crinkling the corners of his eyes when he gave his wry half-smile had grown more pronounced, he looked no different than he had when I'd first seen him in the Mahrkagir's festal hall.

And the way that they looked at each other was the same.

I wanted that.

I'd never thought about aging; never thought about growing old with anyone. It seemed so much of my life had been a scramble to survive. Now, for the first time, I did. I thought about Sidonie. And the thought of her—of us—growing *old* together filled me with infinite tenderness. I wanted it, I wanted it all. All the ardent beginnings and the confused between-times and the bittersweet dregs.

All of the aches and sorrows, all of the soaring joys.

All of it.

I kept my thoughts to myself; it wouldn't be seemly to be doting on her while I was engaged in the business of avenging Dorelei. And I didn't want to dishonor Dorelei's memory. Still, the thoughts were there.

It made me impatient, though. Our progress was slow. Several of the mounts and two pack-horses we'd been able to procure in Skaldia were elderly beasts, past their prime and lacking in stamina. There was no point in trying to push them, and we lacked the coin to trade for better. Betimes, I admit, I longed to clap my heels to the Bastard's flanks and take flight. I could have gained days on the others. But it was an ungrateful thought—and a wholly self-absorbed one—so I struggled to suppress it.

Our course veered southward. Here, there was no mistaking the fact that it was well and truly spring. The days grew warmer and longer, and the last lingering traces of snow vanished. We passed field after field, farmers walking behind teams of oxen as they plowed the fallow soil. The rich, earthy scent reminded me of spring in Clunderry.

Elua, it *had* been almost a year.

The thought banished my impatience. A year ago, I had been in Clunderry, awaiting the birth of my first child. After the long winter, the world had seemed fresh and new, full of promise. The apple trees had been in bloom; I'd been pestering the master of the orchard about the proper way to capture the swarming honeybees. I remembered the uncanny sight of the skin on Dorelei's immense belly surging at the prodding of a restless hand or foot. Rubbing her swollen feet when they ached. Hours of idle discussion about what to name our son or daughter.

Aniel.

We'd settled on it the night . . . that night. My throat tightened at the memory, eyes stinging. Urist was right. I needed to do this and see it through to the end. I owed it to Dorelei and our lost child.

After weeks of frustratingly slow travel, we came at last to the port town of Westerhaven. It was another of those places invigorated by the opening of the Straits, a fishing village that had become a center of trade. The smell of the salt tang of the sea in the air and the sight of gulls circling made my heart beat faster.

Most of the Flatlanders we'd encountered in our journey were friendly and courteous, and Westerhaven was no exception. Phèdre—who had little difficulty with the guttural Flatlander dialect—stopped a man on the street, who directed us to a pleasant inn. We'd made camp whenever we could along the way to save our dwindling funds, but we reckoned we'd have to stay in town for a day or so in order to forge the connections we'd need to sell our mounts and book passage to Alba.

The innkeeper was a young fellow with ruddy cheeks and a shy wife. He beamed as a handful of us entered his establishment; Phèdre, Joscelin, and I, and Urist leaning on his walking-stick, his leg stiff from the day's ride.

"You come for the ship!" he said in cheerful, mangled Cruithne. "We have wonder."

"What ship?" I asked.

He pointed obligingly in what I took to be the direction of the harbor. "The Cruarch's ship. Five days now. No trade, no visitors. Just waiting. Maybe no?" He shrugged apologetically. "D'Angeline and Alban together, I thought maybe so."

I frowned. "The Cruarch's ship?"

The innkeeper nodded, flaxen hair flopping on his brow. "Red sail, black pig."

"Do you mean to tell us," Phèdre asked in Cruithne, slowly and carefully, "that the flagship of the Cruarch of Alba is in the harbor?"

He smiled happily. "Yes! Just so."

We exchanged glances. "I'll go," I said hurriedly.

I fairly dashed from the inn, mounting in a rush. The Bastard caught my mood, snorting as we plunged down the streets of Westerhaven, heading in the direction of the sea. Pedestrians scattered before us; I called out apologies in some tongue or another.

It was true.

Drustan's flagship was docked in the narrow harbor. The red sails were furled, but a pennant bearing the Black Boar of the Cullach Gorrym was flying from the topmast. I reined the Bastard to a halt. Fortunately, the harbor-master was nowhere in sight, and those sailors present looked more amused than not.

"Hey!" I shouted at the ship. "Are you bound for Bryn Gorrydum?"

There was some commotion aboard the ship. At length, a fellow who appeared to be the captain emerged; a southerner by the looks of him, one of the Eidlach Òr. He shaded his eyes and peered at me. "Prince Imriel?"

"Yes!" I called. "There are others with me, too."

Even at a distance, I could see his mouth twitch in a smile. "Aye, we've been awaiting you, your highness. Hold, I'll come down."

I dismounted and waited, lashing the Bastard's reins to a piling. The captain descended and approached, striding along the dock, one hand extended in greeting. He had fair hair going grey, and a beard darker and curlier than the hair atop his head. His grip was hard, the palm of his hand leathery and firm.

"You've been awaiting us?" I asked, bewildered.

"Oh, aye." His smile deepened. "Some days now. Their ladyships had a true dream, they did. All of 'em. Weeks ago, it was. But 'twas Master Hyacinthe confirmed it and cast his eye upon you in his sea-mirror, and Lord Drustan ordered us to set sail when he did. So here we are, and here you are, too. You made slower progress than we reckoned. By the by, my name's Corcan."

"Corcan," I murmured. "Well met. What dream?"

"Ah, that!" His weathered brow furrowed. "'Twas your own . . . well, she's not your sister, is she? Not rightly. The lass, the Princess Alais. Her, and Drustan's sisters. The ladies Breidaia and Sibeal. What I heard, they all saw it. His lordship's ship with a bear's skull for a prow, bound for Alba. Green vines twining round the mast, and a lily blooming atop it." He shrugged. "Fanciful stuff, eh?"

"No," I said quietly. "It was a true dream."

Corcan shrugged again. "Suppose it must have been. Any mind, we're here for you. Will it suit you to sail on the morrow?"

"Elua, yes!" I thanked him and rode slowly back to the inn. The Bastard, objecting to the rein, bridled and pranced, picking up his striped hooves and setting them down with deliberate care, making them ring on the cobbled streets.

There was a stable attached to the inn, and a bright-eyed young lad who looked no older than six waiting to take the Bastard; the innkeeper's son, I guessed. I thanked him and elected to do the honors myself. By the time I entered the inn, with my packs slung over one shoulder and the bag containing Berlik's skull dangling from my right hand, everyone was assembled and waiting. I found myself grinning. It had been a long time since I'd had a piece of sheer good fortune to share with anyone.

"Well?" Urist asked impatiently.

"It's true," I said. "Drustan sent the ship for us. We sail in the morning."

The inn erupted in cheers; we all had need of a piece of good news. I explained about the dream and Hyacinthe spotting us in the seamirror when we drew near enough. Caught up in the excitement, the friendly innkeeper offered to stand a round of ale for everyone in the inn, although Joscelin soon persuaded him to let us bear the cost. We could afford it, now. It was good ale, too; strong and hearty.

"See?" Phèdre said complacently when the initial furor had died. "I told you we'd find a way."

"I'd say the way found us this time," Joscelin observed.

She smiled at him. "It all amounts to the same thing in the end, doesn't it?"

SEVENTY

WE SET SAIL on the morrow.

After a considerable amount of ale and a night's sleep, I nearly thought I'd dreamed the presence of the Cruarch's flagship and my encounter with its captain. But when we made our way to the harbor an hour or so past dawn, half-knackered mounts and all, the ship was still there. Alban sailors were making ready for the voyage, and Captain Corcan greeted us with a bow. With their aid, we got the the horses and our gear loaded, and then ourselves.

When the scarlet sails unfurled to reveal the Black Boar, I nearly wept.

'Tis a strange thing, how one may remain strong in adversity, shoring up one's courage against fear. I hadn't realized I felt that way. We had been uneasy in Skaldia, reluctant to put any faith in Adelmar's sudden generosity, but that had proved genuine, albeit for reasons that were likely self-serving. Since crossing into the Flatlands, there had been no overt danger. We were a small company, but one with skilled and seasoned warriors in it. The Flatlands were relatively peaceable and held no animosity toward Alba or Terre d'Ange.

Still, it wasn't the same as being among friends and allies. As being *safe*.

And we were safe now. These waters lay under the aegis of the Master of the Straits, and he was watching over us. Whatever part of me had remained braced against unforeseen danger finally relaxed. I felt raw with relief and gratitude.

The feeling stayed with me throughout the day. We sailed southward in open water, between the coasts. The wind at our back was mild and steady, like a promise of Hyacinthe's assurance that we would come to no harm.

We wouldn't reach Bryn Gorrydum until well into the following day. By the time the sun set, laying a blanket of ruddy light on the waters, my mood had begun to turn pensive. I spent some time by myself, gazing at the light reflecting on the sea, and thought about how far I'd gone and how much I'd changed since first I'd sailed to Bryn Gorrydum.

A long way and a great deal.

And I thought, too, about how I'd given up on my quest. I'd been honest about that when I told the tale. Joscelin had laughed softly when I told him it galled me to think that neither of them had ever given up hope and accepted failure. He reminded me that he had done that very thing long ago in Skaldia, in Waldemar Selig's steading. That Phèdre had shamed him into persevering in much the same way that Berlik had goaded me.

Would you have come here with a humble heart if I had not?

I didn't think I would have; and in a strange way, I was glad I had. That part, I hadn't tried to explain to anyone. Phèdre would understand, I thought. But if I told anyone, it would be Sidonie. I didn't want secrets between us, and I didn't want to hold any part of myself back from her. And I thought, too, that she would understand. It was part of the shadow of guilt that lay between us for the secrecy and lack of faith that had set this all in motion. If I'd learned nothing else, I'd learned the value of truth and trust in matters of love.

And that, I owed to Dorelei.

So it was that I went to my berth that night with a humble heart. The waves held us up like a cradle, gently rocking. Safe. I fell asleep swiftly and slept soundly, and by the time I awoke the following morning, we were within sight of Alba's shore.

It still seemed too good to be true. The grass was lush and green with the spring rains, and the trees sported pale leaves. Near the coast, fishing boats bobbed. It was a clear day—Hyacinthe's doing, mayhap—and a blue sky arched overhead, sunlight sparkling on the waves.

Today, I felt . . . what?

Sadness and joy, commingled. There was so much I would have done differently if I had known what would come to pass; and yet, such things are never given to us to know. Not even the magicians of the Maghuin Dhonn, who were given a greater vision than most, were able to tease out the threads of the future without making a horrible, tangled mess of it.

And yet . . .

I'd done my best. I had tried. In the end, I had avenged Dorelei and given Berlik the redemption for which he yearned. They were two sides of the same coin; the bright mirror and the dark. I was bringing him home. I was bringing peace to her spirit.

My heart soared when first we glimpsed the fortress of Bryn Gorrydum, the city sprawled around it, the harbor lying before it like a pair of open arms. The wind shifted to drive us straight into its embrace. I felt a gladness at once bright and somber, powerful and strange. This time, it seemed the gods and goddesses of Alba and Terre d'Ange were in accord. I felt their presence in the leaping waves along the prow, in the bright sun that shone overhead, in the beat of the blood in my veins, urging me toward the Alban shore.

When I saw the reception awaiting us, I understood.

Of course there was a reception. All of us crowded into the prow, watching as the dock drew near. Hyacinthe was there with Sibeal; he must have brought word from the Stormkeep himself when we set sail. Drustan mab Necthana, his crimson cloak flapping in the breeze that bore us toward him. Alais was with him, and Breidaia and Talorcan, watching us approach.

And beside the Cruarch . . .

Sidonie.

Even at a great distance, I knew her. I saw the gleam of sunlight on her hair, and I knew. A spark of gold; the spark that had kindled happiness in me. The golden cord that bound us together tightened around my heart, the only bond I'd ever borne joyfully.

Urist nudged me. "Isn't that your girl?"

I didn't answer, my heart too full.

"I believe that would be the Dauphine of Terre d'Ange, sent to represent Queen Ysandre," Phèdre said in a careful tone.

I didn't need a warning to know that this was a state affair and not a lovers' reunion. I could read it in Sidonie's carriage. Her personal guard was arrayed behind her, clad in their livery of Courcel blue, marked by paler blue stripes. When we drew nearer, I could read it on Sidonie's face, grave and serious. Like her guards, she was dressed in Courcel blue. It seemed darker against her fair skin. Her hair was upswept and coiled, a slender crown of gold with sapphire points almost lost against its hue. It had been almost a year since we'd last seen one another. She looked less a girl, more a woman.

Our eyes met.

A thing may be true and not true. An affair of state; but a lovers' reunion, too. I didn't need to see her smile of profound gladness to know it was there behind her solemnity. And I didn't need to smile in reply. What was between us was larger and deeper than what lay on the surface. The cord drew taut, the knot was tied. Captain Corcan gave the order to strike the sails. We glided into port. Sailors went to oars, slowing and guiding our progress. Others tossed out lines, expertly caught and tied.

The Cruarch's flagship had arrived.

I was the first to disembark. It was fitting. I walked slowly down the ramp. My legs should have felt unsteady after a day at sea, but I wasn't aware of anything but the moment. My Vralian attire was worn and shabby, but I had my sword hanging from my belt, I wore the engraved vambraces Dorelei had given me, and the Cruarch's torc around my throat. I carried the leather bag containing Berlik's skull with both hands, holding it before me.

"Welcome, Prince Imriel." Drustan's tone was unreadable.

"My lord Cruarch." I bowed deeply and held it. "My lords and ladies of Alba." I straightened and proffered the satchel like an offering. "I come bringing vengeance for my wife, Dorelei mab Breidaia."

Drustan took the leather bag from me. He undid the strings, removed Berlik's skull, and held it aloft. White bone gleamed under the sun. The jawbone grinned at death's endless jest, but the empty eye-sockets beneath the broad expanse of brow were filled with sorrowful darkness. A sigh ran through the assembled company.

"Well done," Drustan said quietly.

I bowed again; to him, to Breidaia and Talorcan, Hyacinthe and Sibeal. To all of Dorelei's kin, including Alais, who stood with them. And then I turned to Sidonie, and bowed to her as I would have to the Queen of Terre d'Ange.

"Well met, Prince Imriel." Her voice was calm and steady. When I rose, she lifted her chin to meet my gaze. "On behalf of her majesty Queen Ysandre, I extend the sympathies of Terre d'Ange on the loss of our kinswoman Dorelei mab Breidaia. I extend our gratitude to you and your companions for seeking justice on her behalf."

Those were the words she spoke.

I love you.

Those were the words I heard.

I gave Sidonie the kiss of greeting, austere and correct. We could wait. We had learned to wait. It was enough to feel her lips beneath mine, soft and warm. A promise. The blood beat in my veins, a steady pulse of joy. "Thank you, your highness."

Those were the words I spoke.

I love you.

Those were the words she heard.

We knew it; we both knew it. I daresay there was no one there who didn't know it on some level. Albans do not love gossip the way D'Angelines do, but they are not insensible to it, either. Still, we conducted ourselves with absolute propriety.

The others descended the ramp; Urist, leaning on his walking-staff. He got a somber hero's welcome, shrugging it off uncomfortably. So did Brun and Kinadius, although Kinadius welcomed it more gladly. I didn't mind; so far as I was concerned, he deserved it. He was young and stouthearted. He might have loved Dorelei as she deserved.

Somehow, Phèdre managed to get Montrève's household off the ship with unobtrusive grace, mindful that they were peripheral to the occasion. Quiet greetings were exchanged, and even Alais was restrained.

We rode in procession through the city, winding toward the fortress. Drustan presented Berlik's skull to Talorcan, Dorelei's nearest male kin. I saw a shadow cross Talorcan's face as he accepted it. Kinadius was right, there was bitterness there. Still, Talorcan held it aloft as he rode. People from all of the Four Folk of Alba gathered to watch as we passed, murmuring among themselves. Whether it was ritual or spectacle, I could not say. Of a surety, word would go forth this day that one did not offer violence against the kindred of the Cruarch of Alba without paying the ultimate price.

Or, mayhap, that there was nowhere on earth to flee Kushiel's justice.

I rode beside Sidonie as befit my status as a Prince of the Blood. She was mounted on a white palfrey with a pretty gait. The Bastard kept pace with Sidonie's mare, matching her step for step. It made me smile inside. Out of the corner of my eye, I saw the merest hint of a dimple crease Sidonie's cheek, and I knew she was thinking the same thing.

Once we were in the fortress proper, the somber tension eased somewhat. In the great hall, Talorcan approached me after speaking to Urist.

"I understand you were the one to kill the bear-witch." He extended Berlik's skull. "We ride for Clunderry on the morrow. As her husband and avenger, the honor of burying his head at Dorelei's feet belongs to you."

I accepted the skull, the smooth bone cool against my hands. "Thank you, my lord."

Talorcan nodded stiffly. "And you. I am grateful."

I watched him turn away. The last time I'd seen him, I'd been bound by Alban charms. I hadn't been able to read him well. Now I could. He was a steady and thoughtful young man, but he was proud, too, and his failure was eating at him. Until now, nothing in his life had tested his mettle so profoundly. I hoped he would learn to accept it with grace.

Alais came over and hugged me without speaking, wrapping her arms around my waist. I held her hard with one arm, Berlik's skull awkward in my other hand. After a long moment, she sighed and let me go.

"That's him?" She eyed the skull.

"It is," I said.

Alais lifted one hand and touched it. There was a shadow behind her eyes, too; a shadow of a different kind, filled with blood and screaming. She had been there in the hall of Clunderry when Berlik burst into it in bear form, killing Dorelei with one swipe of a massive paw. I hadn't witnessed it. Alais had. Her beloved dog was buried at Dorelei's side. I could only imagine her nightmares. "I'm glad he's dead," she said. "I knew it. When I had the dream, I knew. We all did. Still, 'tis different, seeing it."

I touched her black curls. "I know, love."

Sidonie.

Sidonie surprised me. When was that not true? I watched her approach. She looked different, here; a D'Angeline among Cruithne, only her dark eyes giving any hint of sharing their heritage. She did, though. She took Berlik's skull from my hand and gazed at it for a long moment without comment. I watched her face. Her lashes swept upward. "Was it hard?" she asked softly.

My throat tightened. "Yes."

Sidonie nodded. "I thought it would be in the end."

I swallowed and cleared my throat. "You're . . . here. Alais' dream?"

"And my aunts', too." She gave Berlik's skull back to me. "Father sent a messenger dove from the temple, he was that certain of it. Mother and I agreed that one of us should be here to represent the throne of Terre d'Ange."

"Are matters between you . . . ?" I hesitated.

She shook her head. "'Tis a temporary truce in the Battle of Imriel."

It was so good to hear my name on her tongue, I almost didn't care what words preceded it; but eventually, they penetrated my wits. I tucked Berlik's skull under one arm and took her hand in mine. We both bowed our heads, gazing at our entwined fingers. I was near enough to feel the heat rising from her skin. There was a fine gold chain around her neck, and I could see a brighter glint in the depths of her decolletage, nestled between the swell of her breasts. A gold knot; a ring. Her gift, my pledge.

"Clunderry," I murmured.

Sidonie's fingers tightened briefly on mine. "After Clunderry."

I turned away from her to meet Phèdre's gaze, filled with a complicated mix of affection, rue, and an unexpected thoughtfulness that looked a great deal like respect. I took a deep breath and squared my shoulders, and went forth to greet Hyacinthe and the others.

SEVENTY-ONE

IT WAS A STRANGE FEELING, retracing our path to Clunderry. All of us went, save Hyacinthe, who returned to the Stormkeep. It was only three days' ride, and the days passed swiftly. I remembered my first glimpse of the place so well; the Brithyll River widening to form a weedy lake, the castle, the village, the mill's sails turning lazily. An idyllic place, a happy place.

I had no memory of leaving it.

Or at least, I had only snatches of memory, fever-ravaged. Pain. A jolting cart, anxious faces. Voices, distant and echoing. The Bastard's bony head leaning over the cart that carried me, snorting through flared nostrils. Someone cursing him.

Elua.

None of us had been there since it happened; not me, not Urist, not even the Lady Breidaia. It hurt too much. And yet, Clunderry was as it had been. Life went on apace. The folk turned out to greet us, bowing low at the sight of our entourage led by the Cruarch himself. I recognized and remembered them. Trevedic the young reeve; old Cluna, the midwife. Kinada, Kinadius' mother; his sister, Kerys. They were all there, from Hoel, the lowly cook's apprentice who'd been crowned on the Day of Misrule, to Murghan, the one-armed steward who had been rumored to share Lady Breidaia's bed.

And there were others, too. The *ollamh*, Firdha, had come. Leodan of Briclaedh, my cattle-raiding neighbor. My southern neighbor Golven of Sionnachan, who had lent me his beekeeper, Milcis. Others I didn't recognize; others I did.

Eamonn was there.

Eamonn and his wife Brigitta, representing the Lady of the Dalriada. Her youngest was there, too; the boy Conor. Not a boy, not anymore. A young man with dark, watchful eyes, his harp slung in a case over his shoulder. The blood of the Maghuin Dhonn ran strong in his veins. I wondered how many people knew it.

The only person missing was Dorelei.

I missed her.

It had been a whole other life here in Clunderry, and it had been a good one. I'd been happy, and even if the happiness hadn't been entirely real, many parts of it had been. I was touched by the number of folk who welcomed me back with sincere gladness and pride.

Alais, of course, they welcomed with delight; there were a great many folk who had grown fond of her. But I was glad to see that they seemed genuinely honored that Queen Ysandre had sent her eldest daughter to attend, reckoning it a fitting tribute. In their eyes, Alais had become a daughter of Alba, and did not represent Terre d'Ange; but Sidonie did.

She did it well, with a quiet dignity beyond her years. The composure that had seemed unnatural—and betimes irritating—in a child suited her as a young woman.

We had arrived well before noon and the better part of the day was taken up in arrangements and preparation. It would be a simple ceremony, but there would be a great feast afterward.

I kept to myself that day, and after our initial arrival, folk left me alone. Even Eamonn was subdued, although he greeted me with a great, crushing embrace.

"I'm so sorry for what happened, Imri," he said hoarsely. "Dagda Mor! We were all sick at the news. Mother holds herself to blame for allowing you to accept Berlik's oath."

I shook my head. "'Twas no fault of hers. I made the choice myself. How are matters in Innisclan?"

"Well enough." Eamonn glanced over at Conor, talking quietly with Alais. "We were grateful to hear that you asked the Cruarch to have mercy on the innocent."

"You went a-hunting the Old Ones, though," I said.

"I did." His face turned grim. "Found a few, too. Conor summoned the harpist. I didn't think he would come, but he did. Don't worry, I didn't kill anyone. But I let it be known that anyone sheltering Berlik would be put to death without any questions asked."

"No one sheltered him," I said. "He fled."

"A long way, I hear," Eamonn said.

I nodded. "A very long way."

While the others met and mingled, I went for a walk around Clunderry's holdings. I would as soon have gone on my own, but Urist caught me slipping out of the castle and refused to allow it. I daresay he was the only companion I could have borne.

We walked slowly together, Urist leaning on his stick. All the fields had been plowed with neat, straight lines. Tender shoots of grain were emerging from the furrows. We passed the threshing barn. I remembered taking part in that backbreaking labor, coming home to Dorelei with dust and chaff clinging to my sweating skin. We strolled through the orchard, which was just past its peak blossoming. A gentle rain of petals fell from the apple trees as we walked beneath them, and the skeps of coiled straw were buzzing with honeybees.

"That would have pleased her," Urist said.

I smiled. "It would."

The distant pastures with their low stone fences were dotted with grazing cattle. We crossed the Brithyll on an arched wooden bridge, the heel of Urist's walking-stick echoing hollowly over the water, then circled around the reedy lake. Several families of ducks followed us curiously, trailing fuzzy ducklings.

I wasn't sure Elua's shrine would still be there, but it was, there beneath the arbor I'd helped build. Although nothing was blooming yet, the roses and lavender and columbine I'd transplanted myself had been tended with loving care. The effigy of Blessed Elua stood beneath the arbor, smiling toward the castle, his arms outstretched. I took off my boots to approach, then knelt and gazed at his face. I thought about what a priest of Elua had told me about love many years ago, the first time I kept his vigil on the Longest Night.

You will find it and lose it, again and again. And with each finding

*and each loss, you will become more than before. What you make of it is
yours to choose.*

It was true.

"I have chosen, my lord," I whispered. "Please, no more losses."

Although there was no answer, the steady throb of my heart was answer enough. I knew where love lay, and I would do my best to hold fast to it. I rose and donned my boots. Urist waited patiently, leaning on his stick. In the west, the sun was beginning to sink, low and golden, shadows stretching long across Clunderry. Behind the mask of his warrior's markings, there was compassion and understanding.

"Come on, lad." Urist clapped my shoulder. "Let's give our lass her due."

"I'm ready," I said.

Dusk was a time of day that Dorelei had loved. That wasn't why it had been chosen, of course; that had somewhat to do with twilight blurring the boundaries between the worlds of the living and the dead. She had, though. The world went soft around the edges; that's how she'd described it.

We walked in solemn procession, all of us. The *ollamh* Firdha led the way, with Drustan beside her. I followed, carrying Berlik's skull. The Lady Breidaia was on my right, Talorcan on my left. Behind us came Alais and the Lady Sibeal, and behind them, Sidonie, flanked by Phèdre and Joscelin, my foster-parents. Behind them came everyone else, and I could not begin to guess at the order. There were too many people.

It was the first time I'd visited the burial mound.

It wasn't large. There were only a few stone markers there. Dorelei's was the newest, the carvings on it still sharp-edged and clean. There was the Black Boar of the Cullach Gorrym; there, too, was the swan of House Courcel. There were runes written on it that only an *ollamh* could read. Still, it was old enough that the grass had grown over her grave, rendering it invisible. And there along the sloping incline, a deep hole had been dug, smelling of fresh-turned earth. A pile of loose soil lay beside it.

Firdha gave the invocation, calling upon the gods and goddesses of Alba to bear witness. Drustan stepped forward with a libation vessel, pouring *uisghe* on the green grass that grew above Dorelei's grave. He passed the vessel to his sister, and to his sister's son, and they made offerings, too.

"Let it be done." Firdha nodded at me.

I took a deep breath and stepped forward. I'd been given new clothing in Bryn Gorrydum, and I was attired in the old Cruithne style, as I had been at our Alban nuptials. A crimson cloak lay over my shoulders, and my chest was bare save for the golden torc and the scarred furrows of Berlik's claws. I took the libation vessel and made an offering, and then I knelt on the sloping greensward and placed the skull in the hole that lay beneath Dorelei's feet, dug deep into the hillside. Berlik's skull gazed out at me. I scooped up a double handful of soil and let it trickle over naked bone.

"Be at peace, Dorelei my love," I murmured. "Be at peace, my son."

Somewhere in the distance, a harp sounded.

A ripple of disturbance ran through those assembled. I got to my feet, gazing at them. Conor mac Grainne's head was cocked and listening, but his harp-case lay untouched over his shoulder. It wasn't Conor who was playing. It was farther away, wilder, filled with aching sorrow and regret.

Talorcan stirred, glowering.

"No!" The word emerged from my lips unbidden. "All of Alba grieves," I said more gently. "Let it be so this evening."

In the pause that followed, Sidonie's calm voice rose to fill the void. "Terre d'Ange grieves with Alba," she said. "Let it be so."

The harp echoed, wild.

Everyone looked at Drustan. The Cruarch cast his gaze heavenward, then lowered it. He looked at me. I looked back unwavering. "All of Alba grieves this evening," Drustan said quietly. "Conor mac Grainne, will you give voice to this grief, as you gave voice to joy on the eve of the nuptials betwixt Imriel de la Courcel and Dorelei mab Breidaia?"

He knew, I thought.

Conor flushed. "I will, my lord."

He unslung his harp-case and played for us; a sad, simple dirge. Or at least so it began. The longer Conor played, the more I heard in his playing. He played with eyes closed, his cheekbones bright with color. There was the tune he'd played for Drustan before, the twining harmonies evoking the death of his youngest sister, Moiread. There was the tune Ferghus had played for us, the song of the Maghuin Dhonn's last sacrifice. And there, too, slow and unrecognizable, was the Siovalese children's tune about the little brown goat.

The distant harp echoed it all.

It was strange, haunting and beautiful. I do not think there was any magic in it, save the magic of the harpists' skill. The harps called to one another, echoing over the woods and fields. One by one, the guests came forward to take part in the ritual.

I watched Sidonie make her offering, tipping the libation vessel. She stood for a moment, head bowed. I could see the burden of our shared guilt and sorrow weighing on her. But she gathered herself, stooping with deft grace to grasp a handful of soil and sprinkle it over Berlik's skull.

Bit by bit, the hole filled. The shadows deepened and the distant harp fell silent. Conor's fingers stilled on his harp-strings. Drustan nodded to him. He came forward to place the last handful of earth on Berlik's grave. The master gardener pressed and smoothed the earth, then set a piece of green sod, carefully preserved, over the place, tamping and watering it.

It was done.

Torches were lit. I let the procession turn and pass me by, lingering. Drustan gave me a curious look, but said nothing. I watched them wind toward the castle, then turned back toward the burial mound.

"Be at peace, Berlik," I said quietly. "Watch over them for me."

The lines of the burial mound were blurred by the deepening twilight. The world had grown soft around the edges. I stood there, breathing the moist spring air, listening to the ordinary sounds of night in the countryside emerge; the last tentative chorus of birdsong, the chirping of crickets, the occasional cattle lowing in the pasture. I remembered the way Dorelei's laughter had sounded, ringing across the land she had loved.

I stooped and touched the earth of Clunderry a final time.

"Good-bye," I whispered.

SEVENTY-TWO

I F THE CEREMONY HAD BEEN sober and grave, the feast that followed was its opposite.

There had never been a proper wake for Dorelei in the usual Alban tradition. Her kin had been scattered, hunting Berlik; I'd lain at death's door. Tonight stood in its stead.

Clunderry's great hall—which wasn't terribly large—was filled to bursting. The household staff had labored for two days in preparation for the event. Platter after platter of food emerged from the kitchen. Mead and *uisghe* circulated freely. We sat at long tables, eating and drinking until the small hours of the night.

Telling stories of Dorelei.

Fond stories, funny stories. It hurt, but there was healing in it, too. Lady Breidaia nearly broke my heart telling how Dorelei had privately confessed her astonishment that I'd been thoughtful enough to send for a beekeeper after she'd dreamed I fed her honeycomb.

"You were a good husband to her," Breidaia said, eyes bright with tears. "You would have been a good father to the babe."

And then I laughed until my sides ached at a tale that Kinadius and Kerys told about a piglet, a runt destined for an early demise, which Dorelei had saved from the axe. How they'd rescued it from the pigsty in the dead of night. How the three of them had managed to hide it for weeks, shuttling it from one room to another, two steps ahead of the suspicious maidservants.

"It used to follow her like a dog," Kerys remembered.

"Ah, gods!" Kinadius laughed. "I had to sneak out before dawn every morning to steal milk. She'd let it suckle on an old scrap of blanket dipped in milk. That pig ate better than we did. When we finally got caught, the pig-keeper said, 'Well, she's a runt no more, is she?' "

"Where was I when this happened?" Talorcan mused.

"Doing somewhat more important, I hope," his mother said tartly.

When my turn came, I told the story of scouring the castle on the Day of Misrule to find a pair of men's breeches vast enough to accommodate Dorelei's pregnant belly. How the breeches had been so long I'd had to roll the cuffs for her. How Dorelei had laughed so hard at the sight of me kneeling in her green kirtle, I'd no sooner finish rolling one leg when the other would fall, until at last she caught her breath long enough to tell me to pin them in place.

Alais smiled. "You *did* look that comical, Imri."

"Not as comical as Urist," I said.

"True," she agreed.

Sidonie eyed me, bemused. "You wore her *gown*?"

I flushed. "For the Day of Misrule, yes." I lowered my voice. "I'm sorry. If this is—"

"No, don't." Sidonie cut me off, shaking her head. "It isn't. I wanted to be here, Imriel. Dorelei deserved that much, as blood-kin and . . ." Her shoulders moved in a faint, rueful shrug. "And the other debt. She seemed kind. You did your best to build a life together with her. Truly, I want to understand what you lost."

"Thank you," I said softly.

"Mmm." Her black eyes gleamed. "I'll own, I didn't expect the kirtle."

My heart leapt, then settled. Not now, not yet.

When the well of remembrance began to run dry, the mood in the hall shifted. There was a call for me to tell the tale of my quest; the story of Berlik's death. I didn't want to tell it—I'd told it enough and there was no joy in it for me—but there were too many folk there yearning to hear it. It would have been cruel to refuse.

So I let Kinadius tell the first part, about their tireless efforts and how they'd found Berlik's trail at last, leading northward across the Flatlands and into Skaldia. And I let Urist tell about our sea voyage and the shipwreck.

Then came my part.

It felt strange, telling it here in Clunderry. It almost seemed as though it had happened to someone else. Vralia was so far away. I tried to bring it to life for them; the deep cold, the endless snow. All of them listened raptly, even those who had heard it before. Conor held his harp on his lap, silently fingering the strings as though setting it to music in his mind.

I daresay there were a few—Talorcan, to be sure—who were hoping for a climactic finish to the tale, a dramatic battle in which I defeated Berlik, shouting my vengeance to the skies. Instead, they got the truth. My despair and acknowledgment of defeat; and then the roar of a bear in the night. The quiet ending to my long, long hunt, Berlik kneeling in the snow with his head bowed for the sword.

"Why did he do it?" Kerys wondered aloud when I finished.

"To atone." It was young Conor who answered, his voice so low it was scarce audible. His head was bowed over his harp, coarse black hair hiding his eyes. "For all his people."

There was silence in the hall.

"And now it is finished," Drustan said at length.

It had grown late enough that his words were fitting. One by one, guests left the great hall for their chambers. Clunderry was full to the rafters that night, but no one complained. I stayed to bid good evening to all of them, as did Dorelei's nearest kin. I watched Drustan speaking quietly with Phèdre and Joscelin on the far side of the hall.

"Have you talked to your father?" I asked Sidonie in a low voice.

"About us?" Sidonie frowned. "We've discussed it. He's of a mind to speak to you himself, later. I agreed to let him without intervening."

"Is it bad?" I asked.

"No." Her frown didn't entirely vanish. "But it's not good, either."

"You know, it's not as bad as I thought," Alais offered. "You, I mean; the two of you. Not Father, I've no idea what he said."

"My thanks," I said wryly.

Alais ignored my tone. "The strangest part is seeing you being *nice* to one another."

"Oh?" Sidonie raised her brows in amusement. "We're not always."

It sounded perfectly innocent, and I knew perfectly well it wasn't.

My heart leapt again and a long-suppressed wave of desire rolled over me. I took a deep breath and willed my blood to subside. Alais looked suspiciously at her sister, but Sidonie's expression was guileless. I cleared my throat and changed the topic. "What of you and Talorcan?"

"When he went after Berlik, we decided to postpone the decision another year." Alais looked over at Talorcan, troubled. "No one knew what would happen. Now . . ." She shrugged, dropping her voice to a murmur. "I'm not sure."

Sidonie and I exchanged a glance. For the first time, it well and truly struck me that if we wed, I would be inextricably bound to the political process that linked Alba and Terre d'Ange. She was Ysandre's heir; Terre d'Ange's problems were her problems, too. And her problems would be mine. As the Dauphine's husband, I would inherit a great deal more responsibility than I'd ever wanted.

What a piece of irony *that* was.

"We'll worry about it later, my heart," Sidonie said to Alais. "Tonight's for Dorelei."

They waited until the last guests and family members had departed; then I bade them good night, lingering. Drustan stayed last of all, until it was only the two of us left in the hall. I thought he might speak to me then. He sat on one of the long benches, pouring the last dregs of a jar of *uisghe* into a cup.

"Shall I stay and talk with you, my lord?" I asked.

"No." His face looked tired beneath its woad mask. "Not tonight."

I was weary, too. "Then with your permission, I'll retire."

"As you will," he said, but when I made to go, Drustan called me back. "Imriel." I turned, and he fixed me with an impenetrable gaze. "We'll speak later, in Bryn Gorrydum. This isn't the time or the place. But I do want you to know that I'm grateful for what you did."

I nodded. "Thank you, my lord."

"Clunderry remains yours in name," Drustan said. "Will you keep it?"

I hesitated, then shook my head. "No. Let the deed revert to Lady Breidaia if she will have it; and if she will not, I ask you to hold it until you may bestow it on someone who loves this place as it deserves." I touched the torc around my neck. "I will always be honored to have been Imriel of Clunderry. But that was another life, my lord. Tonight it ended."

Drustan nodded. "Good night, then."

With that, I was dismissed. I made my way to the chamber I'd shared with Dorelei all those long months, our child growing inside her, me bound with Alban charms. By the dim light of a guttering lamp, I could see that everything had been preserved as it had been. Still, it felt very different; not least of all because I'd agreed to share it with Hugues and Ti-Philippe. They were asleep; Hugues on a straw pallet on the floor, Ti-Philippe sprawled on half the bed.

I was glad they were there, even if Hugues snored. There were too many memories in that room. It would have felt empty and lonely without them. Even with them there, I felt the ache of Dorelei's loss.

Still, my quest was over.

I crawled into bed and slept.

We stayed another day at Clunderry to bid farewell to those guests who had come to take part in the ceremony. In the wake of yesterday's strong emotion, everyone seemed purged and calm, like the world after a storm has passed. I did my part, thanking all of them for their kindness. I found myself acutely aware of Sidonie's presence. My wrists and ankles itched with the memory of my old bindings.

The Dalriada lingered the longest, for which I was grateful. I'd scarce had a chance to talk with Eamonn.

"Can you not stay another night?" I asked him.

Eamonn shook his head with regret. "I've got to supervise the building of the library. I shouldn't have taken the time as it was, but I needed to see with my own eyes that you were alive and well."

"And to express your mother's sorrow," Brigitta reminded him.

"Aye," he said. "That, too."

I embraced them both. "Come visit when your library's built."

They smiled at one another. "We'll try," Eamonn said. "Seems we might be busy. Quite a few prospective pupils have expressed an interest."

"You could come visit us," Brigitta suggested. I glanced at Sidonie without thinking. She was talking with young Conor and her aunt

Breidaia, but she turned her head to meet my gaze. A spark leapt between us.

"Seems you might be busy yourself," Eamonn said. "Just . . . try to stay out of trouble for once, will you?"

I smiled ruefully. "I'll try."

Our last night at Clunderry was a quiet one. With most of the guests and their entourages gone, there was more space. I did sleep alone that night in the chamber Dorelei and I had shared, and it was empty and lonely, but the memories weren't as painful as they would have been the previous night, on the heels of all those tales. The ache of guilt and sorrow was still there. It would always be there. It was the nature of loss.

We left on the morrow, another bright spring day. I turned in the saddle many times as we rode away, glancing back at Clunderry, until it had vanished wholly from sight. Sidonie fell in beside me, her personal guard trailing us.

"Do you think you'll come back one day?" she asked me.

"I'd like to," I said. "Mayhap for the Feast of the Dead."

She nodded. "In the hope of seeing her?"

"Yes," I said. "But not soon."

"No," she murmured. "I imagine it would hurt too much."

We didn't speak much for a long time afterward, although there was a great deal to be said. All of our conversation since I'd arrived in Alba had been constrained by propriety. We had a world of talking to do. I had told her about Maslin's role in saving me, but not about the many conversations we'd had, the friendship we'd managed to forge. A thousand thoughts that had crossed my mind during my travels. And I wanted to hear every blessed thing that had befallen her since I left.

But it could wait. Right now, the silence felt good.

For once—for always, I prayed—we *had* time ahead of us. Whatever his thoughts on the matter, Drustan didn't seem inclined to interfere between us, at least not here and now. No one did. Throughout the day, a tacit acknowledgment of our relationship seemed to emerge.

And at night . . .

We made camp in a meadow alongside the narrow road we were following, although camp was a poor term for it. It was a procession of state with the Cruarch of Alba and the Dauphine of Terre d'Ange, and whenever we halted for the night, what sprang up was less a campsite than a small city of tents, dominated by two larger pavilions. Drustan's was wrought of crimson silk, flying the Black Boar from its center pole, and he shared it with the immediate members of his household. Sidonie's was Courcel blue, flying the silver swan of our house and the lily and stars of Elua and his Companions.

The wagons in our train even carried a table that could be cunningly disassembled, ornate stools on which to sit, and fine linens and utensils, along with a plethora of supplies. There were two skilled cooks and a number of attendants.

"It's a long way from dining on salt cod and sleeping in the bottom of a boat," Ti-Philippe had commented on our outward journey.

The mood was subdued that first night after Clunderry, a lingering sense of gravity persisting. We dined and talked quietly among ourselves. The sun slipped slowly beneath the treeline in the west, making the campfires burn brighter. Some distance away, one of Sidonie's guards began playing a lap-harp, tentatively picking out a few of the melodies Conor had played. The air was turning cooler, the world going soft around the edges once more. A few people were yawning, but no one moved.

"Shall we to bed?" Joscelin asked Phèdre.

"In a moment." She was listening to the harpist, her chin propped on one fist. "It's early yet."

"Dawn comes early, too," he reminded her.

It was Sidonie, seated on a stool beside me, who rose. Our shoulders had been nearly brushing all evening. I felt the warmth of her presence leave when she stood. I glanced up to meet her dark gaze. The waiting silence between us deepened. She held out her hand to me, tilting her head imperceptibly in the direction of her pavilion.

I stood and took her hand.

There hadn't been much conversation at the table, but enough to feel the hush when it ceased. In the lull, we walked away. The grass was damp with dew, a little slippery beneath the soles of my boots. Sidonie's hand was warm in mine. There was a lamp lit in her pavilion, making the blue silk glow from within, unearthly in the lowering darkness.

Behind us, I could hear the low murmur of conversation resuming at the table.

"Good evening, your highnesses." Claude de Monluc, the captain of her guard, greeted us with a crisp bow.

"My lord captain." Sidonie inclined her head.

He drew back the a silk flap that served as the pavilion's door. "I'll see you're undisturbed."

"Thank you." My voice sounded strange to my ears.

We entered the pavilion, and he secured the flap behind us. Inside, it was luxuriously appointed, with carpets spread over the grass, trunks containing Sidonie's garments and possessions, and a thick goosedown pallet adorned with pillows and a sumptous coverlet. A fretted lamp hung from the center pole, casting lacy shadows on the silken walls, and a portable brazier warmed the air.

Sidonie and I were alone.

It felt like a gift, somewhat rare and precious. For a long moment, neither of us moved. At last Sidonie released my hand. She withdrew the knotted gold ring on its long chain from her bodice, unclasping the chain. Fine gold links slithered and fell unheeded to the carpet as she removed the ring.

"Thank you for keeping your pledge," she said softly, taking my hand once more and sliding the ring onto my finger.

"It kept me alive," I told her. "I would have given up without it."

Her breath caught in her throat and she made a small, unexpected sound, as though my words had hurt her. The threat of tears made her eyes bright. Sidonie gave her head a familiar, impatient shake, then reached up to sink both hands into my hair, pulling my head down and kissing me with all the ferocity in her.

It was like a dam breaking. All the desire I'd suppressed—we had both suppressed—flooded over me, around me, through me. I held her hard, both arms around her waist, hands pressing her back, returning her kisses as though to devour her whole. I wanted her so badly, my knees felt weak.

I couldn't get enough of her, couldn't get close enough. We sank down onto the soft pallet together. Sidonie's mouth was on my throat, biting and sucking, her fingers working at the buttons on my shirt.

Lower, tracing my scars. I wriggled out of my shirt, pinned her, worked at her stays. Her back arched as I freed her breasts, suckling them, the grip of my fingers hard enough to leave bruises.

"Here . . ."

"No . . . ow! *Yes.*"

Fabric, too damned much of it between us. I almost couldn't wait. A fold of her gown, caught beneath me, tore when I tried to ease it over her head. My phallus was so hard it ached, thick and throbbing, straining the knots on my Alban breeches. Caught in a spiral of rising urgency, we struggled and laughed and kissed our way to nakedness.

"Now." Her nails dug into my buttocks, her voice raw. *"Please."*

Kneeling between her thighs, I spread them wider. "Now?"

Her hips bucked. "Yes!"

I slid into her with one long, practiced thrust, sliding the length of my body up hers and bracing myself over her.

And somewhat changed between us.

It wasn't that the urgency diminished. It simply . . . changed. Both of us went very still. Our bodies were joined. She held me. I filled her. The profound, staggering intimacy of the act of love struck me anew, the way it had never struck me with anyone else in the world. I laughed softly.

"Imriel . . ." Sidonie's eyes were open and filled with wonder.

"I know," I said. "I know."

When the gods themselves make love, I think it must be like this. All of love's glorious mortal follies, all the tangled clothes and awkward limbs, went away. For a long time, I filled her without moving. I could feel her heart beating. Our breath intermingled. When I did move within her, it was as though the hand of Blessed Elua himself impelled me. Our bodies moved together; rising and falling, rising and falling.

Why do we fit so well together?

A woman's pleasure is different from a man's. It surged like a ship atop the waves, and I drove it, furthering it, our gazes locked on one another. Each trough was deeper, each crest higher than the next, onward and onward and onward. It felt as though I could last forever. It felt like it would never end. I wished it wouldn't.

Still, we were mortal.

I held off and held off, as long as I could, making the moment last, until I could hold no longer. My entire body shuddered as I spent myself in her in one long, exquisite series of spasms.

We lay entangled together, neither wanting to move.

"That was . . ." I murmured, then realized I had no words for it.

Sidonie touched my cheek. "Yes. It was."

SEVENTY-THREE

WAKING THE FOLLOWING morning in Sidonie's bed, with her naked and warm and tumbled in my arms, was one of the gladdest moments of my life. The sun had risen and filtered blue light filled the pavilion. I held her and watched her sleep until she awoke and smiled at me, her eyes sleepy and heavy-lidded. For the first time in longer than I could remember, I was quietly, peacefully, and utterly happy.

"Good morning, Sun Princess," I said.

"Mmm." Her smile deepened. "We could make it better."

I daresay we would have, but at the sound of our voices, there was a discreet cough outside the pavilion. "Your highness?" a woman's voice called. "Shall I attend you?"

I groaned. Sidonie kissed me. "Duty beckons."

Even so, it was strange and wonderful to be there with her, openly and unquestioned. Margot de Monluc, who was wed to Sidonie's Captain of the Guard, entered and greeted us both with cheerful respect. She bustled about the pavilion, bringing a ewer of fresh water and arraying Sidonie's attire for the day.

"Well, that will want mending," she observed in a good-natured tone, folding away the gown I'd torn last night. I found myself growing warm, but Sidonie was unperturbed as ever.

When Margot had departed, I donned my clothes, then sat cross-legged on the pallet and watched Sidonie comb out her hair beside me. "I'm surprised Amarante didn't accompany you," I observed. "I would have thought to see her here."

"I released her from my service before I left for Alba." She looked at my face and laughed at my shocked expression. "Elua! Released, not dismissed."

"Why?" I asked.

Sidonie concentrated on a thick tangle. "You know she lacked a year's service to Naamah in order to take her vows as a priestess?" she asked. I nodded. "Well, I would have freed her to do it a long time ago, except she wouldn't have gone. Not until we knew you were safe." She set down the comb. "Whatever lies before us, I don't want Amarante drawn into it."

"You think she would have been?" I asked.

She shrugged. "I've been working to get the support of the priest-hood. Her mother is the head of Naamah's Order. Even the semblance of influence might set tongues wagging. It's not fair, since it's naught to do with Amarante."

I hadn't thought about that. "How difficult is this like to be?"

Sidonie's brows furrowed. "Well, my mother's dead set against us marrying."

I picked up the comb and began working on her tangles. "Love, I don't need to marry you to be with you. Phèdre and Joscelin never wed. I'd be happy to spend the rest of my life as your consort."

"I know. Last night . . ." She shook her head, disturbing my handi-work. "It would be enough if I weren't my mother's heir. But I am. It's complicated."

"Politics," I said softly.

"Always." Sidonie sighed. "Let's not talk about it yet."

I eased the comb through a golden snarl. "Your wish is my command."

"Now *that* would be fun." Her voice was light, but there was a seri-ous undertone. She turned her head to glance at me. "Would you do it? Give yourself over and submit to my will for a night, Imriel?"

"A whole night?" I asked.

"Just one," Sidonie said. "Every once in a while."

I raised my brows. "What would you give me in turn?"

"Any other night you wished." Her gaze was steady, but her color rose.

Another wave of desire rolled over me. Fighting the urge to haul her onto my lap and kiss her all over, I shuddered and handed her the comb. "I think you'd better finish this yourself, and I think we'd better not talk about *this*, either, or we'll end up delaying the entire procession."

Sidonie took the comb without comment, watching as I rose and crossed the pavilion.

"Yes," I said at length, looking back at her. "To you, yes."

She smiled wickedly. "Good."

By the time we emerged from the pavilion, the campsite was bustling with activity. Drustan's pavilion had already been taken down, as had many of the smaller tents. Ti-Philippe glanced up as we approached the makeshift dining table, his face splitting in a broad grin. I ignored him studiously, helping myself to a plate of cold pheasant and farmer's cheese. As it happened, I was ravenous.

In truth, I didn't mind the smiles, not really. Not from folk I loved and trusted. I would have expected Sidonie to respond to them with cool aplomb, but in fact, she seemed quietly amused by it. I wondered if, by the time we'd been together as long as Phèdre and Joscelin, I'd be able to predict her reactions.

I wasn't sure I would.

I wasn't sure I wanted to, either.

The only shadow cast over that morning came from Talorcan. He came from the picket-lines and passed by the table. Upon seeing Sidonie and me seated side by side, he paused, a muscle in his jaw working.

"Could you not have waited a few more days?" he asked me in a low voice. "The sod has barely settled above the bear-witch's grave. Did my sister deserve so little respect?"

It was unexpected. I glanced up at him, seeing the sorrow and grief and bitter failure in his dark eyes. "Talorcan, there was no—"

"Do you say Imriel should have refused me, cousin?" Sidonie inquired.

Dark blood suffused Talorcan's face. "Of course not."

"Then it is I who owes you an apology," she said gravely. "Not Imriel. For I was the one to extend my hand to him. I assure you, in the name of Blessed Elua and his Companions, and all the gods and goddesses of Alba, there was no disrespect intended. If there was a semblance of it, I do apologize."

The muscle in his jaw twitched. "No apology is needed," he said curtly.

"Tal, my prince." Urist, seated on the opposite side of the table, heaved himself to his feet, leaning on his walking-stick. He clapped the Cruarch's heir on the shoulder. "Take a walk with me, will you? I've a mind to tell you a tale."

We watched them walk away.

"You know," Joscelin said wistfully, "betimes I miss the days when the worst of our problems could be solved at sword-point."

I glanced at Sidonie and smiled. "I don't."

After that, though, there was peace; at least of a sort. Whatever Urist said to Talorcan—and I daresay it had to do with the promise he'd made Dorelei—there was no more animosity between us. He made an effort to tamp down his hurt and his anger; and I didn't blame him for it, anyway. In his place, I would have felt the same. Still, I kept a careful eye on him, concerned for Alais' sake. They were courteous with one another, and betimes there seemed to be genuine warmth between them.

At other times, there didn't.

So many uncertainties, so many things to ponder! We tried, Sidonie and I, to find a time to talk freely without the world listening. But there was little privacy on the road by day, and hushed conversations in her pavilion by night turned quickly to somewhat else. We had been parted for far, far too long.

All too soon, we arrived at Bryn Gorrydum.

I would have been content to have the journey last longer. It was an in-between time, a happy time. Such times never last. True to his word, Drustan had held off speaking to me about my relationship with his eldest daughter until we reached Bryn Gorrydum. But that first night, he did. It was a quiet affair, a dinner amongst family and friends. When Sidonie rose to retire, Drustan shook his head at me.

So I stayed.

Everyone else left, taking their cues from the Cruarch of Alba. I slid down the bench to sit opposite Drustan, pouring *uisghe* for us both. I'd celebrated my Alban nuptials in this great hall. I'd composed a heart-felt poem in Dorelei's honor. I'd fought with staves against some fellow named Goraidh and won. And on the night we'd wed, I'd lain sleepless, creeping at last from the bed we shared to read the letter Sidonie had sent to me. Here in this very hall, I'd removed the croonie-stone from around my throat; laughed and wept and realized I truly did love her, madly and hopelessly and always.

I sat across from Drustan and folded my hands on the table.

He cleared his throat. "Sidonie."

I nodded. "I love her, my lord."

"I can see that." Drustan shook his head impatiently. It was a gesture Sidonie had inherited. I'd never noticed before; he didn't do it often in public, any more than she did. "The both of you make it quite obvious. By the Boar, Imriel! *You will always be family*. I said that to you. Do you recall?"

My heart ached. "I do, my lord."

He fixed me with a hard gaze. "You knew then, didn't you?"

"Yes," I said steadily. "And mayhap I should have spoken to you, but I was grievously hurt and racked by guilt. Of a surety, I should have spoken to you before Dorelei and I wed. My lord, I will tell you what I told your wife. I have known since Sidonie was sixteen. We doubted. We were afraid; too young, too uncertain. We should have trusted Blessed Elua's precept. We did not. That was our mistake."

"And now you stand to make a hypocrite of me," Drustan murmured.

"My lord!" I protested.

He held up one hand and drained his cup. I refilled it. "I will not oppose your union," he said in his direct manner. "Neither will I support it. I would have you understand why."

"I'm listening," I said.

"I think you're a fine young man, Imriel," Drustan said. "You've overcome a great deal in your life. You were raised by two people I trust beyond all doubt. You served Alba well; in truth, better than Alba served you. And I would indeed be a hypocrite of the worst kind if I believed that you were worthy of my niece, but not my daughter." His mouth twisted wryly. "Urist was kind enough to point that out to me."

"Urist has been good to me," I said.

"He's come to respect you," Drustan said. "Which is another point in your favor. I value Urist's judgment. If he says you were a good lord of Clunderry and a good husband to Dorelei, I believe it to be true."

I swirled the *uisghe* in my cup. "And yet."

"And yet." Drustan nodded. "Imriel, Ysandre was scarce older than you are now when she took the throne and inherited a realm poisoned by treason, poised on the brink of utter conquest." His voice was gentle. "You've seen battle, I know. I do not think you can imagine the scope of this war. Ysandre is strong and determined. She was always prepared to defend the throne from those who sought to usurp it from within, and to defend the borders of Terre d'Ange from those who sought to assail it from without. But never in her darkest dreams did she suspect one of her own people would betray the very beating heart of Terre d'Ange into the hands of the Skaldi."

I took a gulp of fiery liquid. "I know, my lord. I know what my mother did."

" 'Tis one thing to know it, and another to live through it," Drustan said quietly. "This land is my heart and soul. I love it beyond all telling. If one of my clan-lords betrayed Alba in such a manner, I would raze the very earth on which he walked to purify the land of his touch. I would know no peace until he was destroyed utterly. I'm not D'Angeline. I do not share the profound depths of Ysandre's horror at the thought of Melisande Shahrizai's son wedding her heir . . . but I understand it, all too well. No force on earth can diminish the shock of that betrayal. It goes deeper than words. And for that reason, out of respect for my wife, I cannot give you my blessing."

There wasn't much I could say in reply. I refilled our cups and drank.

"Do you understand?" Drustan asked.

"Yes." I set down my cup. "I do, my lord. But 'tis a piece of irony. It was Ysandre herself who fought so hard to see me found. To heal the rifts within the realm and House Courcel with love and forgiveness." I smiled bitterly. "What are Sidonie and I doing if not that very thing? Of a surety, Ysandre had no qualms about letting Melisande Shahrizai's son wed your sister's daughter when it suited her political needs. What do you call that if not hypocrisy, my lord?"

"I'm not defending it, Imriel." To his credit, Drustan looked disturbed. "But this isn't a matter of reason. All the reason in the world cannot change her heart."

"A man's heart may change in a day," I said, thinking about what Adelmar of the Frisii had said when I'd challenged Berlik's sincerity as a pilgrim. He'd spoken sardonically, but as it happened, he had been right. "What might change Ysandre's, my lord?"

Drustan shook his head. "That, I fear, you must discover for yourself."

I gazed at him for a long moment. "Will you give us your blessing if I do?"

"I will." His voice was firm.

"Then I'll find a way," I said simply.

He drank the last of the *uisghe* in his cup, then rose and extended his hand. I stood, and we clasped hands across the table. "I pray you do."

I made my way up the stairs to my bedchamber. I'd carried Dorelei up those stairs on our wedding night, to the very same chamber that Sidonie and I had been given to share. The thought gave me a pang, but not enough to deter me. I murmured a prayer to Dorelei's spirit, asking her forgiveness as I pushed open the door.

A single candle was burning low on the bedside table, guttering in a pool of wax. Sidonie lifted her head from the pillow, lying propped on one arm. Her hair was loose, honey-gold locks spilling over her creamy shoulders. I stood in the doorway and gazed at her, the tide of desire rising in my veins. A faint smile touched her lips. "Well?"

"Not good," I said. "But not bad, either."

She turned back the covers. "Come here."

I went.

SEVENTY-FOUR

ONCE AGAIN, we made our farewells.

I had a long talk with Alais before we departed, just the two of us. I knew Sidonie had spoken to her, too, and later we would discuss it, but I wanted time alone with Alais. She was the sister of my heart, and in many ways, my oldest friend. If she hadn't been there after Dorelei's death, I wasn't sure I'd have found the will to recover.

We climbed up one of the watchtowers to the parapet of Bryn Gorrydum, empty and windswept. It was one of the few places where one could talk undisturbed. For a time, we simply strolled together.

Alais had changed. How not? She was seventeen, a year older than when I'd left her. It wasn't just age, though. Alba had changed her. She was at home here in a way she'd never been in Terre d'Ange. And Dorelei's death had changed her. She had been a serious child with a charming streak of spontaneity, then a prickly adolescent. Now, she was a thoughtful young woman.

"I worry about you," I told her.

"Me?" Alais flashed a smile at me. "You're the one draws trouble wherever you go."

"No good comes of disobeying Blessed Elua's precept," I observed.

"Talorcan." She sighed, gazing out at the Straits. "I know. He's grieving over his sister's death and angry at his failure. Still, what would you have me do, Imri? I *am* fond of him. And Alba . . ." Her voice trailed off. The wind plucked at her black curls. "Alba, I love."

"Enough to wed a man you don't?" I asked. "And seek to change the laws of succession?"

Her chin rose. "Mayhap."

There was an almighty stubbornness in her violet eyes; and Elua's priests acknowledge all manner of love. If Alais chose to act out of love for Alba, I had no footing to gainsay it. I took her shoulders in my hands. "I want happiness for you, that's all."

"I am happy," Alais said in a low voice. "Imri . . . we're not all given the same sort of happiness. This is where I belong, where I'm meant to be. Why and how and what I'm meant to do . . ." She shook her head. "That's my task, figuring it out."

"Don't try too hard, love." My throat tightened. "Madness lies that way."

"I know." Alais' face was grave. "I won't forget, I promise. After what happened, we are all mindful of it. Conor said . . ." Her words broke off again and she flushed.

I grinned. "Oh, Conor, is it?"

"Don't tease!" Her flush deepened. "About you and Sidonie . . . I'm sorry to have taken it amiss, before. I know there was no hurt intended." I let go of her shoulders, and Alais took my right hand in both of hers, gazing at the gold knot on my finger. "You're good together. I didn't think you would be, but you are. And Imri . . ." Her voice grew small. "I think she's going to need you. I think she's going to need you very badly, one day."

A chill chased the length of my spine. "Is that a true dream?"

"No." Alais shook her head. "It's only a feeling. If I ever have a dream, a true dream, I'll send word." She lifted her head to gaze at me. "You *are* a hero, you know. At least to me."

I kissed her brow. "I'd as soon be a brother."

"That, too. Always." She smiled, her expression lightening. "Next spring, will you come to Alba and bring me a puppy?"

"One of Celeste's kin?" I asked.

Alais' eyes were bright. "Yes, please. You choose. I trust you."

I hugged her, holding her close, feeling her cling to me. "Of course."

"Just be safe," Alais whispered in my ear. "Both of you. Promise?"

"I'll try," I said. "You, too."

She nodded. "I'll try."

On the day of our departure, there was a considerable crowd gathered. I was touched to see that almost all the men of Clunderry's garrison who'd ridden together in the hunt had come . . . Kinadius, Deordivus, Domnach, Brun . . . Urist, of course. It was harder parting from him than I'd reckoned. We'd been through a great deal together.

He gave me a swift, hard embrace. "Take care of yourself, lad." His black eyes glinting, he poked my brow with a callused fingertip. "Wish we could have gotten some proper warrior's markings on you."

I smiled. "Try to give that leg a rest, will you?"

And then there were no more farewells to be made, only the Cruarch's flagship loaded and waiting. We filed aboard the ship; Sidonie and her retinue, Montrève's small company. Hyacinthe had not come, but I had no doubt he was watching in his sea-mirror, for a friendly breeze sprang up at our backs as the ship's prow swung toward the open sea. We crowded into the stern, waving as the harbor dwindled behind us.

"I can't believe I finally got to go on a great adventure, and you never even drew your sword," Hugues said to Joscelin, sounding a bit mournful.

Joscelin gave him a sardonic glance. "I was jesting the other day. Be glad of it."

"*I* am." Phèdre took Joscelin's arm. "I'm glad that we went, and glad to find it wasn't needful. You've had enough fighting and death for one lifetime, love." Her gaze touched on me then, filled with soft emotion. "And above all else, I'm glad that you're alive and well and coming home, Imri."

"So am I." I laughed aloud for the sheer joy of it. "Elua! So am I."

It was another swift journey, sped by the hand of the Master of the Straits. I shared the state cabin with Sidonie that night and we made tireless love in the plunging darkness, finding after some trial and error that it worked best if she rode astride me, rocking gently, the rise and swell of the waves beneath the ship echoing our bodies' motion, soft gasps and moans echoing the splash of the rushing water, the creaking of the wooden hull. Things were still slow and sweet between us, our reunion touched with lingering tenderness and the awe of that first night. The sharper pleasures life offered could wait.

There was time, and time was a luxury.

We reveled in it, and in each other.

In the morning, Sidonie and I went to watch the coastline of Terre d'Ange appear on the horizon. A pair of her guards trailed us at a discreet distance, but no one disturbed us. The night's chill still hung in the air. I stood behind her in the prow of the ship, my cloak wrapped around us both, gazing over her shoulder.

The last time I'd left Alba, I'd wept. I'd felt numb at the sight of home. Now it was all different. There was still sorrow. There would always be sorrow. I bore scars that would never let me forget what had happened at Clunderry. But for once in my life—for the first time I could remember since I was a child—despite the difficulties that lay ahead of us, there was a calm, abiding sense of peace.

Pointe des Soeurs beckoned in the distance. The rising sun sparkled on the wavelets. Gulls circled the topmast, squalling. The world was a good place.

"What are you thinking?" I murmured in Sidonie's ear.

"Too many things I'd rather not yet." She shifted. "Ask me somewhat silly and banal."

"All right." I tightened my arms around her. "Was Maslin a good lover?"

Her cheek curved in a faint smile. "Somewhat else."

"Aha!" I grinned. "All right, then. Do you think Amarante will return when she completes her year's service to Naamah and takes her vows?"

"I hope so." Sidonie leaned back against me. "I promised I'd see a new temple dedicated to Naamah if she did." I peered around at her, and she glanced up with amusement. "I know it's not the most politically astute gesture, but what's the point of being the Dauphine if you can't do that sort of thing? In a year's time, I hope matters will be more settled. And at least as a priestess serving in a temple, she wouldn't have to deal with D'Angeline lordlings in a snit claiming she's naught but a Court attendant enjoying royal favoritism."

I winced, recognizing my own words. "She told you that?"

Sidonie shook her head. "Mavros did, trying to stir trouble."

"Did it work?" I asked.

"What do you think?" she said equably. "I knew why you were in a foul mood those days. I was, too. I think he was just bored and anxious on your behalf. It makes him contrary." She was silent a moment. "I'm glad you didn't inherit that particular streak of Shahrizai perversity."

I smiled wryly. "An endless penchant for games?"

She nodded. "I trust you. I couldn't if you weren't who you are."

A few strands of golden hair blew across my face. I freed one hand to tuck them under a jeweled hair clip. "Betimes I wonder," I mused. "How much of it is me and how much of it is that which shaped me? Is it House Courcel's bloodline with its stubborn—albeit occasionally misguided—sense of honor? Abhorrence of my mother's deeds? What I witnessed in Daršanga? Phèdre and Joscelin's influence?"

Sidonie turned to look into my face. "Does it matter? You are who you are. I love you."

"Then it doesn't matter." I kissed her. "And I love you."

"Of course . . ." Her black eyes sparkled when I lifted my head. "I do expect a *certain* amount of perversity."

"Oh, yes." I traced her lower lip with my thumb. "The part where I do wonderful, horrible things to your helpless body." A steady pulse of desire beat in my veins, at once tender, predatory, and langorous, somehow all the more intense for knowing I had the patience to wait for its fulfillment. "Someday, love, we'll have to figure out what tangled Kusheline bloodline runs in House L'Envers' heritage to manifest in this way."

Sidonie laughed; that unexpected, buoyant laugh that had turned my world upside down three years ago. "Do you care?"

I kissed her again. "Not really, no."

It was true. However unlikely it was, we fit. Whatever the reason, I was glad of it. Time changes things; but so does love. Love, above all else. I didn't fear the darkness in me, not anymore. Love illuminated it, made the darkness dazzling. Tenderness and violent pleasure could be one and the same. The bright mirror and the dark, each reflecting the other, creating an infinity between them.

I understood it now.

The shore of Terre d'Ange drew nearer. Sidonie turned once more to watch, content to remain in the circle of my arms. She was mindful of the statement it would make, and unafraid to make it. The lines had been drawn in the Battle of Imriel. I could make out figures along the harbor; the banner of House Trevalion. I wondered if Bertran would be there.

A world of intrigue awaited.

I thought about the forces arrayed against us; Ysandre's adamant opposition. After speaking with Drustan, I understood it in a way I hadn't before. If there was some way I could rip my heart from my chest and show it to her, convince her, I would do it. I doubted it would be easy or pleasant. The spectre of my mother lay between us, lit by the lamp of the Unseen Guild. As a boy, I had wanted nothing more than to bring her to justice. Now the thought was a burden I didn't wish to take up.

Still, there would be others against us, too. For a surety, Barquiel L'Envers; and many, many others. My mother had left a long trail of hatred in her wake. One way or another, I would have to reckon with it.

But there would be allies, too.

Somewhere behind us, Captain Corcan was shouting orders; Alban sailors were scrambling to obey. I could hear Ti-Philippe making himself useful, and Hugues getting in the way. Phèdre and Joscelin came to join us in the prow, watching the shore approach. Joscelin ruffled my hair lightly, as he hadn't done since I was much younger, the corners of his summer-blue eyes crinkling as he gave his half-smile. He leaned on the railing, one foot propped, the hilt of his longsword protruding over his shoulder.

Phèdre laid a hand on his arm. "Home," she said softly.

"Home," Joscelin agreed.

I wanted to gather them all up, hold them all in my arms and in my heart, never let them go. I never wanted to lose anyone I loved, ever again. Phèdre glanced at me, the scarlet mote of Kushiel's Dart floating in her left iris, the Name of God in her thoughts, a world of love and pride and concern in her smile. I smiled back at her, tightening my arms around Sidonie. Somewhere in the distant future, Alais' warning hung over us.

A bad feeling, nothing more.

One day it might be.

"Imriel." Sidonie's voice was calm and breathless. "I can't breathe."

I loosened my grip. "Sorry."

A lilt of humor leavened her tone. "Well, I don't mind, sometimes."

The flagship's crimson sails descended with a soft rush. Out oars, and the ship glided into the harbor of Pointe des Soeurs. Lines were tossed ashore, the ship secured. Somewhere belowdeck, there was a familiar stomping that sounded like the Bastard expressing his displeasure at the sea passage.

There was an entourage awaiting us, led by Bertran de Trevalion. A certain look of trepidation crossed his face at the sight of Sidonie and me, but he managed to swallow it, and gave the sweeping bow accorded the Dauphine of Terre d'Ange. Enemy or ally? Mayhap neither. His mother had tried to have me killed; his father had wished me good hunting. Who could say? There might be many in Terre d'Ange who would take no side, waiting to see how the drama played out.

To be sure, I was curious myself.

The captain lowered the ramp. Claude de Monluc gave a crisp order, and Sidonie's personal guard formed a double line, flanking the ramp. I let go of Sidonie and gave her a courtly bow, extending my arm.

"Are you ready, my lady?" I asked.

She took my arm. "I am."

Terre d'Ange and the future awaited us.

Together we went forth to meet them.

EXTRAS

www.orbitbooks.net

About the Author

An avid reader, **Jacqueline Carey** began writing fiction as a hobby in high school. This interest became a driving passion after university, during six months spent working abroad in a bookstore in London. The experience inspired her to pursue writing as a career in earnest. Jacqueline has received B.A. degrees in psychology and English literature from Lake Forest College and, during her early writing career, worked at the art centre of an area college – also gaining a strong background in the visual arts. Jacqueline enjoys doing research on a wide variety of arcane topics, and an affinity for travel has taken her from Finland to Egypt.

She currently lives in west Michigan, where she is a member of the oldest Mardi Gras krewe in the state. You can visit Jacqueline's website at www.jacquelinecarey.com

Find out more about Jacqueline Carey and other Orbit authors by registering for the free monthly newsletter at www.orbitbooks.net

If you enjoyed

KUSHIEL'S JUSTICE

look out for

THE DARKNESS THAT COMES BEFORE

by

R. Scott Bakker

CHAPTER ONE

CARUTHUSAL

There are three, and only three, kinds of men in the world: cynics, fanatics, and Mandate Schoolmen.

— ONTILLAS, *ON THE FOLLY OF MEN*

The author has often observed that in the genesis of great events, men generally possess no inkling of what their actions portend. This problem is not, as one might suppose, a result of men's blindness to the consequences of their actions. Rather it is a result of the mad way the dreadful turns on the trivial when the ends of one man cross the ends of another. The Schoolmen of the Scarlet Spires have an old saying: "When one man chases a hare, he finds a hare. But when many men chase a hare, they find a dragon." In the prosecution of competing human interests, the result is always unknown, and all too often terrifying.

— DRUSAS ACHAMIAN, *COMPENDIUM OF THE FIRST HOLY WAR*

Midwinter, 4110 Year-of-the-Tusk, Carythusal

All spies obsessed over their informants. It was a game they played in the moments before sleep or even during nervous gaps in conversation. A spy would look at his informant, as Achamian looked at Geshrunni now, and ask himself, *How much does he know?*

Like many taverns found near the edge of the Worm, the great slums of Carythusal, the Holy Leper was at once luxurious and impoverished. The floor was tiled with ceramics as fine as any found in the palace of a Palatine-Governor, but the walls were of painted mud brick, and the ceiling was so low that taller men had to duck beneath the brass lamps, which were authentic imitations, Achamian had once heard the owner boast, of those found in the Temple of Exorietta. The place was invariably crowded, filled with shadowy, sometimes dangerous men, but the wine and hashish were just expensive enough to prevent those who could not afford to bathe from rubbing shoulders with those who could.

Until coming to the Holy Leper, Achamian had never liked the Ainoni—especially those from Carythusal. Like most in the Three Seas, he thought them vain and effeminate: too much oil in their beards, too fond of irony and cosmetics, too reckless in their sexual habits. But this estimation had changed after the endless hours he'd spent waiting for Geshrunni to arrive. The subtlety of character and taste that afflicted only the highest castes of other nations, he realized, was a rampant fever among these people, infecting even low-caste freemen and slaves. He had always thought High Ainon a nation of libertines and petty conspirators; that this made them a nation of kindred spirits was something he never had imagined.

Perhaps this was why he failed to immediately recognize his peril when Geshrunni said, "I know you."

Dark even in the lamplight, Geshrunni lowered his arms, which had been folded across his white silk vest, and leaned forward in his seat. He was an imposing figure, possessing a hawkish soldier's face, a beard pleated into what looked like black leather straps, and thick arms so deeply tanned that one could see, but never quite decipher, the line of Ainoni pictograms tattooed from shoulder to wrist.

Achamian tried to grin affably. "You and my wives," he said, tossing back yet another bowl of wine. He gasped and smacked his lips. Geshrunni had always been, or so Achamian had assumed, a narrow man, one for whom the grooves of thought and word were few and deep. Most warriors were such, particularly when they were slaves.

But there had been nothing narrow about his claim.

Geshrunni watched him carefully, the suspicion in his eyes rounded by a faint wonder. He shook his head in disgust. "I should've said, 'I know who you are.'"

The man leaned back in a contemplative way so foreign to a soldier's manner that Achamian's skin pimpled with dread. The rumbling tavern receded, became a frame of shadowy figures and points of golden lantern-light.

"Then write it down," Achamian replied, as though growing bored, "and give it to me when I'm sober." He looked away, as bored men often do, and noted that the entrance to the tavern was empty.

"I know you have no wives."

"You don't say. And how's that?" Achamian glanced quickly behind him, glimpsed a whore laughing as she pressed a shiny silver ensolarii on to her sweaty breasts. The vulgar crowd about her roared, *"One!"*

"She's quite good at that, you know. She uses honey."

Geshrunni was not distracted. "Your kind aren't allowed to have wives."

"My kind, eh? And just what is my kind?" Another glance at the entrance.

"You're a sorcerer. A Schoolman."

Achamian laughed, knowing his momentary hesitation had betrayed him. But there was motive enough to continue this pantomime. At the very least, it might buy him several more moments. Time to stay alive.

"By the Latter-fucking-Prophet, my friend," Achamian cried, glancing once again at the entrance, "I swear I could measure your accusations by the bowl. What was it you accused me of being last night? A whoreson?"

Amid chortling voices, a thunderous shout: *"Two!"*

The fact that Geshrunni grimaced told Achamian little—the man's every expression seemed some version of a grimace, particularly his smile. The hand that flashed out and clamped his wrist, however, told Achamian all he needed to know.

I'm doomed. They know.

Few things were more terrifying than "they," especially in Carythusal. "They" were the Scarlet Spires, the most powerful School in the Three Seas, and the hidden masters of High Ainon. Geshrunni was a Captain of the Javreh, the warrior-slaves of the Scarlet Spires, which is why Achamian had courted him over the past few weeks. This is what spies do: woo the slaves of their competitors.

Geshrunni stared fiercely into his eyes, twisted his hand palm outward. "There's a way for us to satisfy my suspicion," the man said softly.

"Three!" reverberated across mud brick and scuffed mahogany.

Achamian winced, both because of the man's powerful grip and because he knew the "way" Geshrunni referred to. *Not like this.*

"Geshrunni, please. You're drunk, my friend. What School would hazard the wrath of the Scarlet Spires?"

Geshrunni shrugged. "The Mysunsai, maybe. Or the Imperial Saik. The Cishaurim. There are so many of your accursed kind. But if I had to wager, I would say the *Mandate*. I would say you're a Mandate Schoolman."

Canny slave! How long had he known?

The impossible words were there, poised in Achamian's thought, words that could blind eyes and blister flesh. *He leaves me no choice.* There would be an uproar. Men would bellow, clutch their swords, but they would do nothing but scramble from his path. More than any people in the Three Seas, the Ainoni feared sorcery.

No choice.

But Geshrunni had already reached beneath his embroidered vest. His fist bunched beneath the fabric. He grimaced like a grinning jackal.

Too late . . .

"You look," Geshrunni said with menacing ease, "like you have something to say."

The man withdrew his hand and produced the Chorae. He winked, then with terrifying abruptness, snapped the golden chain holding it about his neck. Achamian had sensed it from their first encounter, had actually used its unnerving murmur to identify Geshrunni's vocation. Now Geshrunni would use it to identify him.

"What's this, now?" Achamian asked. A shudder of animal terror passed through his pinned arm.

"I think you know, Akka. I think you know far better than I."

Chorae. Schoolmen called them Trinkets. Small names are often given to horrifying things. But for other men, those who followed the Thousand Temples in condemning sorcery as blasphemy, they were called Tears of God. But the God had no hand in their manufacture. Chorae were relics of the Ancient North, so valuable that only the marriage of heirs, murder, or the tribute of entire nations could purchase them. They were worth the price: Chorae rendered their bearers immune to sorcery and killed any sorcerer unfortunate enough to touch them.

Effortlessly holding Achamian's hand immobile, Geshrunni raised the Chorae between thumb and forefinger. It looked plain enough: a small sphere of iron, about the size of an olive but encased in the cursive script of the Nonmen. Achamian could feel it tug at his bowels, as though Geshrunni held an *absence* rather than a thing, a small pit in the very fabric of the world. His heart hammered in his ears. He thought of the knife sheathed beneath his tunic.

"Four!" Raucous laughter.

He struggled to free his captive hand. Futile.

"Geshrunni . . ."

"Every Captain of the Javreh is given one of these," Geshrunni said, his tone at once reflective and proud. "But then, you already know this."

All this time, he's been playing me for a fool! How could I've missed it?

"Your masters are kind," Achamian said, rivetted by the horror suspended above his palm.

"Kind?" Geshrunni spat. "The Scarlet Spires are not *kind*. They're ruthless. Cruel to those who oppose them."

And for the first time, Achamian glimpsed the torment animating the man, the anguish in his bright eyes. *What's happening here?* He hazarded a question: "And to those who serve them?"

"They do not discriminate."

They don't know! Only Geshrunni . . .

"Five!" pealed beneath the low ceilings.

Achamian licked his lips. "What do you want, Geshrunni?"

The warrior-slave looked down at Achamian's trembling palm, then lowered the Trinket as though he were a child curious of what might happen. Simply staring at it made Achamian dizzy, jerked bile to the back of his throat. Chorae. A tear drawn from the God's own cheek. Death. Death to all blasphemers.

"What do you want?" Achamian hissed.

"What all men want, Akka. Truth."

All the things Achamian had seen, all the trials he'd survived, lay pinched in that narrow space between his shining palm and the oiled iron. Trinket. Death poised between the callused fingers of a slave. But Achamian was a Schoolman, and for Schoolmen nothing, not even life itself, was as precious as the Truth. They were its miserly keepers, and they warred for its possession across all the shadowy grottoes of the Three Seas. Better to die than to yield Mandate truth to the Scarlet Spires.

But there was more here. Geshrunni was alone—Achamian was certain of this. Sorcerers could see sorcerers, see the bruise of their crimes, and the Holy Leper hosted no sorcerers, no Scarlet Schoolmen, only drunks making wagers with whores. Geshrunni played this game on his own.

But for what mad reason?

Tell him what he wants. He already knows.

"I'm a Mandate Schoolman," Achamian whispered quickly. Then he added, "A spy."

Dangerous words. But what choice did he have?

Geshrunni studied him for a breathless moment, then slowly gathered the Chorae into his fist. He released Achamian's hand.

There was an odd moment of silence, interrupted only by the clatter of a silver ensolarii against wood. A roar of laughter, and a hoarse voice bellowed, *"You lose, whore!"*

But this, Achamian knew, was not so. Somehow he had won this night, and he had won the way whores always win—without understanding.

After all, spies were little different from whores. Sorcerers less so.

Though he had dreamt of being a sorcerer as a child, the possibility of being a spy had never occurred to Drusas Achamian. "Spy" simply wasn't part of the vocabulary of children raised in Nroni fishing villages. For him the Three Seas had possessed only two dimensions in his childhood: there were places far and near and there were people high and low. He would listen to the old fish-wives tell their tales while he and the other children helped shuck oysters, and he learned very quickly that he was among the low, and that mighty people dwelt far away. Name after mysterious name would fall from those old lips—the Shriah of the Thousand Temples, the malevolent heathens of Kian, the all-conquering Scylvendi, the scheming sorcerers of the Scarlet Spires, and so on—names that sketched the dimensions of his world, infused it with terrifying majesty, transformed it into an arena of impossibly tragic and heroic deeds. He would fall asleep feeling very small.

One might think becoming a spy would add dimension to the simple world of a child, but precisely the opposite was the case. Certainly, as he matured, Achamian's world became more complicated. He learned that there were things holy and unholy, that the Gods and the Outside possessed their own dimensions, rather than being people very high and a place very far. He also learned that there were times recent and ancient, that "a long time ago" was not like another place but rather a queer kind of ghost that haunted every place.

But when one became a spy, the world had the curious habit of collapsing into a single dimension. High-born men, even Emperors and Kings, had the habit of seeming as base and as petty as the most vulgar fisherman. Far-away nations like Conriya, High Ainon, Ce Tydonn, or Kian no longer seemed exotic or enchanted but were as grubby and as weathered as a Nroni fishing village. Things holy, like the Tusk, the Thousand Temples, or even the Latter Prophet, became mere versions of things unholy, like the Fanim, the Cishaurim, or the sorcerous Schools, as though the words "holy" and "unholy" were as easily exchanged as seats at a gaming table. And the recent simply became a more tawdry repetition of the ancient.

As both a Schoolman and a spy, Achamian had crisscrossed the Three Seas, had seen many of those things that had once made his stomach flutter with supernatural dread, and he knew now that childhood stories were always better. Since being identified as one of the Few as a youth and taken to Atyersus to be trained by the School of Mandate, he had educated princes, insulted grandmasters, and infuriated Shrial priests. And he now knew with certainty that the world was hollowed of its wonder by knowledge and travel, that when one stripped away the mysteries, its dimensions collapsed rather than bloomed. Of course, the world was a much more sophisticated place to him now than it had been when he was a child, but it was also far simpler. Everywhere men grasped and grasped, as though the titles "king," "shriah," and "grandmaster" were simply masks worn by the same hungry animal. Avarice, it seemed to him, was the world's only dimension.

Achamian was a middle-aged sorcerer and spy, and he had grown weary of both vocations. And though he would be loath to admit it, he was heartsick. As the old fish-wives might say, he had dragged one empty net too many.

Perplexed and dismayed, Achamian left Geshrunni at the Holy Leper and hurried home—if it could be called that—through the shadowy ways of the Worm. Extending from the northern banks of the River Sayut to the famed Surmantic Gates, the Worm was a labyrinth of crumbling tenements, brothels, and impoverished Cultic temples. The place was aptly named, Achamian had always thought. Humid, riddled by cramped alleys, the Worm indeed resembled something found beneath a rock.

Given his mission, Achamian had no reason to be dismayed. Quite the opposite, if anything. After the mad moment with the Chorae, Geshrunni had told him secrets—potent secrets. Geshrunni, it turned out, was not a happy slave. He hated the Scarlet Magi with an intensity that was almost frightening once revealed.

"I didn't befriend you for the promise of your gold," the Javreh Captain had said. "For what? To buy my freedom from my masters? The Scarlet Spires relinquish nothing of value. No, I befriended you because I knew you would be useful."

"Useful? But for what end?"

"Vengeance. I would humble the Scarlet Spires."

"So you knew . . . All along you knew I was no merchant."

Sneering laughter. "Of course. You were too free with your ensolariis. Sit with a merchant or sit with a beggar, and it'll always be the beggar who buys your first drink."

What kind of spy are you?

Achamian had scowled at this, scowled at his own transparency. But as much as Geshrunni's penetration troubled him, he was terrified by the degree to which he'd misjudged the man. Geshrunni was a warrior and a slave—what surer formula could there be for stupidity? But slaves, Achamian supposed, had good reason to conceal their intelligence. A wise slave was something to be prized perhaps, like the slave-scholars of the old Ceneian Empire. A cunning slave, however, was something to be feared, to be eliminated.

But this thought held little consolation. *If he could fool me so easily . . .*

Achamian had plucked a great secret out of the obscurity of Carythusal and the Scarlet Spires—the greatest, perhaps, in many years. But he did not have his ability, which he'd rarely questioned over the years, to thank—only his incompetence. As a result, he'd learned *two* secrets—one dreadful enough, he supposed, in the greater scheme of the Three Seas; the other dreadful within the frame of his life.

I'm not, he realized, *the man I once was.*

Geshrunni's story had been alarming in its own right, if only because it demonstrated the ability of the Scarlet Spires to harbour secrets. The Scarlet Spires, Geshrunni said, was at war, had been for more than ten years, in fact. Achamian had been unimpressed—at first. The sorcerous Schools, like all the Great Factions, ceaselessly skirmished with spies, assassinations, trade sanctions, and delegations of outraged envoys. But this war, Geshrunni assured him, was far more momentous than any skirmish.

"Ten years ago," Geshrunni said, "our former Grandmaster, Sasheoka, was assassinated."

"Sasheoka?" Achamian was not inclined to ask stupid questions, but the idea that a Grandmaster of the Scarlet Spires could be assassinated was preposterous. How could such a thing happen? "Assassinated?"

"In the inner sanctums of the Spires themselves."

In other words, in the midst of the most formidable system of Wards in the Three Seas. Not only would the Mandate never dare such an act, but there was no way, even with the glittering Abstractions of the Gnosis, they could succeed. Who could do such a thing?

"By whom?" Achamian asked, almost breathless.

Geshrunni's eyes actually twinkled in the ruddy lamplight. "By the heathens," he said. "The Cishaurim."

Achamian was at once baffled and gratified by this revelation. The Cishaurim—the only heathen School. At least this explained Sasheoka's assassination.

There was a saying common to the Three Seas: "Only the Few can see the Few." Sorcery was violent. To speak it was to cut the world as surely as if with a knife. But only the Few—sorcerers—could see this mutilation, and only they could see, moreover, the blood on the hands of the mutilator—the "mark," as it was called. Only the Few could see one another and one another's crimes. And when they met, they recognized one another as surely as common men recognized criminals by their lack of a nose.

Not so with the Cishaurim. No one knew why or how, but they worked events as grand and as devastating as any sorcery without marking the world or bearing the mark of their crime. Only once had Achamian witnessed Cishaurim sorcery, what they called the Psûkhe—on a night long ago in distant Shimeh. With the Gnosis, the sorcery of the Ancient North, he'd destroyed his saffron-robed assailants, but as he sheltered behind his Wards, it had seemed as though he watched flashes of soundless lightning. No thunder. No mark.

Only the Few could see the Few, but no one—no Schoolman, at least—could distinguish the Cishaurim or their works from common men or the common world. And it was this, Achamian surmised, that had allowed them to assassinate Sasheoka. The Scarlet Spires possessed Wards for sorcerers, slave-soldiers like Geshrunni for men bearing Chorae, but they had nothing to protect them against sorcerers indistinguishable from common men, or against sorcery indistinguishable from the God's own world. Hounds, Geshrunni would tell him, now ran freely through the halls of the Scarlet Spires, trained to smell the saffron and henna the Cishaurim used to dye their robes.

But why? What could induce the Cishaurim to wage open war against the Scarlet Spires? As alien as their metaphysics were, they could have no hope of winning such a war. The Scarlet Spires was simply too powerful.

When Achamian had asked Geshrunni, the slave-soldier simply shrugged.

"It's been a decade, and still they don't know."

This, at least, was grounds for petty comfort. There was nothing the ignorant prized more than the ignorance of others.

Drusas Achamian walked ever deeper into the Worm, toward the squalid tenement where he'd taken a room, still more afraid of himself than his future.

Geshrunni grimaced as he stumbled out of the tavern. He steadied himself on the packed dust of the alley.

"Done," he muttered, then cackled in a way he never dared show others. He looked up at a narrow slot of sky hemmed and obscured by mud-brick walls and ragged canvas awnings. He could see few stars.

Suddenly his betrayal struck him as a pathetic thing. He had told the only real secret he knew to an enemy of his masters. Now there was nothing left. No treason that might quiet the hatred in his heart.

And a bitter hatred it was. More than anything else, Geshrunni was a proud man. That someone such as he might be born a slave, be dogged by the desires of weak-hearted, womanish men . . . By sorcerers! In another life, he knew, he would have been a conqueror. He would have broken enemy after enemy with the might of his hand. But in this accursed life, all he could do was skulk about with other womanish men and gossip.

Where was the vengeance in gossip?

He'd staggered some way down the alley before realizing that someone followed him. The possibility that his masters had discovered his small treachery struck him momentarily, but he thought it unlikely. The Worm was filled with wolves, desperate men who followed mark after mark searching for those drunk enough to be safely plundered. Geshrunni had actually killed one once, several years before: some poor fool who had risked murder rather than sell himself, as Geshrunni's nameless father had, into slavery. He continued walking, his senses as keen as the wine would allow, his drunken thoughts reeling through scenario after bloody scenario. This would be a good night, he thought, to kill.

Only when he passed beneath the looming facade of the temple the Carythusali called the Mouth of the Worm did Geshrunni become alarmed. Men were quite often followed into the Worm, but rarely were they followed out. Above the welter of rooftops, Geshrunni could even glimpse the highest of the Spires, crimson against a field of stars. Who would dare follow him this far? If not . . .

He whirled and saw a balding, rotund man dressed, despite the heat, in an ornate silk overcoat that might have been any combination of colours but looked blue and black in the darkness.

"You were one of the fools with the whore," Geshrunni said, trying to shake away the confusion of drink.

"Yes," the man replied, his jowls grinning with his lips. "She was most . . . enticing. But truth be told, I was far more interested in what you had to say to the Mandate Schoolman."

Geshrunni squinted in drunken astonishment. *So they know.*

Danger always sobered him. Instinctively, he reached into his pocket, closed his fingers about his Chorae. He flung it violently at the Schoolman . . .

Or at who he thought was a Scarlet Schoolman. The stranger picked the Trinket from the air as though it had been tossed for his friendly perusal. He studied it momentarily, a dubious money-changer with a leaden coin. He looked up and smiled again, blinking his large bovine eyes. "A most precious gift," he said. "I thank you, but I'm afraid it's not quite a fair exchange for what I want."

Not a sorcerer! Geshrunni had seen a Chorae touch a sorcerer once, the incandescent unravelling of flesh and bone. But then what was this man?

"Who are you?" Geshrunni asked.

"Nothing you could understand, slave."

The Javreh Captain smiled. *Maybe he's just a fool.* A dangerous, drunken amiability seized his manner. He walked up to the man, placed a callused hand on his padded shoulder. He could smell jasmine. The cowlike eyes looked up at him.

"Oh my," the stranger whispered, "you are a daring fool, aren't you?"

Why isn't he afraid? Remembering the ease with which the man had snatched the Chorae, Geshrunni suddenly felt horribly exposed. But he was committed.

"Who are you?" Geshrunni grated. "How long have you been watching me?"

"Watching you?" The fat man almost giggled. "Such conceit is unbecoming of slaves."

He watches Achamian? What is this? Geshrunni was an officer, accustomed to cowing men in the menacing intimacy of a face-to-face confrontation. Not this man. Soft or not, he was at utter ease. Geshrunni could feel it. And if it weren't for the unwatered wine, he would have been terrified.

He dug his fingers deep into the fat of the man's shoulder.

"I said tell me, fat fool," he hissed between clenched teeth, "or I'll muck up the dust with your bowel." With his free hand, he brandished his knife. "Who are you?"

Unperturbed, the fat man grinned with sudden ferocity. "Few things are as distressing as a slave who refuses to acknowledge his place."

Stunned, Geshrunni looked down at his senseless hand, watched his knife flop on to the dust. All he'd heard was the snap of the stranger's sleeve.

"Heel, slave," the fat man said.

"What did you say?"

The slap stung him, brought tears to his eyes.

"I said *heel.*"

Another slap, hard enough to loosen teeth. Geshrunni stumbled back several steps, raising a clumsy hand. How could this be?

"What a task we've set for ourselves," the stranger said ruefully, following him, "when even their slaves possess such pride."

Panicked, Geshrunni fumbled for the hilt of his sword.

The fat man paused, his eyes flashing to the pommel.

"Draw it," he said, his voice impossibly cold—inhuman.

Wide-eyed, Geshrunni froze, transfixed by the silhouette that loomed before him.

"I said draw it!"

Geshrunni hesitated.

The next slap knocked him to his knees.

"What are you?" Geshrunni cried through bloodied lips.

As the shadow of the fat man encompassed him, Geshrunni watched his round face loosen, then flex as tight as a beggar's hand about copper. *Sorcery! But how could it be? He holds a Chorae—*

"Something impossibly ancient," the abomination said softly. "Inconceivably beautiful."